THE
GOLDEN
NET

For PAM

The Golden Net

BY
RUBY REDINGER

CROWN PUBLISHERS • NEW YORK

PRINTED IN THE UNITED STATES OF AMERICA

PART ONE

Chapter One

PROFESSOR Esther Cornthwaite prepared the tea with the usual slow deliberateness that never failed to madden the three waiting men. The prematurely hot May day had not given them a thirst for tea, but they watched resignedly as she poured boiling water into the silver urn. They knew that their resignations from John Willard College would be more acceptable than the suggestion that she dispense with this method of conducting the meetings of the department of English.

The room in Main Hall had that indifferent atmosphere of all classrooms when invaded by teachers without students. Used for seminar courses only, it was furnished with a long table and numerous straight-backed chairs. A blackboard covered the back wall, and on this remained the evidence of the 1:30-3:00 Seminar in Byron, Shelley, and Keats:

Upon entering, the four people had glanced cursorily at this; three had found the marks meaningless, and one had winced to think that he had forgotten to erase them.

Professor Cornthwaite now judged the tea ready for pouring. She filled the four cups that waited before her on the table in a semicircle. Then she replaced the urn on the oval tray, where also stood a matching creamer and sugar bowl, both brimful, although it was a long-accepted fact that no member of the department used cream. With a nod she indicated the obvious fact that spaced at even intervals down the long table were a platter of severe soda crackers, a glass plate of pale lemon slices, and another platter of the crackers.

This done, she folded her firm, shapely hands in her lap and waited motionlessly, a symphony—as Whistler would have seen her—in gray: gray heavy silk dress of a perennial style, gray scholar's skin, darker gray hair. The hair was arresting. Intricately coiffed, it was abundant and vital, seeming to have sprung directly from the brain, which was indeed the fount of Professor Cornthwaite's strength.

It was Professor Grant who moved first. He stood, lifted a cup and saucer, placed them more properly in front of her, and then offered her the sugar, the lemons, and finally the crackers. He did all this without mishap, for it was a perfected routine, but accustomed as he was to it, he never stopped fearing that one day she would say, "Thank you, my Good Man." Hastily he took up a cup for himself, omitting all garnishes because it was simpler that way.

The other two men, as if to conceal their reluctance, now rushed for their cups, almost colliding. Instructor Duncan stood respectfully aside while Assistant Professor Scott speared a lemon slice and helped himself to the sugar. Because Grant had reseated himself, they did too. There was something about Grant that made him a comfortable person to follow, although Owen Scott would have hotly scorned the suggestion that he aped Grant in the slightest particular. At present, however, he was mostly concerned with his diagram on the blackboard. Should he explain it? He decided against it.

Paul Lewis Grant thought yearningly of the chapter he wanted to finish writing that evening and of the frosted brown bottle of ale waiting for him in his own iceless. But as he was a man to do the work before him, he switched his mind to the business at hand. Being an obedient mind, it responded without resistance, and obligingly clicked off the facts he desired. Remembering that he had given the applicants' papers t oScott to digest before this meeting, he leaned forward and half-whispered across the table, "You brought the papers, Scott?"

Without turning his head, Scott nodded in the casual manner that he assumed, resisting the old tortuous impulse to let go and answer Grant bombastically. He pushed his emptied cup away from him and struck a seemingly relaxed pose. There was a natural grace about his long slender frame, and he managed to look comfortable in his uncomfortable chair. Shifting slightly, he more directly faced Esther Cornthwaite, who merely stared noncommittally at him over the rim of her cup. Even before this blankness, his handsome angular face suggested respectful deference and willingness to cooperate upon any and all matters emanating from Professor Cornthwaite, Chairman of his department.

While he thus posed for Esther Cornthwaite, he inwardly continued his explosive retort to Paul Lewis Grant: And why *wouldn't* I bring the papers? Have you ever found me incompetent? Perhaps Ritson *will* reject my manuscript. . . . Literary history proves that the really good is often rejected. So you have published more than I. Well, you've had a good half-dozen years' start on me. Besides, you don't have a wife and maybe a baby on the way. . . . And why aren't you married?

He glanced at Grant. He looked virile enough. Although not short, he gave the impression of solid squareness. His movements were gentle, as if he were carefully checking the flow of physical strength. This accounted for the seeming restraint in everything that he did and said, a restraint that annoyed Scott because it gave him the uncomfortable impulse to be aggressive and noisy.

Kimball Duncan sensed Scott's taut nerves, and his own feeling of

4

tension mounted. It's just a department meeting, he told himself, and I'm bored stiff.

Bored? He winced with self-disgust. He was scared. As usual.

Suddenly defiant, he stretched out his long legs. That would show them. He still had the power of free movement.

His chair creaked, and Professor Cornthwaite, who never heard him when he tried to talk to her, looked unerringly at the source of the noise. His scowl gave way to an expression of innocent attention. To his great relief, she questioned no further, but put down her cup with the air of finality that presaged the opening of the meeting.

She spoke: "Well, gentlemen! The chief business for this afternoon is, as you know, the apportioning of next Fall's courses and the discussion of the final candidates for our vacancy."

As always, her voice brought the men to immediate and serious attention, not because it was especially pleasant, but because it was a low monotone that required the concentration of those addressed. She had so successfully sublimated her impulse to adjust her speaking to her own deficient hearing, that she barely spoke at all. Fortunately, she had developed also a Spartan verbal economy.

She reached behind her and pulled from between herself and the chair the voluminous black leather purse with its scarred gold-plated clasp and worn straps, a familiar bit of local color on the campus. Opened, it revealed a black gaping chaos; but apparently it was intelligible to Miss Cornthwaite, for without a fumbling search she brought to light a small folded note paper. This she smoothed out before her on the table and, after a brief glance at the set of hieroglyphics, continued:

. "Provided that conditions remain normal—"

"So you think we may be at war by September?" asked Duncan, determined to acquire verbal ease.

Both Grant and Scott, longer-time members of the department, shifted uncomfortably. They were aware of Professor Cornthwaite's profound conviction that world affairs had no bearing upon those of John Willard College. She had been speaking merely in the spirit of the true scholar, who knows that the future can be predicted only in terms of probability.

The silence was condemning, and Duncan felt the humiliation of the introvert whose rare overture to the outside world is rebuffed. Grant had sudden sympathy for this somber young man with the dark fathomless eyes, and murmured: "Provided that there be no Act of God, such as Famine, Pestilence, or Earthquake."

Not having distinctly heard what had passed, Professor Cornthwaite waited for Grant to report. When he said nothing to her, she concluded that the interruption had been of no consequence, and again struck the opening note:

5

"Provided that conditions remain normal, we are scheduled to offer these courses in the Fall: Freshman Composition I and II, English Fundamentals, Survey of English Literature, American Literature III, Eighteenth Century I, Chaucer, Milton, Later Nineteenth Century I, Development of the English Language I, and Modern Novel."

Each man stared at the middle of the table, as if the courses had fallen there upon a platter. Each waited politely for Miss Cornthwaite to do the honors of serving, but all were quickly appraising this cut and that piece, pretending for the moment that they had absolute freedom of choice. The first passing was automatic: each, including the hostess, took a section of Freshman Composition I. One might prefer a different appetizer, but if he valued his chance at future invitations, he would not suggest a substitute.

Professor Cornthwaite worked in the manner of the ancient pyramid-builders, laying a broad, firm foundation and building solidly up to the peak. To her, the broad, firm foundation of all English teaching and learning was Freshman Composition.

Now she said, "There will be five classes of Freshman Composition, for, of course, our new member, as yet to be chosen, will teach a section. To avoid confusion, let us refer to this person as X."

Scott was making notes on the back of an envelope. This reminded Duncan, and he felt anxiously in his vest pocket, relieved to be able to pull forth his little black notebook. He had noticed that men never failed to work with paper and pencil at all meetings. Sometimes he puzzled as to what they found necessary to write down, but chiefly he blamed himself for inattentiveness. Perhaps, one day, he would get the hang of all this.

As he leafed through in search of a clean page, he was ashamed to see the inconsequential fragments of notes that he had gleaned from two whole years of meetings—all kinds of meetings: committee, department, general faculty. He hurried past these sad reminders, desperately hoping that Grant had not glimpsed this evidence of his inadequacy. Finding an unused sheet, he flattened the notebook out on the table and wrote:

Schedule of courses, Fall, 1941
Fresh Comp I — 5 hrs.

"You have noticed," Professor Cornthwaite was saying, "that there is a trailer section of Freshman Composition. That means, gentlemen, that one of us must teach two courses in Composition. . . ."

Without waiting to hear more, Duncan added Freshman II to his schedule. It was inevitable that the course should fall to him. So it had been for the past two years, always Freshman Composition and English Fundamentals. So it would be until he made a move toward getting a Ph.D., or grinding out articles for publication, or talking with the casual superiority of Scott, or acting with the efficiency of Grant. Nothing less than the sudden and mid-term death of either Scott or Grant would ever throw a literature course his way.

"Mr. Duncan, will you please take the trailer section?"

He nodded, keeping his face expressionless. At least it was kind of her to put it in question form. He pretended to write this into his note-book; actually he added English Fundamentals. That completed his schedule, unless the old girl had thought up some new monstrosity for him, such as Sub-Freshman Comp or Remedial Reading.

Professor Cornthwaite consulted her sparse notes. "Of the writing courses, there remains English Fundamentals. I am wondering, Dr. Scott, if you would be willing to undertake this very important course."

Both Scott and Duncan looked up unbelievingly. Scott recovered and frowned judiciously. English Fundamentals was the basement that Professor Cornthwaite had built to catch those students who were passable but not proficient in Freshman Composition. The course had to be handled delicately, for its creator had let it be known that if it proved ineffective, she was capable of devising additional and still more subterranean remedial classes. Scott didn't care to say outright that the course belonged to an instructor, not an assistant professor, but he was determined that she wouldn't get around *him* with that very-important-course-tactic. He had to be careful, however. Grant was watching.

"It *is* an extremely important course," he said, raising his voice, for he desired her to hear him. "I do not feel quite competent. . . ." He had meant to convey an appealing shade of modesty, but he couldn't be loud, conversational, and intimate at the same time.

She had heard him, and she resented the raising of his voice. Also, she disliked his remark. True, her sixty-four-year-old memory was not infallible, but judgment wasn't a faculty that weakened in proportion to its stretch over a period of years. Had she judged Scott incompetent, she should not have asked him to teach the course. "I have had no occasion to doubt your competency," she told him sharply.

Grant was amused. He knew that Professor Cornthwaite's great contribution to Philology was her superb analysis of what man said *after* he thought; she was neither inclined nor equipped to disengage the thought from the word. It had not, therefore, occurred to her that Scott did not mean literally what he had said.

"Gentlemen," she was saying calmly, "these are my reasons for suggesting that Dr. Scott take English Fundamentals: Dr. Grant could, of course, teach it, but it would have to be in place of Chaucer or American Literature. For reasons obvious to all of us, such a procedure would appear more foolish than wise."

She paused, challenging dissent. Scott calculated quickly. Grant's title to the American Literature was as inviolable as Cornthwaite's to the Development of the English Language; but his one (and now practically buried) article on the *Troilus* didn't mean that he had the right to teach Chaucer forever. Should he, Scott, now make a bid for that

7

course? True, he had had no occasion to read Chaucer seriously since Graduate days, but with a little brushing up this summer. . . .

But Professor Cornthwaite had waited long enough. "I am glad that you agree with me. Next, we *could* give the course to X, but I am sure that again you will agree with me that because of its peculiar nature, it is much better taught by someone who has had previous acquaintance with the students concerned.

"Finally, we could give Fundamentals again to Mr. Duncan, who taught it all this year and last. You will recall, gentlemen, that Mr. Duncan has taught only Freshman courses for the two years that he has been with us. I have been pleased with his ready acceptance of his rôle. I feel now, however, that he deserves to be released from at least one paper-grading course and that he needs an enlarged scope for his ability. In fact, I had it in mind to offer him the new course which at our last meeting we voted to add to our curriculum—the Modern Novel."

Duncan opened his mouth, but no words came. Professor Cornthwaite favored him with a brief direct look. "If," she said then, "there is no strong dissent, we shall consider the matter settled."

Good! thought Grant. Cornthwaite, as he had told himself many times in the half-dozen years he had taught under her, was no fool. He felt sorry for Scott; but the boy Duncan had something valuable within him, although what it was, or in what direction it was going, was as yet unknown.

Scott too signaled across the table, as if to say that he thought it tip-top that Duncan old man was at last to have something worth sinking his mental teeth into, and that now they really were brothers under the skin. Inwardly, however, he was having another tempest, rankling over Fundamentals and regretting the lost chance to bag Chaucer. Well, at least he would have the Eighteenth Century; there would be no question about that, he being the acknowledged Eighteenth-Century Man. It was good to be teaching his specialty. That would inspire him to write more, and even to revise the manuscript if Ritson sent it back. Perhaps at this very minute there was a letter waiting for him at home. . . . Never mind. If Ritson said no, some other publisher, sooner or later, would recognize that Owen Scott had a way of interpreting that most sophisticated and intellectual age with a profundity foreign to— well, say to students of American Literature, which, at its best, was merely *nascent* literature. . . .

The remaining blanks in the schedules were filled in rapidly and with little disagreement. Grant questioned X's schedule, which stood: two Freshman Compositions, Survey, and Later Nineteenth Century. He reminded Professor Cornthwaite that this was a heavy program, especially to a newcomer who would have to exert energy in adjusting his life to that of the college.

"Life at John Willard is not that strenuous," she retorted. "Furthermore, if X is worth his salt, he'll handle the program competently."

Grant felt anticipatory sympathy for X, who was evidently to be tested even more rigorously than Duncan. He didn't argue, for the courses had, after all, been distributed fairly, and Cornthwaite had certainly not manufactured any new ones for the occasion. And although he himself did not believe that any individual had the right to impose Spartan discipline upon another, he admitted that X would be none the worse for his ordeal.

Duncan had heard little of this final program-planning. He was swimming in his own sea of thought, and he was already near to going under. Did he really want that course? Could he handle it? By now he was used to Freshman Composition. He had memorized the grammar text, and the class time was taken up with exercises, which he graded by use of the Teacher's Key. But the Novel . . . Even if he could find a textbook, it wouldn't be the kind he could memorize. They'd expect him to lecture. . . .

Professor Cornthwaite peered once more at the small scrap of paper still before her on the table. "Gentlemen, we have yet to discuss the applicants for the instructorship in our department. Dr. Grant will please make the report."

In his unhurried way, Grant told how, by pre-arrangement, he had been able to meet each one of the three final candidates at the College English Convention held at Columbus two weeks ago. They were: Sidney Meyerson, 30, a New York University M.A. nearing his Ph.D.; Etta Wilson, 34, a Cornell Ph.D.; and Marcia Anderson, 26, an Ohio State Ph.D. In letters addressed to Professor Cornthwaite, all three had been highly recommended by their respective superiors and colleagues. Both Mr. Meyerson and Miss Anderson had had teaching experience— Meyerson in both literature and composition, Anderson in only one composition course. Miss Wilson, however, had preferred to be a research assistant and was now for the first time interested in teaching. Each was at present actively engaged in research and gave evidence of continuing to be so.

Thus far, Grant's tone implied, the score is even. He asked Scott to show the applicants' papers. Scott took the papers from his briefcase and spread them out on the table, so that there were three separate piles, each topped by a sheet to which was clipped a 3" x 4" photograph.

Sidney Meyerson had alert light eyes and energetic blond hair that sprang back from the high, broad forehead in a widespread pompadour. Yet the slight smile on the full but delicate lips gave the impression that he found droll amusement in application photographs; and the one eyebrow cocked higher than the other suggested a quizzical detachment from all possible reactions to his obviously intelligent face.

Etta Wilson frankly wore her shell rimmed glasses. Her smooth hair, parted in the middle, lay flat across her forehead, turned abruptly and continued straight down her long cheeks until it again abruptly turned and disappeared. Her pose was a severely full front view and an assurance that no blemishes were hidden.

Marcia Anderson looked wantonly different. Her photograph was the most artfully finished of the three, and the shadow effect around the eyes, as well as the full, unsmiling lips, gave the face a languid and melancholy expression. The dark hair fell loosely to the shoulders. A short pearl necklace also showed, the middle bead breaking the oval line as it fitted into the shadowed hollow of the throat. Scott was sorry that the photograph ended there.

"Well, she certainly has the looks of the trio," he said involuntarily, "although I suppose that Etta has the brains."

Professor Cornthwaite chose to hear this. "I believe," she said, addressing Scott directly, "that you have already perused *Doctor* Anderson's papers. Did you find therein any conspicuous evidence of a lack of brains?"

Scott reddened. He had not, as a matter of fact, given the papers much time. True, he had looked at them long, but without seeing them, for he had been obsessed with the idea that one of those three people would be chosen largely on the basis of Grant's impressions formed during the convention. He himself had not been able to go this year. Had there been waiting for him some Grant from an eastern college? Could there have been for him the meaningful handshake, the pointed exchange of questions and answers made casual-seeming, the significant farewell-but-more-will-come-of-this? The possibility still taunted him.

"She's young, of course," said Duncan of Marcia Anderson. "Twenty-six, you said?" He hoped that they would remember that he was twenty-eight. He brightened as he considered the prospect of no longer being the baby of the department. But as he looked again at the photographs, his hope dimmed, for what chance did Marcia Anderson have against that apparent determination of Etta Wilson?

"Gentlemen," said Professor Cornthwaite sternly, "we are not conducting this discussion in an orderly manner. Let us examine the applicants one by one, starting with Mr. Meyerson. Dr. Grant, please contribute your impression of these people."

Grant spoke with reluctance. He did not like this seeming to hold people in the palm of his hand. He gave freely of the facts and chose carefully from his impressions.

"Sidney Meyerson has two articles forthcoming: one on Shelley (this grew out of the Master's thesis), and the other on the Literature of Propaganda in the Renaissance. At present he is working on Thomas Wolfe, something to do with the development of objectivity in his writings."

"But what's his *specialty*?" Scott asked.

Grant smiled, remembering Meyerson. "He doesn't believe in specializing."

Scott pursed his lips. "Jewish, isn't he?"

Grant nodded. No one in the room needed to be reminded that

there was at present no Jewish member on the John Willard faculty. Although the College had not formulated a policy concerning racial credentials, no department was eager to provide the first test case.

"Mr. Meyerson lacks a solid base to his scholarship," said Professor Cornthwaite conclusively.

No one disagreed. Grant reached out and removed Meyerson's papers from the table. He was a little sorry. Although Meyerson had not been his own final choice, he had liked him. Too he wondered briefly about Professor Cornthwaite's sublime objectivity. Had she been aware of the real issue? Did she deliberately never descend from her Parnassian heights, or was she rooted up there?

So there goes Meyerson, thought Duncan as he watched the papers disappear into Grant's briefcase. This was how they did it; this was what they had done to him two Mays ago. But why on earth hadn't *his* papers been quickly stuffed away?

Well, good-by Sidney Meyerson; hello Etta Wilson!

"Dr. Wilson," Grant told them, "is a Philologist. Last year she published a kind of experimental text for the teaching of linguistics to undergraduates." He raised his voice slightly. "Perhaps Professor Cornthwaite would give us her opinion of the value of this work. . . ."

Esther Cornthwaite considered. "Well, of course, the subject is an exceedingly complicated one to be presented in the simplified manner that Miss Wilson attempts. However, considering her object, I should say that her book is successful. Yes, successful." She hesitated, but was obviously considering further. "Needless to say, her approach is only one of many, and I personally favor . . ." She appealed with her fine hands, managing to look helpless, even a little coy. "You see, gentlemen, how personal opinion intrudes when one thinks in terms of one's own specialty! *Any* approach is permissible when based in sound scholarship. And I'm sure that Miss Wilson's scholarship . . . She is, of course, young, and her subject is an old, old one. You know, the life so short, the craft so long to learn. . . ."

The others restudied the photograph in new light. Miss Wilson's stern determination had suddenly become the unbridled energy of the very young rushing headlong toward the tranquil temple of Knowledge, already capably inhabited by Professor Cornthwaite.

The old devil, thought Grant fondly. He was not sorry to see Miss Wilson's star sink. Not that he hadn't recognized her superior intelligence, but the department needed a teacher, not a research person. However, he couldn't resist adding, "It should be said that Miss Wilson made it clear that she desires this position chiefly because of the opportunity of working with you, Professor Cornthwaite. She hoped that you might collaborate upon a new text."

Esther Cornthwaite accepted this as her due. Inwardly she quailed at the idea. She felt past the age for collaborations. However, she would, of course, have to recognize this tribute. A letter, yes, a tactful

11

letter would do it: (My dear Doctor Wilson: The members of our department have regretfully decided that a teaching position at John Willard College would not provide the proper scope for your great ability in research. In fairness to your scholarship, we must in this instance be the losers . . . *etc* . . . *etc.* . . .)

Good-by Etta Wilson; hello Marcia Anderson!

So this is how it happened to me, thought Duncan; I was Nordic, and I wasn't a serious threat to anyone already here. . . .

Grant explained that Miss Anderson had written her thesis on William Blake ("A Study of Thought and Expression"). While at the convention, he had talked with her advisors, and they had spoken highly of the thesis, which they said was original and creative as well as scholarly. Miss Anderson was now revising it for publication. He himself had been impressed with Miss Anderson's intelligence and personality. In short, he was certain that she would be a valuable addition to the department, not because she was the only applicant left for consideration, but because of her own worth. He would have said as much had she been considered first.

Professor Cornthwaite nodded approval, implying that they were dotards for not having reached this obvious conclusion long ago.

Scott relaxed. This Marcia Anderson would be ornamental and not, he imagined, seriously competitive. Anyone who looked like her would have a man in her life, and that took at least three-fourths of the drive out of a woman's ambition.

Duncan was almost happy. "I think that we have made an excellent choice," he told his colleagues. He shut his notebook and slipped it into his vest pocket. As he did not want to be the first to leave the room, he busied himself with contemplating the photograph of X, who had miraculously become Marcia Anderson. Out of the tail of his eye, however, he was watching the others. He felt the need to attach himself to someone.

Scott was the first to go. He knew that Grant was lingering to talk to Cornthwaite, and that she would delegate him new important duties. . . . The power behind the throne! He liked to think of Grant as that; there was something ignominious in the sound of it, particularly when you considered, in this instance, the throne. So let him stay; let him tidy up the tea things!

He made a half bow to Professor Cornthwaite and hurried out of the room. Duncan looked ready to tag after him, and he didn't want that. The kid was all agog over the Novel course, and he didn't feel like talking about it now. . . .

Duncan knew he had been shunned. He was hurt and angry. Some day . . .

He turned his attention upon Grant, who was already in a huddle with Cornthwaite. He preferred Grant to Scott; so why should he mind what Scott did? When he had cleared his throat noisily, he called out, "Well, so long!" Grant waved but hardly looked up. Duncan wandered on.

Grant agreed to present the application to President Cameron and Dean Holcomb. If he hurried, he might manage it yet today. He was halfway down the hall before he remembered. Returning, he found Professor Cornthwaite stacking the tea cups.

"I'm sorry," he said in some confusion. "I completely forgot. May I help?"

But she waved him away.

Again alone, she resumed the clearing-up, a task which she did not enjoy. But she was above requesting a man's services, and she would not leave the work for a cleaning woman. When all was orderly, she walked slowly to the Summit. There was no reason for her to return to her office, yet she could think of nothing else better to do. It was the Spring, she supposed. She saw young David Whitney and Carol Leeds strolling toward her across the Heart. She liked the boy, he having earned the only *A* she'd given in the Language course for the past five years. The girl too had brains, so she had been told, but she didn't look the bookish type. She favored them with a nod, quickening her steps for fear they would say something to her that she wouldn't hear.

As she neared the Summit steps, Kimball Duncan bounded down them, almost toppling her over. He mumbled something and rushed on. She stopped to watch his long figure with the still longer shadow slanting after him. He carried a bundle of sticks and what she had learned was his paint box. Queer lad, always to be painting and conveying sticks from place to place. . . . She saw him pause at the tip of the Heart, glancing at David and Carol, who stood talking, their backs to him. He seemed about to join them, but at that moment they moved on. He walked rapidly down the Hill, a curiously solitary figure. She watched until his bobbing head disappeared, and then went into the Summit, hoping to dispel that feeling of loneliness he had given her.

President Cameron's door was closed, but she heard the murmur of voices behind it. And that appreciative chuckle was of course Holcomb's. Grant's voice now. Hearing his voice, she went on into her own office, shutting the door after her and feeling confident that things were being handled in exactly the right way.

She threw open the wooden shutters to the one long window in the room. Wind was working up, and it carried a river smell. Rain wasn't far off. Good. It would end this unnatural heat.

Mechanically she sat down in the cushioned swivel chair before her spacious mahogany desk. From her purse she withdrew the box of crackers that she had salvaged from her tea. First helping herself to a cracker, she stowed the box away into the deep bottom drawer of her desk. She munched and stared about her, seeing the familiar things and not seeing them. She liked the room and felt more at home in it than in her set of living rooms on the Heights. Its cherry woodwork was almost a hundred years old, but the pale Kem-Tone on the walls was only two years old. She was slightly suspicious of the Kem-Tone, although it blended smoothly into the moss green carpet that was thick under her feet.

On the wall to her left hung the only picture, a large reproduction of Holbein's *Erasmus.* On the right wall were grouped three large framed and colorful linguistic maps portraying the global language families. These were signed *E. Cornthwaite,* and were the originals of those reproduced in the three volumes of *History and Development of the English Language,* by E. Cornthwaite.

These volumes stood on the desk between the bronze bookends that were minute copies of Rodin's *Thinker.* She was not past feeling satisfaction as she looked at them. They by no means represented the sum total of her published works, but they were what most pleased her. She had intended to bow out of active scholarship with them, but her publisher was nagging at her to do a fourth volume, on the development of American English. She did not like the inescapably modern aspect of this subject, and she wasn't sure that the whole idea of American English wasn't little more than a fad. But in a moment of weakness—when there arose that old familiar fear that if *she* didn't do it, someone less capable would and get the credit—she had committed herself. And very uncharacteristically, she hadn't done a thing about it as yet, even though she had agreed to have ready a tentative table of contents and chapter-summaries by September. Well, there was her Summer gone. Really, she was very tired. . . .

For long minutes now her mind had been skirting the matter of Etta Wilson. Had she, E. Cornthwaite, acted out of jealousy or egotism? Perhaps. Strange that those fierce feelings did not die down with age. Did women continue to feel so possessive of their men? She shuddered visibly at this idea. But as for Etta Wilson, it was not so much *fear* of her as it was reluctance to face her dogged enthusiasm. Besides, if she did the study of American English (and of course she *was* going to do it) , she intended to do it alone; and she certainly would have no time to collaborate upon another study. Finally, Etta Wilson was quite plainly not what her department needed. As a matter of fact, she would have been more selfish had she spoken *for* Etta Wilson: there could be pleasure in having a disciple about. . . .

A door suddenly opened upon President Cameron's voice, which was bidding Grant and Holcomb farewell in the dry precise way so well-known to her. She thought of poking her head out her door to let Grant know that she was present. It would not displease her to know the results of the meeting immediately. But she sat still. Let him come to her with his report. She was sure that it would be a favorable one. Marcia Anderson was a good choice. Even Cameron and Holcomb would see that, and so would J. W. MacMillan and the other trustees. Her record spoke for itself, even though her picture was a little surprising. Surprises were good for people. At least she didn't look tiresomely aggressive, not the type that would attempt to reform departmental procedure the day she arrived. Perhaps she . . .

Deliberately she shut Marcia Anderson and all other departmental business out of her mind. There was no work that she had to do, and she was in no mood to write her letter to Etta Wilson. But her hands were tired of their idleness. To satisfy them, she opened the long middle desk drawer and brought out a square pasteboard box. Inside was a manicure set folded up in the shape of a miniature suitcase. Unfolded, this revealed an array of instruments and bottles of varying shaded liquids. The bottles had never been opened; they were there only because they had come with the set.

She selected a long slender file and pushed the box and set away from her. From another drawer she took a paper-backed copy of *Mystery of the Sleeping-Powder Murders,* which she propped up in front of her, its back touching the backs of the *History and Development of the English Language.* She had never been unaware of the beauty of her hands, and now she filed her fingernails carefully and deftly as she read. She was not engrossed in what she was reading, but her mind was occupied, and that was her object. She did not like an idle mind any more than she liked idle hands. She had long ago given up the pastime of thinking about people. That merely confused life's meagre relationships. She found detective stories much more satisfying.

Suddenly she leaned nearer to the page, as if to reread a sentence. Then she chuckled, and as she realized that she was laughing over a passage that the author had not intended to be humorous, her chuckle deepened until her shoulders shook and she had to stop the filing. Automatically she reached out for a pencil and made a marginal note.

Chapter Two

IT WAS good to be going home to Judith, Scott thought. His head ached with those devilish thoughts he hadn't been able to speak out at the meeting. As after all meetings, he was on edge, and he longed for a pleasant, inconsequential evening with just the two of them, just the two of them. . . . He hoped that she would sense his mood and not say the wrong things.

As he turned up his walk, he had the old nagging thought that he and Judith could live much more happily in some other house. Theirs was the right side of a duplex that stood between two other gray stucco duplex houses. These three were faculty houses, and when he had read about them in the John Willard catalogue, he had thought that it would be most fitting for him to live in one. But that had been almost five years ago, when William G. Holcomb was Dean Holcomb and not his next-room neighbor.

The walk abruptly forked as it neared the two identical brick porches. Scott mounted his own little brick platform and rested his briefcase on the never-used wood bench that directly faced an identical bench on the Holcombs' platform. Twice he ran his hand down into the metal mailbox, although he was sure that Judith would have taken in the afternoon mail.

He stood for a moment, well aware that he was postponing the time of knowing whether the letter had come or not. A second-story window in the Summit caught the sun and sent it back into his eyes. He squinted and looked the other way, seeing the homes farther down the Heights, homes more spacious than his, not faculty houses. He couldn't afford to rent one of them; besides, none was for rent. And there was nothing down in the town worth renting. He certainly wasn't going to *buy* in Riverville! Two more years at most, and he'd be moving eastward. Until then, he and Judith would have to put up with the Holcombs. . . .

He jumped when Judith suddenly opened the door. "Aren't you ever coming in, Professor Scott?"

"Naturally," he said shortly. Couldn't a man stand on his own front porch without . . .? But once in the narrow hall, he instinctively sought her eyes to be assured that he was home again. Even in the gloom of the unwindowed hall, he saw their deep blueness, that unexpected light under the near-black hair and lashes which still in this familiar act of daily homecoming never failed to surprise him. Her eyes were almost on a level with his, and he had hardly to lower his head to kiss her.

"Darling," she said, turning him around and pointing to the hall stand, "the letter from Ritson Publishers! It's here!"

He hadn't wanted it announced that way. "Swell," he said. He picked up the long thin envelope, flapping it casually against his other hand. Walking into the living room for a better light, he carefully read his own name and address. He could feel Judith waiting.

"Let's drink to it, good or bad news." He made his voice bright. "Fix us drinks, will you, Judith?"

"But I want . . . Well, all right." Her voice was not reproachful.

When he heard her in the kitchen emptying the ice-cube tray, he tore open the envelope. He read deliberately, his heartbeat mounting with each word. The first two paragraphs of praise took him up the hill of hope. Then came the gradual descent. The manuscript was excellent, but. . . . There were five *but's,* all signifying that publication was at present out of the question. He went limp and cold inside, but he reread the letter, this time with a foreign objective interest. Who is this persisting fool Owen Scott? Well, we can afford to be patient; let us be neatly polite to him, urbanely encouraging.

When Judith came back, the letter was out of sight. She handed him his Old Fashioned, reading his face. "I'm sorry," she said.

That was all she said about it, and that was just right. He began to feel better. After all, it had been exactly what he had expected, and now the worst was over. He lighted Judith a cigarette and one for himself. With their drinks and cigarettes, they sat on the low blue couch, their bodies touching.

A sense of well-being slowly seeped in through his limpness. The room was satisfying. Judith had made it pale yellow and gray and blue. She had worked a miracle with a large plain mirror so hung as to give an illusion of spacious width. Beyond, he could see the blond dining table already laid for dinner. It would be a good dinner, attractively served. His home was smart, modern, comfortable. Like Judith herself. The drink was beginning to cut through the coldness, helping him to feel sorry for himself.

"Judith, there's a chance that this manuscript will never be in print; so I want to tell you about the dedication that I had planned. . . ."

"Of course it will be printed!" she said.

He knew that her words were no more than an automatic response to his, but he absorbed them eagerly and sought for more. "No. Damn it, Judith, that writing represents my best! If they don't want *that*, well . . ." He shrugged.

Judith tucked her hand through his arm. "We've been wrong somehow, darling. We'll go over it sentence by sentence, making sure that every thought is crystal clear. You'll revise and revise, I'll type it again, and then . . ."

The human warmth of her felt good to him. His body listened even while his mind rejected. He set down his emptied glass and leaned his head against the soft back of the couch. Judith's voice was lulling, and he grew drowsy, until into his awareness came another sound, muffled but disturbing, like the buzz of an unseen bee.

He stiffened as he identified the sound from the Holcombs'. "Good God! why does she have to vacuum at this time of day?"

Judith laughed tolerantly. "Out-of-town company in the morning."

"Company! Any *children?*"

"Two, darling. Do you have good courses for next Fall?"

"*Two!* I tell you, Judith . . ."

"I'm sure they won't be the noisy type. Tell me about the courses. Did you have any trouble with Cornthwaite? Did you get the new Novel course?"

"Judith, let's get away from here. I can't live through another baseball season! I tell you, if I hear another baseball game from *his* radio . . ."

"Now, don't work yourself up! They're not *that* bad. And we should be grateful that they never complain about our typing late."

17

"*He* doesn't have to do his own typing." He groaned. "*Two!* For how long?"

"Oh, I don't know. Come on, tell me something. Did you choose the new person?"

He nodded. "Now she's banging dishes!"

"Man or woman?"

"Woman."

"Oh. What's she like?"

He shrugged. Then the memory of the photograph flashed into his mind. Instinctively he sought to conceal it from Judith. "The usual type, I guess. You know. Name's Marcia Anderson."

Judith saw her: intelligent, a little severe, beautifully plain. She saw herself being friendly to this Marcia Anderson who didn't have Assistant Professor Owen Scott for a husband. "We'll have her to dinner as soon as she comes—" She broke off with a little laugh.

"What's funny?" He didn't really care, but he didn't want her voice to stop.

"You might be embarrassed. *It* will show a little by then, you know."

"Show?" His tired mind struggled. Suddenly he sat up straight. "Judith, you don't mean—"

"Yes." She didn't turn to look at him.

"How wonderful," he said to give himself time to decide how he really felt.

She caught the flatness of his tone. "It's a first publication, darling, and I dedicate it to you." Her words ran together. She reached desperately for a cigarette.

He suddenly felt conventional alarm. "Should you smoke? And drink?"

"Tonight's special. Or so I thought."

He saw her hand tremble. He caught it under his own, gently taking the cigarette from her. "It's truly wonderful," he said, putting feeling into the words. She stayed tense for a moment, and then relaxed against his shoulder.

He held her tightly, cursing himself. Why couldn't he feel the unqualified happiness that he had always supposed he would feel at this moment? But now all he could think were the wrong things: Judith losing her beautiful slenderness, then her pain, then the hospital and the bills, and finally the inevitable wailing when he was trying to study or write. It wasn't that he didn't want a child, he told himself; he just wasn't ready for one now. But when would he be, if not after five years of marriage? He gave it up; his mind wouldn't work straight.

"We'll not have to revise this manuscript," Judith whispered.

He wished she'd be done with that silly analogy. All right, so she could produce something more acceptable than he. . . .

Hell, I'm a cad, he thought.

He bent his head down against her breast. She drew her fingers

18

through his hair the way he liked. After a minute, she said, "Darling, I have to look at the things in the oven."

His fingers tightened on her arm. "Don't go, Judith. This is the only thing in the whole world that's right, just now." He did not try to explain his fierce desire to stifle the flow of time, to stop it at this moment.

She forced herself to sit still. Her mind agonized over the sweet potatoes growing soggy in their burnt jackets, the milk evaporating from the baking ham, the salad wilting in the iceless. For herself, it didn't matter. She could have fun over a spoiled dinner, especially one spoiled for a good reason. But Owen was different. He would forget the reason with the first taste of soggy potato. She clenched her free hand against her desire to rush to the kitchen. . . .

Together they heard the Holcombs' door open and shut. He's home, they thought. The Holcombs' radio snapped on. He's getting the news, they thought. Against their will, they strained to listen to the indistinct and tinny voice.

"There's a lot of static," Judith said. "It must be going to storm."

The voice was abruptly snapped off. He has been called to dinner, they knew. To Judith, these familiar sounds tolled the time with cruel significance. It isn't fair, it isn't fair, she thought wildly; I had it all planned to the minute; I couldn't know that he would want this.

But she sat still, now and then touching his hair. At last he grew heavier against her, and she knew that he was asleep. Carefully she got up and placed a pillow under his head. Then she ran to the kitchen to see what she could do.

The bundle of sticks that Kimball Duncan carried was his portable easel. He set it up on the bank where the Tuscarawas River turned to meander away from Riverville. He shoved the leg pins into the soft earth so that the easel stood firm. His paint box already was open upon a large flat stone which months ago he had dragged there for this purpose. From a groove in the lid of the box, he pulled out one of the three 12" x 16" canvas boards. The mere sight of the blank canvas vitalized his mind and body, and from then on, he worked with a rhythm foreign to his movements at other times.

Quickly he clamped the canvas to the easel. From still another groove, he drew out a light wood palette, delicately stained with colors long since used. To this he attached two tin cups, the one filled with linseed oil and the other with turpentine. Now he stood over the box, deciding what colors to mix. This was the part he loved best. His fingers moved sensitively over the three rows of tubes, as if counting them. It was a very complete array of colors. Unnecessarily complete, he knew; but the love of color had tainted his soul. He bought well over the margin of what he needed, and he often chose exotic colors and imported brands that even he was sure he would never use.

Today he worked solely with the earth colors, for he was striving to reproduce a small portion of the river that flowed by the bank across from him. He wanted to re-create the water's muddy opaqueness, its eternal motion and its eternal sameness. He would put in it too a part of the lush willow whose snake-like roots slithered down to the very edge of the water. He knew that if he were successful he would create a picture at which people would look and feel with Heraclitus, who had arrived at a whole philosophy by merely observing that the river into which he stepped today was of different waters from those that swirled around his legs yesterday. Or perhaps they would feel with the people of Riverville, who said, "Here is an unnavigable river. What can we do about it?" No answer had been found. It is costly to make a river disappear. So now he was intrigued by the river's complacent way of continuing its existence in the face of such uselessness.

But he put aside these thoughts as he worked, knowing that if they controlled his mind they would also control his brush and mar his work. He sought to become that moving useless river. For a long while he stood motionless and stared at the water and the giant willow, but he did not immediately see and feel clearly. His mind refused to submit. Unbidden, it pictured the girl Carol Leeds. It cast her image in the water, then on the bank, and finally she stood suggestively against the tree trunk

He blinked hard and fast, and tried again. Now he smoked, but impatiently tossed the cigarette away before it was half gone. He stripped off his wristwatch and tucked it into the paint box. He wanted no mechanical indicator of time, which for him at this moment must stop. When at last he was enabled to enter into the spirit of the water and of the tree, he turned to his canvas and worked feverishly, and the great inarticulate level of his being became finally an integral part of himself.

The rising wind brought him out of his absorption. The easel swayed; his hand lost its sureness of touch. He thought of van Gogh painting against the mistral, and worked doggedly on. But the spell was broken. At last he freed his canvas and slid it back into its groove in the paint box lid. Packed up, he climbed the short steep cliff to the Heights. There he stood for a moment, slowly returning to watchtime, man-time. When he moved on up the Heights, his walk was again jerky, uncontrolled.

Nearing the top of the hill, he sought the Scotts' house. Through the front window he could see a light in a back room, perhaps the dining room. He slowed down, thinking that it might be pleasant to tap lightly on the door. ("Hi, Scott. Good evening, Mrs. Scott. Just dropped in for a minute. . . . Oh, no, thanks, don't bother about a drink. . . .") Someone inside walked across the front room, abruptly blocking out the light. He hurried on.

He skirted the President's home, which sprawled before the tip of the Heart. Instinctively he tiptoed and bent his head as he went by the well-known study windows. There was always the danger of being seen and stopped with: "Well, Young Man, how is it with you and the Profession?" Teaching was to President Cameron the Great Profession, and Kim was sure that the inadequacy of his replies to the periodic inquisitions must by now be painfully apparent.

He cut across the Heart and went around the left side of the Summit. He was awed to see the light in Cornthwaite's office. The woman was evidently indefatigable. On the second floor was another light. That would be Professor Webb's, and this light did not surprise him. The Professor's great philosophical work-in-progress was college tradition, although no one had so much as seen the manuscript. He had been told how for years Professor Webb, when asked about his treatise, would merely shake his head sadly.

Gravel crunched loudly under his feet as he passed the small, quiet chapel, blue-white in the dusk. The big slab of gray stone that was MacMillan Hall, men's dormitory, loomed ahead of him. Two lighted windows on its top floor made him think of leering yellow eyes. For a moment he closed his own against them. He hated the ugly heaviness of this building as much as he loved the grace of the Summit.

More than that, he feared it. He did not find it hard to pretend that it was an evil monster whose jaws snapped him out of freedom.

The trouble was, he admitted as he went up the steps and shoved open the mammoth door, no jaws snatched him; for he entered this big, barren hall of his own free will. He walked out of it every day, but he also walked right back into it.

He was glad that no one was in sight, and went quickly up the wide, rubber-padded steps. Safely in his room, he locked the door and tenderly deposited the easel and paint box in a corner. The wet canvas he set on a straight chair. Then he wondered what to do.

The mirror attracted him. He stood before it and studied himself. His face was always a mystery to him. He fingered it gently, as if to block it out for drawing. But that told him nothing.

Was he a hypocrite? He left the mirror and paced over to the window. A drizzling rain had commenced. He hoped it would work itself up into a savage storm. He turned his back on the window and sat down on the edge of the bed.

The meeting that afternoon. He thought of himself throughout it —his docility, his submissiveness, his fears of the people—and he sneered at himself. Then he thought of his eagerness, his awkward and futile attempts to attach himself. He thought of Grant's self-sufficiency, of Scott's cozily lighted house. . . . The sneer faded. He felt sorry for Kimball Duncan.

For two years he had been a willing shadow, but now the willingness was gone and he felt stifled. Soon he'd . . .

He thought suddenly of the Modern Novel course. That was it! By

God, he'd show them how he could teach literature. He'd prove . . .

He rushed to his writing table, pulled a sheet of paper to him, and wrote:

Modern (Contemporary?) Novel Course
American (and European?) Novels

Then he was stuck. He struggled hard with ideas for ten minutes, but when he was ready to make a note he discovered that he had filled the paper with pen marks that looked suspiciously like the brush stroke with which he had mastered the motion of the river only this afternoon. He threw down the pen in disgust, and a bubble of the black ink appeared on the point. This he cleaned off with the paper, which he then crumpled and dropped into his wastebasket.

He drew out fresh paper and again used his pen, but this time to write his own kind of language. Rapidly he outlined what he had memorized at the English meeting, unfalteringly depicting the essential structure of Marcia Anderson's face. To him, contour was no more than a surface shape made by what lay beneath it, and so it was that in studying the photograph he had allowed the highlights and shadows to lead him to the seven bones that shape the face. He had done this as instinctively as Grant would winnow fancy from facts, as Scott would separate motive from deed, as Cornthwaite would divide footnotes from text. While the others had been hindered by the reduction of the face to the simple pattern of black and white planes, he had caught beneath it the set line of the lower jaw-bone and the prominence of the cheek-bone as it arched back to the ear.

As he worked with the black ink, he unconsciously endowed it with color. He was not deceived by the shadowed eyes. He deemed them lighter in color than they showed, perhaps of a transparent ochre that deepened and lightened with emotions. He knew too that the hair would not have the flat darkness of the photograph. It could have in it the red of gold ochre and burnt sienna when mixed direct on a white grain canvas, the red of fresh coffee caught up in a spoon under light.

The nose was one of the twelve types classified by his da Vinci: thin in the middle, with high narrow, but slightly flaring, nostrils. With his pen he shaded in the two slight furrows from the wings of the nose to the angle of the mouth. As the lips were unsmiling, these lines were almost straight, thus giving the face its appearance of melancholy. He knew, however, that when the lips moved, so would the lines; hence it would be a face subject to many changes of expression.

He looked at his work with dissatisfaction. It was a difficult face to reconstruct, even from a photograph, for it was made of contradictions. He saw that essentially it was a face made mobile and flexible for the expression of moods. It was softness and hardness, fire and snow. He threw the sketch into the wastebasket.

But a sudden thought made him pick it out and study it again. It was, he had discovered, a face not unlike his own. His was longer and narrower, and the coloring would be different, but the expressions were similar. . . .

Perhaps Marcia Anderson would be someone to whom he could talk.

Carefully he put the sketch away and, whistling softly, went to the bookshelf over his bed and took down a volume, *The Journal of a Young Artist.* He was feeling better. He propped himself up on the bed and leafed through the book, reading a paragraph. here and there. Over one entry he nodded somberly and reread it aloud: *True artists can never be happy; they are conscious, in the first place, that the majority of people do not understand them. . . .*

Marie Bashkirtseff understood almost as well as he; at times she might be he talking to himself. But he never failed to find something new in her *Journal,* something to which he had been blind in an earlier reading. Idly he turned back a page and read; then he frowned and tried to ignore the passage, but the words were already a part of his memory, as if his mind had served as target for a game of darts: *Have I really any talent for, or shall I really ever be anything in Art? What is my unbiased opinion concerning myself?*

These are terrible questions. . . .

He slammed the book shut and tossed it down to the foot of the bed. What did Marie Bashkirtseff know about anything?

He heaved himself off the bed and got a cigarette. When he inhaled, his stomach growled. He was hungry.

The rain was pounding now. He snapped off the light and saw slanting rows of silver beads slung across the black window. He opened the window wide. Rain splashed on the sill and sprayed his hand.

He stared over the gleaming roof of the chapel into the dark, dripping campus. Cool air stirred, but there was no wind. It was not a real storm. There was no fury, no majesty; only monotonous rain.

Chapter Three

WHEN Paul Lewis Grant left President Cameron and Dean Holcomb, he was determined to make the rest of the evening his own. The meeting had, he supposed, been a success. Cameron had been appreciative of Marcia Anderson's record, and Holcomb had given an academic whistle when he saw the photograph—a reaction which had so irritated Grant that he had said shortly and without truth, "She doesn't look like that." Cameron had promised to present the matter to the trustees the very next day, Saturday afternoon.

"So soon?" Grant had asked. "I thought they were to meet *next* Saturday."

"They were." Cameron had looked apologetic. "But Mr. MacMillan has to be in New York then."

Now remembering· this scene, Grant again felt annoyance. He wasn't sure that Cameron could give Marcia Anderson's papers time enough tonight to present a good case the next day. Besides, he was tired of helping the college revolve around the activity of John Willard MacMillan.

In fact, he was tired of many things, he decided: tired of Marcia Anderson as recorded on paper and in the photograph, tired of the very appearance of the Heart surrounded by the college buildings, tired of everything that remotely suggested John Willard College.

Deliberately he had not stopped by Cornthwaite's office, although he felt that she was there, perhaps even waiting for him. He was willing to be her Good Man up to a certain point; after that, he . . .

But the next moment he was amused over his own petulance. He had true reverence for E. Cornthwaite, as he had understanding of their relationship. Quite simply, he was her ears, and when he wasn't depressed by end-of-the-year tiredness, he was amused by her strategy of pretending to be bored by all interviews and therefore delegating them to him.

End-of-the-year tiredness. He was glad to have identified his mood, and now he walked under it as if it were a thing apart from him. A few good hours writing the new Melville chapter, and it would be gone from him. First, however, his own cooked supper of bacon and eggs.

Before he reached the bottom of the hill, he turned sharply to the right, taking the steep path that was the short cut between the Heights and the town proper. This brought him into the part of Riverville that had been laid out to accommodate John Willard College before the Willards decided that a better site was the broad level top of Willard Hill. The streets here were short and closely filled with square frame houses of a drab gray from want of fresh paint. In a front window of almost every house was a sign inviting roomers or boarders. The roomers were railroaders who worked in and out of the Riverville Shops; the boarders were employees of the John Willard Tractor Company.

Grant was the only faculty member living in this neighborhood. He felt mildly defiant about this, and was prepared to answer all queries with a firm statement that his choice of residence was strictly his own affair. However, no one had ever asked him about it.

He turned off Academic Avenue to his own street, College Row. His rooms were in Millicent Winters' house, fifth from the corner. Besides himself, she kept four roomers, transient railroaders. He alone had two rooms. He even had a small iceless and an electric plate, installed at his own expense, so that he could have his ale on hand and

24

cook simple meals when he wanted to eat in and alone, as usually he did. Millie didn't mind about these arrangements. That was the great thing about Millie—she didn't mind about anything, and was a friend to all the world, and more than friend to various of her roomers, so gossip had it.

Drawn up before the house was a long, low-slung roadster, too big and expensive-looking for the street. Millie evidently had company, and he let himself into the hall quietly, hoping to escape to his room unseen. But Millie appeared almost immediately, posing effectively against the thick, fringed drapes between the hall and parlor. "Oh, so you're home," she said, her voice made intriguingly husky for the benefit of the owner of the roadster. With an air of elegance, she touched her smooth, low-knotted hair that was carefully kept a shade too golden to be true. "We've been waiting—"

But her scene was cut short, for someone on the other side of the drapes called out bluntly: "Hey! Is that Paul?" The speaker followed his words with a hearty thrust at the drapes that jostled Millie out of her pose. She was annoyed, but managed a polite smile for the sake of Professor Grant, who was her favorite, although most remote, roomer.

"Matt," Grant said, shaking his brother's hand. His voice sounded flat to his own ears, and he put enthusiasm into it. "Good to see you."

Matt winked as Millie drifted away. "Been hearing about the late Mr. Winters, Dentist. Watch out, Paul. I think she's ready to supplant his fond memory."

Grant laughed. "Thanks, but I'm holding my own." He rested his briefcase against the stairs, again aware of his heavy tiredness.

"Well, it must cost you some effort, that's all I got to say." Matt lighted a cigarette with not quite steady hands, eyeing his brother critically over the flame. "You look done-in. Let's go eat and pep you up. Come on—come *on!*"

"All right," Grant said, but made no move. Matt's impatience set him obstinately against hurrying. He watched him unthinkingly drop the dead match on Millie's carpet, and pace about the small room, seeming suddenly bored with being there. He was a tall man whose clothes hung loosely on him as if he had recently lost weight. "All right," Grant said again, "but what's the rush? You're not starting back to Chicago tonight."

Matt laughed grimly. "Like hell I'm not. I've got to make time. That's the way *my* job is. I don't just sit on my fanny, y'know, and grade papers."

"Yes, you've said that before. Well, come up with me while I change and I'll give you a bottle of ale. Then we'll go eat."

"*Now* you're talking!" Matt swooped down upon the briefcase and thrust it into Grant's arms. "For a minute there, I thought you were going to cold-shoulder me."

Grant was mildly surprised. Matt's concern seemed genuine, and he was sure that it did not spring from brotherly affection. "We'll go eat," he said suddenly, "on the condition that there's no talk of Oaklands."

"*Oaklands!*" Matt cried innocently. "Why, I've got nothing to say about Oaklands. I came to talk to you about Janice!"

In the roadster they drove the ten miles up Canal Road, passing through the Quiet Zone of Willard Memorial Hospital and then by the airport, where the yellow passenger planes looked like toys on the rolling stretch of land against the somber evening sky.

They parked easily in the allotted space at the side of Riverside Inn, there being only a half-dozen cars besides theirs. The Inn flourished for its drink and transient dance orchestras, not its food. Later the parking space would be jammed, but Grant fervently hoped they would be well away by then.

"Come on," said Matt, spotting the bar as they entered the large square room with its rows of tables flanking the dance floor. "A quick one before meals, that's what the doctor ordered."

He had three quick ones, while Grant nursed along his whiskey and soda. "What about Janice, Matt?"

Matt beamed. "She sends her love to her old Uncle Paul!"

"Is that what you came to tell me?"

"Never miss a trick, do you?" Matt cried admiringly. "It's this way. Janice graduates from high school this June, and Helen and I have decided to send her to John Willard so you can keep an eye on her. We thought . . ."

Grant listened uneasily. He knew his niece only well enough to be sure that she wouldn't appreciate his or anyone else's guardianship. "College is an impersonal place," he said cautiously when he saw that Matt was waiting for some kind of answer. "My being her uncle couldn't—" He stopped as Matt frowned and looked sullen. "All I mean, Matt," he went on, shrugging, "is that I could keep only a *casual* eye upon her."

"What the hell!" Matt said generously, his sullenness gone. "That's just what we want. Helen will sure be glad to have that settled. Nothing's too good for Janice, that's all I've got to say." He snapped his fingers to order new drinks, and then put his hand heavily on Grant's shoulder. "You're the kind of brother every man should have."

Grant moved slightly. "How's Helen?"

"Helen? She's oke, I guess. I don't—we don't . . . I'm on the road a lot, and then when I'm home, she has her clubs and things." Matt reached out for his new drink and drained the glass. "Say, Paul, why is it?" He leaned toward Grant. Beads of sweat stood out on his forehead and nose, and his eyes were red-veined. His whole face puckered as if he were about to cry. "What has happened—to Helen and me, I mean? I can remember when we . . . D'ya know what I mean, Paul?"

26

Grant checked an impulse to look away from the maudlin self-pity he saw. And yet he was moved by his question, sensing that it had welled up from a depth of consciousness of which Matt himself was unaware. "Nothing has happened," he said finally, knowing that it didn't matter how he answered. "Or if something has, it probably happens to any two people who live together for twenty years."

Matt nodded, glumly satisfied. It was Grant himself who protested his own glib answer. He'd stake his life on the supposition that there were people fundamentally different from Matt and Helen, inhabiting a world fundamentally different from theirs. "Let's find a table," he said abruptly.

They ate without talk. The hot food sobered Matt, and when he did speak over coffee, his voice was harsh and defiant, as if he were determined that the moment at the bar be forgotten. "We could afford to send Janice *any*place, you know."

Grant laughed. "Why not send her *any*place, then?"

Matt ignored this. "She's literary, like you. That's why we decided she ought to be near you." He took a cigarette from his flat silver case and put it in the corner of his mouth, where it dangled unlighted while he talked. "She's goddam smart and ritzy about it. She reads and scribbles and won't talk. She's—well, she's queer."

Grant said nothing to this. Matt's angry thrusts seemed pathetic, and he was willing to humor him. "You must be doing very well, Matt. That's an elegant car."

Matt shrugged, but something of the old shrewdness was back in his eyes. "I'm doing all right, I guess. Did I tell you how J.W. took to my idea of extending the advertising through the East? I have to run up to New York next week, and J.W. himself will be there until we get the thing organized. We'll have a placard in every subway before *I'm* through!"

Grant was puzzled. "But how can you hope to sell tractors to New Yorkers?"

Matt hooted. "Who said anything about *selling* tractors in New York? That's a college professor for you! Listen"—he leaned forward, serious now—"the object is to get the name of the product before the eyes of the public, into the mind of the public, into the *subconscious* of the public!" Then he slumped back in his chair and pretended to watch the people who were now filling the room. He needed time to think.

The Janice proposition had almost fallen flat. Paul hadn't seemed pleased to know they were willing to send her to John Willard. "It'll make him feel more like Family," he had told Helen, "and soften him up on Oaklands."

Oaklands still ran in his mind like a theme that wouldn't go away. He saw Oaklands, not as it was, but as he would someday make it.

The large, gracious white house, always newly painted, the terraced grounds, the endless rose garden. . . . J.W. had acres and acres of roses. J.W. was a big man. Matt Grant was still small fry. Still, but not for always.

Oaklands was the place to start. The house in Chicago didn't count. That was for living. Oaklands was extra. After Oaklands . . .

He scraped back his chair and turned to see what had caused the new stirring in the room. White-coated men were taking places on the orchestra stand. They tuned up and swung into a number. Couples left tables and squeezed into the small plot of dance floor.

There was a woman in blue across the floor from them, and she disappointed him by not getting up to dance. On the floor there was no one worth— And then he saw the girl in brown. He hated brown on women, but she did something to it. Maybe it was her hair, copper-like. Or the long-legged body under the close brown crêpe. She was dancing with a big dark fellow, Latin type, who held her the way he'd hold her himself if he had the chance. . . .

He jerked his mind away from her and got busy lighting a cigarette. Remember Oaklands! He caught his brother's eyes and smiled genially. "Know what I've been sitting here thinking? About how sometimes I feel guilty because right off the bat J.W. named me a salary that was probably twice the size of yours, when, after all, it was through you I got the job as his advertising manager. What I mean is, well, wouldn't it help if I bought out your share in Oaklands? I'd give—"

"You've broken the condition, Matthew!"

Matt squashed out his cigarette, frowning. "Be serious. I'll give you a big price. Far more than it's worth. Your kind of job will never bring you that kind of money in a lump sum. Besides, you'd have no more bother—no taxes, no investments, no nothing!"

Grant seemed amused. "Tell me once and for all why you're so dead set on becoming sole owner of the place."

"Why"—Matt spread his hands—"it's the old homestead—where I was born."

"Where I was born too."

"But you won't invest in it! Not that I blame you, for I know that you can't do much of that sort of thing on your salary. That's just the point!" He leaned forward and spoke urgently. "This is your chance to save Oaklands. Don't you see that, Paul? Sell out to me and I'll not stop at anything to make it one swell place." He raised his right hand. "I promise—I swear it!"

"Put your hand down, Matt. The waiter thinks you want him."

Matt sucked in his cheeks. "Cut the comedy, Paul. You can't laugh yourself out of everything."

"I'm not laughing inside," Grant said. "Oaklands was once a good farm, something real—even before you gave it that fancy name. Then

28

you hired tenant farmers who don't care what happens to the place, played the lordly role of absentee—"

"Paul!" Matt looked hurt. "I took on responsibility, that's all. You weren't interested in keeping up the place, and so I—"

"Keeping it up! Making it a show place, you mean. You build a summerhouse while the soil grows barren, and there's a blight on half the trees. If you have this great desire to invest, why don't you—" He broke off what he was saying, disgusted over his rising temper. Why did Matt and Oaklands set him off so easily? What did it matter? Why didn't he sell out and be rid of the problem? The anger went out of him, but he still felt stubborn. "Let's both sell out—to an honest-to-God farmer."

"Not on your life," Matt said shortly, and dropped the topic. But he wasn't discouraged. Paul wouldn't hold out forever, and he'd see more of him with Janice in Riverville.

Business over, he didn't know what to say to Paul. He turned to watch the dancers, hoping to find the girl in brown. He did. She was standing near him, waiting with the other dancers for the orchestra to begin a new number. A waltz started, and the dark fellow grabbed her to him. They danced like pros. Just then the dark fellow swung her around, and Matt saw her full-faced, for she moved her head slightly and looked straight at him, as if she had felt his eyes on her. A thrill or a chill ran up his spine. He wasn't sure which it was, because there was something creepy about the way her eyes had covered him from head to foot without a change of expression on her face.

He tried to catch her eye again, but she was no longer interested. He turned to his brother to make a crack about Riverville women, but saw that he was watching too, and this tickled him. "Not that one. Take it from old Graybeard. She's dynamite."

Grant gave him a look of quick interest. "What makes you say that?"

Matt wasn't sure what had made him say it; so he laughed loudly. "You forget *her*. Now, if you're feeling that way, there's one across the room—the one in blue—who's more your type. The only trouble is, she looks taken."

Grant looked and grinned. "She is. That's Mrs. Scott."

"I knew it," Matt said glumly. "And I suppose that collar-ad beside her is Mr. Scott. So you know them?"

"He's a colleague."

"Well, then! Let's join them."

Grant hesitated, thinking the Scotts appeared quite satisfied with only one another's company. But at that moment Scott saw him and waved with such friendliness that he changed his mind. Nothing could be worse than to go on talking with Matt about Oaklands, and probably Matt was equally eager for release.

They started across the now vacant floor. Hot, bright lights had come on while the orchestra had intermission, but the room was hazy with smoke clouds. Grant watched for Carol Leeds when Matt wasn't looking. He found her at a table back of the Scotts'. She was staring at her escort with the same devouring look that he had seen her give Matt. He was more disturbed by the strangeness of that look than he was by the fact that according to campus regulations she was out-of-bounds.

Scott was standing with outstretched hand. He was truly delighted to see Grant, for this meant that he wasn't home grinding out another aricle.

Grant introduced Matt, who immediately wanted to order a round of drinks.

"Oh, no, thanks," said Judith Scott, pointing to the bottle of champagne that was already on the table, snugly tucked into its bucket of ice. "You must join *us*."

They declined the champagne, but Matt pulled over two chairs from another table. "I hear," he said with a wink, "that we're brothers-in-work."

Scott's eyebrows went up in reappraisement of Matt, whose appearance had first suggested to him moneyed success and the go-getter. "You're joining our faculty?" he asked, politely keeping incredulity out of his voice.

Matt slapped his knee. "That's a good one! Oh, how my brother will love that one! No, I'm the little cog in a big wheel. I simply promote tractors."

"He's being modest," Grant said, seeing Scott and Judith look puzzled. "He's J. W. MacMillan's advertising manager."

Scott was impressed. J.W. was a big man, and his advertising manager would be no small one. He was impressed enough to feel proud when he noted the way Matt kept looking at Judith.

"Would you care to dance, Mrs. Scott?" Matt asked finally, although he felt only a little excitement at the prospect. True, her surprising eyes alone made his heart thump, but he sensed that tonight at least she was Scott's in every feeling and thought.

"Thank you, but no. . . ." Judith involuntarily reached out her hand to Scott.

Grant saw the gesture and felt like a clumsy intruder. To his surprise, he had little trouble in giving Matt the hint that they should go. As they they stood up, he glanced again in Carol Leeds' direction. She had been watching their table, and her eyes met his, but his impulse to nod or raise his hand was stifled because there wasn't even a flicker of recognition in her expression. It was as if she had never seen him before, let alone sat in his class that very morning and listened, or pretended to listen, to his lecture on Ralph Waldo Emerson.

Grant awoke Saturday morning with the unpleasant feeling that last night lay crumpled in the wastebasket. With deliberateness he fixed and ate a bacon-and-egg breakfast. At least he would have his bacon and eggs, although postponed. It was, he told himself, a new day.

The morning was bright and rain-washed. He wanted to linger in it, but forced himself to hurry. With a certain sense of guilt he recalled not stopping to report to Esther Cornthwaite. She had a right to expect him early today.

When he reached the Heart, he took the border walk, for the ground was still soggy from the rain. Students lounged around the steps and stone pillars of Science Hall, this being intermission time for the labs, the only classes held on Saturdays.

Among them he spied Carol Leeds, and was relieved. At least she was safely back in school routine. She was sitting on a raincoat that had been thrown over a step for her. He deduced that the raincoat belonged to David Whitney, who stood over her, a bovine expression of worship on his usually intelligent face.

Carol looked bored. But she also looked very young and harmless, quite different from the way he remembered her at the Inn. He felt, however, that the difference was no more than an illusion created by the tweed suit and the clear sunlight.

He was somehow shocked to see her with Whitney. What did she want with John Willard's model English major?

Professor Cornthwaite listened affably to his brief report upon his meeting with Cameron and Holcomb concerning Marcia Anderson. On his way out, she handed him a letter to post; and that was the only sign that she was slightly piqued by his not having come to her office immediately after the conference.

He placed the letter tenderly in the mail basket, and going up the broad winding stairs, he amused himself by imagining, word for word, the politic message being sent to Etta Wilson.

The second floor was quiet, almost hushed. Dean Haskins had closed her door against the world for a Farewell Conference with a Senior Woman, and across the hall Dean Holcomb was for the same reason closeted with a Senior Man.

Grant's office was the first of the three small square rooms that branched off the main hall. As he pushed his key into the lock, he noted that the office next to his was closed and silent. That did not mean, however, that Professor Webb was absent from it. Professor Webb was always in his office, although no one ever saw him enter it or heard evidence of his being there.

From the farthest room came the clear smooth tones of Medora Day as she dictated to Miss March. He stood listening for a moment, envying the even flow of the dictation. He wondered if Dr. Day's being a psychologist had anything to do with her fluency and lack of inhibition before a secretary.

Before he had his door open his telephone was ringing, but the sound didn't hurry him. He was too used to it. As E. Cornthwaite would not tolerate a telephone in her office, his had become the official extension of the English department. He threw his briefcase down on the already paper-laden desk and flung open the wooden shutters to the one window in the room. This opening did not admit much daylight, for it was choked by the thick branches of the huge elm that had stood guard over the Summit all its life. Between the branches he could see patches of cerulean sky.

Then he reached for the phone and listened resignedly as the Director of Admissions asked him please to proofread the English course-descriptions for the new catalogue. "I hate to bother Professor Corn—well, you know how it is. And we *do* go to press on Monday!" The voice carried a tremolo of hysteria.

"Of course, Cunningham," Grant said soothingly, although he couldn't help glancing at the stacks of papers waiting to be graded. "Hold tight until I get there."

Before he left his office, he searched his desk for the scraps of yellow paper on which he wrote memos to himself. He found two bearing the day's date, and he stared at them with a sense of defeat. It was as he had feared—two meetings that afternoon, one for the *Gazette* and one for the Scholarship Committee.

He shrugged. The papers would have to be done at night. Melville would have to wait. . . .

Melville was always waiting for the summer. And this summer, if he didn't coddle himself with the idea that he needed a rest, and if he could make himself stay in New York libraries during the hottest season, perhaps he'd make enough progress to justify his asking for a leave of absence in which to finish his book.

Downstairs, Arnold Cunningham had taken over the long registration room which ran the width of the building. Grant noted with amusement that he had also captured all available secretaries.

"Here!" Cunningham thrust a sheaf of typed material into his hands. "Sit right here—no! not there. Those papers lying there must *not* be disturbed. Oh, Miss Schroeder, are you *sure* that President Cameron hasn't been in. . . ." He darted off, a slight man, his usually sleek dark hair rumpled, his shirt plastered against his back with sweat, although the day was not hot. His trim pin-striped coat hung over the back of a chair, and his fine calfskin briefcase lay open on a table, empty and deflated.

Grant read through the papers given him, corrected two small typing errors, and returned them to Cunningham.

"*Thank* you, Professor Grant! If only all were as conscientious as you! Professor Day has read hers, Professor Webb . . ." He looked his hopelessness. "We go to press on *Monday!* And Cameron! Every year he insists upon writing a new Our-Educational-Philosophy squib, and so of course he hasn't brought the newest one in yet. If he—" He broke off to glare at the Registrar, who had made an abrupt entrance.

Clayton Dexter was a tall, graying man with cool blue eyes that followed a dotted line to whatever concerned him at the moment. He did not greet Grant, not because he was unfriendly, but because his business at the moment did not concern greeting Grant.

"I should like my secretary, please!" he announced crisply.

Cunningham arched his back. "*If* you don't mind. . . ."

Because the oncoming battle did not concern him, Grant quietly withdrew.

Intending to eat in the Cafeteria, he turned into Main Hall, but stopped when he found Scott on the steps, smoking and looking at odds with the world. Ritson's letter of rejection was again nagging at his mind.

"How about lunch?" Grant asked. He hoped that Scott and Judith had not quarreled after their special celebrating the night before.

Scott didn't say yes or no, although he tossed away his cigarette. "But not in the Cafeteria. Too many students—too noisy."

They walked across the Heart in back of the President's home to the green and white Cottage, where, under the excellent supervision of Miss Schultz, noonday lunches were prepared and served by home economics majors to faculty and secretaries. When they were settled at one of the larger tables near the back of the cozy room, glasses of water and hand-written menus appeared before them with startling promptness, and Alice Mueller stood posed with pad and pencil, a graven image of Waitress Waiting for an Order. She wore a set smile and a worried frown, her open, freckled face beaded with sweat. Not only was this her first day at serving, but a mere look from Dr. Scott, whose Romantic Seminar I she was taking, rocked her heart and weakened her knees.

The men ordered, and Miss Mueller rushed away without having used her pad and pencil.

Scott was beginning to enjoy himself. Several weeks ago he had sensed Miss Mueller's malady and—well, after all, he was only human. He hoped that Grant had noticed it.

"Ritson rejected my manuscript," he said in an unusual burst of frankness.

Grant frowned sympathetically. "Too bad." Scott had never offered to show him his work, but he had a feeling that it was good—perhaps, however, too specialized to interest many publishers. "I wonder," he said, "if you'd like me to speak to Tudor. He's with the Academic Press, you know."

Scott didn't know and was interested, but he said shortly, "No, thanks." He had seen the ubiquitous Kim Duncan coming their way, and he had no desire to be caught by him receiving favors from Grant.

Kim was looking above and beyond them, in headlong flight for

33

some unseen table. Grant reached out and caught his coat. "Why not join us?"

Kim simulated great surprise. "If you're sure I'm not intruding. . . ."

Miss Mueller, arriving with Grant's order, was unhappy to see a newcomer. Impatiently she listened to his order, and was about to speed away again, when Scott said genially, "And don't forget *my* food, Miss Mueller."

She looked suddenly terrified, her mouth forming a silent O. Then she managed a whisper: "I've forgotten what you ordered, Dr. Scott."

Scott pleasantly repeated his order and chuckled when she had again disappeared. Grant and Kim were vaguely surprised at his good nature, and thought it quite decent of him to be so considerate over Miss Mueller's mistake.

Grant, the only one with food before him, was urged to eat, and by the time Miss Mueller had accomplished the serving of Scott and Kim, he was ready for dessert. She looked so desperate that he immediately relinquished the menu and refused dessert in any form. She returned to the model kitchen with a sense of salvation.

Kim put on a listening face as he ate his lunch without tasting it; but his mind was busy planning a verbal campaign which he meant to launch the moment the food was out of the way. He was determined not only to contribute to but to direct the after-lunch talk, and thereby not be left sitting as dumb as a stone.

The tables were now all filled. Dean Haskins appeared at the door and stared fixedly at a corner table occupied by a newspaper. Her look apparently bore through the paper, for Professor Colley suddenly emerged from behind it. He rose and beckoned to her.

She thanked him briefly and sat down, immediately studying the menu in an engrossed manner that was meant to sever the personal contact. But Colley stood above her, reading aloud a news item which provoked him to uproarious laughter. Miss Haskins was not amused. Colley subdued the laugh to a chuckle, but he still thought he had a good thing and stood surveying the room for a more appreciative audience.

Grant saw him start toward them and warned the others. Scott groaned. It's now or never, Kim thought, and shot forth his carefully planned question. "Dr. Scott, do you believe that the theory of the best-possible-world, such as expounded philosophically by Leibniz, more popularly by Pope, and satirically by Voltaire, actually influenced eighteenth-century life?"

Scott stared. He tested the question warily, suspecting a trap, a joke, a trick. "The answer rests," he said with guarded ambiguity, "upon that old, old problem. . . ." Both Grant and Kim were listening with what seemed to be genuine interest. He reached for a fresh cigarette and swiftly reviewed in his mind that portion of his rejected manuscript which illuminated the old, old problem. "Yes, that problem of what is the relation between *any* idea and what appears—"

But Colley had joined them, leaning down upon the table so that it tipped slightly. He thrust his newspaper into Grant's hands. "I want you to read that little item—that one right there—"

". . . beween any idea and what appears to be consequent action," Scott went on rapidly. "If we take, for example—" But he had to give it up, for Colley, as if sensing a contest, had put more power into his voice.

"You see, the point is that in Sociology II—just yesterday, mind you —Pete Wilson—you all know Pete Wilson—said exactly the same thing!" He straightened and laughed until his round, full face was red and shiny.

Grant read obediently, found nothing funny, but laughed and handed the paper across to Scott, who accepted it gingerly, read briefly, smiled thinly, and passed it on to Kim. Noting Kim's apathy, Colley started to explain again. "You see, the point is that in Sociology II . . ."

Grant looked idly over the room, telling himself that he should get back to his office. Then he grew interested in Iris Taylor, who stood in the doorway also looking over the room, apparently in search of someone. She seemed a slim boy in her slacks and v-necked blouse with the sleeves rolled above her elbows. Her thin, vital face was drawn with tiredness, and she was oblivious to the various people who looked up and waved or called out to her. That meant she was working on a play, and as Grant was sure it was Kim she wanted, he raised his hand. She spotted their table then and came directly toward it.

As she passed by him, Vincent Diaz arose quickly and gestured an invitation for her to share his table for two. She made no response, for she hadn't seen him. The Spanish teacher went back to his chair and his soup, but the back of his neck had turned pink.

"Kim," Iris said abruptly, shoving Colley aside, "there's something wrong with the forest set. Please come look at it."

Kim glared up at her, disgusted with this new interruption. He had a good Herman Melville question to spring on Grant whenever that nuisance Colley went away. "There's nothing wrong with that set. You must be using the wrong gelatins."

"No. I know more about lighting than you do. Somehow, Kim, you failed to get the right effect."

"Effect!" Kim looked dangerous. He had already forgotten about the Melville question. "So I don't know about effects! Oh, of course not. I only painted the thing. But *you*—"

"Sit down for a cup of tea, Iris," Grant said. "You look fagged."

Iris saw the others then for the first time. "Hello," she said absently. Her sea green eyes stayed on Colley, who stood by watching, a forced smile on his lips but a cold light in his pale eyes. "Did I edge you out? Sorry."

Colley stuck a hand in his pocket and jingled coins. "That's all right, little girl. You and your boy friend run along and play." He strolled away to a new table.

Iris screwed up her face. "Guess I hurt his feelings." She turned back to Kim. "Look. It's supposed to be a *thick* forest—luxuriant, gloomy with shade. And you've got exactly three trees. When I sensed something wrong, I counted them, and . . ."

"*Sensed!* Before you presume to judge Art, you had better develop a sense of illusion." Kim snorted. "I suppose you're going to have real birds hopping about on the stage. If you think"—he got up and kicked his chair back into place under the table—"you're going to make me betray my convictions to satisfy some muddle-headed Realists, you're very much . . ."

Amused, Grant watched them across the room, both arguing violently. Scott said, "What a pity Duncan can't manifest equal enthusiasm for English literature."

Grant moved uneasily, for the same thought had flashed through his own mind. But he had no desire to speak of it to Scott, whose tone had indicated that the presence of Kimball Duncan in the department was somehow impeding the progress of English literature. He laughed. "At least he seems to have developed a sudden interest in eighteenth-century literature."

Scott looked at him sharply and decided to say nothing. He still was suspicious of that absurd question. He glanced away and then was sorry he had done so, for Dean Holcomb stood in the doorway, and the sight of his neighbor filled him with bitter thoughts.

But Miss Schultz herself appeared to tell the dean how sorry she was that serving-time was over. Holcomb withdrew, looking sad.

Hah! thought Scott. That would teach him to invite company with two children.

Miss Schultz had remained to collect sugar bowls. At their table she suddenly bent low to look out the window, and announced, "President Cameron!"

"President Cameron" was echoed throughout the room, and many turned for a look. They saw his tall, spare figure move down the hedged driveway with dignity. Those who didn't like him thought grudgingly, well, he looks the part, even if . . . The trustees meeting was in everyone's mind—the meeting at which salary-increases and promotions would be discussed.

There goes the case of Marcia Anderson, Grant thought with relief.

Heads now turned in a new direction, for Professor Cornthwaite had progressed into the Cottage, unnoticed in the general concern for the President.

Belatedly Miss Schultz spied her. She squared her shoulders and went forward. "I'm *so* sorry, Professor Cornthwaite, but . . ."

"Splendid!" said Esther, and seated herself at an empty but uncleared table for four.

Chapter Four

JOHN Willard MacMillan stole a look at his wristwatch and saw that he should be getting home to dress for dinner, but one did not so simply take leave of the bookstore when Christian Deardorff was moved to talk.

"It was Esther Cornthwaite," said Deardorff, leaning across the small counter, the only space in the shop free from books and upon which he somehow managed to do all his book-wrapping, "yes, Esther Cornthwaite it was who said ten years ago—*ten* years ago, mind you— after she had returned from her summer visit to Europe, 'Mr. Deardorff,' she said, 'there is something ominous in those marching Italian children, no matter how blue the Italian sky and how bright the Italian sun.' "

J.W. nodded, wondering if he should have to leave without selecting a book. "I can believe it. Mother has always said that Esther is a woman with rare insight, when she so chooses to be." He allowed his eyes to wander over the rows of books back and above Deardorff's head.

Deardorff straightened, blocking his view. "Insight!" He waved his shirt-sleeved arms. "Insight is not so rare. It is *outsight* that is beginning to count, and that is what Esther Cornthwaite had as she watched those marching children!"

"Perhaps so." J.W. smiled agreeably to end discussion. It would be annoying to have to leave without finding the proper book.

His chance came when Deardorff reluctantly moved to his desk to answer his telephone. He edged over then to the Art section, for a moment surveying the noncommittal backs of the books. Most of them he knew by sight; most of them, in fact, he had at home in his own library, in more expensive editions. He did not linger over the tall books of reproductions: painting he valued, but only in its original form.

Because slender volumes attracted him, he pulled one off the shelf, but replaced it without looking into it when he saw that it was marked $6.00. He had to find a volume for $3.00 or less. He could spend only $3.00 today on his fortieth birthday because when he was nine years old, his mother had given him $3.00 to select a "birthday book" for himself. To teach him the value of money, as well as the way to choose his own books, she had repeated this gift until he was twenty, and from then on he had fulfilled the tradition for himself.

Enjoying his need to be unusually selective, he thoroughly explored the shelves within reach, and then bent low to inquire into the lower ones. It would not do to walk out with any $3.00 book; it had to be one which he would especially desire and be willing to admit into his own

37

library. Standing straight again, he brushed the dust from his hands and went after the ladder on rollers, moving carefully so as not to disturb Deardorff, who was showing signs of great impatience at not being able to break through the monologue on the other end of the wire. Deardorff was capable of being impatient over a $500 book order if he did not approve of the books.

Up on the ladder, J.W. first tugged at a small gray and brown book that was almost lost from sight, so tightly was it wedged in between two larger books. When he saw that it was Gauguin's *Noa Noa,* marked $2.75, he frowned. He had little patience with Westerners who fled from their own civilization to paradisical islands outside the pale of order. Yet when the cover flopped open, the simple opening line from Baudelaire *(Dites, qu'avez-vous vu?)* had the witchery of the thin wail of a train across the distance. He read on, recalling Gauguin's paintings. When he had seen them, he had felt a mild contempt for their strange paradoxes—the colors of surfeit and forms of want, the pagan sensuousness and Christian asceticism. . . .

Reading *Noa Noa* would be like a contest between him and the man Gauguin: he would stand in judgment while Gauguin would strive to persuade him that there was some sensible reason for his distorted view of life. Perhaps this was the book, after all. Like the other birthday books, it was something out of the way, a bit of mental luxury.

He was hot up on the ladder. He wiped his coatsleeve across his wet forehead, and this long unused habit of childhood set him back in time. He was a boy of twelve, of seventeen, of twenty, about to descend into the jumbled little shop, his heart-beat quickening with his new discovery. Clutching the chosen book, he would stand waiting, half fearful of Deardorff's disapproval. The bookseller would peer briefly at the volume and nod if he agreed, or shrug if he disapproved, his pointed satyr face waiting to be asked why or why not. . . .

Remembering, J.W. smiled almost sadly. It had been many years since a book had affected his heart-beat.

It was not until he had climbed down and replaced the ladder that Deardorff slammed the receiver back in place. "Mrs. Murdock," he said prettily, "would like some Plato and Aristotle and the other Greeks in beige with brown or gold lettering."

J.W. laughed sympathetically. "I trust that black type will do?" He did not think it quite proper to say more, for Justin Murdock was, after all, a fellow-trustee, a successful fruit-farmer, and the possessor of a goodly sum which he had indicated he might decide to leave to John Willard College.

"Well, who knows," Deardorff said wearily, scribbling a note to himself, "but that one day *someone* will accidentally look into these very volumes in the Murdock library and feel the breeze from Athens. Sending books . . ." He broke off abruptly to bellow, "Is it a book that you want?"

The young girl hovering in the background whispered that she thought so, that is, if this was Deardorff's Bookstore.

Deardorff said that if she could read, she could have seen his sign hanging in plain sight over his door; and that if she couldn't read, she had no use for a book.

The girl's round freckled face paled. "Professor Scott said to come here for more Shelley and Keats."

Deardorff tucked his thumbs under his arm-pits and drawled, "Isn't that thoughtful of Professor Scott!" Then he asked sharply, "More than what?"

"Why, more than is in our text," she said.

"Now, you don't say!" He paced away from her, wheeled suddenly, and rushed back upon her. "And did your professor tell you how I was to know exactly what is in your precious text?"

"No, but he said you'd be queer." She had startled herself more than Deardorff and became rooted to the floor.

But her words were alchemy, for Deardorff stepped around her and took off a table a fat blue volume containing the complete works of both Shelley and Keats. When he held it up for her to see, she nodded speechlessly, and he wrapped it up for her without another word.

While he was making her change, a tall young man entered, warming everyone with a general good-afternoon smile, and then saying in some surprise, "Why, hello there, Miss Mueller!"

For a moment the girl looked as if Keats or Shelley had appeared in person. "Good afternoon, Professor Scott," she gasped. Then, throwing her change loosely into her purse and clutching her new purchase to her, she fled.

"Come back soon," called Deardorff after her. "I have an edition of Keats' letters that I want to show you."

J.W. retreated into a corner, observing that Scott had not recognized him. Unaccountably, he was glad. He did not want to be drawn into foreign, and probably strained, conversation. He set his back to them, examining the leather-bound volumes that Deardorff kept in a glass but unlocked case. He heard Scott ask for what sounded like a specialized study on the baroque style in eighteenth-century English poetry.

"I'll have to order it for you," Deardorff said unenthusiastically.

"What a nuisance!" said Scott. "I had especially wanted to use it tomorrow—a little paper I'm doing, you know."

Deardorff reached for a battered pad and pencil and put down the publication data that Scott gave him. "It will take two or three weeks," he said, ripping off the sheet and tucking it into a large ledger.

"Well, if that's the best you can do—"

"That's the best that the publisher and the United States mail service can do," Deardorff corrected grimly. "Now, let's see. I'll have that sent to Owen Scott—"

"*Professor* Owen Scott, 528 Riverville Heights. Thank you. Thank you very much, Mr. Deardorff." Scott hurried out of the shop.

"Good day, *Professor* Scott!"

J.W. came out of his corner. "Some day, you old silenus," he said, "you're going to lose all your customers."

Deardorff ignored this, tapping his forefinger upon his forehead. "*He's* the professor-type."

J.W. put *Noa Noa* down on the counter. "I'm taking this," he said. As he watched Deardorff absently wrap it, he asked, "Did you mean that as an insult?"

Deardorff rested his hands on the unfinished package. "In this instance, yes! He's made himself into a rubber stamp marked PROFESSOR and his sole intent is to impress himself upon the world as just that." He leaned forward, wagging his finger. "Do you know that in the four years he has come into my store, he has never asked for a book that did not relate to his special studies! Special Studies! Ugh!"

J.W. was only mildly interested. As Chairman of the Board of Trustees of John Willard College, he knew that Scott was professionally competent. As a man, he envied him his tallness of something over six feet. Beyond these objective items, he did not care to probe.

But the bookseller was intent upon following his own thought, saying as he pulled at the large spool of brown wrapping cord, "Oh, he has brains enough, but, you see, it is not a matter of intelligence. Now, an explosion—yes, a complete disruption—might save him, because then the pieces might fall together differently. . . ." Suddenly he was shaking with his strangely private and silent laughter. "Cause and Effect, Cause and Effect," he muttered.

"What do you mean?" asked J.W.

"Professor Scott and our little Miss Mueller. Maybe he *is* only a rubber stamp, but now and then . . . Don't you see? Miss Mueller starves for Shelley and Keats because of Professor Scott. She'll read them, all of them—thinking of Professor Scott, it's true; nevertheless, she'll *read* them. Cause and Effect. The arrow has found its mark."

"The arrow?"

Deardorff nodded, knotting the cord over and over again. "The arrow. That's what I was starting to say when Miss Mueller came in. When I send book orders to Mrs. Murdock, I'm shooting an arrow high and wide, but sometime it's bound to fall. We all shoot arrows, even Scott, although probably quite accidentally in his classes. . . . Well, there you are." He handed J.W. the package and reached for the large ledger.

"No, this doesn't go on my account," J.W. said. He put the money on the counter.

"Why, of course! It's your birthday book!" Deardorff clapped his hand to his forehead. "Why didn't I remember! Well, well, so it's another happy birthday, Jack?"

"I hope so," said J.W., pleased and liking the "Jack."

"By the way, what book did you get?"

"*Noa Noa*," J.W. told him quickly, wishing that he didn't have to say it at all. "Marked $2.75."

"Hmm." Deardorff made his change. "Better that you had read it some years sooner, but—" He shrugged.

"I suppose," said J.W. at the door, "there's no use asking you to dinner tonight."

Deardorff closed his lips and grinned.

"Christian Deardorff, are you forever going to make the public come to *you?*"

Deardorff lifted his pointed face. "You know what Socrates said about going into public life."

"Don't be so smug," J.W. said, laughing. "Besides, Socrates didn't hide in a musty bookshop. He taught in the Market Place."

"Well," said Deardorff, his brown eyes merry, "I'm on the Square of Riverville!"

J.W. crossed the Square, automatically looking up at Benjamin Willard, who with bronzed impassivity sat in the center of it, surrounded by a small plot of grass and severely placed iron-wrought benches. It seemed to him that Benjamin had a sceptical eye on *Noa Noa*. He didn't blame him, for already *Noa Noa* seemed a foreign package under his arm, a book to be slipped, unread, far back in one of his bookshelves.

He walked rapidly, down Main Avenue and then on to Ray Street. When he had passed the neat black and white sign that marked the limits of the town, he turned into a dirt and cinder road that was protected by a large and solid sign of PRIVATE. The sun had dried off last night's rain, and his feet lifted little clouds of dust with each step. Feeling the need to hurry, he walked as a man would along a city block. To each side of the cinders that covered the middle of the road, he saw tire marks that had not been there when he had walked to town shortly after noon; they had been made, he decided, by Sam when driving to the station to meet his mother and back with her.

Ahead he could see only trees and fields and sky, but when he turned abruptly right there was his own home, deep-set and sprawling, with the sun now to its back. To come thus suddenly upon the large white frame house still gave him pleasure, and often when he brought with him out-of-town guests he would be amused at their disappointment over finding that the Willard home was nothing more than could have been built by any prosperous farmer, the type of which they had already seen many in passing through the outskirts of Riverville. The grounds, however, distinguished it, for the house and newer garage were surrounded, not by fields and gardens, but by expertly landscaped grounds. Too, there was the rugged oak with the plaque stating that this was the original site of Benjamin Willard's log cabin which he had built for himself when, after founding Riverville, he had withdrawn from its limits to watch it grow.

Now as he neared the gate, he saw Tamburlaine surveying the road from his position of advantage inside the white picket fence. He saw his smooth reddish brown body quiver and strain forward, but because he was a Boxer with an Obedience Degree, he remained propped up by his forelegs, tensely waiting.

"Tamburlaine!" called J.W. softly.

The dog leaped the fence with a single well-spaced bound and slithered to a stop at J.W.'s feet, sniffing at his knees: is this a suit which I may mark? Yes! J.W. braced himself and closed his hand softly around the cool moist bulldog nose. Tamburlaine disengaged himself and grunted reprovingly: but you have come too late for a good walk.

"You tell that Tamburlaine to go about his business!" Kate shouted. "You're late enough as it is."

J.W. laughed and gave Tamburlaine a final pat, then hurried to the porch, where his housekeeper awaited him, Quaker-like in the perennial black dress and white starched apron. Her smooth gray hair was parted severely in the middle over a calm brow, but she had an iron jaw line, which he had long respected.

"I'm sorry," he said meekly, handing her *Noa Noa*. "Please put this in my study, Kate. Mother upstairs?"

Kate pursed her pale thin lips to indicate that of course she was, for hadn't it been planned that she be home by now? "And you'd better be getting up to see her," she said tartly.

He nodded without resentment. Kate had a philosophy of promptness and order that was akin to his own. "There'll be no need to change the time of dinner," he assured her.

He took the stairs two at a time, thinking, I'll do it when I'm fifty too. But at the top he was out of breath. Pausing to rest a moment, he heard the inevitable music coming out of Russ's room, and his good spirits went down a notch. The record was worn from constant playing, and every now and then the violin slid off key. It was sentimental music that pretended to power and significance.

"Russ!" he called sharply. "I hope that you're not going to be late." There was no answer, but the music was stopped abruptly. Grimly satisfied, he moved on down the hall. It wasn't the music itself that annoyed him so much as his son's inconsiderate liking for something that he found trifling.

He tapped on his mother's door. "Jack. May I come in?"

"Of course," she said, and he heard the characteristically definite voice with pleasure.

She sat before the dressing table and watched him in its mirror, bending her head slightly to the side for his kiss.

"You've changed perfumes again," he said.

She went on carefully penciling her eyebrows. "Happy birthday—

42

not that you deserve it! I thought you'd surely come home early to talk with me. After all, it's been nearly a year." She made her mouth petulant, but rather awkwardly, for she was not ordinarily a petulant woman.

"I meant to, but I was selecting my birthday book. And you know Deardorff!"

"Oh." He could see that she was pleased to know that he had not forgotten the birthday books. She gave a final pat to her gray-brown hair, which she had arranged in an upsweep, leaving severely exposed her well-shaped Willard face. Finally she turned to face him fully, and they both smiled, relieved that the first personal encounter was over, for neither was at ease in circumstances that conventionally called for a display of emotion.

"Russ tells me," she said, "that you're sending him off to Princeton in the fall."

J.W. withdrew a trifle. "*I'm* not sending him by force. He seems willing enough to go." He waited for a moment and then smiled down at her. "How's New York and all your good work?"

His mother refaced the mirror. "They're fine—but irrelevant at the moment. And don't use that let's-change-the-topic smile on me!"

"As for Russ," he said, distant again, "I—"

"As for Russ," she broke in, "you *wish* him to go, and you know how people hesitate to displease you. Why not send him to John Willard, at least until he decides what he really wants?"

"Look, Grace," said J.W., calling his mother by her first name as he did when being serious with her, "do you honestly think that Russ would be happy at a college reeking with his ancestors?"

"Including me?" asked Grace, now a bit coy.

"Certainly including you! Who else made the College co-educational; who else gave it Grace Hall; who else . . ."

"Stop!" She laughed and waved her hand, the amethyst dinner ring with its diamond band twinkling. "The best thing I've done was to find Esther Cornthwaite for the College. She's coming tonight, isn't she?"

"Yes, of course." J.W. smiled. "As she put it, the body, if not the mind, needs at least one social excursion a year. And, Grace," he went on, "this reminds me that Cameron spoke to me just this afternoon about having your portrait done. They would like it to hang in the Summit, with that of Amos."

Grace stood, holding the violet satin dressing gown to her. "Really?" she asked, quite pleased. "How ridiculous!"

"We'll arrange for it during the year. You decide what painter. . . ." He stopped as they heard the doorbell chime. "That'll be Uncle Otis. He's always first. I've got to dress!"

"It's good to be with you again, Jack," she said, following him to the door. "How are you in your lonely life?"

"When will you ever get the idea out of your head that I'm lonely!

Kate and Sam take wonderful care of me. Besides, if you knew how busy I am—"

"Oh, I know that you're *busy*." She continued to regard him thoughtfully. "Why, you have new gray in your hair!" She said it as long ago she had said, "Why, you have a new tooth!"

J. W. took a shower and rubbed himself down briskly, annoyed with himself for being late and yet amused to think of Otis MacMillan poking about downstairs, waiting for those unpredictable Willards who had attached their name to that of MacMillan.

So this, he thought while brushing his hair, is how it is to be forty. He felt trim and competent, and after a none too easy day. This morning had been the interview with the government man from Washington to talk over possible conversion of the John Willard Tractor Company. He turned away from this memory; it needed more thought than he had time for now. Then had come the tennis game with Russ. Not that he usually played tennis at high noon on Saturday, but Russ was seldom home, and soon, when he went off to Princeton, he would be at home hardly at all. . . . Another thought that he didn't like. And then finally the trustees meeting, which had been neither one way nor the other. Still he was in fine shape, ready, even glad, to confront an evening of Family.

Adjusting his black tie, he leaned forward to peer more closely into the mirror, searching for the new gray in his hair that his mother had observed. He rather hoped that he would not find it; but he did. He neither liked nor disliked it, but he wished that he had noticed its coming. Surprises did not please him.

Downstairs he found Otis MacMillan chafing his hands before the fireplace, although there was no fire. Seeing J.W., he cleared his throat gratingly, but when he spoke his voice was still hoarse. "Happy birthday, Jack boy!"

"Thank you, Uncle Otis. May I get you anything?"

Uncle Otis shook his head, hunching his shoulders under the shiny tuxedo coat. Beneath the fringe of yellow-white hair, he set his thin face into shrewd lines. "Well, J.W., what did you think of the meeting this afternoon?"

J.W. shrugged impatiently, not caring to discuss the meeting at a social time. When he noticed the vase of pink and white peonies that Kate had set in the exact center of the mantle, he frowned critically and pushed it tentatively to the side until he found the spot in which the vase did not obscure any part of the life-size painting of a young girl above the mantle.

"Murdock's a fool!" persisted Uncle Otis.

"Oh, I don't know." J.W. looked over the liquor tray, making sure

44

that things were right for the Martinis he would mix when the others arrived.

Otis cleared his throat. "And Cameron certainly is a poker-face! Why, he—"

"Here comes someone." J.W. had listened gratefully to the sounds of a car, and now there were footsteps across the porch.

"Probably my son-in-law," rasped Otis, tugging at his large watch. "Always late, he is."

He was right. Harry Frazer blustered his birthday greetings while his wife, Marie, looked on with an aloof smile which suggested that her husband was being effusive enough for both of them. "Vincent coming?" she asked in her bored voice.

"Perhaps he's here now," said J.W., hearing new steps.

But it was Philip Willard who stood at the door. "Uncle Philip!" greeted J.W. "I was afraid that you couldn't make it this year."

"How could I forget the birthday of the great tractor magnate?" Philip smiled, his chin disappearing for a moment into the folds of smooth but not flabby flesh. "Where is my sister?" he demanded.

"Descending upon you," called Grace, coming down the stairs. The full effect of her presence spread through the room as she stood for a moment on the wide and curving bottom step. Marie swiftly followed the lines of the mauve crêpe dinner gown and, although twenty years younger than Grace, suddenly felt at once overdressed and dowdy in her printed silk.

Grace moved to her brother. "Must you be so distant? We could have made the trip together."

He ignored her reproach and bowed slightly over her hand, saying in the manner that no one could be sure was serious or mocking, "As charming and beautiful as always, my dear."

She accepted this as her due and swept toward the others. "Otis," she said, lightly touching the old man's wiry arm, "I'm so glad to hear that you've retired."

Marie laughed harshly. "That's what *you* think, Aunt Grace! Actually, he runs Harry ragged, pestering him to death. . . ."

"Oh, I wouldn't say that, honey," Harry said hastily. "I'm sure I couldn't run the Dairy without his help."

Otis grunted, and Grace patted his arm comfortingly. "Why, there isn't a MacMillan hen that would lay a proper egg without you on the job!"

When Russ came down the stairs, Tamburlaine brushed against the screen, wanting in. The boy threw out a casual hello and went on to the door, opening it for Tamburlaine, who trotted over to the fireplace, aware that he had everyone's attention.

"Did you enter him this year?" Grace asked.

"We certainly did, Grandma," said Russ. His face looked freshly scrubbed and he had had trouble with his tie. J.W. restrained an impulse to reach out and straighten it for him. "He placed first and got his Obedience Degree!"

"Of course." Philip smiled and waved his hand. "A Willard wouldn't raise a canary without entering it, and, what is more, the canary would place first. If you . . ." He stopped, watching Kate as she opened the door. "I hope this is Esther. I want Esther."

Esther appeared, and Vincent Diaz emerged from behind her. "So sorry to be late," he murmured, bowing to Grace.

"My fault, young man," said Miss Cornthwaite. "My hair," she explained calmly.

As one, they looked at her hair, understanding how the coiffure could account for almost any length of time.

"My dear Esther!" said Grace, coming forward.

"My dear Grace!" returned Esther, allowing her black velvet cape to fall into Kate's receptive arms. She stood majestic in black chiffon, with flowing sleeves and panels.

"Ah, the Victory of Samothrace," murmured Philip as he crossed the room to her.

J.W. excused himself to mix Martinis. Esther nodded approvingly and settled in the middle of the sofa. She fixed upon Russ. "So you're about to enter Princeton, my boy. For what will you prepare?"

"For the war, I suppose," he said, and then laughed uncertainly when the silence told him that he had given a too serious answer.

Slowly they turned to him. He stood with his hands in his pockets, pulling his coat tight across his slender hips, his eyes now directed over their heads, his face smooth and calm but intently listening. He's older than we remembered, they thought.

"Russell!" cried Grace.

"What's wrong, Grandma? I'm tired of being made an ostrich. It's silly to send me off to Princeton or to anyplace!"

J.W., busy over the liquor tray, neither spoke nor looked up.

"Gad!" said Otis suddenly. "The boy's right. What place will colleges have in the tomorrow that's coming?"

"Nonsense!" Esther Cornthwaite folded her fine hands in her voluminous black lap. "Colleges are about to come into their own."

"Besides," said Philip softly, sitting next to Esther, "your father will see to it that his factory is converted into an essential industry."

Russ flushed angrily. "I'm not looking for a way out, Uncle Philip!"

J.W. glanced up at this with a tolerant smile; but it was a deliberate expression, as if carefully chosen out of several possible ones. Then deftly he shook orange bitters into the gin and vermouth.

Philip sighed. "Oh, to be so young and so very eager. . . . Esther, your hands are still the most beautiful that I have ever seen. And do you know that I've discovered a positively lyrical passage right in the middle of Volume II of your treatise on the Language—positively lyrical!"

46

The most beautiful hands fluttered slightly. "I've no idea what passage you mean, Philip. That reminds me, however, that I wish to thank you for the volume of your new poems. I'm sorry to say that I find your work increasingly obscure."

Philip laughed soundly. "My dear," he gasped, "as usual, you say in one sentence what the reviews took . . ." He held his hands far apart to indicate the space used by the reviewers.

"You exaggerate," said Esther stolidly. "Your book didn't receive that much attention."

"Obscurity," said Vincent Diaz, crossing his short legs and making slow circles with his pointed shiny toe, "is a sign of decadence."

"Before I regard that as an insult," said Philip, still smiling, "I had better know whether you mean decadence of the individual or of a whole nation."

Diaz moistened his full lips and began, "I should say—"

"You're looking more and more Nordic, Vincent," said Marie, who had not followed what was being said.

"A compliment, Aunt Marie?"

Marie shrugged, not liking the "Aunt."

"More like my mother, perhaps?" Diaz persisted, allowing his gaze to rest on Otis MacMillan.

"No!" Otis exploded, taking the bite. "My daughter was decidedly blond."

"I never knew her," mused Harry.

"She missed you by running off to Argentina," Marie said dryly.

Diaz fingered his striped tie. "I'm trying to look like the well-dressed American professor. I have succeeded, I understand."

Grace regarded him and then said decisively, "You do not look like a teacher at all!"

Philip leaned forward to take his Martini from the tray that Russ had lowered before him. "I admire people who do not look their vocations." He raised his glass slightly to Diaz.

"Thank you," purred Diaz. "And I should not have guessed that *you* were a poet."

"The apricot brandy's for you, Uncle Otis," said Russ.

"Esther, perhaps you'd prefer the brandy to a Martini," J.W. called across the room.

"Splendid!" said Esther Cornthwaite, who had not heard what he said.

Grace went swiftly to Russ and took a Martini from the tray, carrying it back to Esther. "She'd be furious," she said in an undertone to J.W., "if she had heard you!"

"Well!" said Harry, when they all held glasses. "Let me propose a birthday toast to J.W., the one and only!"

"Stop it!" hissed Marie. "Don't you remember?"

"Wh-what?" stammered Harry.

"To Eileen," said J.W., lifting his glass to the large painting over the mantle. As they respectfully sipped, Eileen looked down upon them, fay-like in her blondness, but a curiously human appeal showing in her unshadowed blue eyes.

"I'm tired of consorting with ghosts!" Grace said suddenly. All but her son and his son looked at her, surprised, agreeing, but not daring to say so.

"You're speaking of my mother, Grandma," said Russ.

"So I am, but I'm not blaspheming her," Grace said. "Besides, a painting is hardly a mother, and you've never known any other!" She spoke to Russ, but sent a defiant look to J.W., who was suddenly not looking at any one.

Russ stooped beside Tamburlaine, turning his face into the shadows, away from the room.

"Sentiment in the tractor magnate is compelling," Philip said blandly. This seemed to arouse J.W., but before he could speak, Philip was staring intently into his glass and saying, "You know, I find the colorlessness of gin a bit odious."

"But this is a beautifully smooth cocktail. I congratulate you upon it," Diaz said to J.W. He drained his glass and moved over to the painting. "And upon this. It is a lovely work."

"Why, thank you." J.W. joined him, glad to be done with personal talk. "It was executed in Paris. I wanted Eileen to have the experience of sitting to a French artist."

"Ah, yes. And did she enjoy it, the experience?"

J.W. smiled reminiscently. "Like a child. I was with her at all times, for Bonsard, the artist, discovered that she kept a much more natural expression when I was in the room with her."

"Then it was at you that she was looking as she posed?"

"Yes, come to think of it, it was. Why?"

"I was wondering," said Diaz slowly, "about the questioning look in the eyes. What was she thinking or asking, and whom was she asking?"

J.W. regarded the portrait again, singling out the eyes. "I suppose," he said somewhat shortly, "that the artist was overimaginative."

"I see. Of course." Diaz turned slowly from the portrait, surveying the room, the high ceiling, the long windows, the hardwood floors. "A fine house too. Is it Early American?"

J.W. laughed. "Nothing like. It's not even so old as the Summit."

Diaz looked humble. "I am so innocent of American styles and customs as yet!"

"You see," explained J.W., "the family built and moved into this house in 1910, when they turned the Summit over to the College. The furnishings are a great conglomeration. We've never tried to make our home a museum. . . ."

"Really, Jack, it's nothing to brag about," Philip said, shrugging with distaste. "This house, I mean. If one is a Willard, why not live like a Willard? Now, if you kept a proper butler—as everyone expects you to—there would, for example, be someone on hand at this moment to pass me the canapés."

"But, Uncle Philip," said Russ, looking up, "there's a platter right in front of you!"

"My boy, you're as literal as your father!" Philip sighed resignedly and bent forward to select a canapé.

J.W. smiled. "I'll take that as a compliment." He began to refill glasses. "Esther?"

She seemed not to hear, and did not object when she picked up her glass and found it full.

Philip held out his glass. "But this conglomeration is a symbol of the times. A shuffling of furniture, a shuffling of the classes. However, it is nothing more than make-believe, I assure you. One may stand back from his own class to criticize—like me—or to help another class —like my dear sister—but it is, in the end, a childish game of let's pretend."

"Philip!" Grace was angry and hurt, for she took her volunteer social work seriously. "Sometimes I loathe the way you make light of everything."

Otis growled. "F.D.R. He's the shuffler."

Philip eyed the old man, amused. "Be at peace. As I said, the distinctions are ultimately rigid. You businessmen will . . ."

"I'm not a businessman!" Otis snapped. "I'm a dairy farmer."

Harry glanced up in surprise, and Marie asked why her father had to harp on the fact that he was a farmer.

"Because," said Esther Cornthwaite abruptly, " 'farmer' has a more innocent sound in Washington."

"Why, Esther," said Grace, "what an amazing remark!"

"Not so amazing, my dear Grace. I'm a student of words, and even Etta Wilson could detect the difference in the connotation of 'farmer' and 'businessman.' "

"Etta Wilson?" they chimed. "Who's that?"

Esther smiled mysteriously over the rim of her glass. "The coming Esther Cornthwaite," she said, suddenly solemn.

J.W. laughed. "Only this afternoon Deardorff told me that she"— he nodded toward Esther—"had outsight as well as insight, and now I'm ready to believe him completely!"

"Ah yes, Deardorff," sighed Philip. "I intend to spend tomorrow with him—which means that I'll ask permission to sit the day through in his grimy little shop and listen!"

"He *is* an enigma, that Deardorff," said Diaz.

"No, no!" objected Philip. "Just the spectator type, but—"

Kate announced dinner, and the group arose, finding partners. Diaz and Philip followed Grace and J.W. through the hall and into the large square dining room, Diaz nodding with intelligent interest as Philip expounded Deardorff. Esther Cornthwaite took three steps and stopped suddenly. "The heat is intolerable," she reproved everyone in general, "and it has almost overpowered me." Russ offered his arm, and she took it willingly.

"What you said a few minutes back about your sister's social work interests me." Vincent Diaz spoke to Philip Willard in an intimate tone which caused everyone at the table to strain to hear. "It *is* superficial, that sort of thing, isn't it? I mean, its very existence indicates a national malady, doesn't it?"

"Hitler says that in *Mein Kampf*," Russ said loudly, surprising them again.

Diaz turned to him. "Why, yes, I believe that he does. I read all things to keep—how do you say it?—the open mind. That is, I believe, the favorite American attitude."

Russ looked belligerent. "Well, I read it to learn more about the enemy!"

You never told me, thought J.W.; we never talked it over.

"—but you refused to discuss the matter fairly!" Grace was saying down the table to Philip and Diaz. "Whether or not social work is a symptom, you cannot deny that it leads to national progress! How else should we obtain shorter working hours, fair labor laws, and all the rest?"

Philip touched his napkin to his lips. "But to what are we progressing, Grace? Do you know what Pierre Laval said, as reported in this morning's newspaper?" He pushed back his chair to allow more room for gestures. Diaz eyed him eagerly, already nodding understandingly. "Said Laval, standing on a balcony overlooking the Champs Elysées down which German infantry marched behind a band, 'Every noon as that parade passes I say to myself, "that, Leon Blum, is your work, the fruit of the incompatibility of your war policy and your 40-hour week which stimulated conflict among the classes and masses." ' *That* is what Laval said."

Grace glanced uneasily at J.W., whose silence meant that he was either bored or displeased with the talk. "Of course, one distrusts balcony speeches," she said; then turned to Marie. "And how is your bridge, my dear?"

Diaz looked confused and appealed to Philip. "Laval is right. It is the . . ."

Philip held up a plump hand of warning. "To dine here, you must learn to be at ease in Zion. One never pursues an idea further when my sister asks, 'How is your bridge, my dear?' " Abruptly he turned from Diaz and spoke to Esther across the table. "You are filled with sibylline wisdom tonight. What is the cause of the world's chaos?"

"Stature," said Esther readily. "Short men, such as Hitler and Mussolini. Compensating aggressiveness."

Diaz, a short man, reddened and did not again attempt to impede the progress of conversation.

Philip was the last to leave. Standing on the porch, he tucked his white silk scarf under his coat lapels and shuddered. "This raw country air!" He looked enviously at J.W. "How you *do* thrive on it!"

J.W. laughed. "Don't go out in it. Why not stay the night here?"

"Thank you, no. My things are already settled in a Bijou cubbyhole." He shuddered again. "Horrible place!" He gestured a farewell and went down the steps to the waiting car, climbing in beside Esther Cornthwaite.

Russ sat on the steps, his chin on his knees, moodily watching the red taillight round the horseshoe drive and disappear down the road.

"How about a walk?" J.W. asked him.

Russ nodded somberly. J.W. called Tamburlaine, and the three went striding down the road to Riverville. Occasionally Tamburlaine made side excursions after a scurrying field mouse. Russ kept his silence, and J.W. respected it for some minutes. He watched his son walk with shoulders hunched, and he thought with irritation: he has the MacMillan posture. Aloud he said, "Rather a boring evening for you, Russ."

Russ shook his head. "I like watching people."

"Which one did you watch most?" J.W. asked, curious.

"You."

J.W. was surprised and unexpectedly embarrassed. "Well, what did you discover?"

"That you don't tell what you believe," Russ said slowly. "All the others do, in some way or other."

"Perhaps you're right," he said. "I'm not much good at social chitchat."

When they reached Ray Street, Tamburlaine, long familiar with the walks, bounded ahead; but J.W. stopped Russ and pointed to the south where stood the John Willard Tractor Company, now only a darker blur in the night. "There it is, Russ," he said. "There's my belief."

Russ looked puzzled. "Tractors?"

J.W. laughed. "Tractors only incidentally. Chiefly work, work, and more work!"

They walked again, skirting the yard of the plant and circling the depot, and finally following the river. Soon they made a steep ascent and were on the Heights. J.W. began to wish that the boy would say something. He had grown too moody. Only a few short months ago they had been good companions; now the silence between them was a dividing one.

"Later I'll talk to you more about Princeton," he said heartily, taking the boy by the arm. "We'll discuss living quarters and clubs. You'll find the name of Willard quite well known there." He said it a bit proudly.

"That will be fine, Dad," said Russ.

J.W. fancied that the boy moved slightly away from him, and he hastily released his arm. "And starting this summer, I'll take you into the plant, and you'll begin to learn the business. That's the way I did it, you know. College for nine months, tractors for three. My grandfather started me at the very bottom, just as I'll start you. No plush seat for us! That's the real way to work, so that you come to know all the departments and the men and what is best for them, for what is best for *them* will make the best tractors."

When Russ said nothing, J.W. was irritated. He had hoped for more enthusiasm. "Well," he said, forcing a laugh, "it didn't sound very exciting to me either, when I first heard about it. But you'll grow into it, just as I did. Why, do you know that, except for my honeymoon, I've never taken a longer vacation than two weeks!"

"Mother died when I was born, didn't she?" Russ asked.

"Yes," said his father, impatient at the irrelevant question. "Died in childbirth."

"Died in childbirth." Russ repeated the words, seeming to listen to them anew. "That sort of thing goes on all the time, in peace as well as war, doesn't it?"

"What sort of thing?"

"People killing each other."

"War is mass killing. There's a great difference," J.W. explained impatiently. He pointed again, this time to the twin towers of Main Hall. "There's a part of your life too, Russ. John Willard College. Do you realize that it's the John Willard Trust Fund that keeps the place going?"

Russ stared into the campus, his face blank.

"Let's turn back," J.W. said shortly. "Tamburlaine!" The dog bounded back to them and led the way down the Heights. "Work well and spend well. If I have a motto, that's it."

Say what you're thinking! he wanted to shout at his son. You can't withdraw from *me*. Not from me, who conceived you, who understood your silent secret mind before it began even to store up memories. Not from *me*.

"What are you thinking?" he at last demanded.

"Why—why," Russ stammered, as if startled at being interrupted. "Nothing much. Well, about beliefs—yours and Uncle Philip's and Uncle Otis'. They're all different." He spoke wonderingly. "They ought to add up to something, but they don't. They're all too different."

"There's no reason why they should add up to something," said his father. "Freedom of the individual, that's what it is. Freedom to believe and work and spend as one chooses. Anything else leads to Hitlerism! Reread the Preamble to the Constitution, about the Pursuit of Happiness, and you'll find it all there. . . ."

Russ took a book and went upstairs to his room.

Grace was sitting idly by the fireplace, still in her mauve dinner gown.

"May I get you a book, Mama?"

"No," she said wearily. "I'm going up to my room now. I've just been indulging in the luxury of feeling sorry for myself."

J.W. lighted a cigarette, concerned with his own thoughts. "But why?"

"I've kept myself busy all my life, and it's not easy to reach my age and be told that my life has been of no value. I—"

"If you're referring to Philip's inanities—!" He clicked his lighter shut and angrily shoved it into his pocket. He was suddenly exasperated with the evening's crisscross of ideas, beliefs, theories. "He talks for the sole sake of his most admiring audience—himself."

"Perhaps so. . . ." She studied her hands. "But Vincent Diaz seemed to agree. I noticed that."

"Diaz!" J.W. paced across the room. "He's only the fair-haired boy trying to make himself agreeable to the most sparkling of our guests."

"Perhaps so," Grace said again. "But he seems so—so un-American."

J.W. laughed grimly. "He's American enough to know how to make his MacMillan niche secure. He knew enough to come to John Willard for a job; he knows enough to come here for dinner."

"Well, he *is* part Family," Grace admitted. "I wonder if he's a good teacher."

J.W. shrugged. "He certainly should be able to teach Spanish. He was brought up speaking it."

"Yes, I know. But what I mean is . . ." She hesitated, searching for words.

He didn't wait for her to find them. "You're overimaginative tonight because you're overtired."

She looked up at him quickly. "And you're overcross. You didn't quarrel with Russ, did you?"

He shook his head but turned away.

"Be patient with him," she said, rising and touching his arm. "Why, he has changed even since I last saw him. Things move rapidly these days."

"You talk as if he had been out knocking against the world."

"The world has come to knock against him. He's examining the pieces, one by one, and is bewildered because he can't fit them together." She reached out to him again. "Now, Jack, don't hurry or force him, don't plan for him—"

He moved abruptly away from her.

"Get off your high horse!" she said sharply. "I'm still your mother, and I guess I can still give you a few 'don't's' on special occasions. On the whole, you'll have to agree that I've stayed remarkably out of your life."

He returned to her and patted her hand, his face still unrelenting. "You go to bed, Mama."

She laughed resignedly. "Oh, all right. And I'll not bother you for another year." Her hand on the banister, she stopped suddenly. "I almost forgot! I took a call for you, from Mr. Justin Murdock, who wanted to know—or, rather, his *wife* wanted to know—if it would be proper for them to write to a Miss Somebody Anderson inviting her to room with them when she comes to the college in the fall."

J.W. looked amused. "He must mean Marcia Anderson, the new English instructor we appointed this afternoon. Why on earth did they think they had to ask me? What did you tell him?"

"I told him," Grace said innocently, "that if his home was one of high moral standing, I saw no reason why such a letter would be improper."

"Grace, you didn't!"

"I most certainly did." She laughed and went on up the stairs, saying over her shoulder, "One last 'don't', Jack dear: don't lose your sense of humor."

He waved her a good-night, smiling fondly. Then he went into his study for *Noa Noa,* meaning to read in bed, for he was tired. He picked up the book and stood scanning random pages. The words called forth no response from him, not even a critical one. Wondering what irrational mood had tricked him into buying it, he replaced it on the smoking stand. He thought for a moment, then took up a newspaper and went upstairs.

In his room, he remembered that he had intended to stand alone before the painting of Eileen, thinking of her. But, he told himself, to go down again deliberately would make the gesture artificial.

Chapter Five

MARCIA Anderson stood under the sign of gilt letters on black that read RIVERVILLE. The narrow eave of the little brown and tan depot was no protection against the September sun, which beat steadily down upon her. This is a significant moment, she was thinking; this is the climax to what started for me that day in Dr. Ware's office. . . .

But the girls who had been in her coach strolled about on the cement platform, quite indifferent to her significant moment. One girl

54

sat down alone on the wooden bench, carelessly crossing her long, slim legs. Her rose suit had a sophisticated cut, and her coppery hair was in a long and severely straight bob with bangs. She paid no attention to the others, but stared listlessly ahead of her.

Marcia watched her against her will. She was challenging in some way. Her obvious and flat boredom did not wholly hide a certain taut energy, an expectancy. How would Martin see her? Not being astute, he'd make a Renoir of her because of the color. She wasn't soft enough for a Renoir. More like a Manet, but Martin wouldn't—

Deliberately she thrust aside thoughts of her father, although not without effort, for they flowed at their own will through old and deep channels in her mind. Angry with the girl in the rose suit for having set up the association, she turned and stared purposefully up the road, as if expecting someone. She felt that the other girls were covertly watching her. She wasn't ready for them and studiedly avoided their eyes.

If she were Virginia, she'd strike up a friendly conversation with them. *Dear girls, I'm your new teacher* . . . and all the rest of it.

Well, she wasn't Virginia. She was Marcia, who stayed in her own locked room of self because that was where she wanted to be. Thus Martin—when he chose to notice her—would say, in his damnably amused way, that sooner or later she'd have to unlock the door or perish, for life. . . .

Charlie came in a dust-cloud and with a roar. She knew he was Charlie because the girls screamed his name when he drove up in the stationwagon marked JOHN WILLARD COLLEGE. All but the girl in the rose suit clambered into the car and made a great fuss over him. She got in last and said nothing.

When Marcia stepped back from the farewell spray of dust and gravel, she wondered if it might not have been wiser to speak to the girls, after all. She was now the only sign of life near the station house. Perhaps she should have allowed Professor Grant to meet her. But she had written him that his meeting her was quite unnecessary. That high-handed gesture had been prompted by her desire to deal from then on directly with Esther Cornthwaite. She was through with an interlocutor. . . .

She found herself squinting against a glare. She traced it to the reflected sun on the great network of tracks ahead of her. Beyond the tracks was a cluster of buildings, one a huge round structure bearing a clear sign: RIVERVILLE SHOPS.

A sudden breeze carried a stagnant river smell. . . .

This place, she thought in sudden fear, has nothing to do with me, nor with William Blake, poet, engraver, mystic-philosopher. Scholarship could not be here.

She sat down on the wooden bench, dragging the calfskin bag to rest near her feet. The matching zipper case she held carefully in her lap, for it was tightly packed with her Blake papers—papers too precious to be trusted to her trunk.

Why not face it? She did not want to be a teacher. Those girls . . . especially she in the rose suit. . . . She had told Grant that she wanted to teach, but she had said it simply because that obviously was the thing to say. You taught to make a living while carrying on scholarship. Dr. Ware had explained that.

Scholarship was a high and spacious temple in which one worked fervently but alone with the great ideas of the past. It demanded independence of vision, and solitude to keep the vision pure. Dr. Ware had first said it in her emphatically precise way that made it seem irrevocably true. . . .

. . . Dr. Alice Ware sat with her profile to Marcia, the side on which the straight short graying hair was drawn into a tortoise shell barrette high on her head. The ends of her hair pointed away from her neck, for she had the habit of sweeping her hand through them without remembering to smooth them back into place.

"I don't know," Marcia answered at last.

Dr. Ware jumped up from her chair with characteristic abruptness. She came around to the front of her desk and faced Marcia squarely. "To decide one's vocation is not to make an arbitrary choice, you know!"

"Yes, I know," Marcia whispered, fixing her gaze upon Dr. Ware's flat brown oxfords which so securely clamped the floor.

"I doubt if you do," Dr. Ware said scornfully. She turned sharply and strode to the window. "How do you feel about ideas?"

"Why, they're—they're fine."

Dr. Ware sat down again. "For some time," she said more gently, "I have read your papers with great interest. You have the feeling for ideas that others have for words or color or sound. You like to find them lurking beneath surface art forms; you like to compare them, to track them down to their roots. . . ." She swung around in her swivel chair, her profile again to Marcia. "I have observed too that yours is a solitary nature, an independent one. I have discerned in you no bias that would hide from you the objective truth." Then she turned back and leaned urgently toward Marcia. "Why don't you become a scholar?"

"But—what is that?"

Dr. Ware frowned impatiently. "Let us say now that *objectivity* and *search* are the key words. . . ."

As Dr. Ware talked on, all the petty confusion in Marcia's mind gave way before the encroaching image of Scholarship, the white temple with its vista of blue sky and its sonorous voices beyond human intercourse, beyond Martin—

"Of course," Dr. Ware was saying sharply, "there is always the possibility of marriage." She looked suspiciously at Marcia, gauging the possibility.

Marcia shook her head, keeping back the words: *I am Marcia, alone, always alone.*

Dr. Ware shrugged. "It is not by accident that Learning and Scholarship began in monasteries. Well!" She smiled briefly. They were making progress. "You must first get your degrees. The B.A., the M.A., the Ph.D. There is no real money problem?"

"No. . . ." Marcia said reluctantly. How explain that she did not wish to use her father's money?

Dr. Ware did not wait. "You're lucky, my dear." She stood, her hands on her narrow hips. "After *my* B.A., I had to— Well! That's irrelevant. We'll talk more, not here, but in my room. . . ."

That had been the beginning. So here she was. At least the briefcase upon her lap was very real. And carefully packed in the bag at her feet were the suit and blouse she would wear for her initial conference with Professor Cornthwaite in the morning.

Resolutely she stood up, meaning to ferret out the station-master to probe him concerning the many means of transportation of which the John Willard catalogue boasted. She took one step and then stopped to watch the black coupe that came jogging down the road. When she saw the sign TAXI tucked in the windshield, she set down her bag and waited.

The driver stopped without bothering to park, and slid out, leaning against the door and surveying the station platform with disinterest. He left Marcia until last, and when he came to her, gave a long low whistle.

She ignored it. "If that's really a taxi, may I hire it?"

He shook his head and kicked at a piece of gravel, showing thin brown legs, for his trousers were rolled almost to his knees. Instead of a shirt, he wore a tight-fitting jersey sweater of green and white horizontal stripes. "Wish you could," he said, grinning, "but I'm here to meet a Dr. Anderson."

"What a coincidence," she said dryly, "for I'm Dr. Anderson."

He whistled again but with new alertness, shook down his trouser legs, and within a minute had stowed away her bag and opened the door for her. "I'm Richard Tibbet," he announced as they drove off. "Junior year."

"Oh, a student." She relaxed her voice. "And are you also the Riverville Taxi Company?"

"On the side. It helps buy books and pay lab fees. Ever been here before?"

"No. I want to go to—"

"I know—the Murdocks'. Mrs. Murdock called me to meet you." He jerked his head to the left in the direction of a long, flat red brick building. "That's the John Willard Tractor Company."

"I see," said Marcia, without interest. "Perhaps I'll be having you in class."

"Nope." Richard was firm. "I'm through with English." He jerked his head again toward the factory. "J. W. MacMillan's the president. He's all the big chief trustee of the college."

"When did you finish with English?"

Richard grinned. "When I got through with what was required! I'm a Physical Ed major," he explained, settling the matter. "You don't look so much like a teacher. You didn't talk much like one back there either." He gave her a quick sidewise glance and smiled shyly.

"Thanks," she said, laughing.

"This is Main Avenue. Runs right into the Square. If I turned down Ray here, we'd come to the road leading to J.W.'s private home. Want to ride past it?"

"I think not," Marcia said.

"OK," he agreed, a little disappointed.

"But I'll make it a point to look at it soon," she assured him.

"Oh, it won't knock your eyes out. Now, Otis MacMillan lives out by his dairy farm in a regular show-off dump. We don't go by it—unless you want to," he suggested eagerly.

"No, thanks. Not this time."

"Well, here's the Square. That's Benjamin Willard, founder of Riverville, sitting in the middle." Richard twice circled the round plot of grass, pointing to the street corners. "That's Witherspoon's Department Store. Bijou Hotel, where you eat on special occasions. Next is Herby's, where you eat when you're hungry. And that," he said with satisfaction, indicating the fourth corner, "is Deardorff's."

"And what's Deardorff's?" asked Marcia.

"Our bookstore."

"Oh, I see."

"Deardorff's has always been here," he said, trying for more enthusiasm. "Corny once said that the census of Riverville is 8,000 *and* Christian Deardorff!"

"Corny?"

"Professor Cornthwaite." He grinned again. "Heck, I forgot that you're a teacher, but I guess it's all right, because you haven't really started yet. Now, this takes us right into the Heights," he explained, heading away from the Square. Carelessly he shifted into second as they climbed a short but abrupt hill. He pointed to the row of housebacks above them. "This section built up after they moved John Willard up here with the Summit. The houses face part of the campus and Riverville Park; that's why they have their backs to the town."

"Without doubt, you're a native, aren't you, Mr. Tibbet?"

"What? Oh, no, not me—I. I'm from Dayton." He jerked to a stop and then turned sharply to the left. "This is the Heights. Rides smooth, doesn't it?"

Marcia looked out her window at the sloping park grounds, and then the other way at the passing houses set in the shady shadows of their own trees and well back from the street and wide concrete sidewalk that had diamonds in the sunlight. This is more like it, she thought. "And is that the Summit?" she asked, feeling her first excitement. She pointed ahead to a large gray stone house that seemed to stand in the middle of the street.

"Nope. That's President Cameron's home, 1910—although, of course, other presidents besides Cameron have lived in it. The Summit," he reproved her politely, "sets back of the Heart and is red brick, 1859."

"Oh, of course," said Marcia, remembering the photograph in the catalogue. She bent forward to peer above and ahead. The sky was clear and blue with rolled cottony clouds, and the direct sunrays made all objects brilliant. "So 'yonder sparkle is the citadel's circling its summit!' " she said softly to herself. " 'Thither our path lies; wind we up the heights.' "

"What did you say?" asked Richard.

"Nothing," she said guiltily. When she saw that he looked hurt, she confessed, "Oh, that was just a bit of Browning."

"*Robert* Browning? Say, he has some pretty good stuff, hasn't he?" He brought the car to a stop, saying, "That's the Murdocks' over there, the tan brick." But he made no move to get out. Staring at his hands resting on the wheel, he suddenly came forth with:

" 'I sprang to the stirrup, and Joris, and he;
I galloped, Dirck galloped, we galloped all three;
da *da* da da *da* da da (a couple lines here I forget)
And into the midnight we galloped abreast.' "

He nodded with satisfaction. "Good stuff. You can make it sound like a real gallop." As he slid out and around to open the door for her, he asked, "Is that what English teachers do, quote all the time?"

She laughed embarrassedly. "I'm sorry you caught me at it."

"Forget it!" he said magnanimously. He fished her bag out and carried it over to the Murdocks' walk.

"That's fine," said Marcia, following. "Thank you—for everything." She adjusted her briefcase under her arm and opened her purse.

"No charge," he said, blushing. "Be seeing you!"

Mrs. Murdock led the way up the rust-carpeted stairs. She was a large woman and quite covered the stairway, straining forward and breathing asthmatically as she climbed. At the top she turned into a large bright room with white ruffled curtains and gladiola-patterned wallpaper.

"It's lovely," Marcia said.

Seeming pleased, Mrs. Murdock moved about the room, touching the maple dresser, the chintz-covered chair, the hob-nail spread over the maple poster bed—as if Marcia would not be likely to find those objects by herself. "You understand," she said in the explosive way that still startled Marcia, "I have never before had a roomer. As a matter of fact," she confided, lowering herself carefully into the chintz chair, "I don't consider you a roomer, Dr. Anderson. You don't look exactly as I had you pictured, but— I wouldn't sit on the bed, if I were you!"

Marcia jumped up hastily.

"Of course, the bed's yours from now on," admitted Mrs. Murdock, "but if you don't want the mattress to sag—"

"Oh, I'm sure you're right," Marcia said, moving to the spindly chair before the desk.

Mrs. Murdock smiled approvingly. "As you can see, that desk is new. I bought it purposely when I knew that you were coming with us. I *knew* that a teacher would need a desk!"

"That was thoughtful of you," said Marcia. She had noticed the desk when she first entered the room, seeing its three pigeon-holes, its one small drawer, the pale green blotter with the leather corners, the china heart-shaped stamp box, the painted quill pen rising out of its crystal container filled with colored pebbles. At least, she thought, I'll be able to use it for letter-writing. Aloud she repeated, "That *was* thoughtful of you."

Mrs. Murdock looked toward the beruffled curtains, and sniffed. "You'll get good air here."

Marcia sniffed too, and it occurred to her that the fresh clean smell was unsullied by smoke. "I may smoke here, may I not?" Mrs. Murdock seemed so startled that she explained hastily, "I acquired the habit when I spent so much time studying."

Mrs. Murdock took a moment to associate nicotine and cerebral activity, and appeared slightly happier. "Why not?" she said daringly. "I want you—" She stopped short as a downstairs door closed softly. Familiar with the house sounds, she identified it immediately and shouted: "Stephanie, oh, Stephanie!" Then she arose and whispered to Marcia that Stephanie was not exactly a daughter, but a sister's child, early orphaned, whom the Murdocks kindly cared for and would no doubt some day adopt. "Our Stephanie," she said loudly when footsteps sounded in the hall, "is a John Willard sophomore, and all summer she has been looking forward to having you here. She loves English."

Stephanie appeared, a large, big-boned girl, but firmly built with no superfluous flesh. "This is our Stephanie," cried Mrs. Murdock, throwing an arm around the girl's shoulders. "Stephanie Kail," she added. "And, Stephanie, this is our Dr. Anderson!"

Stephanie stood as straight and stiff as a young poplar tree, and seemingly as unaware of her aunt's arm. Her response to Marcia's greeting was so miserly that Mrs. Murdock began to talk quickly: "Perhaps you'll have Dr. Anderson for a teacher. Won't that be wonderful?"

Stephanie moved away from them. "Except that I don't like English."

Her aunt frowned an appeal. "Why, Stephanie, you—"

"I hate to write," Stephanie said flatly, "and I hate grammar."

Marcia smiled. "There's always reading."

Stephanie shook her head. "I hate—"

"Justin, oh, Justin!" Mrs. Murdock shouted. "I heard the door," she explained, giving Marcia a bright look. "He'll want to meet you right away. *Justin!*"

"Heard you the first time." The voice was somewhat insolent in its indifference.

"He's mad," Stephanie observed. "He's mad because you made him break up his afternoon."

"Well?" A tall broad man stood in the doorway. "Here I am." He had a long mournful face that lent ominous significance to his statement of the obvious.

Beginning to feel nervously responsible for the family conclave, Marcia held out her hand to him. He pumped it without interest.

"You've been in the orchards again!" Mrs. Murdock exclaimed, staring at his mud-caked boots.

He gave her a long look. "That's right, Madge. That's where I generally work."

"He insists upon puttering around in those orchards," Mrs. Murdock said apologetically, "even though he *owns* them."

Her husband opened his mouth, but seemed to decide that words were futile. "What interesting work," Marcia said cautiously.

He sent her a quick, suspicious glance and then became engrossed in the study of his boots. "You know, this is the first time I've been upstairs in these things. Next thing, I'll be allowed to smoke my pipe in the house."

Marcia started, and Mrs. Murdock said hastily, "Oh, Justin, I was about to tell Dr. Anderson about the Faculty Tea Sunday afternoon. I was thinking that we could all go together—"

"Go ahead and think it," he said agreeably, "but I'm not a-going."

"But, Justin!" Mrs. Murdock controlled her voice. "The trustees are especially invited, and I can't go without you. You *know*—"

"Can I leave now, Aunt Madge?" Stephanie had edged outside the doorway.

Mrs. Murdock frowned. "*May* you leave, you mean, don't you, Stephanie? You *must* watch your grammar now, with an English teacher in the house."

Stephanie flashed Marcia a dour look and left them. As she went down the hall and then the stairs, they heard her chant, *"May* I leave, *may* I leave. . . ."

Mrs. Murdock sighed. "She has moods."

Mr. Murdock grunted. "That what you call 'em?" He gave his wife another look. "Guess I'll go back to my *puttering.*"

Mrs. Murdock stared at the vacant doorway. "It's a problem," she said, listening to her husband's footsteps.

"Yes, isn't it?" Marcia said with polite vagueness. She was tired and yearned to shut out the Murdocks and all potential students who hated writing, grammar, and reading. "I believe that I'm beautifully settled now, Mrs. Murdock. My trunk and box of books should arrive—"

"Books!" Mrs. Murdock roused herself only to look perturbed again. "But I got in some lovely ones just for you—Plato and so forth —and all with beige covers!"

But shutting out the Murdocks did not help. She moved aimlessly about the room that did not seem to belong to her. Stephanie had made her think of the bored girl in the rose suit. And there was Richard Tibbet, who was definitely through with English. . . .

She opened the briefcase merely to look at the papers. Blake was real, very real. And so was Dr. Alice Ware. . . .

Soon after the interview in her office, Dr. Ware invited Marcia to her one-room apartment. They made coffee on the electric plate back of a tall bookcase. Dr. Ware had partitioned the room off with bookcases.

They sat on the floor, and Dr. Ware smoked and talked energetically, but forgot to drink her black coffee until it was stone cold.

Smoking and coffee-drinking were her two vices, she said. Yes, a little cursing was another one, perhaps, but she considered it a minor one and helpful to blood pressure. After all, curse-words had only emotive meanings. . . .

And that reminded her of an old friend, a great scholar of linguistics—Esther Cornthwaite. She thought that Marcia should meet Esther, when she was adequately prepared.

Marcia listened avidly, fondly waiting for the brusque *hell's* that more and more supplanted the *well's* that Dr. Ware used when in her office.

"It's time now," Dr. Ware said one summer evening after Marcia had received her M.A., "to talk seriously about the kind of work you're going to do. Most women spend their lives on the sort of thing that eventually becomes a footnote in an important book. They leave the big, daring things to the men. They're afraid of making mistakes." She studied Marcia intently. "Are you going to be one of those little animals that dig away patiently all their lives only to end up two inches away from where they started?"

Marcia said, no, she didn't intend to be one of those little animals; she was going to work with William Blake.

Dr. Ware stared at her, then shook her head gravely. "That isn't wise, Marcia. Blake is big in his own way, but he scares people. Save him until later. Find something *neat* for now; then go back to Blake when your reputation is made, at your own leisure—"

"Blake is for me," Marcia said calmly.

Dr. Ware shrugged and laughed. "And that's that! All right. You're very unwise, of course, but I guess I admire you for it. Hell! I knew what I was doing when I plucked you!"

Marcia smiled at the memory. Not even Dr. Ware had quite understood what Blake meant to her.

She remembered her discovery of him in an anthology of English poetry. The anthology was still among her books—her most personal memento. The selection had been meagre, and the lines had been shorn from their context:

> Bring me my Bow of burning gold:
> Bring me my Arrow of desire:
> Bring me my Spear! O clouds unfold!
> Bring me my Chariot of fire.

Instantly they had articulated a yearning within her, although she did not know their meaning.

They led her to more of Blake. Long she wandered hazily through his grotesque world, bewildered by its weird inhabitants and their violent acts of love and hate. Yet her response remained intimate, for their tumult seemed an echo of some buried force within her, which, now discovered, arose to mock her outward self: *Who art thou, Diminutive husk and shell broke from my bonds?* It was this husk that lived with people. . . .

Slowly she came to understand that Blake's was the epic of the heaven and hell of consciousness, triumphant over time and space. *Then Eno, a daughter of Beulah, took a moment of time and drew it out to seven thousand years. . . . She also took an atom of space and opened its centre into infinitude. . . .* The gigantic figures of Los, Urizen, Beulah, Enitharmon, and all the others were but the conflicts of self, hurled into life when the One Man fell from the heaven of Unity and plummeted to the hell of Division. *From everyone of the Four Regions of Human Majesty there is an Outside spread without and an Outside spread within, beyond the Outline of Identity both ways, which meet in One, an orbed void of doubt, despair, hunger and thirst and sorrow. Here the Twelve Sons of Albion, joined in dark assembly . . . became as three immense wheels turning upon one another. . . .* And their battles were waged within the mind, the heart, the loins—*in the auricular nerves of human life, which is the earth of Eden.*

Intellectually she worked painfully through the labyrinth, but there stayed with her a conviction that had little to do with her mind. She was firmly convinced that Blake had written expressly to her, and that she alone could understand him. She condoned his eccentricities, disregarded his occasional lapses into incoherence, admired his arrogant originality. *I must create my own system, or be enslaved by another man's.* Didn't that make him worthy of her loyalty and devotion?

She had not mentioned her peculiar conviction to Dr. Ware, but motivating her at all times was his promise of inner richness despite outward barrenness. *Return, O wanderer, when the day of Clouds is o'er.*

"What on earth are you going to do with him?" Dr. Ware had asked.

And she had answered confidently, "Explain him."

Yes, Blake was real. She felt more at ease than she had since she had arrived in Riverville. She would make a place for him even here.

Soon she snapped on the light to dispel the gathering shadows, and reverently laid out the blouse and suit for her morning conference with Esther Cornthwaite.

The Summit was noisy with registration. She had to push her way past students who crowded the hall. She felt safely anonymous, until she saw the girl who had disturbed her at the railroad station yesterday.

She was in yellow today—somehow a daring color on her. The challenging boredom was still in her face, in her very attitude. *Well, here I am. What are you going to do with me?* She was about to light a cigarette, when someone called from the landing. "Miss Leeds—Carol, may I speak with you a moment?"

Carol Leeds looked up at someone Marcia couldn't see, and smiled briefly. "OK, Dr. Day." She sauntered toward the steps, the unlighted cigarette still between her fingers. There was a swing to her walk, as if her body flaunted a freedom denied to others, yet her steps on the stairs were heavy.

Marcia went slowly on down the less crowded side hall, angry that she should have seen the girl before she had seen Professor Cornthwaite. *What are you going to do with me? You're here to teach me, after all. What do I care about your precious scholarship!*

To steady herself, she rested in the dim corner under the stairs. She wanted to be exactly right for Esther Cornthwaite. . . .

A group of students had stopped nearby. A big hulking fellow intently studied a card in his hand. "I've got Corny!" he bawled out suddenly.

Someone whistled sympathetically.

Another boy frowned over his card. "Who's Anderson?"

"The new English instructor," a small girl with pigtails told him. "I wish she were a man."

Marcia turned abruptly, seeing for the first time rows of open mailboxes. With a sense of unreality, she found her name above one. She pulled out two papers and moved into the hall again to see them. One was mimeographed instructions about the forming of the Academic Procession for Convocation, signed *Arnold Cunningham, Marshal.* The other informed her that classes would begin immediately after Convocation.

She wanted to throw them far away from her, but she folded them carefully and slipped them into her purse. Then she stepped across the hall and knocked directly above the staid lettering:

E. Cornthwaite
Chairman, English Department

It was Paul Lewis Grant who opened the door. He shook her hand and drew her inside before she could explain that she must have knocked upon the wrong door.

But it was the right office, for he was introducing her to Professor Cornthwaite, who stood royally behind her desk. Marcia forgot Grant and looked at Esther greedily. Dr. Ware had not misled her. The hair was magnificent, the pale but clear-featured face was calm and quiet with wisdom, the proferred hand was a beautiful scholar's hand. Marcia sought for the proper words of homage—but the hand had lightly disengaged itself and was waving her to a chair.

She sat down and glanced at Grant, thinking that he was about to leave. To her disappointment, he looked mildly apologetic and, when Esther was settled in the chair behind her desk, seated himself.

"I welcome you, Dr. Marcia Anderson." Esther folded her fine hands before her on the desk. She said a few more introductory words while she formed an opinion of the young woman sitting before her. She trusted records, she trusted Alice Ware's judgment, but above all she trusted her own opinion. "I am sure that you will find . . . John Willard maintains high standards. . . . Nothing more important than Freshman Composition. . . ."

Marcia strained to hear. She was still patient and had no thought of interrupting with a word about Dr. Alice Ware or William Blake. But she tried to make her eyes speak: *You have arrived, a Scholar. I intend to work with ardor and steadiness. I am a willing, suppliant priestess before you. . . .*

"If I dwell upon Freshman Composition, it is because I am thoroughly convinced of its supreme . . ." Esther cut through the smart clothes and concentrated upon the essential elements: hands, facial expression, eyes. The hands were good enough, and the second finger of the right one bore a writer's callous, of which she approved. The face was mobile, perhaps too expressive of personal feelings. At the moment the eyes were intent, almost pleading. The eyebrows and forehead were Classic, the mouth Romantic. If those two opposing factions of temperament could meet in harmony, Marcia Anderson, after a rigorous apprenticeship of a decade or so, might stand a fair chance of becoming a scholar. ". . . certain that you are aware of the grave responsibility of teaching Freshman Composition."

Marcia moistened her lips. "Yes, of course. But my true interest is in William Blake. I was hoping . . ."

Esther arose, not abruptly, but deliberately, to show that she could not possibly have heard Miss Anderson's words. She had decided that the eyes *were* pleading, and that the appeal was directed to her. Ironically she recalled Etta Wilson. Had external facts betrayed her? Would not Etta's dynamic energy have been soothing in comparison to this youngster's deep, silent pleading?

Marcia stood too, uncertainly, wondering what was coming next. Grant had also risen. She felt weak with strain and frustration, and she had the hysterical thought that someone was about to announce the singing of a hymn.

But Esther was regarding her kindly, although as if from a great distance. She picked up an ancient purse. "I leave you now with Dr. Grant. I must attend a meeting."

Marcia turned to Dr. Grant and in a brief glare tried to convey her feeling of contempt for people who invaded other people's conferences. But he avoided her look and said to Esther, "If it's at all possible, I should be glad to attend that meeting in your place."

Professor Cornthwaite gave him a long, steady look and said that as he well knew that was quite impossible.

He half smiled. "I understand." He moved around Marcia to the door, which he held open until Esther had proceeded into the hall. Then he closed it gently and turned back to Marcia. "Sit down, please. We start over again, it seems." He smiled genially, as if they shared a joke.

She was not amused. She walked to the window and stared uncompromisingly out of it. He watched her, hardly blaming her for her anger, although its intensity surprised him. For once he was annoyed over Esther's petty strategy of leaving an interview to him. She had no right to walk out on this girl, who had obviously come in the spirit of a votary before a shrine.

"Perhaps you'd like to ask me some questions," he suggested hopefully. She merely shook her head briefly. "Is your schedule of courses satisfactory?"

She faced him then, meaning to say yes, but his guileless smile exasperated her into lashing out at him with the angry disappointment she was feeling. "I think I should be teaching Blake. Obviously you people here don't care about one's specialty, but I don't see why Blake couldn't have been included in my program." This thought had not occurred to her before the present moment, but the more she said, the more convinced she became that she and Blake had been treated with vile injustice. "How else can you encourage scholarship, if not to allow a teacher to teach his specialty?"

It was Grant's turn to stare thoughtfully out the window. He was wishing he had a way of letting her know that he understood the cause of her outburst. But he could not be sure of the right words for, after all, he hardly knew her. He said finally, "I think it's fortunate that you don't have to teach Blake so soon."

"You mean that you think I'm unequipped?" she asked coldly.

"No, no. If anything, you're *too* equipped. That's the point. You see, you'd take your graduate-school notes to class, and you'd be dis-illusioned when your students didn't absorb them with avid interest and clear understanding." He grew interested in what he was saying and walked to Esther Cornthwaite's desk and back again, talking slowly and earnestly. "You'd be so conscious of the long study by which *you* had come to know Blake that you'd begin to believe that no mere college student could possibly come to know him too. Teaching isn't only a giving-out process. The teacher must *share. . . .*"

He had more to say about teaching. She stopped listening to watch him, and because she was still more a student than a teacher, she speculated on how it would be to take a course under him. She decided that it would be pleasant. But then she thrust aside that favorable impression and said flatly, "I don't agree."

He stopped abruptly and laughed. "I don't blame you for resenting a lecture on your first day here. I tell you what—I'll investigate the possibility of your teaching a course that will at least include Blake."

She was unbelieving. He was being politic—that was all. But she said politely, "Thank you. And now if there is nothing more. . . ."

"Of course, of course," he said quickly, and held the door open for her.

He watched her until she was lost in the student mob. She had not looked back, although he had stood in readiness.

He himself went into the hall and banged Esther's door shut with unnecessary force. As he went up to his own office, he realized that he was more than annoyed to have been put in such an awkward position with Marcia Anderson. It had been decidedly unpleasant to watch her surprise at seeing him in Cornthwaite's office turn into disappointment and finally anger.

As for E. Cornthwaite, she was probably sitting calmly in the Library. It would serve her right, he reflected, if Marcia Anderson stopped in to look over the Library before she left the campus that morning.

"Where's the Library?" Marcia asked Richard Tibbet, who had miraculously appeared before her the moment she stepped outside the Summit.

"Science Hall, second floor, right wing." He pointed to the white building gleaming under the bright hot sun, and planted himself in front of her. "Want a guide?"

"No, thanks." She walked around him, uncomfortably aware that he stood staring after her. He acted as though his meeting her with the taxi had given him some kind of claim on her.

But when she stood before Science Hall, she decided that she was still too angry to enjoy investigating the Library. She hurried on to the Murdocks', sweltering in the suit she had worn as an offering to Professor Cornthwaite.

Her trunk and box of books had come in her absence and now stood uncompromisingly in the middle of her room. She ripped off her jacket and set to work on the trunk, unpacking feverishly, bitterly consoled by the physical exertion. Automatically she noted how expertly Virginia had packed her dresses. One could always count on Virginia! But this thought gave her little pleasure.

When she at last came to the small trunk drawer that her mind labeled "personal," she moved more slowly. For a moment she absently ran her fingers over the top covering of corrugated paper. Then she pulled this off and reached for the small oblong oil painting. Carrying it to the dresser, she studied it, although she knew it well. Somehow she was always surprised to find Martin and Virginia looking the same. She had often unpacked the picture, for Martin had given it to her when she had left for her M.A.

Always there was her father, his spectacles pushed back upon his forehead, the small, carefully trimmed moustache, the slim cigar between the fingers of his left hand. And always there was Virginia, her shoulder touching his, her tightly waved blond hair in styleless dips over each temple, the faint and somehow maddeningly tolerant smile, the open book on her lap . . . Martin and Virginia Anderson. At home.

They looked very much as they had when Marcia came home from that first conference with Dr. Ware. Martin had started the double portrait that day. She had come in to find them both in the living room, and this had surprised her, for it was the time of day that her father was usually in his studio. He hadn't heard her, but was absorbed in the trick mirror arrangement he had set up so that he could manage his own portrait. . . .

. . . Virginia, though, looked up immediately. "Oh, it's Marcia!" she said, turning only slightly, as if her neck were stiff. She laughed guiltily, and her eyes pleaded: *You see how it is, don't you, Marcia? I can't move, for I mustn't spoil the pose. We didn't expect you home this early. . . .*

Marcia deliberately turned away. Her father saw her then in one of the mirrors and nodded absently.

"Martin," Virginia said, "I need a rest."

"You deserve it, I guess," he said reluctantly. "It's going well, don't you think, Ginny?"

"Yes, indeed," Virginia said with comfortable assurance, but her worried eyes were on Marcia.

Martin still studied the mirrors. "What's new, Marcia?"

She knew that the question was automatic. He didn't really care what was new with her. He didn't care about anything beyond doing that stupid portrait with Virginia. "Nothing," she said, shrugging. "Why should there be anything new?"

It was Virginia who persisted. "But you're home early."

Marcia laughed softly. "Obviously." She picked up a magazine and sat down on the couch, but her whole self had cringed before the sound of her own voice. It was curt and harsh, not the voice that belonged to her outside this house.

Virginia smiled, as she always smiled when she didn't know what to say to Marcia.

Martin paced abstractedly, unaware of them both, for his thoughts were still on his work. He was neat, even dapper, in his Oxford gray business suit. So different from Virginia, who was styleless. He had stopped by his smoking stand to reach for a cigar. Suddenly he turned, looking at Marcia as if she had just then entered the room. "But you're home early!" he cried, and to Marcia the words, which from Virginia had been innocuous, now vibrated with interest and concern.

She put aside the magazine, pretending casualness, but from deep within her came the desire to tell him about her talk with Dr. Ware and her new plan to become a scholar. If she—

"It's chilly," Virginia said, slipping on the old yellow sweater that was always within reach.

Virginia, always Virginia blocking her way to him. She stood up. "I have to change. I'm eating at the dorm tonight."

"Oh, Marcia," Virginia said sadly. "Again? We're having a beautiful roast."

Marcia held back the bitter laugh. Virginia *would* think to keep her home with a roast. Soon she would be away and free of them. "I've already promised," she said, hurrying by Martin, whom she now hated again. Why hadn't he insisted that she talk about her plans? Why—

Virginia had followed her to the stairs. "Marcia," she said, putting her large firm hand over Marcia's as it clenched the banister. "Marcia, the portrait is for you. He intended to surprise you with it, but I think you ought to know now."

Marcia moved her hand, but for a moment she looked into the mild blue eyes. She saw the fine lines around them. She couldn't remember having seen them before, and they made a curious stab into her feelings. For the first time it came to her that Virginia was the right mother-age. . . .

"Thank you for telling me," she said abruptly, and went on to her room, closing and locking the door behind her.

She carefully laid the double portrait face-up on the dresser. She leaned over it, resting her elbows on the edge of the dresser. For what it was, it was good, she had to admit. It was the sort of thing that Martin loved to do. He had been like a boy over the success of the trick mirror arrangement. It was as small and complete in detail as a Watteau, but more brilliant. And it was as definite as an etching. Oh, yes, is was good, for what it was. . . .

She straightened, half enjoying the familiar hurt that always came with seeing the little painting. . . . She would have to ask Mrs. Murdock about picture hooks.

She went back to the trunk drawer and returned with a slender folded leather case. Opening it, she set it on the dresser alongside the double portrait. It showed the photographed portrait of a young woman with a delicate profile and sensitive, full lips.

Marcia picked it up and gently brushed some imagined dust off the top of the case. She started as Mrs. Murdock shouted outside her door, "Dr. Anderson! May I speak with you just one minute?"

She unlocked the door. "I was going to ask you about picture hooks. I wonder if you happen to have—"

"Of course," Mrs. Murdock said heartily, edging into the room. "I came to tell you"—her face saddened as she remembered her message— "that Mr. Murdock and I will *not* be able to attend the tea with you tomorrow. The orchards, you know," she added vaguely. "Oh, are these the pictures?" she asked, going over to the dresser.

Marcia nodded. "This one," she said, pointing to the double portrait.

"Why," Mrs. Murdock said in awe, carefully touching its surface with the tip of her finger, "it's painted! How extraordinary—to have an original painting to hang up just like any picture! Is it your father and mother?"

"It's my father and *step*-mother," Marcia said quietly. She had been waiting for that question. She pointed to the photograph in the leather case. "This is my mother."

Mrs. Murdock shook her head mournfully, but she asked with quick curiosity, "Dead—or divorced?"

"She died when I was two," Marcia said distantly. "Perhaps we could find the picture hooks now."

Chapter Six

MARCIA followed a tall couple into the Camerons' long, high-ceilinged living room, which was shuttered against the sun and lighted by candles. A small gray-haired woman sat pouring at the lace-covered table. People clustered around her and then glided away, their movements undulating in the candlelight. Noticing Marcia and the tall couple, the woman came toward them in a mist of rose-petalled chiffon.

"How lovely!" she said over and over, touching their hands lightly. The tall young woman called her Mrs. Cameron, but she was calling no one by name. She looked twice at Marcia and puckered her forehead slightly, but said or asked nothing. She directed the women to go up to her very own room to leave their things, and made it sound like an exciting game.

Marcia had nothing to leave, but she willingly followed the tall young woman, who went up the stairs with surprising slowness. When she turned into a room off the hall, she cried, "Iris! So you were sent up too."

The girl called Iris was standing and smoking by the white-curtained window. "Judith! I was afraid you'd decide not to come." As she crossed the room, Marcia saw that she wasn't so tall as her slenderness and the amber feather on her small gold hat made her appear. Iris' friendly smile included Marcia, whom she evidently thought to be with Judith.

Before Marcia could deny this, Judith was saying, "I'm determined not to stay in, although sometimes I think that Owen would prefer it." Somewhat stiffly she sat down in the straight chair before Mrs. Cameron's wicker desk, and Marcia saw then that she was pregnant.

"Bah!" Iris turned to look into the mirror of the dressing table. "Owen should have no say in *this* matter." She caught Marcia's eye in the mirror and politely included her. "Don't you agree?"

"Oh, yes," Marcia said, and when Judith glanced at her curiously, she added hastily, "But of course I don't really know. I mean, I don't know anyone here."

Iris turned quickly. "You aren't with Judith?"

Marcia smiled. "No. I merely took refuge with her. I've just joined the faculty. Doc—Marcia Anderson, English Department."

"I'm so sorry," Judith said, rising. "I thought you must be someone I should know because Mrs. Cameron seemed to know you."

Iris laughed. "That means nothing. She forgets everybody's name and therefore pretends to know everyone. Menopause," she explained to Marcia. "Well, I'm Iris Taylor, Drama, and this is Mrs. Owen Scott, the wife of one of your colleagues."

"We've given you a horrible welcome," Judith said with concern. "I'll find my husband. He'll be eager to—"

"I *thought* I'd find you up here powdering," said an assured voice from the door.

"Good afternoon, Dean Haskins. Did you come up to powder too?" Iris asked innocently.

Judith smiled at this, but the Dean did not. "No, I did not come up to powder," she said with unnecessary insistence, for her smooth, full face was obviously free from all make-up. She turned to Marcia then, frankly examining her, and Iris began the ritual of introduction. Dean Haskins concluded it with an expert handshake, as if she had long ago decided upon the proper number of shakes due an English instructor. "Of course I shall introduce you around," she said, leaving no doubt.

Marcia murmured her thanks, but she regretted losing Iris as a guide through that labyrinth of tea-drinkers.

"However, you must excuse me a moment." The Dean whispered in a tone which confided that even deans are only human. "As a matter of fact, I stepped up here to go to the bathroom."

Iris waved her hand. "Right down at the end of the hall." And when the Dean had left the room, she grimaced. "See her sniffing the smoke?"

"At least," Judith said as Marcia wistfully followed her and Iris to the stairs, "Dean Haskins will make your introduction *official*."

Dean Haskins was soon back, bringing with her a distinct lily-of-the-valley fragrance which had not before been noticeable. As Marcia walked dutifully by her side, she idly wondered whether the Dean had helped herself to Mrs. Cameron's cologne or carried a vial of her own in her purse.

Judith nudged Scott. "There she is, with Dean Haskins."

Scott looked up. She was as good as the photograph, even with a hat on. Quickly he took in what hadn't been supplied by the photograph. Not bad.

"You didn't describe her very *accurately* to me," Judith said, laughing a bit.

He was puzzled. Marcia Anderson wasn't important in their lives. "Why should I have?" He glanced at Judith for an answer, and then looked more carefully. She was jealous! He had a sudden feeling of unexpected pleasure over the discovery. "She *is* good-looking, isn't she?"

"Shouldn't you be meeting her?" Judith asked.

"Not on the assembly line! Haskins is giving her quite a work-out." He shrugged. "No hurry. I'll be seeing enough of her soon—working together, you know, day after day. . . ." He moved to a small table and

72

put down his cup and saucer. "Think I'll circulate a bit. You be all right?"

When Judith nodded, he wandered aimlessly across the room, but out of the corner of his eye he watched Cameron and J. W. MacMillan. J.W. sat in the Queen Anne chair by the radio, wearing that expression of his that suggested only politeness kept him from showing boredom. Cameron was standing and talking earnestly in his slow, precise way. J.W. briefly glanced up at him now and then, but most of the time he seemed to be attracted by something across the room.

Scott ducked around Kim Duncan, who seemed attached to the wall like a leech. No use getting stuck with *him*. He found a vantage point and looked around him curiously. What was interesting J. W. Mac-Millan? His gaze lighted on Marcia Anderson, shifted to J.W., returned to Marcia. So that was it! An intriguing little sidelight—although he'd never before thought of J.W. and women. Somehow the usual urges of mankind seemed too common for that suave exterior.

He tried to think of a reason to join J.W. One didn't appear before him simply to talk about the weather. One was very appreciative of his mere presence and made every word count—

He jumped as something hit him between the shoulder blades. Colley popped into sight. "Gave you a start, eh?"

"Not at all," Scott said, moving away. "I was just going—"

"Have you seen old Cliff Hughes?" Colley trotted along with him.

"Who's he?" Scott asked without interest.

"Why, an alumnus—back to teach Philosophy. Webb's protégé, but Cliff and I were always very close—"

"Well, he was before my time," Scott said sharply. These people who thought you should know every detail of John Willard history! He knew very little of its past, and he hoped he wouldn't have to know much of its future. . . .

"Back with his Ph.D., too. A bit puffed up about it, I fear. That's what degrees do—make people forget that it's human nature that counts. I never got around to picking up that last scrap of paper," Colley said confidentially, "and believe you me, I'm glad of my plain little old title of *mister*! Keeps me—"

"Sometimes it's an advantage to have *both* titles," Scott said. "Where is this Hughes?"

Colley scanned the room. "Over there—sitting on the arm of the chair right back of your wife."

Scott found him. Long and lean like himself, but very fair. Girlish mouth, but alert eyes and high forehead.

Scott's eyes wandered to Judith, who was standing near the chair, apparently unaware of Hughes, although he appeared very much aware of her. It gave Scott a queer feeling to watch her apart from him. She was beautiful in spite of— Well, he just couldn't get used to her pregnant. Sometimes he was proud, sometimes embarrassed.

Why did she just stand there? Why didn't she join some of the other women?

He saw Hughes stand suddenly and say something to her. She gave a little start, as if surprised to find someone near to her; then she turned and smiled fully at Hughes.

Scott felt his muscles go tense, as if he wanted to go to her. That smile, unguarded, complete. Different from what she gave him of late?

But he didn't move. It wouldn't do for a husband to rush across the room to his wife because some blond Adonis happened to speak casually to her.

He thought he could safely ask J.W. about his son—what was his name . . . Russell?

Judith smiled again to reassure the gravely concerned young man. "I really don't want or need to sit down, thank you."

"But I thought—" He stopped, blushing faintly.

She laughed easily. "I know: Everyone does. But I assure you that it's sometimes more restful for me to stand up."

"Really?" he said seriously. "I don't know much about—" Again he stopped, seemingly torn between scientific interest and personal embarrassment.

"You're new, aren't you?" she asked, meaning to help him on to another subject. Then she was afraid he might think her question referred to his newness in the world at large, and so she hastily added, "To John Willard, I mean."

"Well, yes and no," he said earnestly, with no indication that he had caught a double meaning. "I'm an alumnus, but I'm back to teach. Philosophy." He cleared his throat. "Clifford Hughes is my name."

She exclaimed over his achievement and introduced herself. "I wonder how it feels," she said, "to meet your teachers as colleagues. This must be quite an interesting occasion for you, Dr. Hughes."

He blushed again. So her guess about the "Doctor" had been right. He pondered her question. "To tell the truth, it's not all pleasure. Do you know," he said wonderingly, "some of them are actually *jealous* of me!"

"That's only human nature," she said, beginning to like him very much. Maybe he didn't have a sense of humor, but there was no tortuous subterfuge to him. "Have you met Miss Anderson? She's even newer than you." She found Marcia being introduced to the Librarian, Mr. Breen, and pointed her out to Hughes.

"I met her briefly," he said without noticeable interest.

Judith was relieved. At least *all* men didn't swoon at Marcia Anderson's feet! Then she told herself that she was being ridiculous—and petty.

"There's Professor Webb!" Hughes announced suddenly in such awe that she looked quickly to be sure that he meant the only Professor

74

Webb she knew. Yes, there he was, standing in the midst of people, but still a barren island unto himself. "I thought he was on sabbatical," she said.

"He is," Hughes said, his voice tender. "But he never leaves the campus, you know, and he forgets that he doesn't have to attend things. He'll probably show up at Convocation tomorrow, unless I remind him that he doesn't have to." He nodded wisely. "All great men are absent-minded. Their minds are on really important matters."

That's the polite way of putting it! she thought. Not even Hughes could convince her that the dry and crabbed old man out there holding his teacup and forgetting to drink his tea was anything but a dry and crabbed old man. Curiously she glanced back at the young man as he gazed raptly upon Webb. She wondered suddenly if Owen had ever looked so eager and so—so straightforward, if he had ever proffered love and loyalty to an old teacher. . . .

She said gently, "Why don't you go rescue him?" She was afraid that Hughes would feel duty-bound to stay by her side for the rest of the afternoon.

He started guiltily. "If you really—" She nodded, and he gave her his first smile, a grateful one, and went toward Webb.

Alone again, she wondered what to do. She could join the group of wives standing at the other end of the room, talking and laughing easily. But the group looked forbidding in its closeness, and she'd feel an outsider. It was when she attended an affair like this one that she realized how completely she and Owen had lost all social contact with his colleagues. Owen had no social being. No . . . that wasn't quite fair. Owen was too busy, as he was always telling her. . . .

She was passing J. W. MacMillan, who smiled pleasantly and half arose. She shook her head to show that he was not to bother, and went on, amused at the concern the single men showed over her condition. She wondered why J.W. didn't remarry . . . a handsome piece of masculinity going to waste.

Idly she imagined what it would mean to be his wife. Wealth, prestige, ease . . . no straining to get ahead, get ahead. Get ahead—to what?

Deliberately she paused to speak to Miss Browne, of the Physical Education Department, whose long, supple body quite made up for her plain, square-jawed face.

J.W. tried to place the attractive pregnant woman. He had it—Mrs. Owen Scott. And Scott was the one whose height he envied and who had come up to ask him some inane question about Russ. He smiled slightly, amused to recall in what various forms homage had been paid him that afternoon. . . .

He allowed his eyes to find Marcia Anderson again. She had been brought up to him by Haskins. She hadn't looked carefully at his face and had perhaps failed even to catch his name. They would meet again, but it would be in his own way, leisurely and with no peremptory Dean Haskins looking on. . . .

She didn't have the appearance of a teacher. That was what intrigued him, he supposed. Her thin black velvet dress was smart, yet not at the expense of beauty. His mother would approve of the way she looked. . . .

A substantial background? He tried remembering that part of her application papers, but could not.

And her face. What was there to be said about her face? Say it went with the clothes. That was sufficient.

No, he could not imagine her in a classroom. She would be best in evening clothes. He began to see her in a simple white evening gown . . . at his own table . . . on his porch, sipping coffee and brandy . . . in his garden. . . .

He thought suddenly of the Cézanne landscape he had brought home from New York last week. He hadn't gone in search of it, but had found it quite accidentally, and even then he had had no intention of buying. But when he had gone away from it, he began thinking about how from then on he would be aware of its absence from his study, until he had at last hurried back to buy it. . . .

"In a way," Marcia answered President Cameron absently. She hadn't heard his question, but she thought by now it didn't matter whether or not she gave the right answers. She turned slightly, uncomfortably aware that someone was staring at her.

"You either are, or you aren't, you know," President Cameron reproved her mildly.

Are or aren't what? she wondered. "I didn't want to appear presumptuous," she said, looking up at him humbly. He was a tall man with gray hair that still glinted red, like a dying fire. He kept his profile turned to her in the manner of an Egyptian painting.

"Equivocal answers are the Bane of Mankind," he continued, unappeased.

"Oh, I agree," she said quickly, wishing that Dean Haskins had not withdrawn her capable guidance. But the Dean had judged her duty completed when they had reached the President.

"Humility is a most desirable Asset," he said calmly. "Still, we must temper it with Daring." The eye turned to the ceiling. "I remember—"

"A call for you, dear." His wife touched his arm.

He nodded his thanks to her and an apology to Marcia, who thought that she had never seen the nod used so efficiently. Mrs. Cameron watched her husband disappear into a small room off the larger one. Then she turned to Marcia. "How charming you look this afternoon, Miss . . ." Her forehead puckered slightly under the gray curls. "How *is* your mother?"

"If you mean my step—"

"Oh!" Mrs. Cameron laughed delightedly, her restless hazel eyes already on a new object. "Excuse me, my dear Miss . . . I must give tea to Professor . . . Professor . . ."

"Professor Grant," Marcia told her, watching Grant start toward her but stop when he saw his hostess coming to welcome him.

The sight of him reminded her of the disappointing meeting with Esther Cornthwaite. He was doing his best to look at her over Mrs. Cameron's head, but she pretended to be unaware of his efforts. He had a bulging briefcase under his arm, and she thought it a silly affectation for him to bring it to tea. Mrs. Cameron took it from him prettily and carried it to the lace-covered table. There she plied him with tea and sandwiches, which clearly he didn't—

"Dr. Anderson?"

"Why, yes," she said, looking up into eyes that were cool, watchful, unrevealing.

"I'm Owen Scott. Dr. Scott, of the Department of English. Eighteenth Century." He inclined his head and smiled in such a way that she did not know if he were being condescending to her, or to himself for being the man he said he was. "You don't know me, but . . ."

Instinctively she gave the room a surreptitious glance for his wife, Judith, who was determined not to stay in while she carried his child.

Judith leaned back against the couch. "Jealousy?" she repeated, wishing she had chosen a different topic for tea-talk. "What do you mean—'deceivingly basic'?"

Dr. Medora Day turned sideways then to look at her, and Judith was immediately reassured. The clear brown eyes showed neither surprise nor calculation. They were accepting, even absorbing, and Judith felt herself drawn into them. The cluttered, heavy room faded from her senses, and in its place arose four quiet walls of soothing enclosure.

"I mean," Dr. Day was saying, "that jealousy is attached to so basic a drive in our nature, that we accept it as normal—that is, we are not shocked to find it in ourselves. As a result, we crowd other feelings into it . . . feelings that we're afraid to call by their true names. Jealousy then becomes a convenient cover-up for what we don't want to acknowledge." Dr. Day smiled and looked away, as if to assure Judith that she was safe from further discourse unless she desired it.

Her turning away broke the spell for Judith, and her fundamental distrust of psychologists reasserted itself. "I see," she said politely. But she still thought that if she felt jealousy for Marcia Anderson, even without apparent cause, she felt exactly that—instinctive jealousy. "It's very interesting—your theory," she said then, afraid that she hadn't been properly appreciative.

"Oh, theory in itself means nothing," Dr. Day said, picking up her purse and gloves. She pulled briefly at the brim of her brown felt hat. "I must be getting along. Mother, you know, loves us to have tea together in the afternoon." She gave a little apologetic laugh. "I hate to disappoint her."

Judith watched her make her way through the tea-drinkers, a small, inconspicuous figure in brown. It occurred to her that Dr. Day made tortuous little detours to avoid meeting people.

Then she saw Owen and Marcia Anderson. So they had met—without waiting for her! After a moment of watching him, she arose and went toward them.

Marcia was glad when she saw Judith coming. Scott was setting her on edge. "No, I haven't published yet," she answered him.

He became a shade friendlier. "Well, I can hardly call what I've done *publishing*. Just the usual thing—about half a dozen articles. I have to be cautious, you know. You have to be when you're on the really big ones like Swift and Pope."

So William Blake wasn't one of the big ones! "I suppose you do," she said politely.

"But you have one great advantage with Blake: he's so fantastic that—"

"Hello!" she said warmly to Judith.

"I'm so glad that you two managed to get together at last," Judith said dryly.

Her tone puzzled Marcia. "I don't understand how Dean Haskins missed him," she said.

Judith moved to Scott's side and linked her arm in his. "Oh, he preferred to be missed, didn't you, dear?"

And he probably did, thought Marcia, for some obscure reason of his own.

Scott patted Judith's hand. "As I was saying," he went on to Marcia, "Blake is so fantastic that you're perfectly safe in saying *anything* about him. A wide open field."

"That's right," she said with forced lightness.

"You were wise," he said shrewdly, "to find such a happy hunting ground. How'd you ever get started on Blake?"

"Darling!" Judith said. "Let's have no more shop talk."

"I'm disappointed not to see Professor Cornthwaite here," Marcia said quickly, trying to direct the remark to Judith.

Scott raised his eyebrows. "Surely you don't expect royalty to bother with teas!"

"But it isn't that she doesn't like tea, is it, dear?" Judith laughed up at him as if over a shared secret.

Uneasily Marcia wondered what had happened to change Judith's impersonal friendliness.

Scott laughed tolerantly. "Judith is right. I'm afraid you'll soon find out how much Cornthwaite likes tea. At least once every two—"

Marcia turned as Scott broke off abruptly, and saw Grant approaching them. To her surprise, she felt relieved, as if rescue were at hand.

"Glad you've met," he said after he had greeted them. "I'm sorry I didn't arrive in time to introduce Dr. Anderson myself."

"Yes, I noticed your lateness," Scott said, *and* the briefcase. What do you intend to do—steal the silverware?"

Grant laughed, but Marcia was suddenly angry with Scott, although she herself had had the same feeling about the briefcase only a few minutes earlier.

"Have you met all the English people?" Grant asked her.

"Well, I'm not sure. . . ."

"Kimball Duncan?" Judith asked.

Marcia shook her head. "I don't recall that name."

Grant surveyed the room. "There he is—standing against the wall, not far from the piano."

Marcia looked at the tall young man and was intrigued by his long, olive face. He stood in conspicuous solitude and somehow avoided seeing them, although she was sure he was very much aware of their looking.

Judith laughed. "I imagine Dean Haskins missed him because she mistook him for a picture hanging on the wall. He hasn't budged since we entered the room."

Scott shrugged. "A queer youngster."

Marcia turned back to Judith, whose voice had again been warm and natural. It was Grant's joining them that had made the change, she decided. His mere presence seemed soothing to jangled nerves. She glanced at him with new curiosity, and found him watching her.

"You should meet Duncan, I think," he said.

Scott watched the two of them walk off together. Judith's hand tightened on his arm. "Can't we leave now?" she asked.

"Why not?" he said absently, but made no move. How vulnerable was Grant to a good-looking woman? Would he dare slice off a part of the Eighteenth Century for her to teach?

"Truly I'm tired, Owen. Let's go."

He felt the warmth of her hand upon his arm. Strange what her touch could do to him still. Steadied him, quelled the devil-doubts. The evening was theirs—an evening before Convocation tomorrow morning and then nine months of the old grind.

"Right away," he said gently, smiling. But the smile faded as he again noted the new quiet beauty of her face. He had grown aware of it soon after they knew about the baby, and it seemed to him that she had a private happiness in which he had no share.

He moved so abruptly that she withdrew her hand. "I suppose," he said with sharp irritation, "we'll have to make some pretense of thanking Mrs. Cameron before we go."

79

Kim did nothing to keep up the talk. After all, they had taken long enough to come to him; so why should he trouble himself.

"If you'll excuse us," Grant said finally, "we'll search for a quiet corner. Dr. Anderson and I have some business to discuss."

Kim saw Marcia look at Grant in quick surprise, but she murmured a disgustingly conventional good-by and obediently went off after him.

Well, all right, he thought, staring after them. If they already had secrets from him, all right. What did he care about them? Or anyone else in the room . . . in this stagnant pool of staid sobriety and propriety. . . .

He watched Judith Scott speak to Mrs. Cameron. What wouldn't he give to paint her as she was now! After Vermeer. The Dutchman had known how to paint a pregnant woman—not blatantly or bizarrely, but inconspicuously in the midst of an everyday scene that had the quiet rhythm of growing life. . . .

He'd do it in the manner of Vermeer! Fine wishful thinking.

The moment of freedom was gone, and again he looked restlessly around his prison. Marcia Anderson and Grant were being waylaid by Dean Holcomb, that little man who wore his smug geniality like a cloak of office. Haskins joined them, as if afraid to miss something, erect as steel in the pin-striped suit with the proper white at the throat. Career female in frigid mold.

Beyond them, by the radio, sat MacMillan. Slight but distinguished gray at the temples, alert eyes, aristocratic nose, inflexible chin, impeccable tailoring. Made up to look the part: Successful American Man, Twentieth Century.

Even Iris. . . .

There was a sulky feather on her hat, and it drooped over her forehead, putting mystery into her green eyes. She took a step, and heads, mostly male, turned to watch. If she came to him, he'd tell her he liked her hat.

She didn't, but stopped by Webb and the new blond fellow. A dehydrated vegetable and a ripening one; and in a couple of decades, the old one would be dry dust, and the younger one would shrivel into the dehydrated state.

He wished that Carol Leeds—

The moment her name floated to the surface of his thoughts, his mind illuminated her image in the blazing brightness of a photographer's bulb. Sweat came out on his nose. The palms of his hands prickled as though a thousand little diamonds were pressed against them.

He wished that Carol Leeds would make a sudden entrance. She could stir even the moribund. Her coming would be like that of the wind and rain on a dull, lethargic summer day. Her fathomless eyes, her shining hair—

He had never seen her wear a hat.

Marcia Anderson shouldn't be wearing a hat. He returned to studying her. It made her look too well groomed. Only plain or ugly women needed to look well groomed.

He decided that his sketch of her face was good. Even with the hat on, she was all those things he had read into the photograph. How, then, could she be content to sell herself to this institutionalized life?

Perhaps she didn't know. He'd find a way to warn her. . . .

Iris was watching him, spying upon him. There was that humorously amused expression on her face. He knew it well and hated it. It was a devastatingly objective look.

He'd show her. He'd show the whole damn stuffy room—

Marcia and Grant were at last finding their quiet corner on the other side of the radio, near MacMillan.

The radio. If he hadn't felt forced to come to the tea, he'd now be listening to the afternoon symphony program.

Carol Leeds couldn't enter the room, but music could. Why, he could make it pour in like a mighty, cleansing river.

As if set off by a spring, he went across the room in long strides, colliding with the soft, pudgy Colley, taking a sharp detour to avoid the startled Cameron, but at last turning the little knob right under the fine nose of J. W. MacMillan.

The sudden mellow tones of the violin in full volume stopped all voices. Mrs. Cameron stood stock-still, holding the copper urn over a waiting cup. MacMillan tried to show only bland amusement. Grant and Marcia turned slowly, stared at the source of the sound, then at him, the cause.

Iris alone moved. Out of the corner of his eye, he saw her detach herself from the two vegetables and come toward him. The silly grin on her face told him that sheer will power kept her from running. When she reached the radio, she bent down and casually modulated the volume. "You had it a little too loud, Kim," she said sweetly. She flashed a smile at MacMillan, Grant, and Marcia. "I do hope you don't mind. I asked Kim if he thought we could arrange to hear the program today. You see, this is one of my favorite—compositions."

Under her breath and the music, she said to him, "Couldn't you get yourself fired in a less spectacular way?"

Grant was listening to the music critically. "What is it?" he asked her.

"What is it?" Iris smiled blankly. "Oh, the name escapes me. Kim, what *is* it?" She poked him in the back.

"Name eludes me too," he muttered, furious with her. She had stripped his gesture of all meaning, had made of it a farce.

"Prokofieff," J. W. MacMillan said then. *"Second Violin Concerto in G Minor."*

"Of course!" Iris cried.

Marcia nodded dreamily. "The Andante movement." She smiled

sympathetically at Iris. "It's one of my favorites too."

Kim put his elbow on the top of the radio, rested his chin in his hand, and half closed his eyes. Sensitive Young Man Absorbed in Music. But the need for a support was real. He was weak. The gesture had consumed almost all of his nervous energy and courage. He was glad when the others stopped looking at him and went about their dull business.

Grant laughed suddenly, and the sound was discordant against the music. He seemed to realize this and lowered his voice almost to a whisper. "These teas become livelier each year. I really do have something important to tell you. Shall we try the porch? Or," he added after a second look at her face, "do you prefer to listen to the music?"

"Well . . ." Marcia hesitated. Her eyes hurt from looking at faces, and her lips were stiff from smiling. The music cast an opiate charm over her tired mind, lulling even her interest in what Grant had to tell her.

"All right, then," he said easily. "I want to speak with Mr. Dexter before he leaves. After I do that, I'll wait for you on the porch."

When Grant left, the man who had identified the Prokofieff arose from the Queen Anne chair and joined her. She was embarrassed because she could not remember his name.

"It seems," he said, smiling down upon her, "that we share Prokofieff."

"Yes," she said, although it occurred to her that anyone who especially liked the concerto would not deliberately talk through it.

His face sobered, as if to fit the mood of the Andante. "I know this movement well." He did not deem it necessary to explain that he knew it well because his son played it so frequently that he, J.W., was ready to smash the phonograph. "It is compelling music."

"I've met so many people today that I can't recall . . ." She paused, but he didn't help her. "Are you in the History Department? Or is it Economics?"

He seemed amused. "Neither. J. W. MacMillan."

"Oh." She struggled with the name, then with startling clarity remembered, not her introduction to him that afternoon, but Richard Tibbet's pointing out the red brick building. "Then you're the president of the John Willard Tractor Company down by the station."

He nodded gravely. "But I'm not here in that capacity today."

She remembered more. *He's also the big chief trustee. . . .* "Of course not," she said quickly, blushing.

It was, he knew, the first time that she had lost her composure that afternoon, and he was not displeased to be the cause. He pretended to become reabsorbed in the music.

She too pretended to listen, but by now she could be conscious only

82

of his standing so near to her that their arms touched lightly. She felt childlike with him, and tried to be angry because of it. He hadn't even mentioned the capacity in which *she* was present. . . .

But the anger wasn't real, for she felt oddly protected by his nearness. It was as if she no longer had to think for herself, maintain her poise, or care that Professor Grant probably was convinced she was a fool.

"Do you want the next movement?" Iris called out to them.

He waited for her to speak, and she said no. Iris snapped off the radio and led Kim away.

J.W. smiled again. "An unexpected pleasure." For a moment he hesitated over final words to her. He knew that he would see her again, but he had no intention of being hurried. Russ was too unsettled . . . the conversion of the factory too recent. . . . If public opinion were not at the moment set against the Germans, he should have said *auf Wiedersehen* to her.

As it was, he inclined his head briefly and said, "Good afternoon, Miss Anderson."

She watched and heard him say essentially the same words to Mrs. Cameron, and she was deeply dissatisfied.

She found Grant waiting on the porch. "Let me be brief," he said immediately. "It is now arranged for you to teach Blake."

"Pardon?" She struggled with what he had said, for it seemed alien to her mind.

He regarded her queerly and repeated his statement.

"Oh." She leaned against the warm stone pillar. She had completely forgotten about her sudden desire to teach Blake, although she still felt keenly the disappointment of her interview with Esther Cornthwaite. "But there is no such course in my schedule."

"It's a new course that Professor Cornthwaite agreed to set up. We discussed it only today. In fact, that's why I came here late."

"Professor Cornthwaite discussed this with you today—Sunday!" She laughed shortly. "Frankly, after my conference with her yesterday, I thought . . ."

He seemed to understand what she had thought. "E. Cornthwaite is no simple mechanism, but you'll look far and wide before you find a better administrator."

When she said nothing, he went on briskly, "We'll call this the Later Eighteenth Century and offer it in place of the Later Nineteenth, for which there is no real need this semester. It's yours to plan, of course, but I thought you might make it a history of the rise of Romanticism, with Burns and Blake the major. . . ."

She only half listened. She was annoyed, not pleased. Why did he have to make her feel even more foolish by satisfying her childish demand? "Isn't Scott the Eighteenth-Century man?" she asked abruptly.

Grant nodded. "But he has never done much with the later part. He'll be relieved to be rid of it."

That's what you think! she almost said; then reminded herself that, after all, she was new here. She said instead, "This doesn't give me much time for preparation."

He was sympathetic, but also implied that he couldn't bring about *two* miracles.

And after that there seemed little else to say. People were still coming out the door, and they stood watching them. Then she began pulling on her gloves, studying them carefully. "Please don't think me ungrateful. You see, yesterday I—"

Kim and Iris appeared. "How would you like to see your office?" Iris asked her. "We'll walk around the Heart; then Kim can take you up in the Summit."

At that moment she had little interest in her office, but the invitation was a means of breaking away from Grant with some dignity and grace. "That will be fine," she said brightly, and turned to Grant. "Thank you again. I'm delighted with the course."

Grant watched the three of them go down the steps and around the walk. She has a nerve, he told himself. Who did she think she was to come here as a beginner, demand a course, then, after he had with no little trouble arranged it for her, accept it in the spirit of doing him a great favor?

Hearing Cunningham's voice nearing the door, he hastily went down the steps. He didn't want company. But once he had escaped, he had the feeling that everyone had deliberately gone off and left him alone.

He strolled toward the Heart, thinking that he might as well go see his newly arrived niece, Janice.

Underneath his disgruntled, restless mood he knew that he was angry because his second meeting with Marcia Anderson had come off no better than the first. He was growing suspicious of his reactions to her. As he thought back, he began to understand that he had been waiting all summer to see her again, although during that time he had not consciously given her more than a casual thought or two.

Then he recalled Holcomb's reaction to her photograph, even Scott's at the English meeting. . . . Mentally he checked over her record one more, and was consoled. It was a superior record, one that certainly justified the hiring of her. He felt even better when he remembered that E. Cornthwaite had had as much to do with the decision as he.

He slowed down as he rounded the President's house, for the three of them were not far ahead of him. She was carrying her hat in her hand and the sun put unexpected reddish lights in her hair. He had to stop as they stopped to light cigarettes. They walked on, and she laughed at something Iris said. He found himself listening to the sound with the preciseness of a scientist discovering a new element. It was the first time he had heard her laugh.

When they reached the Summit steps, Iris said, "I'll leave you here. I want to make sure the Barn wasn't looted during the summer." She showed Marcia how the grape arbor to the side of the Summit led directly to the Barn. "And back of the Barn is Grace Hall, women's dorm. I live there. So does Haskins," she added ruefully. "Otherwise"—she gave Kim a wicked look—"students and Carol Leeds reside there."

Marcia placed the name. The girl in the Summit hall . . . at the railroad station. "Isn't she a student?"

"Certainly," Kim said primly. "Furthermore, everyone speaks very highly of her class work."

"There are a few low things to be said also," Iris murmured. "Unfortunately," she said to Marcia, "she happens to be the best theater material that has ever come my way, and so I tolerate her." She shrugged, but Marcia thought her eyes too serious for the flippant gesture. "Well—see you tomorrow in academic garb, I'm afraid."

Marcia threw away her cigarette and followed Kim up the Summit steps, wondering if he knew that Iris was in love with him. Probably not, she decided, for he impressed her as an intensely self-absorbed individual.

The Summit interior was cool and quiet. She followed Kim up the wide stairs to the second floor, where he stopped to say with spirit, "You can see how finely built this house is. And all the rooms are done in different woods. That's why they're called the Oak Room—that's Cameron's office—the Cherry Room—Cornthwaite's—and so forth." He stamped hard on the floor. "You don't find anything like that today!"

She was mildly surprised at his enthusiasm, for he did not seem to have any great love for John Willard. "You have quite a feeling for this place, haven't you?"

"For the Summit—yes." He waved his long arms. "It is a fine old house. I have great feeling for all fine things." He grew belligerent. "But they have ruined it to make it part of the institution. I abhor all things institutionalized!"

He went angrily up the darker and narrower stairs leading to the third floor, seeming to forget that she was with him. She followed gropingly, aware that the temperature was rising with each step.

"It's *hot* up here!" she said when they reached a large finished attic with a sloping ceiling. Beaver-board partitions separated a row of desks to create the illusion that each desk was in itself an office. The air was close and incongruously filled with the smell of turpentine.

"Yes, it's hot," he agreed morosely. "We call it the Inferno—Dante's *Comedy*, only backwards. Paradise is the first floor, where the really Big People are, and where it's cool in the summer and fairly warm in the winter. The second floor is Purgatory, where the Almost Big People are, and where the temperature is indifferent at all times. And this is Inferno, scorching in summer, freezing in winter."

"And who are the other lowly sinners thus doomed?" she asked, sitting down in someone's desk chair.

"Diaz is where you're sitting—"

"Diaz? Don't tell me there's someone here I've not met!"

"That's right. He wasn't at the tea and he won't be at Convocation. He doesn't have to attend anything, because he's related to J.W."

"J.W.? Oh, yes. . . ." She heard a few strains of the Prokofieff. "What does he—Diaz, I mean—teach?"

"Spanish." Kim pointed to the next partition. "That'll be yours, the next is mine, and the next will go to Clifford Hughes, I think."

"So." She got up and went into the cubbyhole which he had said was hers. The desk had been emptied for her, but it needed dusting. She removed her glove and absently printed out her name on the top of it. "Well," she said wearily, "I've always liked attics, but I never seriously considered earning my living in one." She sniffed the air. "What are they doing, painting the place?"

Kim looked guilty, then defiant. "That's my turpentine. I paint up here in rainy and winter weather. I'm an artist, you know."

She said nothing but went over to his desk. The beaver boards around it were covered with reproductions of paintings held in place by Scotch tape. She saw nothing original. "Perhaps you'll show me your things someday."

He flushed slightly. "I don't bring them out—much."

She nodded understandingly. "I know. The more something means to you, the greater is your fear of having it criticized."

This set him off. He strode from one desk to another. "I have no fear—only contempt! Why should I allow myself to be judged by mediocrity? I have no desire to become a *popular*"—he spat out the word— "painter like Denvers or—or Anderson. I have no—" He stopped, his mouth still open. He closed it slowly and eyed her fearfully. "Anderson," he repeated as if tasting the word. "Martin Anderson. Marcia Anderson. You're not . . .?"

She had felt only momentary anger over the contempt in his voice as he spoke of Martin Anderson. She smiled calmly. "Yes. I'm his daughter." Going to her own desk, she stood with her back to him and idly drew her fingers through the printed letters of her name until they were no longer legible. "But don't be embarrassed or—anything. I feel as you do about his work."

But he was embarrassed. "Good Lord, I didn't know . . . didn't mean . . ."

"It's too hot and close in here to breathe," she said abruptly. "Let's go."

"We can get fresh air up on the Widow's Walk." He seemed eager to keep her with him. She waited below while he went up the ladder-like steps in the middle of the room and pushed at the trap door in the ceiling. When it opened and flopped back upon the roof, he reached down for her hand.

They walked over to the iron railing that enclosed the level square in the center of the roof. "Amos Willard got the widow's walk idea from the East, I guess," he said. Then he directed her to lean over the railing. "See the year-date in colored slate—1859?"

She looked obediently, but she was more interested in finding the parts of the campus and Riverville which she had already come to know. The Heart was deserted and even the town seemed quiet and motionless. A glint of gold attracted her, and she saw that it was the yellow river touched by the late afternoon sun.

"That's where I paint in good weather," Kim said, following her look. He sighed tragically. "I like it up here. I come up whenever I feel cramped. Up here you can see beyond all this"—he flicked his hand to indicate the Heart and its buildings—"stuffiness."

Just then Grant appeared on the walk below. With him was a slight, dark-haired girl. "Grant," Marcia said, "doesn't seem stuffy." She felt a flare of curiosity over why he should single out a student for such special attention.

"No. But"—Kim was bitterly confident—"he will be in time. I can't understand why he doesn't leave this place!"

"Why don't you leave?" she asked absently, still watching Grant and the girl as they walked toward the tip of the Heart.

Her question strangely disturbed Kim. He pounded the railing, forcing her attention back to him. "Why?" he shouted.

"If you are an artist, why not paint?"

He glared. "I tell you, it isn't so simple as you might think! After all, I *do* have an M.A. in English. Don't ask me why I have one—ask my mother. You see, it all began when . . ."

At first she listened valiantly to the story of his life, but after some minutes her mind wandered. The tea had left her with a medley of impressions, and seeing Grant had set them all in chaotic motion. To her own surprise, she thought first of J. W. MacMillan. There was something unreal yet tantalizingly familiar about that memory. Confused, she put it aside, for it seemed to have nothing to do with her present life—with Alice Ware, Esther Cornthwaite, or William Blake.

The Blake course—that was definite and real. She'd have to unpack her notes and prepare an introductory lecture this evening. But she wouldn't start the course with Blake. She'd save him until last; work up to him, then present him in a burst of glory. . . .

What should she wear to her first class? The pink wool? But that wouldn't do under her academic robe at Convocation in the morning. It would have to be the black suit, with the white blouse—

The white blouse! Now she remembered that she hadn't seen it when she had unpacked her clothes yesterday. Virginia had forgotten to pack it—even though Virginia knew very well that it was her favorite white blouse.

How like Virginia! It was even possible that she had omitted that particular blouse purposely. . . .

She imagined how she would tell Virginia about it if she were face-to-face with her. Her voice went up hysterically; Virginia's stayed low and calm, maddeningly so. . . .

"What?" she asked Kim with a start. "I'm sorry, I didn't . . ."

His somber eyes were fixed upon her so intently that she feared he must have seen the fury in her mind. But he said, "You do understand, don't you?"

"Oh, yes," she said quickly, relieved. "I do indeed."

"I knew you would. I knew that from the minute I first saw you— even your photograph." He held out his hand. "I'm glad that you have come, Marcia Anderson. Together we can fight for Art and Freedom."

She took his hand, feeling guilty. She hadn't been fighting for Art and Freedom: she had been having a temper tantrum.

But he had seen none of that in her face. Puzzled and vaguely sad, she turned back to the railing and stared out over the darkening land.

```
┌─────────────────────────────────────────────┐
│                                             │
│             PART  TWO                       │
│                                             │
└─────────────────────────────────────────────┘
```

Chapter One

WEARILY Marcia went to the window and slid up the blind. The grim dawn was turning even the snow gray. It filtered into her room, making the electric light vapid.

Back at the sagging maple dask, she put the books, the three small card files, and her thick thesis manuscript on the floor. Then she leafed through the notes and outlines she had made during the night. It was unnecessary activity, for she already knew that she had not found the right way to present William Blake to her class. Weeks ago she had been confident, but now, with only a few hours between her and class time she felt so hopelessly buried under her knowledge that she couldn't breathe, let alone lecture coherently to that blur of apathetic faces. . . .

So Grant had been right. But not for the reason he had said. It wasn't *her* fault. Impatiently she switched off the desk lamp and went back to the gray window, resting her aching forehead against the cold pane.

It was the students—their indifference. Already she saw the stifled yawns, heard the restless shuffling of feet, sensed the never-voiced yet ever-present question: *What is this going to get us? What's the use of all this stuff?* She could fight anything but indifference.

You had to earn a right to know Blake. She had. Now she was willing, even eager, to plant the seeds of knowledge in receptive soil, but she hardly thought it her duty to furrow the land first.

What would those students do if she were to talk seriously on one single thought from Blake—for example, the line that became a refrain in his work: *For everything that lives is holy?* Why, they'd laugh. They laughed at everything. The laugh, the giggle, the smirk—those were their badge of honor. They—

The radiator sizzled and then clanked. A door opened and someone pattered down the hall. The day had begun. She looked out the window and saw that the gray had brightened into a pink glow.

She sat down at the desk and jerked at the lamp chain. Deeply dissatisfied, she found fresh paper and made perfunctory notes: Born 1757; proceed with life thru dates; define Mysticism briefly & throw in vision or two for illus. and *humor;* . . .

Richard Tibbet considered the risk of turning on the light. M-107 was filled with the bleak grayness of the December day, and he hated gloom. But Dr. Anderson had already begun to speak, and he did not want to interrupt. The less conspicuous he remained in this class, the better. Last year he had bragged about being through with literature courses forever, and here he was in one again. . . .

"William Blake was born in 1757," Dr. Anderson was saying, "and died in . . ."

Richard carefully wrote down the dates. He liked them. They were as definite as doors opening and shutting. If all literature could be reduced to dates, he'd be happy.

"In 1771, Blake began his apprenticeship as an engraver. . . ."

Carol Leeds deliberately stared out of the window. Dates, dates, dates . . . so what?

She was bored, and made no effort to pretend otherwise. God save her from women teachers! Why? Well, she liked men teachers better. They often bored her too, but she had a game of pretending that they didn't. Most women students did that instinctively; but she *knew* when she was doing it, and that was why she was better at it.

. . . You sat with shrewd, calculating eyes. They thought them thinking eyes, thinking upon the large, powerful ideas coming from their large, powerful minds. You parted your lips, ever so slightly, as if tasting of the large, powerful ideas. They talked on and on, making the ideas smaller and smaller to fit into your pretty little female mind. You were so interested that your breathing quickened, and you absently moved an arm so that your sweater stretched tight across your breast. Their eyes wavered, returned, wavered again. You crossed your legs, their eyes lowered swiftly. . . .

But no use putting on that act for Dr. Anderson.

Even so, she crossed her legs. She might have rung a bell, the way David Whitney looked around. He always responded with the promptness of a well-tuned mechanism. She gave him a languid smile.

He smiled briskly and winked.

He would wink! The height of daring! She allowed her smile to die out and then stared gravely at him, knowing that her very still body was eloquently articulate. That always discomfited him. It did now. He looked for a moment and then flushed and turned abruptly away. She saw him fumbling with his notes.

Let us see you shine now, Mr. David Whitney, our little fair-haired English major. Prig! prig! prig!

In a way, she was practicing on David for the benefit of Mr. Kimball Duncan. For the same reason, she was also enduring Mr. Duncan's Novel course. Faculty. That was something new for her. It was good to feel that inner stir of excitement as she thought of him. Maybe he'd be too easy. But he was faculty. Something new. . . .

However, she'd have to keep it from Dr. Day. There were some things that even Dr. Day wouldn't understand, and Dr. Day had a way of detecting those very things so carefully hidden out of sight.

Something tugged at her interest, and she listened. . . .

". . . when Blake was a very young boy, he began to see the Prophets in the fields and God at the window. . . ."

So. There was something more to Blake than dates. But she carefully kept her face expressionless. It wasn't wise to show interest.

. . . You learned that most of the little external inducements to bring you outside yourself were fakes, and that responding to them was dangerous. It was like being invited to come out for a walk by someone you trusted and who told you that you didn't need a coat, but when you were out, you found it cold and were chilled to the marrow. . . .

Richard Tibbet put down his pen. There was something in him that wouldn't allow him to record the fact that William Blake had seen God at the window. Fact? He doubted it.

His thought relaxed, and his eyes stayed greedily upon her face. That was all he had of her. He had no right to know what she was thinking underneath the words, what she did outside this one class—nothing.

But he didn't like her hair pulled back. He wondered why she had changed it. To look more like a teacher?

"Mr. Tibbet!"

He blinked. "Sorry. I didn't hear the question."

"I asked," she said with cutting deliberateness, "if you had read the assigned biography of Blake."

"No, ma'am."

"I see. Mr. Whitney?"

Mr. David Whitney not only had read but was ready with judicious observation. "I think," he said carefully, "that the author's treatment was excellent, considering, that is, the extreme difficulty of his subject. After all, Blake wasn't the common garden-variety type of person, and—"

"Pardon, but I wonder if such a person ever did or does exist, the common garden-variety type, I mean!" Mr. Street, a psychology major, sat forward tensely. "If you don't mind my interrupting, Doctor, I should like to challenge Dave to point to such a person!"

David frowned, but obligingly looked contemplatively around him, seeking the common plant. When his glance fixed upon Richard Tibbet, Richard stared back defiantly, and David changed his mind. "Why make an issue of this? I agree that I used a generality, but we're talking about Blake, an individual, not generalities!"

Mr. Street nodded to show that although he didn't intend to cause further interruption, he certainly wasn't taken in by that bit of sophistry.

"Well," continued David, "I think that the author's weakness lies in his not defining mysticism. Avowedly, Blake was a mystic, but what exactly does that mean?"

What exactly does that mean, mimicked Richard's mind. Common garden-variety! Boloney!

"Yes, it is now time to define," Dr. Anderson said almost gratefully. "There are two phases to Blake's mysticism which we must consider. First, his visions; second, his conviction of the ultimate nature of life. Now, concerning his visions, we must—"

"Were Blake's visions *theophanies?*" asked David earnestly.

O Gawd! thought Carol Leeds.

"Hallucinations," said Mr. Street pleasantly.

"I propose," said Dr. Anderson as Mr. Whitney and Mr. Street engaged in a brief duel of glaring, "that we disregard the visionary element, for I believe that the essential meaning of mysticism is independent of it. Now, what is the belief upon which mysticism rests? For it *is* belief or faith, not knowledge. All mystics believe that there is in each individual a power to penetrate and actually experience ultimate reality, call it what you will—Over-Soul, God, First Principle—it is the creative principle of all life—"

"Sex," someone giggled.

Dr. Anderson's face froze. "As I said, call it what you will. Blake thought . . ."

She's mad, she's really mad, Richard thought with wonder; she's serious about this Blake guy. . . .

Blake? One moment he was near enough to touch her; then, abruptly, he was gone. Carol watched and waited as well as listened. . . .

"To be more accurate," Dr. Anderson went on, "Blake believed that the individual naturally possessed this power himself, but that it was too often thwarted by reason, sensible knowledge, repression, false beliefs, superstitions. All these things he saw as restrictions and therefore evils barring out the good. . . ."

Carol opened her hands. There were nail marks on her palms. But that buried force was evil! Hadn't she proved that time and time again? It couldn't be good. Could it? But Blake belonged to the dead past—

". . . of all ideas or beliefs, mysticism is the one that has no history, for its truth depends upon individual experience. Thus, for those who experience it today, it is as new and vital as it was for those who—"

Someone yawned audibly.

". . . those who experienced it in the pre-Christian era," Dr. Anderson finished rapidly. The stony quality returned to her voice. "Please continue reading the shorter poems. Don't bother with the Prophetic Books. They require more time than we have. . . ." She hesitated, and her hesitation made distinct the unspoken words *and more interest and understanding.* She added finally, "Don't become confused over the idea of mysticism itself. Read the poems for the sake of the poetry alone." She nodded dismissal.

In other words, thought Carol, you take the dross and I'll take the gold! She shivered. Here she was without her coat again. . . .

Richard Tibbet stayed in his seat. He watched Dr. Anderson gather up her notes and put them into her briefcase. She didn't see that one of her notepapers had fallen to the floor. He almost called out, and then changed his mind.

Although she and the rest of the class had gone, he still sat. This mysticism—funny if there should be something in it, something that he could take off to war with him. He didn't know. Besides, he didn't understand it. But he needed a lift to war, and he was willing to— Cut out the war thoughts, he told himself sternly; you don't like them, you'll meet them when you have to, and that's that. . . .

Common garden-variety. Who said?

That wasn't fair, not when he had this feeling for her. Marcia. He looked at the name in his mind. Still strange to him. Marcia . . . mysterious . . . mysticism. . . .

The next class was coming in. Someone stooped to pick up the piece of paper.

"Hey!" Richard leaped to his feet and rescued it.

What to do with it? Keep it. Forever. Her handwriting. Going down the hall, he examined it. Small, crowded, hard to read.

Call her. "This is Richard Tibbet, one of your students. I have found an extremely important document which I have reason to believe belongs to you. If you would be so kind as to meet me. . . ."

Marcia hurried down the hall—away from the class and her own sense of defeat. When she saw Carol Leeds standing in the outer doorway smoking, she walked more slowly, hoping the girl would move on before she had to pass her.

To take more time, she glanced into Scott's office. She'd ask about the baby. She saw him standing at his window, but something in his attitude made her keep silence. He was looking at nothing outside himself. Quickly she went on, embarrassed to have looked in upon such personal discontent. Yet only a week ago, when the baby had first come, he had seemed happy enough. . . .

Carol was still there, but she didn't turn to look as Marcia passed. Relieved, she took the walk to the Summit. Not that she wanted to go back to the Inferno. Kim, Hughes, and Diaz would be there, and she didn't want any more talk at the moment. She was sick of words! She—

"Dr. Anderson, are you a mystic?"

Marcia started. "Why, Miss Leeds, I didn't know that you—"

"Cigarette?" Carol pulled a pack out of her deep fur pocket. When

Marcia refused one, she tossed away her own half-smoked one. "Sorry. Suppose it wouldn't be quite proper for a female instructor to walk around the Heart smoking." Her smile seemed mocking. "Dr. Day does it, though."

"I refused because I don't enjoy smoking in the cold air," Marcia said shortly. The girl didn't have to *try* to irritate her. The mere presence of that blank face in class did it successfully enough. "I imagine that the Heart is very beautiful in the summer. I've seen it only in—"

"Well, are you, or aren't you?"

She turned then to look at Carol. The girl hadn't expected this and was caught off-guard. The little twisted smile was gone from her lips, and her eyes were serious. The disconcerting smile came back quickly.

"No," Marcia said, "no, I'm not a mystic."

"That's what I thought," Carol said. She took another cigarette for herself and lighted it deftly against the wind.

Marcia was puzzled. Carol's voice had been childlike in its disappointment, as if she had been hoping for something against her reason. "But one doesn't have to be a mystic to enjoy Blake," she tried.

"That's what you said in class," Carol said rapidly, "but it doesn't satisfy!"

Marcia stood still. It seemed incredible that anyone—Carol Leeds especially—could respond so vitally to anything that she had said in class.

Carol had stopped too. "What I mean is that I don't want simply to *enjoy* him, to read him for only the poetry. I want—"

"Excuse me," said Richard Tibbet, "but I believe that you dropped this paper back in class."

Marcia accepted the paper impatiently, aware that Carol was walking away. Richard sensed that he had chosen the wrong time. "It looked important; so I thought, well, I thought—"

"Thank you," she said with a hasty smile, and caught up with Carol.

"One of your worshipers, you know," Carol said. Her voice had lost its seriousness.

"What is it that you want of Blake?" Marcia asked, although she knew it was too late.

"Skip it. If you're not a mystic, why do you bother with him?"

"You don't have to be a mystic to—"

"Oh, never mind. You've said all that before." Carol smoked moodily. After a moment she shrugged and asked flippantly, "What do you think he'd say about someone who had come from the gutter? Oh, I don't mean a real gutter," she said in answer to Marcia's look. "But I mean someone who's just plain—well, rotten inside."

Marcia still stared, not because of the words, but because she could not believe that she was listening to someone talk about Blake as if it mattered what he thought. Carol's face, the dim figures passing by them, the background buildings all seemed suddenly unreal, and her mind went blank.

Carol laughed, as if she had expected no answer. "He was crazy, anyway. That's what one of the books said." With an angry little jerk of her arm she tossed her cigarette into the Heart. "Thanks—for everything," she said with sarcastic emphasis. Then she turned and sauntered away.

Her leaving set Marcia's mind in motion. "The book's wrong!" she cried, but Carol either did not hear or did not want to hear.

Marcia went slowly up the Summit steps, an answer to Carol's question forming in her mind.

To begin with, Blake wouldn't admit the existence of such rottenness as Carol meant. Belief in it came from a sense of shame, wrongthinking. . . . She saw his words: *In every voice, in every ban, the mindforged manacles I hear.*

At the top of the stairs on the second floor, she stamped the snow off her feet to give vent to her fury. Why hadn't she been quick enough, why hadn't she had sense enough to give that simple answer!

"Damn!" she said under her breath, and stamped again.

Dean Haskins opened her door to investigate the unseemly noise. She clucked disapprovingly. "There is a mat right back of you, Dr. Anderson, provided for the express purpose of . . ."

The Inferno air was thick with smoke and turpentine odor. Kim was working at his easel, standing much too close to the small canvas and frowning deeply in the bad light. He was happily unaware of Diaz, who glared at the back of his grimy blue smock. When Diaz saw Marcia, he shrugged, put on a long-suffering smile, and turned back to his desk.

Hughes slammed a book shut and lighted a cigarette. As the first stream of fresh smoke passed before Kim's eyes, he groaned. Diaz shot him another look. "Don't you find painting under these difficulties a hazard to your eyesight, Mr. Duncan?"

"No." Kim refilled his tin cup with turpentine and set it on the window sill.

Marcia quietly moved over to her own desk and sat down, but did not remove her coat. Her eyes ached from no sleep and she was still too angry with herself to work, even if she were to be given a private, soundproof, and well ventilated office.

Hughes had begun to clean out his desk. He pulled out drawers, banged them shut, and crumpled paper savagely. He was always slamming things these days.

Suddenly there was soft music. Kim turned sharply, Marcia listened unbelievingly, and even Hughes was surprised into silence. Together they saw the small portable radio on Diaz's desk, and cried in unison, "No!"

"But yes." Diaz smiled. "Mr. Duncan pursues Art, Mr. Hughes is incredibly noisy, and I have my little radio."

Kim wiped his hands on the front of his smock. "Let's take a vote."

Hughes laughed shortly and pointed at Diaz. "If there's one person in the whole country who wouldn't be affected by a vote, even a unanimous one, it's he. Yesterday he . . ."

Marcia slipped by them, only half listening to the part of Diaz's soft answer that floated down the stairs with her. ". . . said merely that no number of votes will make a thing right if it happens to be wrong. Are you afraid that . . ."

Before she reached the first floor, Kim was calling after her. She waited, and he came clattering down the stairs, thrusting on his overcoat as he ran. "Marcia! Why did you run out on me?"

"I ran out on Hughes and Diaz," she said bitterly. "They find a way to get into that same argument every day. I'm sick of it."

Kim held open the big door. "Well, I'm sick of this place. Let's go to Herby's for coffee."

They walked around the Heart and down President Cameron's slushy driveway before he asked suddenly, "What argument?"

She gave him an amused glance. "You're there to hear it as often as I am, Kim. You know, you're lucky. Pick up a paint brush and you're oblivious to everything else. . . . They seem to argue mostly about the democratic procedure. Diaz says how stupid it is, and Hughes gets pale and—"

"Oh," Kim said, not interested, "then it isn't personal." They crossed the Heights and he helped her down the still icy short cut.

"But it is somehow," she said as they went on. "I believe Hughes is losing weight over it. He's deadly serious about it and Diaz merely eggs him on. That's the awful thing about it."

Kim shrugged. "That isn't very polite of Diaz, but what's so awful about it?"

"Diaz is just pretending to care one way or another, and that means," she said slowly, "that he's indifferent. I think Hughes senses that." She shivered and drew her big fur collar more closely around her face. "There's nothing worse than to have to fight indifference!"

That struck a response in Kim. He grabbed her arm excitedly. "Right, Marcia! That's exactly what I've been feeling. Tell me! Why are a few of us made sensitive while the great stupid majority is blunt and dull? Is it to torture the few? Is there somewhere a grinning deity. . . ."

Here it comes! she thought, but she listened patiently and, as always when he raved, with mixed feelings. He echoed a confused part of her own thoughts, yet when she heard it said aloud, she could catch the undertone of fear, and she never failed to be grateful that he, rather than she, was the one talking.

"Howdy, folks." At the sound of the door, Herby had lowered his widespread *Billboard*. From under the slanting eyelids that gave him his perennial sleepy look, he watched them slide into one of his red leather booths. "Just been reading about a pal of mine I ain't seen in many a moon. Always did wonder what had happened to him. Well, he's dead."

"Too bad," Kim said, impatient of the interruption. "Coffee, please, Herby. One black and one with sugar and cream."

"One straight and one fancy!" Herby shouted as if to an invisible helper. Without rising, he reached to the back of him for two coffee mugs and filled them from the big urn to the side of him. He began a lugubrious whistle, which was a grotesque accompaniment to the soap-opera voices coming from the radio on the counter.

Kim scowled. "Radios everywhere! Invented solely to prevent thinking, a part of the conspiracy against the individual. . . ."

Marcia only half listened. Radios . . . the Cameron radio . . . Prokofieff. Her idly directed thought became suddenly intense.

She was annoyed. That memory of J.W. standing at her side pursued her meaninglessly, and with unwanted objectivity she had already noted that it grew most persistent when she was dissatisfied with her work.

She lighted the cigarette Kim had given her but had forgotten to light for her, and was thankful to see Herby coming with the coffee. He set the mugs down and plopped a spoon in each. "In '28, when we were on the Big Time, I said to George—that's my friend what died— I said, 'Georgie, vaudeville's singin' its swan song, and the smart thing is to quit right now.'" He shook his head sorrowfully as they took their first sip of coffee. "Well, I did, but Georgie didn't."

"Is that what killed him?" Kim asked politely and set down his mug with great deliberateness.

Herby reflected seriously. "Could be. It's like I said. Vaudeville sang—" He was stopped by the ringing of his telephone. "Better answer. Probably bad news. . . ." He glided off.

Kim began eagerly, "Marcia, what I mean is—" He broke off and stared at her. "What on earth have you done to your hair!"

"I'm wearing it up—obviously. What's the matter?"

"What's the matter! What are you trying to look like—a teacher?"

"Well, I am a teacher," she said, half angry.

He was scornful. "You're an artist. Here—this is the way you should look." He reached into his overcoat pocket for a carefully folded piece of paper, which he smoothed out and put in front of her. "I made that from your photograph. That's how I knew even before I met you that you were my kind, that at last there would be someone around here who would understand me."

She studied the sketch silently, feeling that she had encountered a mirror when she least expected or wanted one. After a minute she refolded the paper and gave it back to him. "You forget, Kim. It's my father who is the artist. I'm not one."

He slipped the paper into his pocket and said with careless wisdom, "Art isn't what you do; it's how you do it." He brooded over these words, then asked suddenly, "Marcia, what would your father think of my work?"

She frowned slightly. "It's hard to say. His approach is very business-like and technical, as I've told you. He insists upon sharp, clear out-lines, and hates vagueness or mystery."

He shuddered, and for a moment they were silent with different thoughts. "I'm not an artist," Marcia said again. "I'm a scholar, or trying to be. No one here really cares. Professor—"

"I know, I know. That's what I feel. Every time I—"

"Professor Cornthwaite," she cut in quickly, "is completely oblivious to me. Grant has said that he'd like to see the manuscript I'm working on now. Kim, do you think he really *means* that? I can't bear to—"

"Of course he means it," Kim said confidently. "Grant always means what he says." He waved his cigarette to dismiss that topic. "Marcia, there's only one other thing in life as important as Art—and that's Love. I honestly believe"—he leaned forward—"that if you had come along earlier, I'd have fallen in love with you."

"My misfortune to arrive late," she said, smiling, but feeling weary inside. "So there *is* someone else who understands you."

Kim frowned. "Not that exactly—I mean, I don't know. I don't talk to—her. I look at her. She's a symbol of everything that's different, of everything I want."

"Iris?"

The delicate frown became a scowl. "Why did you have to guess *her?* I like to work with Iris, but she's too—too definite." He stared into his cold coffee. "It's Carol Leeds."

Marcia was startled, thinking of her strange talk with the girl. "But, Kim," she said, and then did not go on, for she could think of nothing to say.

He did not look up and so did not see the concern in her expression. "She's free. She's scornful of the mediocre, as we are. You can tell that in the way she looks at people. She's beautiful, as all worthwhile things must be." He turned the mug around and around. "And for those reasons, people don't like her. Why is she as she is?" He looked up defiantly. "She's a complete egoist. That's what you have to be, you know, to live fully. That's what"—he jabbed his thumb at himself— "*I* am."

Marcia protested politely. "Not any more than is natural, Kim. We all—"

"But I am!" he insisted. "I tell you . . ."

He proceeded to tell her until Marcia happened to note the time. "Don't you have a class coming up?" she said, holding out her arm for him to see her wristwatch.

He paled. "Oh, Lord! I'm going to be late!" He clutched his coat and sprang out of the booth. "Oh, Lord!"

As they ran across the Square, it occurred to her that, for a complete egoist, Kim was surprisingly afraid of being late to class.

Scott roused himself. That must have been the bell. He'd wait until the halls cleared. Maybe he wouldn't even go to class today—but he supposed he would. God, how he hated to drag through another unprepared class! Odd how he was always wanting to teach the Eighteenth Century and then when he got it, how he'd always slide through on his old notes. What made a man do that?

He reached for a cigarette and moved to the window. Medora Day was passing. . . . Why didn't *he* have an office in the Summit?

Well, it was understandable why he was sliding through classes now. This wasn't an ordinary time for him, not with Judith in the hospital, the bills growing, the baby to think about. . . . John Worman Scott, his son. He said that over to himself several times a day, but he still couldn't get much meaning out of it. Decent of him to give in to Judith's father's name without even an argument. But had he really cared, one way or the other?

Kim and Marcia came running around the President's house. Childish. Romance? He doubted it: Kim was too young for her, or so he seemed. His eyes narrowed as they watched Marcia Anderson. Enemy? Well, she had taken a slice of the Eighteenth Century for herself, hadn't she? Actually, he had never bothered much with the later part. But just the same, he didn't care to have *any* Eighteenth-Century course taught by anyone but himself. Made him feel that he was losing hold.

Maybe he was. That's what happened when a man's private affairs sapped his strength. He should have fought that Fundamental course. He should have insisted that the Later Eighteenth-Century course at least be renamed so that it wouldn't so obviously appear to be the Eighteenth Century. But he had been passive, allowing them to do as they pleased with him. . . .

Kim had waved and dashed across the Heart, and Marcia walked on alone, more slowly. She had a controlled, almost prim walk, as if she were keeping something back. He wondered briefly about her sex life, and then shrugged, not really caring. She was too aloof. . . .

Judith had something of the same aloofness. There had been excitement in breaking it down. It came back now and then, when she was angry. She never stormed and raged, but became calm and remote. He dreaded that . . . and hadn't she been that way more frequently of late? But never mind. Babies were supposed to adjust that sort of thing, weren't they?

Even so, he'd like Judith back wholly and completely, and of her own free will. Call it pride. . . .

He was suddenly aware that the hall was very quiet. He looked at his watch: three more minutes and the class had a right to walk out on him. Again he was tempted, but even as he considered not going, he ground out his cigarette and picked up his book.

Alice Mueller sat tense. Professor Scott was in one of his bad moods.

He balanced the textbook in his hand and leaned against the front of the table-desk. "Has any exceptional student read the assignment for today?"

Hands went up, and he selected one. "Now, Miss Mueller, we'll start with the simplest facts first. What *was* the assignment?"

"The first epistle of Alexander Pope's *Essay on Man*." Afraid that she would shout the words, she mumbled them.

"I must apologize for my defective hearing, Miss Mueller. I didn't quite understand you."

She repeated her answer, and when he nodded to indicate that she was correct, she went weak with relief. She quailed under his sarcasm, yet was morbidly fascinated by it. To be made a victim was proof that he took particular notice of her.

"And now," he was saying, "quote me the final couplet of the first epistle."

There was a reaching for books.

"No, no! Without looking into your books. You people must develop an awareness for significant lines! Nothing will help you do this, if not Pope, who is the most quotable English poet. Why, when I attend the Literary Convention, a group of us Eighteenth-Century scholars talk *in* Pope for a period of two hours or more."

The class was obediently awed.

"Ah, yes," Professor Scott said reminiscently, "we restrict our entire conversation to lines from Pope."

Alice Mueller closed her eyes, imagining this feat. She saw Professor Scott leading the discussion, the other great scholars faltering after him.

"It would be interesting," suggested David Whitney, "to know just what one has to be or to do to become eligible to attend the Literary Conventions."

With effort, Professor Scott brought himself back to the present. He frowned. "It's quite an arduous process, Whitney. First, of course, is the attainment of the doctorate, and then . . ."

The class relaxed.

Alice Mueller leaned back in her seat and studied him. Had the baby changed him? The thought of the baby both embarrassed and saddened her. It made him seem almost ordinary, somehow. . . .

She thought of Mrs. Scott, that disturbing shadow which occasionally moved across the background of his life. A tall and beautiful shadow; therefore, cold and heartless. Probably she hadn't wanted the child. Probably she failed to make him a good, comfortable home. . . .

"I'm afraid that we went off on a tangent," he was saying. But his humor had improved. He glanced at his watch. "I see there's hardly time enough to begin a discussion. Too bad. Well, be sure to check that couplet before our next session!"

She stood in the hall, seeming to search through her notebook, but watching him as he paused by his office door. "Professor Scott!" she called.

"Yes, Miss Mueller?"

She moved toward him, wishing that she wore stockings instead of the socks, a dress instead of the shapeless sweater and skirt.

He waited, smiling impatiently. She groped for words, steeling herself against running away. What had she thought she dare say to him? "I want to change my major—to English," she said breathlessly.

"Really?" He seemed pleased. "Then see Professor Cornthwaite."

Oh God, she thought, why didn't I say something else? Corny scared her. "But couldn't *you*—couldn't you—"

"Just remember to talk up so that she hears you." He was being kind, and his kindness was as impatient as his smile. "Anything else, Miss Mueller?"

"No. Oh, no. Thank you. Thank you very much, Professor Scott." She turned sharply and walked away from him, her legs stiff. Cold sweat trickled down her arms.

When the door had shut out Alice Mueller, Scott stopped smiling and threw the textbook down on the desk. He lighted a cigarette, but 'he first intake of smoke nauseated him. He ought to do something about lunch; he wasn't eating right these days. Where should he go? Not with people. Home then, for another canned meal. He grimaced at the thought, and then felt pity for himself.

He left Main Hall, walking hurriedly. He could make a few notes on the Swift chapter before hospital hours. Jonathan Swift, a devil of a fellow to match. . . . Most likely, it was the Swift chapter that had made Ritson reject his manuscript. Well, he had a new idea for catching him. What would Judith think of it? But Judith wasn't interested now. . . .

He knew exactly how she would look when he walked into that foreign and antiseptic room. She would smile her new smile of gentleness and tenderness that was not for him. She would ask and answer questions absently, her mind elsewhere, her eyes veiled to him.

No decent meals, no one to talk to. And all because of John Worman Scott. . . .

"Hey! Dr. Scott. Watch out!"

He stopped short. There was a squealing of brakes. Richard Tibbet rolled down the window and leaned out. "Sorry, sir, but I turned into the drive before I knew that you were going to stop there."

Scott smiled weakly. He saw Esther Cornthwaite in the back seat, and he felt foolish. He hadn't known that he was standing still in the entrance to the President's driveway! "Sorry, Tibbet. I had my mind on something else." He tipped his hat to Esther and raised his voice. "Fact is, I was thinking about Swift. I'm revising my manuscript, you know."

"Splendid!" said Esther, beginning to back out of the car. "I'll walk from here, Richard. Thank you. My briefcase, please."

Richard handed the briefcase through the open window and drove away.

"I'll walk back with you and carry your briefcase," Scott suggested amiably. It wouldn't do any harm to impress her with his new idea on Swift.

But Esther settled the briefcase firmly under her own arm. "I may need a ride up the Heights in icy weather, but I'm still perfectly capable of walking unassisted on level ground. Thank you, however. Now, you run along and think about Swift, young man."

Scott tipped his hat again, but this time rather curtly, and strode off. She had no sense of value. That kind of treatment might do for Kim Duncan, but— He shrugged. He wasn't going to be upset by trifles. She wasn't *that* important!

What *had* he been thinking about? Oh, yes. John Worman Scott. Well, well, so he had the initials *J.W.* He hadn't noticed that before. Maybe that meant he'd be successful. He had a feeling too that it was a good sign that John Worman Scott had slipped in a few days before Pearl Harbor. All in all, John Worman Scott might be a good thing to have happened.

The front room had a close and musty smell to it. He threw his overcoat into the couch.

The room mocked him. *She isn't here . . . she won't come back alone.*

As always since she had been away, he looked to see himself in the mirror over the mantel as he passed it. He didn't want to, but something made him do it. It was beginning to seem to him that there was nothing but that mirror in the whole house.

The kitchen was cluttered with stacked dishes, yet barren-seeming. He reached into the cupboard and pulled down a can. Tomatoes. He shrugged and opened the drawer for the can-opener. He let the can-opener clatter back into the drawer when he heard the knock at the back door.

It was Mrs. Holcomb with a covered tray. "I thought perhaps— well, here is some lunch."

Surprised, he took the tray and held it while she darted down the steps and around to her own steps. She wore the eternal wrap-around apron in which she did her eternal cleaning, and her hair was up in curlers.

"Thanks!" he shouted. "Thanks very much."

He sat down at the table and bit into the sandwich. Ground meat of some kind. He didn't like ground meat of any kind. Judith knew enough not to make ground meat sandwiches for him. But there was also a bowl of steaming soup.

Suddenly he was eating the sandwich very fast. He was famished, had been for days. He started thinking over those past, vacant days. . . .

He lighted his second cigarette and then remembered that he had meant to do something on the Swift chapter. There wasn't time now. He'd have to hurry to get to the hospital at the beginning of the visiting hours. . . .

He wanted to hurry, but he made himself sit there and smoke slowly. He wanted to hurry, but he also wanted to see how she'd look when he walked in late.

Esther Cornthwaite sat wrapped in her ancient beaver coat. She was not cold, but there was a wheeze within her when she breathed, and she had the notion that the coat would somehow eliminate it. Besides, to remove it might indicate to the Maintenance Department that she was well satisfied with the temperature of the room, and she saw no reason to coddle the Maintenance Department. "As Montaigne observed," she proceeded, severely eyeing her Freshman Composition students, "wars are fought over matters of grammar. . . ."

Janice Grant did not stir restlessly as did many of the other students, but she was intensely bored. After a few shuffling sounds, however, the room became respectfully quiet, for by now it was well known that Professor Cornthwaite had developed a sixth sense to detect inattentiveness.

Contemptuous, Janice watched the students around her settle into listening poses. They submitted out of fear. She submitted because she had learned that Professor Cornthwaite was important.

Yet as she now looked about her, she was aware of a faint hope that she would find a face marked as neither Important nor Unimportant, but as belonging to an improbable third class of humanity. This person she would admire without qualification, and be admired in return. . . .

But she discovered no sign hitherto missed. She was not surprised. She was observant, and weeks ago she had carefully estimated the social stratum, the I.Q., and the chances for success of each student around her.

For a while she had thought that Paul Lewis Grant might be such a person, for he had been kind and had not (as she had feared he would) reminded her that he was her uncle and superior in age and profession. But when she had come to understand that his kindness was impersonal, she had somewhat regretfully placed him in the Important class. In fact, she felt a certain scorn for his kindness, which she had observed he gave without discrimination; and although she had been a little hurt, she thought that—

"Today," Professor Cornthwaite was saying, "I have chosen to read to you an essay entitled 'Knowledge is Power.' Please listen carefully, for the sentence structure is admirable, the choice of words excellent. . . ." As she talked, her calm gaze came to rest upon Janice, who returned it unblinkingly.

But her heart thudded. "Knowledge is Power" was her theme, and she listened critically to its words. She was humble about her writing talent. That talent was her key to the world, and some day she would turn the key. For a moment she heard not her own words, but the crashing of the world as it fell in two at the turning of her key. And at the dim end of the long jagged corridor dividing the halves, stood her mother and father, awe and pleading on their usually indifferent faces. . . .

" '. . . Knowledge, then, is the only true source of power. All other sources, even money, are exhaustible. Scientists control nature through knowledge, psychologists control people through knowledge. . . .' "

Janice relaxed, hoping that the unimportant ones around her had guessed the essay to be hers.

Silent for a moment after reading the last word, Professor Cornthwaite rearranged the papers neatly on the table before her and folded her hands over them. "As I remarked earlier, this composition shows genuine writing ability and"—her eyes flickered toward Janice—"intelligence." She gave the word a strange emphasis. "I do, however, find the subject matter distasteful. I cannot quarrel with the theme, for knowledge is indeed power. But let me admonish you, when it is acquired for the sake of power, and not for the sake of wisdom, it becomes as evil an instrument as gunpowder." She arose. "I assign to you not only the reading of, but the reflecting upon *The Tragical History of Doctor Faustus*, by Christopher Marlowe. Good day."

Sobered, all students but Janice left the room with unnatural quietness. It was not frequently that Professor Cornthwaite was moved to stirring comment upon their unworthy literary efforts.

Janice was glad to wait until the room was cleared of all but her and Professor Cornthwaite, for she needed those few minutes to quell her fury.

So her idea was distasteful. Knowledge for the sake of wisdom . . . blah blah. She hereby withdrew her respect from Esther Cornthwaite, who had revealed that underneath that impressive exterior she was nothing more than a fearful old woman, a Sunday-school teacher. . . .

She left her seat and went slowly up the aisle to the front of the room. "I want to thank you," she said in a properly shy, but carefully distinct voice. "I see now how wrong I was about knowledge and power."

"For your sake," Professor Cornthwaite said, drawing the great coat around her in the manner of a toga, "I'm glad to hear those words from you. To admit an error is an experience as instructive as commendable. As for your composition, I am understanding of the fact that your idea controlled you, rather than you it, when you committed it to paper. Ah yes, it is in writing that the danger lies, Miss Grant, for writing is part muscular activity, and with all such activity there occurs what the Moderns term a conditioned reflex." She smiled kindly down at the slight girl. "Because of that reflex, many honest men write more than they intended. . . ."

Janice stood at humble attention, her face grave, her eyes large with gratefulness for these few rare moments. But not the whole of her listening attitude was pretense, for her mind took in the words and efficiently stored them. It was possible that later she would find a use for them. All things were grist to the writer's mill.

Chapter Two

GRANT evened the sheaf of papers and carefully put them back into the box. Automatically he picked up his pipe and went to the window. The elm was budding and the sky was bright. But he was still under the spell of what he had finished reading, and it seemed that the world was filled with drifting fog, through which moved primeval yet eternal forces of love, hate, fear. . . .

Dimly he heard footsteps on the stairs. He made a sudden gesture, as if clearing away the fog. Then he went into the hall. She was starting down the second flight of stairs. "Dr. Anderson!" She stopped and looked questioningly over her shoulder. "I have read your manuscript. If you have a few minutes to spare. . . ."

She glanced at her watch. "Why, yes." She followed him into his office, seeming eager yet reluctant. "Mrs. Murdock prefers me out of the house during Saturday cleanings."

He laughed heartily, feeling like a dentist putting his patient at ease. "I'm homeless on Saturdays too, for the same reason. We—oh, sit down, please, and won't you take off your coat?"

She ignored his reading chair and took a straight one, holding her coat on her lap. He took the coat and folded it carefully over the back of the reading chair. "Sorry I have no cigarettes—only an extra pipe."

She barely smiled and lighted one of her own cigarettes. "I was beginning to think that you had forgotten about my manuscript."

"Forgotten? Of course not!" He handed her a huge ashtray. "It's a long one, you know, and I read it twice."

"Twice?" She smoked calmly, but he thought her tense. "Do you mean you had to read it twice to understand it?"

"I'd have read it twice"—he grinned—"if it had been about Little Boy Blue. That's my plodding method. But to answer you specifically —yes."

She looked away and appeared to be examining his bookshelves.

"I thought it perfectly clear. My advisors thought the original thesis perfectly clear."

"We mean different things. Each sentence, taken by itself, is admirably clear. But when the sentences are put together to form a whole. . . ." He shook his head.

"It's not a completed manuscript," she said with quick resentment. "I told you that when I gave it to you. It's fragmentary as yet. There is no whole."

"In a way there is. You create a world." He leaned against his desk, staring down at her intently. "Before anything else, I want to tell you this: it is *powerful* writing. As I said, you create a world."

She jabbed out her half-smoked cigarette. "You don't like that world?"

He hesitated, then said slowly, "It's a world of instinct. Whether I like it or not is of no matter. I belong to that world with all the other animals—human and otherwise. Don't think I glibly dismiss it. However"—he shrugged—"I happen to cling to faith in reason. Perhaps I should look shamefaced as I admit this—but there it is. You make Reason your villain, Instinct your hero. Frankly, I don't like that—frankly, I don't believe it's true."

"Frankly," she said grimly, "that happens to be Blake's world. Am I suppose to falsify his ideas merely to satisfy"—she gave him a faintly contemptuous look but finished politely—"those who disagree with them?"

"Blake's world?" He walked to the window, as if he had forgotten her. "I wonder."

"How well do you know Blake?"

"A good question." He laughed and came back to the desk. "My knowledge of Blake is definitely limited. I'm not trying to hide that fact. Oh, I've tried him at various times, but the longer poems leave me groping. Not that he hasn't some superb lines—and some symbolic pictures charged with explosive meaning. Take this—

A dog starved at his Master's Gate
Predicts the ruin of the State.

Now that I—"

"That's from a minor poem," she said impatiently.

He nodded. "Perhaps. But minor or major, it's a poem I can understand, with a meaning I can communicate, and a—"

"About reason and instinct," she said, "aren't you ignoring the fact that certain modern psychologists would agree with me?"

"Ah, the irrefutable argument! I was sure it would appear." He smiled, but when she showed her irritation, he said quickly, "You mean they'd agree that Reason is a villain?"

"You know very well what I mean. That instinct is the reality, that reason is false—or rather, our conception of it is false. We think of it as something separate and independent, when, in truth, it's only a part of instinct."

"All right," he said, "let's agree that we have a kind of instinct which allows us to interpret and to plan. We'll call it instinct, for we no longer care for the sound of the term *reason*."

She lighted another cigarette in silence, but her look said, I am not amused.

"Ill-timed levity," he murmured, then frowned and drummed on the desk. "This is what I mean. The psychologists you refer to analyze the irrational by means of the rational, explore instinct by means of reason, and then announce the enlightening result: there is no rational, there is no reason. Well, if that is true, then there is also no hope for the existence of the science of psychology—of the science of anything—or of scholarship."

Still she said nothing, but her expression changed slightly, as if she had become interested in spite of herself. "You see," he went on quietly, "this is more than a theoretical problem. A few hysterical men in Europe today are shouting, 'Down with Reason!'—and we already know some of the results. It becomes a question of—"

"You're a moralist!" she cried accusingly.

"The way you say that suggests I should cringe and protest violently, or you'll think I've lost my—my special kind of instinct."

"But you can't be a moralist and a scholar. What about objectivity? What under the sun are you doing with Herman Melville?"

"If you mean by moralist," he said more seriously, "one who interprets facts according to a controlled idea, I suppose I am. But so-called facts—well, is there an absolutely objective fact? When we say that a thing has meaning for us, haven't we already interpreted it? Isn't that *why* it has meaning?" He thought to himself for a minute, then laughed. "Let's go talk to Professor Webb about this."

"I'd rather go talk to Professor Day."

He was still thoughtful. He stood staring at the box that held her manuscript, as if it also held the answers to their questions. Suddenly he brought his fist down hard upon the box. "Objectivity! Are you trying to tell me that you think *this* is written with the kind of objectivity you mean?"

"I don't think it," she said confidently, "I know it."

"Hah! Woman, I've never read a more personal work in all my life. That's why it has its peculiar power—that's why it's not good scholarship. If I had—"

"You don't talk straight!" She moved quickly to the desk, but to the side away from him, and put her hands on the box. "First you say there's no such thing as objectivity; then you criticize this for not being objective."

"There are degrees of it—just as you admit to degrees of instinct. What you lack is a controlling idea. I was moved as I read, but meaning

escaped me. I sensed that it was there, but my mind couldn't find it."
He talked rapidly, his face stern, because he did not enjoy having to
talk to her this way. "You keep a veil between the reader and Blake.
You *hint* at tremendous meaning in him, but you never *say* what it is.
You write about him as if he were a god who had revealed himself
only to you, and you brag a little about that revelation, but you never
share it with your reader."

She stood quietly by the desk. He heard his watch ticking. He
wanted to mop his face with his handkerchief. Instead, he stuck his
pipe in his mouth and looked at her all the more severely because
his mind was pleading with her to understand that he was talking this
way out of respect for her intelligence.

She had picked up the heavy box of manuscript and was holding
it to her protectively. She looked alone and unhappy—but not sullen
or childishly hurt, thank God! It was a harsh test for her, he knew.

"In brief," he said to snap the strained silence, "we can call everything I said up to a minute ago—all that about reason and instinct—
personal opinion. I have my idea; you have yours. But what I just said
about your work's being too personal and obscure stands as my"—he
laughed apologetically—"*objective* criticism."

She returned the box to the desk and went over to the chair for
her coat, which she had slipped on before he could reach her. Then
she turned to him. "I still think . . . I'm not convinced that you're
right, but if my work gave you that *impression,* then I must have mis-
handled my material. Perhaps," she said with sudden hopefulness, "it's
merely a matter of style."

He thought it was more than style, but he nodded. Right then he
would have nodded to anything. He was proud of her, and he wished
he knew how to put his feeling into words without seeming patronizing
or condescending.

"Here! I'm going with you," he said as she went to the door. He
snatched up his coat and followed her into the hall, banging and locking the office door after them. He took the box from her and guided
her down the stairs, for the building was almost dark.

When they reached the first floor, he released her arm. Instinctively
each of them stepped away from the other and, losing the sense of
direction, collided at the door. Instantly he was aware of an almost
overpowering impulse to take her into his arms, and it was with effort
that he moved away from her.

Not so fast, Professor Grant, he told himself sardonically; remember,
you champion reason, not impulse.

But as they walked through the Heart and then down the Heights,
he could not help wondering if back in that dark hall she had felt
what he had felt. He gave her a sidewise glance. Her profile was unrevealing.

She wasn't making small talk, and he didn't blame her for not trying. When he saw that they were nearing the Murdocks, he said, "You know how to get even, don't you? Demand to read my Melville; then give it to me straight."

"You're humoring me," she said, not smiling.

In front of the Murdocks' she took the box from him. "Thank you. I—"

"But I think there's still much to be said about reason versus instinct." He glanced over her head at the unlighted house. He didn't like to think of her sitting alone in her room, going over what had been said. "Why don't we continue the discussion over dinner?"

"Thank you, but I've lost my appetite. Besides"—she smiled briefly—"I think you're still humoring me." She took a step up the walk, then turned back. "I've been intending to tell you that Professor Cornthwaite invited me to tea Sunday—tomorrow. Should I go?" She spoke rapidly and with some embarrassment, as if she were no longer sure she wanted to ask his advice.

"If you can bear to drink more tea," he said, smiling, "go—of course. Why not?"

She hesitated. "Professor Cornthwaite has actually avoided me. I don't understand the invitation."

"Perhaps it's subconscious atonement. Seriously, I think she is very tired this year—even ill, possibly."

"Perhaps." But she looked unconvinced. "I'll go . . . I suppose." She stared moodily down the Heights, then said with a sudden flash of anger, "You said reason helps us plan. But it doesn't! There's no constant element—not one! Why, when I was on my way out of the Summit today—just a split second before you called me—I was think- ing that I didn't want to drink tea with Professor Cornthwaite to- morrow because I wanted the whole day to work on Blake. Now . . ."

"You take a long vacation from Blake," he said quickly. "When you come back to him, your mind will be fresh. And go tomorrow; something might come of it."

"Well, thanks," she said, "for *all* the advice." She gave him another brief smile and went on up the walk.

He watched until she had shut herself inside the house; then he started down the Heights, thinking it strange that the street was deserted on Saturday night. But all Riverville, it seemed, was deserted, for even in Millie's neighborhood there was that same atmosphere of complete vacancy, as if even the houses were uninhabited. Growing curious, he looked around him and, with some amusement, counted four couples and several lone individuals on the street with him.

He turned up Millie's walk, telling himself with grim determina- tion what a lucky man he was to have before him an uninterrupted evening with Herman Melville, dead since 1891.

Marcia put the Blake manuscript away in a drawer, out of sight. Then she sat down and laboriously recalled every word that he had said.

He was wrong. He had to be wrong. If he should be right . . . She shuddered to think of what had been wasted if he should be right —not only the time and energy, but the feeling.

At last she stirred and lighted a cigarette, the striking of the match loud in the silence of the house. The Murdocks were to their Saturday-night movie. Her window was dark because there was no light from next door. The quietness grew oppressive, and it seemed to her that only she was left in Riverville. Everyone else had moved to a happier town.

The trouble was, she finally admitted, Grant had been at least half right about her teaching Blake, and that gave her the uncomfortable feeling that he might be right about everything else. . . .

She turned on a light and walked aimlessly around the room.

Perhaps he wanted more footnotes. Perhaps he was afraid of *original* scholarship. Perhaps he was afraid because he was jealous! She wasn't convincing herself, and she knew it.

What she desired above all things, she understood then, was not to belittle Grant, but to prove to him that she was right and he was wrong, and she wanted to do this by honest means.

Suddenly eager, she hastily retrieved the Blake manuscript from its short exile. She should take a long vacation from Blake! That was the one unfair thing Grant had said, for if she stayed away from Blake now, she would never go back to him.

She took Chapter One out of the box and sat down with it at her desk. As she read, she made a few pencil notes in the margin. Grant himself had agreed that the trouble might be merely style. . . . She frowned as she turned a page, and her new zeal ebbed, for she could find nothing wrong with the style. As he had said, each sentence by itself was clear. . . .

If the style didn't need changing, then nothing needed changing. There could be no alternative to that conclusion. Therefore, her next step was to complete it and send it to a publisher. Publication would be a fact that Grant could not deny.

She reassembled Chapter One and returned it to the box; then brought out note cards and began to write. She had written a sentence and rewritten it three times when she threw down the pencil. The trouble wasn't within her, but sounds from Stephanie's room. She couldn't help recognizing them as sobs, huge gasping ones.

Stepping tentatively into the pink and cream room, she saw the girl stretched out on her bed, face down, her shoulders jerking convulsively. She seemed too long for the bed. "What *is* it, Stephanie?"

The sobbing ceased, but Stephanie did not lift her head. "Nothing," she mumbled into the bedspread.

Gingerly Marcia sat down on the edge of the bed, thinking that she should put out her hand to touch her, but she had no desire to do so. "What is nothing?" she tried, making her voice gentle.

This released more tears, but at last Stephanie gasped out, "I'm just lonesome, I guess."

Marcia couldn't think of anything to say. She sensed that there was something important underneath Stephanie's feeling that she should be getting at, but she didn't know how to probe. And she didn't want to. "Go freshen your face," she said finally in desperation, "and come with me to Deardorff's."

Stephanie sat up, surprised. "Why?"

"We'll go book-hunting together," she said brightly.

Stephanie stared, and Marcia was afraid she was going to announce that she hated books; but after a minute, she got off the bed and went to freshen her face.

Marcia went to her room for her coat, trying not to see the Blake papers spread out on her desk. "The luxury of staying single," Dr. Ware had once said to her, "is that you have to contend with only your own problems."

Angrily she jerked her coat off its hanger. She was beginning to think that she could tell Dr. Alice Ware a thing or two.

No one was in the cluttered little shop except Deardorff, who was working at his desk at the back of the room. He paid them no attention.

"There are hundreds of personalities in this room with us," Marcia whispered to Stephanie. "Every book has a life of its own. . . ."

Stephanie slowly looked around her, her face expressionless.

"You browse for yourself, Stephanie. If you find a book that you like, I'll make you a present of it."

Stephanie nodded but made no move to browse.

"Look *into* the books, Stephanie, while I speak with Mr. Deardorff."

She left Stephanie then and went back to Deardorff. "Good evening," he said without looking up, "but I'm busy."

"Oh, I wouldn't think of disturbing you with a sale!"

He glanced up. "So it's you. Sorry, but I can't get Blake's *Daughters of Albion* illustrations. They're probably out for the duration."

"I was afraid of that. I wasn't really concerned about that tonight, though. Do you happen to have *Noa Noa?*"

"Nope. Sold my only copy about a year ago." He sighed. "What do I get for doing all my own work? Stiff wrists!" He stretched his arms above his head and wiggled his fingers. "I could order a copy for you, I suppose."

"No, thanks," she said. "It was just a whim. Why don't you try selling some books so that you can hire an assistant?"

"As for selling books, well, there they are for anyone to buy." He gestured toward his book-lined walls and the crowded tables. "Who's that?" he asked, seeing Stephanie.

"She's with me," Marcia told him. "Stephanie Kail, the Murdocks' niece."

"O-ho! She's the one with the Aristotle and Plato clad in beige and gold—"

He stopped short to listen to a faint cracking sound. Marcia turned with him, and together they saw Stephanie awkwardly bending back the stiff covers of a new book. Horror spread over his face. After a minute, he closed his eyes and tapped his forehead. "What was I saying?"

"About Plato and Aristotle," she said quickly, understanding that it was out of deference to her that his wrath was not descending upon Stephanie. "I appreciated those books even though—" She held her breath as she saw Stephanie draw forth another book. Crack . . . crack . . .

Deardorff threw down his pencil and clenched his hands. He took a step forward, but Marcia was ahead of him. "Look," she said, her voice low and urgent, "I know that what she's doing is all wrong, but I'm trying to get her interested in books and reading. If you scold her, she'll never touch another book. Please believe me, it's important!"

He stepped back, muttering, "What do you take me for, an ogre?"

"I'll pay for any book that she damages," Marcia pleaded.

"It's not the money!" He was indignant.

"I know," she said swiftly. "I understand how you feel. Every sound makes my flesh crawl too."

His brown eyes were speculative; then they twinkled. "You are an evangelist in the clothes of a bibliophile. I am glad that I discovered it early!"

"I am not!" she denied, but he had moved away from her, his shoulders shaking with silent laughter. She watched him adjust his ladder against the shelves. He climbed up it and came down with a large thick volume.

"Delacroix's *Journal*," he said, laying the book on the shelf and pointing for her to examine it. "If you like books, you'll appreciate that binding and printing job." He watched over her shoulder as she opened it to the title page. "And the reproductions of his paintings . . .!" Words failed him.

He went back of the shelf, constantly watching her face as she leafed exploratively through the pages.

"It's beautiful!" She turned another page and then said firmly, "I want it."

"It's expensive!" His voice was startled.

"I know, but I owe it to myself. I haven't bought a book in ages!"

"It's old," he said, "and dirty. Look!" He rubbed a finger across the top and held it up to show her the dust smudge.

She shrugged to show that meant nothing to her.

"There'll be a cheaper edition out soon. There always is, you know."

"Not until after the war," she said. "Besides, *this* is the book that I want." Suddenly she understood. "You don't want to sell this book!" she said accusingly.

"Well . . ." He rocked on his heels, looking over her head.

"A fine bookseller! How do you prefer a customer to act in this situation?"

He grinned then. "My duty is to sell it to you. I see that clearly."

She laughed. "Thank you! And thank you—about her." She nodded toward Stephanie.

His eyes twinkled again. "No doubt you told her to find a book that she wanted, and you'd buy it for her."

"Yes, that's it exactly. Why?"

"I'll wager you anything you suggest that she found no book." His face was glum. "A creature who opens books in that manner couldn't even know *how* to read!" He went to Stephanie's side. "Well, young lady, what do you think of all these books?"

Stephanie looked frightened. "They're . . . interesting." She appealed to Marcia.

"Did you choose a book, Stephanie?" Marcia asked.

"I—" Stephanie closed her mouth and shook her head.

Deardorff chuckled.

"We'll go now, Stephanie," Marcia said shortly.

"Goodby, Evangelist," called Deardorff, watching from his doorway. "Come back soon."

Stephanie looked miserable.

"I need something to eat," Marcia said. "Would you like to stop at Herby's with me? And, please, do cheer *up!*"

Stephanie nodded and put on a sickly smile.

The Square was busy and crowded with Saturday night. They walked slowly along the side of the store windows. Witherspoon's long window had a dimly lighted display of evening clothes. Two mannequins, a man and a woman, stood charmingly oblivious to their audience. The man was in tails, and the woman wore a long white gown, severely plain except for a shimmering silver arrow that started at the hem and outlined one side of the smooth, slender body. Back of them were a couch and a low table bearing ashtrays, a decanter, and waiting glasses.

Involuntarily Marcia stopped to stare at the white gown. It was so unlike Riverville, so unlike John Willard College. In such a dress, one would not worry over Blake, or bother to prove Professor Grant wrong, or—

She became aware of Stephanie's questioning look. "I don't like the blackout," she said, moving on quickly. "I miss the lights, don't you?"

"Well, I guess so." Stephanie seemed undecided.

Herby's was crowded, and they had to wait a few minutes for a booth to themselves.

"I'll have a ham sandwich," Marcia told Herby when he came to clear off their table. She had to shout above the juke-box music coming from the back.

Herby balanced dishes in one hand and swiped at the table with a damp rag. "No ham. Hamburger's the nearest I can come to it."

"All right, then. And black coffee. Would you like a soda, Stephanie?"

Stephanie nodded.

"What kind? Chocolate?"

Stephanie nodded.

Stephanie sipped slowly at her soda. She didn't like chocolate; it made her a little sick. Dr. Anderson was putting mustard on her sandwich, but she was watching her too; so she drew on the straw again. She thought she was allergic to chocolate. Perhaps if she explained that, Dr. Anderson wouldn't be hurt if she didn't finish the soda. "I'm allergic," she said.

"Allergic?" Marcia stared. Stephanie's lack of response in Deardorff's still rankled in her mind. "To books?"

Stephanie blushed, remembering too late that she had not made it clear that the allergy had to do with chocolate. "It's a good soda," she

"Well, I'm glad." Marcia took a bite of sandwich and told herself that perhaps there was some hope. Stephanie was smiling. "Stephanie, why don't you go to the movies with your aunt and uncle?"

The question was a surprise, almost a shock. She pushed the straw around in the brown bubbles and watched them pop, all the while trying desperately to get at the locked words. It was like trying to see the separate colors of a spinning pinwheel. Aunt Madge was there, and Uncle Justin. She too, but not really. The knowing that it was their time alone, those Saturday nights; and the strange pride in refusing to share it . . . "They always *ask* me to go with them," she said.

Marcia jumped. She had given up expecting an answer. "Why *don't* you, then?"

She went back to poking with the straw, now flattened between her tight fingers. It helped. Not liking to beg. Simple. "I stay home alone," she said, and then closed her mouth firmly, for she felt that she had been talking too much.

"Yes, I know," Marcia said, keeping dryness out of her voice. The girl looked tortured.

Stephanie released the straw and it drooped like a broken flower stalk. She could stop the pinwheel. Dr. Anderson had pushed aside the half-eaten sandwich and was concentrating on coffee. Her face could be a flower, she thought, under sun and under moon; then she blushed.

She sat very still, making the strange events memories. The coming into her room, the taking her to Deardorff's, the asking her those questions as if she *cared*.

There was a rushing wish to tell the few good things about herself. Chemistry and Math. She had private knowledge that she could be ahead of everyone else in Chemistry and Math *if* she wanted to be. "I have a Chemistry test tomorrow," she said quickly and loudly before fear stopped her.

Marcia smiled understandingly and picked up her purse. "Then you want to go home to study, don't you?"

Stephanie nodded.

Chapter Three

THE sunroom shimmered in light, but there was a raw feeling to the air, as if some of the still wintry wind had come in from outside. I need weather-stripping at the windows, thought Esther Cornthwaite as she pulled up the Venetian blinds. But her mind did not linger on this fact. She found satisfaction in this bright room of hers. She liked waking to the light slipping in between the blind slats, for it brought with it a spirit of renewal. It was only when she arose from the studio couch that she would be forced to remember the stiffening muscles and the unfirm flesh.

From blind to blind she moved noiselessly in her carpet slippers, her left hand holding the gray kimona close to her chest. She heard her own breathing and objectively noted its heaviness and slight wheeze. The wheeze had become almost a friend, but she supposed that she ought to see a doctor about it.

Out of habit she paused at one of the front windows, looking into the spacious, uncluttered lawn. The sidewalk and street were comfortably far off. Across the street, the park grounds seemed to meet the sky. She liked that; she liked living on a hill. Her eyes went swiftly over details, for she saw nature only in large pieces, which either pleased her or displeased her. This piece had pleased her for many years.

But today her pleasure was automatic. This was an annoying Sunday. Why had she invited Marcia Anderson to tea? There was a most disturbing out-reaching about the girl. . . .

She moved restlessly, taking up a slender green volume, the only book in sight. *The Collected Poems of Philip Willard.* It had arrived in Friday's mail without a word of explanation. But she understood. She looked once more at the dedication: *For Esther.* It was not hand-written as always before, but printed. She had waited many years for that dedication.

She leafed through the pages, catching words and phrases here and there. She knew the poems well by now, for she had read them care-fully. As poems, they did not please her, but she had set her scholar's mind to the task of detecting personal allusions. She had been curious —objectively curious—to know if the volume contained any trace, besides the dedication, of Philip's remembering. There was nothing to be found—unless she counted the verse about violets, "the rich bursting of greensilver stems. . . ." But her scholar's mind keenly and surely rejected this as evidence. In its own mystic way, Philip's poetry was as impersonal as her *History and Development.* His violets were symbolic, not real. What they symbolized she didn't know, and didn't care. She firmly disapproved of the way Philip distilled the essence from realities and used only the shells for words.

But there had been real violets that day. The setting? Quite idyllic —a picnic under a tree. Yes, years clarified a memory. This one was now composed of three simple parts: Philip's eccentric request that she take down her hair; her refusal; the clash of wills.

The entire episode was significant only for the gross stupidity ex-hibited by both agents. If—

She closed the book firmly and impatiently thrust it into the depths of a magazine stand. To burrow into the past did not become her.

With alien eyes she surveyed her room. How would it appear to Miss Anderson, who had been inconsiderate enough not to decline an invitation to Sunday tea? Relentlessly the light outlined the heavy library table and the two bulky wing-backed chairs. Grace MacMillan had once seen to it that the chairs were covered with a bright striped material, but the sun had long since faded the colors to a dead gray.

The table became annoying. She discovered that wherever she looked in the room, her eyes were called back to that long, unadorned expanse of mahogany. The table needed something on it. She went into a back room and returned with two books. After a minute of pondering, she placed one at each end of the table, and was satisfied.

In her small kitchen, she prepared tea and toast, and sat down to it after placing a pen and pad of paper beside her plate. At the moment she had no idea of what use the pen and paper were to serve her, but it was habit of long standing to secure them when she was confronted by a problem. Even years ago the habit had amused Grace MacMillan—

Grace! Grace would be in Riverville this week-end. Quickly she took up her pen. "Dear Clarice," she wrote, "please communicate to J. W. MacMillan that I request the pleasure of his and his mother's company this afternoon at tea in my rooms. I should appreciate their arriving at 2:55 p.m. This is important, Clarice. Do not delay. Thank you. E. Cornthwaite."

She took the note to the sunroom and pinned it to her pillow on the studio couch.

Going back to her kitchen, she shut the connecting door and settled down to her tea and a fresh slice of toast. She ate with new relish, having full confidence in Clarice's ability to carry out her instructions. Clarice could be relied upon to remain blissfully invisible. She would soon slip in to tidy up the sunroom, and her fine instinct would tell her not to enter the kitchen. She would find the note easily, for she was used to finding notes pinned to the bedpillow. She would do her work efficiently, go, and soon quietly return to leave an answering note on the library table.

She was ready in her gray when the car drew up to the curb and stopped. She nodded with satisfaction: it was exactly the right time. Marcia Anderson had not yet come.

As Grace and J.W. came up the walk, she hastily, almost furtively, stooped to bring Philip's book out of the magazine rack and placed it on the library table.

When she told them that Marcia Anderson was coming, J.W. laughed and said, "So that's it. What does that make us—shields? And if so, against what?"

"I'm merely doing Miss Anderson a great favor," Esther said coolly. "It's not every instructor who is given the opportunity to meet the MacMillans socially."

He was not disturbed by her irony. "But think of my position— three women and tea!"

Esther shrugged. "You didn't have to come, Jack. In fact, you may still withdraw, if you wish. I give you permission."

"I never retreat," he said, taking one of the wing chairs as Grace and Esther settled themselves on the couch.

"To tell the truth," Grace said, "I made him come. He's been working much too hard, and if I had left him alone today, he'd have gone directly to the office."

He held up a cigarette. "May I defile the temple?" he asked Esther. When she nodded, he lighted the cigarette. "You can see," he said, tilting his head back to watch the first smoke he had made, "how Mother endeavors to slow down production. She really ought to be reported."

Grace smiled happily. "Now, don't pretend to be annoyed, Jack. You're in a marvelous mood. Do you know," she said turning to Esther, "there's something very familiar sounding about the name Marcia Anderson?"

"Perhaps it reminds you of *Martin* Anderson," J.W. suggested.

"Why, of course!" Grace said. "Martin Anderson has been commissioned to do my portrait, the one to be hung in the Summit," she told Esther. "Are they related, do you know?"

Esther didn't know. She tried to remember Marcia Anderson's application papers. But even if they had said *Father*: Martin; *Occupation*: Artist, she would have dismissed it with something like disdain.

"Well, I rather hope they are," Grace said. "It would be interesting. By the way, Esther, what do you think I should wear for the portrait?"

J.W. listened, amused. To ask Esther—of all people—such a question! He wasn't worried, however, for he knew that his mother would ultimately make her own choice, and that it would be exactly right. Grace had been born with a knack for clothes, and he was glad. He liked women to dress not only well, but interestingly. Eileen's taste had been unformed—a little too flowery and ribbony—but it would have developed. . . .

Marcia Anderson had the knack too. He remembered very well how she had looked at the tea, for her image, accompanied by the Prokofieff, was often in his mind. He was amused to note how the inescapable law of association had made him tolerant of the music. In fact, when certain that Russ was out of the house, he had played his records and discovered an unexpected liking for the last movement. Fast and loud, with an obvious yet exciting rhythm, it matched his new mood.

He was beginning to think that he had been in a rut before the war. At first he was annoyed to have to stop making his tractors and produce what someone else told him to produce. But then he had begun to enjoy the increase, the step-up, the feeling that he was doing something important, even indispensable. It gave him ideas for expansion afterwards.

Matt Grant had helped him to get into the right spirit. When he had wanted to be cautious, Matt had thrown caution to the winds. When he had suggested withdrawing their new advertising campaign because, after all, they weren't making tractors now, Matt had insisted upon strengthening it. "Look here, J.W.," he had said, "keep your name before the public! We'll get out new placards to announce the conversion, and, man, the subway riders will soon be thanking you for winning the war! Why, you'll be a patriotic symbol in no time!"

And it was happening. A newsreel camera had caught him in Washington. . . .

Matt was all right! He knew all the angles. A little vulgar and swaggering, perhaps, but dynamic. If he could fill John Willard College with people like Matt Grant, he could step-up production there also. Why was it that academic training took all the vitality out of people? There were exceptions, of course—Esther Cornthwaite, for one—but in spite of the brains, teachers were flat, tame. . . .

Marcia Anderson? Well, he hardly thought of her as a teacher. He admitted, however, that she had something besides flatness and tameness, or he shouldn't be thinking about her at all. Then he smiled to himself. Of course, she had something else! She was a woman, and a striking one. There was hardly anything else needed—"Sorry, Mother, but I didn't hear you."

"Well, I should think you didn't!" Grace said reprovingly. "I was asking if you knew that Philip had a new book of poems out? Collected poems, if you please."

J.W. laughed. "Isn't it like Uncle Philip to collect his own poems? No doubt he has a preface bidding his public a nostalgic farewell—when he knows perfectly well that he'll be publishing new poems again next year."

"He has no such preface," Esther said seriously. She gestured toward the green book on the library table. "Well, there it lies!" When her words provoked no action, she said to Grace, "Why not look at it while I put the tea-kettle on?"

Grace grimaced and shook her head. "Philip's poems somehow shock me. I'll wait until I receive my own copy; then I'll take it to bed and fall asleep over it, and in the morning persuade myself that I've read it through. I feel disloyal, but that's the way it is with me."

J.W. reached out for the book and held it tentatively in his hand, as if weighing it. "I wonder how much this sort of thing costs Philip."

Esther paused in the doorway. "Whatever do you mean?"

"Well, he finances these publications, doesn't he?"

Esther drew herself up. "You *are* in a mood today, my boy, but I wouldn't call it a marvelous one!" She disappeared.

He looked questioningly at Grace. "Of course, I wouldn't mention this outside the family, but he *does* pay for this stuff himself, doesn't he?"

Grace stroked the arm of the couch, studying her fingers. "I shouldn't push the matter, if I were you, Jack. Especially before Esther. I think that I'll go out with her," she said, standing. "I'm afraid that she needs unruffling."

He turned back to the book, puzzled. Why was Esther so concerned over it? He leafed through it, pausing over "Trinity."

> Tri-pointed Thought
> Why art thou so dear to man!
>
> Logic Triangular,
> Sublime and ultimate usurper of Isis . . .

He looked out of the window, trying to remember what he knew about Isis. How like Uncle Philip to write about Isis!

Into his sight moved a girl in slacks and a dark short coat. She had a jaunty walk and frankly stared into the houses as she passed them. Obviously she did not belong on the Heights. He knew where she did belong—in one of those little houses that he himself had caused to grow in a row down by the tracks. A year ago he would have resented her arrogant intrusion into Riverville's Sunday, but now he smiled gently at her. She was one of his own workers. . . . Idly he played with the idea of suddenly appearing before her: *I am J.W. MacMillan, your employer. And also your father in a certain sense, don't you see? Have I made everything right for you?*

He turned back to the book, amused at his fantasy. Ridiculous, of course, yet pleasant. . . . Well, each to his own fantasy. Here was Uncle Philip's, for example, on page fifteen: "Death's Outlet Song":

I am mute before my past as before eternity,
For it is all and nothing.
Built upon decay,
But built, sanctioned, sold.
I stand before the dark of chaos . . .

He frowned. The words struck a discordant note. His gentle amusement over Uncle Philip's fantasies shifted into anger. What right had Philip to expose publicly even his own small segment of Willard life?

He half threw the book back upon the table. . . . *but built, sanctioned, sold* . . . Absurd melodrama, betraying Willard reticence. Uncle Philip was a traitor, even though only an armchair one. . . .

Marcia Anderson was there on the walk. He wasn't ready for her. He sat still, forcing down his annoyance over Philip's trivial poem.

She was out of sight now, and the door chimes were sounding. He didn't move, for he did not intend to open the door to her. Let her see him only after she was inside, when she was still unprepared.

He heard Grace tell Esther that the door chimes had sounded for the second time.

Marcia was surprised at the presence of the MacMillans. She had expected remoteness from Esther, but not actual armament. She tried to be cool in her greeting, but, in spite of herself, her voice thawed before Grace's warm friendliness.

J.W. came up to her and touched her hand. "We are doomed to meet at teas." He lowered his voice. "And this one must be endured without the accompaniment of Prokofieff, for Esther, of course, has no radio."

She was startled, for his manner seemed to justify the significance she unwillingly gave to the same memory. She sat down in a faded wing chair, annoyed, yet flattered. She had wanted to be very much self-possessed for this occasion, and now she wasn't. Yet his intent interest was strangely soothing, as if he had said aloud: *I find you very charming and attractive. I do not care in the least whether your Blake scholarship is sound or unsound.* . . .

"I must ask you," Grace was saying, "if you are related to Martin Anderson, the portrait painter."

Marcia smiled at her, relieved to be free to turn away from his look. "Yes. He's my father."

They exclaimed, and Grace told her that Martin was to do her portrait, and how she had made him promise to come on John Willard Day for the hanging of it.

"Really?" said Marcia, accepting a cup of tea from Esther. She was amused to think how little persuasion Martin had probably needed. That was just the sort of thing he thrived on—a ceremonious hanging of his own work.

"What's he really like, your father?" Grace asked eagerly. "I've seen him only once, and he intrigued me considerably."

"Well," Marcia said, "he isn't what you expect of an artist—"

"Oh, I noticed that," Grace said. "That's what I like about him."

Marcia laughed. "He'd enjoy hearing you say that. He's more a technician than a painter. That's his own description. I believe that he's something of an authority on paint itself—the chemical side. He smokes very strong cigars, raises Chinese vegetables. . . ." She went on, enjoying herself and hoping that she made Martin sound a bit ridiculous.

J.W. sat across from her in the other wing chair. He had passed her a cigarette and had lighted it for her. Then he had leaned back to watch her through the lazy smoke from his own cigarette. She felt his eyes linger on her hair, her earrings, the silver antique broach that Martin had given her. . . .

When she had said all that she had to say about Martin, Esther asked about the people he had painted. Weren't there anecdotes? Marcia told several, but she was well aware of Esther's strategy to avoid the subject of why Marcia Anderson had been advised to come to John Willard. It occurred to her that had Esther Cornthwaite taken the proper interest in her, she should not have had to endure that discouraging and humiliating session with Grant yesterday; and her resentment once again kindled and flamed.

Abruptly she concluded what she was saying and asked the question that was to give Esther her last chance. She made her voice firm. "Miss Cornthwaite, you remember Dr. Alice Ware, of course?"

Esther frowned in slight perplexity, as if trying to place the name in the far distant past. "Yes," she said at last, "yes, I believe I do."

Marcia persisted. "But I thought you were old friends. Surely you heard from her recently. About me."

Esther looked delicately pained. "Yes," she said. It was a patient, tolerant monosyllable. "You must tell us how your father started raising Chinese vegetables. What an odd hobby!"

"I haven't the slightest idea," Marcia said curtly. She placed her hand over her cup to keep it from rattling in its saucer. She was trembling with fury.

"Oh, your cup is empty!" Esther said. "Let me pour you more tea." She came forward with the teapot.

"No," said Marcia. "No, thank you."

"Splendid!" Esther said, leaning forward to pour.

Suddenly it seemed imperative to Marcia that Esther should not complacently pour tea into her cup against her will. Her arm jerked back, but Esther poured on.

"O-ho," Esther exclaimed, staring in amazement at the puddle of tea by Marcia's feet. "How stupid of me!"

"It was my fault," Marcia murmured. She was uncomfortably aware that Grace and J.W. had leapt to their feet. "I'm so sorry." She leaned down and dabbed in the puddle with her handkerchief.

"Did it go on your skirt or stockings?" Grace asked. "Tea can make a hideous stain. . . ."

"I think not." Marcia rubbed her handkerchief fiercely into the carpet, seeing J.W.'s immaculate leather shoes and Grace's gray suède ones. The feet seemed posed in a solicitous manner, and this angered her.

She sat upright, her face flushed. Her handkerchief was black with dirt and she made a soggy wad of it in her fist to conceal it.

"Esther," said Grace firmly, "you *must* have your carpet cleaned this spring!"

Esther was indignant. "Grace, that carpet was cleaned—now let me see—ah yes, when the Revised Edition of the *History* came out!"

Grace sighed. "That was six years ago," she explained to Marcia.

"Yes, I know," Marcia said too quickly and too seriously. When J.W. gave her a short, amused glance, she set her lips defiantly. Well, she *did* know, and she was certain that she knew the content of that work better than any MacMillan.

"Look!" cried Grace. "Miss Anderson's handkerchief is quite ruined!"

Oh, blast my handkerchief! thought Marcia, struggling against the maelstrom of farce.

Esther was incredulous. "Really?" Her face lighted. "Why, of course. It's soaked in tea. I'll replace it immediately."

"Please don't—" Marcia gasped. But Esther was already gone from the room.

J.W. said to Grace, "Don't you know by now that there's no use trying to domesticate Esther?"

Grace sighed. "But she's lovable, don't you think?" she asked Marcia.

Marcia thought that Esther was behaving lamentably beneath her dignity. "It is a great experience to work under Professor Cornthwaite," she said coolly.

"A most laudable sentiment," said Esther, returning.

J.W. and Grace laughed at this, and Marcia smiled thinly.

"Choose any one you please," Esther told Marcia, placing a cretonne-covered box in her lap. "These I've never used," she said, lifting up the cover to reveal neat piles of white handkerchiefs with fine lace edgings. "They are the accumulation of years."

Grace peered over her shoulder. "Oh, they're from the Albuquerque niece, aren't they?"

Esther nodded. "Poor Jennifer. I've never seen her, nor she me, but ever since she was old enough to ply a needle, she has labored under the delusion that a schoolteacher-aunt should like nothing better than a lace-trimmed linen handkerchief. So every Christmas and birthday . . ." She made a helpless gesture with her hands.

Marcia selected one quickly and returned the box to Esther. "It's lovely," she said. "Thank you."

She was again aware of J.W.'s eyes. No doubt he was enjoying this very much! No doubt he knew exactly how foolish she felt! She reached for her purse and put the handkerchief into it. Then she looked up at him defiantly. He was smiling down at her, but tenderly. She felt suddenly childlike, not unpleasantly so. . . .

. . . She had fallen asleep curled up in Martin's big leather chair that smelled strongly of cigars and paint. She liked it because of that. She had awakened, cramped and warm. When she had brushed her hair back from her wet forehead, there had been Martin, smiling down at her, tenderly. . . .

While Grace was putting on her coat, Marcia picked up the green book and examined it curiously. "*Modern* poetry!" she said softly.

"It *is* surprising to find it here, isn't it?" J.W. said, coming to her side.

She looked back at the title page. "Philip Willard. I don't know him."

He was a little disappointed. "He is my uncle," he said.

"Willard," she repeated. "Oh, of course. I should have known."

He said nothing but watched her leaf through the pages. He wondered if she had seen "Death's Outlet Song," and if so, what she thought of it. . . . She turned back to the front of the book, seemed to study something, and then put it back down on the library table.

"I can't help remarking," she said to Esther, who reappeared with Grace, "how surprised I am not to see more books here. I had thought that your rooms would be literally lined with them!"

Esther looked directly at Marcia for the first time. She sensed something different in the girl's attitude . . . as if she were no longer reaching out to her. She, Esther Cornthwaite, no longer held her interest. "I find books a nuisance," she said suddenly. "They collect dust and get in one's way."

Marcia looked unbelieving.

Well, let her riddle this one! Esther thought. "I have known musicians to refuse to hear their favorite compositions played. They insist that they can hear the music in their own heads, at any time, and in more nearly perfect renditions. That is the way I feel about books." She gestured toward the table. "I need keep only one or two of my greatest friends by me."

Interestedly Marcia picked up one of the other volumes from the table. "This?"

Esther nodded cautiously. She strained to see the title, but couldn't. What books had she put out?

"I should never have guessed that you'd take Schopenhauer seriously," Marcia said.

Esther smiled sagely. "Schopenhauer prevents weakness and softness. Yes, I read through his *World as Will and Idea* every birthday." She paused effectively, and then said to Grace, "I clipped out the latest review of Philip's book. It should interest you. If you'll excuse me for a moment . . ."

Marcia stared after her. Grace and J.W. suddenly laughed outright.

"Child," said Grace, taking Marcia's hand, "you deserve to see something!"

Tiptoeing, she led her through the small hall. "Here," she said, opening a door, "are a few more of our Professor's friends!"

Marcia saw a square room furnished with nothing but books. Books filled the shelves that lined the walls, and books were stacked on the floor.

"This used to be her bedroom," Grace said, "but—well, you can see what happened!"

"I'm glad," said Marcia, turning slowly around to look. "There was something all wrong about those few books on the table out there."

Grace smiled. "I think I understand. That's why I decided to show you, though I must admit that it wasn't very sportsmanlike of me. Well, we had better hurry back. Softly now . . ."

Shamelessly Esther watched the three of them stand at the end of her walk. They were taking a very long time to part. It was over. She had brought them together, and now it was over. Why didn't they disperse?

They were going toward the parked car now, and Marcia was with them. J.W. swung open the door, and there seemed to be some hesitation as to who should get in first. Marcia did. Then Grace. Finally she heard the slam of the door. J.W. hurried around to his side. The car moved. She leaned forward. It was gone.

Without warning a hot flame of jealousy flared up within her. It was so short-lived that she could easily persuade herself that it had never been.

Marcia Anderson—with all her youth, eagerness, intelligence, and, yes, even the fantastic William Blake—could have been hers to sit at her feet.

But she hadn't wanted her. She had planned not to have her.

Very well.

Absently she picked up the Schopenhauer. Then she opened it, suddenly curious. She read, her lips forming the key words. "Rot," she said softly after a few sentences.

But it had made a good story. She looked up and chuckled. Really, it had!

Marcia relaxed against the soft seat. There was an intimate warmth about the inside of the car. Outside it was snowing lightly.

"It will have to be the Bijou dining room," J.W. said across her to Grace.

"I'm afraid so," Grace said. "We promised Kate that we'd eat out this evening."

"Will the Bijou be all right?" he asked, looking down at her.

She smiled and nodded. She felt snug and warm and protected.

J.W. turned at the top of the Heights, in President Cameron's driveway. As they sped smoothly back down the Heights, Marcia watched for Esther's windows.

"Philip Willard's poems are dedicated to 'Esther,'" she said as they passed them. "Is that . . .?"

"Oh!" cried Grace. "That's our Esther, of course. What a pity we didn't notice, Jack!"

He smiled. "So that explains her unusual concern over the book."

"*What* a pity we didn't notice it!" Grace said again. "How disappointing for her."

It seemed then to Marcia that she and the MacMillans had been looking into Esther's life, and had come away saying, "What a pity, what a pity. . . ." She felt a strange satisfaction, as if an unjust score had been evened.

"Something might come of it," Grant had said. Well, something had. A handkerchief and dinner with the MacMillans. It was more than he could have guessed, and she felt triumphant over that, as if she were also settling a score with him.

Only one thing bothered her. If she had known about dinner, she could have dressed. She thought fleetingly of the white gown in Witherspoon's window.

Esther sat very quietly, thankful that she had no Monday afternoon classes. "You rest before you leave here," Dr. Bingham had advised. "Stay in my waiting room as long as you please."

But that was not why she had stayed. She had a desire to ring for the doctor and explain to him that she had remained for a reason other than to rest. She smiled grimly at her whim, understanding it. She had never been one to take orders.

However, she did not ring. She had no wish to disturb Dr. Bingham further. He was harassed enough. Besides, she liked him. Once during the examination he had lifted her hands in his and murmured, "What fine hands!" He had said it as he might have said, "What fine lungs!"—in that completely impersonal manner that she most appreciated in compliments.

With his freckled face and rumpled hair, he was so young-looking that at first she had thought of writing Philip that he ought to staff his hospital with doctors of a respectable age. But Dr. Bingham at once proved that he knew exactly what he was doing, and he was admirably down-to-earth in his approach to the human body. This alone had been enough to win her, for she had an inflexible dislike for doctors who attempted to glorify that most inconvenient and uninteresting mechanism by calling it Nature's greatest Work of Art, or some other equally absurd figure of speech.

"Of course," he had said when she was once more fully clothed, "we'll have to go much more thoroughly into this—X-rays and all, but off hand, I'd say that your heart needs to go to bed—and I *mean* to bed—for at least a year."

"But I came to see about the wheeze," she had said crossly.

He had shrugged. "That's unimportant compared to the other."

"And after the year of hibernation—then what?" she had asked.

He had turned his back to her then, taking off his stethoscope. He was very thin. She watched his shoulder blades move under his white coat. "Then—nothing strenuous. Nothing whatever."

"You mean—"

"You must resign your position, of course."

"And if I don't do all these things?"

"I'll wash my hands of you. Any doctor would." He turned to eye her suspiciously. "But you're going to be sensible, of course."

"Of course," she had echoed smoothly.

"Damn it, you're lucky!" he had said then, boyish and cheerful again. "Semi-invalid, with everyone waiting on you, center of attention, and all that. Me, I have to go to war. Drafted yesterday."

126

As she sat in his waiting room, she thought about Dr. Bingham and the war. That made her and him a little alike, didn't it? Perhaps he had a better chance of coming out alive, but at that, it was only a chance. And whatever odds he had in that respect meant little when set against his age. He was at the beginning; she was at the end.

Resign? Humph! She'd rather be dead— She smiled wryly. She probably would be!

It was the probable suddenness of it that most annoyed her, she decided. All her life—Life! Couldn't one think through a simple thought without having to use those words, *life* and *death?* Well, to come back to the point, she was used to planning carefully in advance for everything. To plan was her peculiar essence. *Essence . . . being . . . living . . .*

If she'd stop *looking* at the words in her mind, she wouldn't be so aware of them! But how could she stop being aware of words? After all, words had been her whole life. *Life*—there it was again!

She reproved herself severely and nervously opened and shut her purse. The familiar action quieted her. What an old companion was that purse! And how ugly, she admitted, seeing it for the first time.

Again to come back to the point, what if it should happen to-morrow? In what would they array her? The purple? Hardly. She wouldn't mind, but the anonymous "they" might. The gray? Suitable enough, but how often it had appeared at the bi-monthly teas! She hoped she wasn't being morbid, but she did think that the occasion merited something new.

She thought of Miss Brown, her dressmaker. But first there would have to be an elaborate exchange of letters, and then Miss Brown was very, very slow. Usually, it didn't matter, but this once she felt the unfamiliar need for haste.

That left Witherspoon's . . . Did she dare? Why not? If John Donne could sit alive in his winding sheet and if bishops could order their tombs, why couldn't E. Cornthwaite go in search of her burial dress? She rather enjoyed the prospect.

And after that, there were a few other things she must get done. She wanted to leave everything neat and tidy. . . . People passed before her. Philip . . . nothing there. Grace . . . much there, but nothing to be done. Grant . . . ah, yes, something to be done. She was not pleased to contemplate her relationship with him. It had risen out of her cursed inability to acknowledge dependence upon anyone . . . and so she had treated him like a lackey while leaning upon him. She was fairly sure that he understood, but she wanted to make certain. A seemingly casual word . . . soon.

Alice Ware . . . to be seen this summer—that is, if summer did not prove too late. Unlike Philip, Alice was an uncaught thread. Marcia Anderson? Something there perhaps, but nothing essential. Besides,

Marcia was too new to her, hadn't taken root in her. . . . But she would try to think of a little something, if she were given the time.

Rushing time. She looked at her watch. Richard Tibbet would be waiting for her in the car by now. She had better go out to him.

She closed the door gently behind her. Good-by, Dr. Bingham. There was no need for her to subject herself to more of this sort of thing—X-rays and so forth, as he had said. He could justifiably wash his hands of her. . . .

Someone rounded the corner at the other end of the corridor. Mrs. Scott. She did not want to see her or anyone else, but there was no way to avoid it, short of jumping out of a window.

"Good afternoon," she said, quickening her steps.

But she needn't have worried, for Judith Scott seemed no more inclined to stop to talk than she. There was something magnetic about her as she passed, and to her surprise, Esther felt compelled to turn to watch her. She saw her go into the office next to Dr. Bingham's. Fine looking. Youth. Vibrant health. To be envied.

With Scott for a husband? Well, she didn't know much about that, but she had her doubts. And a baby. Wonderful, of course, but a nuisance too.

Inwardly she laughed at herself. No matter how much she tried, she couldn't be sorry for herself.

She hesitated before the elevator. It was one of those self-operating things, and she dreaded it. Sooner or later, someone was bound to come along who was going down too. She backed against the wall and waited patiently. . . .

Before going to Witherspoon's, she would stop at Deardorff's. In fact, from now on, she would go to Deardorff's as often as possible. If there was anything that she would like to take with her, it was perhaps Deardorff, with his impersonal and never-prying talk and interest.

And there was one more thing in the back of her mind—that unfinished volume of the *History and Development*. Well, she would finish it. There was no force in the world unjust enough to make her leave behind a fragmentary work to be concluded by some Etta Wilson. . . .

The elevator door had slid back and there was Richard Tibbet grinning out at her. "I *thought* maybe you were stuck up here!"

"My boy," she said as she stepped into the little cage, "I had just this moment concluded my business here!"

When Judith Scott left the hospital, she decided to walk back to town. The clear, brisk day called to her, and she felt that she could walk a hundred miles without tiring. The doctor had said that she was in perfect health, that she needn't come back.

She had known all along that the doctor had been wrong about her after-birth disturbances. Not the baby, but her fight against unhappiness had caused them. As soon as she had determined not to struggle, her physical health had come back. Yes, that was the answer. Give up struggling; stay calmly resigned. . . .

But the quarrels! Once she had never quarreled, but of late something drove her on and on. . . . The quarrels shocked her. Owen didn't seem to mind them. When they had made up, he would say, "It was worth it for this, wasn't it?" She would lie awake trying to remember how it had started. . . .

She was nearing the Square, and she was sorry. She hadn't enjoyed the walk as she had intended.

If only she knew the *cause* of them. Or why Owen seemed to have no genuine affection for the baby. Or why—*why!*

Now weary, she walked slowly across the Square, wondering what to do with the free afternoon she had made for herself. She went into the first doorway and was ironically amused to find herself in Witherspoon's. Owen was the kind of man who thought that a woman's soul could be speedily put in order by a new dress.

Well, why not try it? She had bought nothing for herself since the maternity dresses.

She looked idly through the dress racks. She would avoid blue. She had too much of that.

Someone came out of the fitting booths. "Just look into this long mirror here for the *full* effect."

Judith looked up to watch. She recognized the little gray-haired clerk. Miss Doty—absolutely no sense of style, but very gentle and pathetically eager to be helpful. At this moment, Miss Doty clasped her hands ecstatically. "A perfect fit, my dear, and you wear it beautifully!"

Judith had to agree. Even from the back, the white evening gown was stunning. Why didn't *she* get something like that instead of a practical dress? Maybe she would. . . . She moved a little to see the front of the dress in the mirror, and then she saw that the wearer was Marcia Anderson.

Marcia saw her in the mirror also. She turned so abruptly that she almost upset little Miss Doty. "Why, hello!" she cried too effusively. "I'm considering being very extravagant, as you can see. I really haven't any need for this sort of thing, but I can't resist it. I seldom go any place where I need it. Teachers don't, you know. But I—"

"Oh, my dear," said Miss Doty brightly, "if you have the dress, you'll be *bound* to go some place. The dress first, and then the going! Isn't that the way it is, Mrs. Scott?"

Judith smiled politely. "Perhaps so." Why was Marcia Anderson explaining all that to *her?* What was she feeling guilty about?

"Well, I don't know. . . ." Marcia turned back to the mirror, nervously adjusting the dress here and there.

129

"You should take it," Judith said. "There's no doubt about that. It must have been made for you."

Marcia looked pleased. "Do you really think so?"

"*Yes,* my dear," breathed Miss Doty. She wagged a finger. "And you'll see—first the dress, and then the going!"

Judith moved back to the dress rack. Every single dress on it looked very dull and uninteresting. Why *did* Marcia Anderson want that dress? A very special dress usually meant a very special person. What man? She could think of no one worthy of such a dress in all Riverville. Unless . . . She turned slightly to look again. Marcia and Miss Doty were in conference. She *was* damnably attractive. Why didn't she get married? She shrugged and went back to the dresses, although she had already gone through the rack. Well, she supposed that she'd now become a wife in earnest and note carefully how Owen spent his evenings. . . . Sudden tears blinded her. Was this, then, the reason for the quarrels? She was deeply hurt, but at the same time she also felt a restful satisfaction in at least finding an answer.

She blinked rapidly and became engrossed in a singularly unattractive dress. Miss Doty had tiptoed to her side. "I'm so sorry that you have to wait, Mrs. Scott. Just a few minutes longer and—"

"Oh, that's quite all right," Judith said. She saw that Marcia was joining them. Why didn't she take that thing off? She was flaunting it indecently.

"I'm going to take it," Marcia told her. Her face was flushed and she seemed excited.

"I'm sure that you're not making a mistake," Judith said coolly.

Miss Doty clasped her hands again. "It's just perfect!" Then she tried to look efficient. "You might tell me what sort of thing *you* have in mind, Mrs. Scott, and I'll be thinking it over while I conclude this sale. A nice little daytime frock?"

Judith shuddered. A nice little daytime frock! "No," she said suddenly. "Something for evening. Perhaps not quite so *decolleté* as that"—she gestured briefly toward Marcia, who blushed—"but something definitely for evening."

Miss Doty looked very happy and nearly flew away. "Wait!" Judith called her back. "It must be blue, you know. My husband insists upon my wearing blue. Because of my eyes."

Instinctively Marcia drew back from Judith's voice. She's jealous, she told herself in amazement; she's jealous of *me!* She was shocked, then hurt. How unfair!

"Miss Cornthwaite!" Judith was saying as someone approached them. "I was concerned about meeting you at the hospital. I do hope that you're not ill."

"I'm never ill!" Esther said heartily. "Dr. Anderson, quite a fetching costume."

"Thank you," said Marcia absently, too engrossed in her new view

130

of Judith to be surprised over Esther's presence. Didn't she *know* that her husband was too wrapped up in himself to be interested in any other woman? She glanced at Judith, and saw that her face was set, controlled. Her own hurt went away, and she was saddened.

Miss Doty reappeared, flustered. She had never seen Esther Cornthwaite before. "I'm *so* sorry," she said breathlessly, "but we're short on this floor today. If you don't mind waiting a few min—"

"Not at all, my girl," Esther said. "I have to the end of my life for this purchase."

Miss Doty looked uncertain. "Well, perhaps if you'll tell me what you have in mind . . ."

"I have in mind," Esther told her, "something for a funeral. Something quietly sepulchral."

They were all startled. "Yes . . . yes, indeedy," said Miss Doty, but she stood quite still.

Judith made a sudden movement. "I believe that I haven't time, after all. I'll come in again, Miss Doty. Thank you."

Marcia said good-by and stared after her. If it could only be said between them, talked out and away. . . .

"I must hurry too," she said to Miss Doty. Esther seemed to be watching her intently, and again she felt embarrassed and foolish, as she had when she had first seen Judith in the mirror. If only she were out of this dress and in her suit! And what on earth was Esther Cornthwaite doing in the Dress Department?

Esther still regarded her with disconcertingly bright eyes. She seemed in a rare mood. "I wonder," she said suddenly, "if that attire will go with Blake."

"Yes, indeedy!" said Miss Doty, again at her ease. "It will *go* with anything. That's the beauty of white!"

Chapter Four

GRANT left Esther Cornthwaite's office puzzled. As he well knew, she was not one to waste time or words; yet for the life of him he could not fathom the purpose of their conference, although she had sent him a special note requesting him to appear. Delayed by the faculty meeting, he had arrived late, and she had been annoyed and told him so, adding a lecture on Time. He had clenched his pipe between his teeth and openly glared at her while she talked. The faculty meeting had depressed him. She couldn't know that, of course, for she had not attended.

Three times during their seemingly aimless hour together she had said that her reason for calling him in was to remind him that the committee met tomorrow morning in her office to judge the Competition essays; and three times he had said with ill-concealed impatience that he had been aware of the scheduled meeting for the past two weeks, and that he intended to give the entries a final reading that evening—*if* he ever reached home.

She was immune to the caustic hint, and became uncharacteristically solicitous over his progress with Melville. Then she praised him for not allowing his research to get in the way of his teaching. She knew the temptation to neglect teaching duties for the more personal interest of one's own scholarship—ah yes, indeed she knew!—and she had observed how nobly he had resisted it. In fact, she had observed further that when his call came, he would make a fine administrator.

Surprise jostled his irritation, and he had listened with mixed feelings. She made him feel incredibly young—the apprentice before the master. Although it had occurred to him that he was being fattened for some well planned slaughter, it was pleasant to hear her insist upon his value to the department, to the college, to the academic profession, to humanity—

At that he had stood up, quietly but firmly, and said that he appreciated her sudden interest, but that if he were to hear a—er—call to administrative work, he'd probably ignore it, for his concern was with teaching and scholarship, not administration.

She had merely smiled and nodded wisely, as if to imply that they all said that before becoming administrators. He had left then, feeling very unoriginal as well as puzzled.

Thinking it over as he cut across the Heart, he decided that at least the mysterious conference indicated she would be appreciative of his need for time to finish his book, and that should make her receptive to his desire for a leave of absence next year. If he—

Clifford Hughes appeared by his side with such miraculous suddenness that Grant suspected he had been lurking about purposely to waylay him. He wanted to hurry on, but there was something about Hughes these days that made him loath to turn away from him. The young man's unrelieved gloom seemed to forebode an oncoming catastrophe, and as if in defensive preparation, his sensitive face had hardened and his shyness was almost lost. "What are you going to do about it?" he demanded without preliminaries.

Grant suppressed a groan. "What am I going to do about *what?*"

Hughes came to a sudden stop. "J.W. MacMillan's remarks about the *Gazette* editorials! You heard them as well as I. You heard him say they were too anti-war. You heard him give that spiel about freedom of speech—how it's fine in peacetime but unpatriotic in wartime. Lord, man, you're the *Gazette* advisor! Are you going to sit by and allow that kind of censorship to be slapped on the paper?"

To be polite, Grant had stopped too. Now he put a hand on Hughes' arm and gently prodded him on. "Let's keep walking, eh? What is it you think I should do, Cliff?"

"Fight," he said readily, "in the open. Oh, I don't care so much about a showdown with MacMillan as I do about waking up some of these teachers! I watched them during the meeting, and I tell you they might as well have been fishing. They have no *awareness*. They made no association between John Willard College and the John Willard Tractor Company; they didn't bother to see how a John Willard editorial might possibly reflect upon John Willard business interests; they—"

"Who are 'they'?" Grant asked.

"Everyone. Well, practically everyone. . . ." Hughes stared across the Heights into the still barren park. "Webb. Did you notice him at the meeting? There he sat in mystic contemplation!"

Grant smiled. "But he's on sabbatical. That ought to excuse him."

"That's just it!" Again Hughes came to a standstill, and Grant stopped with him, for they were now opposite the short cut. "It means so little to him that he even forgets he doesn't have to come. That absent-mindedness of his used to—amuse me, but now. . . ." He tried to sneer, but it was more like a spasm of pain that contorted his face. He looked away and muttered, "He has no more right to be a Brahmin than the rest of us."

They stood in silence. The early spring air was cold without the sun, and when a gust of wind blew at them, Hughes absently turned up his coat collar. His face was in profile, and Grant thought that if its expression had been less intense, it might have been out of Botticelli. He thought too of many things to say, but rejected them. He had no remedy or even anesthetic for disillusionment—unless it were more living. But who wanted to be told that? "Cliff," he said finally, "something else came up at the meeting—the Army training program."

Hughes moved impatiently. "Yes, I heard that too. J.W. and the Government are planning it." He laughed ironically. "It's damn good of J.W. to help the Government."

"Never mind *how* it's going to happen," Grant said. "It will be the largest educational movement in history, and it won't end with the war."

Hughes shrugged. "So what? The bigger it is, the greater evil it can be. Can good result from a plan rooted in war? And will such a program essentially change John Willard?"

"Perhaps the answer to both questions is no." Grant took Hughes by the arm again and they crossed the street. "But I'm not guessing; I'm going to wait around to find out for myself. Walking on with me, Cliff?"

Hughes shook his head glumly, as if to say he now saw no reason to walk on with him; so they halted by the path. "This is what I mean," Grant went on slowly. "Some things have a power to develop far beyond their beginnings. A college is one such thing. What you've missed, Cliff, is the life this place has that is independent of Willard interests. You couldn't stamp that out if you tried, because, as yet, every teacher here has the right to go into his classroom to teach as he sees fit. And it seems to me"—he hesitated, finding little encouragement in Hughes' face, but he finished saying what was in his mind—"it seems to me that one trained in Philosophy has a remarkable advantage. He can teach methods of thought as well as the vital ideas of the—"

"Ideas!" Hughes thrust back his head and pointed up at the pale sky. "The realm of Ideas—there it is, in the clouds. Let us make sure that it never touches earth." Embarrassed, he put his hand in his pocket and said more quietly, "Historians are wrong. We're medieval still, content with the bad because we're suckers enough to believe it when we're told that the only good is stored up in heaven." He gave Grant a sharp look. "So you're not going to fight?"

Grant laughed apologetically. "If you mean, am I going to start educating my colleagues—then, no. But if you mean, am I going on educating students—then, yes."

Hughes was silent for a minute. He lighted a cigarette, drew heavily on it, then changed the subject with contemptuous deliberateness. "How's the book coming? Herman Melville, isn't it?"

"Yes—Melville. It's coming, but very slowly."

"Scholarship," Hughes said, "must be a very satisfactory means of escape." He said a careless good-by and strode away.

Grant watched after him. "Damn!" he said to the universe; then turned down the path, his coat flapping in the steadily rising wind.

Janice sat in the parlor talking to Millie, who called out to Grant when he entered the hall. She excused herself then and left the room, her long green housecoat and heavy perfume scent trailing after her.

Janice came to his side. "She's a character. Do you sleep with her?"

He brought out his pipe. "No, Miss Grant, I do not. Nor do I mean to pry, but I should like to know why you ask."

Janice shrugged her thin shoulders. "After all, this *is* a convenient set-up—you living here and she being the type."

"I see." He struck a match and put it to his pipe. In the match glow Janice's face seemed pale and unreal, and it occurred to him that his feeling for her was as shifting as the shadow pattern caused by the flickering light. He admired the intelligence and even the boldness, he distrusted the too mature intent behind every casual word, he pitied the loneliness that he sensed. At the moment he quite simply disliked her. "Did you ask the same question of Mrs. Winters?"

She giggled. "Of course not!" She steadied his wrist with her hand and blew out the match. Her touch was soft and warm, grotesquely childish in contrast to her shrewd eyes. "But you needn't worry, Paul. Even if I found out—something, I'd never mention it."

Her eyes, he was thinking, reminded him of Matt's. The only difference was that Matt sometimes forgot to look shrewd. He had never seen Janice forget. "Knowledge is power. Is that it?"

"What do you mean?" She was curiously angry. "Why do you say that to me? You didn't see my—" She stamped her foot. "Don't *talk* to me in that tone of voice."

He smiled without humor. "I was merely following your mind. And the next step *could* be blackmail, couldn't it? As you said, this is a convenient set-up."

"Paul!" She stared up at him, her eyes wide, her lips parted. *"Uncle Paul!"*

He stared back for a minute, wondering if she felt as tragic as she looked. "I'm sorry," he said then, and meant it. He went on more gently, "I know you and understand,"—it wasn't true, but it seemed the natural thing to say—"but someone else might wonder about your extraordinary interest in private lives."

Janice was dramatically quiet, and when she did speak, her voice was humble. "I have to know about private lives for my writing. Oh, Uncle Paul, I have to know *everything* for my writing."

He moved to turn on the floor lamp, and the light came feebly through the thick silk shade. As always when Janice talked with humility about her writing, he was softened, although at the same time he suspected that she knew of this effect and produced it for her own purpose. "What did you want to see me about, Janice?"

"Well, it's about my writing. . . ." She sat down on the edge of a chair, seeming suddenly shy. "Have you read the sketch I submitted to the Literary Competition?" When he nodded but said nothing, she laced her fingers together and studied them. "Did you like it?"

"It's good writing," he said.

"Do you think it has a chance to win?"

"I can't talk about that tonight, Janice. The entries will be judged tomorrow morning by Professor Cornthwaite, Dr. Anderson, and me. You'll be told of the results very soon after that."

"Oh, but Uncle Paul. . . ." She bit her under lip and blinked fast, as if to keep back tears. "You don't know how important it is for me to know *now*. You don't know what writing means to me! At least tell me how *you* intend to vote, Uncle Paul—please!"

"Actually, I'm not sure how I'll vote, but"—he pointed his pipe stem at her—"even if I were sure, I'd not tell you, for that would be unethical."

She was very still for a minute, and then, to his surprise, looked up with an amused smile. "All right. I know from your voice and the way you're using that pipe that you wouldn't tell me if I begged until I was blue in the face—which I certainly don't intend to do." She stood up and came to him. "What I really want is to make certain that you're not prejudiced by the way I wrote about Helen and Matt in that story. I don't know yet how sentimental you are or aren't, and I don't like the idea of my losing out just because you decide that it isn't *nice* of me to write of my mother and father in that way. You see, you're the only one on that committee who will know that those characters are moth—Helen and Matt."

"You'll not lose because of that, Janice."

Her eyes narrowed as she watched his face intently. "Promise?"

"I promise," he said quietly.

"I guess I can trust you." She went into the hall, but at the door she hesitated. "Why don't we go eat dinner together?" she said indifferently.

"I'm sorry, Janice, but it's late already, and I have work to do."

She laughed shortly. "With Mrs. Winters? And another thing"— she took a step toward him—"I want it understood that I didn't write about Helen and Matt as I did to get even with them. They're— they're simply good story material to me." Her voice had risen shrilly. "Do you understand?"

"I understand."

He waited until she had reached the street; then he closed the door softly and went up the stairs, feeling even more helplessly sad and weary than he had when Hughes left him.

He began to stack the papers he had spread out on his desk. There was no need to reread all of them. It was between Janice's story and David Whitney's essay. He had known that before he had settled down at his desk.

Once again he picked up Janice's sketch, "The Boy." The portrait of Matt was unmistakable. He had recognized it at the first reading. It was powerfully and relentlessly drawn, and it was, he admitted, accurate in essence. How often he himself had seen in Matt that swagger and drive, that lack of grace and sensitiveness, the lust for what could be touched and seen and finally bartered for still bigger things. . . . There was the Helen he knew too, with closed understanding and an apathy of spirit unknown even to herself, and therefore almost pitiful. . . .

He sighed and pushed the papers away from him. There was no cruelty in the characterizations themselves, but only in the external fact that they were the work of the daughter. His own reaction was confused, for he felt a small, ugly triumph over this portrait of his brother. . . .

It was Janice, he decided, who had confused him. She had so much of Matt in her, and yet she had wandered into *his* world. . . .

He shook his head slowly. He couldn't judge that sketch of hers objectively. It had made him feel. There was no doubt of that, for he had his own muddled mind as evidence. But that didn't equip him to vote for it.

He reached for David Whitney's essay. He nodded approvingly as he read it once more, even while it irritated him anew. "Conquest of Self" was an exposé of the human soul, which was, according to Whitney, a severely departmentalized organ that functioned most efficiently when the departments were coordinated. This startling theory was strengthened with well chosen excerpts from Plato, Spenser, Milton, Shelley, and Emerson, which were documented with exasperating correct and honest footnotes. The essay was the flight of the earnest English major into the flower-studded fields of literature, psychology, and philosophy in search of sweetness and light.

As he stuffed the papers into his briefcase, he annoyed himself by recalling the expression on the face of the author of "Conquest of Self" while talking to Carol Leeds on the steps of Science Hall, and he found cause to hope that all the departments of Whitney's soul were perfectly coordinated.

Esther Cornthwaite's usually neat desk was cluttered with papers. She was writing hurriedly and barely looked up when Marcia and Grant came into the office. "Please be seated," she said, "and excuse me while I conclude this paragraph. I can't afford to lose the thought."

Grant was surprised. Marcia, he thought, looked annoyed. She didn't realize that Esther had never before kept people waiting.

Marcia gave him a purely social smile, then sat down and stared out the window. He had been planning to say something casual and jocular about their session over her manuscript, but her manner changed his mind. Clearly it was better not to mention Blake for a while. He pulled his chair nearer to hers. "I haven't seen you all week. How was the tea?"

"Enjoyable." She turned and smiled again, but it was as if she were amused over a memory he couldn't possibly share. "Surprisingly so."

"Good," he said, and the topic died. She returned to staring out the window. Although she wore a black dress relieved by only a pearl necklace, she seemed colorful to him. He decided that it was her face that—

"If you please," Professor Cornthwaite said suddenly, "the judging will commence." When they had turned to her, she said gravely, "We must perform carefully the task before us. The winning of the award is a rare distinction."

"What is the award?" Marcia asked.

Esther looked at Grant, who explained, "Fifty dollars and publication in the John Willard Day issue of the *Young Spectator*. I believe that's a knock at the door," he added quickly.

"Of course it's a knock," Esther said. "Please see who produced it."

Mr. Westaway, News Editor of the *Gazette*, had produced it. "Hi," Grant said.

Mr. Westaway wasn't being familiar. "Professor Grant, the *Gazette* asks permission to be represented by a reporter at the judging of the Competition."

Grant looked at the bright young man and sighed inwardly. "This is a new procedure, isn't it?"

Westaway nodded. "This step is motivated by information we have received concerning certain remarks made in yesterday's faculty meeting about the *Gazette* editorials."

"I see," said Grant, and he wished Clifford Hughes could see. By God, the students had awareness, if nobody else! "Come in and tell Professor Cornthwaite."

Esther regarded Mr. Westaway as he stood unflinchingly before her. A stenographer's notebook was in his hand, and a silver clip and bulge inside his sweater signified a ready pencil. "Young man," she said at last, "there is neither news nor the making of news in this room."

"There soon will be, ma'am," he said confidently and sat down in Grant's chair.

Grant saw Esther appeal to him. Briefly he explained the circumstances. Not having been at the faculty meeting, she still didn't understand. He told her more details, at last mentioning J.W. by name. This moved her to action.

"I'm certain," she said, "that Mr. MacMillan had only the good of the college in mind."

Grant smiled. "That's not the issue. Students, it seems, are wary of even a suggestion of censorship."

She gave him a considering look and then said in a mildly incredulous tone, "You are serious."

"The only point at hand," he said, "is whether Mr. Westaway be granted permission to remain with us."

"So?" She re-examined Mr. Westaway. "It is both presumptuous and revolutionary, of course. However, I have no real objection. Stay, young man, stay. But do not continue to sit in front of me. I have no desire to confuse you with the judges." She waved him to a chair in the far corner.

He moved willingly. Instinctively the three of them turned to watch him flash his pencil, open his notebook on his knee, and wait politely.

Marcia had listened and watched unbelievingly. She tried to remember the faculty meeting. What had J.W. said that was of the ominous significance that Westaway and even Grant pretended? She could think of nothing. In fact, she hadn't listened closely. His unexpected appearance had reminded her of the Sunday evening she had spent with him and his mother, and that in turn had set up a different train of thought.

Obviously, Grant had never eaten dinner with the MacMillans. Obviously, Esther had.

She heard him tell Esther that he had chosen David Whitney's essay, "Conquest of Self." She glanced at him sharply. What *was* the matter with him today? She recalled Mr. Whitney's essay with the same exasperation she had felt when reading it.

"It has sweetness and light," he concluded without enthusiasm.

Marcia shuddered, but Esther nodded approval. "We are agreed," she said and looked at Marcia for confirmation.

"I selected Janice Grant's 'The Boy,' " Marcia said firmly. "To me there was no question. Mr. Whitney's essay shows him to be an accomplished English major. But Janice Grant's sketch shows her to be a *writer*. I think—" She stopped and glanced nervously at Westaway, whose pencil was hurrying over his notebook.

Esther had listened with scholarly tolerance. She searched for "The Boy" among the papers on her desk. When she had found it, she read here and there in the manuscript, her lips silently forming an occasional word. She began to shake her head. "It has no form. It is neither essay nor story. It has no structure."

"But it has feeling, and isn't that alone what gives life form?" Marcia sat forward, forgetting Mr. Westaway's recording pencil. "Don't you feel the frustration of the Boy as his sensitive reaching out for life is thrust aside by the gross indifference of the father, by the heavy apathy of the mother. . . ."

Grant looked up at her. She had caught all that Janice had meant, even without knowing Matt and Helen. "Yes," he said suddenly, "the sketch is lucid and direct. Nothing comes between the scene and the reader. It's good writing."

"That's what I've been trying to tell you," Marcia said dryly. Then for the first time she remembered that the writer of "The Boy" was his niece. "We should have concealed the names," she said more gently, "so that the matter of family relationship would not intrude."

Grant half smiled. If she knew how much family relationship was intruding in that brief sketch! She thought mere modesty was holding him back. "I can be impartial," he said.

Esther seemed perplexed by his wavering. "A freshman has *never* received the award!"

"Tradition!" Marcia's scorn was really for Grant. His cautious attitude reminded her of his reaction to her Blake. "Mere empty tradition!" she said vehemently, as if ready personally to break all links with the past. "I tell you, Janice Grant is a born writer."

"Born?" Esther queried politely. "Do you really think that, Dr. Anderson? I should say rather that Miss Grant came to us with a certain flair for writing, which, under careful supervision, has developed into what we see before us." She turned back to Janice's manuscript and thoughtfully tapped it with a fine forefinger. "The writer of this is my student in English Composition," she said then as if to herself, but quite distinctly.

"It seems to me," Grant said after an effective silence, "that tribute should be paid to such supervision as well as to the result. With your permission, I should like to withdraw my original vote and cast it for 'The Boy.' "

"Your action savors of caprice, Professor Grant," Esther said, but she did not seem displeased. She shrugged faintly. "As unanimity is our object, you leave me no other course than to follow, somewhat reluctantly, your most irregular procedure. Therefore, in the interest of our common purpose to promote writing of fine quality among our students, I too cast my formal vote for—"

They were aware of a stir and a breeze, and then they saw that Mr. Westaway had left them.

Marcia threw her coat over her shoulders and went out on the Summit steps. Grant followed her and cupped his hands around the match flame as she lighted a cigarette. The wind was high and tricky.

"I keep thinking," he said, "that there's more we should say about Blake."

She shrugged. "There's nothing more to say."

He was beginning to believe that she was right. He felt at a loss. She was neither friendly nor unfriendly. Staring out into the Heart, he watched students cross from Science Hall to Main Hall and others from Main Hall to Science Hall.

She watched too, wondering why she didn't ask him outright about J.W. MacMillan. "Professor Cornthwaite doesn't seem ill to me—or even tired. She certainly takes the Competition seriously."

He laughed. "That's her fifty dollars, you know."

"No, I didn't. If I had known, I probably shouldn't have spoken up as I did."

"I'm sure she appreciated your speaking up—as I did."

She looked at him as if faintly amused. "I can't understand how you came to select Whitney's essay. You distrust originality in *any* form, don't you?"

That told him what he had feared—that she was still half angry over his criticism of her Blake. "This wind is bad. Why don't we go to Main Hall Cafeteria for coffee?"

She tossed away her cigarette. "Sorry, but I promised to see Dean Haskins. I must be doing it, for I have another meeting coming up."

He reached out to hold the door open for her, and as she went inside, she said belligerently, "Meetings, always meetings! I'd welcome a class as a diversion." She walked quickly to the stairs, clearly not expecting him to come with her.

He released the door and stayed on the outside, feeling somehow responsible for all her meetings. He wondered what—

"Paul!" Janice ran up the steps, and for the first time he thought her pretty. The sharp air had brought color into her cheeks, her eyes were bright and eager, her dark hair windblown.

"Well, it's over," he said, smiling, "and although you should be made to wait for the official announcement, I see no real harm in telling you that your—"

"Who *is* she?" she asked breathlessly.

He was puzzled. "Who is who? Dr. Anderson?"

"Dr. Anderson," she repeated slowly, her eyes intent upon the door which had only a minute ago closed behind Marcia. "I've heard about her—but I didn't know she looked like that."

"I thought," he said dryly, "that you were interested in the Competition."

She frowned impatiently. "I won, didn't I?"

He studied her face for a moment. "Where were you hiding—in Mr. Westaway's pocket?"

"But I knew I'd win if you didn't ruin my chance. That's why I came to see you last night. I told you that."

"Oh, of course. Well, forgive the boring repetition on my part. But tell me"—his voice became elaborately casual—"why you are so interested in Dr. Anderson."

"I don't know. . . ." There was a softness in her face which he had not seen there before. "I was watching you two here . . . I like the way she looks, the way she sort of shrugged you off when she went inside. . . ." Her face became alert, and she put a small, urgent hand on his arm. "You tell her about me—right away, Paul! You point me out to her and say I'm your niece and the one who wrote 'The Boy.' You promise to do that as soon as. . . ."

To make talk, Marcia admired a white china cat that was curled up with a blue ball on a corner of Dean Haskins' desk. The Dean clutched at this topic and told about her collection of china cats from England, the European Continent, Canada, and a few rare places in the United States.

"You must travel a great deal," Marcia murmured.

The Dean smiled happily. "Oh, I do—that is, when there is no war. In the summers, you know." Then she became brisk, as if settling down to business. "It has been my custom to render a written account of each of my travels. In fact, my Essays have appeared from time to time"—she waved her hand in the direction of the window—"here and there. . . . But occasionally I do something more than the Essay. Something with more feeling, more depth, more *inner* meaning. . . ."

Marcia nodded, and Dean Haskins continued: "It so happens that I have a little something at hand which you perhaps would be interested in reading." She then reached into a desk drawer and brought forth a sheaf of papers. "This is my play, about John Milton. 'A Closet Piece,' I have called it."

Marcia accepted the manuscript. "I'll be glad to read your play, Dean Haskins," she said, wondering why she had been thus selected.

The Dean was elaborately unfolding a handkerchief. "I do believe that my little play has excellent possibilities as a John Willard Day production." She gave the handkerchief a final shake so that it wafted a delicate lily-of-the-valley scent. "Perhaps if you find merit in it, you might suggest it to Miss Taylor."

"Of course," said Marcia. "However, Miss Taylor has already chosen and cast the play for this year."

But Dean Haskins, it seemed, had investigated enough to know that Miss Taylor was not at all satisfied with the chosen play. "She'd much prefer something original, I understand, and, after all. . . ." The Dean waved the handkerchief at the manuscript in Marcia's hands. "By the way," she said, glancing at her wristwatch, "I believe that we're both due at the same luncheon meeting. Why don't we walk over together?"

As they walked to the Cottage, the Dean explained more specifically what Marcia might say to Iris Taylor. Listening, Marcia began to understand that the seemingly casual episode of giving her the play to read had been carefully planned. She even came to feel that the Dean had calculated her admiring the china cat, which had led to the traveling, which led to the essay-writing, which led to the play. . . .

Did the Dean's shrewdness extend to larger spheres? Marcia was not adept at strategy, and her leading question was awkward. "What did you think of the faculty meeting?"

Dean Haskins looked surprised and then shrugged slightly as if to say, "My dear, what does one usually think of faculty meetings!"

"I mean," Marcia hurried on, "Mr. MacMillan's coming in unexpectedly was exciting, wasn't it?"

"Exciting?" The Dean measured the word doubtfully.

"Well, at least it broke the routine. And what he said was quite interesting, didn't you think?"

"I see what you mean. Yes, of course." The Dean reflected a moment and then evaluated, "An admirable man, J.W. MacMillan."

Marcia smiled. Both Esther Cornthwaite and Elizabeth Haskins couldn't be wrong! "Then you didn't think there was any harm in what he said?" she asked quickly, no longer concerned with strategy.

"Oh, I heartily disapproved of what he said, if you're referring to his remarks about the college newspaper."

Marcia stared. "But you just said—"

"That he is an admirable man. And he is, you know. Didn't you admire the subtlety and the suavity with which he made his point?" She smiled at Marcia and then nodded toward the Cottage. "Did you notice that Colley and Hughes—and, yes, there's Holcomb—have already gone in? We've timed it perfectly. I abhor being first and having to wait. If we walk a bit more slowly, I shall be able to complete what I was saying. Now, I have a sweeping contempt for all men," she went on pleasantly. "They are arrogant, smug, and intent upon keeping women in a prehistoric stage of evolution. However, as men appear to be inevitable, I must admit that I prefer those with power and a facility for using it. For several years I have studied J. W. MacMillan closely and critically, and I have never once seen him at a loss. An admirable man!"

Clifford Hughes pushed back his plate abruptly. "What's the purpose of this meeting?"

"Well, son, it's like this." Colley tilted back his chair and attached his thumbs to his vest pockets. "If a committee doesn't meet at least once a semester, it automatically goes out of existence. Besides, we've never had a real get-together since our new additions—namely, you and the Doctor here."

Marcia steeled herself. The way Colley called her Doctor! Little-girl-playing-at-something-big. She put down her soup spoon. "May I ask the purpose of the *committee?*"

Dean Haskins smiled but said nothing.

Colley caught the smile, and his face clouded. "The good Dean here doesn't approve of our little Student Personnel Committee."

"Oh, that's an extreme statement," said Dean Haskins politely. "I merely think it superfluous. Furthermore, I disapprove of meeting at a time when Dr. Day cannot be with us. It is well known that she has interviews scheduled daily at this hour."

Colley was hurt. "Now, I can't be expected to remember all those details." He appealed to authority. "You know how it is, Holcomb."

"What? Oh." Dean Holcomb meditated into his milk glass. "Yes, yes—"

Dean Haskins coughed gently.

"—of course, I understand Dean Haskins' point of view. Thoroughly. If we— Oh." He took the menu from the girl who was hovering at his side. "Dessert," he said with satisfaction.

Colley beamed up at the girl. "You certainly have given us fine service, Alice! I intend to speak to Miss Shultz about it."

"Mildred," said Dean Haskins to the girl, emphasizing the name, "would you please bring me more hot water for my tea when you return?"

Colley flushed. "Why, of course it's Mildred! Guess I confused her with little Alice Mueller. They look enough alike," he confided to Marcia, "to be twins."

Dean Haskins turned to Hughes. "I had never noticed a resemblance, had you?"

Hughes didn't respond, for he had half turned to watch Professor Webb, who was taking the table next to them. Seated, the Professor slowly searched through his pockets.

"He's forgotten his glasses again," Hughes said softly.

"Now, Alice Mueller, there's a girl for you!" Colley tilted back again. "I remember her when she first came to us. Even then there was no doubt in her mind about what she wanted to be. A dietician. And ever since—"

"Does lemon pie appeal to you?" Dean Holcomb asked around the table. "Miss Shultz's lemon pie is never a disappointment!"

"No dessert for me," Dean Haskins said delicately.

"Come, now, Elizabeth!" coaxed Holcomb. "Your figure doesn't require such careful vigilance."

Elizabeth tried to look displeased. "What an absurd conclusion! It so happens that I have *never* cared for confections."

Dean Holcomb leaned forward intently. "What about *you* and lemon pie, Dr. Anderson?"

Marcia shook her head, trying to listen to Colley, who had fastened upon her. "—and that shows that all this high-falutin' vocational guidance is unnecessary, for there she was, a freshman, knowing exactly—no pie, thanks—exactly what she wanted without anyone *guiding* her. And her record indicates what a perfect choice it is, for she has done *beautiful* work, *beautiful*—"

"Who has?" asked Hughes. He turned back to them when he saw Vincent Diaz join Webb. "What's this all—no, thanks. I don't like *any* kind of pie. Who does beautiful work?"

"Alice Mueller." Colley looked appreciatively at his expanding audience. "I was just telling the Doctor here how she—"

"Why don't *you* have lemon pie, William?" suggested Dean Haskins.

Dean Holcomb looked wistful, but he shook his head. "No, I shouldn't enjoy eating it alone." He resigned the menu to the patient Mildred.

"But," said Marcia to Colley, "Alice Mueller changed her major to English." He looked so startled that she added hastily, "Of course, you probably knew that."

He reflected. "Let me see . . . did I? No—now wait a minute! I'm beginning to remember something . . . yes! Little Alice did stop in to see me some time ago, and she mentioned that she was contemplating such a change. That's it, all right—" He stopped as Diaz's soft yet distinct voice came smoothly to their table.

". . . the admirable thing about Plato is that one can find anything in the *Republic*, from communism to dictatorship."

"Except democracy," said Professor Webb sadly. "Except democracy. He leaves no doubt that he thinks democracy a form of anarchy, symbolic of the disintegration of the human soul."

Diaz seemed delighted. "Exactly!"

Hughes stood with such suddenness that his chair toppled over. "You didn't used to talk that way!" he cried accusingly to Webb.

Diaz looked up, smiling faintly. "Do you find your own meeting boring, Mr. Hughes?"

Hughes ignored him. "If you start with Plato's premise, you can't find *everything* in him! You know that. You taught me that!"

"I had assumed, Clifford," said Professor Webb earnestly, "that Mr. Diaz *knew* Plato's premise."

Hughes stared at him for a moment, then shrugged. "I'm a fool," he said as he righted his chair and sat down.

No one disputed this, and only Colley found the appropriate word. "Well," he said. "Well!"

"Clifford, I think that you misunderstood my remark to Mr. Diaz." Webb's voice startled them all. He had risen with ghostly quiet to stand at Hughes' back.

Hughes flushed but didn't look up. "Sorry I made a scene."

Webb rested his long thin hand on Hughes' shoulder. "We have much to talk over, Clifford."

Hughes' mouth twisted. "Yes, sir."

The hand was withdrawn, and Webb faded away.

Dean Holcomb cleared his throat. "I dislike to break up our meeting, but I have another appointment. . . ."

Dean Haskins remembered an appointment too. She lingered only long enough to give an admonishing pat to the play manuscript by Marcia's place. "My only copy, you know. I trust it to your good care!"

"A week from today," Colley shouted after the departing deans. "Same time, same place!" He turned back to Marcia and Hughes. "There's nothing like—"

Hughes muttered something and left abruptly.

"I was saying," Colley went on to Marcia, "there's nothing like a little old luncheon meeting to draw people out."

"Apparently not," she said, and excused herself.

In the evening Marcia worked sporadically at Blake. The empty luncheon meeting lingered unpleasantly in her mind, and Cliff Hughes' tenseness was puzzling. But underlying her uneasiness was, she knew, a nagging curiosity about J.W. MacMillan, whose words at the faculty meeting had aroused disapproval in Grant and even Dean Haskins. . . .

She was grateful when Mrs. Murdock shouted up the stairs to tell her that Iris Taylor had come to see her.

Iris glanced at the paper-littered desk as she came into the room. "Hope I'm not interrupting something important."

"Just Blake."

"Blake? Oh, William." Iris sat down on the edge of the bed, as if she didn't intend to stay long. "It's indecent the way you consort with him. You've got me thinking he actually stalks the campus." But she said this mechanically, and lighted a cork-tipped cigarette at the wrong end. When Marcia told her about the cigarette, she laughed apologetically and took a fresh one. "I'm off the beam tonight, but I did come for a legitimate reason. I want to thank you for turning Haskins' manuscript over to me."

Marcia stared. "You don't mean you can use it?"

"Why not? It has possibilities—although they're not the ones Elizabeth intended. I can stylize the Cromwell and Charles First scenes. . . and I'll underplay the Dean's obvious Royalist sympathies." She was beginning to seem more like her real self. She crossed her legs and leaned forward, her elbow on her knee and her chin in her hand. "Yes, it can be made timely stuff."

Marcia was doubtful. "It bored me horribly when I read it this afternoon."

Iris nodded vaguely, her green eyes dreamy. "Dave Whitney is a natural for Milton, and Carol Leeds must be Mary. What she won't do with Mary! She'll make her another Nora, with more meaning than Ibsen's—and what a doll's house to break!"

Marcia listened in surprise. She thought it noble of Iris to talk so generously of Carol Leeds' acting. After all, considering that Kim—

"I'll show it to Kim tomorrow. He has an instinct for what's good theater. He—" She gave Marcia a quick defiant look. "We work together very well."

"I know you do," Marcia said hastily. "Kim often mentions it."

"I can imagine," Iris said dryly, "*how* he mentions it." She shrugged and forced her attention back to the play. "I'll use very few props. The stage must be somber, austere. For the first scene Mary must wear gray. . . ." She reached for an ashtray and put out her cigarette violently. "I'll be glad when that bitch is off the campus."

Marcia pretended not to know who was meant, but Iris laughed shortly. "You know, of course. Everyone knows. He's so stupid and obvious about it." She lighted a new cigarette and stared at it. "But even if I handed that wolfess her diploma in person, it wouldn't change anything. Even if she went to China, it wouldn't change anything. That's the way Kim is. He thinks she. . . ." Her words trailed off with the smoke.

"He thinks she symbolizes everything he wants—beauty and freedom," Marcia finished for her.

She looked up suspiciously. "Did he tell you that?"

Marcia nodded reluctantly, sorry she had spoken. "But it doesn't mean anything—his talking to me that way. We simply—"

"Oh, I understand. Your souls had a speaking acquaintance in another world." She smoked moodily, the impatient anger leaving her face. "He promised to go over the Haskins thing with me tonight, but of course he didn't appear."

"I don't think he's with Carol," Marcia said. "You see, he—"

"You don't have to explain him to me," Iris said sharply. "I *know* he isn't with Carol. It would be easier and simpler if he *would* go sleep with her. God knows, she wouldn't object. But he has to be different." She shrugged and smiled wryly. "Right now he's in one of two places—either down by the river brooding on a rock, or up on the Widow's Walk, brooding on the stars. And as you are of kindred soul, perhaps you can explain to me why he has more to brood over than anyone else."

Marcia was almost angry. Iris' contempt seemed directed toward her as well as Kim. "You can't judge by mere appearances. There are various reasons to brood, and just because Kim broods more dramatically than most people, you shouldn't—"

"I told you that you don't have to explain him to me!" Iris sighed then. "Sorry. I don't know why I'm talking to you this way. Well, maybe I do. I've noticed how he trails you around, and I thought you might have something wise to say—unless. . . ." She gave Marcia a searching look. "Are you in love with him?"

"No!" Marcia said emphatically, thinking of J.W.

"You needn't be insulting about it!"

Marcia laughed guiltily. "I didn't mean it that way." She set her mind to being wise. "You have to accept Kim as he is. You can't disregard his very nature—"

"Yes, he has a wonderful nature," Iris said grimly. "It fills the whole world. My own is beginning to feel cramped."

"If you think that way," Marcia said confidently, "then you don't love him. So there's no problem."

Iris seemed startled. "Perhaps you're right," she said slowly. "Maybe *I'm* changing. I know that a year ago I would have been rushing around to find him—but I refuse to do that now. Still. . . ." She was quiet, then said suddenly, "About Carol Leeds. I think I stopped being jealous months ago. Chiefly I'm worried. That girl isn't—well, quite normal. I can't tell you exactly what I mean, but I sense—" She jumped as Mrs. Murdock shouted up the stairs that there was someone else to see Dr. Anderson.

"It's a man," Mrs. Murdock whispered ominously as Marcia came down the stairs. "And he won't come in."

The man was square-faced and muscular. Marcia had never seen him before.

"Are you Miss Marcia Anderson?" he asked hesitantly.

"Of course she is," said an oddly familiar voice, and J.W. stepped into view. There was a large dog too.

Marcia stared. "Won't you come in—all of you?"

"Not the *dog!*" whispered Mrs. Murdock hoarsely and fled.

"No, thank you," J.W. said. "We were just passing, and I wanted to leave this book with you."

She took the book in her hands as if she had never seen one before. He smiled, seeming to enjoy her surprise. "A friend told me that you were inquiring about it. Keep it as long as you wish. Oh, yes"—he nodded toward the square-faced man—"I want to introduce you to Mr. Whitelock, Tamburlaine's handler."

"Pleased," Mr. Whitelock said, then moved discreetly into the background.

"And of course you must meet Tamburlaine," J.W. said gently.

She took Tamburlaine's proffered paw. "Pleased," she murmured, because that was the only word in her mind. Tamburlaine nozzled against her hand.

"He takes to you," J.W. observed. "That's no mean compliment, for he's quite irritable when in training."

She felt flattered and tried to give Tamburlaine more attention, but he left her when he heard Mr. Whitelock's soft whistle.

J.W. was saying, "Forgive this little interruption. I'm sure that you were very busy."

"Not at all," she said hastily, for his tone belying his words, suggested that she couldn't possibly have been busy enough to think his coming an interruption; and she was eager to agree with even his unspoken thoughts.

"Who was it?" Mrs. Murdock had reappeared on tiptoe.

Marcia moved away from the door. "Only Mr. MacMillan," she said carelessly.

"Oh! You should have made him come in—his dog too!"

On the stairs, she looked at the book for the first time. *Noa Noa.* Deardorff, then, was the friend who had told him she wanted the book. She was glad to think of Deardorff as his friend.

Opening it, she saw that the inscription was simple: *May, 1941.* Yet it made her heart beat fast.

She ran up the rest of the stairs but halted at the top. Iris! She had forgotten about her. It would be more pleasant to be alone. . . . She fanned her face with the book, for she was sure that it was flushed. Then she strolled nonchalantly into her room.

Iris had been pacing. She stopped when she saw Marcia and said, "What I mean is that Carol Leeds doesn't have normal reactions."

"Oh, she'll be all right," Marcia said gaily.

"Thanks, my friend," Iris said dryly, giving her a curious look. "Who *was* that caller?"

"Just a man with a book." And Marcia held up the book to prove it.

Iris shrugged and gathered up her purse and cigarettes. "You and your books. You're darn lucky."

"Must you leave?" Marcia asked perfunctorily.

Iris looked guilty. "I was thinking I'd walk down to the river. . . ." Suddenly she laughed. "And if I don't find anything there, I'll have just time enough to make it up to the Widow's Walk before Charlie closes the Summit."

Marcia thought her unwise, but said nothing, and they went downstairs in silence. On the porch, Iris said, "Thanks for the confidence hour. I indulge very seldom—so don't be alarmed." She started down the steps, but looked back to say, "Come to think of it, I'd better not underplay the Royalist sympathy too much. After what Papa MacMillan said at faculty meeting, a play glorifying Cromwell would probably make the Department of Drama extinct."

Marcia managed a laugh, but she was exasperated. Why couldn't people talk without mentioning that meeting! When Iris had turned down the Heights, she went quickly upstairs to make sure that *Noa Noa* was still there.

It was—and so were the Blake papers. The papers seemed a silent rebuke, and as she put them away, she justified herself to them. Events, not she, were the cause. If she hadn't seen him after the September Tea, she could easily have forgotten him. If she hadn't seen him after that Sunday at Esther Cornthwaite's, she could still have forgotten him. But he had appeared tonight. . . .

When she caught a glimpse of herself in the mirror, she saw with surprise that she was smiling triumphantly.

Chapter Five

MARCIA couldn't recognize the voice calling her name, for the rain beating down on her umbrella deadened the sound. J.W. never called her *Doctor* and he wouldn't be walking through the campus on this wet morning; but even as she thought these things, she turned in eager hope.

It was Richard Tibbet. Unprotected, he stood in front of Science Hall as if in sunny dryness. "Hello," she said, walking back to him and wondering why he hadn't said whatever he wished to say when she had seen him in the Library only a few minutes earlier.

"Hello," he said gravely. His usual grin was missing, and with a strangely formal gesture he put his hand up to his hat.

"Don't take that off!" she cried, seeing the water between the crease and around the brim. "You'll drown us both. Here—stand under this." She held the umbrella over him.

To him it seemed that the umbrella closed in around him like a tent with no air holes. "I'm going home today. I report to training center next week."

She stared at him. She knew about the war, of course—but why Richard Tibbet? He belonged on campus. He was one of those blank-faced, apathetic students who had filled seats in her class for the sole purpose of misunderstanding William Blake. . . . "Can't you do something about it?"

He grinned then, briefly. "When the United States Army says come, you come."

"I know," she said quickly, feeling rebuked. "I merely meant. . . ."

He consoled her. "I'll get my grades for this semester, because it's so near the end of the term."

"Grades? Oh, I'm glad that you'll get them."

"Yep, I'll get them all right." He stared down at his wet shoes and saw that hers were wet too. Everything was awkward. He had only a minute more, he knew.

"Then," she went on because she felt that she should keep talking, "you'll be a senior, won't you?"

He nodded and water dripped off his hat. He hadn't meant to talk about grades. "I want to thank you for Blake," he blurted out, and it seemed that he shouted.

She looked at him, puzzled; then smiled. Obviously he was saying that to be polite, and she was touched. "Some day, Richard, if you should ever look into Blake again, you may be surprised. He is not so impractical and out of this world as you—many students think."

He had heard only the *Richard,* had seen only the smile. He had never dreamed that he'd want to tell her, but he did. He did! Going off to war was special, and he felt that at this moment she could understand anything—*anything.* He held out his hand and when hers met it, there was in the touch nothing of younger and older or of student and teacher. "I want," he said, "I want you to know—" He stopped abruptly, for the moment was gone. "Good-by," he said roughly, and ran up the shining steps to Science Hall.

But he heard her call after him. "Write to me, Richard. Remember to write."

He had left his bag by the door. When he stooped for it, a thin stream of water slid off his hat brim. He half lifted the bag and then set it down again. He was weak, and the discovery shocked him.

He leaned against the door and lighted a cigarette. He had been faithful about not smoking when training for track. But he wasn't in training now.

Oh, no?

He didn't find his own joke funny. He moved nearer to the steps and saw that she was almost to the Summit. Her bright plaid umbrella was like a sun. She put it down and disappeared. He stepped back into the dry spot by the door.

There wasn't a damn thing for him to like in the whole, wide dripping world.

But it was good to smoke. He watched the rain slant across Main Hall. It wasn't bad rain. May rain, after all.

It was the same world that had been before he had met her there on the walk. It could easily have been a very different one, for he had almost made a fool of himself by telling her. Something had saved him.

He'd eat at home tonight. His mother, the hot meal, the kid brother green with envy because he couldn't go off to war. . . . All waiting.

For everything that lives is holy.

Why not?

Maybe he'd start a letter on the train. . . .

Marcia stood in the Summit hall, letting her umbrella drip. She watched the growing puddle and wondered why it had to rain on the day Richard Tibbet left for war. Uneasily she thought of the significant words she should have said and hadn't, words proportionate to the occasion.

She thought too of the pleading in his face and the desperate clasp of his hand. With surprise she remembered how only a few weeks ago she would have withdrawn from his out-reaching, been embarrassed by it, even afraid of it. It as as if her own feeling for J.W. had given her a new understanding.

No, not understanding. It was not a process of the mind. It was an awareness of a human feeling that was more powerful than individuality. Like a rich vein of ore in the earth, it was inexhaustibly present to all who wished to draw upon it. . . .

There the image burst like a bubble, for she could not imagine J.W.'s condescending to tap any feeling shared by a whole world of people.

She was not sorry when the door swung open and stopped her thoughts. Scott came in, glistening in his long black raincoat and rubber hat. "Aha!" he cried, pulling off the hat and making a mock bow. "I hope I am the first to congratulate our new heroine."

"What on earth are you talking about?"

"Seen the latest *Gazette?*"

She shook her head. "Is there something important in it?"

"Not particularly important, but I think you'll be interested." He pulled a crumpled copy from his pocket and opened it out for her. "And now, my dear Dr. Anderson—Oh, hello, Colley. Is Cameron free now?"

"Guess so." Colley carefully closed the door to President Cameron's office, and when he saw Marcia, he saluted. "So she came, saw, and conquered!"

Scott laughed at her puzzled look. "This will explain it," he said, putting the *Gazette* into her hands.

She saw the big headlines: ANDERSON CHAMPIONS FROSH; then unbelievingly scanned the column headed *Says Tradition Empty.* According to Mr. Westaway, Dr. Marcia Anderson alone had seen to it that justice was done all entries in the Competition.

> The climax to the dramatic judging scene came when Dr. Anderson spoke out boldly in defense of the entry of Janice Grant (Freshman). Exposing the unfairness of the customary procedure of the Committee in giving serious attention to only those contributions of upperclass students, Dr. Anderson succeeded in . . .

"Ridiculous!" she said.

"Shh." Scott put a finger to his lips. "You might be quoted, you know."

"Very, very clever," Colley said. He looked shrewd and knowing.

She saw that he meant it seriously. "You don't think that I purposely—"

"Have *you* seen it?" Scott called to Grant, who was coming down the stairs.

He nodded and looked pleased. "I read it in proof."

She turned to him. "Why did you let it go through?"

He laughed. "Westaway was on the scene, remember. And if that's the way he saw it—well, that's the way he saw it."

"It's absurd!" she said impatiently.

"Shh," warned Scott again. "In any event, congratulations. You've secured a following for at least four years!"

"Three," she corrected dryly. "You forget the accelerated program."

"Superb for a beginner," said Colley. "A little obvious, of course, but—"

"A momentous conference, no doubt." President Cameron presented his fine profile as he glided by.

"Good afternoon!" Scott said eagerly and broke away. He glided a few steps with the President. "I was about to knock at your door. Our appointment, you know. . . ."

"Very, very clever," said Colley wistfully as he walked to the door. He thrust it open and stood there for a moment before he called out in a note of personal triumph, "The rain has stopped!" When he stepped back, he collided with the President, who stood poised with watch in hand.

The President was dismayed. He studied his watch, then Scott, and then the watch again. "I don't understand it. Miss Bale must have failed to mark down our appointment."

"I see," said Scott, backing away.

"I apologize humbly. This meeting I'm going to now is very important, or I'd—"

"It's quite all right," Scott cut in sharply. "Quite."

"My dear fellow. . . ." The President put away his watch. He sighed deeply as he went out the door that Colley was holding wide for him.

Colley followed briskly. "I hope you feel with me that the chat we had today was very worthwhile, very worthwhile. . . ." The door swung shut.

Scott shrugged and came back to Marcia and Grant. "How about a cup of coffee?"

Grant looked apologetic. "I promised Cunningham that I'd read over the catalogue material. I was on my way when—"

"You have to take on the damnedest jobs for Cornthwaite, don't you?" Scott looked at Marcia. "What errand are *you* on, heroine?"

"Well. . . ." She hesitated. She had meant to grade papers in the hour left before her first class, but she knew he wouldn't believe this. "It's too wet to go to Herby's. Will Main Hall Cafeteria do?"

Scott smiled faintly. "Very wise of you to appear in Main Hall now. Your public will be appreciative."

"Wish I could join you," Grant said, and watched them go off together until the door closed behind them.

Marcia wished so too. She didn't feel up to sparring with Scott alone.

"He's really a flunky, isn't he?" Scott said as they went down the steps.

She knew that he meant Grant, and she was instantly furious. With effort she made her voice guileless: "Oh, you mean Colley?"

"No, I didn't mean Colley," he said shortly, and dropped the subject.

It was after three o'clock when she was able to return to the Inferno, which was miraculously empty. Enjoying the luxury of sole possession, she draped her coat over Hughes's chair and turned on Diaz's radio in the hope of soft music. The rain had forced Kim to paint inside, and the turpentine smell still cloyed the air. She lighted a cigarette and went over to examine the canvas upright on the easel.

It was, she finally decided, a portrait of MacMillan Hall. She called it a portrait to herself because the front of the building was made to look like a face—a malicious, greedy one. It was a night scene, with yellow lights coming from the windows and a small daub of a man standing before the house. His arms were raised in what might have been a defiant or a fearful gesture. She couldn't tell which Kim had meant.

Martin wouldn't like the work, she knew. He'd call it a careless blur. Reluctantly she admitted that he might be right. . . . Still, there was a certain power in it, despite the obscurity. . . .

Obscure yet powerful. She remembered then that Grant had said something very similar about her Blake manuscript. Annoyed at this recollection, she grew aware that the radio was not yielding soft music, but the Afternoon Bird Club. She clicked it off and sat down to her themes, grading them with uncharacteristic severity.

She turned sharply as she heard a step creak. Someone was on the stairs, anonymous in the shadows. An unfamiliar voice called out, "Dr. Anderson?"

"Yes." She arose and peered. "Come up the rest of the way."

A slight dark-haired girl stepped into view. "I'm Janice Grant." She looked at Marcia with intent black eyes that seemed too large for her thin face.

Marcia smiled. "Professor Grant's niece. I'm glad that you came to see me. Let me pull up a chair for you." She got Kim's chair for Janice, and reseated herself at her desk.

Janice sat down and demurely folded her hands in her lap, but she was clearly in no hurry to explain her visit. Her observing eyes took in Kim's easel, the other desks, Marcia's coat, papers, and book. Finally they stayed on Marcia's ashtray. "I like the way you hold your cigarette when you smoke," she said.

Surprised, Marcia asked her if she wanted a cigarette. She shook her head. "I don't smoke now—but I'll begin soon." She leaned back in her chair, as if her survey of the room had made her feel at home. "I came to thank you."

"*Thank* me? For what?"

"You know." Janice smiled knowingly. "For making them choose 'The Boy.' I read all about it in the *Gazette*."

Marcia made a gesture of protest. "Oh, but I didn't—"

"I realize," Janice said easily, "that you can't admit you forced them to select my sketch, but I want you to know that I'm aware of what you did for me."

The girl's manner was so self-assured that Marcia almost responded with a thank-you, but she caught it in time and reminded herself that she was the teacher and Janice a student. "You are a fine writer," she said firmly, thinking that she must sound a little like Esther Cornthwaite, "and I was aware of bestowing no favor upon you. Your writing justly deserved the award."

Janice nodded. "I can write, of course, but it's important that I win prizes. I always won them in high school—that is, the ones worth going after." She grew silent and thoughtful, and her fingers worked with the slightly curling ends of her hair. "But I don't want you to think that I came to see you only because of that. I had decided to come before I even knew about the Competition. I—"

"Yes?" Marcia said encouragingly as for the first time Janice seemed unsure of herself.

"I can't tell you about it now," she said, "but maybe I'll tell you sometime later—maybe." She glanced at the themes. "Are you busy?"

"In a way. . . ." Marcia said hesitantly. She glanced at her watch. "I have these papers to grade, and then in a few minutes I must go over to the Barn. I promised Miss Taylor to watch a rehearsal."

"Oh." But Janice made no move to go. Suddenly she said, "There's another reason why I came, and I can tell you this one."

Marcia laughed. "It would seem that this is a *very* purposeful visit."

Janice did not like the laugh. "The reason," she said with dignity, "is that my Uncle Paul told me to come to you. He said that of all the teachers on campus you were the one most worth cultivating."

Marcia decided that she was misquoting Grant. He wouldn't speak of *cultivating* a person. Yet she found the basic idea attractive. She was, in fact, surprised to find how flattered she felt. "Any teacher here is worth cultivating, I'm sure," she murmured modestly.

Janice smiled a strangely private smile and seemed to relax again; and for a moment Marcia had the unpleasant feeling that she had calculated the effect of her remark about Grant. But she quickly stifled the unworthy feeling. After all, the girl was only a freshman. . . .

"Will you come visit me at Oaklands this summer?" Janice asked.

"Oaklands? What is that?"

"Our summer home. It's quite pleasant, and you can hardly tell that it used to be a farm."

Marcia began to stack the themes, suddenly wanting to be free of the girl. "Thank you very much," she said, smiling, "but I intend to spend the summer writing."

"Oaklands is perfect for writing."

Marcia stood up. "I'm afraid that I'm too used to working at home to risk a change. I usually—"

"You think it over." Janice stood too. "May I go to rehearsal with you? I'm going to write a play one day."

"I believe that Miss Taylor prefers not to have students sit in on rehearsals—outside of her classes and the cast, of course."

Janice shrugged. "That's silly, isn't it? But if she feels that way, I suppose you can hardly take me with you." She moved to the stairs. "Are you here at this time every day?"

"Not every day," Marcia said quickly out of an instinctive feeling of self-preservation.

"Well, I'll find you when I want you."

She smoked a part of a cigarette to make sure that Janice would be well gone, then left the Inferno. She found Dean Haskins standing on a step in the middle of the stairs leading to the first floor. She looked uncompromisingly stationary, and her intent gaze was fixed

155

upon President Cameron's door as if she hoped to force it open by sheer mental force.

"Excuse me," Marcia said, finding it impossible to squeeze between the wall and the Dean.

Dean Haskins did not move, but said distinctly, "The little windbag!"

"Pardon?"

The Dean turned then and looked coldly at Marcia. "Not Cameron. Holcomb."

Marcia laughed embarrassedly. "I thought you meant me."

Dean Haskins blinked. "Dr. Anderson! I'm so sorry."

"Think nothing of it," Marcia said lightly, and tried to escape.

But the Dean walked on down the stairs with her. "I wanted to make certain that they had been to the meeting this morning."

"I happened to be in the hall when President Cameron *said* he was going to a meeting," Marcia said cautiously.

"Holcomb too?"

Marcia shook her head. "I didn't see him."

"He went, you can be sure."

"Perhaps so," Marcia said, hoping that it was a neutral remark.

The Dean still accompanied her, and to be polite Marcia stopped with her outside the Summit. It was not raining, but the air seemed a web-like mist. "You have no coat," she reminded Dean Haskins.

"No matter," said the Dean with unusual carelessness. She was silent for a moment; then spoke rapidly: "It was a meeting of the Administrative Staff. I knew that it was coming up. I saved the time purposely." Her voice arose a pitch. "But I didn't even receive a notice."

"That was a terrible oversight," Marcia said with suitable emphasis, "but I'm sure that it was an error."

"Error?" The Dean eyed her suspiciously. "What kind of *error* could it have been?"

"Oh—clerical," said Marcia sweepingly.

The Dean considered this and found it possible. "I shall make inquiries tomorrow."

Marcia regarded Dean Haskins with real concern. Her face was pale and stiff with anger. "I'm on my way to a rehearsal of your play," she said. "Why don't you come with me?"

The Dean seemed startled. "Do I dare?"

Marcia laughed. "Why not? Aren't you the playwright?"

"Why, so I am," said the Dean slowly, and she looked both pleased and surprised.

They sat in the last row of the rough-hewn benches. The stage was in a flat light, and two boys were pulling a table and chair across it.

"About six inches more to the left," called out Iris, then went on talking to a shadowy group of figures down front.

Marcia made out Kim sitting alone some rows in front of her and Dean Haskins. He was hunched down in his seat, his arm thrown over the back of the bench. He found a cigarette and lighted it with one hand, without changing his position. He blew out the smoke noisily. It was clear that he felt very much at home. "We'll use the gray backdrop, after all," he said suddenly.

"Right," said Iris without looking up. "Call Leeds and Whitney!" she shouted to someone.

The prop men gave the table and chair a final pat and disappeared. Lights flickered.

"We're not bothering with lights today!" Iris said. The lights steadied.

David Whitney appeared on the stage and seated himself at the table, pretending to write. Carol Leeds came out of a wing and walked around him and the table critically. "It won't do," she said loudly. "I want to do this scene in profile."

Her voice worried the Dean. "It's so—resolute," she whispered. "How can she be Mary Milton?"

"Fix it, then," Iris told Carol.

Carol made David adjust his chair so that when she stood at his back her profile was clearly seen by the audience. The change had disturbed David, and he went back to his imaginary writing with obvious effort. " 'Mary,' " he said, " 'do not stand at my back. Your presence distracts me.' " He enunciated with stolid determination.

"I can't react to that," Carol said curtly. "Tell him to get the tempo!"

The Dean sighed. "She's temperamental. Really, she doesn't seem Mary Milton's type. . . ."

"That's right, David," Iris said calmly. "You're annoyed—exasperated, remember. Mary is a fly buzzing around you."

David squinted at Iris. "But I—" He sighed and resumed his writing pose, adding a scowl. " 'Mary, do not stand at my back.' " With his left hand he made a gesture as if to swat a fly. " 'Your presence. . . .' "

Carol grimaced and made a mute appeal to Iris. But Iris signaled for her to go on.

Carol's face went blank and then slowly took on a soft, hurt expression. Gently she leaned over Mr. Milton. " 'But I'm interested in what you're writing. You never tell me about it, you know.' "

" 'This is not to your taste,' " David recited.

" 'You always say that!' " pouted Mary. She was quiet for a minute, and then she coaxed, " 'Tell me the title, just the title. . . .' "

As she listened, Marcia began to understand why Iris could set aside personal feelings in order to have Carol Leeds act. Mary Milton had emerged from a few indifferent lines and a slight movement, an individual distinct from anybody else who had ever been. The magic spread, touching even David Whitney, whose very stiffness and ponderousness began to seem right. The barren stage was suddenly richly filled. . . .

"Cut it!" Iris called after a few minutes.

Carol's face changed instantly. She leaned against the table, one hand insolently on her hip. David got up and stretched.

Iris tossed a script onto the stage. "Just read lines. I want to hear how they come out of you. Some will have to be reworked, I'm sure."

"What does she mean?" the Dean demanded indignantly. Marcia pretended not to have heard.

David and Carol sat on the table and held the script between them. " 'I had to choose between my husband and my king,' " Carol read tonelessly. She crossed her legs.

" 'Nonsense!' " boomed David.

" 'So they are going to kill the king—my king—it will seem strange to be without king—it will seem strange to the queen to be without husband—it will seem strange to the children [Lord, what lines!] to be without father— I think that I could write more truth about the king, my king, than you.' "

" 'Absurd!' " boomed David.

Someone down front giggled. Dean Haskins stirred uneasily.

" 'I have heard say that he was a good fa-ah' "—Carol's voice went up with a stifled yawn—" 'ther. I have heard—' "

"Cut it!" called Iris. "That's all. Same time tomorrow."

Carol threw the script to one side and asked someone to hand her a book she had left on a front bench. When she had it, she opened it and began to read, still sitting on the table. Whitney said something to her. She didn't look up from the book, and he finally wandered out of sight.

"House lights!" someone shouted.

Orange and blue walls sprang out. Rising from her seat, Dean Haskins drew attention to the colors and remarked disapprovingly, "We owe all *this* to Mr. Duncan."

"Really?" Marcia glanced where Kim had been sitting, but he was no longer there. Following the Dean to the back of the small theater, she looked around her with new interest, now that she knew he was responsible. She liked what she saw, and it occurred to her that even Martin would approve of it. The orange and blue had been applied skillfully, for even with the full lights on, the effect was not garish, but warm and stimulating.

Before they stepped out the door, Dean Haskins halted her with a gentle yet firm touch on the arm. "By the way," she said with only slight embarrassment, "I want to thank you, Dr. Anderson." She cleared her throat. "We women must stand together. If we don't . . ." She made a small gesture to indicate that there were not words dire enough to describe what would befall women who did not stand together.

While Kim waited outside, he lighted another cigarette, although he didn't really want it. His hands fumbled with the match, for they were cold and numb. And then he saw the Dean and Marcia come out of the Barn. He hadn't known that they had been inside.

The Dean, thank God, merely nodded and walked on alone, but Marcia was joining him. "Kim, I just heard that you did the Barn. Why, it's marvelous!"

He shrugged to what she said and wondered how long she would linger. "Anyone could have done it—anyone with a brush and a can of paint."

She shook her head decisively. "No. Only you could have even thought of it in the first place. It has something—" She hesitated to say that it had something his paintings lacked. "Kim, if ever you show your work to Martin, don't fail to show him the Barn."

"Show him the Barn?" he repeated incredulously. If it had been another time, he should ask her what she found exciting about the Barn, but tonight was not for that. "Staying around long?" he asked casually.

"No," she said quickly, fearing that he wanted to talk. "In fact, I should be hurrying, for I'm expecting a phone call at the Murdocks'." She backed away. "Walking down the Heights?"

"No, I'm waiting—for Iris."

"Well, I'll go on then. . . ."

He nodded eagerly. "Yes, you go right ahead. It may be hours before Iris comes out. You know how she pokes around in the Barn."

As she walked around the Heart, she corrected herself: she wasn't expecting a call—she was hoping for one, as she had been ever since he had brought her *Noa Noa*.

She walked fast, although she was very tired. There was a queer pounding energy within her that seemed to force her to keep moving rapidly. Later, when it was clear that he wasn't going to call or come, the energy would desert her, leaving only the tiredness, and she would go to bed, exhausted but unable to sleep.

Kim paced moodily, not liking himself. He seldom told downright lies. When he heard the Barn door open, he knew it was Iris, and because he knew too that he would tell another lie, he felt angry with her.

He turned and saw that she had stopped, taking it for granted that he was waiting there for her. She leaned wearily against the building, closed her eyes, and held out her hand like a sleepwalker. "Cigarette."

He gave her one and lighted it, looking critically at her face in the match flare. "You're working too hard on that damn closet piece—which ought to be kept in a closet."

She opened her eyes. "I thought we agreed that it had possibilities."

159

He snorted. "I hadn't counted on Whitney."

She grinned sleepily. "He'll be all right—if we can keep him from acting."

"Leeds is all right," he said casually.

She yawned. "Uh-huh."

"She's great, and you know it!"

"I cast her, didn't I?" She moved to the walk. "Coming to Herby's for something to eat?"

He was prepared for this and said glibly, "I'd like to, but I promised to wait for Marcia."

"Oh." She turned to stare at the dark Summit. "She in her office?"

He shrugged. "Guess so."

"Oh." She flipped away her cigarette. "Well, have a good long talk with Marcia."

He watched her walk away, half angry that she had believed him, or pretended to believe him, so easily. When she was out of sight, he turned back to the Barn, which now seemed very quiet. He knew that she was alone in it, waiting for him. She.

And as always when he was about to see her, he had a moment of panic from the fear that she would be somehow wrong, an inaccurate copy of the image in his mind.

She was still sitting on the table, reading. He didn't particularly like her choice of meeting place. The stage, after all.

She didn't look up, although she must have heard him. He walked down the middle aisle with slow, deliberate steps, his eyes taking her in greedily. He even wished that he might sit down to watch her and that there would be nothing more to their meeting than that.

He went up on the stage and sat down in Mr. Milton's chair. "What are you reading?"

"William Blake." She looked up then and smiled. Her eyes grew dark and soft, and her legs swung gently against the table.

She's glad to see me, he thought; but a part of his mind protested the truth. He knew damn well what that rare smile of hers meant: *You came as I intended. You could not stay away.* "Blake's Marcia's man," he said to shatter his own thoughts.

"Marcia's? Oh, Dr. Anderson." Her face hardened and her legs stopped swinging. "So he belongs to her." With a violent motion she sent the book spinning across the stage. "Well, she can have him. He's crazy, anyway."

Kim stared. "Now, wait a minute! I merely meant—"

"That's just the way she acted! I, the great Anderson, can understand the great Blake, but nobody else can."

He crossed the stage and picked up the book, because he didn't know what else to do. To his surprise, when he put it down on the table beside her, she reached out and covered his hand with hers. He stared down at the hand. It was long and thin, made longer still by the pointed deep-red nails. Her dress was tight across her breast. His eyes went to her face. The eyes were dark again, the moist lips slightly parted.

Mockingly he thought of Art and Freedom, of her as he held her in his mind.

She leaned toward him, the slow movement stirring the scent of her perfume. The copper hair was fire-gold against his dark suit.

Roughly he pulled her off the table. There was no resistance in her body as it molded into his, and even as he tried to lose himself in the soft, eternal yielding, he thought of a sucking whirlpool of endless depth. He made his lips as savage as hers, but as the sharp nails dug into his neck, there leaped into his mind the image of cruel talons reaching out of the whirlpool. . . .

He jerked himself free.

She opened her eyes, laughed, then raised her hand and struck him across the mouth.

He did not feel the slap. "Call me Kim!" he said harshly and seized her wrist. "Call me by my name, Carol!"

She tried to wrench free, but he held her with the strength of fury. Then she sneered. "Must we play nursery games?"

He shouted: "Call me by my name, I said."

"Oh, for God's sake." After a moment, she said tonelessly, "Kimball Duncan." He let go her wrist, and she sauntered across the stage, chanting in the flat voice she had used to read Dean Haskins' lines: "Kimball Duncan, Duncan Kimball, Kimball Duncan, Duncan . . ."

"Damn you." He strode off the stage through the wing, through Iris' office, and out the back door.

He went down by the river to brood, but the very passivity of the old familiar rock angered him. He tramped through the mud along the river; then he tramped through the town, avoiding the Square and Herby's, avoiding the lighted houses and people. He went outside Riverville's limits and took a cinder road, following the wire fence that bordered the Murdock orchards.

Suddenly there was a hoarse shout through the night. "Say, you! Have you seen Stephanie?"

He stood still and stared around him, at last spotting a shadowy figure on the other side of the fence. "What's that?" he shouted back impatiently.

"Stephanie Kail. She's lost. Have you found her?"

"Good Lord, no!" He strode on, not caring who Stephanie was or who the man was or why he should have been so careless as to lose her.

When he was out of breath, he slowed down. Some of the fury was spent. He took out his handkerchief and mopped up the sweat on his face and hands. Then he turned back toward town.

Calmly now he began to think of Carol, who was perhaps still in the Barn waiting for him to return. He had acted the fool. The slap now stung across his face, and he touched the place with bitter satisfaction. He had deserved it.

Carol was growing clear in his mind, not as she had been in the Barn, but as he often saw her walking in the Heart, the sun in her hair, someone else at her side, he out of sight watching . . . he, the perceptive eye that gave her being.

It was the old cycle commencing again, he knew; but mere awareness could not halt it. He hurried.

Yet he was not sorry when he found her gone. She had left on the stage lights, and one part of his mind thought that inconsiderate of her. Charlie would blame Iris if he found the lights on.

Exhausted, he slumped down in Mr. Milton's chair. Soon he put his head down on the table, with his arms as a pillow, and went to sleep.

Dimly he heard his name, and for a moment he thought she had come back. He got to his feet and cried out in fear and eagerness, "Carol!"

"It's Marcia."

He should have known. The voice was low and urgent, very different from Carol's. Marcia emerged out of the dark auditorium, close to the stage. He stared down at her. "What are you doing here?"

"Looking for Stephanie Kail. Have you seen her?"

He groaned and pressed his hands to his head. "Who in blazes is Stephanie? Why is she lost? Why is all Riverville out looking for her?"

"You know Stephanie," Marcia said impatiently. "The Murdocks' niece. She runs away. She hid here once, but"—she turned slowly to look around her—"I guess she didn't come here this time." She glanced back at him and smiled wearily. "Are you still waiting?"

He said nothing, and she told him that he ought to put off doing whatever he was doing until morning. Then she went back up the aisle. Her footsteps sounded very tired.

When the door closed behind her, he mechanically went through the process of switching off lights and locking up.

Back at the Murdocks', Marcia sat in her room listening to the stillness of the empty house. She thought of Mrs. Murdock making the usual round of hope, the worry biting deep within her. The drugstore? No Stephanie. Herby's? No, of course not. Stephanie wasn't the kind to linger there with a group, putting nickels in the jukebox.

She thought of Mr. Murdock, tramping through the dark wet orchard. They had found her there once before, in the dead of night.

She thought she could hear the soft thud-thud of their questing feet, and she knew of no lonelier sound.

"Why do you suppose she does it?" Mrs. Murdock had asked Marcia that evening, subduing her despair to polite bewilderment.

Why?

And Stephanie, the loneliest of them all, some place. . . .

She could stand the silence no longer. She flung open her door and went across the hall to Stephanie's room, which was, as always, in prim order, kept that way through vigilance by Mrs. Murdock.

She sat down at Stephanie's desk, so like the one in her own room. Its dainty pigeon-holes were crammed with papers, and she explored shamelessly. They were mostly old themes. Stephanie—even Stephanie —had not the heart to throw away the sweated literary labor of her freshman year.

At first she thought that the themes had uniformly earned a *C* grade. Then she found a *B* one and a *D* one. Curiously she opened the *B* one—"A Summer Picnic." Beneath the stilted phrases, she was sure that she detected Mrs. Murdock's conception of the formal essay.

She began to scan the *D* theme, but when she understood that in it Stephanie had been trying to express her feeling about her uncle's orchards, she read carefully. One sentence especially attracted her: "When I feel the dirt in my hands, and even under my fingernails, I feel happy, and then I know peace."

The instructor had called this a stringy sentence. Marcia thought that it was something more. *When I feel the dirt in my hands . . . I feel happy, and then I know peace.*

Thoughtfully she replaced the themes. When she heard the downstairs door open, she went into the hall and for a moment stood listening to the low voices.

Mrs. Murdock's: "Stephanie, you're filthy!" The voice covered tears.

Mr. Murdock's: "What do you expect! Factory yards aren't the cleanest places in the world."

Mrs. Murdock's again: "Now be quiet, Stephanie. We don't want to disturb Dr. Anderson. She was out looking for you too. Take those dirty shoes off, and come into the kitchen. I'll fix some hot milk. . . ."

Nothing from Stephanie.

Marcia went into her room and closed her door softly.

Chapter Six

WHEN he was sure that the ceremony was over, Kim slipped into President Cameron's office. It was empty, he thought. The newly hung portrait of Grace MacMillan was on the wall opposite the desk. Standing, he regarded it intently for a minute, and then pulled a chair up to it. He sat down and leaned his head back, studying the portrait through half-closed eyes.

It was a very conventional job, he decided. Good technique; obvious conception. "Humph!" he said in contempt.

Still he lingered. The technique, he began to see, was more than good—it was superb. That definiteness of execution! What wouldn't *he* give for such brush control!

What a pity that such technical skill had to be linked to mediocrity. . . . It *was* mediocre, wasn't it? Yes, of course—and yet . . . He had been aware of a mounting tension within himself as he looked. Now, why was that . . . ?

Ah, he had it! The reds, the unexpected reds. On one of the long slender fingers (what flesh tint!) was an amethyst ring that glinted red as it caught the light. That wasn't quite right, was it? Never mind —it was right in effect! The hand was relaxed on the passive mahogany arm of the chair, but that sparkle of red hinted at secret concern, smothered worry. . . .

Excited now, he looked eagerly for other touches of the surprising red, and found them in the depths of the folds of the mauve gown, in the almost hidden rug at the feet, and the deep velvet of the top of the high-backed chair that framed the smartly coiffured hair.

There was tension too in the line, he saw finally. The tilt of the head wasn't just what one expected from the relaxed pose of the body. It suggested strain, as did the uneven palette-knife strokes of the background. . . .

He stood up and stretched. Probably he was reading far too much into it. No one with such damnably perfect technique could have the depth to imply that much meaning.

He wondered what Marcia thought of it. He'd go find her and talk it over. . . . *But,* he warned himself, be careful of what you say, you blockhead! This is her father, remember. . . .

"You seem to be taking a very serious interest in this portrait, young man."

Kim started. The man had approached him noiselessly. He flourished a cigar, and Kim was afraid that he was about to stroke his moustache. Otherwise, he looked like all the other men Kim had seen on campus that day, each one some student's parent, each a business or professional man, varying only slightly in success. He put this one down as a business man in the upper brackets of success.

"Are you enjoying John Willard Day?" he asked politely.

"I'm not sure yet. I've been here only a very short time, you see. Now, this portrait"—he waved the cigar toward it—"how does it strike you?"

The man's assured air and his meticulous dress irritated Kim. "Oh," he said, shrugging, "good technique; mediocre conception."

"Quite a sweeping judgment, young man." The man moved to an ashtray. "However, quite professional also. Do you paint?"

"Yes, I dabble. You know how it is," Kim said carelessly, feeling quite sure that the man knew nothing of the kind. He carefully put the conversation on an impersonal basis again. "This"—he indicated the portrait—"was just hung today, you know."

"I do know," said the man. He walked over to President Cameron's desk and picked up gloves and—Kim noted with some disgust—a cane. "I attended the hanging," he said, coming back to Kim. "In fact, I'm the executioner."

Kim thought the pun in very bad taste. "Really," he murmured. *"Really?"* he said a moment later in a very different voice.

"Really," the man echoed. The little moustache twitched with an amused yet friendly smile.

"Then you're Martin Anderson! Marcia's father!"

"Both," laughed Martin. "And from Marcia's description, I have a hunch that you're Kimball Duncan. Mr. Duncan." He held out his hand.

Kim shook it weakly. "You—I—you must think—"

"I think that you gave that portrait very serious attention," Martin said easily. "I was sitting—shall I say—mousy-like behind that desk —tell me, does anyone ever *use* that mammoth, glassy thing!—and I saw you study it with great intelligence." He put his gloves and cane back down on the desk. "I'd appreciate your telling me exactly what you felt as you looked at it. You see, I haven't quite made up my own mind. That's why I was in here, all alone. I wanted to see the thing when the room wasn't crowded with people. There's nothing that can turn a portrait into a still life more quickly than a live person standing next to it!"

"I think that it's admirably executed," Kim said hesitantly. "I think—" He stopped as Martin frowned impatiently. "Well, here it is. You won't like it, and it doesn't make sense, but the longer I looked at it, the uneasier I felt. Restless, even anxious. . . ."

"Good!" Martin stared at his own work. "Gad! I believe the thing's a success."

"But why?" cried Kim. "I mean, look at the subject! I've seen her —this very day, for instance—and she looks exactly as you've made her look—successful, wealthy, composed—"

"And very much in this world," Martin said gently. "Come here and look at this—shall I say—companion-piece." He took Kim's arm and led him to the portrait of Amos Willard. "You've seen it before, of course?"

Kim nodded. "Typical nineteenth-century American."

Martin smiled. "So you have no fondness for it?"

"It's so—so prosaic and *definite.*"

"Hmn. If you mean *definitely prosaic*, then that's sufficiently condemning." He reached to the desk for his cane. "However, I think that you mean something quite different. Look at that"—he pointed with the cane—"the richly brocaded dressing gown, the little velvet lounging cap with its silken tassel, the fine plush chair, the tapestry in the background. . . . Ah yes, one imagines Amos Willard, and not the artist, suggesting this array and this setting. . . ."

Again the cane pointed, and Martin's voice sharpened. "Now see the face. It shows tiredness, in spite of the assumed repose. And the hands—the one lax in the lap and the other limp on the arm of the chair. No doubt Amos Willard thought that they went with the dressing gown and the slippers and the little velvet cap, but the artist tells us that they are *tired* hands, those of a physically exhausted man."

Kim stirred. "I hadn't noticed. . . ."

"All right," said Martin briskly, "so the subject is tired. *But* he is happy, assured, self-confident. The head position, the mouth, the alert eyes tell you that. He has had a busy day, and he'll have another one tomorrow. He knows it, and his knowledge of that is the only true kind of repose in the picture. Everything else in this portrait tells of great busy-ness, great hurry-hurry. . . . Yes, my boy, it is as you said—typical nineteenth-century American, but not as you meant it. It is, in fact, nineteenth-century America in a nutshell—rather, in one portrait! And if an artist can portray all that with *definiteness*, does he not merit at least approval?"

Kim sank down into a chair, but Martin paid him no attention. He took a small glass from his vest pocket and re-examined Amos Willard through it. "Of course," he said finally, "the artist had to pay for all the hurry-hurry. There's a fine network of cracks here already, and they will soon spread. Probably Amos Willard did not allow the poor fellow much time. . . ." He tucked the glass back into his pocket and sighed, "Ah, well. . . . Now, my boy—where are you? Oh. Are you tired?"

Kim sighed. "I'm merely overwhelmed by the way you can read a book into every line. But you still haven't told me why you put tension into a portrait of Grace MacMillan."

"Let me say simply that it's easier to sit at the beginning of a fortune, as did Amos Willard, than at the end of it, as does Mrs. MacMillan."

Kim was puzzled. "But the fortune is still a—a fortune, isn't it?"

Martin shrugged. "As far as I know. But I didn't mean that. This is a very different time from that of Amos Willard. Is the characteristic sign of our time a hurrying for getting more? No! More likely, it's a struggle for what has been got. That's what I mean by those palette-knife strokes. Is Grace MacMillan an escapist? No, nothing of the sort. That's why the delineation is so—so blasted definite, as you would say. (However, I *never* smear and blur my work.) Is she intelligent? Sensitive? Yes, decidedly so. Hence, the tension." He drew on his gloves, looking pleased and satisfied.

Kim stood, feeling like a sleep-walker.

Martin drew a flat silver watch from his pocket. "Shortly I must dine with the MacMillans. However, there is time for me to look at your work, if you would be kind enough to show it to me." He replaced the watch and smiled genially at Kim. It was clear that the idea of dining with the MacMillans did not displease him.

The sudden descent into the personal jolted Kim out of his comfortable daze. He wanted to shout that he would never show his things to Martin Anderson. Then he imagined a scene between Martin Anderson and Marcia. (My dear, I *asked* the boy to show me his work, but he refused like—shall I say—an idiot.) "I don't like to trouble you," he murmured.

"Not at all, not at all!" Martin touched his arm. "Lead the way, my boy."

"It's up two flights," Kim told him. In his mind, he saw the pitiful pile of canvases, and for a horrible moment he thought he was going to cry. He cleared his throat roughly. "In my office."

"You keep them in your office?" Martin was incredulous.

"Of course," Kim said casually. He certainly wasn't going to explain how he had brought them from his room that morning, hoping that Martin Anderson would give them a few minutes. . . .

He led the way morosely.

"Why not do a portrait of your daughter?" J.W. asked suddenly.

Martin sipped his brandy and sighed appreciatively before he answered. "That's a fond plan of mine—for the future. Everything has a time."

What does he mean? Marcia wondered half angrily.

"You must pose in white," Grace said to her.

J.W. smiled. "I agree. In fact, the dress you now wear."

"Indeed," Martin said dryly. "Place a lily in her hand, and we'd have one of those Pre-Raphaelite messes. May I suggest—"

"Please suggest nothing," Marcia said with a nervous laugh. "I assure you that it's quite embarrassing to be discussed as pure *objet d'art*." But she was suddenly happy. Her dress had been justified. He liked it. What had that fluttery little Miss Doty said? *First the dress, and then*—

"I suppose," Martin was saying irritably, "that I should be worrying about the time. I always miss a train when . . ." He did not finish the sentence as he looked at his watch.

When Virginia isn't with him to watch the time for him, Marcia thought, her happy mood shattered.

"Please reconsider my invitation," Grace said eagerly. She liked Martin Anderson and she was well pleased with her portrait. "I promise to allow you to paint from dawn to sunset—and this is beautiful country."

Martin laughed softly. "My dear lady, never have I roamed through nature with kit and portable easel. Landscapes bore me. Seriously, I have work waiting for me at home."

Go home, then, to Virginia. I have plans of my own. Instinctively Màrcia averted her face, leaning toward Tamburlaine, who lay at her feet. Her thoughts were unguarded tonight; so, perhaps, was her face.

"Oh, there is no need for hurry," J.W. said calmly. "Marcia and I shall drive you to the station when we leave for the play."

You see? I have plans of my own. "I'm sorry," Marcia said to her father, "that you're not staying. (*That is easy to say, now that your going has become unimportant to me.*) I had wanted you to see Kim's work."

"But I did see it, my dear." He smiled reminiscently and lighted a cigar.

"What did you tell him?" she demanded, thinking that he looked unusually pleased with himself. Life is too easy for him, she thought; and that is not fair when for me it is . . . "I hope that you were at least tactful."

"Oh, I was—I was. I told him merely that he lacked a bounding line. That's very evident in his work, and I suspect that it also applies to his life." He gestured briefly with his hand, the movement dispersing the thin blue stream of cigar smoke. He enjoyed his attentive audience. "How do we discern a tree from a stone? By their respective boundary lines! One tree from another? Even more particularly, by their boundary lines. And man too must have his boundary lines. Ah, yes, 'the great and golden rule of art, as well as of life, is the sharp and wiry bounding line.' "

"How interesting," said Grace slowly, "and true also!"

"Are you quoting?" Marcia asked suspiciously.

Martin stared at her, genuinely surprised. "Don't you *know*, my dear?"

"Why should I?"

"Indeed I *am* quoting—and from *Blake!*" He chuckled and looked at Grace and J.W. "Blake is Marcia's boy, you know."

"Really?" J.W. said with polite interest. "*William* Blake, of course? He has some charming things."

Charming! The adjective shuddered in Marcia's mind. Blake was about as charming as the war.

But she forgot her irritation in watching Martin curiously. How did he know Blake? She hadn't been sure that he even knew she was working upon him.

That passage he had quoted. Where in heaven's name was it? Why hadn't she ever noticed it—

Guiltily she brought her attention back to what was being said. She should be worrying about Kim. He must be suffering over what Martin had told him.

". . . explains why your Kim smears rather than paints," Martin was saying. "He makes everything misty. Even his palette is muddy. No clear-cut line, no clear-cut color, no—"

. "Perhaps," Grace said suddenly, "the young man believes that there are some things that cannot be seen so definitely—as either black or white, I mean. Perhaps there is an intermediate—"

"Ah!" cried Martin, holding up his hand. "You're about to tell me that the intermediate something is that beautifully ambiguous color of gray. I refute that. The merging of black and white can result in nothing other than—shall I say—muddiness." He flicked ashes with an air of triumph. "By the way, Marcia, I saw that poor excuse for an office that you have. Really, you should speak to the authorities about it!"

Grace wanted Marcia to see the roses. There were hundreds of them. They started by the water-lily pond and, in the shadowy twilight, seemed to stretch to the horizon.

"I have never seen so many before," said Marcia, stooping to touch a pale yellow one. "It's almost too much to take in."

"I feel as you do," Grace said. "I like to know flowers individually." She laughed tolerantly. "The number is Jack's idea, not mine."

She led the way to a small marble bench, and for long minutes they sat without words, although Marcia felt that Grace had something to say to her. It is a strange evening, she thought, in which every word uttered, every gesture, and even the silences are important.

Grace spoke then, but merely to say: "I wish we had cigarettes. We should have brought the men, if only to carry things."

"But they wanted to look at some picture or other, didn't they? I'm glad to be out here. Frankly, I'm tired of Art."

"The painting is of Eileen," Grace said with quiet significance.

"Eileen?"

"Yes. Jack's wife, dead eighteen years."

Marcia said nothing, but her hand tightened over the cool marble.

"She belongs to the past," Grace went on softly. "I hope that you'll help Jack to remember that. In fact,"—she laughed—"I brought you out here purposely to tell you just that!"

Yes, yes, Marcia thought excitedly; that is what I must do—what I have been wanting. Do away with Eileen and get even—

Then she was confused. How could she have those thoughts when she had not known about Eileen until this minute?

And she was strangely tired, as if she had been working and scheming over long years. "He doesn't want me," she said; then added hastily when she realized that she had spoken aloud: "He doesn't seem to need *anyone*. He is so self-assured, so—"

"Oh," Grace said easily, "you mean that armor he wears? It's all in one piece, you know, and if you're lucky enough to pierce it in just the right place, it will fall off"—she snapped her fingers—"like that."

"Have you ever made it fall off?" Marcia asked.

Grace laughed apologetically. "To be honest—no."

When they came back to the house, J.W. moved quickly to Grace, deep concern on his face. "Mr. Anderson estimates that Eileen's portrait won't hold up for more than seventy-five years!"

"That's quite long enough, Jack!" Grace said firmly. "I doubt if you'll hold up that long yourself."

"Mother, don't be facetious! It must go to Russ, and then to *his* children—"

"Now, now!" Martin came forward, looking faintly apologetic and tucking away his little glass. "As I told you, Mr. MacMillan, I could make only a very rough estimate. I do not have the proper equipment with me to allow thoroughness. Besides, you should never have asked me to examine that particular painting critically."

"Why not?" Grace asked curiously.

"My dear lady, it has ceased to be merely a portrait executed by a certain artist within a certain time and place. It has become, instead, a beloved object. You are not critical of the dimness or of the camera angle of an old family photograph, are you? Well, it is the same with this portrait."

"But how did you know that about this portrait?" J.W. asked slowly.

Martin shrugged. "By no supernatural means, I assure you. But look"—he gestured toward the portrait, and all but Marcia obediently looked—"is it hung to its best advantage? No. Rather, it is hung where it can be easily and frequently seen. Have you carefully furnished the room to correspond to the color scheme of the picture? No, of course not. To do so would have seemed artificial to you, a betrayal of an old friend. . . ."

Marcia moved apart from the others. J.W. had not noticed her since she and Grace had returned. She looked up at the portrait and observed mechanically that Eileen had an appealing prettiness.

I dislike her, she thought then. The intensity of her feeling shocked her, as had her thoughts in the garden. But she could not help herself. *If she were a living presence in this room, I should hate her.*

She turned sharply away from the portrait toward Martin, who was still speaking of it to J.W. and Grace . . . stirring the embers of memory and re-creating for them the living presence.

"Stop it!" she said harshly.

He paused, hand in midair in an unfinished gesture, and looked at her quizzically. She was aware that J.W. and Grace had glanced at her in surprise. "I mean," she said with effort, "that you must conclude that lecture if you really intend to make your train."

"Oh—thank you, my dear." Martin smiled tolerantly, accepting her change of mood easily, as always he had.

She dared then to face J.W. He was regarding her with a faintly puzzled expression. She knew that he felt something that he could not understand, and he did not like what he could not understand. When she smiled, he returned the smile immediately, relieved. He would not be accepting of her moods. She would have to remember that.

In the Barn lobby, she and J.W. stood out of the thick of the crowd and lighted cigarettes. His aloof silence forced her to talk. "I saw the script and it seemed such an ineffectual thing. But the production was moving, didn't you think?"

He smiled indulgently. "Oh, yes—quite."

I'm bored, she thought. I wish I were backstage with Kim and Iris. She said defiantly, "Iris deserves all the credit. I've never taken her seriously enough. She's a genius!"

"Miss Taylor? Perhaps so," he said mildly, "but of course she had superb material to work with. The one who was Mary Milton, for example—Miss—who was that?"

"Carol Leeds. But she couldn't have done it alone. You have no idea how wooden those speeches were. I saw—"

"—the script," he finished with her, laughing. "I admit that your Iris is very good. I mean merely—"

"Good!" she flashed at him. "Do you realize that her allowing David Whitney—he was John Milton—to be a natural comedian saved the play! Do you realize—"

Mrs. Cameron had come up to them and lightly touched their hands. "My dear Miss . . . and Mr. MacMillan, why are you hiding back here? Isn't it remarkable? I never dreamed that Elizabeth Haskins had it in her! You know?"

"We were just talking," J.W. said with a faint smile, "about the *magic* of Miss Taylor's production."

"Magic?" Mrs. Cameron pondered this and brightened. "Oh, I know what you mean. The way that table and chair began to seem like a whole roomful of furniture. And that weird music for the Cromwell scene! What *was* it—I couldn't place it at all?"

"Prokofieff," Marcia said readily.

J.W. was gentle. "You mean Shostakovitch, I believe."

"Oh, didn't I say that?" Marcia said coolly, although she was furious with herself for her mistake. "I merely—" She turned as someone grasped her arm.

It was Hughes, and he asked abruptly, "Have you seen Kim Duncan?"

"No," she told him. "He's probably backstage with Iris."

Hughes shook his head. "He hasn't been there this evening. Iris sent me to look for him." He gave J.W. a brief nod and walked away.

171

Marcia watched after him, again vaguely worried over Kim.

"I asked you," J.W. was saying to her with a trace of annoyance, "if you wouldn't care to leave now. It's disagreeably hot."

Outside near the door Dean Haskins stood receiving a steady stream of congratulations. Her handclasps were firm and rhythmically spaced, yet there were worry creases in her usually smooth brow.

Marcia and J.W. did not join the line but went to her side, and Marcia whispered, "It was wonderful! I knew that we could count on Iris."

Dean Haskins abruptly dropped the hand she had been shaking, and turned to Marcia an honestly perplexed face. "But I didn't intend anyone to *laugh* at John Milton!"

J.W. offered his hand. "Congratulations, Dean Haskins."

She started and stared at him as if she were already seeing the avenging ghost of Mr. Milton.

As they walked to his car, J.W. asked if she would care to drive to the Inn. He asked this casually, as if already indifferent to her answer.

I'm bored, she thought again, and infinitely weary. Even as she thought this, there flashed into her mind the imagined scene of her leaving him at the Murdocks' and his driving on alone to return to the house that was complete and self-contained without her. "Yes," she said, matching his casualness, "I believe I should like that."

Before they had found a table, a large man with a pale face and tired eyes but blustering manner bore down upon them. He clapped his hand down on J.W.'s shoulder. "Old J.W. himself! You're going to join us—and no argument!"

J.W. moved from under the hand and then shook it briefly. "Thank you, Matt, but I'm not alone. Miss Anderson—Mr. Grant."

Matt gave her a quick appreciative look and grinned. "I'm not complaining. Besides, I doubt if there's an empty table left—so what can you lose?"

J.W. smiled apologetically at Marcia. "We'll not stay long," he murmured as they followed Matt.

It was not until she saw Paul Lewis Grant awaiting them by a table that she realized they were joining him. Matt was so different from him that she had thought nothing about his name being Grant.

"This is Miss—I'm sorry—Anders, is it?" Matt said to his brother. "And I believe"—he laughed loudly—"that you already have some acquaintance with Mr. MacMillan."

"Good evening, Dr. Anderson," Grant said. "Hello, MacMillan."

"*Doctor!*" Matt sat down heavily. "Good God. How do you get to be a patient?"

Grant laughed. "Not that kind, Matt. Dr. Anderson and I are colleagues."

"Oh. Your kind." Matt was visibly less impressed. He gave Marcia a curious stare. "Well, well. My brother knows the best-looking women in Riverville, but he's awfully quiet about them. I have to find them for myself—from Millie on up."

Millie? Marcia wondered, not looking at Grant. "Why," she said to Matt, "you must be Janice's father."

Matt winked. "Unless they've been stringing me along all these years." He shouted for a waiter. "Refills for Paul and me. Now, what are you drinking?" he asked Marcia, then leaned across the table and whispered hoarsely, "How about a nice little old Between the Sheets?"

Before she could answer, J.W. had raised his eyebrows and asked her if she would consider a Manhattan. She merely nodded, annoyed at his stiffness.

"Kim Duncan is lost," she said to Grant. "I think we should—"

J.W. laughed. "But aren't you exaggerating? Adults don't lose themselves so easily."

"You don't understand," she said coldly. "Kim and Iris always work on productions together, and the fact that he didn't go backstage tonight at all is very—" Music blared forth suddenly, and she did not finish what she was saying. I'll give him one more chance, she thought; if he asks me to dance, I'll— "The orchestra is rather horrible, isn't it?"

He agreed conclusively.

She shrugged mentally, and said to Matt: "Your daughter is a fine writer. She won the Literary Competition, you know."

Matt looked embarrassed. "Yep. I got that magazine rolled up in my pocket right now."

"And, Matt, Dr. Anderson knows whereof she speaks," Grant said, laughing. "She coerced the committee."

She smiled reminiscently. "But I still don't understand why you allowed the *Gazette* to run that absurd story. It put me in a ridiculous light. Scott and Colley—" She remembered that J.W. could not follow what was being said, and explained to him: "You see, the *Gazette* insisted upon having a representative present because—" She was stopped by the discovery that the *because* led directly to him. "The Competition award is a very important distinction," she said lamely.

Matt was bored and showed it. He scraped back his chair. "Personally, I'm going to dance with my brother's colleague—if colleagues dance, and if she'll risk it."

She gave him a grateful smile and said she'd risk it. They went off together before J.W. and Grant could get to their feet.

With a queer, surprised feeling, Grant watched them reach the floor and Matt take her into his arms. When he saw that J.W. was surprised too, he felt better.

173

They smiled politely at each other. "That's a remarkable portrait of your mother," Grant said amiably.

J.W. looked modest. "Martin Anderson is a remarkable painter. A remarkable man, in fact. We were fortunate enough to have his company at dinner this evening."

"Yes!" Grant agreed heartily. "Yes, he is that." And he was suddenly full of good feeling, for now he understood the natural course of events that had led to her coming to the Inn with J.W. MacMillan. He hadn't known that he had been wondering about it, but he did know that he was vastly relieved to have the answer.

The music stopped, but Matt kept his arm around her. "There'll be an encore," he said close to her ear.

She pulled away from him and said loudly, "Your daughter is a remarkable writer."

He grinned and dropped his arms to his side. "O.K. I believe it now."

"That she's a writer?"

"No. That you're a teacher."

A waltz started and lights were lowered. But he held her far away from him. "All right, teacher?"

"All right," she said coldly, but her anger was for J.W., who sat placidly at the table.

Matt grew talkative. "But what's *in* writing? I mean, there's not much of a financial future in it for her, is there?"

With effort she brought her thoughts back. "Perhaps someone said that to Shakespeare."

"Shakespeare! So she's that good, eh?" He looked pleased, but he was still doubting. "Even so, I never heard that Shakespeare got much more out of it than fame after he was dead and buried."

"He was able to build a very fine house."

"He was, eh? Didn't know about that. Maybe I'm wrong, but the writing game doesn't seem to get you any place. Now, take my brother, for instance. . . ."

When they came back to the table, Matt said, "Know what I been thinking, J.W.? Why not buy up this place? It's a lousy joint now, but you could make something big out of it."

Marcia laughed a little, thinking Matt was joking; but J.W. shook his head seriously. "Mitchell won't sell out—for some reason or other."

"Hurrah for Mitchell!" Grant said, startling them. He smiled innocently. "What a pity, I mean. What a pity that Mitchell should deprive us of that magnificent neon sign—*Tractorland!*"

Matt gave his brother a black look, and J.W. laughed thinly. Marcia felt uneasy without knowing why, and told J.W. that she was ready to leave.

"Of course." He signaled to the waiter. "I'm taking care of this table," he said, putting some bills into the waiter's hand.

The waiter was incredulous. "Even including before you arrived?"

J.W. smiled. "Even including before—"

"Tractorland!" Matt jerked himself out of a deep study. "Paul, you've got something. What publicity! Why, I can see that sign"—he pointed excitedly and closed his eyes for clearer vision—"Willard Tractorland—drink horsepower liquor . . . dine on food from Willard plowed fields . . . dance. . . ."

In the close privacy of the car, J.W. was pleasantly aware of her nearness. He wondered if he had felt this way with Eileen. He could not remember.

For a fleeting moment he wished that he were not a man of large responsibilities, that she were not a highly civilized woman. If, for example, he were Gauguin. . . . He smiled inwardly at his nonsense.

It occurred to him then that she was very silent. At the Inn she had been talkative, but now as they drove back to Riverville, she seemed withdrawn in her own thoughts. She was a little like Russ in her change of mood and, as with Russ, he was annoyed. "What are you thinking?" he asked.

"Nothing," she said too quickly.

He laughed. "Let me guess. About the brothers Grant?"

"In a way," she admitted, and was silent again. She had been thinking about Janice Grant. Now that she had met her father, she was beginning to understand. Matt was in "The Boy." Grant had known, of course, and that was why he had been reluctant to select it.

Matt didn't care about Janice's writing . . . didn't care about Janice herself, really.

Poor Marcia . . . no, no, poor Janice; and she, understanding, would be kind to Janice, never withdraw from her, always—

"Fool!" J.W. muttered as he abruptly swerved the car to avoid hitting a man who had walked directly into the path of his headlights. The man seemed oblivious to his narrow escape.

"It's Kim!" Marcia cried, looking back.

"Kim—again?" J.W. slowed down. "Well, shall we stop?"

"There's no need to stop," she said, disliking the impatience in his voice. "What do you mean—Kim again?"

"My dear Marcia," he said tightly, "you have compelled everyone around you to worry about Mr. Duncan all evening."

She said nothing, but thought how often she felt critical of his words and attitude. At that moment she was very clear-minded, and considered with scorn her confused reactions to him. She was as sufficient unto herself as he to himself.

She'd see him during the two weeks more before vacation, if only to assure herself that he had no hold over her. Then she'd go home to work seriously on Blake—

"Russ comes home tomorrow," he said. "He has two weeks to spend with me before going into the Army."

She found all casual words suddenly elusive. She took a cigarette from her bag, but made no move to light it. "You must be very happy about that," she said. "Not about his going to war, of course, but about his coming home." Now the words rushed from her. "You'll want to spend every possible minute with him. I'm sure that—"

"Yes, I intend to." He drove in silence for a while. Then, startling her with the unneeded emphasis in his voice: "Russ and I are very close, you know."

I didn't say you weren't! she thought angrily. The cigarette was bent double in her hand. She let it fall to the floor and stared out the window into the darkness.

Perhaps she'd stay in Riverville during the summer. She could work on Blake there as well as at home. After Russ was gone, he—

"I wish," he said with a sigh, "that I could look forward to a restful summer."

"Can't you?" She groped for another cigarette, obsessed with the thought that if she kept her hands busy, he would not be able to see the effect of his words upon her.

"I have to divide my time between Washington and Chicago—Washington"—he laughed modestly—"for the Government, Chicago for my own business."

He glanced at her profile, and was well satisfied. As he had thought, he was secure without his having to be Gauguin, even without significant words. "Oh, you need a light for your cigarette. I should have noticed. . . ."

Martin Anderson, Kim told himself, was a little man who knew nothing about Art. He had told himself this a hundred times, and he was beginning to believe it.

When he saw the lights of the Inn ahead of him, he realized how far he had walked, and his feet began to drag. He'd stop at the bar for a drink and a rest.

He cut through the cinder parking yard, winding in and out among the empty parked cars. But near to the Inn was a coupé not empty, for through its back window he could see two heads. As he moved on, instinctively quiet, he heard the soft sounds of a skirmish within. He shrugged contemptuously over the eternal male and female tug-of-war and was about to pass by when he heard a sound that rooted him to the ground.

It wasn't the monosyllable *Don't!* that stopped him, but the voice

176

itself. It went racing through his blood and struck at his nerves. He stood tense, his eyes narrowed watchfully.

The car door opened, and Carol stood on the running board, but someone inside was holding her arm. She wrenched free and ran toward the Inn. Kim heard a soft "Damn!" and saw the man slip out after her. He overtook her at the building.

Carol faced him then with a flare of bravado. "Enough's enough, Mike," she said laughingly, adjusting the shoulder strap of her pale green gown.

But Mike wasn't playing. "So this is where I get off! Is that it?" He took her by her bare shoulders.

She twisted out of his grasp. Her voice was crisp and cool. "Stop it! I mean it, Mike. I'm not in the mood."

"Not in the mood!" Mike mimicked. "Why, you little bitch! You've turned it on and off long enough to suit yourself. Now you're going to suit *me!* Do you hear! Why, you little—"

Kim moved then. Even as he stalked his prey, he marveled at his carefulness. He walked cat-like, maneuvering until he could see Mike's face. When he knew exactly what he was going to do, he allowed his foot to scrape over the cinders.

"Watch out, Mike," he heard Carol whisper. "Someone's coming."

It seemed incongruous to him that Carol should be solicitous about Mike's safety, but he had to keep his mind busy with other matters. Mike had shifted position and was now standing directly in front of the Inn window. He shifted too, so that he faced the window. Then he said, "I am going to knock you to hell."

They stared at him. Carol said in a rasping whisper, "Get away from here, you fool!"

"Know the bastard?" Mike asked her, not taking his eyes off Kim.

Kim didn't wait for her answer. He was growing impatient. Drawing back his arm, he tightened his muscles and then swung mightily. It was a strong, sweeping thrust for Art, against Martin Anderson, and perhaps also against Kimball Duncan. It landed neatly on Mike's jaw.

Mike staggered but didn't fall. He righted himself and touched his jaw, finding the fresh spurt of blood from the corner of his mouth. "Jesus!" He worked his jaw, then said stiffly, "Didn't think you'd come through with it." He was almost admiring in his surprise. With an air of settling down to business, he began to rip off his coat.

Carol put a restraining hand on his arm. "Never mind, Mike. People are looking out the windows. Remember, I'm not supposed to be here. Mike, honey, you don't have to fight for me—*Mike!*"

He pushed her away and put his carefully folded coat down on the cinders. "This isn't for you, baby. That's off—remember? This is for my honor."

Kim waited almost gratefully. He could have walked away, he could have made ready to fight back or even to duck; but he did none

177

of those things. He put his hands in his pockets and stood there, half smiling.

Mike was elaborately ready. He faced Kim squarely and looked for his hands. "For Chrissakes, put out your hands!"

Kim shook his head. "Thank you, no," he said apologetically. Someone in the gathering crowd whispered shrilly, "One of those fanatics."

The joy died out of Mike's face. "What the—" Then he shrugged, raised his clenched fist, and struck a perfunctory blow upon Kim's jaw.

Kim didn't pitch forward into blackness as he had hoped he would, but he lost his balance and fell back, hitting his head against the unyielding wood of the Inn. He slid on down to the ground, thinking how clean was Mike's blow in contrast to the sly buffets he had been receiving from the mocking world.

He opened his eyes directly under the moon. He was lying on his back, but there wasn't room for him to stretch out his legs. He could feel motion, although he lay perfectly still.

In spite of pain, he turned his head and looked up into the face of Paul Lewis Grant. His mind worked in awkward jerks, but he finally concluded that his head must be resting on Grant's lap. He struggled to rise to a sitting position.

Grant gently thrust him back. "Take it easy, son, take it easy."

"What—happened?"

Grant grinned down at him. "You attracted some attention. Fisticuffs."

Kim groaned, remembering. "Where—" The one word exhausted him.

Grant understood. "We're in the rumble seat of my brother's car. You're on your way to the hospital."

"Carol—"

"She's in the front seat with my brother. Insisted on being taken to Dr. Day's. We'll see that she gets there after we've made you comfortable."

Kim groaned again. Nothing made sense. Why should Carol go to Dr. Day? Why should he be rushed to the hospital? Kimball Duncan, the conquering hero! "Hospital—no!"

"But yes," Grant said cheerfully. "There was an M.D. among the revelers, and he assured us that it was safe to move you. You need rest to recover from shock."

Shock! He closed his eyes. So he was being hurtled into the hospital to rest after a blow on his unimportant physical head, although day after day his spirit was shocked and never allowed rest.

Chapter Seven

MARCIA decided to take Delacroix's *Journal* to Kim in the hospital. She put the book out in readiness, then dressed carefully. But when she was finished, she saw that she had chosen the wrong dress. With desperate haste in her movements, she changed to a different one, smoothed her hair, and reached for a hat. Even before she had it on, the hat dissatisfied her, and so did her hair. She threw aside the hat, pulled the pins out of her hair, and combed and brushed it out, watching herself in the mirror with a half embarrassed, half guilty expression.

At last she was more nearly satisfied. She picked up the Delacroix and stood for a final moment before the mirror, thinking: Why can't he see me now?

There was, of course, no chance that he would miraculously appear before her on her way to the hospital. He was snugly at home with his son.

Never mind. I will have him in the end. The thought had been involuntary, and it shocked her, as did her own image. Her face had hardened with a shrewdness she had not known she possessed. She stood still until she had forced her facial muscles to relax.

Then she hurried downstairs and all the way to the Square, where she waited impatiently for the bus. There was no need to hurry and she was exhausted from rushing, but she had to pacify that destructively high tempo within her.

Janice Grant was in the hospital waiting room, reading a magazine. "You can't go up yet," she said to Marcia. "Uncle Paul's with Mr. Duncan now." She put aside the magazine. "I went up to your office Monday and Tuesday, but you weren't there." Her voice was accusing.

Marcia felt her high-pitched nerves quiver, but she reminded herself that she felt a deep sympathy for the girl. "This *is* the end of the term, you know," she said, smiling. "I have had many papers to grade."

"Well, don't you grade them in your office?"

Marcia ignored this. "What did you want to see me about, Janice?"

"It was just—" Janice seemed suddenly shy. Nervously she twisted the ends of her hair. "I wanted—are you going to come to Oaklands this summer?"

"I certainly appreciate your inviting me, Janice, but I have other plans—as I told you."

Janice sat forward. "But you *promised* to come!"

"Oh, but I didn't, Janice. Don't you remember? We left it that I was to think it over."

"You as good as promised."

"I'm sure that I did not," Marcia said firmly.

For a moment Janice looked angry and hurt; then she shrugged resignedly. "Well, at least I tried my best. Uncle Paul ought to do his own inviting."

"What on earth do you mean?"

Janice smiled, seeming pleased over Marcia's surprise. "He'll be there in August, and he especially wanted you there then. He said you could write together and—" She stood suddenly and whispered, "He's coming! Don't say anything about this. It'll embarrass him. You know how he is!"

No, I don't know how he is! Marcia thought, turning to watch him walk toward them. Was it a habit of his to invite, by proxy, members of the English Department to spend the summer with him?

"He's better today," he told them cheerfully. "The shock is wearing off." He pulled his pipe out of his pocket and fondled it, looking from Marcia to Janice. "What are you two talking about?"

"End of the term," Janice said easily. "Finals and stuff. Dr. Anderson has been giving me points on cramming."

Grant laughed and looked back at Marcia. "End of the term is an ordeal for a teacher too. You look tired."

I do not, she thought angrily; I look beautiful. He held a light to her cigarette and no doubt noticed her unsteady hands. She stepped away from him and glanced around for an ashtray. Silently he pointed to a large sign on the wall: NO SMOKING. She said defiantly, "Well, I didn't see it."

He regarded her quizzically. You needn't stand there looking like a wise old owl, she thought. Aloud she said, "I want to be rid of this. I should go up to see Kim now."

He laughed and held out his hand. "I'll take care of it for you."

She thought it would serve him right if she boldly mentioned his invitation. But as he took the cigarette from her, their fingers touched, and for that moment her hand felt at rest. She looked into his clear brown eyes and was calmed. "I'm sorry I didn't see the sign," she said quietly, and walked across the lobby to the elevators.

In the outside lobby, Grant found a sand urn and, somewhat reluctantly, stuck Marcia's cigarette into it. Then he put his hand into his pocket, as if to protect the lingering touch of her fingers from Janice's too interested scrutiny. He was wondering if anything besides the end of the term had made her nervous.

"Let's take a long walk in the country," Janice said eagerly. "I wore my walking shoes."

"Well, I didn't. Besides, I have grades to—"

"Oh, you and your work!" But the next moment her face had changed and she bit her under lip as if to keep it from trembling.

"I'm lonely. It isn't fair of you always to leave me alone."

He reflected that in her own queer way, she probably was lonely. "All right," he said, "it's a walk, then."

She took his arm and as they went out under the hot sun said almost gaily, "Do you want to know what Dr. Anderson and I were *really* talking about? Why, she invited me to go home with her during the summer, but I had to tell her I had other plans. . . ."

Marcia was startled by Kim's appearance, although she did not know exactly why. He did not look especially ill.

"Hello," she said again, for he had not turned his head to see her.

"Hello," he said dully.

She sat down in a straight chair near his bed. He seemed incredibly long and flat under the white covers. His arms were outside the covers, close to his sides, and there was a lifeless quiet about them that suggested they had been placed there by someone else.

It was his apathy, she decided, that worried her. It was so unlike him. "I brought you something." She held up the big book, and he turned then to regard it with indifference. "It's Delacroix's *Journal*."

He winced and closed his eyes.

"What's the matter!" she cried, alarmed. "Do you have a pain?"

He said, with his eyes still closed, "Not the kind you mean." He opened his eyes and stared at the ceiling. "If I can't paint, I don't want to read about those who could."

She knew then that he was brooding over his talk with Martin. "I'm sorry, Kim. Don't—"

"Swell of you to lug that tome here, anyway." For the first time he was looking directly at her. "I like your hair. I told you—" He smiled crookedly. "I haven't any bounding line."

"*Don't* take Martin seriously!" she said impatiently.

"So he told you," he said quickly. "The hell of it is—maybe he's right."

She stood up and laid the book down on the table by his bed. "I know how you feel about Delacroix, but I'm going to leave it. You may want it later. It might even help bring back your—your interest." She looked down upon his unhappy face. "You go to sleep, Kim."

"Soon. That's all I want to do now." He looked away from her and said casually, "I suppose they're making a fuss about Carol Leeds. What are they going to do about her?"

"There's a meeting tomorrow morning," she told him reluctantly. "Student Personnel Committee."

"A *committee*! Oh, my God." He turned his face away from her. "What has a committee to do with Carol Leeds!"

"Well, what are we going to do about Carol Leeds?" Colley asked, rubbing his hands together. But his bluffness struck a wrong note. The others moved uneasily. Only Dr. Day was unperturbed. She sat behind her desk with a patient and waiting air.

Dean Haskins frowned. "It is very difficult to know how to judge her actions."

"Judge!" exploded Clifford Hughes. "Who said anything about judging!"

"I didn't," Dean Holcomb said hastily. He became grave. "However, there are matters of the most serious importance to be considered. For example, the effect of all this upon the reputation of John Willard College."

"As I see it," Grant said, "the essential problem is whether or not Miss Leeds be granted her degree. Normally, she would graduate tomorrow. Right?"

"That's right," said Colley with an impatient nod.

"Facts!" said Dean Holcomb. "That's what we need."

"Well, sir," Colley said with relish, "I can give them to you." He reached into his briefcase for a manila folder, which he opened and held up to show its contents. "This is her record. From an academic standpoint, it is very good, as you all know. . . ." He proceeded to report her grade averages over the past four years.

Holcomb cut in sharply. "Actually, Colley, there's nothing in the academic record that's pertinent to the case at hand, is there?"

Colley hesitated and then reluctantly agreed.

"Perhaps it should be mentioned," Marcia said, looking directly at Dean Haskins, "that she has a remarkable acting talent."

Dean Haskins blushed faintly, but she said, "I fear that neither talent nor intelligence has anything to do with this situation, Dr. Anderson. It is a question of will power!"

"But as a college," Grant said suddenly, "we should be concerned about Miss Leeds' future as well as the present moment. If we deliberately bar her from a degree, we're influencing her future far more than we can have any knowledge of today."

"You cannot possibly exaggerate the importance of Professor Grant's remark," Dr. Day said calmly. It was the first time she had spoken, and they turned to regard her with mild surprise. "You would be influencing Carol Leeds' future in a far more serious way than merely vocationally."

"Now, listen!" Colley sat forward. "I'm only the chairman of this little old committee, but if no one objects, I'd like to have my humble say. This is what I think." He stopped short, as if suddenly not sure of what he did think. Then he went on, more slowly, "I'm a tolerant man, but I know right from wrong. Now, what do we have? Well, in the first place, we have Carol Leeds, a John Willard coed, found on the premises of the Inn. That in itself is a transgression of a college rule. Furthermore, she was with a man and practically naked—"

"Fully clothed," Grant corrected. "That is, she wore an evening gown. Of course, such dresses are not meant to be particularly covering. For instance, on that same night and at the same place, Miss Anderson wore—" He stopped suddenly and looked confused when Marcia flashed him a look.

Colley pursed his lips. "Of course, there's no rule forbidding faculty to go there, but it seems to me . . . well, the Inn's not a very savory place. . . ."

Grant grinned suddenly. "Perhaps I should explain that Miss Anderson, my brother, and I were at the same table. In fact, we were all the guests of Mr. MacMillan."

Marcia couldn't help smiling. Holcomb said hastily, "Oh, as I said from the start, Grant, we consider ourselves very fortunate to have had you there so that you could make your first-hand report to our committee."

Colley became reproving. "This has been a most unworthy digression. *Tempus fugit.* Personally, I think Carol Leeds is a common little street-walker—I beg your pardons"—he nodded at Dean Haskins and Marcia—"but we should no longer mince words—"

"Ladies have been talking about these things for some years now," Hughes told him. "As long as we're being personal, I should like to know what has put you on the other side of the fence, Professor Colley. I thought you were always the *student*-sympathizer."

Colley pointed dramatically. "I am, Cliff, I am! That's just it—and right now I'm sympathizing with all the other John Willard students who have Carol Leeds as an example! What effect do you think her actions will have upon them—and now I'm talking about the normal college student!" He looked defiantly at Hughes, then Marcia, and finally Grant, who he sensed were silently opposing him. "Good old Joe College and Betty Coed, I mean—the average, healthy, happy American girl and boy as you and I know them!"

"Why do—Joe College and Betty Coed have to know about this?" Hughes asked. "I thought we were the only ones that were in on it—besides Duncan, of course."

Colley shook his head sadly. "You can't keep a thing like this down, son."

"*You* couldn't, I'm sure," Hughes muttered.

"I'm afraid that I agree with Mr. Colley," Dean Haskins said, looking pained to admit it. "About the effect upon the other students, I mean. It appears to me that we have no choice but to make Carol Leeds an object-lesson."

Dr. Day picked up the Chinese red cigarette box on her desk and handed it to Hughes. "Why don't you smoke, Mr. Hughes?"

He helped himself to a cigarette. "Thanks!" he said in a pleasantly surprised voice. "I've been wanting one."

Dr. Day set the box back down on the edge of the desk, leaving it open. "Help yourselves, please." She took one for herself and tapped it gently on the desk. "Professor Colley, haven't you created an abstraction—Joe College and Betty Coed, that is?"

"I certainly have not!" he said indignantly.

"That's true," she admitted. "Advertisements have done it for you, especially the June ones. Wristwatches and so forth, you know."

He tossed his head. "I don't know what you're talking about."

"I'm trying to talk about human beings—and you're not," she said a bit sharply. "I'm confident that you have never met this mythical creature, the normal college student, in the classroom. Bring me any student you select, and after five minutes alone with him, I'll convince even you that he is a seething mass of problems and eccentricities. However, he adjusts well enough so that this remains fairly hidden, and, conveniently but misleadingly, he becomes known as typical or average or normal."

Dean Holcomb looked troubled. "Is this really true, Dr. Day—about *any* college student? Really—"

"Yes, it is!" Marcia said suddenly, surprising both herself and them with her emphasis. She hadn't meant to speak, but her memory of Carol, of Janice, and even of Richard Tibbet flung the words out of her. "Students break down into individuals right before your eyes! They—I mean—" She floundered. "I mean that's what makes teaching so difficult."

Dr. Day gave her a kind smile and then turned to Holcomb. "To emphasize my point, perhaps I did exaggerate slightly"—she paused as Colley said "Humph!"—"but only slightly."

Dean Holcomb frowned, as if looking into a new world, the sight of which did not please him. "It doesn't paint a very rosy picture, does it?" His voice became almost pleading. "It doesn't speak too well for American youth, does it?"

"If it *is* an indictment," Dr. Day said slowly, "then it is one upon their backgrounds—"

"John Willard students come from excellent homes," Dean Haskins reminded her.

Dr. Day smiled. "I didn't mean any single home—or even homes in general. I was thinking of large cultural forces. But, of course, those need not concern us now."

"But they should!" Hughes cried. "That's exactly where my thinking has taken me. Even psychologically speaking, an individual doesn't live in a vacuum, and if we teachers don't realize that, then our work isn't worth a single damn!"

"Oh, I agree," Dr. Day assured him. "I meant merely that we today, in this meeting, cannot consider—"

"Now you're talking!" Colley folded his arms in front of him. "This has been most enlightening . . . fine shop-talk for Dr. Day. But, personally, I can't see where it's taking us."

"I'm coming to the point, Professor Colley," Dr. Day told him mildly. "But first we must realize that the point in a situation such as this cannot be reached readily. You have sought out the facts, and you have found them to be pitifully few and unrevealing. I too have facts to offer. Ordinarily I should not consider revealing confidential material, but I see now that without it you may make a tragic mistake. What you do *with* it is your responsibility."

She knows exactly what she's doing, Marcia thought suddenly: she purposely let us talk ourselves out, to show that we had absolutely nothing worth saying. . . .

"*Your* facts," Dr. Day went on, "have brought forth an excellent academic record and a dubious one of personal conduct. Does not that strange discrepancy arouse your curiosity?"

"We're your most willing listeners, Dr. Day," Holcomb said, as if from afar. He still looked perplexed.

"Carol Leeds," Dr. Day went on, "was born an illegitimate child. She was early adopted by honest, upright people with excellent intentions but little insight. When she was twelve or so, they deemed it time to tell her of the adoption. This they did, at the same time emphasizing the sinfulness of the mother and the desertion of the father. They did this, of course, to set an example before the child." Dr. Day smiled briefly. "An object-lesson, as you would say, Dean Haskins. In addition, these adoptive-parents are of a taciturn and undemonstrative nature. So there, as Professor Colley would say, we have Carol Leeds, who from the time of childhood has been weighed down with two emotional convictions—one that she was unwanted by both the real parents (the mother had given her up for adoption, and the father, as I said, deserted) and the adoptive-parents, who, although loving her, were by nature unable to make her feel affection. The second conviction was that she herself, as a consequence of her mother's 'sinfulness,' was in some way evil."

Dr. Day paused, and Dean Holcomb cleared his throat. "Is that *all?*" he asked, clearly surprised. "This is the *whole* story?"

"In other words, Dr. Day, can't you rake up a few murders and ancestral ghosts to please us?" Hughes said with heavy irony.

Dr. Day looked at Holcomb. "Yes, that's all as far as a certain kind of fact is concerned. Now we come to that part of the explanation which some of you, I fear, will not be so willing to admit as fact." She hesitated, then went on slowly but evenly. "Dean Haskins was more nearly right than she knew when she said that the matter had nothing to do with intelligence or talent. The emotional convictions of which I have spoken set Carol Leeds' whole pattern of conduct. We—all of us —live out our problems, you know. Ironically, our nature is such that we actually *seek* situations similar to those which begot our problems in the first place. Carol Leeds is no exception. She has consistently followed a pattern which reconciled her desire to strike out against a world that had proved itself hostile and her conflicting but very intense search for affection. Quite naturally (under the circumstances, you understand), she turned to men and the sexual experience. Over and over again she 'proved' to herself her own sinfulness, while at the same time, by her indifference to conventions and morals, she hit back at the world. Also, the experience itself became a substitute for the affection that she craved."

Colley came to life. "So! She's just what I said she was—a common street-walker. And we're right back where we started!" He pointed an accusing finger at Dr. Day. "I still say that Carol Leeds is a morally responsible individual, and that she deserves no more privileges than the average—well, as you're finicky about that term—than anyone else!"

"If I understand you correctly," Dr. Day said to him, "you feel that Carol Leeds should be made to *pay* for her actions, which in the eyes of society are, of course, wrong." When Colley nodded emphatically, she went on, and there was a slight edge to her voice. "Well, she has paid! Three years ago she had an abortion. It was badly bungled and not given the proper care. She can never have children."

"I daresay," said Dean Haskins tightly, "that she does not consider that a tragedy!"

"But she does," said Dr. Day calmly. "You will have to take my word for that."

"It seems to me," Colley said, "that we have to take your word for many things! You knew about—all these matters right along?"

"Yes," said Dr. Day.

"Three years ago!" Dean Haskins stiffened. "Why, she was already a John Willard student. Why didn't I, as Dean of Women, know about it?"

"I withheld that information for an excellent reason," Dr. Day said firmly. "Carol Leeds became my client, and the ethics of my profession, as well as my own personal ethics, would not permit me to betray her confidence. In fact, I chose to say as much as I have said only because I feel that she is at a turning-point. You can help lead her to self-respect, or you can convince her that she is as worthless as she fears she is. It must be understood what is said here will not in *any* way go beyond this room."

"Your trust in our discretion is not misplaced," Dean Haskins said indignantly. "But I am not satisfied. I still think that we should not ignore the matter of will. 'Where there's a will, there's a way.' Why could not Carol Leeds have *willed* herself to be guided by reason rather than those disturbing emotions?"

Dr. Day raised her hands in a gesture of helplessness. "What you don't seem to understand is that Carol Leeds has been *compelled* to act as she has. Not even the strongest advocate of free will would claim that it functions when there is no possibility of choice."

"Ah, yes," Colley said, "by like procedure you could come to excuse

Hitler. You know, frustrated when he was in the cradle and so on. . . ."
He chuckled and looked around expectantly, but no one laughed with
him. He sobered. "I wonder . . . perhaps we ought to investigate this
from the Duncan angle. After all, student-faculty relations are ticklish
affairs. We can't allow this sort of thing to go on in our halls!"

"Kim was defending Carol Leeds that night!" Marcia said hotly.
"Or so he thought—and he's suffering enough for it."

Dr. Day closed the red cigarette box with a little bang. She came
around to the front of her desk and faced them. Marcia saw that she
was at last angry. "Mr. Duncan is an extremely unimportant piece of
this pattern."

Colley shrugged. "All right. We have to take your word for it
again. But what are we going to *do?*"

Dean Holcomb arose, glancing at his watch. "I have a luncheon
meeting. . . ." Then he said with surprising firmness, "It appears to me
that under the circumstances we must allow Carol Leeds her degree."

"Yes," said Dean Haskins slowly, "that seems to be the wiser
course."

"I'm sure that I need not admonish you," said Dean Holcomb,
pausing at the door, "with the importance of regarding what has
transpired during this meeting as highly confidential. *Highly* confidential!"

"Dr. Day has already admonished us, William," Dean Haskins said
and swept by him.

"But what *has* transpired?" Colley asked.

Dean Holcomb did not stay to answer.

Colley looked limp. "I mean, aren't we going to *do* something?"

Grant smiled. "I should like to remind you that great consequences
sometimes arise from complete passivity. I need mention only St.
Francis, Jesus, and—more recently—Gandhi."

Marcia lingered after the others had gone. "We won," she said
rather shyly.

Dr. Day stood rubbing the sides of her neck and then the back, as
if soothing tense muscles. "So we did." She laughed softly and gestured
for Marcia to take a cigarette. "But I must admit that there for a
while I wasn't too certain of victory."

She sat down in her desk chair, and leaning back against it, relaxed.
Marcia watched her with something like awe. Fleetingly she remembered her as she had known her before, at the September tea and at
other meetings—a small, inconspicuous woman, quiet, if not shy, before other people. "You were marvelous," she said, thinking of her as
she had been today.

"Thanks," Dr. Day smiled. "Glad you caught the act—as they say."
Then she was serious. "But it was important, you know."

"Oh, I know," Marcia said quickly. "It's terrifying. My head's swimming. I had Carol in class."

Dr. Day nodded. "She spoke frequently of you this year."

Marcia looked up in surprise. "Of me? But—"

"Yes. And she talked about Blake, too. She seemed to think that he had written especially for her, although she also often complained that he didn't make sense." Dr. Day reached out for a cigarette. She lighted it and said, "I couldn't help her much, for I don't know Blake."

Marcia winced. "I think that she tried to talk with me—once. But I was so *unknowing!*" Dr. Day looked sympathetic, but Marcia was not satisfied. "In spite of what you said, I keep thinking that there must be some one clue that will help. I mean, we can't possibly know every person we meet as we now know Carol Leeds. How then. . .?"

"You're right, of course. We know very few people this way—fortunately, I think. There's little that we can do, unless it is to learn how to give without exhausting ourselves. If we—" The telephone on the desk rang sharply. "Excuse me, please."

Marcia moved restlessly about the room as Dr. Day talked over the telephone. She knew that she would never again enter this office without a feeling of tenseness, a feeling of standing on the brink of a dark chasm. . . .

"That was Mother," Dr. Day said, clicking the receiver back into place. "She expected me home for lunch fifteen minutes ago."

"Oh, I'm sorry," Marcia said. "I've kept you."

"It doesn't really matter," Dr. Day assured her. However, she began to move quickly about the room, straightening chairs, dumping ashtrays into the wastebasket, making things orderly on her desk. "I couldn't quite have made it anyway. Mother is a little fussy about such things—she's an invalid, you know—and she likes me to walk in the door at the exact moment I said I would."

Marcia tried to be helpful. She picked up a pencil she found on the floor and handed it to Dr. Day. But Dr. Day was busy with something else at the moment, and she murmured rather irritably, "Just leave it on the floor, please." She was really very much in a hurry.

Marcia stood by the door, out of the way. "Now that Carol is going to graduate properly, what will happen to her?"

"What? Oh. Well, for the summer she has an excellent opportunity with a summer stock company in Maine. Miss Taylor arranged it for her."

"But can she get along without you?"

Dr. Day looked up at that, and she seemed suddenly tired. "I don't know," she said slowly. "I have a good relationship with her now, but if something upsets that or keeps her from coming back to see me after she leaves here, well . . ." She shook her head. "I'd feel much more hopeful if I knew I was going to continue seeing her regularly."

"What seems especially pathetic to me," Marcia said as they went

188

down the steps together, "is the way Carol Leeds seems to *flaunt* her freedom. And now I find that she has *no* freedom, that she is completely bound within herself, to herself. . . ."

"Yes, yes," Dr. Day said absently. "But, of course, that is the way it is for most of us." She glanced at her watch and made a little sound of annoyance. "I'm going to be at least a half hour late! Mother will be *furious!*"

Carol lighted her last cigarette and threw the empty package at the wastebasket. It missed and fell to the floor. She kicked at it angrily but did not pick it up. Now she'd have to go out after cigarettes.

It wasn't that she minded the furtively curious stares people gave her. She rather enjoyed them. But she didn't want to miss a message. Damn them all! At least they'd let her know whether or not she graduated tomorrow, wouldn't they?

Yes, she thought they would—and she also thought she'd graduate. Dr. Day wouldn't let her down.

If she were expelled, the summer stock company would be closed to her. She grabbed up a gay pillow and flung it savagely against the wall. Kimball Duncan! If he hadn't acted the fool, nothing would be wrong for her now. She could kill him. Maybe she would. Maybe she'd—

She forced herself to think of Dr. Day and was calmer. It was the waiting that was getting on her nerves, she told herself.

Deliberately she kept her mind on Dr. Day. How wise she was . . . how kind she was. . . . She thought of the summer without her and was suddenly afraid. . . . But she'd write, and perhaps even manage to get back to Riverville once or twice—

She went tense again as she heard a timid knock upon her door. When she had called out sharply, a fearful freshman opened the door a crack. "Professor Colley is downstairs waiting to see you," she said apologetically.

"Colley!" Carol frowned. "O.K. Scram now."

Why Colley? She shrugged and put out her cigarette, then ran the comb through her hair and straightened the seams of her stockings.

Colley was waiting in the cheerless lounge, his round face grave and portentous. After one look at it, she walked back to draw shut the large folding doors. Then she faced him and waited for him to say the first word.

"Miss Leeds," he said, "I come directly from a meeting of the Student Personnel Committee, at which we discussed your—escapade, and I—"

"Where's Dr. Day?" she cut in flatly.

"*I'm* the chairman of the committee, Miss Leeds."

She put her hand on the door. "I'm not talking with anyone but Dr. Day."

His pale blue eyes flickered over her. "Dr. Day was busy," he said quickly and in a softer tone. "She asked me to see you."

Carol didn't believe that; yet it was true that she hadn't heard from Dr. Day. For a moment she felt cold and lonely.

Colley didn't seem able to keep his eyes off her. She was used to the kind of look he was giving her, and it steadied her. She walked across the room, her thin dress molding her thighs, and seated herself in a high backed chair. "Why don't you sit down, Professor Colley?"

He moistened his lips and did not move. "I want you to understand, Miss Leeds, that we know—everything."

"Do I graduate or not?" she asked quietly and crossed her legs.

His look dropped to her ankles. "Yes, but"—with effort he raised his eyes to her face—"that does not expiate your sins. *We* have forgiven you, but you must face your own sense of shame. The way will—"

"What are my sins?"

He took a step toward her and pointed an unsteady finger. "They are sins of the body. I see now that they show in your face, in every move that you make. You are following in the path of your mother. You—"

"Did Dr. Day tell you all this?" she asked without expression.

He had moved to her side and pressed against the arm of her chair. "Before it is too late, you must leave this path of sin. I have pity." He reached for her limp hand. "Let me help—"

Too quickly for him to step back, she was on her feet and ground her sharp high heel into his toes.

When she got off the bed and dragged herself across the room, she saw that the sun was still bright. She had expected it to be night. She leaned against the dresser and sneered into the mirror. She looked like the end of a binge. Then she shrugged. Why not meet David as planned?

She took a cold shower and dressed with meticulous care. When she was ready to leave the room, she looked fresh and cool and poised.

She sauntered across the Heart, her thoughts still formless, until she caught a glimpse of Dr. Day coming out of Science Hall, her briefcase in one hand, several thick books under the other arm. Instinctively she slowed down and allowed Dr. Day to go on ahead. She followed her carefully, as if she had a plan.

When she reached the front of the President's house, Dr. Day was starting down the Heights, and she suddenly stopped. What could she accomplish by following her? If she had a gun, a stone, a . . . But she had nothing—only the old, old fury of betrayal.

Her hands and face were wet. She took out her compact and fixed her face. Then she walked on, slowly, aimlessly. She had over an hour before meeting David.

At the Square she boarded a bus and got off at the hospital because it was the last stop near Riverville. She stared at the austere building for a minute, remembering Kimball Duncan. She went inside.

Cautiously she asked her questions of the receptionist. She was wary with a new sense of having to be on guard, for now it was Carol Leeds alone. The receptionist was polite and matter-of-fact. Yes, Miss Leeds could see Mr. Duncan.

As she walked on, she felt new strength. She was safe. What had happened to her was not apparent to other people. Her knock upon the shuttered door to which she had been directed was firm. Kim himself called out.

She pushed open the door slowly, enjoying the shock on his face as he saw her. Silently she sat down in the chair pulled up to the bed, her eyes tyrannically on his. She was looking at him through the hate which she felt for him only slightly less than for Dr. Day, but she knew that he could not read this in her face.

"I've been worrying," he said at last. "God knows, I meant to help you, but I caused trouble."

"I'm going to graduate," she said softly. "There is no trouble."

He stared unbelievingly, not because of what she had said, but because of the new tone in her voice.

"I came to thank you," she went on, "for allowing me to know a great love. . . ." She hesitated, running out of words. She had not planned this until she had entered the room. Hastily she brought together in her mind everything she knew to be meaningful to him, and she drew upon her long discipline of acting to keep the contempt out of her voice. "I had to be with that horrible man—Mike—to understand the bond between you and me. Perhaps it is our art. You have painting, I have the theater. Art is our meeting place, above the world, and together"—she stood up—"we could have known glorious freedom."

"Carol!" But beyond her name, he could say nothing. The moment was too dream-like for thought.

Her face was sad. "But I found out too late. I have caused—"

"Too late! What do you—"

"I have caused unhappiness to many people—especially you. I must go away for a while. I want to atone for—"

"Carol! This isn't like you!"

"I have changed." She smiled. "I'm leaving tomorrow."

"No! Not until I'm out of this place—not before we have a chance to talk. Carol, please!"

She backed away from his outstretched hand. "Don't try to find me, but wait for me. Trust in me. You will hear ugly rumors about me. But you know how the world lies about people like us—don't you, Kim?"

He nodded mutely, hypnotized by her words.

"Trust in me, and wait for my letter."

His mind struggled feebly. "Letter?"

"Yes. When I know that it is right for us to be together, I shall write to you. Do you promise to wait for my letter, Kim?"

Again he nodded.

Her face hardened. "*Say* it, Kim."

"I promise," he whispered.

Carol swung down the highway. She was not completely satisfied with what she had done to Kimball Duncan, but it was good enough. He'd suffer while waiting for that letter, which would never come. He was the kind to suffer, she knew. She had seen agony in his eyes many times.

She turned up the dirt and cinder road marked PRIVATE. It still amused her to meet David on MacMillan land. The only annoying thing was that she couldn't tell it to the College, to J. W. MacMillan himself. A short way up the road she took a footpath that led across a field of stubble and down a small but steep hill. At the bottom was a grassy spot hidden from both the highway and the private road.

She ignored shade and flung herself down in the sun, her hands under her head, her face to the sky. Shadows were lengthening, but it was still blazing hot. There was the drowsy hum of unseen insects, and occasionally she heard the louder roar of a car passing along the highway.

She was very tired and longed to let go her mind, to make it as lax as her body against the firm ground. But she had to hold it tightly to keep it from slipping back to the hurting thoughts. Dr. Day, whom she had trusted, who had pretended to be her—

She glanced at her watch and frowned irritably. David was already five minutes late. Not that she was eager to see him, but she was eager to have the meeting over with. Perhaps it would be their last one.

He bored her. She yawned to prove it. She hung on to him chiefly because he was John Willard's fair-haired boy, the model English major. . . .

Thoughtfully she turned on her side, plucked a grass blade and put the sweet white root between her lips. She had already smashed his smug goodness, but need she stop with that? Slowly the thoughts formed in her mind.

She lay quite still, for she heard him coming down the little hill, whistling softly as he always did. He stood over her for a minute and then, after carefully looking around him, knelt and gently pulled the blade of grass from between her lips. He kissed her quickly, still not at ease in a clandestine meeting.

She pushed him away and sat up. Hurt crossed his face, but he was too used to her strange moods to make a point of it. "Didn't you bring the sandwiches?" he asked.

"No." She leaned back on her hands.

He sighed in mock desperation. "A loaf of bread, a jug of wine, and thou. Well, I'm not complaining. I have the most important of the three—thou." He stretched out, resting his head in her lap. "Ah, Carol, this is it—this is everything!"

She stared down at his contented face, and sensed that he was thinking not only about her and their being together, but about David Whitney, *magna cum laude,* most likely to succeed. . . .

"David," she said abruptly, "I thought perhaps you'd be interested to know that I'm pregnant."

He jerked up and twisted around to stare into her face. "You mean . . .?"

She laughed. "I mean exactly what I said."

He got to his feet and walked away from her, then back, not seeming to know what he was doing.

Calmly she studied the dazed look on his face. "What are you trying to say, David? That you don't want to marry me?"

He dropped down beside her and took her hand in his. "No, no, Carol. You know I want to marry you. It just isn't the way I thought it would be. Somehow—well, somehow it sounds cheap—and sordid."

"You didn't think that while you were having your fling," she said coldly.

He flushed deeply and tightened his hand over hers. "Don't say it that way, Carol."

"We'll leave tomorrow. Maybe we'll go to New Jersey."

"Tomorrow?" He frowned in a puzzled way, as if there were something about tomorrow he should remember. "Tomorrow"—he remembered and looked at her incredulously—"why, tomorrow is Commencement, Carol!"

"Did I say that it wasn't? We'll leave immediately after it."

He stared for a moment; then he shook his head, and his voice took on firmness. "I can't, Carol. My mother and father will be here. I'll—"

"You'll think up something to tell them. You know how to lie, David. You lied well enough when you were scheming to meet me—remember?"

He looked away from her and was quiet so long that she began to wonder if she had miscalculated. But then he said, "I'll arrange it. I guess you have a right to have it your own way. Mother and Dad will understand when we explain it to them. They're swell people. You'll—"

"You're explaining nothing to them, David, my lad. This is to be a *secret* marriage. Maybe some day I'll want to shout it from the housetops—particularly from the Summit—but if you think I'm entering a summer stock company as *Mrs.* David Whitney, you're crazy. I start in three weeks, and I start as Carol Leeds—which is a damn good name, in case you're doubting it."

"Three weeks," he said dully, as if he had heard only that. "Three weeks. That's when I go into the Navy."

193

She laughed shrilly. "Do you think I had forgotten? Do you think I'd want to marry you if I weren't sure we had only three weeks?"

He looked at her, searching her face. "Don't you love me, Carol?"

The simple question made her laugh again. "What do you think, David Whitney, *magna cum laude?*"

She watched him find the truth, then thrust it aside. His face had paled. "I think—you do." He drew her to him roughly. "You've got to."

"Do I?" She wrenched free of him and lay back in the grass. "This is very funny, my love. Where's your sense of humor?" She looked into the sky and her voice was reminiscent. "Remember that paper you wrote—on the Soul? You read it to me, made me listen to all that noble tripe. It bored me then, but now it makes me laugh. I'm laughing— hear me?" She sat up suddenly and leaned toward him, her face taunting. "I hope that you are filled with a sense of shame, David Whitney. You're a hypocrite, with a sinful mind and body, and I'm not going to let you forget that for one minute of our three wonderful weeks."

When she returned to Grace Hall, there was a note pinned to her door. It said that Dr. Day had been trying to reach her all afternoon and evening, and that she was to call her at her home as soon as she received the message.

She sneered and crumpled the note in her hand. Inside her room she tore it into shreds and scattered them over the floor. Then she dragged out her suitcase and began to throw clothes into it.

In spite of her great weariness, there was an exultancy within her, and she wondered why she had ever thought she needed Dr. Day.

Chapter Eight

"I'LL STAY here," Grace said, her eyes suspiciously bright.

Russ kissed her lightly. "Goodby, Grandmama. You take care of Dad."

She laughed unnecessarily. "You'll never meet anyone else who's better able to take care of himself."

"I know, but—well, last night we had"—his voice cracked—"an argument."

"What else are fathers for, I should like to know!"

He tried to smile with her. "Grandmama, if anything should happen to—me, you be sure to tell him how I feel about him—and the family and everything. Will you promise?"

"Of course," she said confidently, although she wasn't at all sure how he felt about anything.

"If I—" He stopped as they heard J.W. on the stairs. "I'll have to be leaving," he said to his father.

J.W. glanced at his watch. "Yes, I suppose so, if you're still insisting upon this absurd plan of walking to the station alone."

"That's the way I want it, Dad."

On the porch, J.W. said, "Is it against your mysterious code for the father to carry the son's bag?"

Gravely Russ handed the bag over to him.

They went down the farther side of the long horseshoe drive. "Difference of ideas between people of the same blood means very little, you know," J.W. said lightly. "I always did think that elaborate mental work was superficial—although of course it makes life more interesting. A man has a few instinctive beliefs, and anything else is embroidery."

Russ was thoughtful. "Then why did you send me off to college?"

J.W. frowned. "Well, as I admitted, it does make life more interesting."

"But it might have been simpler for everybody if you had skipped the embroidery—as you call it—and put me right into the factory."

"The Willards," J.W. said mechanically, "have always gone to a liberal arts college before getting into industry. Why, even the first Willard—the one who designed the Willard plow—was trained for the clergy. It's a tradition with us. You can't deny blood! You belong to me—to the family. Anything else can't matter."

"It matters in this way," Russ said doggedly. "So long as I think as I do now, I can't come back to work for you. I don't want you to make plans that I can't fulfill."

J.W. was exasperated. "Good Lord! You won't be working *for* me! You'll soon be part owner, and one day you'll—"

"I know that," Russ said quietly. "That's why I don't want to come back. I don't want to own things."

"You're pretty young to decide that," J.W. said against his better judgment.

Russ stayed silent until they reached the end of the drive; then, unexpectedly, he said, " 'Property is only what a man hath mixed with his own labor.' "

"Oh, stop quoting!" J.W. set down the bag and reached for his cigarette case. "Smoke?" Russ shook his head, and he hurriedly lighted one for himself, although he didn't want it. "Marx again!"

"John Locke," Russ corrected him seriously.

"All right, Locke then! Now, listen, you're not going to own anything without working. What about me! Why, I haven't had a vacation since—"

"You work very hard, Father," Russ said soothingly, but he added, "and so do the men under you. Therefore, they—"

"Never mind rehashing what we went through last night!" J.W. tossed away the cigarette. "Well, we're being a bit premature. No use

195

crossing bridges and so forth, you know," he said with an effort at lightness.

But Russ hadn't heard. He stared into the horizon until J.W. made an impatient move. "Do you realize, Dad," he said then, excitement showing in his face, "that life is made so that everyone shares all the truly great experiences—birth, copulation, death! Isn't that a clue to —*something?*"

J.W. smiled tolerantly. "And in what book did you find *that?*"

"I didn't find it in a book." Russ looked away, hurt. "I have to go now."

Yes, J.W. thought, that was true—the one reality. Suddenly he was afraid. He thought it best to be jocular. "Well, don't you go copulating around," he said, feeling heavy-handed.

Russ didn't smile. Silently he picked up his bag, and then held out his hand. "Good-by, Father."

"Good-by, Russ," J.W. said, glad that it was coming to an end. He didn't want the scene to be lengthened, for he knew that the memory of it would annoy him for many days to come. "Take care of yourself, and all that."

Russ nodded and turned quickly.

J.W. stood watching. *He'll come back the way I want him. He shall not be lost to me.* And to this thought he added hastily: *Nor shall he be killed.*

He became alert as he saw Russ suddenly put down his bag and turn back. Russ was coming back to apologize, to promise that he would return as he should! The thought rushed through his mind, displacing the fear.

Russ was breathless. "I had to tell you, Dad, that I *love* you. I don't know how to say it, but you were right when you said that the ideas didn't make any real difference between us. I mean, I'll always love you even though—" He stopped, as if suddenly aware of his father's immobility. "You understand, don't you?"

"Of course," J.W. said.

Russ seemed to be waiting for something. He swallowed thickly. "That's all, I guess. . . ." He went back to his bag, and when he had it in his hand, he turned and waved self-consciously. Then he struck out in his familiar, jerky stride.

J.W. didn't move until Russ had long been out of sight. He walked slowly back to the house, staring at it absently as he approached it, then suddenly seeing it very clearly. It was a solid-looking structure.

How solid was his life? His work, yes—but his home?

Russ would be back, of course—in spite of the war, in spite of his absurd talk. Even so . . . even so . . .

"Grace!" he called abruptly the minute he was inside the house. "Grace!"

She was alarmed. "What has—"

"Nothing has happened," he said impatiently. "Russ went off—all right. Grace, will you stay here this winter?"

"For heaven's sakes, why?"

"I need a woman in the house," he said bluntly.

"Well! I'm hardly flattered. After all, Kate's here."

"She won't do. It has to be family."

"Don't make your appeal so sentimental," she said ironically. "You're overwhelming me!"

"Seriously, will you?"

"Seriously, I have important work to do in New York."

"But you could turn it over to someone else—temporarily." He spoke then in a gentler tone. "It's important to me. *Please*, Mother."

She made a dramatic gesture. "How *could* I resist that 'Mother'!" Then she was serious. "If you'd explain, Jack, I'd feel more—"

"I need a chaperone," he said, feeling foolish.

"A chaperone!" She looked puzzled, then thoughtful, then eager. "It isn't Marcia Anderson, is it?" He nodded briefly, and she said, "Well, I *had* hopes, but I gave them up. I didn't realize that you were seeing her."

"I haven't seen her since John Willard night," he said; then went on quickly as his mother looked ready to ask questions: "I'll appreciate it very much if you can arrange to remain here." He became busy lighting a cigarette. He didn't want her to discover and probe into the empty feeling which Russ's going had given him. His lighter slipped through his fingers and fell to the floor.

"I've never before seen you drop anything," she remarked idly as he stooped to pick it up. She sighed. "I'm sorry that you and Russ quarreled today of all days."

"Russ and I never quarrel," he said shortly. "You'll stay?"

"Yes—yes, of course. I'm far too interested to miss it. By the way," she added brightly, "have you informed Miss Anderson of your new project?"

He ignored her irony. "Thank you," he said and kissed her lightly. But he still felt it imperative to be safely away from her. "It's later than I had realized. I must return to the office now."

Outside again, he called Tamburlaine three times before he remembered that Tamburlaine was not home. Disappointed, he strode down the drive alone.

Tamburlaine decided that the fat fly with the sparkling wings wasn't worth his sticking his snout into that evil-smelling stuff again. Without any consideration for him, all the cottage screens had been sprayed with the stuff to keep out the July bugs.

He moseyed over to investigate Esther Cornthwaite's long pointed oxfords. The tweed skirt was rather interesting—but nothing happened. Then he went over to the cot to try Alice Ware's green slacks.

He had to sniff up the whole length of the cot, for she lay stretched out. She was reading in a small paper-backed book, but her hand dropped gently upon his head and her light, quick-moving fingers set to tickling him behind his ears. He squatted down, pretending to be hypnotized, for he liked her exceedingly.

Esther halted her letter to Paul Lewis Grant to watch. After a minute, she asked, "Alice, what pleasure do you get out of it?"

"What's that? Oh." Alice yawned and allowed the book to fall on her flat stomach. It went gently up and down with her breathing. "You may as well know the worst. I've read detective stories for years. Relaxes the mind."

Esther leaned slightly over the arm of her rocker to see the cover, which bore the picture of a fleshless hand dripping blood. "I wasn't referring to your reading matter," she said, "but as you have now called it to my attention, I should inform you that you are reading a mystery, not a detective story. There's a subtle distinction, you know."

Alice grinned. "I know, but I shouldn't make a point of it. That's the difference between you and me. How about settling for 'whodunit'?"

Esther looked her contempt and went back to her writing. Alice did not resume her reading but lay quietly, her hands tucked under her head. "Well, Esther, have you decided?" she asked suddenly.

Esther stared at her and then closed her brown leather writing portfolio with a gesture of annoyance. "I'm not adept at telepathy, Alice. What do you mean?"

"Whether we should have lived like this—together, I mean—for the past thirty-five years."

Esther was genuinely puzzled. "I certainly hadn't given it any special thought."

"Why did you ask me up here, then?" Alice sat up abruptly and swung her legs over the side of the cot. "Hell, Esther, I've left you in peace for a month because I respected your desire to finish that damn manuscript. But now that you've sent it off to the publisher, I deserve to know! How many summers have I invited you to Michigan with me, only to have you politely decline! Something unusual must have prompted you *this* summer. Wasn't it to decide once and for all whether you might not have been wrong?"

"Nonsense!" Esther said firmly. "I'm merely—concluding a few things this summer."

Alice grimaced. "I hope *you* know what you mean. I don't." She lighted a cigarette and shrugged. "Well, I don't much care if I know or not. I like Maine, I like Tamburlaine, and I like this MacMillan man who has furnished both. Who is he, by the way?" She grinned suddenly. "You're not a kept woman, are you, Esther?"

"He is," Esther said with dignity, "a very good friend." She hesitated and then added, "He is Philip Willard's nephew."

Alice looked fully enlightened. "O-ho!! That's the Philip who broke your heart just before we tried that apartment together."

"Alice, you're fictionizing!"

"So I am," Alice admitted. "I was young and very much in awe of you then, but even in those days I had the sneaking thought that some man had made a lucky escape. You were granite in those days, Esther." When Esther said nothing, she asked again, gently, "Well, Esther, are you sorry—about us?"

"No," Esther said quietly, "I'm not." She cleared her throat and briskly screwed on the cap of her fountain pen. "You still bang doors and bring in stray people. And don't pretend that *you* are sorry. Granite could hardly be an agreeable companion."

"Well, I've been lonely. . . ." Alice murmured.

Esther nodded quite sympathetically. "Yes, I can understand that. You are meant to be with other people. That was always apparent to me."

"Well, don't say it in that tone of voice. You make it sound like a disfiguring birthmark!" Alice blew smoke out of her mouth angrily.

"Do you recall what Chaucer's Wife of Bath says about the very unsanitary habit of smoking?" Esther said, gently fanning the smoke away from her face. "I've always wondered why you didn't marry or find another apartment-mate."

"I don't know," Alice said slowly. "Let myself drift, I suppose . . . filled up my life with students." She laughed shortly. "Maybe I couldn't find anyone who quite measured up to you."

Esther was silent. Alice hunched forward, her elbows on her knees, the cigarette dangling between her fingers. "Granite is—granite, but you don't forget it once you've met it. And I guess there's not too much of it in the world." She made her voice brisk. "I haven't been unhappy, though. Students can be satisfying if you keep them evenly balanced between the personal and the impersonal. I mean, if you allow them to get into your feelings, then you're likely to be left flat." She went to the screen door and tossed out the cigarette. "Marcia Anderson, for example," she said, coming back to the cot. "Now she came the nearest to reminding me of you. You know, it rather hurt me when you didn't take to her."

Esther looked pained. "What do you mean—didn't take to her?"

Alice talked on as if she had not heard Esther. "Marcia didn't write much about it to me, of course. She has pride—your kind. But from what little she said, and from reading between the lines, I gather—"

"She happened to arrive at the wrong time," Esther said with sudden frankness.

"Time! You've harped about time all summer. I don't understand it . . . don't like it. Hell, Esther, you're in your prime. You should rest on your laurels, gather your followers around you. No one else in the world would miss the opportunity!"

"Don't talk such absurdities, Alice. To my knowledge, I have instigated no movement, and self-designated followers can be a nuisance. As for Marcia Anderson, I'm leaving her my papers. It's not much, understand—only a small token. Does that please you?"

Alice stared. "What do you mean? You give me the creeps talking about concluding that, leaving this—"

"If it's necessary," Esther went on, unperturbed, "you explain to her that the papers are only a token. They're merely things that I never had time to polish for publication. A few may be of real service to her, although, of course, she'll find nothing among them concerning that unfortunate William Blake!"

"I hope," Alice said ironically, "that you'll be considerate enough of Tamburlaine and me not to become extinct until we're out of this place. Really, it would be quite inconvenient! What's that you've been writing"—she pointed to the portfolio—"your last will and testament?"

"No," said Esther calmly. "This is a letter to Dr. Grant. The chairmanship will be his. At least, that is the way I want it. I'm not giving it to him now, of course, but there are certain records that he should know about." She sighed. "So many details! I'm sure that I'll forget—"

Alice stamped her foot. "I can't stand this! It's downright morbid!"

"Nonsense! It's only preparedness. By the way, Alice, if I should forget—my books are to go to the John Willard Library, my money"—she chuckled—"Alice, do you know that I don't know to whom to leave my money! Do you want it?"

"Good Heavens, no! I'd feel obligated to leave mine to you. In fact, you're putting me into a frenzy to get home and start sorting things out. I'm totally unprepared, and I do have a touch of anemia."

"Very well, Alice." Esther's face brightened. "Oh, of course—the niece in Albuquerque. She shall have it, but first I want a fund set aside for the Literary Competition Award. Now," she asked anxiously, "can you remember these things, Alice?"

Alice sighed resignedly. "All right, I'll remember them. But my knowing about them won't make them legal. You'll have to have a will proper made up—and how you're going to enjoy that!" She picked up her book and stretched out again. "And now, if you'll please excuse me, I'm going to return to my cheerful torso murder. Hell!"

Esther regarded her. "Alice," she said, "I'm dismayed to find that you have retained your habit of cursing. Do you realize that those 'hells' of yours sound lamentably like the Nazi salute? It's your slight nasal twang that does it, of course."

"Oh, fudge!" Alice said, flipping a page of her book.

Esther smiled and watched her a minute longer. Then she opened her portfolio and concluded her letter to Grant.

When he saw the mailman bicycle away, Grant walked down the long and gently sloping lawn to the new mailbox. Set on a post, it was a minute, although not exact, replica of Oaklands. Matt, of course, had supervised its creation, and he had added the large sunroom and right wing as way of jesting reminder that he intended soon to add them to the real house.

The mailbox both exasperated and amused Grant. It was a complicated affair with various compartments for different-sized mail. Impatiently he undid the many latches and explored the tricky interior. Today all his mail was large in size; so he found it without particular trouble. His *Literary Record* lay on the veranda, and the two long white envelopes addressed to him were in the hall that ran the length of the house. The fat envelope was from Silas Seabolm, and as he weighed it in his hand, he grinned, for he was fairly sure that it contained an offprint—which meant that Si had another article in print. The sight of the other envelope—characteristically unadorned in form or with engraving—pleased him. It was the letter from E. Cornthwaite that he had been expecting.

In the sunroom he saw propped up a letter to Janice from her mother. He carefully extracted this and pocketed it to give to Janice, for she would be sure to join him before the end of the afternoon.

He unrolled the *Literary Record* and turned down the dusty road, reading as he tramped along. Soon, however, he closed the magazine, rolled it up again, and shoved it into his hip pocket. Every day he discovered anew that it was a shameful waste to read while walking along a country road alone. He had made a late start, and now the sun was burning directly down upon him. He did what he had often longed to do during June and July in New York—took off his shirt and flung it over his shoulder.

For a while he could walk in the shady border made by high cornstalks. Then he turned off the road and crossed a pathless field, the short, dry grass slippery under his shoes. At the end of this, he spread the wires of a fence and stepped through, entering at last his old reading room. He sprawled down next to his reading stand, a gnarled and worm-eaten tree stump. For a few minutes he did nothing but enjoy being there. It didn't belong to Oaklands, and he smiled to think that he didn't know anything more about who owned it than he had years ago when he had first propped up on the old stump the big book called *Moby Dick*.

He straightened up and lighted his pipe, then pulled out his letters. He opened Esther's first, and he found her letter as puzzling as his conference with her in the early spring. She praised him again, but said that she did not see fit to endorse his request for a leave of absence during the second semester of the coming academic year. The major portion of her letter described the filing system devised by her for the preserving of certain specified records, and the seeming irrelevancy of this information irritated him.

He was irritated, yes; but, he noted with surprise, he was not even justifiably angry over being denied the leave. Musing upon this, he opened, without eagerness, the letter from his friend, Silas Seabolm. Friend? Well, he supposed so. They had taken three years of graduate study together, and they had explored New York City together for that length of time. That made them friends, didn't it? Even so, he wished Si weren't such a punctilious letter-writer. His periodic accounts of himself always made him aware of how little he was getting done and how much Silas Seabolm was accomplishing.

This letter was no different. As he had guessed, Si had dashed off another article. The hastily autographed offprint of it was enclosed. "The Neurosis of Nathaniel Hawthorne." He read it through, admiring the style but uneasy over the subject matter. Si's writing had a darting brilliance that arrested the mind and almost prevented sound judgment of the thought-content.

He put the article aside and glanced again at the inevitable conclusion to Si's letter: "Write to tell me what *you've* been up to. . . ." Sooner or later, he'd send back his inevitable answer: "Well, Si, I'm still plugging along at the book. . . ."

"Hi, there!"

"Hi," he said back and raised his hand in welcome, although he had no special desire for Janice's company on this one day of complete idleness he had given himself. He watched her get through the fence and come toward him, her slight figure seeming childish in the shapeless blue overalls which she had rolled above her bare knees. She carried a fat book and a cigarette.

She sat down beside him, and he pointed to the cigarette, "Since when?"

She shrugged, as if to say that she had smoked for years. He remembered her letter and handed it to her. She gave it a hasty look, grimaced, and put it, still sealed, between the pages of her book. He refrained from saying that it was normal for a daughter to read a letter from her mother. "What are you reading?" he asked, indicating the book.

"Freud—on dreams." She studied him speculatively. "What did you dream last night, Paul?"

"I never dream," he said firmly.

"Hah!" She pointed at him triumphantly. "If you suppress even your dreams, then you're a *real* case!"

"Rubbish." He opened the *Literary Record,* but the book reviews seemed written for the express purpose of telling him how many men managed to break into print before he could finish Melville. He lost interest and watched Janice bend over Freud. Every now and then she glanced away from the page to frown at her cigarette and change its position between her fingers. She did this so frequently and deliberately that he at last grew curious. "What are you doing?"

She held out her hand with the cigarette, her little finger elaborately arched. "Is this the way Dr. Anderson holds her cigarette?"

He regarded her hand thoughtfully, then leaned forward and straightened the little finger. "More like that. She's not so ostentatious about it."

She jerked her hand back. "So you know exactly how she holds her cigarette! So you've noticed every little thing about her. Well, then, why do you suppose she changed her hair style?"

He was startled by her sudden anger, but he felt unfairly trapped too. He shrugged. "How the devil should I know? Besides, I hadn't observed that she changed her hair."

"That's a lie! I saw you see it at the hospital that day, and I knew then that you were falling in love with her."

He could only stare at her. Her face was tense, and she went on in a threatening voice that fell harshly into the quiet afternoon, "You can't have her. She's *my* friend. She's the only one I've found who's worth being my friend. She understands me . . . my writing. . . . I told you how she wanted me to come home with her this summer. . . ." She stopped, out of breath.

"I haven't the least idea what you're talking about," he said finally, "but I do know that I don't like it."

She knew by his voice that he was on the verge of being very angry. She waited a minute, then said in a small voice, "Sorry, Uncle Paul. I got excited, I guess. You see, I've been worrying about this because I don't want you to be hurt."

"Just how am I to be hurt?" he asked drily.

Her eyes were wide and earnest. "She's in love with someone else, Uncle Paul. She told me so."

"She told *you?*"

She nodded emphatically. "But confidentially. It's a secret because —well, the man is married. It's—it's Dr. Scott."

He turned his face from her view and knocked his pipe heavily against the stump. He didn't believe it—he did believe it. Was it common gossip? He was sickened to think what someone like Colley could do with such a rumor. "See here, Janice," he said sternly, "if there's talk on campus about this, I'll know the source, and, uncle or no uncle, I'll have you expelled. Do you understand?"

"Yes, Uncle Paul," she said meekly, and went back to Freud.

He took up the *Literary Record* again. Marcia and Scott. Impossible! Scott wasn't simply another married man. Judith Scott was his wife.

Marcia and Scott. Quite possible. Why should he be surprised to discover that she was in love? Shouldn't it be even queerer if she were not? As for Scott, he was good-looking, brilliant. . . . Unbidden, his mind reeled off scene after scene in which Marcia and Scott appeared together. . . .

He felt depressed. Triangles were insidious and led to cruel results, no matter how unintentional. Feelings couldn't always be controlled, but couldn't either Marcia or Scott have withdrawn before it was too late, if only out of conventional respect for Judith? Perhaps, he thought ironically, Marcia found justification for herself in Blake. Instinct *sans* reason—bah!

Then he was irritated with himself. Why gloss over his jealousy? That was his basic reaction, wasn't it? Admit it, then, and get it out of his system. He wanted a solitary life, didn't he? Hadn't he long ago decided that his kind of work demanded solitude?

Even as he answered himself with a bored affirmative, it came to him that the reason for his surprisingly complacent reaction to Esther's refusing him his leave was that he didn't really want to be away from John Willard while Marcia Anderson was there.

"Blake," Marcia wrote, "is the philosopher-poet of Freedom. To him Freedom is a great positive force, not merely absence of restraint. Energy is good, passiveness is evil; imagination is the vibrant essence of thought, reason its dry shell; love is . . ." Her hand holding the pen grew lax, and she thought of J.W.

After a while she put down the pen. She knew from experience that there was no use in forcing herself to work on. She stood up and stretched in the warm afternoon sun that came through the wide front windows. The ivory clock by her bed said two-fifteen. In fifteen more minutes it would be the time Martin had said to come to the studio on any day she felt ready to have him begin the sketches for her portrait. Should she surprise him by going today?

She decided against it. Let him wait a few more days . . . perhaps forever.

It was a day for walking. Energetically she changed to slacks and walking shoes, but when she was ready to leave the room, she suddenly sat down again at her desk. She didn't want to walk. What was there in a walk other than going out to come back?

Listlessly she read over the meagre additions she had made to Blake during the summer. What she had written was good. She thought of Grant's probable reaction to it. It was bad. She shrugged. It was indifferent.

She lighted a cigarette and smoked moodily, not, however, particularly disturbed over her futile restlessness. It had been with her ever since she had come home.

Finally she wandered downstairs. The rooms seemed sunnier than usual and everything she saw pleased her unexpectedly. It came to her then that this day was in one way at least different from all the others, for Virginia was not at home.

She paused before the connecting door to the studio, hearing no sounds on the other side. She put her hand on the knob, then took it away and went outdoors, where she strolled around the yard. Idly she wondered where Virginia had gone, but she didn't really care.

Without consciously making a decision, she went into the studio, using the outside entrance. No one was in the large room, but she heard Martin puttering around in the adjoining laboratory, where he ground his pigments and prepared his canvases. She banged the door to make some noise, and he appeared, seeming surprised to see her.

"Can't stay long," she said before he could say anything.

"My dear," he said, his moustache twitching, "I'm flattered to have even a moment of your time. My pride has fallen this summer, for I've found that I can't compete with William Blake—or even one of his emanations."

"Emanations?" she said, amused and not displeased. "You really are up on Blake, aren't you?" She walked across the bare floor to the dais and pointed to the straight chair on it. "Is that where I sit?"

The chair was uncompromisingly hard, and she began to feel stiff and unnatural under Martin's professional stare. In fact, she found it difficult to think of him as Martin. He sat some distance away from her on a stool, a large pad upright on his knee and a fat stick of charcoal in his hand. His face was absorbed, even severe, and the look of good-humored satisfaction over life in general and himself in particular was gone. She missed that look, although when she saw it, she never failed to tell herself that it was shallow and conceited.

"Remember," he said suddenly, as if sensing her feeling of unnaturalness, "that I see your face as I would an apple. *Become* an apple, if possible. That might reduce your self-consciousness."

She laughed. "I'm sure that it would. But why an apple?"

"Apples do not arouse the moral feeling. One does not look at an apple and think, Ah, little apple, thou shouldst be otherwise. This is a lesson to be learned before looking at the human face."

"That's good," she said admiringly. She was beginning to feel more relaxed than she had during the entire summer. "I'll have to tell it to Kim."

"Kim? Ah, yes . . . Kim." He looked up and said in a business-like tone, "That laugh was good. Do it again."

"But I don't want to face posterity with a laugh on my face."

He shook his head impatiently. "This isn't for posterity. We have to do dozens of preliminary sketches. The laugh is important, for it teaches me the mobility of your face."

She laughed again, quite easily. "I feel silly."

"Naturally. Thank you." His tone became conversational again. "And how is my friend Kim?"

"Your friend!" she said dryly. "You practically ruined his life." But at that moment she wasn't angry with Martin. "Is it true that he can't paint? Please be serious, Martin."

He shrugged. "But I'm no prophet. He has the—shall I say—true reverence for the art, and perhaps even the necessary humility, although in such a fantastic form that he probably doesn't recognize it."

"Did he show you the Barn?"

"Barn?" he said absently, ripping the sheet off the pad and starting to work on a fresh one. "Has he taken to painting barns? That's quite sensible of him."

"You're cruel and smug," she said, but she also smiled. "The Barn is the campus theater, and Kim decorated the interior. Truly, Martin, it's remarkable—very effective."

"Of course." He nodded shrewdly. "His work there has *functional* beauty. It has a use." He sighed. "My friend Kim doesn't take the Barn seriously, I'm sure."

"How did you know?"

He shrugged again. "Perhaps I *am* a prophet. Why restrict myself?"

She frowned thoughtfully. "But use can't be the test of everything. What's the use of those, for example?" She pointed to the conté crayon and sepia sketches that were thumbtacked to the walls.

"Don't move the torso, please!" He gave the rows of sketches a brief glance. "The use of a picture, my dear, is to hang on a wall and give pleasure—perhaps, occasionally, information."

"You're wrong," she said violently. "Why, if I had to question the *use* of my Blake, I'd not write another word. I'd—"

"Then," he said simply, "*you're* wrong about Blake."

She tapped her foot irritably on the dais. "You and Professor Grant ought to get together."

"Don't distract me with the foot, please! Does he paint?"

"No. He has opinions and holds to them staunchly—although he's neither so blunt nor conceited as you."

He smiled and ripped off another sheet and let it fall to the floor.

"Have you finished?" she asked, disappointed.

"No, no. We need at least five more—and then perhaps ten more tomorrow. But right now I need a rest and a cigar."

"*You* need a rest!" She rubbed the back of her aching neck.

He took off his glasses and lighted the familiar cigar. Then he strolled by the rows of sketches, nodding with satisfaction. "They have their use," he murmured. "Anything not locked away from life has its use. . . ."

Marcia stared around the big, bare room. She didn't know it very well, just as she didn't really know Martin when at his work. Virginia knew every inch of the studio. . . . She painstakingly supervised the work of a carefully selected cleaning woman who did nothing but keep the studio spotlessly clean, although Martin didn't even dream of her existence.

Virginia, always Virginia. The home-keeper, the secretary, the wife. Tomorrow would be unlike today, for Virginia would be home. "Martin," she said, "I'll not have time to sit tomorrow."

"Then you'll have to make time," he said complacently. "I insist upon getting in a second batch of sketches before I leave."

"Leave? Where are you going? When?"

"Crusading, my dear." He slipped on his glasses and went back to the stool. "Day after tomorrow." He transferred the cigar to his left hand and held the pad upright again. "Please remove the frown—no, on second thought, hold it a moment. It gives an interesting line above the eyes."

"What on earth do you mean?"

"It lengthens the forehead and narrows the—"

"Crusading," she said impatiently. "What do you mean by that?"

"Oh." He laughed modestly. "Remember my idea for an art colony?"

"Don't tell me anyone is taking it seriously," she said, but her mind was not on the art colony. So he was quite simply going off, without warning, for her last two weeks at home.

He was indignant. "Of *course* it is being taken seriously!"

"Need I remind you what happened to van Gogh's plan for a communion of artists?" And need I remind you, she thought furiously, that I'll be left here alone with Virginia? Unless—

"There's always a first time. Anything," he said joyously, "*anything* can happen to a plan like this, Marcia!"

"Virginia isn't going with you, is she?"

"If Virginia doesn't go," he said mildly, "there is no colony. She's secretary-treasurer, and that fact alone"—he looked up at her, his face again becoming absorbed and impersonal—"should convince you that the plan isn't so impractical as you seem to think. Another laugh, please, Marcia."

"Sorry," she said briefly, "but I'm not in the mood. Where is Virginia today?"

"Out making the various arrangements." He paused to flick ashes, and she thought she saw the smug satisfaction back in his face. "You know how she takes care of all the unpleasant details for me. . . . By the way, Marcia, you don't mind being left alone for a few days, do you? We'll be back a week before you leave and then . . ." His words trailed as he bent over a new sketch.

"I'll not be alone," she said stonily, "for I'm going back to Riverville tomorrow."

He nodded absently. "I assured Virginia you wouldn't mind." He was studying her face again, but his gaze was disconcertingly impersonal. "You practically live alone even when we're here. It has taken you all summer to wander down here. . . ." He frowned and abruptly tore off the sheet upon which he had been working and crumpled it fiercely. "Marcia! When I suggested that you become an apple, I meant merely that you should try to feel like one, not *look* like one! Stop controlling your face. Defrost it. *Express* something."

She looked away from him. "I never did wear my feelings on my face."

"You were doing all right a few minutes ago." He waved his cigar. "What has happened to your thought? Grown too complicated, over-subtle? Well, then, draw upon one of the elemental feelings—love, hate, jealousy, greed. Any one of those should be a good antidote." He selected a new stick of charcoal and waited impatiently.

She knew that her face stayed like a mask. The hot sun beat through the skylight above her head, but she felt no warmth in her body. I could be elemental, she thought, and surprise the smugness out of him; I could thrust myself between him and her, shatter the snug happiness; I have a right to do this. . . .

Desperately she tried to think of J.W.—the way he looked, the restlessness she felt away from him. . . . But now the memories and even the desire were faint and nebulous. . . .

"No, no!" Martin shook his head despairingly. "No, no!"

"I haven't any more time. I told you that I have to pack." She stood up quickly and stepped off the dais before he knew what was happening. She murmured something more about packing and then, forcing back her impulse to run, walked across the long, long floor to the door.

In her room she packed hastily and carelessly, knowing that she would have to send back for many forgotten things. She paused only when she came to the photograph of her mother. She lifted it tenderly from her dresser and looked long at the lovely face; but even as she looked, a part of her mind told her that it was the face of a stranger.

Disturbed, she put the photograph in the trunk drawer. The thought had been false, of course; yet it had brought a feeling of loneliness which persisted.

The last thing she packed was *Noa Noa*. The book was real in her hands, and as long as she had it, she had also the certainty of seeing J.W. at least once again, for she would someday return it to him.

She could think now of him, and she did so, grateful for a life apart from the house of Martin and Virginia, which still had the power to fill her with sickening rage and desolation.

PART THREE

Chapter One

SCOTT stared down at Johnny in his play pen, amused and exasperated. Johnny had discovered the blue sky. By clinging to the pen railing, he pulled himself to a standing position and looked up, slowly following the endless expanse of sky until he toppled over. Scott grimaced and leaned down to right him. "That's the third time in five minutes! If you haven't learned by now that you fall over when you do a backbend, you don't deserve the name of Scott."

Johnny did not take these words lightly. He sat on his blanket and demurely played with what was left of Donald Duck. Scott lighted a cigarette and strolled across the yard, curious to know if his son would try it again when he thought he was alone. He pretended to examine Mrs. Holcomb's pansy bed, but he watched the play pen out of the tail of his eye. Soon Johnny threw aside Donald Duck and grabbed the railing with both fists.

Scott sprang back. "Aha!" Johnny abruptly ceased all motion, his eyes still bright but now wide with fear and wonder. For that moment he looked like one of Della Robbia's grave cherubs against a field of blue. Scott smiled, and Johnny, taking careful note of the relenting smile, grinned back, shattering the Della Robbia image. He lost interest in the hovering menace and went on with what he had been about to do, his face flushed, the sun making a jaunty halo of the fuzz that covered his head.

"Oh, no, you don't," Scott muttered. He tossed away his cigarette and bent down again, this time scooping Johnny up into his arms. Johnny recognized superior force and merely placed his warm cheek against Scott's. Instinctively Scott turned his head away from the softness, feeling old and grizzled. Johnny must find tobacco breath odious. He thought Judith should stop smoking. . . .

Johnny did his best to postpone leaving the sky. He chattered and pointed to various objects of interest he thought they should stop to examine. God knew why, Scott thought as he walked slowly to the back porch, but Johnny was a happy baby. And because Marcia Anderson was coming to dinner, he thought of William Blake and that absurd poem of his called "Infant Joy."

'I have no name:
I am but two days old.'

On the porch, Johnny sensed the inevitability of progress into the house. He gave up trying to wiggle out of the binding arms around him and snuggled down into them. Scott rested his chin on the fuzz, wondering if Johnny found such utter contentment with Judith. She was efficient with him, of course, but somehow he doubted that she. . . . It occurred to him then that if there were only he and Johnny, he could be the best father in the world.

What shall I call thee?
'I happy am,
Joy is my name.'

When he was in the dining room, he heard Judith slide up a window and call out: "Owen, where are you? It's time for Johnny's nap."

"I'm already on my way up!" he shouted irritably. Good Lord! did she have to direct his every move with Johnny?

"Sorry," she called back. "I didn't realize you were in the house."

"Well! if you'd—"

Johnny howled. Scott strode through the living room and up the stairs. " 'Sweet joy befall thee!' " he muttered, determined to complete the Blake verse.

Judith waited at the top of the stairs. Gingerly he held Johnny out to her. "He's wet now," he said with bitter satisfaction. "It didn't happen until you frightened him to death by yelling down the stairs."

"That was mean of me, wasn't it?" Judith murmured into Johnny's ear, and Scott noticed how the traitorous chubby arms went instantly around her neck and clung there.

"Judith," he said, following her into their bedroom, "how about listening to the new chapter now?"

She started, then laughed apologetically. "I didn't know you were there."

"You certainly were absorbed in your own thought. You practically stepped on me in the hall without seeing me. What's on your mind?"

"You mean why didn't I see you in the hall? I don't know, Owen. Truly I don't. I wasn't"—suddenly she pressed her finger tips against her temples—"thinking anything in particular."

He stared at her raised hands. "What's the matter?"

She moved her hands away from her forehead. "Nothing. Well— maybe a little headache."

"What's on your mind?" he asked again. "There must be something. First you don't see me in the hall, then you have a headache, and you—"

"Owen!" Her voice was suddenly sharp. "What are you trying to do?"

"What am *I* trying to do?" he repeated in a hurt voice. "I merely—"

"You should work in your office, Owen," she said casually, "even when school isn't on. When you stay home all day, we invariably quarrel over—something or other, and that isn't good for you or your work—or Johnny."

"So. You'd like to be rid of me. I think I understand. You'd like to have Johnny to yourself. Isn't that it?"

She flashed him a look that shocked him, for it seemed to him that her eyes had darkened with sheer hate. "You can't make me quarrel today."

He observed that even under her anger she was remembering Johnny, for her voice was quiet and controlled so as not to rouse him. He wheeled about and went noisily down the stairs.

He sat at his desk staring down at the sheet of paper half covered with the large loose scrawl that was his own handwriting. For a while he made heavy jagged marks over the paper; then he threw down the pencil and leaned forward, his elbows on the desk, his head hard against his knuckles. *Judith* had a headache!!

She came silently into the room and sat down near him. She had changed to a long flowered housecoat, and her face had that white and strained look made by dabbing powder over tears. At the thought of her crying, some of his inner fury abated.

"Owen," she said, "I think there's time for me to hear the chapter."

He laughed shortly. "You know damn well there isn't."

She was quiet for a minute. Then she said, a trace of hysteria in her voice, "I'll make time. I'll make time for it, even if Marcia Anderson has to wait until midnight for her dinner."

This was too much for him. He stood up and banged his fist down on the desk. "Why in God's name did you have to choose tonight to have company!" He stalked by her and into the kitchen, from which there was no place for him to go other than the back yard.

Marcia had the house to herself. The Murdocks had left on a late vacation the day she had returned to Riverville. Mrs. Murdock had wanted to cancel their plans, but Marcia had insisted that she would enjoy being alone.

Now, however, as she roamed about the forsaken downstairs rooms, she wondered why she had thought she would enjoy being alone. Light was meagre and cheerless, for Mrs. Murdock had pulled down and closed almost all blinds. A thin layer of dust covered the usually mirror-like surfaces of tables. In the kitchen a faucet dripped desolately. Even the refrigerator was dead, and she missed its occasional soft hum.

She decided that it had been foolish to return early. She had seen no one besides Scott, and she felt unpleasantly detached and deserted. She thought it even possible that no one expected her back at John Willard.

Following an impulse to get in touch with Grant, she dialed his home number before she had invented an excuse for calling him. She thought she must have made a mistake in the number when a husky feminine voice answered, but the voice assured her she was right, and she had only a few minutes' wait before Grant was speaking to her.

He seemed surprisingly glad to hear from her—or perhaps it was her own relief in hearing his voice that made her think his sounded eager. He commented upon the remarkable coincidence of their both returning early, and asked about Blake. Had she accomplished anything this summer?

"Why, yes. That's why I called you," she said quickly, for it seemed plausible. "I didn't get much done—I was busy with other things— but I'd like to ask your advice about publishing houses. I'd feel more secure if I had a definite plan in mind."

"Can you tell me briefly how and to what extent you're revising the manuscript I saw?" he asked.

She hesitated, then said almost unhappily, "Frankly, I'm not revising it at all. I'm merely completing it."

"Oh, I see. Well, then, I don't suggest the Academic Press. You might try Hill-Moran. I know someone there who might be of help. . . ."

She listened gratefully, not because of what he was saying, but because nothing about his tone or manner indicated that he was in the least offended by her blatant disregard of his criticism. It was as if he understood her desire to test her own conviction about her work and that, after having had his say, he was as glad to have her stand by her own judgment as he would have been if she had heeded his advice.

"Thank you," she said sincerely. "Now I feel a much greater incentive to finish it. I'll take down those addresses when I see you."

"Why not make that tonight?" he said. "After all, we're two lone academicians in Riverville; so why not commiserate over dinner?"

She thanked him again. "But I have already promised to have dinner with the Scotts tonight."

All he said was, "Oh," in a curiously flat voice. She felt compelled to end the awkward pause that followed. "I happened to meet him yesterday on the Heights. I was just walking around, looking for someone—well, you know how it is."

He said curtly that he knew how it was. She frowned, puzzled. "I'm sure that if he or Judith had known you were in town, you would have been—"

He cut in with a laugh. "Did I sound as if I were sulking because I hadn't been invited? Sorry. The truth is. . . ."

His voice was normal again, but after she hung up, she sat for a while by the telephone, wondering why he had reacted so queerly to her mentioning the Scotts.

Everyone seemed uneasy about Scott. She herself had been vaguely disturbed by his invitation. What if he had offered it without consulting Judith? In view of Judith's past restraint with her, it did not seem likely that she would find delight in entertaining her. . . .

There was, however, one good thing about her going. It gave her a legitimate reason to walk up the Heights and back, and that provided two more possibilities of seeing J.W.

Judith stared seriously at her image in the mirror. Too pale? Owen didn't like her to use rouge . . . said that color in her cheeks took away from her distinctiveness. She searched through the drawer for the seldom used box of rouge, but when she leaned forward to the mirror with the puff between her fingers, she shook her head. Whether she liked it or not, Owen was right. She flung the box back into the drawer.

She grimaced as she took the thin blue dress off its hanger. Blue—how she was growing to hate the color! Nevertheless, it remained her best color; so it would be foolish of her not to wear it this evening. Slipping into it, she thought how queer it was that she was dressing as critically for Marcia Anderson as she used to dress for Owen. She sat down on the bed as suddenly as if she had been pushed, staring at the rug pattern and giving herself up to the thoughts that crowded her mind but which never told her anything. . . .

She started, hearing the doorbell. She had steeled herself for the sound, but now she felt her nerves quiver. "Owen!" she called downstairs. "Owen, did you hear? Please go—"

"Going," he shouted, and she heard his long strides across the room. There had been eagerness in his voice, she thought.

Marcia decided that she needed genius, not mere etiquette, to carry off the evening gracefully. Scott was listless and taciturn, but Judith seemed unwilling to let the talk stop. He made it clear that small talk exasperated him, and got up and prowled around the room. Judith paid him no attention, and after a minute he brusquely cut into what she was saying: "Aren't you going to show off Johnny?"

"I'd love to see him," Marcia said quickly. "I never have, you know."

Judith said without looking at him, "I hadn't thought of it, Owen."

"Don't be deceived," he said ironically to Marcia. "That's *all* we—"

"Perhaps he's sleeping and shouldn't be disturbed," Marcia said.

"Owen's right." Judith arose hastily. "I merely wanted to be coaxed." She crossed the room and went up the stairs.

Scott paced about. "What did you do with Blake this summer?"

"Nothing much," she said briefly. She hadn't liked the way he had asked the question—sharply, as if he had meant to surprise an answer out of her. But she asked politely in turn, "What did you do with Swift and Pope?"

He grimaced. "Nothing much." Then he gestured toward his desk in the dining room. "How much do you think I could accomplish in there!"

She murmured some sympathy which she didn't feel. He sat down across from her and smiled without warmth. "Of course, we're both probably lying."

"What do you mean?"

He waved his hand. "It's conventional—that kind of lying. Sensible too. I feel safer to make you think that I'm not progressing and at the same time make you feel better. You feel safer to—"

"Speak for yourself," she said with forced lightness. "At least I'm glad to know that you've made such progress."

"You misunderstand. *I* really didn't—" He stopped to look up at Judith, who was carrying Johnny down the stairs.

"He's sleepy," she apologized. "It's near his bedtime. Besides, his nap was interrupted this afternoon."

Johnny was awake enough to be coy with Marcia. He showed her his irresistible blue eyes, then his long lashes. Suddenly he gave a plaintive cry and held out his arms to her.

"Don't believe him," Scott said bitterly.

Marcia laughed and held out her arms. "May I? Or would you prefer that I didn't hold him?"

"I prefer him to do exactly what he wants to do," Judith said, settling him on Marcia's lap. "I don't want him to be shy. I want him to be happy, normal, and—"

"And a complete extrovert," Scott said. "Well, your wish is already granted."

"Whatever he is," Marcia said, "he's perfect." Johnny tried to express his appreciation, but his eyes were glazed with sleep, and soon his head lopped back into the crook of her arm. "Now," she said, watching his face, "I feel that I can understand Blake's 'Songs of Innocence.' They used to seem like nonsense verses to me, but now I—"

"Such as 'Infant Joy'?" Scott asked.

She nodded, suddenly uncomfortable. Scott's face bore an eager, impatient look, as if he were about to make something significant out of the Blake poem. She couldn't imagine what, but she knew it wouldn't be pleasant. "Johnny is an unusually good-natured baby, isn't he?" she said to Judith, who had taken a distant chair. "Wouldn't many babies cry when sleepy, especially with strangers?"

Before Judith could answer, Scott laughed shortly and said, "He deems it more effective to cry when we're asleep—or when I'm trying to work. You mentioned 'Infant Joy'—but don't forget the corresponding 'Song of Experience.' " He turned to look at his wife. "Do you know the one I mean, Judith?"

"The only Blake poem I know," Judith said, "is the tiger-tiger-burning-bright one."

"That's—" Marcia began, but Scott cut her short. "It goes this way, Judith—

> 'My mother groaned! my father wept.
> Into the dangerous world I leapt. . . .' "

Judith had risen before Scott finished quoting. She took Johnny from Marcia. "I really must put him to bed now. If you'll excuse me. . . ."

When Judith was out of the room, Scott offered Marcia a cigarette and took one for himself. As he lighted hers, she saw that the tenseness was gone from his face. "Now, how about one of the Scott Old Fashioneds?" His voice was almost gay. He started toward the kitchen, then hesitated. "Of course, it's against the rules for both the host and hostess to leave the guest alone."

"Go right ahead," she said sincerely, refraining from telling him that she thought she needed and deserved several Old Fashioneds.

She sat smoking and listening to him get out ice and glasses. He was whistling softly, and the whistle annoyed her. She thought that he might have bestowed some of his good spirits upon them earlier.

On impulse she went upstairs to Judith and stood tentatively by the open door of the nursery. Johnny was already tucked in and asleep, and Judith was bending down to pick up Donald Duck off the floor. When she straightened, she saw Marcia and seemed surprised. "I thought you were downstairs talking with Owen."

"I'd much rather watch Johnny go to bed."

Judith looked at her again, a small smile of ironic disbelief on her lips. She slipped Donald Duck under the covers with Johnny.

Marcia spoke quickly: "Owen and I have nothing to say to each other—*nothing*."

For a moment, Judith seemed resentful of the deliberate significance put into the words. Then she snapped off the soft light and came into the hall, pulling the door to. Face to face with Marcia, she smiled again, and although it was still not a happy smile, it was without irony or strain. "We had better go drink Owen's Old Fashioneds," she said, and touched Marcia's arm. It was a natural gesture, and yet Marcia felt in it a kind of mute apology.

Scott walked Marcia down the Heights to the Murdocks', and they both made inconsequential talk because they both wanted not to talk. He sensed her lack of sympathy for him, and this rankled. It was as if she had walked into his life at the wrong moment and then judged him on purely circumstantial evidence. It had been a mistake to invite her into his home. He wasn't at his best as one of the Scott trio.

Besides, who was she to judge? He stole a glance at her profile, and again he thought he detected some change in her since he had seen her last June. Once he had thought her aloof and cold; but tonight she had seemed vibrant and warm, especially toward Judith. By the time the evening was over, he had been convinced that the two women had joined forces in a subtle conspiracy against him.

Judith had been the one to urge the invitation. Why? She used to be jealous of Marcia Anderson. Was that changed now? If so, why? There had never been any cause for the jealousy; so why should Judith suddenly lose it?

He wondered what would happen if he gave her cause for it. If he had to suffer because of her jealousy, why should he be so careful not to give it a real basis?

Careful? He grimaced inwardly. The fact was, he couldn't arouse one iota of personal feeling for another woman when he wasn't sure that Judith was with him completely. And God knew he hadn't been able to be sure of that since—well, since Johnny.

And what reward was his for this remarkable singleness of loyalty and devotion? None, of course—just as there was none for plugging away at his manuscript . . . for sacrificing himself to the classroom, monotonous day after day.

He came back to Marcia Anderson and bitterly measured her probable destiny against his. She could win without half trying. Female, good-looking (Grant, he suspected, had already succumbed to those admirable qualities), brains (which she didn't have to use), freedom, means (she could go home whenever she wanted to throw over teaching) . . . .

He glanced at her again. She was preoccupied and didn't notice. And it wasn't with Blake that she was preoccupied, he thought suddenly. Her face was soft, perhaps even wistful. There was about her too a strange intentness, as if she were watchful, listening, waiting. . . . For what? Obviously, a man. She was in a mood, and it might be any man.

He began to wonder. . . . If he pretended with her and she proved to be susceptible, wouldn't that serve to show her that she was not so sublimely above the petty dilemma of his life as she thought herself? If she—

"Look," she said, pointing skywards. "The September moon with its halo."

"Ah, yes," he said, looking. He felt encouraged to find her thoughts centered on the romantic moon. He allowed his arm to jostle against hers as they walked. When she did not move away, he pressed more closely against her, until there could be no mistaking the significance of the pressure.

He felt coolly triumphant when she looked up, no anger in her face, only a kind of puzzled surprise. But she said, "Who was that man?"

For a minute he did not speak but carefully moved his arm away from her. "What man?" he asked then with icy politeness.

"Who just passed us." She looked back over her shoulder and obviously meant him to do so too. He did and saw a broad, stalwart back of sweatshirt and duck pants. It meant nothing to him, and he said so.

She seemed unreasonably disturbed. "He evidently thought he knew me, and I think I should know him."

"That," he said crisply, "is without doubt the most startling phenomenon to occur in Riverville tonight." Perfunctorily he guided her up the Murdock walk and waited by the steps until she had let herself into the dark house.

He walked a short ways up the Heights, then crossed over to the Park and strolled about, the dry, dead leaves crackling underfoot. He thought again of the evening he had spent between the two women, and it seemed to him that he was the pet lamb in a sentimental farce. This image of himself came so naturally to his mind that it was only as an afterthought that he recognized it to be John Keats's, not his own.

Sentimental farce—that was his life. Even in his work he was forced to kowtow to the woman Esther Cornthwaite.

Sentimental Farce—a good title, if only he had a book to fit it.

After two slow cigarettes, he decided that time enough had passed for Judith to begin to wonder why he was so long in escorting Marcia Anderson home under the September moon.

Judith sat brushing her hair, knowing that she was trying to keep back the thoughts. But they came relentlessly.

She wasn't jealous of Marcia Anderson. Why? Because—quite simply—there was no cause for jealousy. She wondered how long she had known that? Hadn't she all along been pretending. . .? Her brush dropped, and she did not bend to pick it up.

Jealousy becomes a convenient cover-up. . . . When had she heard those words? Cover-up for what? . . . *for what we don't want to acknowledge . . . for feelings that we're afraid to call by their true names.*

Where. . .? Suddenly she was hearing Dr. Day say those words at the September tea . . . just a year ago. To remember was somehow a relief. She picked up the brush and idly fingered the bristles.

The idea was still absurd, of course. . . .

What was she concealing from herself? What had her jealousy protected?

She got up and walked around the room, wishing that she could make herself go into sudden and dreamless sleep. When she heard Owen come into the house, she had a moment of panic, as if she were about to be caught in a guilty act. Automatically she moved to do something to her face, but the mirror showed her nothing but tiredness and a strange guilty expression.

She heard him go into the kitchen for a drink of water. Then a light was snapped off, and his footsteps sounded on the stairs. She had to steady herself against a wild impulse to rush out of the room which he would enter.

He pushed open the bedroom door and found her standing there, staring at him. "Oh. Sorry you waited up. Didn't mean to be so long, but Marcia and I had—things to talk over."

I hate him, she thought; and looked quickly away from his face. "What did you have to talk about?" she asked, knowing that she must say something. He went to the clothespress, his back to her, and she sat down on the edge of the bed.

He waited significantly, then said in a glib voice that was meant to be distrusted, "Shop talk. You know how it is—working with a person, day after day."

"But you haven't worked with her all summer." She watched him, objectively curious to know his reaction; and it occurred to her that Iris must feel this way when casting a play.

He shrugged elaborately and said nothing, intending her to interpret his silence as a confession that she was right in thinking more than shop talk had delayed him.

"Are you in love with her?" she asked dutifully.

He came to her almost eagerly. "No, Judith, no. It isn't that. It's—" He stopped, delicately embarrassed.

"You mean she's in love with you?"

"Well—perhaps," he admitted with modest reluctance.

Ashamed, she looked away from him again. When she said nothing more, he turned irritably and began to rummage noisily through a drawer. After a few minutes he came back to her. "Judith, I did *not* kiss her tonight. I know that is on your mind, and I want—"

She half smiled, and the smile took the words away from him. "I appreciate your scrupulous faithfulness, Owen," she said.

She saw his eyes narrow suspiciously, and she felt pity. She said gently, "I understand." She stood up and touched his arm. "I understand, Owen." Then she moved quickly away from him and began to brush her hair again, for the pity was such a blessed relief from the hate that her eyes had filled with tears.

He stared after her. "I must say that you are *unusually* understanding. Most wives would at least pretend to show some concern. You seem to *welcome* the. . . ."

Determinedly she counted the brushstrokes, telling herself that if she could reach one hundred, she would be safe. The pity was not yet strong, and she knew that it could not withstand all the traps he might devise. I don't hate him, she told herself over and over, like a lesson she had to learn by heart. Love and hate were closely allied. Everyone knew that. Perhaps pity was the pathless middle region. Soon she'd find her way back. . . .

". . . while I'm trying to work at my desk!" His voice went up shrilly. "Do you know what it is to have to write while. . . ."

She noticed for the first time how cruel his face looked. "Don't shout, please," she whispered. "Remember Johnny."

"Remember Johnny! What else do we do in this house?" He sneered. "The Scott slogan—Remember Johnny! Hah! Some day you'll have no one *but* Johnny to remember!" He had opened the room door, but he hesitated by it, looking back at her.

She met his look with an expressionless face. She didn't mean to do that, for she knew it maddened him. He wanted her to shout back at him, to sob hysterically. . . . But at that moment she could do nothing but stare at him and silently will him to go out of her sight and hearing.

He moved at last, slamming the door after him. He walked furiously down the hall, then back, shouting to her: "And why did you have to become so friendly with Marcia Anderson? God, you probably made her think this was her second home, that she could drop in any evening she wished. I've told you before, Judith, that I *can* not have casual company. I can't live like other people. I have to plan my time carefully. . . ."

Mixed with his voice, Johnny's wail arose, like an off-tune violin. She could see him in his crib as clearly as if she were standing over him. His cry was a shriek of terror.

"Shut up, Owen," she said calmly, but she began to tremble.

"You can't always use that child as an excuse to shut me up. You can't always. . . ."

Pity might save her—but Johnny? She stared at the closed door, no longer hearing the loud, relentless voice. *My mother groaned! my father wept. Into the dangerous world I leapt. . . .*

The voice hammered on her mind . . . and then the cry. . . . Her hand reached out and closed over the top of her china powder bowl, an old-fashioned girl in hoopskirts and with an innocuous smile. She threw it with all her strength against the door. It struck hard and fell to the floor, breaking into pink and white fragments. She stared at these unbelievingly. It was the first time she had thrown anything in anger, she told herself. Then she sobbed, hysterically.

Owen's voice stopped abruptly. He tried the door cautiously and hurried to her. She did not resist when he lifted her to her feet.

"Judith, darling!" he whispered. "We love one another too much for this sort of thing. You are everything to me, and I—"

"Yes, yes!" She clung to him. "Go on, Owen. Say more."

"I need you, Judith. I love you."

And I hate you, she thought wildly. "Don't let me go!"

219

"Let you go! Why, I *couldn't*." He stroked her hair. "I think," he said reasonably, "that you've been torturing yourself with needless jealousy. You know now, don't you, that I have absolutely no feeling for Marcia Anderson?"

She quieted. "Yes, I know that now, Owen."

"I think that she's the least important person in the whole world!" he said fiercely. "You know that too, don't you?"

"Yes, yes." She shivered. "Can't you hold me close, Owen—*close!*"

His arms tightened around her. He laughed softly. "Why, I'm falling in love with you all over again!"

She opened her eyes and saw the broken china girl on the floor. *And I'm falling in hate with you, falling in hate. . . .*

He sighed and moved slightly away. "I know how you worry about Johnny, darling. Hadn't we better look in on him? He's still cry—"

"No!" She jerked away and covered her face with her hands. "No! I don't want him to see my face this way!" Not with hate on it! her mind cried out.

"I'll go to him," Owen said kindly, "until you've fixed your face."

Marcia did aimless things in her room, finally changing into a blue lounging robe. She combed her hair carefully, then stepped back from the mirror. And now, she thought ironically, I am ready for him to come.

The doorbell rang. She went downstairs slowly, postponing the moment of knowing that it wasn't he.

"Good evening," he said.

She smiled stiffly. "Good evening. Won't you come in?"

J.W. stepped inside and looked questioningly around.

"The Murdocks aren't home," she said. "Did you come to see them?"

He smiled down at her. "What do you think?"

"But how did you know I was here?"

"Mr. Whitelock," he explained. "He passed you on the Heights. He mentioned the fact to me, and I came immediately."

"Oh." She placed the man who had passed Scott and her. "Tamburlaine's handler."

He nodded, and still looked about him as if he expected to see someone else.

"I promise you," she said angrily, "that I have not hidden the Murdocks. They are really away."

He seemed annoyed. "I had expected them to be here."

"I'm so sorry that they didn't understand that." She walked across the room and turned on a brighter light. He followed her. "Do you still have *Noa Noa?*" he asked gravely.

She almost laughed. "I haven't lost it. I'll get it for you immediately."

He took her hand. "But I came to tell you that it now belongs to you. It's a Birthday Book. I give it to you."

"Thank you," she said blankly.

He looked as though she had not made enough of it. "I never give away Birthday Books—but I am giving this one to you."

"Thank you *very* much."

"Your hands are icy, Marcia."

She looked quickly away from the gentle concern in his face. I find you absurd, she thought calmly. Your propriety and your talk about a book—these are quite absurd. You are remote and untouchable. . . .

But suddenly she violently desired to destroy the remoteness, even if it meant making herself abject before it.

The rush of feeling left her shaken. Abruptly she freed her hand and moved away from him. He came to her quickly. "Marcia! What is it?"

She did not speak, for she knew that her voice would be unsteady. She tried to turn from him, but he forced her to look at him. He studied her face for a moment, then said softly, "You love me, Marcia."

She flushed angrily. "I—"

He kissed her. "You love me," he said again.

"Yes," she said wearily.

He kissed her once more, then guided her toward the door.

"Are you leaving—or are we going for a walk?" She tried to sound amused, as he himself might.

"I am leaving. If the Murdocks were here, I'd be more than willing to stay. As it is, I—" He stopped as she laughed. He smiled politely. "Yes, Marcia?"

"There's one thing," she said, fighting off the senseless laughter, "that you forgot to tell me. Do you love me?"

"But of *course,* my dear," he said generously. "Why do you think I came tonight?"

She stood by the open door long after the sound of his footsteps was lost to her. The night air was warm and caressing, mockingly so. The reasonless desire to laugh was gone; the anger was gone. She felt nothing but the breeze upon her flesh.

At last she closed and locked the door. In her room she lighted a cigarette, and as she smoked quietly, his words began to come back to her, until she could remember every one he had spoken and every change of his expression. She realized then that he had said nothing about seeing her again. He had merely come, given her two placid kisses, and returned to his own very complete home.

As she thought upon this, the old restlessness returned, and it was as though he had not come.

Chapter Two

GRANT looked up from his desk in surprise. He couldn't remember Matt's having been in his office before. "Hello! Anything wrong?"

Matt ignored this. He pushed the door shut behind him and strode to the desk. "There!" He flung down a crumpled copy of the John Willard Day issue of the *Young Spectator*. "Did you read that thing by Janice—'The Boy'?"

"Of course."

"Did you read it before it got into print?"

Grant reached for his pipe. "Yes. It was my job to read it."

Matt banged his fist down on the magazine. "Then why the hell didn't you stop it!"

"I saw no reason to. It's good writing. Besides, a committee awarded it the prize."

"A committee!" Matt mocked. He grabbed the magazine and threw it violently across the room. "That's me and Helen in there, as big as life, and you know it!"

Grant saw the puzzled hurt in his face, and he knew then that the anger was mostly bluster. "It took you a long while to read it," he said gently.

Matt sank down in the reading chair. He stuck a cigarette in his mouth but made no move to light it until Grant held out a match. "I carried the thing around with me for a long while. Finally I put it down someplace at home"—he shrugged—"some magazine rack or other. Then the other day Helen cleaned out the rack, and she found it and read it. When I got home, she made me read it." He stared at the cigarette between his fingers. "Helen's pretty upset."

Grant said slowly, "There's one thing that you have to take into account, Matt—one thing that should help you understand. Janice is a writer—a real one. And even—"

"That's what that Miss Anders or Anderson tried to tell me," Matt broke in impatiently. "But hell—so what?"

"And even when she thinks she's writing with absolute realism," Grant went on, "she colors everything with her own intense feelings. Her reproductions are magnified, slightly distorted. . . ." He tried lightness. "I can imagine what she'd do to *me* in writing!"

Matt wasn't consoled. "She's a queer one," he said dully.

Grant nodded. "Yes, she is."

"What d'you mean?" Matt asked with quick suspicion.

"Janice worries me, Matt. She has talent, intelligence, and ambition, but—"

"What's wrong with those things? They sound good to me."

"They're neither good nor bad . . . in themselves." Grant walked to the window, then turned and regarded his brother with a serious look. "She's—well, she's ruthless, Matt."

"Ruthless," Matt repeated blankly. He laughed uneasily. "Good Lord, you take her too seriously. Why, she's just a kid"—he spread his hands—"just a girl."

"That's exactly why I'm taking her seriously," Grant said dryly. "Matt, last year we had a girl who also seemed just a kid. Then came a time when we had to investigate, and we found that because of a certain lack in her background, she—"

"Background!" Matt shouted. "What's the lack in Janice's background?"

Grant shook his head. "We mean different things. I know that you and Helen intend to—" He stopped as he saw Matt's face tighten, and he knew the futility of his words. They'd serve merely to make Matt angrier and, in the end, put even more distance between him and Janice. "Perhaps all I mean is that you should"—the telephone jangled, and he reached out for it—"see Janice today. Tell her you *came* to see her. . . ."

Matt watched him answer the phone, then got up and walked over to the *Young Spectator* lying on the floor. He gave it an impatient little kick, but a moment later stooped to pick it up, scowling at it. "What the hell kind of institution is this?" he muttered. "First you turn kids away from their parents, then you"—he looked at Grant as he heard him hang up—"investigate like the FBI— What's the matter with *you?*"

"Esther Cornthwaite is dead," Grant said tonelessly, still holding the telephone in his hands.

"Cornthwaite?" Matt frowned and shrugged. "Don't know her."

"Chairman of the English Department," Grant said automatically. He set the telephone on the desk.

Matt whistled. "The old girl herself! Remember her now—saw her once. Met her at J.W.'s, in fact. Looked like she owned the whole show. Hmn. . . ." His eyes narrowed speculatively. "What does this make you? Next in line, aren't you?"

Grant merely looked at him. "What I meant," he said then, as if groping for lost words, "is that you ought to drive Janice back home for Thanksgiving. Let her miss today's classes . . . do her good."

"Wish I could—but I'm heading for St. Louis. You didn't get my point, Paul. This may be just the break you need. You've got to put yourself forward; you've got to—"

"Shut up, Matt," Grant said quietly. He turned his back to Matt and filled his pipe from the tobacco can on his desk. "This news is a shock to me. You see, I rather liked her."

"Sure, sure," Matt said, embarrassed. He waited a proper time.

"But she's dead now and you're alive. So you've got to—"

"You stop in to see Janice for a few minutes today," Grant said roughly.

"Sure." Matt glanced at his watch. "For a few minutes. I'm making St. Louis, you know. . . ." He shook his head, honestly perplexed. "Can't make you out. I can understand your feeling, but feeling won't make your future. If you'd—"

"And at least tell her you'd like her to come home Thanksgiving."

"I'll tell her," Matt said uneasily, "but I'll be in St. Louis and Helen's having a houseful . . . nobody the kid's age. . . . But I'll tell her— I promise." He walked to the door, still seeming dissatisfied, as though he had much more to say. He sighed. "Well, I hope you do right by yourself."

Grant followed him into the hall and watched him down the stairs. Near the bottom, Matt stopped and looked back. "Say, what's the name of that place where Janice stays?"

"Grace Hall," Grant said, and told him how to find it.

After Matt was gone, he stood for a moment in the hall, already sensing the emptiness of the Summit, although he could hear the movements of many people.

Grant looked at the three people he had called together, and told himself once again that it would be more possible for him to fly than to serve as their chairman.

Kim Duncan slouched in his chair, lost in morose meditation. Scott was attentive, but a certain nonchalance in his pose suggested that he was condescendingly present. Marcia sat down in a chair several places away from Scott, although the chairs between were vacant. Beyond a minimum of greeting, they had not spoken. Grant wondered if they assumed indifference for the sake of appearance. . . .

He stopped the thought. That kind of personal thinking would always be getting in his way if he were chairman. He knew these people too well, and they knew him too well. . . .

"How?" Kim cried, startling them. "That's what I want to know!"

Grant guessed what he wanted to know. "Of a heart attack. It happened very suddenly this morning."

This news made no effect upon Marcia and Scott, for they had come already armed with it. Kim, however, gathered it in almost greedily and went back to his brooding.

"I called this meeting," Grant said, "to tell you that I have been asked to assume the chairmanship until a permanent arrangement has been made." He paused as he saw Scott look up with new alertness. "I'm sure," he went on, "that you will agree with me that Esther Cornthwaite's place can never be wholly filled. However, we must make a move to find someone at least to take over the courses that are now left without a teacher. With your permission, I should like to invite Dr. Etta Wilson."

Scott shrugged. "Why not? Her specialty fits in perfectly."

"Who is Dr. Etta Wilson?" asked Marcia. "Am I supposed to know her?"

Grant explained who she was, adding, "As Dr. Scott said, her work in philology makes her particularly desirable now. Furthermore, she is a research assistant and not teaching at the present time, so that she could come on short notice—if, of course, she's still interested in John Willard now that Esther Cornthwaite is not here. In any event, I shall—"

"By the way," Scott broke in, "do you think we'll have any say about the new chairman? I for one don't want just *anyone* brought in from the outside!"

"Why should anyone be brought in from the outside?" Marcia asked.

Reluctantly Grant said, "Perhaps I should tell you that I have been asked to continue as permanent chairman."

"And why," Scott said crisply, "did you not tell us that in the first place?"

Grant smiled. "I haven't yet made my decision, and therefore did not consider it pertinent information."

Scott looked dissatisfied. "What about office space? Who gets Cornthwaite's office?"

Grant noted the suspicion in his face and felt weary. "I believe there's no real need to settle that today," he said, standing.

"Good God, no!" Kim leaped to his feet. "Why, she's hardly *dead!*" Suddenly he seemed embarrassed, as if it had occurred to him that never before had he spoken out with such violence at an English meeting. But he drew himself up and declaimed effectively, if irrelevantly: "You cannot institutionalize Death!" Then he departed.

When they had gone, Grant felt as dissatisfied and unsettled as he had when he had walked into the room. In his mind there no longer existed an English Department, but four very distinct individuals; and in his present mood, it seemed more credible that they be widely separated than bound together in membership.

He strolled down the hall, observing that Scott was in his office talking with Alice Mueller. Marcia, then, had gone on alone.

On the outer steps, he stopped to light his pipe, postponing his return to the Summit. There was no doubt in his mind that Esther had wished him to move into the chairmanship. Those mysterious conferences with her and letters from her were now becoming clearer. So she had known.

Also, he admitted with due modesty, there was little doubt that he could take over the position with less trouble to the College and more immediate efficiency than anyone else.

Put that way, it seemed almost his duty to accept. Yet he still had a strong disinclination for it. In fairness to Melville, he needed less, not more, responsibility.

With distaste he thought of Matt and his opinion. That too, he admitted, strengthened his desire to withdraw. He resented being shoved into a situation in which it would seem that he had accepted Matt's values. . . .

Halfheartedly he waved to Kim Duncan, who was retracing his steps to Main Hall. Seeing him made him think again of the people. Marcia and Scott. And with the thought of them, he had an uncharacteristically violent impulse to resign from John Willard and go to—well, say, the University of Tibet. But his voice was matter-of-fact as he greeted Kim, who had evidently come back purposely to talk to him.

"I wanted you to know how I felt," Kim was saying. "It may save the Department. In fact, it may save the College!"

Grant was puzzled. "Do you mean the coming Cadets—or is it something I haven't heard about?"

"Your becoming chairman," Kim explained impatiently.

"Wait a minute! I haven't—"

"I'd like working under you. Cornthwaite is—was a—marvelous woman, but I didn't always feel like *talking* to her. Know what I mean?"

Grant nodded soberly. "Yes, but I—"

"I almost wish I were staying around here," Kim said casually, but watched closely to see what effect he had produced.

"But I—" Grant took a second look at Kim's intent face. "Well, never mind that. What do you mean—you *wish* you were staying?"

Kim shrugged elaborately. "I'm leaving. I'm resigning."

"Have you written a letter of resignation?"

"Not exactly. I wanted you to be the first to know. Now that you're chairman, it's only fair that you be—"

"Yes, yes," Grant broke in, "but *why* are you leaving?"

Kim took time out to light a cigarette, and Grant saw that his hands were not quite steady. "This place smothers me. I'm not a teacher. I don't know how I've stuck it out this long."

Grant sensed that the words were mechanical. He said simply, "We need you, Duncan—especially now that the Department is short-staffed and the Cadets are coming."

Kim gave him a disbelieving look and laughed harshly. "You don't need me—you don't know how much you don't need me." He dropped the cigarette and stepped on it. "There's something I ought to tell you." He stared across the Heart to Science Hall. His face was deeply flushed.

Grant moved uneasily. "Sure you want to tell me?"

226

Kim ignored this, and said quickly, "The Army rejected me as psychologically unfit."

Grant was silent for a moment. "I appreciate your telling me, Duncan—but we still need you." Kim stayed motionless. Grant went on, "That means, you know, only that they predict you'd break down under military discipline, and—well, that doesn't necessarily indicate any lack or weakness. After all, our society has hardly prepared men for army life."

Kim raised his hands as if in appeal. "But I feel. . . ." He could not find the right words, and he let his hands drop to his sides.

"As for now," Grant said, "what are your plans?"

Kim shook his head. "Haven't any."

"Then why not stay on? That way you'd give yourself time to think and you'd also be helping the Department."

Kim turned to look at him, quick hope in his face. "To tell the truth, I'd rather not change addresses right now. I'm waiting for a letter."

"Oh, yes," Grant said gravely, as if fully enlightened. "Walking back to the Summit?"

As they walked along the Heart, Kim said with his old defiance, "I'll explain to you what I most detest about teaching. Grades! I refuse to think of individuals penned in a small area of achievement. I refuse to grade on the curve. The curve! That insidious deity set up to mechanize the vital impulses of life, that. . . ."

When Kim went on to MacMillan Hall, Grant watched after him, sad, amused, weary. He sighed and started up the Summit steps. The door opened and Marcia came out. He stopped where he was and she came down to him.

"I hope," she said seriously, "that you will accept the chairmanship."

He smiled. "It's a relief to talk with someone who isn't convinced that I hadn't accepted it even before today."

She nodded. "I rather thought you'd be feeling this way."

"What way?"

"You're afraid of the chairmanship," she said slowly, "because it was made possible by Professor Cornthwaite's death."

He gave her a quick, surprised look. She had come nearer to understanding his feeling than anyone else. . . . He had an unfamiliar urge to talk about Matt. If she could know what Matt had said, she would realize even more—

"It isn't only a personal matter," she was saying. "You have to consider the good of the Department. You once told me that one would have to look far and wide before finding a better administrator than Esther Cornthwaite. Well, that's the way I feel about you. You have the ability to—" She broke off with an embarrassed laugh. "But I'm still new here and shouldn't be talking this way."

"Nevertheless," he said, "I thank you for doing so." He thought that they had never been so close, and he was silent, enjoying the mere awareness of it. Then he began to fear her walking away. "Would you have dinner with me?" he asked suddenly.

"I'm sorry," she said, already on a lower step, "but I have another engagement." On the walk she looked back. "I really am sorry." Then she hurried away.

He wondered if her haste meant she thought his invitation a breach of good taste on the day of Esther's death. If so, he was sorry, for that would mean she had not shared his feeling of togetherness and understanding.

In the Summit he entered Esther's office without further delay. Less than a week ago she had told him that in the bottom drawer of file C was a letter for him (under G), which he was to read promptly if for any reason she were suddenly called away.

The room was neat, the desk cleared, the letter in the designated folder. He drew it out and read it, standing by the shuttered window.

> *"Dear Professor Grant:*
>
> *You have, of course, accepted the chairmanship. I wish to congratulate you and also to tender my apology for not finding it convenient to endorse your request for a leave of absence. I am sure that you now understand the circumstance that prompted my decision. I trust that after this untimely interruption, you will arrange for the leave, which you richly deserve.*
>
> *"I am sorry to miss the privilege of reading your work on Herman Melville.*
>
> *Sincerely yours,*
E. Cornthwaite
>
> *"Postscript: I assume that you will occupy my office, for it is more befitting the dignity of the position than yours on the second floor. Feel free to make any change you desire; but I should appreciate your taking vigilant stand against any proposed painting of the woodwork.*
>
> *E.C."*

Slowly he folded the letter and slipped it into his pocket. In one small detail he'd have to disappoint her. He did not intend to invade her office. Let it be given to a stranger who would not have memories or—

He was startled to hear the precise tap on the door. Was there someone who still did not know about Esther, or was it already assumed that he had taken over the office? "Yes?" he called and opened the door to look into the direct gaze of Registrar Dexter, whose hand clutched several white grade sheets in a purposeful way that fore-

228

boded trouble. "I thought I might find you here," Dexter said after only a slight hesitation, "for I knew that you would carry on during Professor Cornthwaite's"—he cleared his throat—"absence."

When Grant merely nodded, Dexter looked relieved and went briskly into his problem. "I'm making a study of grade distribution. In tabulating certain statistics, I discovered that Mr. Duncan gave in one class"—he held up one of the grade sheets—"twenty *A's* and one *F*. Now, although I am aware that there are a few—a very few— legitimate reasons why grades cannot *always* follow the Curve, I do consider Mr. Duncan's distribution—a bit odd." His voice had quivered in payment for the polite understatement. "I wonder if we might discuss this matter further."

"Certainly." Grant touched his arm consolingly. "But let's do it in my office."

As they went up the stairs, he was suddenly remembering the first of the series of strange conferences with Esther, when she had complacently implied that all administrators said no before they became administrators, and he grinned. Had she ever been wrong?

Dexter caught the grin and said in a frosted tone, "This is not an amusing situation, Professor Grant."

"I was thinking," Grant said quickly, "of Mr. Duncan's philosophy of grading. I'm not sure that we can convince him of the proper respect due the Curve. You see, he believes . . ."

When she reached the Heights, Marcia half ran the rest of the way to the Murdocks'. She was later than she had intended. She was surprised and a little ashamed that even Esther Cornthwaite's death had not lessened her fear that she would not be ready when J.W. called.

Not even Mrs. Murdock was at home. Considering the time of day, this was strange, but Marcia was too hurried to give it a second thought. She not only had to get herself ready, but pack a small bag, for she was to stay with the MacMillans over Thanksgiving.

There was a letter from Virginia. She opened it and spread it out on the dresser, reading it in snatches as she filled the overnight bag. Virginia was sorry she could not be home for Thanksgiving, but she was glad that Marcia had such lovely friends as the MacMillans. Martin had assured her that they were very pleasant people indeed. And of course Marcia would be home for Christmas. . . .

And of course I *won't* be home for Christmas! Marcia thought triumphantly. Hastily she refolded the letter into its envelope and threw it upon the desk. It was already arranged that she would spend the whole of the Christmas vacation with the MacMillans.

She was ready and waiting. She lighted a cigarette and listened tensely for the sound of the car, although she knew that she would hear it the instant of the arrival, no matter what she was doing or thinking.

How many times had she gone through this! The feverish dressing —and then the waiting. Sometimes he would come, sometimes he wouldn't. That was all right; that was understood between them. He seldom had an evening free from work, and never could he plan far ahead. When he couldn't come, he would telephone. She would go down to answer when she heard Mrs. Murdock's shout. She would talk to him brightly, and Mrs. Murdock would hover by, looking sympathetic. . . .

She could never risk not dressing for she could never be sure that he wasn't coming. He was very critical of the way she looked.

Occasionally, when with him, she would feel sudden anger over his complacency. Didn't he know about *her* work? Didn't he know that when he left her, she had to prepare for the next day of teaching? Couldn't he understand that some evenings were better for her than others? Apparently not. He merely reproved her gently when she seemed tired.

But the moment he left her, the anger went away, and there was again the relentless yearning to see him. And on the nights he didn't come, she was too uneasy to work. . . .

She glanced at the clock. Tonight was different, of course. The plan was definite. Sam was to drive up for her. She would be with Grace, even if J.W. should be detained. *Jack,* she told herself sternly, not *J.W.* Tonight there would be no telephone call.

The telephone rang. She crushed out her cigarette and waited, and then remembered that there was no one else in the house. Probably it was for the Murdocks. Yet . . .

She hurried downstairs to answer it.

"Marcia?" J.W.'s voice was crisply matter-of-fact, the way it always was when he called to explain why he couldn't see her. "You have of course heard the tragic news by now."

"Why, no," she began, and then remembered. "I mean, yes. I guess I still haven't accepted it as a reality." For the first time that day, it came to her that the death of Esther Cornthwaite would be a matter of personal concern to the MacMillans.

He was explaining how Esther was to be buried in Albuquerque. "Albuquerque?" she broke in. "The niece who makes handkerchiefs?" She shivered slightly. "But she doesn't know Esther—not really!"

"Oh, yes," he said, not understanding. "She and her family are the nearest kin. Mother is going with—well, she's leaving tonight—insists that Esther mustn't go down there among strangers. That's nonsense, of course, but"—he became faintly apologetic—"Mother is quite broken up over it, you see."

"I do see," Marcia said, "and I'm glad that she's going. "

"It may be a convenience, after all, for she is also the executrix of Esther's will. I can't take time enough to go with Grace, but I must help her get off tonight."

"Of course. Can't I be of some help to her?"

"No, thank you. Everything is quite arranged. Marcia, I thought that as long as our original plan was upset, I'd use these few days to go to Washington—"

"But tomorrow, Thanksgiving . . ." She gripped the telephone hard. "I mean, travel will be extremely difficult."

"I'm flying. It's quite—"

"I know," she said coldly, "it's quite arranged."

"But, Marcia! You see, with Grace gone, we couldn't—"

"Oh, you're right, of course. With Grace gone, we couldn't possibly be together, for your powerful feeling for me might lead to rape and who knows what other scandalous—"

"Marcia!" He was shocked. "I didn't expect you to be so callous over Esther's death."

"Callous! You would think of it that way! Maybe I have some thoughts about Esther Cornthwaite that you don't know anything about. She was never real to me. I wanted her to be, but she wouldn't allow it. . . ." She stopped, knowing that it was futile to explain to him. "I'm sorry," she said at last. "Are you sure that I can't be of help to your mother?"

"Of course you're sorry," he said, relieved. "And there's nothing whatever for you to do or worry about."

"Good-by, then," she said quietly.

He hesitated. "You still love me, Marcia?"

She laughed shortly. "I'm afraid so."

The answer did not please him, and he abruptly left the subject. "I'll call you the minute I'm back."

"Yes. Good-by." Swiftly she replaced the receiver before she could hear the little click that would tell her he had hung up. She had come to dread that click, just as she dreaded seeing him walk away from her.

Aimlessly she wandered into the living room and sat down, wishing that the Murdocks would come home. She did not want to be alone with her thoughts. As she sat there, she began to have the sense of someone else's presence in the house. Perhaps Stephanie had slipped in while she was talking on the telephone. . . .

She went upstairs to look, but Stephanie was not in her room. When she called out, there was no answer of any kind. Obviously, no one had come in. But the feeling that she was not alone persisted. Nerves, she told herself. She decided to be active.

Downstairs again, she resolutely put in a long-distance call. As she waited for the return ring, she thought she heard faint movements from the basement, but when she went to listen at the kitchen door that led to the basement steps, she heard nothing more. Probably, she told herself, the sound had been made by a loose piece of coal sliding down the huge coal pile that filled the bin. No doubt that had also given her the sense of someone else's presence in the house.

She hurried back to the ringing telephone. "Dr. Ware?" she asked eagerly, and the emphatically precise answering voice was comforting. "I'm so glad to hear your voice," she said involuntarily. "I'm alone in the house, and—" She stopped herself, remembering that Alice Ware would neither understand nor care about those details. "Something has happened, Dr. Ware, and I thought you might like to know about it before you saw it in the papers. Esther Cornthwaite died today."

There was such a long silence that Marcia thought they must have been disconnected. "Dr. Ware! Operator!"

"I'm here, Marcia," Dr. Ware said at last.

Marcia felt suddenly that the call had been a blunder. "I'm sorry. I'm afraid that I shouldn't have—"

"Oh, I'm glad to know, Marcia. Thank you for telling me."

This conventional politeness was as disturbing as the flat voice. "It was very sudden and painless," Marcia said rapidly. "Clarice—the girl who cleans for her, you know—found—well, it was about ten o'clock this morning. That was—"

"Now I understand this summer," Dr. Ware said slowly.

"This summer?" Marcia was puzzled. "I tried to see you, but you were away all—"

"That's all right, Marcia," Dr. Ware said abruptly. Her voice was normal again. "I want to tell you something, Marcia. Esther left you her papers—things she didn't get around to publishing—well, you'll see them for yourself. She asked me—"

"You must be mistaken," Marcia interrupted. "Esther Cornthwaite never gave me a second thought!"

Alice Ware said sharply. "Who are you to know what Esther is thinking?" Then she laughed grimly. "Hell! It's all in the past tense now, isn't it? Didn't mean to be short with you, Marcia, but it so happens that she *did* leave these papers to you, and she asked me to tell you that they were a token."

"A token?" Marcia was still unbelieving. "A token of what?"

"Of her thinking of you!" Dr. Ware told her decisively. "What is John Willard doing about it? Classes were dismissed, I hope?"

"It was all so sudden," Marcia explained, feeling vaguely apologetic. "And then tomorrow being Thanksgiving, there will naturally be no classes until Monday."

"I see," Alice Ware said contemptuously. "Well, on Monday I shall dismiss at least my own classes." There was another short humming silence, and then she said suddenly, "Goodnight. Come to see me whenever you can, Marcia. It's a lot to lose—well, never mind that, but come."

Marcia stayed by the telephone, thinking of Alice Ware's strange reaction and wondering about the papers that Esther had left her. Again she became aware of the sound from the basement, and this time it could not be mistaken for a sliding piece of coal. For a moment she was frightened, and then it came to her with clarity that Stephanie was downstairs hiding and that the Murdocks were out looking for her.

She switched on the lights and went quietly downstairs. The big, white-washed laundry room was too light and open for hiding purposes. She crossed it quickly to peer in the small, shelf-lined room that stored the products of Mrs. Murdock's energetic canning. Stephanie was here, sitting on an old camp chair. She stared at Marcia for a minute and then said guiltily, "Hullo." Her head lolled back against the canvas chair covering.

Marcia was alarmed. The girl looked ill. "What on earth are you doing down here, Stephanie!"

"Hiding," Stephanie told her matter-of-factly.

"And I suppose that your poor aunt and uncle are out in the cold looking for you all over Riverville!"

"S'pose so."

"Well, you come right upstairs with me."

Stephanie came slowly. In the bright kitchen, Marcia faced her. "Aren't you ever going to grow up? Why do you do these silly things, Stephanie!"

Stephanie tried to shrug. "Maybe I'm dying."

Marcia looked more closely at the girl's pale face. "What do you mean?"

Stephanie began to answer, but stopped short to grimace as if with sudden pain, and the next moment, she was bent double. Marcia backed her into a chair. "Stephanie!" she cried, standing over her. "You didn't do anything really foolish, did you? You didn't *take* anything that you shouldn't have, did you? Stephanie, you must tell me the truth!"

The pain had left Stephanie limp. She held up her head with effort.

Marcia dropped to her knees and clasped her hands around the girl's clammy ones. "You must tell me, Stephanie!"

Stephanie stared down at Marcia's hands. "I guess I did," she said, and sighed peacefully.

Marcia rushed to the telephone and dialed the operator. "The Willard Hospital!" she shouted. "Quickly!"

Stephanie watched, wide-eyed. Suddenly she was at Marcia's side. "Don't call anyone!" she gasped. "I was just fooling."

Marcia leaned weakly against the telephone stand. Dimly she realized that she had a connection. "Never mind," she said, "she was just fooling." She hung up and confronted Stephanie. "That wasn't very funny, you know."

"I know," Stephanie whispered, sobbing now.

Marcia was still too frightened to feel real anger. "But something seems to be wrong with you. What is it, Stephanie?"

"Just the cramps."

"Well, I guess I can cope with them," Marcia said with relief. She led Stephanie into the living room and forced her down upon the couch.

Stephanie looked terrified and held herself up on her elbows. "I'd better go up to bed," she said. "Aunt Madge says that davenports aren't to sleep on."

"Lie down!" Marcia said sternly. Stephanie obeyed meekly. "If it will ease your conscience, you needn't go to sleep. By the way, is this when you always run away—once a month?"

Stephanie's mouth tightened, and she stared at Marcia with fearful eyes. Marcia understood the look and had a sudden wish that she knew how to tell her that she meant only to help her, not rob her of her secrets.

The thought surprised her. It was so different from her earlier thoughts of Stephanie. Before, she had been merely exasperated. Now, she—well, now somehow it was different.

Stephanie allowed herself to be covered with a comforter and even accepted a hot-water bottle. Sipping the warm milk that Marcia had fixed for her, she looked almost happy.

Marcia sat down on the edge of the couch. "What feeling is it that makes you want to run away?"

Stephanie said nothing, and the happy look faded from her face. Marcia felt a rush of the old impatience. Why couldn't the girl talk? Why wasn't Dr. Day at hand? She thought of what had been said about Carol Leeds. . . . "Do you feel that you live in a hostile world, Stephanie?"

The question caught no spark. Baffled, Marcia stood up and looked down upon the girl's unrevealing face. Suddenly she was thinking: she is not Carol Leeds . . . not anyone else in the world but Stephanie Kail. She remembered then the theme she had found. *When I feel the dirt in my hands, and even under my fingernails, I feel happy, and then I know peace.*

She sat down again. "Why aren't you training yourself for some kind of work in—in orchards?"

Stephanie stayed speechless, but life had come into her face.

"I don't know much about it," Marcia went on, "but you could talk it over with your uncle. Surely he knows about the vocational possibilities. I think you'd have to transfer to another college to get the proper courses. You wouldn't mind that, would you? You don't particularly like John Willard, do you?"

"I hate it!" Stephanie said fiercely.

Marcia felt triumphant. "You should transfer next semester—in February. You may lose a few credits, but—"

"Oh, I couldn't," Stephanie said and sank back against the pillows.

234

"If I left, Uncle Justin wouldn't leave the money to John Willard, and then Aunt Madge would be furious. I couldn't!"

"Let that work itself out," Marcia said with more confidence than she felt. "Those are problems outside of you, Stephanie. Let's think of you. Wouldn't you be happier away from here?"

"Yes, *yes!*" Stephanie cried. Then she looked guilty and gave Marcia a sudden, suspicious glance. But when Marcia remained silent, she said: "I love them. I love Uncle Justin. You should see him in the orchards. . . . He knows so much. When I was little, he let me go with him, and he talked. Now he doesn't want me . . . says I only get in the way." She looked again to see how Marcia was taking it. She went on with low, swift words, and her voice was not childish. "And I love Aunt Madge—even all her funny little ways of keeping house that make it so awful for Uncle Justin. But . . ."

"But?"

"But *they* don't love me!"

"What makes you so sure of that?"

"Well," Stephanie said heavily, "you don't see them adopting me, do you? Oh, they've talked about it for years, but they've never done anything about it." She talked now with effort, and Marcia knew that it was the first time she had said these things aloud. "They keep thinking how much better their own child would have been, if they could have had one. Uncle Justin wanted a boy, and Aunt Madge—well, she would have been satisfied with a girl, but not one like me." She seemed suddenly bored with her young-old wisdom. "They don't love me," she repeated, sullen again. "Nobody does."

"I do," Marcia said because it seemed necessary. With surprise she saw how easily she had reached out to touch Stephanie's hand. There had been a time, she remembered, when she did not want to touch Stephanie.

"Not the way you do Janice Grant," Stephanie said, avoiding her eyes. "She's always hanging around your office."

"But, Stephanie, *you* never come to visit me in my office." Stephanie said nothing to this, and Marcia went quickly on, "And your aunt and uncle love you too. Why do you think they are so upset when you disappear? It's very hard on them, you know."

Stephanie's eyes narrowed. "They won't look for me one of these times—you just wait and see!"

"So that's why you do it," Marcia said softly.

"I didn't say so!"

"Stephanie, think how wonderful it would be for you in another college. Then you wouldn't have to run away to be brought home. You'd simply come home for vacations, and they'd be glad to see you. Besides, you'd be working toward something you really wanted."

Stephanie shook her head from side to side. "They wouldn't allow

235

it." But there was a glow of interest in her face. "You don't think they'd allow it, do you?" she asked eagerly. "You don't suppose—" She stopped short, hearing the footsteps on the porch.

Marcia had to force her back against the pillows. "Lie still and look pale again!" she instructed. "You see, I found her," she said brightly to Mr. and Mrs. Murdock as they stood speechless in the doorway.

Justin Murdock grunted and banged the door shut. He took off his hat and hit it against his knee to clear it of the new-fallen snow.

"Justin, you should have done that outside," Mrs. Murdock said absently. She was staring at Marcia. Then her gaze shifted to Stephanie.

"Where?" Mr. Murdock demanded.

Marcia smiled. "She was quite safe, I assure you. I merely—"

Mrs. Murdock sighed tiredly. "I'm so glad," she said simply. "We had almost given up this time, hadn't we, Justin?"

Justin took a few steps forward. "Where?"

"I do hope," Mrs. Murdock said fearfully to Marcia, "that this hasn't spoiled your evening! I thought that you were going—"

"Oh, my plans were changed already," Marcia said, and it came to her then that for the first time in months she had spent a half hour without a thought of J.W.

Mr. Murdock sat down solidly and placed his hands on his widespread knees. "*Where?*"

This time they both waited for an answer, and Marcia said casually, "She was in the basement—quite snug and—"

"Basement!" Justin laughed unpleasantly and looked up at his wife. "While we were tramping around!" He struck his knee. "This is the *last* time, absolutely the *last*—"

"I think that it is," Marcia said quietly, standing. They watched her, as if expecting magic. "Stephanie isn't feeling well," she told Mrs. Murdock meaningfully, "and should be put to bed and kept warm." She smiled down at Stephanie. "Goodnight—and don't forget about next semester!"

Mrs. Murdock followed Marcia to the stairs. She still wore her fur coat, and a print scarf dangled around her neck in an unintended rakish manner. She looked worried and vague, as if unable to fit together the pieces of the puzzle that she had found in her own living room. "I want to thank you—for . . ." The words trailed, and she made no attempt to finish the sentence.

"That's all right," Marcia said quickly.

Mrs. Murdock sighed conclusively, and then went on to a brighter prospect. "If your plans have really changed, why not take Thanksgiving dinner with us? There will be just the three of us and you, and it will be very cozy!"

This is what I get for probing around! Marcia thought ironically. But she was too weary to think of a reasonable excuse. "I should like that very much," she said. "It's very kind of you."

"Oh, not at all," Mrs. Murdock responded generously. Already there was an anticipatory gleam in her eyes. "While we were out"—she lowered her voice to a respectable whisper—"we heard about Miss Cornthwaite. It's too terrible, isn't it! Well, I've been worrying about poor Clarice, knowing how lonely she would be tomorrow without Miss Cornthwaite to wait on. So when Justin and I parted for a few minutes, I dropped in and asked her to come serve our dinner tomorrow!"

Marcia shuddered inwardly. "Is she coming?"

"Of course, I found her very upset—crying as if her heart would break, and all alone, just as I expected—so she didn't really say yes or no. But I'm sure she'll be here when the time comes. Won't it be lovely! Maybe she can tell us—I mean, it's silly, I know, but I just can't imagine Miss Cornthwaite's passing away so suddenly. She seemed such a healthy, vigorous woman. But I'm sure—"

"Are you suggesting," Marcia said coldly, "that she may have been poisoned?"

Mrs. Murdock fingered the scarf. "I know that nothing mysterious ever happens in Riverville, but I can't help wondering." She eyed Marcia hopefully. "You were quite close to her. Did she have enemies?"

"She had only a devoted following. And as for poisoning, Mrs. Murdock, perhaps you came very near to one in your own home tonight!"

Mrs. Murdock went white. "What do you mean?"

"I mean," Marcia said more gently, "that you'd be wise to give Stephanie half as much consideration as you gave to Clarice tonight."

"But there's *nothing* I wouldn't do for Stephanie!" Mrs. Murdock gasped.

"I'm sure of that," Marcia said. "And I'm sorry that I said anything. It really isn't my business at all! Goodnight, and I thank you again for the dinner invitation."

Mrs. Murdock was still staring up at her wide-eyed when she turned the landing.

In her room, her mind went back to Stephanie, and she noted again how the thought of Stephanie no longer filled her with impatience. She felt eager to do something constructive. Next week she'd investigate Stephanie's record at school and talk about her to Deans Holcomb and Haskins and perhaps even Dr. Day. . . .

Learn to give without exhausting yourself. Dr. Day had said that. It was what she was finally doing with Stephanie. Perhaps she did even have a kind of love for her, as she had told her. . . . What had happened to her—this Marcia Anderson, who once had felt the need to be miserly with her feelings?

She shrugged. Not understanding, she determined to be casual about the mystery. What if in the morning when she saw Stephanie, she should feel only the old annoyance?

Before they were half through the long meal, even Mrs. Murdock was ready to admit that her idea to have Clarice had not been a happy inspiration. The girl was red-eyed and wordless, and she served them with an automatic efficiency that indicated she could have done as well in her sleep. Whenever she disappeared into the kitchen, they could hear a soft, sniffling sound that impelled them all to talk loudly, although no one had anything in particular to say.

Mrs. Murdock made a valiant struggle to maintain sprightly table talk, but she was obviously harassed. As last she sighed, as if giving in to some unworthy impulse, and asked outright, "Justin, do we have any poison around the house?"

Mr. Murdock looked up. He was perhaps the least troubled one at the table, for he was a man to find solace in good food. The interruption annoyed him. "What a durnfool question! Pass the bread, Stephanie."

Stephanie surveyed the table and shook her head. "I can't find it, Uncle Justin."

"Of *course* it's not on the table!" Mrs. Murdock picked up the little silver-handled bell at her plate and tinkled it.

Justin Murdock moaned. "Forget it!"

But Clarice came promptly.

"Another roll for Mr. Murdock," Mrs. Murdock directed. "Perhaps you had better made it two or even three," she added as Clarice picked up his bread-and-butter plate.

"Now what's this about poison?" Justin asked.

Mrs. Murdock signaled a warning, and conversation was suspended while Clarice set down the replenished bread-and-butter plate.

"I was just wondering about poison," Mrs. Murdock said when the kitchen door had swung back into place. "You see, I found a dead bird in the yard the other day," she went on quickly, avoiding Marcia's eyes, "and it had all the symptoms of having been poisoned. And I thought that if we did have anything of that nature, we ought to throw it—"

"What do you know about dead birds—or poison for that matter!" Mr. Murdock returned to his food, but without his original relish. The question had disturbed him. Finally he put down his fork and said grudgingly, "Well, there's lye and some insecticide in the garage."

"Oh, Justin! How dangerous!"

Stephanie stared at her aunt, and comprehension came slowly into her face. "But, Aunt Madge, I didn't *really* take any—" She stopped abruptly as Marcia went into a coughing fit.

"It's all right," Marcia said hastily when Mr. Murdock arose uncertainly to his feet. "It was just a bone."

He sat down again. "Turkey bone?" His voice was incredulous, and he stared down at the huge drumstick on his own plate. "Well, you must have some throat, because this is a *big* bird that we're eating!"

Marcia had to laugh at this, and seeing that she had fully recovered, they all laughed. Justin Murdock looked pleased to have made them laugh. "And it's *good* turkey too," he said to his wife. "Cooked just right."

"Thank you, Justin," she murmured gratefully. She sensed that the atmosphere had changed for the better, and seemed content to allow the topic of poison to fall by the wayside.

Even Stephanie perked up. "Uncle Justin," she said with such determination that everyone started, "I should like to transfer to another college. Right away!"

Marcia winced. Didn't Stephanie *know* that this wasn't the time!

"You stay put," Mr. Murdock said mildly, his good-humored tolerance lingering.

But Mrs. Murdock was less confident. She glanced at Marcia, hoping for an answer, but Marcia was studying an olive. "Justin, dear," Mrs. Murdock began tentatively, "if Stephanie really wants to go to another college, perhaps . . . I mean . . ."

This aroused him. "I said she stays put. It's hard enough to keep track of her right here in town." He glowered as he recalled his long, cold search the night before.

"John Willard is really a lovely school, isn't it, Stephanie?" Mrs. Murdock pleaded.

"I hate it," Stephanie said flatly.

"Well, you stay in it," Justin Murdock said conclusively, "or I'm not a-going to leave the money to it!"

Mrs. Murdock flushed and rang for Clarice. "Please eat your own dinner now, Clarice," she told the girl kindly. "We'll not need you until dessert."

Marcia studied Clarice curiously. The girl's grief was genuine, she decided. What strange alchemy had produced it? She could understand why Clarice would please Esther Cornthwaite. She was self-effacing, unobtrusive, and a willing worker. If it weren't for her sniffling today, she would be so much a part of the general background, they wouldn't even be aware of her presence. Yes, that was enough to please Esther Cornthwaite, Marcia thought with some irony.

But what had there been about Esther to affect Clarice so deeply? Marcia gave it up. Esther, it would seem, had affected the whole world in a most surprising way.

Clarice went back to the kitchen, and the sniffling sound began again. "Good Lord!" said Justin, listening.

"Now, Justin," Mrs. Murdock soothed.

Marcia smiled across the table at Stephanie, who had retreated into gloom again. She did not return the smile, but her face lightened.

She looks less lonely today, Marcia thought. She herself was not so unhappy as she had expected to be. The dinner was a dismal substitute for what she had thought the day would bring, but her feeling for Stephanie was the same as it had been the night before. It brought her a strange sense of freedom, of—

"Madge," Justin Murdock said suddenly, "you ask that girl to come in here and eat with us!"

Mrs. Murdock looked relieved, as if she had been thinking the same thing. But she glanced at Marcia and said doubtfully, "I don't know if it—"

"I think it would be lovely," Marcia said.

Mrs. Murdock forgot about the little bell and went eagerly after Clarice. The girl came back with her, alarmed but willing to oblige. Once seated, she ate quite steadily, and even contributed a monosyllable when Mrs. Murdock suddenly held forth in praise of the great tradition of Thanksgiving Dinner.

A little later, Mrs. Murdock arose to serve the mince pie.

Chapter Three

J.W. STOOD in the middle of the ice-encrusted wheel tracks, shadowed his eyes with his hand, and looked across the gleaming snow. "I think we had better turn back, Marcia."

"But we've been walking for only an hour!" Marcia slid down the small bank at the side of the road to explore the depth of the snow. "Look! It's up to my knees!"

"Those clouds," he worried, "indicate heavy snow."

She glanced carelessly at the clouds and then back to him, amused. All morning Grace and she had rummaged through the big house to find the right pieces of clothing to keep him warm on a long winter's walk. The bottoms of his trousers were stuffed into high galoshes, and he wore a huge sheepskin jacket. The folds of a green woolen scarf almost met the fur ear muffs of his plaid cap. She had never before seen him in such miscellaneous array.

Suddenly she giggled and scooped up snow with both hands. She packed it into a firm, round ball and took aim. He didn't see her, and jumped when the snowball hit him in the small of his back.

"Now, why did you do that?" he asked in an injured tone. He pulled off a glove and tried to reach the spot with his hand.

She ran up to him and brushed the snow off his thick jacket. "I couldn't resist it. You looked so concerned and so—so unlike *you*." She turned him around, surveyed him from head to foot, and laughed outright.

He smiled patiently. "Well, what about turning back?"

"Oh, no! At least let's make the top of that next hill." She pulled at his hand, and they walked on, although he was still reluctant. The snow under the mid-afternoon sun had a gold-silver sheen, and that in shadow was faint purple. "Sometimes," she said, "this country seems too tame and pretty, but today I love it. I *love* it today!"

"I can believe that," he said, watching her. "You seem to be in love with everything today. I have never seen you so gay. Any special reason?"

"Yes," she said after a moment's silence. "I'm happy because I *know* that I'm going to see you tonight and tomorrow and the next day and the next. Now, what do you think of that!"

He looked pleased and leaned over to kiss her cold nose. "I'm flattered, naturally."

"You don't understand!" she said impatiently. "Do you know that I feel physically ill every time you walk away from me?"

"That's absurd, of course."

"That's what I mean," she said eagerly. "It's not normal. What do you make of it?"

He put his arm around her as they walked. "I don't intend to make anything of it," he laughed. "Just so you don't feel physically ill when we're together!"

She was thoughtful. "Sometimes I wonder. . . ."

"Good Lord, Marcia! What do you mean!"

"Darling, you can't be serious with those ear muffs!"

He was exasperated. "You're as changeable as a—a pixy. It's that pointed cap you're wearing, I've decided. Where on earth did you get that skiing outfit?"

She shrugged. "Virginia's Christmas present. In a letter I happened to mention that some of the students went skiing around here—so this arrived. That's Virginia for you."

"From what I've heard, Virginia is very responsible for your being a spoiled little girl. That's what you seem like to me today, you know. Now, Dr. Anderson would have been very sensible and turned back when I suggested—"

She stamped her foot. "Virginia owes me plenty!"

"That doesn't make sense, but the remark is quite in keeping with your mood." When she said nothing, he glanced at her uneasily. "You're not angry, are you, Marcia? You can take some teasing, can't you?"

"I'm not angry."

"Then why have you become so solemn?"

"I'm thinking."

"Well, what about? You can't make such a leading remark and then simply stay silent."

"I was wondering," she said reluctantly, "why I *did* throw that snowball at you."

He made an impatient gesture. "But that's over and done with!"

"It's queer," she said slowly, "but now that I think back upon it, I know that I had the feeling of having done it before. It was as if I were repeating something. . . ."

"My theory," he said lightly, "is that you are repeating some day out of your childhood."

She was startled. "What makes you say that?"

He stared at her. "You didn't take me seriously!" When he saw that she had, he frowned. "Marcia, you're too serious about little things. It's abnormal to probe for hidden meanings behind trivial acts. You sound like Russ!"

"Russ? Does he talk about feelings this way?"

He laughed shortly. "Not exactly about feelings. He talks about the great, outside forces—all the freedoms, you know."

"The freedoms? Oh. Russ and I ought to get together, for the two kinds of freedom are related, don't you think?"

"What two kinds?"

"The inner and the outer," she said impatiently. "You can't have one without the other, do you think?"

"Truly, I don't know what you're talking about. Now we're at the bottom of your hill, and when we—"

"You never talk about either, do you?" she asked curiously. "The great, outside forces, or the inner ones?"

He smiled tolerantly. "It's a luxury in which I don't indulge."

She was concerned. "But that's bad for you. I mean, you're human and you have those thoughts; so it's bad for you not to give them an outlet."

"I doubt if it matters," he said pleasantly. "Personally, I don't believe that all the talk there is contributes the least bit toward saving the world. Or annihilating it, for that matter."

"But who's talking about the world! I said that it's bad for *you*. It must give you a kind of mental constipation."

"What an odd figure of speech, Marcia."

She laughed. "What a vulgar one, you mean, don't you?"

"I'm not that prim," he said, irritated. "But from you—well, somehow it was a shock."

"Good. I wanted to shock you. I've been wanting to shock you all afternoon. I feel like a little girl who simply has to shock her prissy schoolteacher." Her mood changed suddenly. "I *wish* you didn't make me feel like a child. I hate it!" She stopped and faced him. "I wish that you would kiss me right now—in a very unchildlike way."

"I should like nothing better." He looked briefly in the direction from which they had come, and put his arms around her. "My honesty, however, compels me to warn you that a car is coming." He tightened his hold upon her. "Do you still want to be kissed?"

She broke free of him and stepped to the side of the road. He followed and took her hand, laughing. "I wanted you to make that decision, Marcia, for if I had suggested we wait until the car passed, you'd accuse me of being prim again."

"Maybe I decided that I didn't want you to kiss me, after all," she said shortly. She watched the cautiously approaching car. "This car is the first we've seen on this road. Why should it come along right now?"

"I wonder." He lighted a cigarette and gave her an amused look over the top of his hand as he shielded the flame of the lighter.

"Why, it's Sam!" she cried, waving at the driver. Sam tooted his horn. Suddenly she stopped waving and turned suspiciously to J.W. "You didn't *plan* for him to come after us, by any chance?"

He seemed pleased with himself. "Don't you think it was an excellent idea, Marcia? Now, won't you admit that you're really too tired to walk back?"

She was angry. "The original idea was to walk—both ways. Hello, Sam," she said as he pulled up to them and stopped.

Sam rolled down his window and, in spite of the cold, mopped his forehead with a handkerchief. "Some road! Glad to find you at last. Was beginning to think that you two had made it clear through to Cincy."

"Good work, Sam." J.W. opened the rear door. "Enter, my lady."

"No!" said Marcia stubbornly. "I'm not going to be driven back to the Murdocks' in this outfit! All Riverville knows that I started out for a *walk*."

J.W. stepped into the car and seated himself comfortably. He smiled. "You're going to find that walk back twice as long without my charming company."

She kicked at the snow. Sam looked on curiously. "I admit," she said crossly, "there's not much point to it now." She climbed in and sat down in the opposite corner. J.W. reached out and pulled her over to him. "Well, all right," she said, "but you let me out at the Square. At least I'm going to walk up the Heights!"

"Sam will call for you at seven-thirty," J.W. said when they stopped on the Square, "and from then on you live with the MacMillans until next year."

His words took away the last trace of her petty annoyance, and she waved cheerfully as Sam drove away. She hesitated a moment, and then crossed the street to Herby's, pulling off her cap as she went. If she went straight to the Murdocks', she'd have time to spare, and she didn't want that.

In Herby's there was no empty booth, but Etta Wilson leaned out of one and beckoned to her. "Please join me," she invited, neatly sliding a pencil into her hair over her ear. "You're just the one I've been wanting to see, Dr. Anderson!"

"I've been walking," Marcia explained, feeling apologetic about

243

her costume. She looked curiously at the table, which was covered with papers and white filing cards.

Etta nodded. "I try to manage a brisk walk each day myself. Ours is a sedentary Profession, Dr. Anderson, and we simply must force ourselves to exercise, for nothing else will prevent premature hardening of the arteries. If we—"

"Howdy," said Herby, and almost swiped his damp cloth across the papers. "You don't want that litter cleared up?" he asked incredulously when Etta seized his hand.

She shuddered, and Marcia ordered coffee for them. Etta consulted her wristwatch. "I have been here seventeen minutes, Mr. Herby."

He shrugged. "No charge for the table space, lady. The point is"— he jerked his thumb toward the back rooms in which he lived—"I'm trimmin' a tree for the kid. The kid expects it," he added defiantly, and went off.

Etta looked after him briefly. "An intriguing drawl," she said to Marcia. "Quite a distinctive mouthing of vowels. From what section of the country does he come?"

"I don't know," Marcia told her. "I'm surprised to see you today, Dr. Wilson. I should have expected you to be on your way home."

"Home?" Etta seemed surprised. "But haven't you found the holiday an admirable time for study here? The withdrawal of the students permits uninterrupted concentration. In our Profession, as you know, we cannot afford to waste a single minute. I have already arranged with Mr. Breen to use the Library eight hours a day."

"I didn't realize," Marcia said, "that you found the John Willard Library so useful. It's good of course, but quite general and not adapted to your specialty."

"You don't understand! I am examining the volumes from Esther Cornthwaite's personal collection. They haven't been catalogued as yet, but, of course, under the circumstances, Mr. Breen saw fit to grant me permission to work with them."

"Under what circumstances?" Marcia asked.

"Didn't you know?" Etta's eyes flashed behind her glasses. "I have been asked to edit the memorial edition of the *History and Development!*"

"Edit?" Marcia said with sudden suspicion. "In what way does it need editing?"

"Porfessor Cornthwaite made her work as inclusive as possible, but naturally certain facts have come to light since she revised the first volumes, and these must be added. And the last volume"—Etta shook her head sadly—"the last volume, Dr. Anderson, shows signs of uncharacteristic carelessness."

Marcia lighted a cigarette and said nothing, but she was suddenly angry with the efficient little woman sitting across from her.

244

"Also," Etta went on, "I have been asked to write a biographical sketch in the form of an appendix. Now, I have here"—she indicated the cards on the table—"the actual *facts* of her life. But . . . those facts are sparse. That is why I wanted to see you, Dr. Anderson, for I understand that you have in your possession—"

"If this isn't a committee meeting," Scott said as he stopped by their booth, "I should like to join you." He wore his raincoat and rubber hat, and his arms were full of packages.

"Please do," Marcia said gratefully. She was beginning to have a foreboding sense of uneasiness with Etta Wilson.

Etta nodded curtly. "Yes, do—if you don't mind my pursuing business with Dr. Anderson. In our Profession, Dr. Scott, we cannot afford—"

"—to waste a single minute," Scott said with her. He set his largest package on the floor, put the smaller ones by Etta, and then slid in beside Marcia. "Yes, Dr. Wilson, I remember well your excellent Philosophy of Time—from previous conversations."

"Snowing hard?" Marcia asked as she saw how wet were his hat and coat.

He nodded. "Almost a blizzard. Where's Herby?"

"Mr. Herby," Etta said grimly, "has peculiar ideas about rendering service. And now, Dr. Anderson, shall we proceed?"

Marcia forced attention. She had been thinking how right J.W. had been about the snow. He was always right!

"I have of course read the will," Etta was saying, "and I learned that you were left a box of personal papers. I should—"

"Not *personal* papers," Marcia said quickly. "They're merely rough drafts of articles that Professor Cornthwaite did not complete for publication."

"But surely," Etta persisted, "there must be something of a more— more *personal* nature."

"Nothing," Marcia said emphatically. "Nothing at all."

"Why this avid interest in the literary remains of E. Cornthwaite?" Scott asked.

Marcia was glad of the interruption, and explained in full. "Hmm," said Scott, interested. "And so for this biographical sketch you want some human-interest stuff, something that swerves a bit from the line of Esther Cornthwaite as Female Scholar personified?"

Etta frowned slightly, but said, "Exactly." She turned to Marcia. "I should very much like—"

"Oh, here's Herby!" Marcia cried with such enthusiasm that Scott looked at her curiously.

Herby set down their coffee and took Scott's order. The big package on the floor arrested him. "Christmas tree?"

Scott smiled self-consciously. "Well, it's almost too little to qualify, and it's artificial. Otherwise, it might be called a tree."

"I'm workin' on a real one right now," Herby said mournfully, "and it's shedding to beat the band."

Etta had been watching his mouth intently. "Mr. Herby," she said suddenly, "where were you born?"

"In a trunk, lady, but it was a nice, respectable birth. Why?"

"No, no. I mean in what part of the country."

"I was told," he said, moving away, "that it was Boston."

Etta stared at Scott and Marcia. "Incredible!"

Marcia laughed. "Perhaps he didn't stay in Boston long. He's from show business, you know."

"No, I didn't know," Etta said thoughtfully. "How interesting! He's a fine example of the typical American hybrid. I must observe more closely his— But let us return to our subject! Dr. Anderson, I should very much like to examine those papers for myself."

"If you think it worth your time," Marcia said uneasily. "However, I assure you that they contain nothing of the nature—"

"I do think it worth my time," Etta said firmly. "When may I call for them? I hope that it will be soon, for in our Profession, we . . ."

The snowstorm had lost most of its fury when Scott and Marcia left Herby's. The air was windless and carried no warmth from the setting sun.

"We shall certainly have a white Christmas," Scott remarked pleasantly.

Christmas softens even Scott, she thought. He seemed in fine spirits.

When they were crossing the Heights, he said suddenly, "If my sleuthing instincts do not betray me, you are hurrying home to remove something from Esther Cornthwaite's box of papers—a something which you don't want to come under the prying scrutiny of Dr. Etta Wilson."

"Well done, Holmes." She did not offer to explain.

"I don't suppose you'd tell me what it is," he said lightly. When she hesitated, he shrugged. "I thought not. Really, I never suspected you of being such a sentimentalist."

It occurred to her then that her silence was making the matter seem more mysterious and significant than it actually was. Besides, Scott might hint to Etta that she was concealing something, and she shuddered to think with what persistence Etta would follow a real scent.

She made a quick decision. "All right, I'll tell you. But you must promise never to tell a word of it—"

"—to Dr. Etta Wilson," he finished with her. He struggled to hold his packages in one arm, and raised his right hand. "I so promise," he said solemnly.

"It's really quite unimportant," she said finally, "but back in Herby's Etta Wilson impressed me as— Oh, no doubt she's brilliant and all that, but I had the sudden feeling that I shouldn't want her to see everything *I'd* written. It would be like—well, like having your own personal letters edited without your consent by someone who footnoted your most innocuous remarks and put *sic.* after all your misspelled words."

Scott nodded understandingly, and kept a patient, waiting silence. Marcia went on, "The 'something' is merely a story written many years ago—or so I'd guess from the state of the papers."

"Yes?" Scott encouraged as she hesitated. "What's it about?"

"It's about," she went on reluctantly, "a girl and a poet. They are in love, of course, and—well, it's quite sentimental. It's called 'Violets.'"

Scott whistled softly. "Not exactly what you'd expect from E. Cornthwaite."

"Not at all," Marcia agreed. "The girl comes to believe that her poet is a kind of reincarnation of John Keats, and she even begins to refer to herself as Fanny Brawne. Oh, it becomes quite mystical. . . ."

Scott grinned. "Worse than Blake, eh?"

"Much worse," Marcia said shortly. "Now remember—"

"I remember," he said quickly, "that I promised not to tell a word of this to Dr. Etta Wilson. Do you wish me to raise my hand again?"

She laughed. "I guess I am being unnecessarily—"

"I understand perfectly," he said with such seeming sympathy that she was mildly puzzled. "And I appreciate your telling me."

They had reached the Murdocks' and he waved cheerfully to Justin, who was shoveling snow off the porch steps. Marcia watched after him as he went on, wondering about his uncharacteristic good humor. Suddenly he turned to call back: "By the way, thanks for your Christmas card. We couldn't send any out this year. It was this"—he held up the little wrapped tree—"or cards."

Justin Murdock leaned on his shovel. "Didn't know Mr. Scott had a large family."

"He hasn't," Marcia told him. "Why?"

"Well, he talked as if he was heading for the poorhouse."

"Teachers' salaries aren't fabulous, you know," Marcia said sternly. She was irritated with Mr. Murdock. She'd given him time enough, and he showed no signs of being in the least sympathetic toward Stephanie. "Besides," she added pointedly, "Mr. Scott is in no danger whatsoever of being left a convenient inheritance."

Justin Murdock looked puzzled, then angry. "Not that it's any of your business, Miss Anderson, but I'd like you to know that we here"—he jerked his head toward the solid brick house—"don't live off one red cent of that inheritance of mine. We live off my orchards, and they're *mine*, I'll have you know!"

"I know they're yours," she said in a different tone, "and I know that it is none of my business. I'm interested only because of Stephanie."

He had made a motion to go back to his shoveling, but now he looked up alertly. "Stephanie! How's that?"

"I've been wanting," she said seriously, "to talk with you—confidentially. I haven't much time now, but if we could go where we could be alone for a few minutes, I think—"

"What's a-wrong with right here?" he asked suspiciously.

She smiled. "It's quite cold, but if you can stand it, I guess I can."

"Well," he said grudgingly, "there's the basement, but I suppose that wouldn't do."

"The basement would be quite fitting," she said, and followed him around to the side door.

"I understand," Marcia said when they were primly seated in the laundry room, "that you refuse to give your mon—inheritance to John Willard College if Stephanie leaves there."

"Seems like a good chance for a smoke," Mr. Murdock said thoughtfully, drawing out his pipe. "Mind?" Marcia indicated that she didn't, and refrained from lighting a cigarette for herself. He took a long while to light up, and then asked, "Who gave you that idea?"

"You did," she reminded him, "at Thanksgiving dinner. Also, Deans Holcomb and Haskins."

He looked threatening. "How come they know about Stephanie's durnfool idea?"

"I told them."

He grunted disgust. "Well, what do they think?"

"Being only human, they're against Stephanie's transferring because of the money. They're positive that you'd withdraw—"

"There's no definite arrangement," he said quickly.

"Don't I know it!" Marcia said bitterly. "That's what makes it all so difficult. But, you see, you have at least *hinted* that—"

"Got them kinda scared, eh?" He looked satisfied and puffed contentedly upon his pipe.

Marcia said quickly, "But Dr. Day thinks otherwise. She—"

"Day?" He frowned. "The head woman?"

"Why, yes, she's chairman of her department," Marcia said impatiently. "And she—"

"I meant this kind of head," he corrected, tapping his skull with his pipe stem.

Marcia winced but said, "Yes, that's the Dr. Day I mean. She has gone over Stephanie's record with me, and she agrees that Stephanie should specialize in some phase of horticulture. But to do this, she must transfer, for John Willard offers no such training."

"Horticulture! So that's what's back of this durnfool notion!" He shook his head and said as if telling her a fact that had not yet come to her attention, "She's a girl."

"Obviously. What has that to do with it?"

He gasped. "What has—! Well, now I ask you—"

"Well, ask me," Marcia said, "and I'll tell you that Stephanie's grades and interest show that she's admirably fitted for such study. I know, because I've checked both her college and high school records."

"You seem to have gone to a lot of trouble over Stephanie," he said suspiciously. "How come?"

"I like her. Besides, she's unhappy in a way that I think can be remedied. An unhappy person like Stephanie," she went on sententiously, "is a waste to society."

He looked disturbed at this. "Funny," he said slowly, "but that's how I've come to think about Stephanie. She just doesn't seem to have any use." He was silent for a minute. "I don't like waste," he explained then.

Marcia made her voice patient, although she felt that they were endlessly traversing the same circle of thought. "She wouldn't be a waste if she were allowed to follow her interest. Stephanie has brains, you know. Have you ever noticed her science grades? And over and above ability, she has an interest. She'd like nothing better than to end up working with you in the orchards."

"She's a girl," he repeated mechanically, but his thoughts were obviously racing ahead of his words. A certain interest had come into his face.

"And you wanted a boy!"

He was startled. "Who told you that?"

"Who told Stephanie is more important, for it has helped make her unhappy. Also Mrs. Murdock has unintentionally made Stephanie feel awkward and even more useless, because—"

"Madge is all right," he said dangerously.

"Of course," Marcia said, quickly changing her tactics. "She's wonderful, in fact. But she has been influenced by your opinion in this matter."

"You mean she follows me . . . lets me take the lead?"

"Exactly," Marcia said. She stayed silent as he puffed away, pondering this new revelation.

After long minutes, he said reminiscently, "Always did think it funny the way Stephanie used to want to tag after me. Used to go out there to the orchards with me. . . . Even now sometimes. Rigs herself up in pants." He seemed to remember Marcia. "Fact is," he said with a self-conscious smile, "I thought you were Stephanie when I first saw you a-coming up the hill today." He sank back into more private thoughts. "Who'd have thought it?"

"I did," Marcia said quickly, "and do. Now, what about the money —I mean, the inheritance, Mr. Murdock? It still isn't any of my business, but if you should refuse to leave it to John Willard because of

Stephanie's transferring, Mrs. Murdock wouldn't approve of the plan."
She laughed shortly. "Furthermore, I'd be extremely unpopular with
the Administration."

He appreciated this. "Got them kinda scared, eh?" He chuckled
shrewdly. His own thoughts led him again into silence, but soon he
slapped his thigh abruptly. "Say, how about a little wine!"

Justin Murdock's dandelion wine was in a keg in a corner of the
little fruit cellar where Marcia found Stephanie the night before
Thanksgiving. He took down two tin folding cups from a shelf and
filled them generously.

"Good," Marcia murmured after her first taste, although she wasn't
sure that she thought so. "I wish I had known about this wine for
Stephanie that night."

"No one," he said warningly, "comes near this keg unless I say so."
He drained his cup as if it had been filled with water, and immediately
held it under the little spigot again.

He drank this cup more slowly. Finally he cleared his throat and
said gruffly, "About that inheritance of mine."

"Yes?"

"Well." He stopped to grope for words. "I got it fifteen years ago,
from an uncle I didn't even know was living. When I got it, Madge
wanted to use it and make a splurge, like old Otis MacMillan and his
gang. We could have, you know—in fact"—his voice rose in defiance—
"we still could!"

"I'm sure of that," Marcia said. "But you didn't want to?"

"I didn't want to," he echoed. "Somehow I— Well, you see, I
wanted—" He floundered. He was not a man to talk about the intri-
cacies of his own desires.

"Perhaps," Marcia suggested, "you had a natural pride in earning
your own living—off your orchards."

He gave her a quick, surprised look. "That's it," he said gratefully.
"Madge was disappointed, but then she got the idea of giving the
money to the college. She'd always wanted to be in the college circle,
but until the money came along, there didn't seem to be any way. . . .
Well. I didn't say yes and I didn't say no. Between you and me, I suppose I'll turn it all over to John Willard some day. But, you know, I
found out that as long as I didn't make it definite, people— Well, first
thing I knew, they had made me a trustee, and then people—even
Madge—sorta did whatever I suggested. . . ."

"I see." She looked at Justin Murdock with new respect. "Money is
power, especially when you don't spend it."

He nodded sorrowfully. "I don't like it, mind you, but it's a habit
by now."

"Yes, but what about Stephanie? Are you going to sacrifice her to
that habit?"

He considered this question seriously and then winked at her. "If Stephanie doesn't find another college, I'm not a-going to leave that money to John Willard!"

"Wonderful!" she said, rising.

"Say!" He was suddenly alarmed. "I wonder if you'd mind going out the side door and in the front. Maybe if we both went up into the kitchen like this, Madge would think it was kinda funny. . . ."

Judith had pulled out the davenport and had set the little tree on a table in the front window. She had fastened on the string of colored lights when the big car roared past. "J.W.'s car again," she said, looking out. "I wonder how he gets so much gas."

"Huh?" Scott called absently from the chair in the corner.

She smiled and went back to work upon the tree. Owen was more absent-minded than she had ever before seen him, but otherwise in an excellent humor. She hoped that it would last through Christmas day. "You're supposed to be helping, you know."

"What? Oh, sure." He joined her and picked up an ornament from the box, but forgot to do anything with it. "Judith!" he cried excitedly, "I've got it! Oh, Judith, this is it!"

"These things are fragile!" she warned, taking the silver ball from his hand. "What do you have?"

"An idea for a book."

She had to force interest, for the thought of the much revised manuscript bored her at the moment. "An idea for another revision, Owen?"

"No, no! This is brand new—something altogether different!"

She was surprised. "This must have come to you very suddenly."

"Not particularly. I didn't want to talk about it until it was definite—and now it's definite. Judith," he said seriously, "this is *it!*"

How often she had heard those words! But now as she looked into his eager face, she felt new hope, although another part of her mind clicked off automatically, *it won't last.* "Tell me about it," she said quietly.

"Yes, I'm ready now." He walked around the room, kicking gently at the open boxes and trailing tissue paper that lay on the floor, and told her first about the story Marcia had found among Esther Cornthwaite's papers.

"That's odd and unexpected, of course," Judith said, shrugging, "but I don't see anything exciting about it."

He smiled. "That's because you don't know how perfectly it fits into the idea I already had!"

She left the tree and sat down on the couch. "What idea?"

"For the book that's going to expose American scholarship," he said casually. But a moment later his smile was gone and his face tense. "Judith, I'm going to crack wide open that narrow, hypocritical world!"

"That's quite an aim," she said dryly.

But he had not heard her. "The idea has been growing in my mind. I first got it when—oh, I don't know exactly when, but perhaps it came when I began to think about Marcia Anderson and Grant." He reached for a cigarette and absently tossed one to her.

She let it stay in her lap. "I don't follow any of this, Owen."

"I'm explaining," he said impatiently. He lighted his cigarette hastily. "What I'm talking about is the overcivilized kind of sex play those two illustrate. Marcia pretends to be wrapped up in William Blake. Grant pretends to be interested in her work. They discuss it, they argue, they criticize. They are very intellectual and impersonal—oh yes, indeed!—but the atmosphere is charged with sex, for the real attraction is of course that of male and female. And that, my dear"—he waved the cigarette at her—"is called scholarship."

Judith was silent; then she half smiled and said, "But she isn't in love with Grant, is she? If she is, she's very fickle, for I thought—"

"I'm not speaking of love," he said, irritated. "*Sex,* Judith, sex."

She nodded wisely. "Oh, I see."

Her lingering smile disconcerted him. "You think I'm exaggerating? Well, then, answer me this: why did Grant read *her* manuscript, when he has never even asked to see mine?" He seemed grimly satisfied when she didn't try to answer. "There you are. Of course, that situation merely typifies *one* kind of hypocrisy that runs through the whole lot of them. They're snobs too."

Judith frowned, puzzled. "*Who* are snobs?"

"They're snobs because they're afraid—afraid to allow anyone new into their little world."

"If you mean the scholarly world," she said slowly, "aren't you a part of it? Why do you want to turn against—"

"A part of it!" He laughed unpleasantly. "You've had ample opportunity to notice how eagerly they reach out for my stuff—how they beg for it!"

She was watching his face. The look which she had recognized to be cruel was on it, making it seem narrower and longer than it really was. The casualness with which he had begun to talk to her was gone, and she did not understand the tenseness that had taken its place. She felt lost and vague. "I still don't follow you, Owen. I can't see what any of this has to do with Esther Cornthwaite's story."

"Hearing about that crystallized my thought, gave me my central figure. Just think of Esther Cornthwaite, Judith! Rather, think of what was under that gloss of cold intellect and smug celibacy. *She* wouldn't pollute herself like a normal, decent woman, but at night in her room enjoyed a vicarious liaison with her poet—who resembled John Keats, if you please—in writing that—"

"How do you know she wrote at night?" Judith asked, but her own flippancy grated on her ears. She shuddered. "You make it sound quite horrible."

"*I* make it sound horrible. You should read Freud." He moved restlessly about the room, talking more to himself than to her. "I'll change that, of course. It's not strong enough. I'll make her the austere scholar who knows how to hold onto her following of male students. Her way to power will be like Queen Elizabeth's—the virgin but iron hand, the—"

"But that's not true!" Judith said sharply. "Esther Cornthwaite wasn't in the least like that!"

"Naturally, for my purpose I need to exaggerate. This will be a satiric novel. I haven't exactly wasted all that time I gave to Swift and Pope. They knew how to attack and keep themselves safe. I can do it too."

Why attack? she wondered, but said nothing. He glanced at her uneasily. "Aren't you interested, Judith?"

"This seems so different from the work you've always planned to do."

He turned from her. "I've tried the other long enough."

She stared at the back of his head, feeling guilty, for hadn't she admitted to herself that she too was bored with the old work? Yet her boredom was different from his. It had grown out of the unwanted conviction that what he did was no longer a part of her real life. It was as if she were turning back to herself and he were going on alone. . . .

He had come back to her, his face and voice pleading. "Judith, I tell you this is *it!* I know that I can write it fast, and I know that it will sell."

"You're happy about this idea, Owen? You'll stay happy?"

He nodded eagerly, and she felt the old worn hope arise out of habit. She smiled tiredly. "I'm glad."

He was satisfied. "I knew you would be when you understood. Now we're going to have Old Fashioneds, for I assure you, Mrs. Scott, this is a memorable evening." And as he went to the kitchen to mix the drinks, he called back to her, "Can't you understand what it means to me to have hold of an idea that might bring in *money!* After all, a man takes a pride in being able to support a family beyond the mere subsistence level. Think what it will mean to be able to do all the little civilized things, such as send Christmas cards. . . ."

Listening, she lighted the cigarette she had been idly fingering. His words struck queerly in her mind. "Order cards if you wish," he had told her, "but sign only *your* name to them. I'm through with wasting money on hypocritical conventions."

Support a family? A million dollars wouldn't help him support a family. Nor could she support them much longer on pity.

When he came back carrying their drinks, he said, "In fact, everything has led up to this—even the time I put in on Freud this summer when I thought I needed that background for Swift. With sex my motif, anything is possible!" He handed her a glass and raised his own. "Let us drink to *Sentimental Farce,* that brilliant, lashing satire by Owen Scott, that most non-academic dissection of the academic world."

She drank with him. "You have the title already?"

He nodded. "And it's devilishly appropriate. For one thing, it's from John Keats himself. Now," he said gaily, raising his glass again, "I propose a toast to Marcia Anderson, for although she doesn't know it, she is—in a small, remote way—responsible for my brainwave."

"Here's to you, Marcia." J.W. lifted his Martini glass.

She stirred on the couch and looked across the room at him. "Thank you. You make me the most toasted woman in Riverville."

He drank quickly and sat down in a chair from where he could watch her face. "You spoil it, however, by not having one last Martini with me. I thought you liked Martinis."

"I do, and I'm sorry not to join you." The morning's buoyancy was gone from her voice. There was dreaminess in it now. Or was it listlessness? he wondered. She laughed suddenly. "I had almost too much dandelion wine this afternoon."

"Dandelion wine! However did that happen?" he asked idly. He wanted to keep her talking so that he could go on watching her. She sat in the corner of the big couch with her feet tucked up under her and her long black velvet gown spread out around her. Her face was indistinct to him, for the only light in the room was from the Christmas tree and the log fire. Occasionally the firelight glanced against the wide gold bracelet on her arm.

"I had it with Mr. Murdock in the basement," she said gravely. She turned slightly to watch the tall and softly shining tree that stood to one side of the fireplace. "Why didn't you invite me to help trim the tree?"

"Kate always does it," he told her. "Even Grace can do no more than look on. Cigarette?" She shook her head. He finished his Martini and set the glass down on the table beside him, fingering it absently. Why had she permitted herself to drink the wine, knowing about the Martinis tonight? He made his voice light. "The Murdocks' *is* a respectable home, isn't it?"

"Quite. There wasn't the least bit of suggestiveness in our wine party, unless"—she laughed—"you could count his asking me to go outside again and re-enter the house through the front door!"

He shuddered. "Crude."

"No," she said seriously, "Justin Murdock is not crude, although once I thought so too. In fact, there's a certain similarity between you two. He has a philosophy of finance which I think would interest you."

J.W. ventured no words. There had been faint irony in her voice, and he had no wish to encourage it.

She was willing to be silent too, and soon he had the uneasy feeling that she was far away from him. "Was the evening boring to you?" he asked.

"Of course not," she said quickly.

"We've always had an elaborate Christmas Eve," he went on, wondering why he was bothering to explain, "but this year, with Russ gone and Esther dead, Grace and I decided that a small, quiet one would be best."

"I liked it," she said. "I liked it very much."

But still he wasn't satisfied. Did she really appreciate the exclusiveness of the evening? Why was she so quiet?

He went to her and sat down on the edge of the couch beside her. He could not tell whether she was glad that he had come.

"We're not on an open road now," he said softly, "and there's no possibility of a car's coming along." He kissed her, but her lips seemed passive. "Marcia," he whispered, still holding her, "I want you to marry me this week—perhaps New Year's day."

She leaned away from him. "My bracelet! It fell—"

"It's not likely to be lost," he said irritably. But he picked it up from the floor and slipped it on her arm. Even then he wondered briefly how it could have fallen off. Her arm had been around him. . . . "Perhaps you didn't hear my insignificant question."

"Yes, I heard." She evaded his eyes and toyed with the bracelet. "It wouldn't do. I haven't even met Russ yet. And I couldn't stop teaching now." She spoke rapidly, and her fingers turned the bracelet nervously. "You once said," she went on, "that you'd want me to stop teaching, and I couldn't stop suddenly—"

"That could be arranged," he said shortly.

"But it wouldn't be fair. It wouldn't be fair to Dr. Grant, it wouldn't—"

"You have many excuses on hand." He stood up and lighted a cigarette.

"Grace went to her room an hour ago," she said irrelevantly, standing also. "I must go now, for I understand that you rise very early on Christmas morning." She came to him and put her hand on his arm. He stared down at the bracelet, noting that it couldn't fall off by itself. "They're not excuses. They're real reasons. You believe that, don't you?"

"Perhaps." He could hardly confront her with his conviction about the bracelet. She'd think him a fool.

She seemed to want to say something more, but after a minute, she went to the stairs. "Good night, Jack." He said nothing, but turned to watch her. Before she was out of sight, a clock chimed. "Midnight," she said, pausing. "Merry Christmas."

He smiled ironically. "Merry Christmas, my dear."

When she had gone, he glanced involuntarily at the portrait of Eileen. How much simpler, he thought wistfully, it had been with Eileen.

Iris glanced at the crack-faced clock on the big desk. "Merry Christmas, Kim."

He jumped. "Same," he said, aware that she was watching him searchingly. "More cheese?"

"No, thanks." She took another sip of the dark red wine and then set the glass down on the box they were using for a table. "This wine's making me sleepy." She curled up on the bumpy black leather couch, pulling her fur coat around her shoulders. There was no heat in the Barn.

He wrapped up what was left of the bread and cheese, sorry that they had finished eating. He had liked that. It was, after all, a slightly less wretched Christmas Eve than he had expected. "Why didn't you go home for Christmas?" he asked her.

"Oh," she said vaguely, "I had work to do here."

That wasn't true, he knew. She had stayed purposely to keep him from being alone with himself, and in his mind he caught a sudden glimpse of himself sitting here with her, keeping sullen silence, stuffing himself with bread and cheese, and thinking of Carol Leeds. He felt guilty and then angry at her for making him feel so, but in spite of the anger, he began to remember other things she had done for him, things understandable only to him and her. . . .

"Why don't you paint, Kim?"

He scowled down at the paint box and easel. "I don't know why you made me drag along that stuff tonight. I don't paint now and you know it."

"You mean," she said quietly, "since that night at the Inn."

She would be the one not to let him forget! But the next moment he felt a grudging admiration for her. Everyone else had made an all too obvious point of not mentioning that night or the Inn or Carol Leeds or even painting when he was within hearing.

"You can't get her out of your mind, can you, Kim?"

"Don't nag at me, Iris." But the kindness and gentleness in her voice had done a strange thing to him, and he felt an unfamiliar need to talk to her about Carol. He wished that he could talk and that her face would show pity. It seemed to him at that moment that her face was capable of showing all the pity that the world owed him. He wished that she would reach out her arms to him, saying, "Poor Kim . . . poor Kim."

She said nothing. He sighed and unlocked the paint box and set up the easel, although he knew that he would not paint. There was not even the desire to paint left; only the pain of remembrance. Carelessly he picked up a brush, feeling no response in his fingers.

"Paint brushes become you," she said. "You look almost happy."

He snorted. "Don't sentimentalize." He threw the brush back into the box and got up and paced around the room, kicking at the easel so that it toppled over, kicking one of his little tin cups across the floor. "If you thought you could make everything bright and rosy by the simple device of bringing me here and telling me to paint, then you must believe in Santa Claus too."

She stared up at him for a minute. "All right—let's go. We should go anyway. It's getting late." She stood up and slipped on her coat. Then she stooped to pick up the tin cup.

He stood by the window. Outside it was so black that his reflection in the glass was quite clear. He could even see Iris standing up the easel. The reflected room seemed cozy and cheerful; the blackness dangerous and without end. He wheeled about, away from it. "You would want to leave now, just when I get all that damn stuff out."

For a moment he thought she was going to be angry, but then she smiled. "I was under the impression that you didn't want to paint, but if you do, fine."

The smile made him suddenly aware of how unhappy her face had looked. As he went back to the pretense of getting ready to paint, it occurred to him again that he had given her a rotten Christmas Eve.

She lighted a cigarette and stretched out on the couch, the coat over her as a cover. "I may go to sleep," she said.

"Well, go to sleep."

She turned on her side to watch him, her arm crooked under her head. He squeezed out Lead White and Venetian Red, and mixed them together. Half suspiciously he noted that he felt some pleasure in this activity, mechanical as it was. Then he covered the small canvas with the pink opaque ground, although he had no plans for using it.

Before he had finished, Iris put out her cigarette and was so quiet that he thought it quite possible she was asleep. He coughed and then called her name. She did not answer. He felt deserted.

He put down his brush and blew on his hands. They were dry and stiff from the cold. He drank some wine, but it gave him no warmth. He sat there and stared around at the objects he knew so well, and he felt scornful of them for Iris' sake. He had raked them together for her from odd places on the campus. The cracked and peeling couch had been cast off by the Dispensary, the ungainly rolltop desk had been cast off by the Finance Office. The Administration had been willing enough to fix up the Barn to impress the visiting public, but it could not be convinced that the Dramatics Department needed an office, or stable props, or. . . .

He thought of how hard he and she had worked together—he sporadically and because it diverted his mind from his teaching; she steadily and because—well, for some other reason. He looked over at her and for the first time since he had known her, he wondered why she chose to do the work she did. She had real talent. Why didn't she make a career for herself? Why did she bother with kids who—

She had bothered with Carol Leeds. He prepared himself to think of Carol Leeds, but nothing happened in his mind. The name had lost its magic. It was as if this ugly, familiar room was a sanctuary against even the thought of her; and this discovery made him feel lonelier than ever.

He went quietly to stand over Iris, his shadow falling darkly across her face. He had meant to waken her abruptly, but now he hesitated. He was used to thinking of her as self-sufficient and assured, but there was a guileless, defenseless look about her face as she slept, as if she might have need of his strength. He liked this thought. . . .

But it wasn't fair that she should be warm and peaceful while he was left alone to struggle with his wretchedness. He sat down heavily beside her. "Iris!"

She stirred and opened her eyes, and when she saw him, she smiled drowsily.

"I'm cold," he said angrily, "and lonely."

"Poor Kim," she whispered. She pushed aside the coat and reached out her arms, drawing him down to the warmth of her breast. "Poor Kim."

He sighed and turned his head so that his lips rested against the pulse of her throat. After a minute he grew aware of the light, and it reminded him of the stage lights under which he had met Carol. Quickly he crossed the room and turned it off, and as he went back to her in the darkness, he had the sudden fear that he might be with her as he had been with Carol, afraid to lose himself. . . .

But her hand was out to him, as if she understood, and he knew then that there was no need for fear.

He awoke with a start, unbelieving of the sleep. He had not meant to sleep. Even before he looked, he knew that he was alone on the couch.

"Hello."

He was so glad to hear her voice that he laughed. She sat at the desk, combing out her hair, and the sight of the long, fair hair brought a rush of feeling that made his whole body too languorous to move. She smiled at him as if this were no different from any other morning and pinned the hair loosely up on the top of her head. "Come over here," he said huskily.

She did. "Breakfast." She stuck a cigarette in his mouth and one in hers, and lighted them. "Orange juice, toast, and steaming coffee. I hope that the three-minute egg pleases you."

"I require a four-minute one."

She shook her head. "That's practically hard boiled, and I'll have nothing to do with it."

"Sorry, but—" Suddenly the light talk seemed blasphemous, and he put his hand tightly over hers. "Iris . . . Iris." He felt her hand grow warm, but she withdrew it gently.

"We ought to be getting out of here," she said.

"Not yet," he pleaded. "Let's plan the day. I tell you what—we'll take the train to some place where we can be married."

"Let's go to Herby's for food. You're light-headed."

"But that's the most sensible thing I ever said in my life!" He stared after her as she went back to the desk to put out her cigarette, although it was only half smoked. He sat up. "Well, I'll not rush you. I'll give you a week. We'll be married on New Year's."

She turned and smiled down at him. "Ready?"

"Aren't you even going to answer?"

She still smiled. "I didn't hear a question."

"Oh Lord, Iris, let's not quibble over a matter of rhetoric."

Her face grew serious and she shivered slightly. "I don't want to talk here, Kim. It's cold and dreary."

Surprised, he saw then that the room *was* dreary in the thin morning light. And he began to feel the cold, inside him as well as out. "What's there to talk about?"

"Please—let's go."

He shook his head stubbornly. "Not until I know what there is to talk about."

When she saw that he meant it, she sat down in the squeaking swivel chair. "I think I'd rather not marry you, Kim."

He sat very still, feeling nothing. "Don't you love me?" he asked mechanically.

She nodded almost apologetically. "I do. You know that."

"Then why. . . ." The shock left him, and the full force of what she had said and what she was doing to him struck against his mind. She had waited until she had offered her protecting love and pity to decide calmly that she could give them no more. Cruel . . . *cruel*. "You can't do this to me!" He leaped to his feet and strode by her, then back to her. "It's unfair, cruel. You can't—"

"Ask yourself what would be fair to me. Ask yourself why you want to marry me."

"I admit," he said with bitter irony, "that I did not think to consider the great unfairness of asking you to become my wife."

"You did not think! You never said a truer word!" She stood, facing him, her eyes brilliant with sudden anger. "Have you ever in your whole life seen beyond that egoism of yours? What is in my mind about us is serious—yet you're in your own way so much that you can't even hear me."

He stared at her, incredulous over this anger in her which he had never before seen. He groaned and dropped down on the couch. "I'm disappointed in you, Iris." He put his head in his hands.

He sensed that she stood rigidly still for a minute. Then she sighed and pulled the desk chair nearer to him and sat down in it. "I'm sorry, Kim. I told you that we shouldn't try to talk today."

Encouraged because the anger had left her voice, he looked up. "But I love you."

"Do you? You came to me last night wanting pity."

He flushed over the truth in her words. "In the beginning—yes. But then it was different. You couldn't help knowing that, Iris."

"All evening you sat here with me thinking about her—Carol."

Again she was right, but not completely. He tried to think how to tell her that after she had gone to sleep, he had not been able to think about Carol . . . not even to see her in his mind. "You're wrong," he whispered. "You're wrong."

For a moment she looked uncertain. "I wish I knew. . . . I'm not jealous of her, Kim. Truly I'm not. But I am of whatever it is she means to you. I don't think you love her—I don't think she's even real to you. Yet you cling to her or the thought of her. . . ." She stood up suddenly. "Oh, Kim, can't you see how wrong it is for you! Everyone knows that she's. . . ."

"Knows that she's what?" he asked dangerously.

Iris shrugged helplessly. "It's hard to know how to say it, but I suppose you might say she has a sick mind."

"So I've got a sick mind."

"But I didn't say anything about you."

He laughed harshly. "You didn't have the nerve to say it right out, but you implied it in a polite way. She has a sick mind, I think about her; ergo, I've got a sick mind. Well, go on—say the rest of it."

She was puzzled. "What do you mean?"

"Don't stand there looking so innocent. You've been waiting for this chance ever since the Army pigeon-holed me for the convenience of people like—"

"Kim! I don't know anything about the Army and you. You forget how much you don't tell me."

"Grant could be decent about it," he went on as if she had not spoken, "but you have to fling it in my face. People like you are afraid of people like me and her, and so you get some witch doctor like Medora Day to put a label on us. You're afraid because you know we've got more than you'll ever have. You're like everyone else around here. This place—"

"Oh, shut up," she said wearily. "If you knew how bored I am with your ranting. If you tell me once more how little and narrow and stuffy this place is, I'll scream. I know exactly when you're going to say it. It's like dropping a nickel into the slot."

"Very, very amusing," he said sarcastically, because he could think

260

of nothing better to say. Her flat, resigned voice hurt. He preferred her frank anger.

"Can't you see that you're *different* from Carol?" she said after a minute, pleading in her voice. "Even I have a vague understanding that she has to be as she is, but you—"

"But I pretend to be what I am—for the hell of it, I suppose."

"Maybe you do, Kim. I hoped that you'd find yourself under that crazy hate of yours, and—"

"And if I became a totally different person," he said contemptuously, "then I might be good enough for even you. Is that it?"

"You wouldn't have to change," she said, weary again. "I meant you'd see what was real and what was not real for you. You hate this place, yet you don't leave. You so easily could. You say you don't love Carol, yet you're obsessed by her. What am I to you? How do I know that you wouldn't soon hate me?"

He laughed shortly. "I love you. That's why I wouldn't hate you. But, as I understand it, that's not reason enough."

She looked away from him. "I don't want to risk it, Kim."

"I hope you realize," he said, grabbing up his coat and thrusting himself into it, "that you're sending me back to her."

"Don't go to her to spite me!" she cried, reaching out to him, but he pushed by her and seized the frail easel. She followed him, taking it from his hands when he tried to fold it without unscrewing the bolts. "Besides, you don't know where she is."

"I'll know. She'll write to tell me. I promised I'd go to her when she wanted me." He jammed the still wet canvas and uncleaned brushes and palette into the paint box. "I expect the letter any day. Being so admirably sane, you wouldn't understand, but a sick mind can keep a promise."

She handed him the folded easel. "Then you are not really free to marry me, are you, Kim?"

He ignored this, and closed the paint box with a savage bang. He strode to the door and jerked it open, hesitating a moment as the raw wind slapped against him. Then he stepped out into it.

But when he had rounded the corner of the building, he halted abruptly, allowing the paint box and easel to drop upon the hard ground, and covered his face with his hands. The anger and fury had gone. He felt light and hollow, and it seemed incredible that the wind did not catch him up and send him spinning over the side of the world.

After a moment he took his hands away from his face and stood curiously attentive to his feeling. This, his anguish, was real. With that thought the easeful pity came, telling him that it was impossible that such pain as his should go unrewarded. If he should return to find her sobbing, then he would know. . . .

He went back quickly. She looked up, startled by the opening of the door. She seemed sad and thoughtful. That was all.

"I sincerely hope," he said, "that your noble pity does not lead you to every man's bed."

Her face went white, but she said nothing. He took a final, hungry look around the room, then again banged the door behind him.

Chapter Four

"SHOULDN'T we be waving flags," Dean Haskins asked, "or something?"

Marcia laughed. "I know how you feel."

The little group crowded against the railing at the side of the Widow's Walk that gave a view of the Heights, and intently watched the approaching double column of Air Cadets. Dean Holcomb sighed as the first pair of Cadets appeared at the tip of the Heart. "Well, they're here." His voice was resigned and joyless.

"Holcomb," President Cameron reproved mildly, "this is the most remarkable Educational Opportunity that History has ever presented to Man."

"Thrilling!" cried Etta Wilson. "A cross-section of the whole country! Think of all those dialects sitting side by side in one class. As you say, President Cameron, *what* an opportunity!"

"Yes, yes," Holcomb said impatiently, "but had you people been presented with the more practical side of this remarkable opportunity—such as billeting and feeding—you might at this moment be subject to slightly different feelings. In fact, you might. . . ."

Kim only half listened. He was watching for Iris, although he had no real hope that she would come. Whenever possible she avoided being where he was. Apathetically he stared across the Heart at the remaining male civilian students who stood together in a lonely group to one side of Science Hall. He knew them well, for he and they together had been shunted from MacMillan Hall to the Bijou Hotel. No doubt they, like himself, were present out of an obscure sense of sportsmanship.

Eagerly he turned when he heard someone coming up the steps. But it was Hughes, who was gingerly leading Diaz to a front position at the rail. "I have brought," he announced, "a Roman citizen to watch the invasion from the north."

Diaz merely laughed, and Hughes joined Marcia. "Did you know that I've been pressed into the service of your department?"

"I'm glad," she said, "but what about Philosophy?"

He grimaced. "That's a luxury not to be afforded in wartime." When she murmured something sympathetic, he said shortly, "Save it. I don't much care. If Philosophy had done its job right, all this"—he gestured toward the Heart—"wouldn't be happening, you know."

"But surely you could say that about *all* subjects, Cliff."

"Not all subjects pretend to hold the keys to the kingdom! That's the important difference. Well, there's no use worrying now." He shrugged and turned to Cameron. "Could you tell us something about the C.O. of this outfit? His attitude will reflect in the men, and we ought to know what to expect."

"The Commanding Officer," said President Cameron gravely, "is a Responsible Individual fully aware of the significance of Education." He consulted his watch. "I see, William, that we must move on to our meeting."

"Yes, yes," Holcomb said wearily, and followed Cameron. At the trap-door opening, they met the Director of Admissions and the Registrar. Cunningham went immediately to the rail and looked down. "Ah, observe that march! If we could achieve *that* formation in our academic processions, I'd be happy. "

Diaz spoke for the first time. "How quaint—and how characteristic of you Americans. Mr. Cunningham would be happy if World War II should produce more efficient academic processions!"

Cunningham reddened. "If you mean to imply that—"

"I mean to imply merely," Diaz said pleasantly, "that Americans strike me as being decidedly confused. I am reminded of someone who is ill but who perplexes the physician because he exhibits an equal number of symptoms of two different diseases."

Cunningham stayed angry, but decided to make nothing of it. Etta Wilson broke the uncomfortable silence. "I hope," she said to Registrar Dexter, "that you have not arranged the classes according to localities. I am looking forward to having representatives of the North, South, East, and West in one class."

Dexter gave her his dotted line stare. "I have arranged them alphabetically. Any objection?"

"I think not," Etta said seriously. "I presume that you mean A, B, C, D, and so on."

"I mean," he said, "that one class is filled with A's, another with B's, another with C's, and so on."

"But," said Marcia, "won't that make it a bit difficult for the teachers to keep the names straight?"

Dexter turned the dotted line upon her. "I did the scheduling according to blocks. I gave *you* the B's," he added, somehow suggesting that the B's were a tricky lot.

"I like B's," she said hastily. "And please don't think us unsympathetic, Mr. Dexter. I can well understand how difficult the scheduling must be."

He softened a trifle. "I can handle it—if I'm allowed to work in blocks, and if teachers don't become hysterical."

Etta rose to this. "*Really*, Mr. Dexter! In our Profession—"

"In *my* profession," he cut in, "I have learned that each teacher fully expects all schedules to revolve around his rising habits, his voice control, or his golfing time. That's why I insist upon the block system, which removes all possibility of the human element. If I can be certain that—"

"Oh, my!" said Dean Haskins suddenly, leaning far out over the railing. "Professor Webb almost collided with the Cadets."

They all looked and saw that the Professor had progressed to the middle of the Heart and there stopped as if stupefied. A briefcase dangled from one hand, and the other arm was crooked over two thick books. He was hatless, but his neck was swathed in a heavy woolen scarf, the fringed ends of which dangled over his back.

"He's trying to get across to the Library," Hughes said, and called down to him.

When Webb spotted the group on the roof, he looked more bewildered than ever. "A fine parade—but why?"

"That parade," Cunningham said gleefully, "is our entering students!"

Webb shook his head sadly. "Truly I see no need for such a militaristic registration." Still shaking his head, he made his way toward Science Hall, which was no longer obstructed by the Cadets.

Hughes sauntered back to Marcia and Kim. "See what I mean about Philosophy?"

"Perhaps, however," Diaz spoke up surprisingly, "our Professor Webb has a point, even though he may not be abreast with events. I myself am curious over the result of this strange wedlock between the Army and American education, the latter of which is noted for its lack of discipline. It suggests difficulties, even"—he smiled and nodded briefly to Dexter, "under your admirable block system."

Before Dexter could speak, Grant emerged from the trap-door opening, followed by a stocky man with untidy light hair who seemed privately amused at what was happening to him and what he saw before him. It was this subtly humorous expression that made Kim think of the application photograph he had seen almost two years ago. "Sidney Meyerson," he murmured to Marcia.

"We were caught in the parade," Grant said, "but I want you at least to meet Dr. Meyerson, our new Department member." He introduced Kim and Marcia, who were standing nearest to them.

Meyerson held out a surprisingly delicate hand with long tapering fingers. "Dr. Anderson," he said in a rich voice. "Mr. Duncan."

His voice carried plainly, and the others looked up with interest. Hughes stepped forward and shook Meyerson's hand. "I'm English too, for the time being. So you've come to help us teach the Cadets?"

Meyerson smiled. "That was my intention, but as Professor Grant and I watched those young men march by, it occurred to me that they no doubt think themselves quite complete without precision work in English grammar."

"I'm worried, too," Marcia said. "We don't have the least idea what to expect."

Grant grinned. "Dr. Meyerson happened to meet the Commanding Officer, and it seems that the other side is equally perplexed."

"You couldn't have met him," Dexter said. "He isn't here officially as yet."

"Oh, there was nothing official in our meeting," Meyerson said soothingly. "We met in the hall of this very building. He was searching for the Dean, and at first he mistook me for one of"—he gestured apologetically toward the group—"you. When he understood that I was merely a wartime emergency, he began to talk freely, and he impressed me as a man bewildered—yes, quite bewildered—over his sudden entrance into the academic world."

"And it seems," Grant said, "that the C.O. has devised a motto to carry his men through the perils of the classroom."

Meyerson nodded gravely. " 'Keep it clean, men; just keep it clean.' He told it to me with a mixture of pride and anxiety."

They laughed, but after a minute, Hughes said, "Actually this isn't funny, you know. However"—he shrugged—"we may as well be grateful for small favors. Isn't it typical of this place that we should receive our first pertinent information from a newcomer?"

Meyerson protested quickly. "Please don't consider what I have said as anything more than entertaining gossip. It was pure happenstance that I—"

"But, Dr. Meyerson, don't be so modest," Diaz said suddenly. "It is quite appropriate that you should be the one to bring us this information, for isn't your race traditionally acquisitive—of knowledge?"

Hughes turned swiftly upon Diaz, but at that moment Grant said with deliberate casualness, "Dr. Meyerson, I believe that you have not yet met Mr. Diaz."

"Perhaps not," Meyerson said, his smile lingering as he offered his hand, "although Mr. Diaz sounds tantalizingly familiar."

Wearily Marcia made herself ready for the possibility of J.W.'s arrival. She admitted that she wished he wouldn't come tonight. She would like a quiet evening to prepare for the Cadet classes. With him she wouldn't be able even to talk about them. She'd have to pretend that there was nothing on her mind other than the unmixed pleasure of seeing him.

As she dressed, she read the new letter from Stephanie. The large, laborious writing was clearly that of a person not at ease with the pen. Quite formally Stephanie reported her academic progress, which seemed satisfactory. But at the end was a postscript: "I have a friend named Bouncer, but I still think of you every day."

She hadn't known that Stephanie thought of her every day. And even if she did, what did that have to do with Bouncer—whoever he was?

Uneasily she slipped the letter into her desk next to the latest one from Richard Tibbet in its weather-scarred envelope marked *A.P.O.* Both required careful answers, and this thought made her more keenly aware of her tiredness. Why couldn't her teaching be confined to John Willard?

She glanced at her watch and was relieved to see that it was past the time J.W. usually called to take her to dinner. If he didn't come tonight, she'd accomplish something worthwhile. . . .

Yet even while she told herself this, she knew that when it was late enough to be certain that he wasn't coming, the relief would change to that gnawing anxiety. . . .

She started at the ringing of the telephone, and when Mrs. Murdock shouted up the stairs for her, she went down to it half fearfully.

But it was Grant. "It's late to be asking—but are you engaged this evening?"

"I don't know," she answered honestly. "Is it some problem about the Cadets?"

"What?" Then he laughed. "Do I have to have a problem to see you?"

She was surprised. "You mean . . ."

"I mean," he said, "that I want to relax over dinner tonight, and I thought you might relax with me. I'd like to celebrate before facing all those uniforms tomorrow. Childish, isn't it?"

"If it's childish, then I'm an infant, for I've been feeling just that way."

"Then I may call for you?"

She hesitated. After all, she couldn't be sure about J.W. He might come after the dinner hour, as he often did. In that event, she could dine with Grant and still be home in time. . . . "If you don't mind my rushing away immediately after dinner," she said finally. "I have a tentative engagement for later this evening."

"Of course not." But he sounded disappointed. "I had hoped to make an evening of it, though. However, I should have asked you earlier. Well, then, shall I call for you—say in an hour?"

She was suddenly aware of manifold complications. What if J.W. came to take her to dinner, although a little later than usual? What if both he and Grant arrived? "Perhaps I could meet you on the Square. You see," she went on quickly, "I have to go to town on another errand, and it would be silly for me to rush back here."

He had to agree that it would be. "Not on the Square, however—in the Bijou lobby."

When she was about to leave, Janice Grant arrived. "I came to talk over some ideas with you," she announced, settling herself on the couch. "If you haven't eaten," she said as Marcia did not sit down with her, "I'll go along with you to dinner."

"I'm sorry, Janice, but I already have a dinner engagement."

Janice didn't stir. "Can't you call it off?"

Marcia checked her anger. "It's with your uncle," she said, hoping that would make it right with Janice.

"Oh." Janice looked thoughtful. "Well, I'll walk down to the short cut with you."

"Fine," Marcia said, although she felt the need to be alone, for she had not yet decided whether or not to leave a note for J.W. It was possible that he'd come after she was gone. *Dear Jack, I have gone out to dine with Professor Grant. Business. Dear Jack, I—*

"You like Uncle Paul, don't you?" Janice asked as they went out on the porch.

"Very much," Marcia said absently. *I have gone out to eat, and I may accidentally meet Professor Grant. . . .*

"Are you in love with him?"

Marcia closed the door with a firm and final jerk. It was too late to leave any kind of note. "Sorry—I didn't hear you."

"Yes you did. Evasion is a very revealing kind of answer." Her smile made Marcia uneasy. "However, it's too bad that you're in love with Paul."

Marcia stared at her. "I don't know what you're talking about, Janice, but it sounds absurd."

"It's beneath you too," Janice went on, the smile now gone. "I thought you were *different*. That's why I decided to have you as a friend." She seized Marcia's arm, making her stop to face her. "You know how much I think of you, don't you? You realize that I have given my friendship to no one else in this world, don't you?"

Marcia wanted to pull away from her grasp, but she stood still. "I didn't know that, Janice. If it's true, it's wrong. You must—"

"Don't bother to talk words to me!" Janice said tensely, but she let go her arm, and they walked on. She stayed silent until they were opposite the short cut; then she spoke abruptly: "The only kind of person I can respect is one who doesn't give in to the so-called normal instincts. Those who do are mere animals of the herd. Those who don't give in have power; they can lead the herd wherever and however they wish."

Oh, come off it! Marcia thought; but she said, "Perhaps I understand how you feel. I used to. . . . But after certain experiences . . ."

"If you believe," Janice said impatiently, "that I feel this way only because I'm young and that I'll change, you're as stupid as any of them."

Marcia smiled. "There you are, Janice. You were wrong about me. I'm not the kind of person you can respect, after all."

But Janice was dissatisfied. "You've been misled, that's all. You've been influenced by Paul. People always go for that surface goodness and kindness of his."

This decided Marcia. "I'm sure that he's exactly what he seems to be," she said coldly. "Janice, I have to go on now. It's already past the time I promised to meet him."

Janice crossed the Heights with her. "So you don't mind about Millie?"

"Millie?" Marcia repeated, and then she was remembering that night at the Inn, when Matthew Grant had made some remark about Millie and she had wondered. . . .

"Yes, Millie Winters," Janice said carelessly. "She keeps that boarding house where he stays. Have you ever seen her?" When Marcia shook her head, she smiled significantly. "Well, when you do, you'll understand. And when all is said and done, Paul is only one of the herd, you know."

"Janice, it's indecent of you to talk about him this way to me."

But Janice merely laughed. "I think I'll call you Marcia. May I?"

Marcia walked on slowly, thinking of Janice's intense avowal of friendship and then the cruelty that had come only a few minutes later. Which was she to believe?

Both are true, for they spring from the same source and have the same purpose.

This thought had arisen in her mind without her seeking it, and she did not understand it. She was still puzzling over it when she entered the Bijou lobby. Grant was sitting in a lounge chair reading. He too is not what he seems, she thought suddenly, remembering Millie. The whole world was a lie, and she herself—

He saw her then and stood, smiling as if he did not think of himself or her as a part of the lie. She went to him, and because she was confused and even frightened, she did not greet him or think to explain her lateness, but said impatiently, "We can't have a cocktail here."

He was apologetic. "They used to serve liquor here, but two years ago the College made an arrangement—"

"I don't care about the history of it. It so happens that I'm very—well, tired, and I'd like at least a glass of wine. . . ." She saw that he was beginning to look amused. "I deserve it—for several reasons."

"I'm sure that you do." And then to her surprise, he took her firmly by the arm and led her toward the dining room. "But now that you are actually here with me, I'm not going to forfeit this engagement for the sake of artificial spirits. Furthermore, as we eat, I shall lecture you severely on the evils of alcohol. . . ."

She was aware then of how absurdly she had acted, but she knew that she did not have to try to explain. She herself wondered, in fact,

. what had been the cause, for his hand on her arm shattered the confusion and made both Janice and Millie seem remote, even unreal.

Grant lifted his slender glass of tomato juice. "May I toast you with my Bacardi?"

"Thank you," she said gravely. Suddenly she laughed. "You have reason to think me a confirmed alcoholic."

He waved his hand. "I know exactly how you were feeling."

"Well—I'm having a Bacardi too." She sipped the tomato juice slowly. "The power of suggestion is strong, for already I feel relaxed enough to tell you that I'm sorry I kept you waiting. I was talking with Janice."

"Then it's amazing that you're here yet. Janice has a way of detaining people." He went on seriously, "She has tremendous respect for you, you know."

"Respect?" Marcia said grimly. "If she had it, she has lost it." She hesitated, not wanting to talk about Janice, yet wanting to, especially to him. "She has divested me of my title. From now on I am to be merely Marcia."

"The nerve of her!" He gave her troubled face a searching glance. "However, you do understand, don't you, that she wasn't divesting you of anything, but elevating Janice Grant?"

"But why does she—I mean, why does she *bother* with me?" Marcia said slowly. "That's the mystery. I can't help her. I almost wish that you had not sent her to me."

He stared at her. "But I didn't send. . . ." Then he shrugged. "It doesn't matter. If she wanted you for a special friend, she'd have found a way. She's as resourceful as she is arrogant."

Marcia caught at this eagerly. "But underneath the arrogance there's something pathetic—some fear or loneliness that she has to hide from herself."

He looked at her surprised. "So you've sensed that too? That's why I always feel sad after talking with her, although usually she has also infuriated me."

"Then that would mean," she went on as if he had not spoken, "that the arrogance is automatic protection, and *that* would mean her actions are equally automatic—that is, not free. If she—" She laughed embarrassedly. "I didn't intend to be so ponderous about this, but the committee meeting on Carol Leeds made me very conscious of the problem of human freedom." She fell silent again, suddenly wondering why that meeting remained so clear in her mind. "You see," she went on uncertainly, "until then—the meeting—I had thought of Carol as blatantly free. . . . That was the way she seemed, you know. Then, after Dr. Day talked to us, I had to think of her as—as. . . ."

He nodded understandingly. "Yes—at least I think I know what you mean. When we had the facts before us, it began to seem that she had never been free or—"

"But they were such odd facts," she broke in quickly. "Hardly facts at all. She must have been unusually sensitive to have been so deeply affected by them." She looked at him hopefully. "Don't you think?"

He shrugged. "They were facts, all right. I'm not particularly wise about such matters, but my guess is that they would have trapped almost anyone."

"Trapped?" she said fearfully.

He nodded. "That's what they did to Carol, isn't it? It's as if she had been born into a net. I suppose"—he laughed—"we all are, but fortunately most of us need not become so aware of it."

She shuddered. " 'Underneath the net I stray. . . .' "

"Not you," he said cheerfully, "Carol Leeds."

"That was Blake," she said almost impatiently. *They bore a net of golden twine to hang upon the branches fine.*

"Well, I'm relieved. You looked tragic. The time for worrying over Carol Leeds is past."

She roused herself. "I'm not worrying over her. . . ." *Pitying, I wept to see the woe that love and beauty undergo. . . .*

She knew that he was perplexed by what he saw in her face, and she tried to put the foolish lines out of her mind. He leaned toward her. "Besides, you know, it's still possible for Carol to. . . ."

Yes, she thought, not hearing the rest of his words, it's possible for Carol *to be consumed in flames of fire and in unsatisfied desire. . . .* She started guiltily. "I'm sorry. What did you say?"

He laughed. "I was, without subtlety, introducing a more pleasant topic. Another Bacardi—or shall we order dinner now?"

"We had better order. . . ." She glanced at the clock, suddenly wondering about J.W. "It's very late," she said abruptly. "I must hurry."

"You may begin to hurry," he said calmly, "after we have dined leisurely."

They ate in silence. She seemed preoccupied, and he was disappointed. "How's the Blake study?" he asked in an effort to make her talk again.

"I've almost finished the version you saw," she said without enthusiasm.

"Good! Are you going to send it to a publisher?"

"I suppose so. At least I thought that was what I was working toward. But now it seems very unimportant. Perhaps your criticism was right. Lately I've felt that my whole study is artificial."

"No, no," he said quickly. "It's the times, not your writing or ideas. I feel the same way about Melville. He is hard put to it to hold his own against the Cadets."

"You probably have very little time to give him," she said sympathetically. "Arranging all the English classes for the Cadets must be a fulltime job in itself. Why don't you take a leave?"

He grinned. "I consider myself indispensable."

"And you are," she said seriously. "Also, you are very unselfish."

He heard the sincerity in her voice and saw it in her eyes, and all his habitual defences went down, so that he had to fight against the strong desire to tell her the long story of how his wish for a leave had been thwarted first by his taking on the chairmanship and now by the coming of the Cadets; and how, even at the expense of not finishing Melville, he was not sorry to have to remain where she was. . . .

She was looking up at the clock again. "I really must go."

"Oh, yes—your tentative engagement," he said unhappily. He signaled the waitress, but when she arrived, he did not ask for the checks. "Surely," he said reproachfully to Marcia, "you are not going to leave without having even tasted the famous Bijou brandy!"

She looked puzzled, but laughed when he ordered two more glasses of tomato juice. The waitress eyed them suspiciously, but, after a stoic shrug, went off with the order.

He smiled sheepishly at her. "I hope you don't mind. I know you're tired, I know you have that tentative engagement, but, after all, we've only begun to talk about what I used as an excuse to meet you."

She smiled. "I don't mind," she said, and marveled to note that she really meant it.

He leaned across the table to light her cigarette. "You misunderstood me a few minutes ago," he said, flicking out the match. "I wasn't referring only to the element of time. I meant that next to the immediate problem of the Cadets, Melville seems remote. Cameron may talk in capital letters, but he's right, you know, in insisting that this program is a great opportunity. But I wonder if they're going to give us enough time in which to do anything with it. We haven't been given a chance to plan, but here is what I think. . . ."

As they walked slowly up the Heights, he was wondering if she were as aware as he of the beauty of the night. It was not only that the March evening had turned gentle and held the eternal promise of spring, but it was their being in it together; and to him, a solitary man, it was this that had given to the time its rare beauty.

"I'm grateful for this evening," she said suddenly. "You make everything seem worthwhile—the way you talk about it, I mean."

He shook his head in protest, although he said nothing. Couldn't she see that it was not he alone who made everything worthwhile, but their togetherness? He wished that he knew how to hurry her awareness of this, but he was afraid of blundering. "There's one thing," he said lightly, "that I can genuinely admire in Janice—her choice of friends. I can think of many obvious reasons why she should be attracted to you. I could—"

"I'll do my best to help her," she said wearily. She wished that he had not mentioned Janice.

He sighed. "I wasn't really talking about Janice." Then he looked at her curiously. "Why are you obsessed with the idea of helping her?"

"Why shouldn't I want to help her?" Involuntarily they had both stopped under a street lamp. "I'm a teacher, and she's—"

"And she's merely one out of many of your students," he went on for her. "Beyond maintaining that relationship, you shouldn't feel responsible for her."

She knew that she could not explain her intimate understanding of Janice. That would mean talking about Matt . . . about Martin. That would mean talking too personally. "You can't discount the personal element," she said vaguely.

"I don't mean to. But relationships have a functional value, and once you transgress them, you're in trouble. A teacher has to observe that boundary; otherwise he'd go mad trying to solve everyone's problems." Looking down into her serious face, he suddenly laughed. "You should know my landlady, Millie Winters. She has a remarkable philosophy of live-and-let-live, and she's a freethinker who—"

"So I've heard," she said coolly, and turned slightly away from him. "If you—" She did not finish what she was saying, but stared intently up the Heights. He turned to follow her look, but all he saw was the shadowy form of a man coming toward them and whistling a faintly familiar tune.

He turned back to her, but before he could ask what she thought she saw, she said rapidly, "If you don't mind, I'll go on up the Heights alone."

"Of course I mind!" he said indignantly. "You can't—" But he was stopped by the panic in her eyes, even while he told himself that he was probably imagining it.

She touched his arm. "Please."

"Whatever you wish," he said, and left her abruptly, for in that split second of time he thought he understood her strange behavior. The man now drawing near to them must of course be Scott. He crossed the street and went carelessly down the dark short cut, not looking back, for even in his white hot and instinctive anger, he did not want to embarrass them.

She stood listening to the two pairs of footsteps, Grant's going away and the other coming; and she had to steel herself against putting her hands to her ears to shut out the sound of the Prokofieff, which at that moment she hated.

J.W.'s face appeared within the area of light—calm, perhaps slightly amused, not surprised to find her alone. "Hello, Marcia," he said, smiling gently. "What are you doing here—and whom did I chase away?"

She realized then how childishly she had acted in sending Grant away, and she said defiantly, "That was Professor Grant, and you didn't chase him away. We dined together to discuss the Cadets."

"You are two exceedingly conscientious teachers." He reached for her hand, but she kept it clenched within her coat pocket.

"We hoped you'd be impressed that way." She was hating her childishness, but she could not help herself. "Perhaps you'll raise our salaries."

He shook his head reprovingly. "Marcia, Marcia. It is I who should be angry, not you. Do you realize that I was forced to chat with Mrs. Murdock for two hours!" He took her arm and they walked on up the Heights. "She kept insisting that you would come back any minute. Truly, I believe that the good soul would have been shocked to know that you were out dining with another man."

"Furthermore," she said suddenly, "I didn't meet him only to talk about the Cadets. I went because I wanted to."

He said nothing, but led her into the darkened house. "Mrs. Murdock has considerately gone to bed," he said then and faced her. "Now that you have confessed, shall I beat you?"

She walked away from him. His tender, amused tone seemed mocking to her. "I almost wish that you would. Or that we could have a great, furious quarrel. There are so many things never said between us."

He came to her and took her cold hands in his. "You're half hysterical tonight, Marcia. You're overtired. That's what teaching does to you. You're not meant for it. Grant had no right to drag you out to talk shop. You're too—too—" He kissed her roughly. "Marcia," he said then more quietly, "I think that Russ will be home for my birthday in May. When you meet him, one of your reasons will be gone."

She was indifferent to his words, although she was aware that they should have much meaning for her; and she wondered suddenly if it were possible that she no longer loved him. The thought gave her a curious sense of relief, and she broke away from him and said almost eagerly, "Jack, you're right. I *am* very tired—and I have an early class in the morning."

He said, "Of course, dear—but it was unkind of you to shorten our evening together."

"Yes, yes," she said hurriedly, not hearing or caring what he had said. He looked at her queerly, but she smiled and opened the door for him, excitedly awaiting her own reaction to his leaving. There was a single, clear idea in her mind: if tonight as he walked away from her, she did not feel that she was losing the whole world, then she would know that she was free.

"Oh, yes," he said, turning back to her on the porch, "I forgot to tell you. I'm going out of town day after tomorrow. I shall try to see you tomorrow evening, but I may be too busy."

"How long do you expect to be gone?" she asked flatly, her new excitement already dead.

He took a step nearer to her, and she saw the slight smile on his lips. "I can't say, Marcia. It may be a day, a week, or a month."

She knew then that he was punishing her for her evening with Grant. But she felt no anger, only self-loathing. "I see," she said. "You'll call?"

"Of course I'll call, Marcia," he said gently, and went away.

She closed the door and leaned heavily against it, morbidly satisfied to have been given an answer.

Chapter Five

SCOTT left the faculty meeting early. He ran down the stairs, lighted a cigarette as he strode across the dark hall, and flung open the door as if in a great hurry. But outside he hesitated. Where to? Home, of course, to tell Judith. There was still some pleasure in the thought of telling her, but it was no longer perfect.

Why couldn't one thing remain perfect for him? Just one thing. That wasn't too much to ask.

He struggled against the malicious darkness that was spreading over his mind. Ritson's letter of acceptance was in his pocket to be touched, to be reread, to be read by Judith. Ritson—he who had politely turned down his belabored scholarly manuscripts—had leaped to take *Sentimental Farce,* which had been dashed off in the sparse hours wedged out of a few months of teaching.

Ritson's letter had made him so carelessly happy that he had thought this was one meeting which he could take in his stride, and he had completely forgotten that promotions for next year were to be announced.

Not that he had expected a promotion. According to the fairly stabilized rate at which one climbed the academic ladder, it wasn't quite time for him to step up again. Even so. . . . And of late he had been much too busy to worry about such things. Even so. . . . Well, when you considered that a relatively young man like Grant could become permanent chairman, and Medora Day, a woman, could become a full professor. . . . When you considered those things, it was not satisfying to contemplate Assistant Professor Scott's remaining Assistant Professor Scott.

His cigarette dropped from his fingers, and he ground it out under his heel. He could hear Judith saying, "But, Owen, nothing is *different*

274

from what it was or from what you expected! Why do you think yourself into such moods?"

He squinted up at the white sun. When he looked away, there were yellow spots before his eyes. Yet it was cold. He shivered, but went on forcing himself to look out into the day, trying to see it as Judith would see it. April was her favorite month.

He had no favorite month. Not even a favorite season. Why not? He doubted if he had even a favorite book or author. Teaching had leveled all that down for him. Judith had habits too. The way she held her fork. The way she slept on her side, like a swimmer. *He* had no habits. Again, why not? It was like discovering that he didn't exist.

Judith was running the vacuum sweeper in the front room and didn't hear him come in. He stood in the hall watching, annoyed. Her profile was intent. He envied her the soothing absorption in work. She grew a little angry as she pushed and pulled the sweeper back and forth over one spot. He saw the tiny dot of white lint that stayed secure in the rug. Finally she shoved the sweeper aside and stooped to pick the lint up in her fingers.

"Hello!" he shouted then.

Startled, she looked over her shoulder and stood up quickly, dropping the lint into her pocket. She started to say something and then reached out to snap off the current in the sweeper. Together they watched the bag sink into itself until after a final gasp and jerk it hung in listless folds.

It's hollow too, Scott thought, and then wondered why he had thought it.

"You're so early!" she was saying.

He bent over the coffee table for a cigarette. "Heard from Ritson today."

Judith was winding up the sweeper cord. For a minute he thought that she hadn't heard him, but then she said quietly, "Good. We can celebrate tonight."

He dropped the cigarette back into the box. "Just how did you know that Ritson's letter would call for a celebration? How did you know that it would be *good* news? God knows, I've had little enough of it! Besides, *you* didn't like the manuscript."

"I didn't like it for reasons of my own. But I knew that it would catch on. It's very cruel and very brilliant, Owen."

"Thanks," he said bitterly. He took the letter from his pocket. "Well, here it is. But as you already know what's in it, perhaps you'd rather not bother to read it."

"Don't be silly. I'm dying to see it!" She rolled the sweeper into the closet, then came back to him and sat down. "But my hands are grubby. You read it to me. Please."

He grimaced but read it aloud, quickly and without expression.

275

"How wonderful," she said, and he thought the words mechanical. He refolded the letter and slid it into the envelope.

Her forehead was puckered. She was trying very hard, and standing there looking down upon her, he felt an alien shock of pity for her. "How wonderful," she said again, and then seemed to realize that she was repeating words. "I mean, how wonderful that they want it almost exactly the way you wrote it! You won't mind changing that one chapter as they suggest, will you?"

"Of course not," he said tightly. He made a move to throw the letter down upon the hall table, but changed his mind. This letter went back into his pocket. It was his letter. She hadn't earned a part of it.

She was watching him. "Owen, why aren't you happy over that letter?"

"Perhaps I would be," he said, "with a little encouragement from you."

"No," she said patiently. "Something spoiled it for you. What happened, Owen?"

He pretended not to hear. "I'm hungry."

She started up at this. "I'll get lunch for both of us."

"Never mind," he said, striding through the dining room. "I'll get my own."

While he was pouring a glass of milk for himself, he discovered that he had a headache. He took two aspirin. He was hungry too. Bread and butter would do. But the butter was in the icebox and too hard to be spread. He banged shut the refrigerator door and explored the blue cooky jar. There were two stale spice cookies. He made a face at them but stuffed one into his mouth and found it surprisingly good.

He ate the second cookie and began to wonder about Judith. She was being very quiet—or had she gone upstairs? He peeked around the door and saw her dark head. She was just sitting.

He carried his milk into the front room and sat down on the couch. He felt better, although he hated the way her hands were lax in her lap. "What about your lunch?" he asked good-naturedly.

"I'll get something soon," she said absently. "But I wish you'd let me fix you something hot."

"Milk is a great food," he said. He sipped a little from his glass and then set it down on the table. He didn't really like the stuff. After a while he said casually, "They announced promotions and that sort of thing at the meeting this morning."

Her eyes were immediately alert. "So that's it," she said as if to herself.

This angered him, but he kept his head. "Need I tell you that I'm still Assistant Professor Scott?"

"But you didn't expect a promotion now, did you?"

He steeled himself. She was already arguing with him in her intolerably reasonable way. "Perhaps not." He yawned and stretched his arms up over his head. It was necessary to impress her with how casually he was taking all this. "But when I heard the names of all those who *did* receive promotions, I began to wonder. . . . Well, you know how it is." He shrugged.

Suddenly she came over to him. He was surprised. Of late she seldom made an impulsive move toward him. Her hand was on his arm, and he felt that her fingers were tense. "Owen, please, *please* don't allow it to spoil Ritson's letter!"

He put on a puzzled look. "But, Judith, I haven't the slightest idea of what you're talk—"

"I know how you feel about such things," she cut in. "I know how easily you get the feeling that you're being forgotten, that other people are going ahead of you. But, Owen, please be reasonable about it—just this once!"

He winced and then spoke loudly to cover it up. "What on earth do you mean, Judith?"

"Don't you remember," she said rapidly "how you promised to be happy if *Sentimental Farce* were accepted? You said that it was the most important thing, that nothing else would matter."

He waited to hear if she had more to say, but she was silent. She had slid to the floor, and sat there curled up, looking like a long-legged little girl. Again the curious pity came, dividing him against himself so that he was like two people. He picked up the glass of milk, steadying both hands around it. "You can't promise *anything* about happiness," he said.

She merely nodded, and the resignation in the final bent of her head filled him with fear. The thought that she had been pleading for something beyond the moment crossed his mind like a shadow, but it was too elusive for him to examine. He was angry too, because of her subtlety. Why didn't she speak out the thoughts she had against him! "For God's sake, tell me what you're thinking!" he shouted. He banged his glass down on the table, and some of the milk leaped over the rim and trickled across the glass table top until it reached the wood, where it began to seep under the glass. He stared at the spreading milk, and Judith turned to watch too. "Damn," he said softly after a minute, and got up to go into the kitchen after a rag.

Back with the rag, he put the cigarette box and tray on the couch and carefully lifted the glass top. Judith watched silently. When he had removed all traces of the milk, he replaced the glass and stood back to survey the result. "Did I smear it?" he asked.

She didn't answer, and he looked at her questioningly. Her eyes were bright with tears. He was surprised. "What's the matter?"

She tried to smile. "It's just that—well, when you do things like that, it's so easy to pretend that we're together the way we used to be."

He grinned, suddenly glad that something had made him go after the rag. "You have trained me well, m'lady."

He went back to the kitchen and threw the rag on a shelf. When he returned, Judith was sitting on the couch. "Tell me," she said, "exactly what happened at the meeting. About the promotions, I mean."

He told her, and she listened carefully. When he finished, she said in her reasonable way, "But, Owen, nothing is *different* from what it was or from what you expected!"

"So?" he asked coldly.

"So"—she shrugged—"I wish you could control your thoughts. Can't you see that you create your own misery?"

"No doubt I manufacture it out of nothing."

"Well, in a way—yes."

"I see." And then he exploded. She had said exactly what he had known she would say. "I'm getting out of here!" He started for the door, his whole being tensely waiting for another sound of her voice.

It came then, self-possessed and remote. "Owen, if you leave here in a rage simply because I tried to reason you into living like a decent human being, I'll not be here when you come back."

He didn't turn to look at her. "Don't threaten me. That's a new low for you, isn't it?"

She was sure that he must have slammed the door after him, but her ears didn't take in the sound. Her throat stung, and she swallowed several times. She stood still, looking about the room, seeing that she had not really finished the cleaning. She wished that she did not have to hold the unfinished room in memory, but she knew that it was already fixed there, as static against time as if she had left off the cleaning of it centuries ago.

She would go upstairs. The decision was like an inspiration, and she moved hurriedly, but when she was upstairs, she could not think what it was she had wanted there.

Downstairs again, she glanced at the telephone. She touched it, went away, and then came back to it. As she called the station, she began to feel that once more she was breathing familiar air, and as she put her question about trains, she remembered that of course she had gone upstairs to pack. It was simple. She had only to stop thought and feeling, and follow long-laid plans.

She packed quickly, even a little furtively. She knew exactly what she was doing, but she was unexpectedly self-conscious, as if she were enacting an anti-climactic scene witnessed by a jeering spectator who kept himself hidden in closets and dresser drawers.

Owen came home at their regular dinner hour, bringing a bottle of wine. He put it down on the kitchen table and kissed her briefly. The kiss was to assure her that everything was the same with them. A different kind of kiss might have indicated an apology or that something had really been wrong between them. Then he told her that they would celebrate *Sentimental Farce,* after all, but at home and alone.

He tiptoed upstairs to look in on Johnny, and she dished up the food. He was very gay at dinner. She tried to remember how she hated his handsome face when it was sullen, but couldn't. Her mind was empty, except for the image of her packed bag upstairs. It came to her that she would be more honest if she were to pick up the carving knife and stab him. She shuddered.

"Are you cold?" he asked solicitously, to show that he was observant of her every move.

She put down her fork. "Owen, I want you to know that I was serious this afternoon—about leaving, I mean."

He was startled, but unbelieving still. He said something in a half teasing way. She began to talk earnestly, until at last she saw by his face that he understood. He pushed back his plate roughly. She faltered then. "I'm sorry to spoil your dinner," she said foolishly.

Without knowing it, she had hoped that they would finish the meal. She hated leaving so many unfinished things. A half-cleaned room, a partly eaten dinner. . . . Everything was fragmentary. "I had meant to be gone before you came back," she said, "but there's no train until ten in the morning."

Still he said nothing. Why didn't he quarrel with her? Why didn't he reassure her how petty and mean he could be? "The book will be a great success, Owen. I know it. That's important to—"

"It's like losing your shadow," he broke in as if he had not heard her.

"I'm sorry," she said because she could think of nothing else to say. She looked away from the fear in his eyes. "It will never be any different. I know that. I don't know how I know it, but I do. You see, I've made so many new starts. . . ."

His hand went out to her. "Isn't there *something* that I can do?"

She shook her head. "I'm sorry."

He stood up abruptly. "Stop saying that!" He paced around the table, striking his fist in his hand. "Give me some reason! For God's sake, give me a *reason!*"

She closed her eyes. "If you don't know now, you never will."

He came to her and put his hands on her shoulders, shaking her roughly. "You used to be jealous of Marcia Anderson. Is that it? Is that *it,* I ask you!"

She freed herself and stood up. "No, that isn't it. But I'd be grateful if it were. I think I'd go down on my knees in gratefulness."

He stared.

"Yes, I would," she went on. "I used to pretend that it was Marcia. And I pretended that it was because you didn't seem to have any love for Johnny. . . ."

"Go on."

"These things are unpleasant, Owen. I'd rather not say them. . . .

Well, all that pretense was only to hide the fact from me that you—"

"—that I'm such an odious person, no doubt."

"—that you were changing me into something I didn't want to be. You see, Owen, you never change, but I have since living with you. I never used to quarrel. Now I do. I hear my own voice get shrill and loud, and I want to throw things. Upstairs in my drawer I've kept— Owen, where are you going!" She ran after him to the door.

"Not to kill myself, if that's what you fear. I shouldn't care to add *that* to your conscience." He stood twisting the doorknob. He gave it a final wrench and let it go. "But if you think I'm going to stay here tonight and carry your bags to the station in the morning, you're crazy!"

"Owen, please don't leave here tonight!" She made her voice a whisper because he was holding open the door and she was aware of the nearness of the Holcombs. "You know Riverville. I don't want any talk—and I'm thinking of you. You can sleep on the couch. In the morning, I'll stay out of sight until you go to your eight o'clock. Please, Owen! It's important—for you—that you go on with everything as usual."

"You have it all thought out, haven't you?" He shrugged. "Not that it matters much, either way. If you don't object, however, I'm getting out of here until you go to bed."

She said nothing. He stepped out on the little brick platform but wheeled about suddenly. "Please understand, Judith, I'm not taking this seriously." She tried to say something, but he waved it aside. "I assume that you're going to your sister's. I shall consider it a visit."

"But, Owen, that's wrong! I—"

"You need at least a month in which to make your final decision. If at the end of the month, you write me that . . . Well, we'll see about that when the time comes. Good night, Judith."

When he was out of sight, she closed the door firmly and fought off a sense of defeat. She washed the dishes and made the couch into a bed. Then she switched off the lights so that he would know it was all right for him to come in, and went upstairs.

She heard him leave in the morning at 7:30. That was earlier than usual. Probably he had slept no more than she had.

The kitchen was as she had left it last night. He hadn't eaten breakfast. She worried a little over that, and then caught herself. The worry was a habit, as automatic as his cleaning the milk off the coffee table yesterday. The habits were a shell, and if she chose, they could go on walking over the shell together for the rest of their lives. But she had chosen differently. . . .

After Johnny had his breakfast and the kitchen was straightened again, she didn't know what to do. For a moment she was tempted to fix something for his dinner, but she decided against it. It would be a false touch. He would hate it, and so would she, when she was on the train thinking about it.

She wandered through the rooms and then went out into the sunny morning. She stood at the edge of the sidewalk. The pavement glittered. She could even see the maid sweeping off President Cameron's porch. It was here that she and Owen had stood when they first came. Together they had looked toward the President's house and the Heart, and he had taken her arm and cried, "This is it, Judith! This is more like it!"

She heard a Holcomb window go up or down, and she moved quickly toward the house. Inside again, she walked softly, feeling like a thief in her own home.

To keep doing something, she went upstairs. Johnny was chatting importantly in his room. She stood, watching him.

He would miss his toys. She hadn't been able to pack many of them, and it might be a long while before everything was settled enough to send for the rest of them. He would miss Owen. It was wrong for a baby to be without its father.

It wasn't too late. She could change her mind. Owen half expected her to. Owen wasn't taking it seriously. . . .

In their room she opened a vanity drawer. There was nothing in it now except some pink and white fragments of china that jostled about with the motion of the drawer. She had kept them as a reminder, but now there was no need for them to stay there for Owen to come upon alone. She could spare him that—although of course he might not understand their presence. There was no way of telling what little things he would remember or what important things he would forget.

She picked up the fragments, one by one, and wrapped them in an old handkerchief. The moment her hand closed around this, she felt a new confidence. She went downstairs and threw the little bundle into the wire basket on the back porch, although the Holcombs had asked the Scotts please never to put china, glass, or tin in the basket. It was an act of ritual, and she stood unnecessarily long over the basket, rubbing her hands gently together.

Grant saw by the chalk-smeared board on the side of the station house that his train was going to be even later than last predicted. Impatiently he hitched his briefcase under his arm and strolled about the platform. He had no great desire to go to New York to read his paper. On the other hand, he had no desire to be in Riverville. There was at least a chance that a break in his routine would jostle him out of the apathy that possessed him for the first time in his life. He had a strong distaste for apathy.

A child's cry pierced the air. It was shrill and eager, and instantly he was aware of the ironic contrast between it and his own feeling. Turning disconsolately to find its source, he saw Judith and Johnny, and at the sight of Judith he had a surprising flare of anger. Why couldn't she take care of her own husband—keep him locked up if necessary?

He shrugged at his own unreasonableness and went over to their bench to join them. Johnny welcomed him with loud approval, but at first Judith looked at him blankly as if he were a stranger. Then a wariness came into her eyes and she said too quickly, "Oh, are you taking our train? How nice!"

"At least part of the way, I believe. I'm going to the Literary Convention in New York." He sat down next to Johnny, who demanded his briefcase. "Your husband told me that you're going to Buffalo to visit your sister."

Judith flushed. "Owen told you that? You've seen him already this morning?"

He nodded and refrained from saying that Scott had seemed unusually on edge and strangely eager to tell him that his wife was visiting her sister. Judith, he though, was unnatural too—tired, abstracted.

Johnny jammed the briefcase zipper and began to howl. Judith put her hand on his bright head. It was an instinctive gesture and she did or said nothing more, although Johnny went on screaming. "Where are you going?" she asked Grant.

He looked away from her and tried to fix the zipper. "To the Literary Convention in New York," he said as if he had not said it before.

"Oh. Owen must have wanted to go."

"I wish everyone could go," he said loudly above Johnny's cry. "This should be Spring Recess, but it isn't because of the Cadets. We could spare only one teacher, and as I had been asked to read a paper, I was the one delegated to go."

She reached out and pulled Johnny on to her lap. He still cried and his face was red. Grant watched uneasily, but Judith merely leaned her head down against Johnny's and whispered, "I love you very much. There's no need to cry. . . ."

The sad calmness of her face was poignant next to the frenzied and distorted face of Johnny, and as he watched, Grant was suddenly certain that she was not leaving Riverville for a casual visit. He wanted to tell her to stay, not to give up so easily; but even as he curbed this impulse, he began to understand that she was not a woman in flight. Her face told him that.

"You're admirably patient with him," he said.

She turned, startled by his voice. He said it again, and she looked back at Johnny. "He never used to cry like this," she said simply, as if to explain her patience.

Again Grant noticed her tiredness. The calmness, he decided, was costing her physical strength. He stood and took Johnny from her, hoisting him up on his shoulder and pointing down the tracks. "The train, Johnny!"

"Is it really coming?" Judith stood beside them. It isn't real, she told herself. She looked at Grant and Johnny, and both of them were a part of the unreality.

She heard a roar and felt hot air against her face. Then there were sounds and motion and the reluctant awareness that she herself had to move. Mechanically she followed Grant to the coach where a brakeman stood shouting. They had to stand aside while someone got off the train. She glanced down at her neatly gloved hands. They were idle and empty. Without warning the strange detachment left her, and she clutched at Grant's arm. "Johnny!" she cried. "You're not used to carrying him. You may bump his head. I can manage. Please, I can—"

Dimly it crossed her mind that Grant understood perhaps too well, for without a word he put Johnny into her arms.

Grant left the crowded lobby and waited on the sidewalk. Madison Avenue was almost dark in the dim-out, and he could see clearly the stars above New York City.

Looking back into the lobby, he glimpsed Silas Seabolm still shaking hands. Si had put on weight and softness, but he had the same delicate nose and fastidious mouth, the same wide blue eyes, and the same round cheeks that had always reminded Grant of a Rubens cherub.

At last Si ran out to him. "And now for Darcy's," he cried in his still boyish voice. "That is, if ever we can find a taxi in this darkness visible."

At Darcy's Si discovered roast beef. Grant didn't care even to think about it after the heavy food of the dinner meeting, but Si had to have it. "Eloise claims she can't get it at all. I simply can't allow myself to miss this opportunity, can I?"

"I suppose not." Grant leaned back against the high oak and red leather booth, almost envious of Si's enthusiasm over roast beef. He sipped his drink, hoping for some synthetic cheerfulness.

When the roast beef arrived, Si was delighted all over again. "Ah, just as I love it—vital red in the center, boardered by two inches of rose pink." He began to cut delicately into it. "Paul, you realize, don't you, that you are our man of the hour? Everyone—even Zander—agreed that your paper contributes significantly to Melville lore."

"Frankly," Grant said, "that paper bored me stiff."

Si's golden eyebrows went up. "Don't pose, Paul. Reading that paper gave you exactly the kind of publicity you need. Why affect indifference? And why be so rudely secretive about your work"—he poised his knife and fork over the meat and leaned forward—"as you have been with me, for instance? Tell me, is the paper a chapter from the book?"

Grant laughed. "It's no more than an expanded footnote."

Si waited eagerly for a moment, but when Grant remained silent, he said irritably, "Really, Paul, your reticence hurts me. There's a reason for my interest. Some years ago I too puttered about with Melville. Of course"— he made a deprecatory gesture with his fork —"my study is not nearly so scholarly as yours. I didn't examine the letters, and I . . ."

Grant only half listened. When Si looked down at his roast beef, he stared absently at the life-size wrestlers painted on the walls, the pale, dead-pan pianist, the drunk at the center table being anxiously watched by the head waiter, the girl in the white evening dress and dark hair falling to her shoulders—

Marcia and Scott probably met at dinner. She always ate out. He'd eat out too, Judith not being home. And even if they hadn't planned it, they'd meet, for that was the way Riverville was. . . .

He jerked his mind back to Si. "Sounds interesting," he said mechanically.

There was nothing real to be said between him and Si, and his thoughts wandered again. Before he had known Marcia, he could not have felt so lonely as he did tonight. When . . .

"Teach Cadets?" he asked hastily when he caught Si's curious look.

Si made a wry face. "Naturally. Who doesn't? But I have petitioned to be released—in the interest of scholarship. After all, a man can't be expected to—"

"Is your program a good one? Do you really know what you're doing with them?"

"There's confusion of course, or so I hear." He shrugged. "I keep aloof."

Grant laughed grimly. "Everyone's keeping aloof. Through all those sessions today, I couldn't help wondering how much of that confusion we might not have eliminated if we had read and listened to papers on the teaching of Cadets."

Si waved his hand. "It's the Government's responsibility to eliminate the confusion. I dutifully meet my Cadet classes, but beyond that I refuse—I simply refuse—to become embroiled in this utterly undisciplined movement toward mass education. I can say with sincerity that I love the lecture hall, but I love better—"

"Who said anything about lecturing?" Grant broke in. "I'm talking about *teaching*."

"Very well, then," Si conceded impatiently. "I love the classroom, but I love better my study. *My* responsibility is to my subject. Besides, why halt scholarship merely to wrangle over something that would end before we finished the discussion?"

Grant shrugged. "You're right—why halt scholarship? Why not

apply it to a living issue for once? If you feel that the Cadets are too temporary, then talk about Veterans." He knew that Si was restless and listening only out of politeness, but he went doggedly on. "For that matter, why not bring into the open the whole machinery back of scholarship—salaries, tenure, leaves? What good is your study, Si, if you can't ever get into it?"

Si tilted his head and gave Grant a quizzical look, as if deciding whether or not to take him seriously. Suddenly he shook with laughter. "Oh, Paul, you gorgeous old rebel! You lovely Socratic gadfly! Tell me, why don't you come East? You could have your pick. Why rot in River-ville? Surely there's nothing there, now that Cornthwaite's gone."

Grant pushed aside his glass. "The only thing wrong with River-ville," he said glumly, "is its size. You can't go downtown even to eat a meal without meeting everybody. If, for instance, a wife leaves—" He laughed at Si's perplexed stare. "If you've finished your coffee, Si, I think I'd—"

"Do you realize," Si said indignantly, "that all evening you have successfully evaded talking to me about your Melville—and now you want to leave! Really, Paul, I hardly know what to think." His face wore a hurt look, but his eyes narrowed slightly. "Why is it that you're so reluctant to talk to me about your work, Paul?"

"No reason, of course!" Grant said hastily, feeling guilty as it oc-curred to him what doleful company he must be. Si had been un-usually tolerant. "It merely happens that of late Melville hasn't been the first thing in my mind. I certainly didn't mean to evade, Si."

"Well, then!" Si exclaimed happily, his eyes again wide and candid. He signaled the waiter.

"Nothing more, thanks," Grant said, "unless you'll have a brandy with me."

Si shook his head regretfully. "Sorry, but I dare not. My digestion, you know." However, he ignored Grant's protests and ordered another drink for him. He smiled tenderly. "One last drink for old times' sake, Paul."

Grant stifled his annoyance and reached for his pipe. The girl with the Marcia-like dress and hair had left without his seeing her face. He thought he was glad of that. He was—

"Your theme?" Si prodded gently.

"What? Oh, yes. Well, I've been interested in Melville's failures. It seems to me that—"

"Failures!" Si cried. "What a novel approach. Go on—go on!"

"It seems to me," Grant went on wearily, "that Melville wanted to be a social critic and satirist, but he was never particularly effective in this rôle because . . ." He did not talk well, he knew. For one reason he had worked with Melville too long in silence and private to talk freely about him to someone else. For another, he was disgruntled over the fact that the someone-else across from him was Silas Seabolm and not Marcia Anderson.

But every time he glanced up, there was Si nodding understandingly and listening with obvious and flattering interest.

Si insisted upon driving him back to his hotel in a cab, although he should have preferred to walk through the dark Village streets to the Square for a bus.

"Until tomorrow," Si said when they stopped before the hotel. "And I advise you to talk to Zander then," he said as Grant got out, "about coming East. He has power, you know. Did you see him holding court today?"

"Thanks for the advice," Grant said, laughing, "but the East will have to plod along without me. Besides"—he hesitated, then made a quick decision—"I'm going back in the morning."

Si was aghast. "But, Paul, things are just beginning! Tomorrow Zander will read his paper on Jung's theory of association and dissociation applied to James Joyce. Even," he went on quickly at the look on Grant's face, "if you're not interested in the subject, it would be only politic of you to hear it. I tell you, Zander has—"

"Thanks again," Grant said firmly, "but there are reasons why I must leave. See you at the next Convention, Si." He smiled, closed the door, and stood back on the walk.

The driver made ready to start, but Si said something to him and then quickly rolled down the window. "Paul," he said gravely, "one more bit of advice: hurry up the Melville. You've been at it a long while."

Grant was amused. "You mean the world is growing impatient?"

Si's voice sharpened. "I mean that one doesn't own ideas until they appear in print under his name. Scholarship isn't the leisurely game that you seem to think it. It's a competitive business, like everything else." Then he laughed and wagged a plump finger, as if to assure Grant that the moment of seriousness had been a kind of joke. "You've grown other-worldly, Paul. I have to watch after you." He sat back in his seat and told the driver to go on.

Puzzled, Grant watched after the cab until it was out of sight. Then, as he went into the hotel lobby, he forgot about Si, for with annoyance it occurred to him that instead of wasting more hours in New York, he might have taken a sleeper back to Riverville that very night.

It was dusk when he finally alighted from the train, and although he was tired and had not eaten on the diner, he strolled up the Heights as if he were taking a casual walk. When he rang the Murdock bell, he understood clearly that he had hurried back for the sole purpose of performing this irrational gesture. To punish himself, he made himself go through with it, and the moment Mrs. Murdock opened the door, he said abruptly, "Sorry to disturb you, but I wonder if you could tell me when Miss Anderson might return."

Mrs. Murdock seemed confused. "But she isn't out, Dr. Grant."

"Oh." He was at a loss, for he had been certain that he would find her out. He had come merely to give himself the bitter satisfaction of finding her gone, as if from that alone he could have known all that he wanted to know.

"Why don't you come in?" Mrs. Murdock invited, swinging the door wide open. "You don't have to wait for her to go out. I mean you can see her right here."

He stepped inside, and Mrs. Murdock shouted up the stairs. Justin Murdock arouse reluctantly from his chair, his newspaper dangling from one hand. "Evening," he said glumly.

"Good evening. I'm sorry to—"

"No trouble at all—not at all!" Mrs. Murdock said gaily. Her smile became significant as she turned to her husband. "Justin and I were just making ready to clean out the basement. I'm sure that you'll excuse us, Dr. Grant."

"Of course," Grant said uneasily.

The newspaper fell to the floor in a heap, but Justin did not pick it up. "Property owner, Professor?" he asked loudly.

Grant mentally discounted his half of Oaklands and said no. Justin nodded grimly. "You're a wise man. It's the renters who get all the privileges." Then he stepped around the newspaper and followed his wife from the room.

Grant stooped for the paper and refolded it. "Anything wrong?" Marcia called out to him as she hurried down the stairs.

"I'm not sure," he said, "but I think I've upset the entire establishment."

She laughed. "I didn't mean that. I was alarmed to know you were here, for I thought you were in New York listening to papers."

"I came back," he said unnecessarily. They sat down and he tried not to stare at her. She wore a long blue robe that made her hair seem as black as Judith Scott's. Scott. "I expected to find you—" He stopped short as Janice came down the stairs. "What are you doing here?" he demanded sharply.

"Well, you needn't ask me in that tone of voice!" Janice said angrily.

Even Marcia had glanced at him in surprise. "Why, Janice brought me her latest story to read. We were discussing it when you—"

"What's more," Janice said to him, "I was here last night and the night before—at Marcia's invitation, if you please."

He almost blushed guiltily, for this had answered the question uppermost in his mind so directly that he was afraid he must have asked it aloud. So Marcia had been with Janice, not Scott, nearly all the time that he had been away from Riverville. "Nevertheless," he said to Janice, but quite genially, "you're imposing upon Dr. Anderson. She probably has to sit up late grading themes after you leave."

Janice shrugged. "If she hasn't sense enough to tell me that she's busy, that's her hard luck."

Before he could speak, Marcia said quickly, "Well, she's right, isn't she?"

Janice laughed. "See?" She leaned over the banister. "I'll come along with you now if you'll take me to the Bijou for dinner. Wait till I get my things." She ran back up the stairs.

"You shouldn't have spoken to her that way," Marcia said in a low voice. "I try to make her feel perfectly free to come to see me whenever she wishes."

"But why?"

Marcia looked impatient. "Must I—" She stopped as Janice reappeared.

Grant turned to Marcia and said resignedly, "You've eaten, of course."

She nodded and smiled. "Besides, I *do* have themes to grade."

He allowed himself to look at her closely, and at that moment her face seemed not only very tired, but sad. "I had expected to find you away tonight," he said daringly. Let her think what she would.

She shook her head. "He didn't even call. He—" She flushed and looked away from him.

"His wife was on my train," he said quietly.

"His *wife?*" She had turned quickly back to him, obvious surprise on her face.

He felt suddenly unsure of himself, but he said, "Yes—Judith Scott."

She stared at him. "But I didn't mean— Why should *Scott* call me?"

"Paul," Janice said impatiently, "I'm starving."

He paid her no attention. "Isn't there a reason why Scott should call you?"

"I'm not waiting another minute!" Janice wrenched open the door and walked noisily onto the porch.

Neither Marcia nor Grant moved. Then he forced his eyes away from hers, as if to break a spell. "I had no right to ask you that. Sorry."

But she said, "There is no reason why he should call me. I don't understand how—"

"Never mind that," he said gently. He believed her implicitly, and it seemed to him then that he had never believed the other. "I came back from New York," he said irrelevantly, "because I was lonely there." That was all he could say, for the door was standing open and he knew that Janice was there on the porch listening intently.

He could see that Marcia understood. She did not protest or look away, but her face seemed sad again. He felt a twinge of resentment over her strange sadness, and he wondered fleetingly whom she had expected to call, if not Scott. But he was in no mood to be disturbed by these trifles. To know that it was not Scott filled the present moment with satisfaction.

So he said merely, "Tomorrow," and went outside to Janice.

"The Bijou stops serving at eight," she said irritably as they turned down the Heights.

"It could be," he said cheerfully, "but if you say so, I'm inclined to doubt it."

She was instantly wary. "Why?"

"Because, my girl, you're the most skillful mangler of facts outside the Nazi propaganda organization." As she made no denial, he glanced at her and found her pathetic. She was unhappy, and he was very happy. "I suppose, however, that you're hardly to be blamed for my being so easily and successfully deceived."

As if sensing the danger to be gone, she moved to him and linked her arm through his. "You *are* rather naïve, Uncle Paul."

He laughed. "You must be right, for only last night a friend passed the same judgment upon me. He, however, was polite enough to call it other-worldliness."

Chapter Six

KIM had little to say, and Marcia had too much time to be aware of Grant's presence at a table across the room. One minute she hoped he wouldn't see her; the next she was sorry that he didn't. Then Etta Wilson joined him and immediately engaged his whole attention by making him look through a stack of her ubiquitous white note cards.

Restlessly she looked around the Cottage, and when she saw Iris appear in the doorway, she beckoned to her. Kim had been watching. "She won't come to this table," he prophesied darkly, "with me sitting at it."

But she did. "Glad you have a big table," she said, sitting down with them. "Cliff Hughes asked us to meet to discuss Diaz." She glanced briefly at Kim. "That's the only reason I'm here."

Kim scraped back his chair. "You can't trap me into a meeting. I don't attend them—on principle."

Marcia wished that he would leave so that she could go too, but he made no other move. She felt apprehensive. For Diaz she had little fondness, but occasionally she met him socially at J.W.'s. "Sorry," she said, looking at her watch, "but I must go. I have a one-thirty class."

"Oh, no, you don't." Hughes had joined them. "Dexter asked me to tell you that the B's have been withdrawn without notice."

She was concerned. "They can't be! We haven't studied dependent clauses."

Iris laughed. "Better write to Washington about it, Marcia."

"Now listen to something important," Hughes was saying impatiently. "A certain Cadet—I promised to keep him anonymous—came to me especially to tell me that Diaz has been, in a most insidious manner, stirring up the whole squadron against Meyerson."

"How do you mean?" Marcia asked sceptically.

Hughes explained earnestly: "In his classes—he has the same group that Sid has—he makes innocent seeming remarks about Sid's being an able instructor in spite of the accident of his race, and he suggests that they shouldn't mind having a class under him. And so on—you know the line. This Cadet who told me has the intelligence to see what's happening, but a few of the others—particularly the already discontented ones—are only too happy to perform exactly as Diaz wants them to—"

"Well, that's none of our business," Kim broke in. "I don't happen to like Diaz, but—"

"Why don't you like him?" Iris asked.

He shrugged, avoiding her look. "Maybe I don't like him because of the way he smirks at you. Whatever the reason, it's personal. And that's the only true kind of hate there is."

"This isn't a matter of hate," Iris said evenly. "What you don't seem to understand, Kim, is that there are a few *impersonal* things which are important to some people."

Hughes nodded emphatically. "That's right. Someone has—" He looked up at the hovering waitress and ordered four cups of coffee to send her away. He turned back to them. "Someone has to be alert to this sort of thing. I want this fought in the open. I want it to go directly to J.W.—today, if possible."

"Not today," Marcia said involuntarily. "It's his birth—I mean, why take it to Mr. MacMillan?"

Hughes stared at her. "Why, I want Diaz fired. Who else could effect his resignation?"

"*You* want him fired!" she said angrily. "What right have you to want that? Besides, Mr. Diaz is a member of the family."

"Exactly," Hughes said grimly. "I want to see which one the MacMillans will protect—Diaz, who is obviously a skunk, or Meyerson, who is a damn good teacher and an honest man."

"I'm sure that Dr. Meyerson is a damn good teacher and an honest man," Marcia went on, although she was aware that she was merely using Cliff Hughes as an outlet for her own rising sense of fear, "but right now you're making a guinea pig out of him. How do you know that he wants to be protected by anyone, or that he wants a civil war waged over his head?"

Kim banged the table. "That's what I say! People are always telling others that they need protecting or that they're maladjusted, or that they have sick minds." He turned pointedly to Iris. "All I hope is that you don't begin to feel *pity* for Sidney Meyerson."

"That remark," Iris said coldly, her hands unsteady as she lighted a cigarette, "is on the same moronic level as most of yours are. If you think I'm going to wither away with disillusionment because I made one error in judgment, you—"

"What's more," Marcia said to Hughes, "you have no moral right to persecute a man merely because he has a few ideas you don't like. For that matter, what about Professor Webb? You don't approve of all *his* ideas. I distinctly remember a committee meeting right here in the Cottage when you overheard him say something about Plato that made you—"

"Leave Webb out of this!" Hughes shouted, half rising from his chair. "You know how he floats in and out of ideas. You can't ascribe a practical motive to him, any more than you can to one of the Summit elms. He doesn't—" He dropped back into his chair as he became aware of the startled waitress standing to one side with a shaking tray of coffee.

In the deep hush, the girl set the coffee before them, and tiptoed away. Kim pushed aside his cup and abruptly left the table. Iris watched him stride out of the Cottage. Then she jabbed out her cigarette. "Maybe Kim had a point when he said that nothing really matters beyond the personal. Against the emotional, half hysterical idiots that we turned out to be, Diaz could win with his mind blank."

"I wasn't being personal—or emotional," Marcia said distantly. "I was arguing about a—a principle."

"I didn't mean to shout," Hughes said grudgingly, "but if you understood Webb, you'd—" He grinned guiltily at a look from Iris. "I'll be good. You're right, of course, Iris. We've got to be objective and reasonable."

"About what are we to be objective and reasonable?" Marcia asked caustically, for she still felt some lurking threat. Instinctively she glanced across the room for Grant. He was gone. But then, how could he have helped her?

Etta was gone too, and someone else was sitting— "Dr. Meyerson!" she cried in triumph to Hughes and Iris. "There he sits, calm and comfortable, enjoying a good lunch and a book. He certainly doesn't appear to need our help!"

They looked, and Iris said, "Why not ask him to join us? Why not talk this out with *him?*"

Hughes said that was a good idea, and went over to Meyerson, Iris and Marcia silently watching. Meyerson came back with Hughes, carrying his book and coffee. "I didn't tell him why," Hughes said under his breath as they sat down.

"How are things going, Sid?" Iris asked brightly.

"Fine . . . fine," Meyerson said pleasantly.

Marcia smiled but said nothing. Even Hughes was without words.

Into the awkward silence Kim reappeared as abruptly as he had left. "I've thought it all over and decided you're right." He held out his hand across the table. "I'm glad to see you, Sid," he said with deep significance.

Meyerson looked faintly puzzled, but shook the proffered hand. "And I'm glad to see you."

Kim drank his cold coffee. "What's happening?"

"*Nothing*," Marcia said emphatically. She picked up Meyerson's book. "Thomas Wolfe! But I thought you were writing a book about Wolfe."

He smiled. "I am. Does that preclude my reading him?"

"Of course not. But I . . . well, I thought. . . ."

He laughed outright. "I understand what you thought. I thought that way for several years. Then it occurred to me that I had been thinking about Meyerson's thoughts upon Wolfe so exclusively that I had almost forgotten what Wolfe himself was like. So I started reading him—and I've made an amazing discovery. He is the same—precisely the same—as he was before Meyerson began to anatomize him."

Kim was listening with growing bewilderment. He signaled Hughes. "Haven't you said *anything* about—"

"What is the nature of your study?" Marcia asked quickly.

"To myself I have called it a study of the growth of objectivity in Wolfe." He looked around the table apologetically. "Sounds forbidding, I know. But I have found it fascinating to watch the progress from self-absorption to world-absorption." He shook his head sadly. "Of course, Wolfe didn't live long enough to achieve complete objectivity, but even in the writing he accomplished, we can see his ego-bound world begin to triumph over itself to become universal."

"Triumph?" Kim said suddenly, sitting forward. There was a disbelieving, yet eager look on his face. "Why not call it escape?"

"It is a kind of escape," Meyerson said readily. "An escape from subterranean darkness to one's place in the whole—or, we might say, escape from selfishness. But I prefer to call it triumph, victory. It is the flower of the buried seed and the reason for the seed. . . ."

Meyerson's deep voice cast a spell. Marcia felt relaxed, as if whatever had threatened her was now remote. She was thinking too that Grant would agree with Meyerson.

"You must be that kind of man—objective," Kim said to Meyerson. "That must be why you can take what happened today so calmly."

Meyerson said nothing, but lighted a cigarette absently. Then he held out the crumpled package. "So sorry. Please join me in a cigarette."

But everyone else was looking at Kim. "What do you mean, Duncan?" Hughes demanded. "What happened today?"

"Don't you *know*?" Kim cried. "I thought it was the purpose of this meeting to find out such things."

"Meeting?" Meyerson said, surprised.

Kim looked at him. "You didn't tell them?"

Meyerson seemed genuinely puzzled. "But they didn't ask me to tell them anything."

Kim closed his eyes and murmured, "Ah, meetings." He opened his eyes and said with ironic deliberateness, "My dear colleagues, when I left your over-zealous presence, I stepped outside the door and before I had traversed beyond the walk, I heard a piece of news which seems to be known by everyone except you. Dr. Meyerson had one hell of a time with his eleven-thirty Cadet class, and although I may be wrong, it is remotely possible that the matter might be considered relevant to our earlier and most aimless conversation."

Hughes glared accusingly at Meyerson. "Why didn't you tell us that something happened, Sid?"

Meyerson blew out smoke slowly. "I am sorry," he said finally, "that the news—as you call it, Mr. Duncan—has spread. I thought it important to keep it in confidence between me and my students. By now it is no doubt grossly exaggerated."

Hughes moved impatiently. "O Lord, tell us!"

Meyerson smiled briefly. "Indeed, I wish that it *were* up to Him to do the telling." He hesitated again, then seemed to reach a decision. "But I do see the point in my telling you, for then you will be equipped to combat the false rumors." He put out his half-smoked cigarette and lighted a fresh one, and Marcia wondered if that were a telltale sign of tenseness under the calmness. "When I entered the classroom," he said matter-of-factly, "I sensed a certain restlessness, although the class stood at attention as usual. I had no more started the lesson—prepositional phrases—when one individual dropped—perhaps threw —his book to the floor. Apparently this was a signal, for immediately five other Cadets put down their books and began to talk loudly among themselves. With the help of the Squadron Leader, I restored order, although I could not induce the six—only six, mind you— Cadets to study the lesson with us. I questioned them, and they told me frankly that they preferred to study under a gentile teacher. I said that I appreciated the frankness, and then"—he laughed—"the bell rang."

Marcia shook her head. "It seems incredible that they . . . I mean, they *are* Cadets, after all."

"They are men in uniform," Meyerson said quietly. "They are a cross-section of our country. As Dr. Wilson often reminds us, they are all the dialects of America. But they are also all the attitudes, the needs, the fears—all intensified in this unnatural lull before battle."

"But in America . . ." she said lamely, then did not know how to go on.

"What is America," he said quickly, "but a cross-section of the world? And when I consider that there were twenty-four men in that class who refused to join those six, I feel hopeful."

"You're being noble about it, Sid," Hughes said, "but we want you to know that you're not alone. We know why this started and I think you do too—and we're going to bring it out into the open."

"Thank you," Meyerson said firmly, "but I have done all that I intend to do about it. On the attendance slip, I suggested that the six be transferred to a different class, as they had requested. What is to be gained by doing more?"

"I can tell you what *I'll* gain!" Hughes cried. "And that's self-respect. I want to regain my pride in being a teacher. If this thing is given a fair hearing, then I'll have it. If not, then I'm through."

Meyerson gave him a quick look. "I can see plainly, Cliff, that this is a personal matter for you." He sighed. "Very well, my friends, but what do you propose to do?" He glanced questioningly around the table. "Is this really a committee appointed by the faculty?"

"Well, no," Iris admitted, "but. . . ."

Meyerson smiled sympathetically. "So what is there to do?" He leaned toward them, and his voice was low but clear against the clatter made by the girls now carrying away the last dishes from the deserted dining room. "Please do not think me unappreciative of what is in your minds. I know you for sensitive, loyal friends. But I know also that you need other traits for what you want to do. You must have unending patience and cold reason and, yes, a little hardness. You must, in short, know how to be effective without harming yourselves."

Hughes pushed back his chair and stood up. "You're a defeatist, Sid. Anyone following your advice would never act. I tell you what. I'm going to Cameron with the whole thing. He's sincere about his Educational Philosophy, and I think he'll go to MacMillan for us."

"I'll go with you," Iris said.

Hughes shook his head. "Thanks, but I'm doing this alone." He grinned wryly. "Sid's got me scared, and I haven't much faith in my ability to be effective without harming all of you. So if you don't mind, I'd prefer to go on from here alone."

Marcia was silently grateful for Hughes' attitude, yet she felt uneasy, as if some danger had been averted only temporarily.

Grant called to her as she reached the President's driveway, and she stopped to wait for him to join her, for she had turned so quickly at the sound of his voice that it was too late to pretend that she hadn't heard. "I'm glad to see you," he said. "I meant to speak to you at the Cottage, but I couldn't wait. I had to leave in a hurry to meet one of Scott's classes. He's ill."

She was embarrassed to have Scott mentioned between them again, and she said rather foolishly, "He shouldn't be ill. I heard that his book has been accepted. I thought that would make him especially well."

He shrugged. "He thinks it's arthritis, but no doctor will diagnose it."

Involuntarily they both had stopped. The driveway seemed strangely private and intimate, although they could hear voices from the Heart and cars on the Heights. His manner was casual, but she felt an onrush of new fear. Don't say it! she pleaded silently; don't—

"Marcia," he said quietly, "you've been avoiding me for a week—ever since the night I came to the Murdocks'. Why?"

"You're imagining things," she said, laughing nervously as she remembered the obvious and crude ways in which she had avoided him. And now that she was face to face with him, she could do nothing but stay silent and let him think her stupid or even damnably coy.

He spoke at last, and his voice was puzzled. "I thought you understood that night, and I thought too that—"

"Ah, Dr. Anderson! Do pardon my interrupting," cried Etta Wilson as she rounded the President's house, "but I had to catch you to make arrangements for going tonight."

"We must not waste a single moment," Grant murmured, exasperated; but then he raised his voice and said cheerfully, "Good afternoon, Dr. Wilson. And to what convention are you going tonight?"

"Convention?" Etta laughed shrilly. "It's not a convention, Dr. Grant, but a family party." She turned to Marcia, her sharp, thin face eager. "I happened to meet Mr. MacMillan—J.W., of course—in Deardorff's this morning, and as we fell to talking, I discovered that his uncle was one of Esther Cornthwaite's personal friends. Oh, they were quite, quite close, it seems. I explained my professional interest in Miss Cornthwaite to Mr. MacMillan, and managed—well, it ended with his inviting me to come to his birthday dinner tonight in order to meet this Mr. Willard. He—J.W., of course—suggested that I see you, for it appears that his man is to pick you up. I thought perhaps I. . . ."

"Of course," Marcia said, as Etta hesitated modestly. Grant had stepped aside, but she knew that he could hear. Well, why should she want it kept a secret? She said to Etta, "We'll stop for you shortly after seven."

Etta was grateful. "I do hope you don't mind, Dr. Anderson. In our Profession, as you well know, one must not miss a single opportunity or—"

"Or waste a single moment," Grant said loudly, coming back to them. "Dr. Anderson and I were revising the entire Cadet program when you came along."

"Really?" Etta cast a brief and sceptical glance around their choice of meeting place, but refrained from comment. "Only one other small matter," she said hurriedly to Marcia, "and I shall leave you to your—revising. Mr. MacMillan made mention of the fact that his uncle is a poet. I'm sure that it is remiss of me, but I cannot think of a poet by the name of Willard. Could you tell me his first name, please?"

"Philip," Marcia said. "Philip Willard. All his published poems are in the Library, for all the volumes were in Esther Cornthwaite's personal collection."

Etta paled. "And I overlooked them, no doubt thinking them irrelevant to my pursuit. However, I shall study them diligently between now and seven, for they should give me significant insight into Philip Willard's character and thus shorten the avenue of my approach. Until seven then," she said over her shoulder as she walked rapidly toward Science Hall, "and thank you for allowing me to intrude."

" 'Intrude' is right," Grant said softly, watching after her, then turning back to Marcia. "I've always understood that no one outside the family attended these birthday dinners, unless he be some exceptional personage like Esther herself. Are you an exceptional personage," he asked lightly, "or one of the family?"

"I—he invites me."

He was silent for a moment. "I believe," he said then, "that I have at least the answer to one question. You expected *him* to call that night?"

She nodded. He took out his pipe and absently fondled it, trying to smile amusedly. "Strange to think of him as a person, as a man who knows you better than I. To me he has always been a symbol." He hesitated, then asked as if it were an impersonal question, "You love him?"

She could only nod again. She knew that he gave her face a quick, searching glance. *Yes, I know that my face shows no happiness from this love, for it is a strange, oppressive love that makes me dread his nearness yet fear his being away. This imperative to love comes from the depth of my being. Beyond that, I cannot explain it. . . .*

With these words in her mind, she no longer avoided his eyes, and as she met them, she had the thought that she must look to him as Stephanie had looked to her when she had responded to questions with only her eyes, which had darkened with desperate, muted pleading. In that moment she understood fully for what they had been pleading; and she held her breath in waiting for his anger, his demanding, or the miraculous acceptance that could sustain itself without knowledge.

He took a step away from her and stood there, his hands deep in his pockets. Already she felt hurt. But when she no longer hoped, he reached out his hand and touched hers. "Weren't you on your way to the Murdocks'?"

She shivered, for as the warm gratefulness went through her, she realized how cold she had been. His touch, his eyes, his words were natural and without anger . . . accepting. "I—yes."

Carlton J. Cameron declined tobacco in any form but took with some alacrity a small glass of white burgundy. J.W. lighted a cigarette and leaned back, deliberately refraining from asking Cameron to come to the point. He knew his man. Also he knew that Cameron must have an urgent point, or he wouldn't have sought him out at his home.

Cameron tasted his wine, relished it, and then said, "I delivered my address in Cincinnati last Monday."

J.W. already knew this. "It was well received, I trust."

Cameron bent his fine head in modest confirmation. "I titled it 'The Responsibility of Freedom,' and I dwelt particularly upon Academic Freedom. I endeavored to show that Freedom in a Democracy must be considered a Positive Thing, not merely a childish refuge from all bonds, and I reiterated the distinction made by John Milton and others between Liberty and License, relating that distinction especially to Teaching. . . ."

As J.W. listened, he allowed his eyes occasionally to rest upon the Cézanne landscape hanging on the wall back of Cameron. From its cool greens and classic design he drew patience. When at last the President's tone indicated peroration, he stifled a sigh of relief.

". . . and so there must be Responsibility attached to all teaching," Cameron was saying. "It is only through accepting such rational Responsibility that teachers can give to Education the Dignity it merits and the Power it requires to combat the Barbarism now stalking the world."

J.W. roused himself from the spell cast by the rolling periods. "Oh, I agree."

"Of that I am very glad," Cameron said after a moment's hesitation, "for you will now understand why we must ask for the immediate resignation of Vincent Diaz."

There was a short silence. Then J.W. said lightly, "Vincent? Why, what has he been up to?"

Cameron gave him a reproachful look, as if he found the question unduly flippant. "Mr. Diaz has deliberately aroused Race Prejudice. There is, in fact, evidence that he has implanted it where it might otherwise not even have existed."

There was another silence. J.W. became very grave. "He shouldn't have done that."

"No," Cameron said dryly, "he shouldn't have done that."

J.W. looked at him quickly. Was the man being ironic? He couldn't be sure. "What do you mean by evidence?"

"Yes—a pertinent question." Cameron sat forward. "We must rid ourselves of *any* Teacher who cunningly distorts the Greatest Opportunity ever given to Education."

For a moment J.W. was puzzled. "Oh—the Cadets?"

"The Cadets, Mr. MacMillan. This very day, six Cadets in one of Dr. Meyerson's classes refused to submit to his rightful authority and requested to be transferred to another class."

"Meyerson . . .," J.W. said thoughtfully, shaking his head. "I was worried over that appointment."

Cameron was on his feet. "Dr. Sidney Meyerson is an excellent teacher."

"Of course, of course." J.W. stood too and walked to his bookshelves, absently moving his finger across the backs of a row of books. "Meyerson told you that he knows Vincent to be responsible?"

"I have heard nothing from Dr. Meyerson."

"From. . .?"

"From a trusted and conscientious member of the Faculty whose name is irrelevant." Cameron's voice became mildly reproving. "I had assumed that my Coming would in itself convince you of the Validity of my Information, as well as the Seriousness of the Situation."

"It does." J.W. returned to his chair. "And I assure you that I'll have a serious talk with Vincent. I'll— Sit down, Carlton, sit down."

Cameron reseated himself. "In that talk you will ask Mr. Diaz for his resignation?"

J.W. smiled briefly. "I hardly suspected this of you, Carlton. You're out for blood, aren't you?" He leaned forward confidentially. "This is the dilemma, which you yourself should have considered. We granted Diaz permanent tenure this year, and according to the contract, we have no right to break it other than for gross neglect of teaching duties or gross immorality."

Cameron crossed his long legs. "You do not deem Gross Distortion of Teaching Privileges sufficient reason?"

J.W. sat back and shook his head. "Not in the contract."

"In a matter of this importance," Cameron said gently, "you would allow yourself to be stopped by a Technicality?"

"I'm not speaking of what I personally wish or desire." J.W. kept his voice calm, but he tapped out his irritation on the arm of his chair. "It's what the printed contract says. Need I remind you of the distasteful publicity that could ensue if Vincent decided to protest the demand?"

Cameron did not answer immediately, but stared intently at the last remaining drop of wine in his glass. "Would a Faculty Petition bear weight with you?"

J.W. waved his hand. "Why go to that trouble? Certainly your word and judgment are enough for me. Besides, what could a list of names add to the case?"

"I see. Perhaps, then, I could appear at the next Trustees' meeting with a statement of the—Case."

J.W. shrugged. "The agenda are already compiled, and it's a full meeting—but if you wish, come along." Suddenly he smiled as if to make his guest more cheerful. "But I think I can safely predict that the others will see it as I do. They will regard any procedure which might induce counter-action as a threat to the good name of the College."

Cameron nodded politely. "I had thought, however, that the Good of our Students might be considered the proper Object of our efforts."

"No one would deny that," J.W. said good-naturedly. "In fact, that's the point, for we don't want to take steps that will keep students away from us, now do we?" He got up again and stood casually over the other man, looking down at him kindly and smiling a little. "You're an idealist, Carlton, and this is a business matter. A scandal of any kind, no students. It's a good thing that you have a few hardheaded realists around to make sure you have something left to be idealistic over."

Cameron smiled faintly. "I am not ungrateful." He swallowed the drop of wine and set down his glass. "A fine vintage."

"Another glass? Yes, have another glass in honor of my birthday."

Cameron arose quickly, offering his hand. "Congratulations! Indeed, I have already taken too much of your valuable time."

"Not at all, not at all," J.W. said amiably, but he was glad to have the end in view, and he did not protest when Cameron picked up his hat. He walked him to the door, not too quickly, yet not slowly. "Glad to have had this informal chat with you. Makes me feel in on things. Anything else on your mind, Carlton?"

They were standing on the porch, and Cameron fixed his eyes on the far horizon. "There is," he said, "the matter of William Holcomb. He has been offered a deanship Elsewhere, and he indicates that although he should be extremely regretful to leave John Willard, he may be forced to do so for the sake of more Adequate Remuneration."

"That," J.W. said irritably, "can certainly wait for the regular meeting." The surge of impatience made him feel at a disadvantage, for Cameron never lost his grave dignity, which, he supposed, was a kind of vocational pose. He forced a light laugh. "Holcomb's method of informing us that he wants a salary raise amuses me. This is the second or third time, and it's beginning to look like a threat."

" 'If you don't succeed at first, Try, Try Again,' " Cameron murmured. "A Homely Maxim." He set his hat upon his head and turned to the steps. "I shall do my utmost to persuade William to stay his Patience. Thank you for your time, and many Happy Returns of the Day." He walked to his car, the last sun rays lighting up the graying red of his hair.

As J.W. mixed the Martinis, it occurred to him that the Toast would have to be changed. For the first time in many years, they would not drink to Eileen. He was glad to have thought of this, for now he could be prepared with a new one.

He glanced across the room at Marcia, where she sat talking with Grace and Marie. Now she appeared natural enough, but earlier he had thought her to be in one of her unaccountable moods. When she had first met Russ, she had become almost as shy as Russ himself, and there had been scarcely any words between the two of them. Russ had gone off to his usual corner by the fireplace, and she had stayed close to Grace. It was as if their meeting had meant nothing. . . .

Yes, it was upsetting to introduce a radically new element into one's life. The necessary change in the Toast, for example. Would it be proper to toast Marcia?

Philip, he saw, kept an appreciative eye on Marcia. It was obvious that he would like to be talking with her, but Etta Wilson had fixed upon him tenaciously. Her somewhat strident voice arose with momentary clarity. ". . . impressed with the profundity of your poem 'Trinity.' Do you refer to Christianity in the line, 'But what dark fantasy shut close the temple doors with Isis not returned'? And when you say, 'She is wild with hate,' do you mean. . . ."

Marie had left Marcia and Grace to join her husband and Otis beneath the portrait of Eileen. A Lieutenant (j.g.) uniform, J.W. decided, was what Harry had always needed. Although his Navy commission took him no farther to sea than a desk in Washington, he had somehow acquired the look of having just emerged from salt air. He gave his wife a brisk nod in his new manner, and went on talking to the old man, who stood chafing his hands behind him and regarding his son-in-law with near indulgence. Otis had the landlubber's awe of the Navy in any form, and besides, Harry's absence had made it necessary for him to return to harness in his own dairy.

Marie soon grew bored with whatever Harry was telling, and she looked restlessly around the room, her gaze slightly incredulous as it stayed upon Etta for a moment, then critical as it shifted to Marcia. Suddenly she turned to stare up at Eileen, and J.W. wondered what was passing through her mind.

He should not, he knew suddenly, toast Marcia. Not only might it embarrass her, but it would perhaps shock Russ.

He moved to see his son. He was still in his corner, but had been joined by Vincent Diaz. That little man dangerous? He was a parasite, of course, and one that would sell his soul twice over for an easy berth. He must also be stupid to have brought himself so conspicuously to Cameron's attention.

Certainly he was too unimportant to be dangerous. He realized, however, that he'd feel more assured if he could overhear the talk between him and Russ. Was it possible that he was witnessing what Cameron would call the Pernicious Influence actually at work?

But Russ was not gullible. Somewhat bitterly he reminded himself that his son had a stubborn, independent mind. If he had ever been an easy prey to influence, persuasion, or even sensible guidance, it had been when he was much younger.

Perhaps, he thought suddenly, some teacher earlier in Russ's life had exerted such an influence. This thought startled him, then angered him. How else explain his son's obstinacy, his pulling away? Some teacher had seized upon Russ with the deliberate intention of molding his mind. Some deceptively mild-mannered teacher had sought to satisfy his own ego by planting the seed of separation between son and father.

His mind obsessed with this thought, he saw anew Vincent Diaz and Etta Wilson, who were teachers, and now they seemed to him mysterious beings with fathomless meaning. And Marcia, he thought in surprise—she was one too! His eyes found her again, and the sight of her instantly soothed him. She was beautiful and all woman. In spite of her moods, he knew her well. For complete reassurance he looked once more at Etta Wilson and saw that she too was mere woman, and a very plain one at that. His imagination had been over—

"My dear nephew," Philip said, coming toward him, "why are you taking so fiendishly long over those Martinis? I have never before in my life needed a stimulant as I do at this moment." He touched his forehead with a white silk handkerchief. "And what perverted sense of humor made you invite that Wilson woman?"

J.W. laughed. "She invited herself, especially to meet you. She's out with tooth and claw for biographical data on Esther."

Philip seemed slightly mollified. "I'm relieved, for I had the horrible suspicion that you intended her to serve as a substitute for Esther." He tucked away the handkerchief and said with a modest little laugh, "The amazing thing is that she seems to have memorized every line I've published." He sighed, but returned to Etta.

"Russ," J.W. called, "will you please serve the Martinis?"

"Of course, Dad," Russ said and promptly came for the tray. "Don't I always?"

J.W. smiled, pleased.

Marcia wondered why they did not begin to drink their Martinis. Harry alone seemed certain of what to do. He faced Eileen's portrait, raised his glass, and said gravely, "To Eileen!"

"Shh!" Marie rasped, then turned deliberately and gave Marcia a significant smile.

Marcia thought the smile in bad taste and was embarrassed as she sensed other heads turn toward her. But too she was aware of feeling triumphant over this silent recognition. She avoided looking at the portrait, although she had a childish desire to do so. Nor did she look at Russ. He's hating me, she thought with strange satisfaction.

They waited for some signal from J.W. He and Grace were talking casually, as if neither had heard Harry. Suddenly J.W. said quietly, "To the memory of Esther."

There was a hush in the room, which was first broken by Etta Wilson, who turned to Philip and said, "It is indeed a privilege to drink to the memory of Esther Cornthwaite." Philip nodded pleasantly, not detecting that Etta's manner had become professional. "Mr. Willard," she went on firmly, "I understand that you have at your command more pertinent information regarding the life and character of Miss Cornthwaite than any other individual who knew her, not only because of your natural intuitiveness and sensitivity as a poet, but because of your long-standing friendship with her. Lest I appear too forward, I should first explain that I have taken upon myself the delightful but responsible task of editing—"

"Ah, yes . . . yes," Philip broke in impatiently. "My nephew explained something of that to me. I am honored to be called upon to aid in such valuable work. Her character? Let me expound my concept to you." He moved to the edge of the couch and set down his glass. "Esther is a classical figure. Do you understand what I mean by that, Miss Wilson?"

Etta nodded politely. "I believe that I do, Mr. Willard. Anything of a *factual* nature, Mr. Willard, will be a great help to me."

But Philip appeared not to have heard, for he said, "Perhaps I can clarify my meaning by offering myself as contrast—for it is only by comparison that we think at all, isn't that true, Miss Wilson?"

Again Etta nodded, and this time the politeness was more noticeably forced. Her expression said: In my Profession, classicism, as well as the methods of thought, is an old, old story.

Philip's enthusiasm was mounting. "However, do not think that I place myself at the opposite temperamental pole. I am no Romanticist. Oh no, indeed. I call myself a *Roman*—yes, a Roman, Miss Wilson. I am one in whose mind the classical ideal is still enshrined and revered, but I am also one who cannot ignore the caress of the sensible world. Confusion"—he touched his forehead and closed his eyes as if in pain —"conflict, torment result. I struggle." He opened his eyes. "If you recall my line, 'I stand before the dark of chaos, where no god has moved his hand to bring forth form,' you will see that I. . . ."

Idly listening, Marcia thought suddenly of Esther's story . . . and of Philip's volume of poems dedicated to her. She looked at him with new interest, imagining his charm as a young poet, before he had become a Roman. How wise Esther had been to harden herself against that charm and so avoid bringing futile ruin to two irreconcilable lives. . . .

She turned as J.W. pulled a chair close to her. She tried to study his face, wondering if Cameron had seen him during the day. "Have you had a good birthday thus far?" she asked.

He smiled. "A busy one."

She resigned herself to not knowing, although she decided that he had not heard anything about Meyerson. In fact, she could hardly make herself believe that the noon meeting had taken place. . . .

He whispered to her under the talk in the room: "And now that you have met my son. . . ."

"I can't stop teaching," she said automatically, "until the Cadets leave. I can't—"

"None of that," he said sharply, although he still smiled. "Not on my birthday. For tonight at least I wish that you—" He stopped and frankly listened as Etta's voice arose with sharp clarity.

"You're wrong, Mr. Willard," she was saying heatedly. "There *is* excitement in scholarship. Esther Cornthwaite knew that. There is excitement in teaching also, and it is accelerated by the new trends. Believe me, Mr. Willard, teaching has become completely unpredictable. Only today one Cadet class was totally disrupted in a riotous manner that might easily have led to rebellion had it not been handled skillfully by the instructor."

"Who was the instructor?" J.W. asked, although he seemed to be watching Diaz. Marcia was then sure that Cameron had seen him and that he had no real need to ask questions.

"Dr. Sidney Meyerson," Etta told him unsuspectingly.

By now Grace was listening too. She looked shocked. "It's incredible that anything like that should happen at John Willard. Why, what kind of man is this Meyerson that his class should rebel?"

"Dr. Meyerson," Etta said promptly, "is a fine man."

Diaz left off talking to Marie and fitted a fresh cigarette into his black holder. He gave no sign of being especially interested in the talk across the room, but Marcia sensed that he was straining to hear every word.

Grace was puzzled. "But then I don't understand. . . ."

"Vincent," J.W. said conversationally, "do you know Meyerson?"

Diaz blinked as if surprised to be called upon. "Pardon?" When J.W. had repeated the question, he shrugged. "Slightly, of course. As Dr. Wilson said, he is a fine Jew."

"You're misquoting me," Etta said indignantly. She looked around her, her definite face expressing as much bewilderment as it was capable of expressing. "I must apologize," she said to Grace, "for unintentionally having started this discussion, which has taken an unwarranted turn. I merely mentioned in a casual way the general episode to illustrate to Mr. Willard one phase of teaching seldom recognized by the layman."

Otis had drawn near. "A Jew, eh? Didn't know we had any."

"But this is serious," Grace said worriedly. She looked questioningly at J.W. "It really needs investigating, don't you think, Jack?"

As he did not answer immediately, Marcia said, "Yes, you're right. And there are many teachers who would agree, for it is believed that the Cadets were deliberately incited to act as they did."

"I'll wager," Diaz said crossing the room to them, "that I can guess to whom you've been talking. Mr. Hughes."

"What makes you so sure?" Marcia asked coldly.

Diaz smiled. "It's exactly what Mr. Hughes would think to say."

J.W. looked up at him. "You mean he's wrong?"

"Who can say?" Diaz waved his cigarette. "For one thing, it would be extremely difficult to prove that A's words are the efficient cause of B's actions. For another, it should be considered what type of man is Mr. Hughes." He smiled down at Philip, who had grown visibly bored with this discussion of the concrete. "Once you advised me to learn to be at ease in Zion. I have found that very valuable advice. Mr. Hughes, however, cannot even imagine ease in Zion. He is a fanatic, a zealot. He must pursue an idea to its ultimate end."

"A criminal offense," Philip said readily. "An idea so pursued inevitably means violence, and violence means pain." He shuddered. "I hate pain. That is why I support a hospital."

Diaz nodded. "Exactly. But Mr. Hughes would involve us in investigations and hearings that could lead only to public scandal." He glanced casually at J.W. and then Otis. "A scandal, incidentally, that would reflect, in the end, upon objects seemingly so remote as tractors and dairy products. Besides—"

"You need not do anyone's thinking other than your own," J.W. said firmly, but Marcia, who knew his face well, saw that his expression as he watched Diaz was one that he might have turned upon a precocious child.

Otis had hunched his shoulders. "Scandal? We can't stand a scandal now—or any time, for that matter—but wartime's the worst time for one. If this fellow Hughes is going to cause one, let's get rid of him."

"Otis!" Grace said sharply. "Mr. Hughes is a splendid young man. One of our former students."

"Besides," Diaz said gently, "it was not his class that caused the disturbance."

"Well, then," said Otis, "it looks as if this what's-his-name ought to go."

"Dr. Meyerson has caused no disturbance whatever!" Marcia cried. "You're twisting everything," she went on more quietly as they all looked at her in great surprise. "You don't know—"

"What's that?" Otis demanded as three melodious chimes floated in to them.

"A dinner bell." Grace arose and looked for a moment at J.W. He nodded briefly, and she said, "And we must go in to dinner promptly, or Kate will never forgive us." She took Otis' arm.

He was still absorbed in the thought of the dinner bell. "So, a new gadget, eh? Think we ought to have one, Marie?"

J.W. touched Marcia's hand and smiled down at her. "Please don't look so distressed. It doesn't become you."

"What do *you* think of all this?" she asked abruptly. "You said nothing—absolutely nothing about the real problem."

"There was nothing left to say. You see, Cameron and I discussed it quite thoroughly this afternoon."

"You mean that it's all settled?"

He looked surprised. "But, Marcia, what was there to settle?"

She started to speak, but looking into his closed face, she knew the futility of words. She took his arm in silence.

She thought how good it would feel to hurl the gleaming dishes against the wall, but of course she merely sat still and ate her minted fruit from the glass cup that nestled in the green cracked ice. Russ was next to her, and although she was sure that Grace and J.W. had purposely arranged for him to sit by her, she was possessed by a strange inertia and could not make herself talk to him. Besides, he was totally absorbed in his food.

Marie leaned forward to look past Otis. "Didn't I hear someone say something about a scandal?" she asked Grace with unusual eagerness.

Grace laughed. "Oh, someone was being fanciful. How is your war work coming, Marie?"

"I gave it up," Marie said moodily. "It seemed so frightfully temporary. . . ."

"Perhaps," Etta was saying to Philip, "you could tell me the year you met Esther Cornthwaite."

"I believe that I can," Philip said thoughtfully, and Etta brought forth a white card and pencil. "It was when I was a young man not beset by the depressive thoughts portrayed in my poem 'Ennui.' You did notice that poem, did you not, Miss Wilson—on page twenty-one of. . . ."

"Harry met a spy last week in Washington," Marie said suddenly. "Tell them about it, Harry."

Harry demurred, then launched into his saga. "As a representative of the United States Navy, I. . . ." It gradually appeared that Harry himself had not met the spy, but had come into close contact with the head of the bureau employing the man who. . . .

Marcia tasted the soup that she saw before her. Russ ate the whipped cream off his, but left the sprigs of parsley and the soup itself. They both looked up as one when Diaz's voice came to them. He was arguing with Philip over the psychological significance of ennui.

They both returned to their soup without words. Marcia thought of the noon meeting, which now seemed more real than the people in the brightly lighted dining room; and so when without warning Russ said distinctly, "You think V.D. is back of the trouble, don't you?" she imagined that she had confused his words with her own thoughts.

But he was looking at her. Although his face was very red, he managed a grin. "I know the subject's taboo, but I could see you weren't satisfied."

"Weren't you?" she asked quickly.

He didn't answer her directly. "It's a funny thing, you know. I have to go fight because a lot of people think the way V.D. does, but, of course"—he gave her a quick, almost defiant look—"Dad doesn't see it exactly that way."

"Of course not," she agreed. "But why doesn't he?" And even as she said it, she thought it a strange question to ask his son.

Russ, however, accepted it as natural. "Because," he said gravely, "he doesn't think ideas of any kind are important. That's why I didn't speak up. There's not much use discussing things with Dad. But he's a swell guy."

She agreed again. "He thinks you are too. He'll be very happy when you're able to come back home to work with him."

He frowned and played with the crumbs from his Melba toast. "In the Army," he said glumly, "they're giving me special training in Mechanical Engineering. They gave me a bunch of tests and then shoved me into it." He sighed. "I was hoping I'd turn out to be a doctor or something that had nothing to do with tractors."

"You don't want to work with your father?" she asked curiously, and then was sorry, for Russ looked painfully guilty.

"I didn't say that," he said angrily. "I mean—well, it isn't personal, although he thinks it is. If you know what I mean."

"You mean that your ideas are different from his?"

He gave her a quick, grateful look. "That's it—ideas. And questions. I ask a lot of questions."

"And you don't like his answers?"

He was pained again. "It's not that—exactly. I've got to know things for myself, haven't I?"

She nodded and joined his morose silence for a moment. "I wonder," she said then, "if there would be any harm in staying with him until you find your own answers."

He pondered this gravely. "I certainly would like to be able to please him," he said finally, and looked slightly less troubled. He gave her another fleeting glance, then stared fixedly at his plate. "Say, I've been wanting to tell you that I'm glad you and Father—that you and Dad—that you. . . ." He gave it up and blushed to the roots of his hair.

"Thank you," she said with meaningless politeness, for she was suddenly confused. She had forgotten that he was J.W.'s son. He was supposed to hate her. "Don't you *mind?*" she asked involuntarily. "If I were you, I. . . . "

He didn't seem to notice that she left the thought unfinished. "I don't mind," he said generously. "I did at first, but I've changed since I've been away. I did a lot of thinking about my mother. I never knew her, actually. She's just Eileen over the mantel. If you know what I mean."

"Yes," she said absently, her thoughts rushing to the photograph of her own mother. But she didn't really know what Russ meant. He should mind very much.

"Funny how you change without knowing it," he was saying. "In what you like too. Before I went away, I drove Dad nuts playing Prokofieff records—the *Second Violin Concerto in G Minor*. Know it? Well, Dad thought it sappy, but I couldn't get enough of it. So when I got back last night, I played Prokofieff the first chance I had. And know what? I couldn't take it."

She now looked at him attentively. "That's remarkable, Russ."

He nodded knowingly. "Just goes to show you. Don't ever tell Dad, but it sounds sappy to me now. Know what I like now? Bach. I didn't know it until. . . ."

She glanced at J.W. He had been watching them, and his pleased and satisfied expression said that he was glad to see how well she and Russ were getting on together.

"You're *certain*, aren't you," she said to Russ, "that your father disliked Prokofieff—found it sappy, you said, didn't you?"

He was puzzled. "Yes—I'm certain. Why?"

She managed a laugh. "No reason—at least none that he would count. Now, what were you saying about Bach?"

Chapter Seven

UNDER cover of her book, Marcia stole a glance at her watch. There was sweat on her nose that was caused by more than the Indian Summer heat. "The final Verbal to consider," she shouted as another airplane droned over the roof, "is the gerund. Mr. Byszewski, please define the gerund."

A dreamy expression had softened Mr. Byszewski's round, blunt face as he listened to the plane overhead. Slowly he brought himself back to the classroom and to the realization that the gerund was one small part of the granite wall of English grammar between him and flying. She should have liked to give him more time, but she dare not break the pace.

"Mr. Brill?"

Squadron Leader Brill flung his arms across the two vacant chairs on either side of him. No one questioned Brill's right to occupy the first row of chairs, for, away from Montana, he was the victim of claustrophobia. "A gerund," he said, searching the ceiling, "is a Verbal, ma'am."

"Yes, we're all agreed upon that point. And now, Mr. Brill, what is a Verbal?"

He gave her a you-can't-fool-me look. "A Verbal is a gerund, ma'am."

"That is partly right," she said, raising her voice against another plane, "but it's not the whole truth. All gerunds are Verbals, but all Verbals are not gerunds. Why is that, Mr. Blythe?"

Mr. Blythe sighed and recrossed his long legs. "I don't know how you people in Ohio consider it," he said sadly, "but in my—"

"What's the matter with Ohio?" demanded Mr. Bittinger from Ohio.

Mr. Blythe turned slightly to give him a pitying glance, but did not deign to answer. He was extremely sceptical of the attempt to educate the West, into which an ignominious fate had tossed him. "However," he continued, "in my civilization, the Verbal is—"

"M-A-S-S-A-C-H-U—"

"Can it, fellows!" Squadron Leader Brill bellowed, and the chanting subsided.

"I think you will find," Marcia said to Mr. Blythe, "that the Verbal is not regional, but a component of the language spoken in all forty-eight—"

"What *I* want to know, Doc," said Mr. Bijeck conversationally, "is just how all this stuff is going to help us fly planes."

Mr. Berenson groaned. "And to think I scorned the Infantry!"

"What you don't seem to understand," Marcia said hoarsely over the sounds of restlessness, "is that your job is not going to be simply to fly airplanes. Flying is very important, but— Yes?"

Mr. Byszewski's hand had shot up, and his face was alight with revelation. "That *flying* you just used there, that's a gerund, isn't it?"

"Why, yes, it is, Mr. Byszewski. Thank you. Did everyone note that example of the gerund? *Flying* is very important, but"—she rushed on —"the war isn't being fought with weapons and ships and planes alone. Speech plays a part too. Most of you, for example, will be giving commands and directions, perhaps writing reports. Men's lives may depend upon the accuracy with which you use words and the order in which you put them together.

"Besides," she went on quickly, taking advantage of the chastened silence, "the English language is the one thing that all of you have in common. There are dialect differences, of course"—instinctively she lowered her voice, hoping that Etta Wilson was not standing outside the open window—"but they are minor. Your language is your heritage of understanding." She opened the textbook again. "Mr. Byszewski has already pointed out for us a good example of a gerund. *Flying* is important. What would be the form of the present participle of the same Verbal—Mr. Bunce?"

"*Flying,*" said Mr. Bunce.

"Right. And what—yes, Mr. Byszewski?"

His jaw was set pugnaciously. "But you just agreed with me that *flying* is a gerund."

"I did, Mr. Byszewski, because the same word may be a participle *or* a gerund, depending upon its function in the sentence. What would be the difference between the two, Mr. Byszewski?"

He eyed her suspiciously. "Between *flying* and *flying?*"

"Between the *functions*, Mr. Byszewski," she said, but she put down the book. "What you need—all of you—is some old-fashioned memory work. Grammar requires the same precision work and drill that you give to other phases of your training. Please repeat after me: Infinitive, Participle, Gerund. Infinitive is used as Adjective, Noun, or Adverb; Participle as Adjective; Gerund as Noun. Infinitive, Participle, Gerund. Infinitive is used as. . . ."

They repeated after her. By the third time, they had found a rhythm which they enjoyed, and successfully drowned out all airplanes and, she was afraid, all other Main Hall classes. It was only by looking at her watch that she knew the bell must have rung. She stopped waving her pencil and signaled Brill. He stood and shouted: "Attention!"

She held her breath, but, as always, they heeded this simple command and arose in almost perfect unison. The room was suddenly very quiet. She gathered up her books and papers. "We'll review this lesson tomorrow," she said in a voice that sounded small to her own ears, "and then go on with Verbal Phrases."

Counting slowly to herself to regulate her steps so that she would not appear to be running from the room, she walked to the door and out into the hall, but once the door had swung shut behind her, she ducked into a short passageway through which she knew they would not come. A moment later she heard them march out of the classroom and down the hall, chanting, "Infinitive, Participle, Gerund. . . ."

Exhausted, she leaned against the wall, dried her face with her handkerchief, and groped for a cigarette. When she had one in her hand, President Cameron and a man she didn't know came around her corner. Before President Cameron could speak, the other man seized her hand and shook it vigorously. "Congratulations!" he cried. "A remarkable performance!" He was short and square-jawed, with bright blue eyes and lank sandy hair neatly parted in the middle.

"We caught the last of your class session," he went on enthusiastically. "Why, it could have been an old time revival meeting." He dropped her hand as suddenly as he had taken it, and smote his big knuckled fist against the wall. "That's what we need, Cameron—a return of the good old pedagogical techniques. I know. My father was a country schoolteacher, and my grandfather before him." He stared at her curiously. "What made you think of having them sing about Verbals?"

She smiled faintly. "Expediency. I take no credit whatever." She put her hand behind her back and allowed the squashed cigarette to drop to the floor.

309

"But you should," he insisted. "Now, don't go running off for a Ph.D. and spoil it! You're a natural, and I don't want to see the talent theorized out of you."

"Miss Anderson," Cameron said with slight severity, "has been in possession of her doctorate for several years. Dr. Anderson, I believe that you have not yet been introduced to Dean Briggs. Dean Briggs, Dr. Anderson of the Department of English."

Dean Briggs gripped her hand again. "Doctor, eh? However, I still have faith in you. Well"—he turned to Cameron—"what comes next on this sight-seeing tour?"

She was puzzled, for she had not known that they needed another dean, but she politely refrained from asking questions. Cameron, however, correctly read her expression. "Perhaps you did not know," he said gently, "that Dean Holcomb is leaving us."

"Oh, I'm sorry," she said involuntarily. Confused, she looked at Dean Briggs. "But I'm glad that you. . . ."

"That's quite all right, Dr. Anderson. I should be suspicious if you weren't still loyal to my predecessor." He gave Cameron a smart rap on the arm. "How about getting back to the—the—what *is* the name of that old house?"

Cameron smiled stiffly. "The Summit, Dean Briggs, the Summit."

As Marcia watched them walk away, she was surprised to discover that she was saddened over Dean Holcomb's leaving. And President Cameron, she thought, looked tired and unhappy.

Grant was standing outside his office when she was on her way up to the Inferno, and she asked him abruptly, "Did you know about Dean Holcomb?"

He nodded, then grinned. "You must have met the new one. You look breathless. Come in for a rest."

His office seemed cool and peaceful, and she needed little urging to sink down into his reading chair. "I never thought much about Dean Holcomb," she said slowly, "but somehow it seems all wrong that he should leave here."

"He's a good man," Grant said seriously, "and he served John Willard well—not conspicuously, but efficiently and thoroughly. I know how you feel about his leaving, and my guess is that he's feeling the same way."

"But then, why *is* he leaving?"

He held a match to her cigarette. "I don't know for certain, of course, but I can imagine what happened." He flicked the match out and tossed it into the wastebasket. He reached for his pipe, but put it down again, then walked restlessly to the window. He seemed very tired, and she found herself faintly angry over this. It was all right that she be tired, that Cameron be tired, that everyone else in the world be tired—but it was his duty to stay untired and cheerful.

"I suppose," he was saying, "that Holcomb wanted a raise and he used the only strategy open to him. No doubt he hinted around that he could get more elsewhere. This would look like a bluff to MacMillan, and so—" He walked back to her and stood looking down at her. "Sorry. I warned you that he was only a symbol to me."

She could think of nothing to say. He moved impatiently. "Please don't look so distressed over Dean Holcomb." He pointed to the yellow-jacketed book which she had laid down on the arm of the chair. "And how are you enjoying *Sentimental Farce?*"

"If you meant," she said dryly, "to switch to a happier topic of conversation, you made a very unfortunate choice. I finished it last night, and I'm bringing it to the Inferno because I don't want to live with it in my room."

He smiled. "So violent a reaction is one form of praise."

"I'm willing enough to praise it," she said, "for it's brilliant as well as hateful. I'll even admit that as an attack upon the narrowness of the academic world, it has a certain value. Maybe it has too much truth in it. Perhaps I resent it because it tells me what a hypocrite I am."

"Good Lord! Surely you're not foolish enough to take it personally, are you?"

"But," she persisted, guiltily aware that under the protection of Scott's book she was talking about herself, "sometimes I sense a hypocrisy about myself that frightens me. It's as if I were living two lives simultaneously. . . . Oh, it's nothing so definite as that sounds. Do you know what. . . . Have you ever experienced that feeling?" She looked away from him and laughed self-consciously. "Of course you haven't."

He answered carefully. "If one were as aware of the feeling as that, then I think he'd be fairly safe."

"Safe from what?" she asked quickly.

"That," he said, regarding her thoughtfully, "is exactly what I don't know."

He seemed to be waiting for her to go on with what she had started, but she began to feel that her sudden desire to talk to him about herself was childish. "Another thing that angers me," she said as if she had not left off talking about *Sentimental Farce,* "is that I have the horrible suspicion that, in some perverted way, Scott got the idea for his main character from Esther Cornthwaite."

He was silent for a moment, and she knew that he was wondering about what had been left unsaid. Then he spoke somewhat absently. "Don't worry about that. The few who are in a position to think of that also know that it isn't true; so it doesn't really matter."

"Yes, I know, but I still feel that he has smirched something he had no right to touch. I'm surprised to feel this way," she said frankly, "for I admit that she disappointed me. You see, when I first came here,

I expected—oh, I don't know exactly what I expected from her, but whatever it was, I didn't get it. I. . . ."

"By the way," he said when she didn't go on, "I've wanted you to know that I was present during your first meeting with her by special request. I knew you thought I was intruding—and I didn't blame you."

She smiled. "I figured that out for myself. You see, there were many other things like that. She was always putting up a screen between us. Then when I went to tea. . . . Well, later I stopped worrying about it because. . . ." She put out her cigarette, hoping that he wouldn't notice the unfinished sentence. *Because I met J.W.*

Why did all her words to him lead back to herself? It was like being trapped in a maze. "Do you teach Verbals to the Cadets?" she asked abruptly.

He stared at her for a moment, then laughed heartily. "You ask that as if it were the tragic question of our age. But"—he added quickly—"I'm not saying that it isn't, in a symbolic way. To answer you—yes, I teach them Verbals. I think I know your doubts."

"I gave them a little speech today," she said. "I was sincere about it, but I knew too that I was trying to convince myself that there was any use in—well, in any of it. If we had more time. . . . It's—hard."

"I know, I know," he said wearily. "As you say, we need more time, more—"

Hughes flung open the door. "I came to say good-by," he told Grant, then added as he saw Marcia, "Glad you're here. I waited for you up in the Inferno as long as I could." He set down his pigskin bag and draped his topcoat over it.

"Well, good-by," she said, puzzled. "But where are you going?"

He gave her a brief smile. "I've been too busy to tell you that I've been drafted. I'm going home for a week, and then—well, then I'm in it."

Marcia looked at Grant. "But isn't the teaching of Cadets considered essential work?"

"I suppose something could be done about it," he said almost shortly, "but Cliff doesn't want anything done." He seemed to rouse himself. "This is a fine farewell party! Let's go drink to—"

"To my future?" Hughes said wryly. But the next moment he looked sorry he had said it. "Thanks. I'd like that, believe it or not. But I'm making a train in a few minutes."

Marcia was still puzzled. Watching Grant, she was suddenly sure that his tiredness was over Hughes's leaving, as Cameron's was over Holcomb's leaving. She looked back at Clifford Hughes. "I thought you were a pacifist, Cliff—a genuine one."

He picked up his coat and folded it elaborately over his arm. "I made a promise with myself over the Diaz affair. I agreed with myself that if it were fought out in the open, I'd stay on; but that if it were smothered up, I'd leave and never come back—never teach again."

Listening to him, she realized with a shock how easily she had pushed back her own thoughts about Diaz and Meyerson since the birthday dinner. Meyerson had had no more trouble, and he and Diaz continued to nod politely whenever they met on campus. She had thought that it was all over. "It seems wrong, Cliff—unnecessary," she said vaguely.

He shook his head decisively. "Not for me, it isn't. To get along here—and maybe it's the same way every place—you have to have either the patience of the Rock of Gibraltar or the strategy of a politician. I don't need to tell you that I have neither." He made a self-conscious gesture, as if in apology for being serious, and forced a grin. "I admit that I don't particularly enjoy going off because of the draft. Heck—I wanted some fanfare. You know—a spread in the *Gazette* at least—Hughes Resigns for Principles." Abruptly he then shook their hands, seized his bag, and was gone.

Grant and Marcia stood listening, and she wondered if there would ever again be angry, violent footsteps on the Summit stairs. "I hope he said good-by to Professor Webb," she said.

Grant merely nodded.

"I still think he's wrong," she went on defiantly. "What did he expect to be fought out in the open? You can't prove whatever it is that he wanted proved, and the only thing gained would have been a scandal. Besides, nothing really happened. What was there to settle?" She waited for him to reassure her. "Well, isn't that the truth?" she demanded when he said nothing.

"There are some who believe," he said then in a deliberate way, "that truth is neither one thing nor another, but merely the way we select and group facts to make them explain what we want explained. From one standpoint, your grouping would be true, but from Hughes', it isn't. What is more"—he hesitated and gave her a quiet smile— "I'm inclined to think that you agree with Hughes."

Words of denial came to her mind, but she did not say them, for she knew suddenly that he would not understand what she was denying. She could see by his face that he was thinking back to what she had tried to say about her feeling of hypocrisy, and he was assuming now that she had felt it because of ideas and viewpoints and attitudes. He was trying to let her know that he understood and sympathized, and she could think of no way to tell him that he was wrong, that she had meant something far beneath the surface of ideas, something as inevitable as life itself. . . .

"I promised to go to the station with Stephanie," she said irrelevantly, and went into the hall. She sensed rather than saw that he made a sudden movement as if to stop her but then seemed to change his mind and let her go in silence.

Mrs. Murdock stood on the porch waving good-by to them. Marcia could see that she was baffled and hurt, and she said to Stephanie, "You really ought to ask her to come along."

But Stephanie was not moved. "I've got to talk to you alone. All summer you've been busy or away, and I—"

"You bring Bouncer home next Christmas," Mrs. Murdock shouted, "so that your uncle and I can meet him!"

Stephanie looker queer at this and abruptly ended her farewell. She started down the Heights at a pace Marcia could hardly match.

"Stephanie," she gasped, "let's at least try to get a cab."

"No, I want to walk," Stephanie said. "It'll take longer." She flung back her head as if in defiance of the scorching sun, and at that moment her face showed the same free spirit as her walk. She looked ready to stride over the world.

The prospect of the long hot walk was not pleasing to Marcia, but she felt unwilling to subdue the new Stephanie in any way. "Are you happy to be going back to school?" she asked hopefully.

Stephanie frowned. "I'm worried about Bouncer."

"What about him?"

"That's *it*," Stephanie said.

"*What's* it?"

"Bouncer is a girl."

Marcia was puzzled. "But you've deliberately led us all to believe that Bouncer is a boy."

Stephanie looked frightened. "No, I didn't—honestly. I wrote Aunt Madge about Bouncer, and when she wrote back, she called her *him* and said she was so happy about it that I didn't have the nerve to tell her the truth. I felt guilty about it all summer."

"There's no need to feel guilty," Marcia said. "However, it might be wise to begin calling Bouncer *she* in your letters to your aunt."

But Stephanie wasn't satisfied. "Funny how I got to feeling guilty because Bouncer's a girl. Why should I?"

"No reason. It's good for you to have a close friend. You think much of this Bouncer, don't you?"

"She's like you." Stephanie gave her a shy look.

"You mean she looks like me?"

Stephanie laughed. "No. She's short with red hair and she's a basketball star. I mean she's like you were with *me*. She takes me seriously and makes me talk about myself. Next to you, she's my best friend."

"Don't you ever date boys?" Marcia asked after a minute.

Stephanie shook her head emphatically. "Bouncer says dating is a waste of time."

"Bouncer knows a lot about everything, doesn't she?"

Stephanie nodded. "Everything."

"I'm glad that you consider me a good friend," Marcia said casually. "Because we're friends, I want you to be the very first to know that"—she hesitated a moment, ironically amused to find herself about to say it as if it were a settled, happy fact—"I'm going to be married soon."

Stephanie stopped to glare at her, startled and unbelieving. "You can't!" She grew angry. "That wouldn't be *fair!*"

"Why not?" Marcia asked gently.

Stephanie had no answer beyond a bitter, accusing look. They walked on, but it was not until they came in sight of the station that she spoke. "It didn't do any good, did it?"

"What didn't?"

"Going away." She looked accusing again. "I only went for you, and you know it."

"No, Stephanie. You went for yourself, no matter what you think. That's the way you live your life—for yourself. That's the way it is for everyone." People were coming out of the station house. It was almost train time. "For yourself," Marcia went on quickly, "not for me—or for Bouncer. Remember that."

Stephanie turned away. The train whistle sounded and she winced, but said nothing. Marcia asked if she were sure she had her ticket. She would not answer.

When the train came, Marcia saw her on it, and when she was seated, stood under her window and waved. The train moved, but not once had Stephanie looked at her.

Feeling exhausted and defeated, Marcia turned away from the empty tracks. Then she saw the man running down the road, waving wildly and shouting, "Detain it! Detain it!"

"It's gone," she called back. But he continued to run as if he could not stop, and she saw that it was Professor Webb.

As he neared her, he slid in the cinders, and she ran forward to help bring him to a halt. "The train!" he gasped.

Again she told him that it was quite gone. "You had better sit down to rest," she said, frightened by his red face and open mouth.

With effort he closed his mouth and allowed her to lead him to the bench. He dropped down upon it, leaned his head against the station house, and panted heavily for a minute. Then he managed, "Clifford. I must not—cannot miss him!"

"Clifford Hughes?" She began to understand. "Oh, you missed him by some hours. I'm sure that he took an earlier train."

Professor Webb was beginning to recover. He held up his head, straightened his tie, and buttoned the coat of his ancient linen suit. Then he turned to Marcia, as if aware of her for the first time. "Impossible, Miss er—ah—"

"Anderson."

"Miss Anderson. We're colleagues, I believe?" When she nodded, he smiled in faint acknowledgment. "I must thank you. If it were not for you, I should have had a bad fall." He looked around him, as if surprised to see the tracks and station. "What was I— Oh, yes! What is this about my missing Clifford by some hours?"

She explained again, but he was shaking his head in rebuttal before she had finished. "Impossible. I was very careful to make a memo of the time his train was to leave. Impossible."

She grew impatient. "Have it your own way," she said shortly. His thin high-bridged nose had regained its natural paleness. It rode high upon his face as if made for rarefied air, and it irritated her. "So you didn't manage to say even good-by to Clifford Hughes."

"As you know," he said reasonably, "I became confused about the time of his train."

"But," she persisted, "even if you had not become confused, you would have missed him, for you came too late for *any* train."

Her intensity surprised him. His cool blue eyes studied her carefully. "My dear Miss Anderson," he said, "I missed this particular train because I was thinking—"

"*Thinking!* You *would* be thinking while he went off to war without even a good-bye from you." She stared at him, remembering Hughes as she had last seen him, and her sudden anger was against her own glib dismissal of what had sent Clifford Hughes away. "That was a deliberate act of cruelty!"

He regarded her kindly. "You are very much like him, aren't you?"

She was taken back. "What do you mean?"

"In violence," he said mildly, "and impulsiveness. I was about to say that I missed this train because I was engrossed in thinking over the long talk I had with Clifford last night. Ah, yes . . . we talked the whole night through. Watching the sun come up took me back to earlier times, when as a young man I attended bull sessions. . . ." He sighed reminiscently, but the next moment he was grave again. "Last night we discussed the causes of Clifford's failure."

She flared up again. "Failure!"

"Failure," Webb went on calmly, "to become a philosopher. In a way, I am to blame."

With that at least Marcia could agree, but she did not trust herself to speak again.

Webb was shaking his head sadly. "You see, I was blinded by Clifford's great love for study when he was a student. He was in love with study, and I thought he was in love with Philosophy. Had he been studying one of the sciences or even a foreign language, he should have had the same love for the study. No amount of study, or reading, or even living can make all men philosophers."

She was unbelieving. "Do you mean that a man must be born a philosopher?"

"It is a matter of temperament," he said precisely.

She shrugged. "Why bother to teach Philosophy then?"

"Frankly, Miss Anderson, I sometimes puzzle over that simple question myself." When she looked surprised, he leaned toward her and whispered, "You understand of course, that I am having my moment of levity. Obviously," he said, resuming his normal voice, "we teach Philosophy to make people think, to make them critical, *et cetera, et cetera*. . . . But we can no more teach a man to *be* a philosopher than we can teach him to be virtuous."

"If not a philosopher, what *is* Clifford Hughes?" she asked.

"He is a Doer," he answered readily. "For that reason, the war is an excellent opportunity for him."

"Surely you are not saying that war is a good thing for *any* man!"

He tapped his long bony forefinger against his knee three times before he replied. "Men who are by temperament chained to the world of doing cannot escape participation in its occasional collisions."

You don't say! she thought ironically. She said aloud, "But do you know *why* he went off to war!"

"But of course I do," he said with some impatience, as if she were a very dull student indeed. "He left because of his failure to become a Philosopher."

She did not argue. "What did he say when you explained this to him?"

The question troubled him. "That is the pity of it. Last night I did not explain it clearly enough. Now," he said sadly, "he has gone away thinking that Philosophy has failed *him*. That is why I felt it my duty to have a final word with him. But I missed him." As if realizing that a cycle of thought had been completed, he stood up stiffly. "I must away to my work."

What *is* your work? she wondered, but she said, "You can write him your final word."

They walked to the end of the platform. The cinder road was deserted. "I'm afraid," she said, "that we'll not be able to find a taxi."

But he was surprisingly cheerful about the necessity of walking. "We shall walk, then!" he declared. "Every New Year I resolve to take a daily constitutional, but always I forget to do so. Now after my walk to and from the station today, I shall have amply made up any lack in the past."

When walking with intention, he had a spry gait. He considered himself on a lark, and entertained her by identifying trees and birds. Once, he explained, he had been a nature-trail guide to earn tuition money.

However, by the time houses appeared more regularly than trees, he lost interest in the outside world and, without saying farewell, caused all but his physical self to vanish from her presence. In this ghostly fashion, they reached the Square, and while crossing it, she heard the explosion. "What is that!" she cried, and with the other people in the street. instinctively stopped to look toward the airport.

She thought she saw a puff of smoke. "Perhaps we could . . ." she began to say to Professor Webb, but stopped when she discovered that he was several strides ahead of her, obviously unaware of any unusual disturbance.

She hesitated and then turned toward the airport. When the Cadets were not at the College, they were at the airport. . . . A fire engine roared past her, and then an ambulance. She began to run.

A jeep sped toward her, coming from the direction of the airport. She made out Squadron Leader Brill at the wheel and Blythe by his side. When they saw her, Brill pulled up to the side of the road and stopped. "Better let us ride you back," he said. "Nothing for you to do at the airport."

Blythe merely stared at her. He was frowning as if puzzled over something. His face was chalky.

"What happened?" she asked fearfully.

"Byszewski, ma'am," Brill said with odd politeness. "Smash-up."

Blythe nodded at this. "Byszewski," he repeated and seemed to think that he had told a long story.

"Is he badly—" She didn't finish asking, for she suddenly knew.

But Brill answered. "Dead, ma'am."

"I'm so—" She had no words. Blythe was looking skywards. She looked too and saw an airplane. She knew what Blythe was thinking. *In our Profession we cannot waste a single moment.* She laughed.

Brill was instantly at her side. "You don't look so good, ma'am. You come with us."

She shook her head and tried to say that she knew they had more important things to do than take care of her, but Brill had her sitting in the jeep before she had said anything.

They drove on, and Blythe looked at her. "He had trouble with grammar."

She nodded gravely. "Yes, I know."

After that they did not talk. On the Heights they passed Professor Webb. He looked exactly as he had looked when she had left him at the Square. He did not glance up as they went noisily by him.

She felt the need to keep busy. Remembering that she should write to both Richard Tibbet and Russ MacMillan, she took their last letters from her desk and reread them, and then tried to answer them. But she had to give up writing when a squadron began to drill in the park across the street.

It grew dark and she switched on the desk lamp. The shouted commands and thudding footsteps became so loud that she went into Stephanie's room to look out the window. The squadron was gone. She shuddered, not liking to know that the sounds were in her head only.

In her room she drew the blinds and turned on more light. Still she could not go on with the letters.

She needed to get out of her room. The walls leaned toward her menacingly. She reached for a jacket and ran down the stairs. The Heights was dark gray, but before she turned off on the short cut, the street lamps flashed on. A rough wind had risen and she slipped on the jacket.

She was not conscious of turning off the main road and stumbling along the dark cinder one, or of time, and it was only when she saw the big house that she was certain where she was going.

Tamburlaine met her in the yard near the porch. Impulsively she knelt beside him and put her arms across his strong back. You are *not* a dog starved at his master's gate, she thought. A strip of light fell across the dark grass. She looked up and saw J.W. at the open door. He came forward, flashlight in hand. He moved so cautiously that she had to laugh.

He found her face with the light. "My God!"

"No," she said, still laughing, "it's Marcia."

She heard him click off the flashlight and hurry down the steps. He pulled her to her feet. The familiar feeling of his arms around her was good . . . what she had been wanting. She stayed quiet in them, thinking: *When in fear, I come to him. I did not think to turn to anyone else. It is right, after all.*

He stroked her hair. After a while he said gently, "Come into the house. You're shivering."

He had already heard about the plane crash. She was very solemn now and tried to tell him about Byszewski. All the while he kept shaking his head and saying, "What a pity, what a tragedy!"

"Do you know how I felt?" she asked eagerly. "Only this morning he was worrying about the difference between *flying* and *flying*. Don't you see how senseless it all is, how—"

"Of course, of course," he murmured, and drew her down on the couch and into his arms. She felt at peace, she told herself. She still marveled at how instinctively she had come to him. . . .

He was saying, "Now perhaps you understand why I want to get you out of all this. It . . . ."

She had come to him as instinctively, she thought suddenly, as she might once have gone to Martin, had there not been always Virginia.

". . . can be arranged, Marcia. It's ridiculous for you to go on when it is affecting your health. Tonight you were actually hysterical."

She sat up abruptly. "I didn't come to hear you say that I should run away from it. You were supposed to say that it takes a certain kind of bravery to go on drilling them in grammar when they are also being drilled to kill and die. You were supposed to say—"

"You should have prepared me for my role," he said with faint irony. "I'm not asking you to run away. I'm asking you to marry me."

"I want to teach veterans!" she said intensely. "It will be a great educational experiment. I don't want to miss it."

He smiled. "President Cameron speaks."

"Oh, don't be so mocking." She stood up and walked away from the couch. She stopped by the fireplace and turned to look back at him. His amused smile lingered, but she thought that he was growing angry, and she had a deep impulse to goad him on. "What would I do when I married you?"

He shrugged. "I don't consider that a normal question. Few women would think to ask such a question."

"Do you mean by that," she asked coldly, "that you don't consider me a normal woman?"

"Perhaps," he said lightly. He came to her and took her hands in his. "Sometimes you are just that—charming and beautiful besides. But other times, such as tonight, you are quite simply a child who won't listen to reason."

He is somehow right, she thought confusedly. She freed her hands. "So you will arrange for me to leave, although there is a great need for all teachers now. You will arrange it, just as you arranged for Vincent Diaz to stay on. What about Clifford Hughes—and Dean Holcomb?"

He frowned down at her, genuinely puzzled. "What about *what?*"

She stared at him for a moment. "Nothing," she said then. "It doesn't matter." And it didn't matter, she told herself honestly, for she had realized that she had asked those questions to keep hidden the real ones. What about Prokofieff? Why did you pretend about that? And *Noa Noa*—have you ever really read that book?

"You *are* wrought up, Marcia," he said with concern. "You've had a very trying day," he went on soothingly. "That accident was extremely unfortunate. You should have come to me earlier."

She said nothing, but thought unexpectedly: I didn't come to you because of the accident. I came for myself. . . .

When she understood how litle real grief she had to offer Byszewski, she was sad and ashamed. "I'm sorry," she said involuntarily. "I'm so sorry. I seem never to know what I mean."

He kissed her gently, taking her words as apology. "Never mind, Marcia. I'm going to take you home now."

"I'd rather walk back. Alone—if you don't mind."

"I do mind, but if that's what you wish, then that of course is what you must do." They walked to the porch, and he whistled softly for Tamburlaine. "However, Tamburlaine goes with you. When you're safe at the Murdocks', merely tell him to come back to me."

When Tamburlaine came, she followed him across the yard, but before they reached the road, she turned to look back. J.W. still stood on the porch, the warm house lights showing behind him. Tamburlaine whined impatiently, but she did not move. It seemed to her that the man on the porch was unknown to her, and there was suddenly no reason for him to be in her life, nor for her to be in his. She could walk away from him tonight and never return, and it would not matter.

He waved. "What is it, Marcia? Shall I come with you, after all?"

"No—no, thanks," she said quickly, already fearful that he had somehow seen within her mind during that moment of freedom.

She had sent Tamburlaine back down the Heights when Janice emerged from the darkness of the Murdock porch. "Wasn't that the MacMillan dog?" she asked eagerly.

"Yes," Marcia said shortly. She hoped fervently that Janice would not linger, for she knew that tonight she could not even pretend to want to talk with her.

Janice sat down on the steps. "You must be *very* close to the Mac-Millans," she said shrewdly, "to borrow their dog."

Marcia ignored this. "Sorry, but I'm going on in now, Janice. I'm very tired."

"I guess you forgot," Janice said calmly, not moving, "that you told me to come over this evening. I've been waiting for hours."

"It has been a strange day," Marcia said absently, her thoughts violently on J.W. now. She had never before been so out-spoken with him. Would he, on thinking it over, be angry? Would she lose even his amused tolerance? Would he—

"Marcia!" Janice got up and stood on a step so that she towered over her. "You didn't even hear what I said. What *are* you thinking about?"

The angry voice roused her. She looked into the flashing eyes that had no right to show anger toward her; and she said what underneath the assumed patience and the strange sympathy she had often longed to say to Janice: "It is none of your business."

Janice jerked back as if she had been slapped. "You have no *right* to talk to me that way!"

"I'm sorry," Marcia said wearily. "Good night." She started up the steps, but Janice moved quickly to bar her way.

"You can't get rid of me so easily! Why do you see J. W. MacMillan so often? Oh, I know that you do. I knew about it before tonight. Mrs. Murdock told me."

"Stop it!" Marcia said with such urgency that Janice, startled, obeyed. "It is you who have no right to talk this way. You have no right—you have no . . ." She gave up repeating the words.

For a moment they stood in silence. When Janice spoke, her voice was hardly above a whisper. "Why can't you stay away from all the other people? Why can't you be just my friend?"

Marcia sensed the rare sincerity in these words, but she was untouched. She felt remote and indifferent. "You use people, Janice. You sought me out when you thought I had done you a favor, and you expected me to go on doing you favors. Well, I can be of no use to you, and so there's no need for you—"

"No!" Janice cried. "Not you, not you. You're different. That's the reason—the real reason I first came to you. I knew I wanted you for my friend when I first saw you, before I knew who you were. *Honestly!*"

Marcia shook her head sadly. "You should have chosen someone more—" She stopped, not knowing whom Janice should have chosen. Why had Janice chosen her? Why had she, Marcia, chosen J.W.?

Janice was crying quietly. She turned her face away, ashamed of the real tears. "Why have you changed?" she sobbed out.

"I haven't changed, Janice. I don't know what you mean."

"You have—you have! You've always been kind. I could always depend on you to . . ."

Marcia reached out her hand to her. "Please, let's forget tonight. We'll—"

Janice shook her arm free. "Never *mind!*"

"We'll talk tomorrow. There isn't anything to talk about, but I mean by tomorrow everything will be natural again. Do you—"

"Never mind, I said!" She had stopped crying. Her face had lost its brief softness and was pale and strained. She came down the steps, and Marcia stood aside, knowing the futility of words.

"Please understand," Janice said with icy deliberateness, but not looking at Marcia, "that from now on I don't know you. But don't think—don't think that I won't find a way to get even."

Marcia watched until she was out of sight; then she sank down on the steps. She had failed with Janice. It was her fault, she knew. Grant would know it too. It had been he who had warned her to keep Janice a student and herself a teacher. . . .

She could not cope with so many levels of being. There was Janice the student, and there was Janice who reached out irrationally to her. There was J.W. bound to her through some desperate need of hers; but too there was J.W. as she had seen him in that moment of clarity apart from her feeling. . . .

As she sat there in the darkness and stillness, it seemed to her that she could think of nothing in which she had not failed; and she wondered if people who saw her the next day would not point to her accusingly: We have at last found you out. Now we know what you are.

PART FOUR

Chapter One

KIM carefully arranged the three apples on the windowsill, then stepped back and frowned critically. The window was bordered with fresh snow that glistened in the sun, and the light was flat and bright on the apples. He rummaged in a desk drawer and brought out some pieces of cardboard, which he set up around the apples to form a shadow box.

Vincent Diaz sighed and closed his book. "Has it occurred to you, Mr. Duncan, that you are destroying what little reading light there is in this attic?"

Kim slipped on his old blue smock. "You have a desk lamp."

"Oh, yes—yes, indeed," Diaz said ironically. "Thank you for reminding me." He pushed back his chair and studied Marcia, who had not looked up from her papers. "I admire you, Miss Anderson, for your ability to mark papers while suffocating from turpentine."

She glanced up briefly. "I rather like the smell of turpentine."

Diaz drummed impatiently on his desk and stared at Meyerson. "Mr. Hughes," he said finally, "you also have a remarkable power of concentration in the midst of fumes and darkness."

Without turning, Meyerson said in an amused voice, "You are confused again, Mr. Diaz. This was indeed Dr. Hughes' desk, but, as I believe you know, Dr. Hughes is at present on the West coast."

Diaz snapped his fingers lightly. "Of course! How stupid of me to forget. I humbly apologize, for I understand how you must feel to be confused with the man who worked so zealously in your interest. It might even be said that he went off to war because of you."

Meyerson said nothing and flipped over a page in the book he was reading. Kim took a step forward and looked ready to shout, but Marcia signaled him to be still. After a minute of the tense quiet, Diaz murmured, "Why, it is quite late. The Culture Club awaits me." He clicked on his radio and set it at full volume. Then he left them.

When his footsteps sounded on the stairs, Kim spat. Meyerson laughed and stood up. "Kim, my boy, you should find a more sanitary outlet for your feelings."

"But why," Kim cried, "do you allow him to make such cracks and get away with them!"

Meyerson stepped over to the radio and turned it off. "Can't you see that he wants me to make something of them? Perhaps it has not occurred to you that the outcome of the little affair last May was not exactly what he had intended it to be. His feud with Hughes was merely academic. I was the real object of his campaign, but he failed because he misjudged personalities. He didn't realize that Hughes would really fight for a principle, and that I . . ." With an impatient gesture he turned back to his desk and picked up a book and some papers.

"He didn't realize that you were as objective as God Almighty," Kim muttered from behind his easel.

Marcia looked worried. "But if he intends to make more trouble, perhaps we—"

"No, no," Meyerson said quickly. "There is nothing for anyone to do except keep calm. He, as you surely know, is very unlike Cliff Hughes and will do nothing to jeopardize his own position."

"He's safe enough," Marcia said drily.

Meyerson smiled. "Yes, I know what you mean. Of course, I have no knowledge of what happened behind the scenes last May, but I agree that to avert scandal, Mr. MacMillan would protect his Vincent Diaz as long as he conveniently could. However, if the thing had exploded and aroused public opinion, he would have wisely chosen the lesser of two threats and brushed Diaz aside without a moment's hesitation."

Marcia moved suddenly, walking to the window, although she knew that there was no significance in his looking at her as he talked. "So you see," he went on, "there is reason for us even to pity Diaz. Certainly it is not enviable to be protected by an impersonal interest that may shift with the breeze of expediency."

Marcia watched the swirling snow. "But what about you?"

"I have better protection," he said gently. "I have my own aware-ness and patience, and those arms should serve me well until the Cadets leave."

"What then?" Kim asked suspiciously. "There's no hope that Diaz will leave with them, is there? He's probably set here for the rest of his life."

"My contract expires with their leaving," Meyerson said simply. "By the way," he went on in a conversational tone, "it is rumored that the Cadets may leave in June. Had you heard?"

"Don't be so certain that you'll leave when they do," Marcia said almost impatiently. "I mean, the contract is a mere technicality, and you don't have to leave unless you want to. I'm sure that Professor Grant—"

"We shall see," Meyerson said, his quizzical eyebrow up, "we shall see. But before I probe the future, I must take care of the present. I have a class waiting. . . ."

"What is so strange," Marcia said slowly, turning again to the window, "is the way everything goes on as usual—in spite of change."

Meyerson had paused by the steps. "Yes," he said softly, "that is the most difficult of all lessons to learn."

She shook her head as he went down the stairs. "He's *too* calm. Why *not* explode? Why not . . .?" She laughed self-consciously as she realized that Kim was watching her curiously. She glanced down at the apples. "I never thought I'd see *you* painting apples!"

"And why not?" he said indignantly. "I hope you're aware of what Cézanne did to the apple. Besides, the apple provokes no moral feeling, and it is wise to learn to paint it before approaching the human face."

She looked at him suspiciously. "You sound like Martin. He said something similar to me once, and I remember thinking that I'd tell you—but I didn't, did I?"

He blushed slightly. "No, you didn't. He wrote it to me in a letter."

"He writes to you?" she asked, surprised.

He nodded. "I—well, I wrote first, about painting . . . my painting. I didn't think he'd bother to answer, but he did. He sent some ideas for exercises; said he was sure I'd thumb my nose at them, but there they were if I wanted to gain a sense of form. At first I said to myself, 'They're not for Duncan.' But I did one and then another and"—he gestured toward the apples—"well, they're the tenth exercise."

She smiled. "I'm glad. It's good to have you painting again." She watched him turn to the easel, and for a moment she felt a flare of envy over the contented look on his face.

"I think we misjudged him," he said suddenly.

She knew he meant Martin, but she asked, "Misjudged whom?"

"Martin Anderson, your father. He's a swell guy, Marcia. He writes me once a week—long, careful letters. I know how busy he is, but he never once reminds me. And everything he says—it's so definite, like black and white." He wagged the long thin bristle brush at her. "Maybe you don't know him very well."

She was instantly angry, for it seemed to her that he was saying something he had no right to say. "I know him quite well," she said sharply, and reached for her coat. At her desk she carelessly swooped up papers and books to take with her.

"You don't have a class now," Kim told her.

"I *know* that! Do I have to have a class to get out of this place?" She turned upon him. "Maybe I *am* suffocating. Maybe Diaz isn't so far wrong when he says you—" She stopped and leaned against the desk. "I'm sorry, Kim. Truly, I am. I meant it sincerely when I said it was good to see you painting again."

"That's all right," he said with an embarrassed grin.

"Thanks. I'm on edge, I guess. I must be coming down with something."

"There's some flu around," he said. "You be careful." He went back to his own business and politely kept his eyes off her as she put down a book and picked up another one. He was puzzled. He didn't believe that she was coming down with flu.

He waited until her footsteps were out of hearing; then he put down his brush and went over to her chair, which he pulled out from the desk and turned so that it faced the window. His own chair he placed in front of the window and sat down in it. His face was grave. Once he seemed about to speak, but shook his head and said nothing. He lighted a cigarette and smoked it for several silent minutes.

"I'll talk soon," he announced suddenly. "Right now my ideas are murky. . . ." He laughed shortly. "They look like one of my paintings. However"—his voice became brisk—"the lines in this last exercise are quite good. Have you noticed those distinct, firm lines?" He nodded as if satisfied, and went on smoking.

Once before the cigarette was finished, he said eagerly, "Today I'll talk about—" He groaned and rubbed his hand against his forehead. "No, that won't do. Damn it all, Iris, this isn't easy! It's torture to keep me at it." He dropped the cigarette to the floor and ground it out with his heel, then kicked it under Diaz's desk. "All right. . . . Well, I'll talk about Marcia. She's in my mind because she was just here." He grimaced. "Profound, huh?"

He went over to the easel and took up the brush, but then put it down quickly. "I agree. I've got to talk without a brush in hand." He turned from the easel. "Facts. I'm Duncan, English instructor, John Willard College. I teach. It's true that I have no great love for—" He wheeled about and stared down at Marcia's chair. "But Iris, I've stuck it out. Isn't *that* something? This is the way I see it. John Willard is my anchor. What's an anchor? Safety device. Do you get my meaning, Iris? Do you—"

"But I'm *here,*" Iris said, standing on the top step.

He stared at her. "How long have you been eavesdropping?"

She avoided looking at him but came on into the room. "I was supposed to meet Marcia—but she isn't here, is she?"

He turned his back upon her and angrily grabbed up the cardboard and the apples. "Look through her desk drawers. Maybe she's hiding in one." He stood awkwardly holding the apples in his arms, furious in his awareness of the difference between the reality and the childish pretense.

"Kim," she was saying quietly, "I really came for Marcia. We were going to lunch together, but she must have forgotten. I was on the steps not longer than a moment, and I stayed that long only because I heard my name. I thought I had a right. . . ." She came to him and forced him to look at her. "I wanted to know what you're thinking . . . doing. I've—I've been lonely."

Her upturned face was in the full light. Other faces—even apples—needed shadowing to hide the small revealing signs of frailties of spirit and flesh, but hers seemed a natural part of the light. There was no barrier or falseness in it, and he knew that there was no reason for him to feel anger or humiliation. "Wait a minute," he said roughly, and dumped the apples and cardboard into a desk drawer.

She watched him silently. He banged shut the drawer. "You'll laugh," he said, "but I talk to you this way every day. I'm a rotten thinker—well, you know that—and it helps if I say out what little there is in my mind. Sometimes I can hear how badly I'm thinking; then I can go back and start over. Sometimes—" He shook his head. "You can see how damn silly it is."

"Why do you talk to *me?*" she asked.

He shrugged. "No special reason. I wanted someone who was understanding, yet not soft; someone with a mind, but not a narrow one. Someone who's honest. . . ." He gave her a quick look. "Of course there's a special reason. It had to be you. Damn it, you know that. How many times are you going to make me say it to satisfy your female vanity!"

Desolately he watched her turn away from him and sit down in Marcia's chair. She slipped off her coat and threw it across her lap, and it was a rich brown against her gold wool dress. She wore no hat, and her hair was brighter still than her dress. The gold and brown tones made him think of Rembrandt, although her face needed a modern painter who knew the secret of flesh tints without the use of the deadening glazes. . . .

"Go on, Kim. Talk to me as if I weren't here."

He shook his head, but she asked, "What were you going to talk about today?"

"Stop nagging," he said harshly. "Aren't you satisfied? Haven't you seen me be fool enough?"

"I'm sorry," she said, and then was quiet. He glanced at her and saw that she was nervously twisting her fingers in and out of a button loop on her coat. Her nervousness reached him as no words had done.

"Marcia," he said abruptly. "I was going to talk about her. The point is to get talking; so I choose anything on the surface of my mind just to make a start. Do you understand?" He waited a moment, his old suspicion returning, but her face stayed serious and attentive. "After I'm started, we—I go on to whatever pops up in my mind. You keep me going. You don't let me stop, and you don't let me evade." He smiled and allowed himself to relax. "You're one hell of a tyrant. You make me sweat blood."

"What does thinking about Marcia have to do with all this?"

He sat down across from her. "Nothing much. She seems high-strung . . . unhappy. . . . I don't know the cause—but the important thing is that at least I notice the change. It has absolutely nothing to

327

do with me, but I can be aware of it. There was a time when I wouldn't have. Why, I can even feel a little sorry for her. . . ." He flung out his hand in an impatient gesture. "That's the awful thing about this—process—or whatever it is—it gets you feeling sorry for the whole damn world!"

"I think I understand," Iris said slowly. "Kim, what made you begin to think like this?"

He shrugged. "You again."

She shook her head. "I made you angry."

"But when that went away. . . . What had made me angry began to seem. . . ." He got up and walked to his desk. "Pity . . . compassion. Maybe that's the real thing, after all. To give because of it, I mean." She said nothing, and he turned back to her. "The only thing wrong is that there's no real reason to pity me."

She smiled faintly. "Now and then there is."

"But I'm going to change! I'm beginning to find myself. I'm beginning to see myself in relation to the whole. That's the way Meyerson would put it. Yes, I think I know now why I belong to John Willard."

She looked puzzled. "But John Willard isn't the whole."

He didn't hear her. "Remember that farce of a meeting we had over Diaz in the Cottage? Meyerson said something then about objectivity that clicked with me. At least I could understand what he was driving at, and when I thought it over, I decided I'd try to be like Meyerson. Oh, I know I'll never come near to him, but if I—"

"But, Kim," she said in a worried voice, "you don't want to be like Meyerson. I mean, I want you to be yourself."

"I want to be like Meyerson, I tell you! I've got to change." He glared down at her.

Suddenly she was laughing. "You change, then. All I know is that I've never heard you talk like this, and"—she instinctively put out her hand to him—"oh, Kim, it's wonderful."

He held her hand tightly. "Iris, I can't do it alone. I need—" He shook his head. "Forget that—but you come to lunch with me."

Iris wanted to make sure that Marcia hadn't left her a note; so on the first floor, they turned down the hall, and Kim idly explored his mailbox while Iris looked into hers. His box was crammed with notices and circulars, for he had paid it no attention for several days. He gave the things a cursory glance and was about to drop them into the wastebasket when he noticed the more personal-seeming envelope addressed in green ink. He tossed the other things into the basket and stared at the green writing, already feeling a presentiment of danger and evil.

"Nothing," Iris said, joining him. "She just plain forgot."

He turned the envelope and saw on its back the name *Carol Leeds Whitney* and the New York return address.

"What's the matter, Kim?" Iris was asking concernedly.

328

"Nothing . . . nothing." He shoved the letter into his coat pocket and grabbed her arm. "Come on. Let's get out of here!" He felt that once out of the Summit and in the bright daylight, the letter would vanish.

But the letter stayed real. Carol Leeds Whitney. The Whitney meant nothing to him, and it did not seem important. It could not change the fact that the letter had come as she had said it would. He thought of the long weeks of desperate hope that she would send for him, then the longer ones of fear that she would, and the final forgetting broken only by an occasional memory that seemed no more real than a dream fragment.

It wasn't fair! His hand tightened spasmodically around the envelope. She had no right to do it. Fate had no right. He was trying. He didn't deserve it. Not now . . . not now! "It isn't fair!" he cried.

"What isn't fair?" Iris stopped him. "You've got to tell me what has upset you, Kim!"

"I can't," he said automatically. "I can't."

She took him by the hand and led him to a sheltered spot in the President's driveway. "What can't you do, Kim?"

"Carol Leeds. It's a letter from her."

"Oh." Iris looked away.

He nodded glumly. "See. It makes a difference, doesn't it?" He pulled out the crumpled envelope.

She stared down at it. "But you haven't even read it."

"I don't have to read it to know what's in it. She's asking me to come to her."

Iris looked impatient. "She's not a witch. You don't *have* to go to her"—she hesitated slightly—"if you don't want to."

He flushed. "I promised her that I'd come."

"Oh, yes," she said with a short laugh, "I remember now. You told me that before." She was silent for a moment. "Have you seen her since she left here?"

He shook his head.

"You made that promise over two years ago, and so now you're going to rush off to her—just like that?"

"I promised," he repeated foolishly.

"Yes, I know," she said dryly.

"Iris, it's all mixed up. Let's go on to lunch and talk—"

"Sorry, Kim, but I can't help you with this problem. I never did have anything to say about her that you could accept. Everything I tried to say, you took personally. Besides"—she turned abruptly and stared at the tracks in the snow leading to the Heights—"I'm tired of talking. It was fine as long as I thought the problems were between only you and me, but now that she's back—well, I had thought that was all over and done with."

"I don't blame you," Kim said quietly. "I know how you—" He

stopped as Marcia came hurrying toward them.

"I'm glad to find you!" she said breathlessly. "Will you forgive me? I completely forgot about our luncheon date, Iris. I suppose you've eaten by now."

Iris forced a smile and said that she hadn't eaten.

"Good," said Marcia. "Then we can still keep it, unless . . ." She looked questioningly at Kim.

"We were just talking," Iris said quickly. "But let's go on to the Bijou, even though it's late. I don't feel like the Cottage. I guess I need a change."

Don't go! Kim pleaded with her silently. Don't go! But she gave him a small smile and said good-by, and there was nothing that he could do then but mutter something in return and pretend that it was all very casual.

He stood still even when they were out of sight, hoping against hope that some miracle would send her back. The driveway stayed drab and empty. He was about to force himself to leave, when he heard light, quick footsteps crunching over the snow. His heart thudded, but it was Etta Wilson who rounded the President's house. He turned hastily to make his escape.

The Summit was mockingly tranquil in the evening stillness. Kim went slowly and heavily up the stairs, propelled by a vague notion of going to the Inferno to paint himself into oblivion.

He had read Carol's letter many times. She needed him and assumed that he would come to her. She reminded him of his promise.

At the top of the stairs he thought suddenly of Medora Day, who knew Carol well, who didn't know him, who was calm and impersonal. With new purpose he hurried down the main hall and turned into the smaller one, but then came to an abrupt stop as he saw Marcia knocking upon Dr. Day's door.

Marcia, he thought, seemed embarrassed as well as surprised to see him. She said nothing, but knocked again, and they both listened intently. Marcia shook her head. "She isn't in."

He was bitterly disappointed. "Why did she have to choose this night not to work! She's almost always here."

"She'll probably come along in a few minutes," Marcia said. They strolled out into the lighter hall. "I want to see her about a—student," she said casually.

He nodded quickly. "So do I."

She smiled. "Poor Dr. Day. She won't get much of her own work done tonight." She walked restlessly across the hall, wishing that Kim would go away. But he was leaning against the wall and looked ready to wait all night if necessary. She went back to him. "Kim, when Dr. Day comes, you go in first. What I want to discuss with her is rather private—private for the student, I mean."

He straightened up as if startled. "Oh, but I'd keep you waiting too long. What *I* want to discuss will take hours. This student has got himself into a terrible jam."

She gave him a sceptical look and wondered when he had begun to take such a personal interest in his students. Almost as if he had read her look, he diverted her suspicion by digging out his cigarettes and offering her one. She refused it and walked again, noticing a light under Grant's door and idly wondering what he was thinking or reading. . . .

Kim lighted a cigarette and resettled himself against the wall. The door downstairs swung open and shut, and they both turned eagerly toward the sound of the footsteps on the stairs. Janice Grant appeared. When she saw Marcia, she hesitated for a moment, then quickened her steps and walked by them with a stonily averted face.

"Hello, Janice," Marcia said.

Janice made no response, and turned into the smaller hall. Her back to them, she knocked loudly and quickly upon Grant's door. They heard the squeak of his swivel chair and his steps across the floor. Instinctively Marcia moved so that she would be out of his sight when he opened the door. Janice announced in the peremptory way familiar to Marcia that she had come to talk. He invited her in, and the door closed again.

Kim had been watching. "What's eating her?" he said to Marcia. "I thought she was one of your shadows."

"I don't know," Marcia said, not wanting to talk about Janice. "I believe I'll not wait any—"

Dr. Day was coming up the stairs. "Good evening," she said pleasantly. Her breath was still frosty, and there were melting snowflakes on her brown coat and hat. "This dry coldness is quite exhilarating, don't you think?" She gave them a smile and went on to her office, key in hand. Marcia and Kim looked at one another and then stood tentatively in the passageway, their shadows falling upon Dr. Day as she turned the key in the lock. She glanced over her shoulder, surprised to find them still there. "Oh, did you wish to see me? I'm sorry— I didn't understand."

Kim nudged Marcia. "Dr. Anderson was waiting to see you."

"No," Marcia said with sudden decision. "It's Mr. Duncan who wishes to see you."

Dr. Day did not appear to find their words or manner odd. She opened her door and clicked on a light. "Come right in, Mr. Duncan."

Kim started to protest, but at the same moment, Grant threw open his door. "I thought I heard voices," he said, looking at Marcia. Janice got up from his reading chair and came to stand at his back.

"Kim was waiting to see Dr. Day," Marcia explained unnecessarily, "and I was waiting with him. Please go in," she went on in a low voice to Kim. "I think that you really want to talk with Dr. Day. I didn't—not really."

"But I didn't mean it to be so damn public," he muttered. Then he shrugged and reached Dr. Day's door just as she looked out again to see what was delaying him. The door closed upon them.

Marcia began to pull on her gloves. Now she felt unaccountably glad and relieved that it was Kim and not she who was behind that closed door.

"We're leaving too," Grant said. "May we walk you down the Heights?"

She glanced at Janice before she answered. The girl did not look at her, but said coldly to Grant, "You have to take me to Grace Hall before—"

"I'm becoming very absent-minded," Marcia said hurriedly. "I was on my way to my desk. I have some papers there to be graded."

She sat at her desk until she was sure that Grant and Janice were out of the building. Then she went down the stairs again and quietly by the corridor leading to Dr. Day's office. If he heard her, Kim might think that she was loitering purposely, and that would make him even more self-conscious.

She wondered what he had to discuss with Medora Day. Their accidental meeting had saddened her, for it made her feel that everyone in the world was sick in spirit and needing to talk with Dr. Day. . . .

What would she now be saying to Dr. Day if Kim had not appeared? *My problem concerns a man*—she would laugh a little here—*yes, you see, mine is the perennial woman-problem. And yet, please believe me, it is different, for although my problem concerns a man as I said, it really has nothing to do with him. I mean, it is wholly mine, not his. Do you understand? I'm sorry, but I cannot explain further. That is what you are to do for me. One moment—there is this much more I can say: he is not the man I would naturally choose, but, even knowing this, I cannot choose to leave him. Where is my freedom?*

She shuddered, ashamed to think how easily she had gone running for help and how narrowly she had escaped saying aloud those thoughts. Now that she had made her mind marshal them together, she saw how absurd they would appear to anyone outside herself.

She walked on quickly, and her fervent hope that she would meet no one made her realize again that Grant was the only one she could bear to face when she felt this nameless guilt and self-disgust that now seemed never to leave her.

But she met Alice Mueller in front of Science Hall. As long as she had to meet someone, she was glad that it was Alice Mueller, who was merely a student to her with no special meaning; and she knew that to Alice she was merely a teacher with no special meaning. She could be certain that Alice would not detain her or eye her critically or speak accusingly or breathlessly wait for her every word; and so she said with confidence and ease, "Good evening, Miss Mueller."

Alice smiled. "Good evening, Dr. Anderson." She looked unusually pretty, as if she were ready for a date. She waited until Marcia had passed; then she cut across the Heart to Main Hall.

Her voice lingered in Marcia's mind. *Good evening, Dr. Anderson.* It had been polite, respectful, and friendly.

Doctor Anderson, who could fathom William Blake, but not herself. Marcia Anderson, Ph.D., who was lost in her own life.

"You have intelligence," Alice Ware had once said to her, "and honesty. What more could you want?"

What more could she want! she thought ironically. But at the same moment she was aware of a clarity of mind that had not been hers for a long while.

At the top of the Heights she paused and looked around at the white world. It came to her suddenly that there was as much spirit of renewal in the fresh snow of the new year as there was in Spring.

"I didn't come to talk about myself!" Kim said belligerently for the second time.

Dr. Day nodded soothingly. "The fact remains, however, that when we talk about Carol Leeds, we also talk about you."

"Why do you say that?" he asked, apprehensive.

She smiled. "I don't say it. You make it very evident."

To come had been a fool thing to do, he told himself. He was hot and uncomfortable. He hadn't taken off his coat, and he was sure that to her he must look like a big bunch of coat cramped into a chair that was too small for it.

He felt that there was some kind of contest going on between her and him. She was trying to make him give in to something. . . .

He hated the silences. They made him say things he didn't mean to say. He didn't feel free even to take out his handkerchief and wipe the sweat off his face. He had to be on guard.

There was a loud voice in the room. "That's what Iris—another person said. That everything she—this other person said about Carol, I took personally." With a sick feeling he realized that this was his voice. He had given in—not much, but enough for her to know.

"Yes," she said, and did not seem triumphant over his giving in. He knew by now that the "yes" did not mean that she had previous knowledge of what he had said or even that she was agreeing with him, but merely that she was accepting his feeble offering. She would accept anything. If he told her that he had walked down the hall with Lucifer, she would look at him in the same calm way and say yes.

The waves of silence closed in on him again. He had to move. He took his hand out of his pocket, bringing with it Carol's letter. He threw it on the desk. "I got this from her today." He hadn't meant to show her the letter, for while waiting out in the hall, he had decided that would be unfair to Carol.

Miserable, he watched her read it. She expressed no surprise over the crumpled condition of the paper or the words upon it. It was a short note, and she did not reread it. She handed it back to him. "You wish me to help you decide whether to go or not to go to her?"

"I can make my own decisions," he said. He thrust the letter back into his pocket. "Did you know that she had married Whitney?"

She nodded. "I knew. While in the Service, David wrote to Professor Grant. Knowing of my interest in Carol, Professor Grant told me."

He almost sneered. "If you had such interest in her, why did you let her go away?" In his excitement he lost his sense of awkwardness. He stood up and stared down at her accusingly. "Why did you stop helping her?"

"I am not a police officer, Mr. Duncan. I cannot send out a warrant for Carol's return to me. I have written her frequently, but I never receive an answer. Even if I sought her out, I could not force my help upon her."

"That's the trouble with your kind of business," he said bitterly. "That's why I have no faith in it. You never *do* anything!"

Dr. Day sighed and leaned back against her chair. "Something happened on that last day. I have my suspicions, but no knowledge. Whatever it was made Carol lose her trust in me." She glanced up at him. "I understand your anger, Mr. Duncan. If I had been successful with Carol Leeds, she would have had no need to send you that letter, and you would not have had to make a decision."

He gave her a long look. "Do you mean," he said finally, in a quiet voice, "that if everything had gone all right for her, she would never have written to me?"

"You know that without my telling you," she said mildly. "You would say it in different words perhaps, but you know that her goal is self-destruction and that she is intent upon destroying everyone else with her. That is why, when with her, you felt a fear of your very life."

He looked unbelieving, then sarcastic. "You mean I expected her to pull a gun on me?"

She shook her head and answered him seriously. "Unfortunately, it was nothing so simple as that."

"Then what was it?" he cried. He turned away from her and walked to the window. "Afraid!" he said, staring out into the black and white night and reliving those moments of sickening fear he had felt with Carol. "I wasn't afraid! I admired her. She was free of this stuffy place. She gave it the contempt it deserves. Why, I envied her! I didn't have the nerve to be the way she was, although I wanted to. And did you ever see her act? She's a great artist. Freedom and Art. Those are the only things that make life worthwhile." He stopped, embarrassed to have said so much. It was easy to talk with his back to her. She sat very still, not moving restlessly in her chair as did most people.

"Freedom and Art," she said softly. "Yes, those are wonderful goals —well worth your keeping."

He thought her words beautiful. He sighed and closed his eyes, wishing Iris could have heard them. At that moment it seemed to him that his existence was almost justified.

"Did you," Dr. Day said suddenly, "have sexual relations with Carol?"

He opened his eyes wide and turned furiously upon her. She had no damn right to ask such a question! He strode to the desk, meaning to tell her so, but the calm, impersonal expression on her face made him aware of the shallowness of his fury. He sat down weakly. "No. She wanted—I wanted— I couldn't, that's all. It was queer—God-awful queer." He stared at the red cigarette box on the desk, remembering. "Something about her at those times made me afraid. It sounds crazy, I know, but I was afraid of . . ." He looked up slowly, meeting Dr. Day's eyes. "I was afraid," he repeated wonderingly. He thought that over for a minute, then sank back in his chair, feeling resigned. The contest was over. He had given in completely. "How did you know?" he asked, but it was not as if he expected an answer.

She gave him none, but merely regarded him quietly. He stayed silent with his own thoughts for long minutes. Then he roused himself and reached out to the cigarette box. "May I?" She said, "Of course," and took one too. He lighted hers and then one for himself. "Everything considered," he said, "it's foolish for me to go to Carol, isn't it?"

"It is," she said agreeably.

"Still," he said, his eyes on the smoke, "I have to go."

She smiled faintly. "I suppose that you do."

He leaned forward eagerly. "Do you understand why?"

She sighed. "Perhaps I do. I believe that you have a sincere hope to be of some help to her. I want to assure you, however, that you can be of no help to her—and I think that fundamentally you know that."

"Isn't it possible," he asked quietly, "she may commit suicide if I don't go? After all, you yourself said that her goal was self-destruction."

She shook her head. "I doubt if that will ever be Carol's way out. Sometimes I think that it is only the very sane and practical ones who resort to suicide. They know when they meet a blank wall or quite simply desire not to exist. Carol's method is the long and tortuous one, for she has imagination and cunning. That is why she may destroy others before she realizes her ultimate goal. Her life follows a pattern which becomes more and more definite. That she sent you the letter is the most positive evidence that she is starting over again and not at all in a suicidal frame of mind. Bluntly, now that David Whitney has eluded her, she is ready for you."

He shuddered. "Did you know that Whitney had been killed in action before you read the letter?"

"No, I didn't. Poor David—poor Carol. Or is it fortunate David? Who knows?"

"I think I can face the facts," he said slowly. "I still want to go."

She nodded. "Yes, I know. Going will be a kind of test for yourself. You will never be satisfied until you put yourself to it."

"You understand," he said simply. He put out his cigarette. "I know that I've already taken up too much of your time—but there's one more thing, one more favor. Will you please tell me more about Carol Leeds—facts, I mean? I want to have more understanding—and I want to know what to expect."

"If you wish," Dr. Day said after a moment. She arose and crossed the room to her file. "Yes, I believe that you are entitled to know the few facts there are. I wish that David Whitney could have known them." She returned with a folder, which she opened out upon her desk.

Kim watched her intently as she glanced over the first page of type-written material. So Carol Leeds was in that folder. Carol Leeds, a case to be discussed across the desk. Her image, which had been blurred to him for so long, suddenly returned with blinding vividness. He closed his eyes against the stab of pain that went through him.

And Kimball Duncan, who was he—a man, or a case confined to a folder? For a moment he felt the old panic, as if he had, after all, sub-mitted to Carol as she had wished. Was there any real difference be-tween her and him?

He reached out and put his hand down on the page that she was reading. She looked up questioningly.

"First, I want to say something." Then he realized that he had nothing definite to say, and felt foolish. "I merely wanted to tell you about some exercises—but they're not important. Sorry I interrupted."

But she seemed interested. "Exercises?"

"Martin Anderson gave me the idea. You see, he's helping me with my painting." He grinned crookedly. "He wants me to gain respect for all lines—the bounding line in particular—and so he sent me some simple little exercises to do. When I finally started to work on them, they didn't disgust me as I had expected and I think they're going to help. Besides, they made me think, and I began to wonder why a per-son couldn't help himself in a different and more important way just as simply—so I . . ." He avoided her eyes and laughed nervously. "Do you follow me? Sanity gained in Ten Easy Lessons."

"I follow you," she said seriously, "and I am exceedingly interested."

He went on with effort. "Well, I began to talk to myself every afternoon. It wasn't exactly to myself, though, because I pretended that a certain friend of—oh, what the hell! You know by now that I always mean Iris. I pretend that she listens and asks me questions. Having her around helps me try to be honest. Of course, I don't expect miracles, but I was beginning to feel more—something, when"—he shrugged—"that letter came. Well, the letter came, and that's that. But about those—those conversations of mine, they're damn silly, aren't they? I mean, what do you think?"

"I think," she said gravely, "that I admire you very much, Mr. Duncan."

He gave her an unbelieving look, but her face convinced him that she was sincere, not merely kind. He smiled. "I believe that now I'm ready to talk about Carol Leeds."

Scott surveyed his newly straightened desk. "You're a neat little soul, Alice," he said. "I could never keep it looking this way by myself."

Alice Mueller blushed. "I brought that wire basket for your mail. You get so much."

"So?" Scott nodded approvingly as he looked at the basket with its two uneven stacks of mail. "All that come today?"

"Yes. And I divided it the way you told me— Important on the right, Unimportant on the left."

He smiled faintly. "Thanks." He pulled the basket to him and looked casually through the Important pile. When Alice was gone, he would examine the Unimportant stack with equal care.

Nothing from Judith. But that didn't surprise him. What was there to be said after her last letter?

When he found the letter from Coningsby College, he ripped it open. Ah! They were favorably impressed by his application. So—it was more than possible that he'd be moving East next year, away from John Willard and Riverville. . . . He refolded the letter and slipped it into his inside coat pocket. What the hell did it matter!

The fat envelope on the top of the Unimportant pile made his fingers itch. It was from his News Clipping Service. *Sentimental Farce* was making a little stir. But as he had pointedly instructed Alice that all communication from his News Clipping Service went on the Unimportant stack, he could hardly open it now.

He glanced at her. "Sorry to keep you waiting."

She blushed again and looked down at her hands. "That's all right, Professor Scott."

He continued to stare at her. She had changed during the past year or two. He wasn't sure, but he thought that she used to be quite plump. Now she was thin enough for there to be faint shadows in her cheeks. She still had freckles, but her face was too pale and serious. "Did you say something?" he asked when he saw her lips move.

She didn't smile. "I asked if we should record grades now."

"Oh, yes. Yes, of course." But he made no move. Her legs had taken on shape. He couldn't remember that they had ever before given him pleasure. They had seemed too thick and blunt—or perhaps they had seemed that way because of those terrible saddle shoes and socks she had worn. She no longer dressed like the other kids. Tonight she had on high-heeled pumps and a blue crepe dress with a low V-neck.

Blue! Oh, God. . . .

He turned abruptly and reached for the pile of themes and his gradebook. Handing the gradebook and a fountain pen to Alice, he said harshly, "You record." But their fingers touched, and he allowed his to linger next to hers. He did this automatically and without feeling. It was habit—the kind of habit that had given him some little enjoyment when Judith had been with him.

He looked at the first theme and felt infinite boredom. "Amberson —80," he read. "Anderson—75."

She wasn't confused by Amberson and Anderson. She knew this class as well as he. They went through the list quickly. ". . . Carlson— 90, Carroll—85. . . ." His eyes went back to Alice. She clutched the fountain pen as if it were an instrument foreign to her. Her legs were crossed to balance the gradebook. She had good knees. He could catch a glimpse of white flesh in the triangular gap between her dress and knees.

". . . Mueller—70." The name arrested him. "Why, that's you," he said in surprise.

She smiled and bowed her head over the gradebook. "Mueller—70," he repeated. "Alice, you ought to do better than that."

"I'm sorry," she said apologetically, "but that seems to be what I always do."

He frowned critically. "You're in the wrong field. You're not the literary type. What're you going to do with Literature when you graduate?"

"I don't—"

"A-ha!" he cried, pointing at her. "I remember now. You transferred from Home Economics, didn't you?" When she nodded, he waved his hand to show that the problem was simple. "Well, then! You get right back there. I don't know anything about Home Economics, but it sounds more like you."

"But I'm a Senior," she said.

He stared. "Good Lord!"

"Don't worry, Professor Scott," she said soothingly, "I'll take care of myself."

"Well," he said, shrugging, "you'll probably marry soon anyway. Most John Willard girls do. They seldom have to make a real vocational choice."

She was shaking her head. "No. I'll never marry."

He was surprised. This was the most personal thing that had ever been said between them. "What makes you so sure?" he asked lightly, even while telling himself that he had better let go the subject. To his relief, she was silent. "In your case," he said, "I—"

"Because I love you," she said suddenly.

Shut up! his mind shouted. But he could think of nothing to say aloud. He shook his head as if to give her some kind of answer, and then picked something up from his desk and put it down again.

"I'd never have spoken like this," she said in a low voice, "if Mrs. Scott hadn't left—gone away."

This steadied him. "Mrs. Scott is visiting," he said coldly.

She said nothing but slowly recapped his fountain pen. She closed the gradebook and held it and the pen out to him. He took them from her, their fingers touching. He shuddered with disgust. He was as sick of touching fingers as she must be.

Turning from her, he threw the gradebook and pen onto the desk. The pen rolled off to the floor, but neither of them made a move to pick it up. He had to look at her again. She was sitting quietly, but her face was strained. He saw the throbbing pulse in her throat. The silence stretched out like a rubber band about to snap. He wanted to rip off her blue dress and press her body to his until it hurt both of them.

He groaned. "Go home, Alice," he said. He put his elbows on his desk and his face in his hands. A half-thought flashed through his mind that he was not impressing her in the right way, but he could not help himself. "Go home."

She rose but did not put on her coat. "Are you ill?"

The real pity and concern in her voice reached him. "Yes!" he said eagerly, looking up at her. "That's what it is—I'm a sick man, I tell you! I ache all over and those damn doctors won't help me. My arms especially"—he held out his arms—"ache just like a toothache. Do you know what it is to ache all over?"

"Yes," she said quietly. "That's the way I feel for you."

He closed his eyes, then opened them. She was still before him. He stood up and took a step toward her. She backed against the wall. There was fright in her eyes, but she made no other move away from him.

Suddenly her unhappy face blurred before him. He stood still. "Get out of here," he said dully. "Didn't you hear me tell you to get the hell out of here?"

She drew in her breath sharply. Then she slipped around him to take her coat off the back of a chair. Near the door she stooped to pick up the pen. She laid it gently on the desk and then went out into the hall, closing the door behind her.

The first thing he noted when he entered the dreary, empty house was that Judith's letter was still on the hall table where he had thrown it three days ago. It was the letter in which she told him that she had applied for divorce.

He flung his coat into the davenport and hurried into the dining room. Good! He had managed to get by the mirror over the mantel without looking into it.

339

He turned on all the lights he could find on his way to the kitchen. Well, he was in the kitchen. Now what?

He hadn't eaten since noon, but he wasn't hungry. He thought for a while and then decided that he would do some drinking. As he went to the cupboard for the whiskey, his enthusiasm kindled. He was going to drink all that he could swallow, but he was going to do it in a very gentlemanly fashion.

When the tray was fixed to his critical satisfaction, he carried it into the living room and set it on the coffee table. Then he sat down on the davenport and nodded approvingly at what he saw before him. He had poured the whiskey into the crystal decanter, and one of their best amber tumblers held his water-chaser. He had no need for ice, but because he liked the looks of it, he had laboriously filled the little silver bucket and brought along the silver ice tongs. He had even a coaster and a cocktail napkin.

He set the gold-edged glass in the exact center of the coaster and filled it. From habit he handled the decanter with great care. He lifted the glass and said, "To a gay evening!" He took a sip of whiskey, raised his eyebrows to show approval, and then emptied the glass quickly.

He pushed the table away from him and stood up. He was curious to know how much he had drunk. Taking out the stopper, he turned the decanter upside down. Fascinated, he watched three big drops of whiskey roll out and fall upon the rug. From habit he worried about a possible stain. Then he remembered and shrugged. He reached down and set the decanter over the spot where the drops had fallen. That would fix it.

Black coffee was what he wanted. He had planned to have black coffee—to finish it off in a gentlemanly fashion. He went to the kitchen, struggled to remember why he was there, and then grabbed up the coffee can. The lid gave him trouble. Because he had to use both hands to pry it off, the can slipped away from his hold and rolled noisily on the floor. He took a step and grimaced with distaste. Coffee grains grated under his feet.

Wonderingly he stooped to run his fingers through the brown coffee. Johnny could use it for sand.

He straightened. That was that. He couldn't have a cup of coffee in his own home. He was a man to be pitied.

The clock was still there on the wall, miraculously running, although no one ever wound it. Good clock. Electric clock, he discovered. That explained it.

It was not yet midnight. He was surprised to find that his drinking had been done in such a short time. If he hurried, he could make Herby's for a cup of coffee.

He found his coat and then the door. The air struck him sharply.

He gasped but went down the tricky steps. He had to go to Herby's for a cup of coffee. He couldn't have a cup of coffee in his own home. He was a man to be pitied.

He sat at the counter at Herby's. Christian Deardorff was sitting on the next stool. He thought this odd and tipped his hat elaborately to him. After he had made the gesture, it occurred to him that he was wearing no hat.

Someone out of sight whispered, "He's from the College. He's a professor!" It was an awed, scared whisper. It amused him, and grew and bounded in his mind like an echo with a life of its own. He laughed over it.

Then he was tired. The upward curling steam from the coffee that Herby had set down in front of him was trying to smother him. He pushed the mug away from him. His hand touched the counter and found it cool. He remembered that it was coolness he wanted.

Cleverly he bent his head forward so that his hot cheek was against the cool counter. He stretched out his arms. One of his hands touched something new. There was a clatter and then a hot dripping upon his knee. He was too tired to investigate.

He heard words. They were muffled but conspiratorial. Again he could do nothing. He was helpless before his enemies. He was a man to be pitied.

Someone was fussing over him. He struggled feebly, then resigned himself to capture.

All the way up the Heights he wondered who had him so firmly by the arm. But walking on the ice kept him too busy to look at the man.

In the strange house—no! *his* house again. The same dreary, empty house. In the house, the man pushed him into the davenport. Then he stooped to pick up the decanter and set it safely upon the tray.

He saw at last that the man was Deardorff. That the man should be Deardorff seemed very funny to him. He laughed aloud, but stopped short at the first lurching of the waiting nausea inside him.

Deardorff stood looking down at him. "I should get you to your bed. Where is it?"

He closed his lips tightly. No one could wrest that information from him.

Deardorff sighed. "I presume that you have a bedroom upstairs." He took his arm again and made him get up.

On his feet, he shrugged. Deardorff was uncanny. There was no use trying to keep important information from him.

They began the long hard ascent up the stairs. With honesty and without subterfuge, he led Deardorff into their bedroom. He pointed to the large bed. "Double," he said. He grew aware of the ridges under the spread. He wasn't a very good bedmaker. He felt humiliated.

Deardorff came at him again. He ripped off his overcoat, then his

341

suitcoat. He did away with the tightness at his throat. He forced him to lie down upon the bed and even stretched out his legs. Then he pulled off his shoes.

He turned his head on the pillow. Deardorff was sitting on the cretonne-covered rocker and rocking away like a little old woman. The rocking motion disturbed him, and he closed his eyes against it. "I'm sick," he said meekly.

"Good," said Deardorff. "You must have a bathroom. Go find it."

Obediently he sat up and with Deardorff's help got to his feet. He noted how gentle Deardorff was with him. He wished that everyone in the world would be as gentle with him as Deardorff. He wished that it would be a gentle world.

When he came back from the bathroom, he was proud. "I cleaned it up," he said.

He lay down again, quiet and thoughtful. Deardorff, his loyal companion, deserved an explanation. He knew what he wanted to explain, but then lost the thought. The words, however, remained, and he said them carefully: "It's the mirrors. When you live alone, every wall turns into a mirror. It is bad to see yourself when you live alone."

Deardorff's rocker creaked back and forth. "I live alone," he said.

He was satisfied. "Then you know." He wanted then to talk about Coningsby. "I'll be moving East next year."

Deardorff wasn't impressed, and this disturbed him. He raised himself up on an elbow. "You don't understand! What's more, I have another book in mind. And for after that, I have a hundred thousand more books in mind!"

Deardorff chuckled and came over to him. "You're all right," he said soothingly. "Why, you're going right up the Golden Steps."

This is the way the world ends.
Scott sat up abruptly. Who said that? He looked around the sunny, silent room. No one. It had been in his own mind and had stabbed him out of sleep.

Now, why was that? He thought for a while, then shrugged. He had more important things to attend to this morning.

Automatically he turned back the blue satin quilt. Then he stared at it. Something was wrong. When had he brought that quilt out of the closet where Judith had it stored on the top shelf?

He looked down at himself and was ashamed to see that he had not bothered to undress himself. Could it be that he was becoming slovenly?

He stood up, stretched, and opened wide his dry mouth. The fresh air rushed in and almost choked him. The room was bursting with fresh air. Frowning, he looked first at one window, then at the other. They were both wide open. Neither he nor Judith ever opened them that wide. He went to the windows and banged them shut.

342

Moving around, he realized how he felt. He was a sick man!
This is the way the world ends.

What *was* that? He shook his head impatiently. It had the rhythm of a nursery rhyme—but a nursery rhyme would hardly say that, would it? He gave it up and began the painful search for his slippers.

Judith was not downstairs, and there was no sign of breakfast. She must have gone out—but why so early? Inconsiderate of her.

He was shaking all over. He pulled a chair out from the kitchen table and sat down. Why was he so much worse this morning? He groaned. He was a man to be—

Suddenly he was remembering some drinking. That explained the horrible dryness. He was relieved at the explanation. But he certainly had to do something about his thirst.

He measured the distance to the refrigerator. Judith always fixed tomato and orange juice for him. He made it to the refrigerator and looked in. There were two tall glasses of tomato juice and one of orange juice. Good girl! He forgave her for leaving him alone so early in the morning.

Carefully he put the glasses on the table and sat down again. He drank one glass of tomato juice without breathing or seeming to swallow. That was the way he felt. He thought that he could simply open his mouth and pour cold liquids down him all day without losing his thirst.

But even the one glass of tomato juice helped surprisingly. He took the second one more slowly, looking around him as he drank. An opened tomato-juice can stood on the sideboard and orange rinds were piled in the sink. It wasn't like Judith to leave the empty can or the orange rinds in sight. In fact, it wasn't like Judith to—

This is the way the world ends.

Damn that line!

Then he remembered everything—not clearly, but distinctly enough to know that it was the truth. Herby's . . . Deardorff . . . bed. He even remembered the spilled coffee. It was gone from the floor now. Deardorff must have cleaned it up.

And Judith wasn't home—wasn't coming home.

Of course . . . of course.

He sat listening to the empty stillness. *This is the way the world ends.* He put his hands over his ears.

The kitchen. Why was he always in the kitchen?

He went into the living room. There was the mirror over the mantel. He looked into it and for once did not run away. He moved toward himself. He looked like hell—but he could look at himself. That was something.

He thought of Coningsby and his plans for a hundred thousand more books. He'd be all right.

Gently he touched his face. He saw himself do it in the mirror. He leaned forward, acknowledging himself.

He was, he decided, a tragic figure.

His next book would—

The telephone rang. He didn't intend to answer, and stood counting the rings. He had no idea there would be so many of them.

Long distance? Judith . . . acknowledging her error . . . withdrawing the divorce proceedings . . . even coming home?

He strode to the phone and shouted eagerly into it, then heard Grant's voice, somewhat apologetic: "Sorry to disturb you at home, but I couldn't reach you at your office—"

"Of course not," he cut in, cursing himself for having answered. "I have no class until this afternoon."

"Yes, I know," Grant went on quickly, "but if you would help us by taking one of Duncan's morning classes, we—"

"What's the matter with Duncan?"

"All we know," Grant said, apologetic again, "is that he isn't here." That's too bad! Scott thought ironically. "I'm a sick man myself."

"I know that, Scott, and I'm sorry. I shouldn't ask this of you if you didn't happen to be the only one free from ten to eleven. Doctors Meyerson and Wilson will take care of the afternoon classes."

"What about Anderson?"

"It so happens," Grant said with the first touch of impatience in his voice, "that Dr. Anderson's schedule coincides exactly with Mr. Duncan's. Frankly, I dislike asking *any* other teacher to take on extra classes, for each has had more than his share lately."

Scott grimaced into the phone, knowing that Grant was referring to his frequent absences. The injustice of it! Could he help his illness? Besides, no matter how low he had felt, he had never failed to give notice. . . . "I'll take the class," he said shortly. "I merely wanted to make sure that you had investigated all other possibilities. It wouldn't be amiss, however, if you were to tell me *what* course it is, where the class meets, and. . . ." As Grant began to tell him, he pulled the telephone pad and pencil to him. Flipping open the pad, he saw that the last entry was a crossed-out grocery order that Judith had evidently phoned in long ago.

He ripped off the sheet and crumpled it in his hand. "Yes, I've got it," he said curtly, and slammed down the phone. He'd have to stop at the Registrar's office for the information.

Coningsby next year. That would show them that he was more than Grant's lackey or wet-nurse to Duncan. He went upstairs and laboriously got himself ready, so that when he left the house he more nearly resembled Professor Scott, Eighteenth-Century Man.

The Heart was gray and slushy. At any other time Kim would have thought it a gloomy sight, but this evening he was comforted by the mere fact of its existence. With new fondness he looked at it and the buildings that surrounded it. Home. This was the only place to which he had learned to belong. If he hadn't had it to return to after New York, he didn't know what he would have done.

He shivered and clutched his coat at his throat. The weather had warmed, but he felt chilled to the bone. He thought it possible that he would never thaw out.

Dr. Day had done her best to prepare him, but now he knew that nothing could have prepared him for the calculating hardness in Carol's face. It had come when she had realized that he had changed, and she had seemed to sense that almost as soon as they had met. He winced when he thought of David Whitney. She had boasted of the three weeks' hell she had made for him, and even of his death, as if she herself had caused it. And he was haunted by the thought that she was right . . . that although there had been thousands of miles between them when David had gone down in the Pacific, she had somehow been responsible.

After leaving her, he had tramped through the streets all night, wanting to shout aloud his discovery of the injustice in the universe. He felt as though the world had shifted under his feet, although before he had become aware of the evil in Carol, he had not known that he assumed the working of so rigid a formula of justice.

Why should she not pay? Why should Whitney have suffered and perished? *Why?*

He flung open the Summit door, reassured by its solid reality, and took the stairs two at a time.

Grant was still working in his office and seemed surprised to see him.

"But you left a message for me at the Bijou," Kim said, sinking into a chair. He was exhausted from no food and no sleep.

Grant sat down behind his desk and looked amused, and Kim wondered what the hell he found amusing in this world. "So I did," Grant said then. "It's customary, you know, to inform someone when you're unable to meet your classes for two days. I merely wanted to be told as soon as you were willing to render service again."

Kim groaned. "Didn't I tell anyone I was leaving?"

"It seems that you didn't. For a day the whole campus was worried. Then Dr. Day suggested that you might have gone to New York. After that"—he laughed—"there was nothing to do but settle down to wait for your return."

Kim roused himself. "You mean she told you *why* I went?"

Grant nodded. "Something about it. For one thing, she knew that I'd want to hear about David Whitney."

"So you know." Kim stared at him. "You know about Whitney, and yet you can go on acting as if nothing wrong had happened."

"For that matter, Duncan, I sometimes wonder how any of us have the heart to go on with constructive work when most of the world is intent upon being destructive. But—"

"Oh, I know," Kim broke in contemptuously. "We're made so that we don't feel other people's troubles as we do our own. That's good old human nature. But I tell you that if you had talked with Carol Leeds about Whitney, you'd feel differently. She's. . . ." He stared around the room, as if he expected to find that she had entered it. "She's like Rappaccini's daughter in the Hawthorne story. Yes, that's what she is." He nodded to himself, satisfied with the idea for which he had long been searching. "She's full of poison, death to everyone who touches her—death to herself."

Grant said nothing. He gave Kim an intent look, then got up and walked around the desk to him. "You need a good sleep. Try to get one tonight, meet your classes tomorrow, and come see me when you feel up to it. I have something to say to you."

"Say it now," Kim said wearily.

Grant shook his head. "It would be cruelty to say anything to you tonight."

Kim laughed harshly. "Good God! If you knew all the talking that I've done and listened to in the last few days, you'd believe me when I say that I'm up to hearing anything."

Grant made an apologetic gesture. "I shouldn't have mentioned it. You go along now to your room and—"

"I don't need sleep!" Kim cried. "I need peace. That's why I came to see you as soon as I got to the Bijou and found your message. I thought—" He stopped, not knowing how to explain what he had thought. *Grant never fails. He is always sane and calm. He will steady the world under my feet.*

Grant stood looking down at him. "All right," he said finally, and went back to his desk chair. "But I hope that you will understand the spirit in which I say what I have to say. I'm very much interested in you, Duncan—as a person. If that sounds patronizing, I'm sorry, for I don't mean it that way. You have a certain kind of vitality that's rare. It's as if you're in actual touch with some phase of reality which others—myself, for example—can see only through ideas. I've given this some thought"—he laughed almost embarrassedly—"for sometimes I think I envy you. It's not an easy thing to explain, but I think you know what I mean."

Kim didn't say whether he did or not, but stared at him in growing astonishment. Grant, Paul Lewis Grant, envying *him?*

"However," Grant went on, "my point is that you have found for that vitality no outlet. It is smoldering within you, and one day, Duncan, it will either explode—or die." He reached for his pipe, avoiding Kim's look. "I think that I now know for a certainty what is thwarting it and therefore your whole life and happiness. John Willard College. You see, I kept waiting for signs that you had made your adjustment, but lately it has occurred to me that while waiting, I have ignored the many signs pointing to something else. One more thing: I may be wrong, of course, but I think that it is not only John Willard. I believe that it would be the same for you in almost any other college."

For a minute there was silence between them. Then Grant said, "I am sure that you know that I do not say any of this lightly."

Kim came to life. "You mean that you want to fire me!" His voice went up. "You're going to fire me because I didn't come running to you for permission to go to New York."

Grant shook his head sadly. "I tried to tell you that you weren't up to this kind of talk tonight, Duncan. I am not going to fire you. I have no authority to fire you. There is no reason to fire you—although, for your own sake, I sometimes wish that there were." He smiled faintly. "Perhaps I should say, however, that it was—to put it mildly—inconsiderate of you to go off without warning. Classes meet whether you're here or not, you know, and your leaving did put an extra burden on teachers who already have heavy schedules—as well as troubles of their own. Did you think of that, Duncan?"

Kim stayed silent. *I admire you very much, Mr. Duncan.* Someone had said that to him years ago. He sneered, because that was the expression that best fit on his suddenly unsteady face. "I always thought this was a stuffy, narrow place—and now I know it. I was willing to stay here forever, but if the place isn't big enough to want me, well, then, by God, I'll. . . ." He allowed the words to trail away. *I'll go forth into the world where there is no justice, where there is no forced bounding line. . . .*

"You can stay here forever," Grant said quietly. "You have permanent tenure. You can stay here until your life rots away, or you can make a clean break and find your life. As for the New York trip, that's unimportant. It merely brought together the thoughts I've had about you and made me resolve to speak to you—even though it meant sticking my nose into a situation which, I admit, no truly efficient administrator would allow himself to see."

"Until my life rots away," Kim repeated wonderingly. "I didn't know *you* felt that way about the place!"

"I don't. I'm talking from your standpoint."

Kim hadn't heard him. "I know exactly what you mean. I used to feel that if I stayed on here I'd end up as withered as—as Webb."

Grant laughed. "There is no one around here less withered than Webb. You're judging by what he would call the most superficial of appearances—the physical. He has a thriving, vital mind—"

"But in the end," Kim said defiantly, "even Cliff Hughes was disappointed in him. You know that!"

"Cliff was disappointed in him as a colleague. Believe me, Duncan, Webb belongs here because he can draw life from this place, and, in turn, give it some of his own. That's what a college, as well as teaching, is, you know—a relationship. If it can't nourish you, and you stay on out of inertia, then you wither."

Kim tried to look as if he were thinking this over. Actually, he had no thought. He got to his feet. "You are telling me," he said with dignity, "that you wish me to resign because I have no life to give to the College. Once you pretended to need me, but now you're telling me to get out."

"I'm telling you no such thing," Grant said, rising also. "Please, Duncan, let's—"

"Never mind." Kim held up his hand. "You wish me to leave. That's the essence of your talk. Well, I shall most certainly leave. I go now to write my letter of resignation." He strode to the door. "I assume, however, that you and the others would find it convenient for me to stay until the Cadets go."

Grant hesitated, as if searching for the right words. Then he sighed and said gravely. "I and the others would appreciate your staying on that much longer."

Chapter Two

WHEN Marcia heard the first strains of the Andante of the Prokofieff, she felt scornful. J.W. must have gone into his study purposely to put on the records. She picked up her book and was seemingly engrossed in it when he returned to the living room.

He stood quietly by her side until it was evident that she wasn't going to look up. Then he reached down and gently took the book from her hands. She pretended to be startled. "I didn't know that you were in the room."

"Not only am I in the room," he said, holding the book behind him, "but there is an appropriate musical background. And you sit reading!"

"It's an engrossing book," she said, laughing a little. *An appropriate musical background. An empty symbol. . . .*

"Really?" He held it out then and read off the title: *"In Praise of Failure: A Study of Herman Melville,* by Silas Seabolm. Ugh—one of those paradoxical titles. Sounds like an Uncle Philip poem." He tossed the book into a corner of the couch and sat down beside her. "Well, what's so engrossing about it?"

"That's paradoxical too. The theme is good, but Seabolm obviously threw the book together. I have the impression—"

"Excuse me one minute," he said suddenly and went into the study to turn off the Prokofieff. When he came back, he smiled and said, "Now it will be possible for me to concentrate upon this profound book review. Do go on, my dear."

She went on without enthusiasm. "It's very unimportant—but I have the impression that he was too lazy to read over his own notes or go back to his source material."

He frowned, as if thinking hard. "He?"

"Silas Seabolm," she said angrily, "the author. And don't ask me the author of what!"

He shook his head reprovingly. "You're very impatient tonight, Marcia."

"I'm sorry," she said tightly, and walked to the fireplace. She avoided glancing up at Eileen, who she imagined looked triumphant. "I can't understand," she said more calmly, "why Professor Grant asked me to read the book carefully."

"So. I'm not competing with Herman Melville or what's-his-name—Seabolm?—but with Professor Grant. It is for him that you do homework rather than listen to Prokofieff with me."

"He is a great Melville scholar," she said irrelevantly. She returned aimlessly to the couch, but did not sit down beside him.

"Grant?" He waved his cigarette. "Until now, the rumor of his fame had not reached—"

"And he is a sincere man," she went on with sudden intensity. "He does not bind people to him with empty symbols. He does not—"

"Please do not be cryptic, Marcia." He leaned forward to put out his cigarette. "Obviously you mean to say something beyond the words you are using."

She stared down at him. "Why did you pretend to me about Prokofieff? Russ told me how you hated that concerto. And have you ever read *Noa Noa?*"

"Russ and you appear to have very much in common." He returned her look for a moment, then shrugged. "I'm glad, of course."

"But you haven't answered my questions!"

"Perhaps," he said stiffly, "I changed about Prokofieff. As for *Noa Noa*, it was a Birthday Book—as I told you when I gave it to you."

"You're evading."

He reached out for her hand and pulled her down beside him. "Very well," he said with easy resignation. "I submit to this inquisition only because of the charm of my inquisitor. Furthermore, I'll confess to using those—did you call them symbols?—as a part of the strategy of courtship." He raised her hand to his lips and kissed it. "And now that you have found out this great villainy, what do you propose to do?"

It was over so quickly and simply that she wondered why she had been afraid to ask. "But"—the thought which only a minute ago had been strong and vital suddenly seemed petty—"but then they have no meaning for me—for us."

"They *had* meaning," he said, "for they served to bring us together. Why should they continue to have meaning? We have no further need of them. In fact"—he laughed—"it will be a relief to dispense with them, don't you agree?"

She said nothing. It had been this way when they had talked about Vincent Diaz. *But, Marcia, what was there to settle?*

He shook her hand gently but impatiently. "For heaven's sake, Marcia, don't sit there brooding. I want to ask you an *important* question. How do you feel about living in Chicago?"

"Chicago?" she repeated blankly.

He nodded. "I intend to start a branch factory there. Later it will, perhaps, become the main one. I'm buying someone out—lock, stock, and barrel. It's a small place and hasn't been converted. By the end of the war, I'll have it running smoothly and be ready to expand. You can see the necessity of my being there to. . . ."

She listened with a sense of detachment. Chicago? Well, why not? Why not Chicago, Peking, Constantinople? It would be a relief to be away from Riverville. "I think that I should like living in Chicago," she said when she saw that he was waiting for an answer.

"Good." He stood up and leaned over her, still holding her hand. "Now I shall go to my conference with a clear mind."

She freed her hand. "You don't really mean *now*, do you?"

"I'm afraid that I do. I learned only a few hours ago that Mr. Luther from Chicago was in Riverville to see me. We are dining at the Bijou. I didn't invite him here because I didn't want to bore Grace and you with our business talk."

It sounded very reasonable, yet something urged her on. "Are you leaving me as a kind of—punishment?"

He frowned. "This is quite genuine, Marcia."

"*This* is quite genuine," she repeated slowly. "But the other times. . .?"

"What other times?" he asked sternly as she hesitated. "What do you mean, Marcia?"

"I think you know what I mean. Your going off always affects me. . . . It's unreasonable, I admit, but I think you know how it affects me, and I think that you have deliberately done it several times. Haven't you?"

He made no denial, and she thought that he was not going to answer; but then he said quite seriously, "Perhaps I have. However, why shouldn't I have done so? If, through sheer accident, I discovered one means of testing your attachment to me, why shouldn't I have made use of it?" He smiled again and shrugged. "It was another part of the strategy. That's all there was to it."

She said nothing, for she understood that he was being sincere and that for him that truly was all there was to it.

"But tonight," he was saying, "you won't mind, will you, Marcia?"

"Of course not," she said quickly.

He kissed her briefly. "I knew you'd understand."

She watched him leave the room, wishing that she had thought to say that she was leaving too. No matter how absurd it might have seemed, she should have said it. If she left first, then he could not leave her. That was the way she had learned to combat Martin when—

"I've just learned," Grace said brightly as she entered the room, "that we're to be alone tonight, Marcia. I'm so glad. I seldom have you to myself."

Grace suggested a demitasse in the living room. Marcia settled down in her corner of the couch, Tamburlaine at her feet. "J.W.— Jack told me about Chicago tonight," she said.

"I'm glad," Grace said quietly, "for now you'll have to make a definite decision soon."

Marcia set the little white and gold cup and saucer down upon the table. "What do you mean?"

"Surely you know," Grace said, "that until you say no, he assumes that you mean yes. My son is like that."

"But . . ." Marcia began, and then was quiet.

"I like you, Marcia." Grace's voice was more serious than Marcia had ever before heard it. "I like you very much, as you know. But what you are doing to my son is not fair, although I'm sure that you do not know it."

"Not fair!" Marcia cried. "But it's he who is. . . ." She stopped, the defiant anger suddenly gone. "I don't understand you," she said distantly.

Grace laughed then, and it was a kind sound that shattered the strain. "Oh, my dear, I've shocked and frightened you, and I am sorry. I blundered with you before, for it was I who spoke before anyone should have spoken."

"It's not so simple as the mere making of a decision," Marcia said slowly. But she could not explain what she meant. She was silent for a minute, then tried again: "He doesn't know me. I have the fear that when he does, he'll not like me. Maybe a greater fear is that he'll never even bother to know me. To him I'm either a child, and he treats me as he would Russ—or, then again, I'm merely a—" She stopped and shrugged.

"Or you're merely a woman to be loved," Grace finished for her. "Oh, I quite understand, my dear. You see, he is very much like his father."

Marcia looked at her wonderingly. "It wasn't wrong for you to marry his father. But I can understand why for you there was no danger. You are so definitely yourself that—"

"You're trying to be too wise," Grace said firmly. "The only difference between you and me is that I've accumulated more years. You're right. It was not wrong for me to marry his father, but then that marriage had great impersonal meaning. It was the union of two families. I participated very willingly—even zealously. It wasn't until after his death that I realized I had ceased to exist as an individual human being."

Marcia shook her head. "I can't believe it."

"I'm flattered," Grace said, smiling. "Nevertheless, what I'm telling you is true. It was difficult for a while. . . . What did I do?" she went on briskly. "Why, I reached out for things that would make me have meaning for myself and in the eyes of other people. I'm not being very clear, am I? I don't quite know what to call—"

"Symbols," Marcia said suddenly. "You reached out for symbols."

Grace thought this over for a minute, then nodded. "Yes, they could be called that, I believe. Color, for instance. I wore one color until I completely possessed it. . . until anyone seeing a purple object, no matter where, would think automatically, there's Grace. And then I found work. That's why New York is important to me. That's why—"

"And you gave up New York because of me," Marcia broke in. "How stupid of me not to have realized that earlier. Now I understand why you—"

"No, no," Grace said hastily. "I am not that selfish, Marcia. That was not my meaning."

But Marcia was not listening. "Rather, *he* made you give it up. I see it now. He is so very proper. He insisted upon your staying here merely to satisfy his sense of propriety." Her eyes flashed. "How like him!"

"How like him," Grace repeated mildly.

Marcia stared at her. "But that's exactly what I've been trying to explain to you—or a part of it, at least. He has no conception of anyone else's individuality, no understanding of what work might mean to anyone besides himself, no—"

Grace stopped her with a laugh. "I know his faults, Marcia. I'm his mother. They don't affect me as they do you. That is the difference —the great difference, you see."

"I *don't* see!" Marcia cried. "I *want* to love him. Do you understand? If only he were different. . . ."

"How revealing," Grace said pityingly. "All you are asking is that he be someone else!"

"I don't know . . . I don't know," Marcia said wearily. She walked around Grace's chair and stood looking up at Eileen. "Would she have made him happy?"

"She was very sweet," Grace said, turning to look.

"And docile," Marcia added bitterly.

"Young, rather—but questioning too. Have you noticed her eyes?" Grace laughed softly. "Remember too that Russ is her son."

Marcia moved away from the portrait, suddenly scornful of herself.

Russ was right. It was merely a picture hanging over the mantel. She sat down near to Grace again. "Doesn't it seem strange to you that Russ accepts me so—so easily?"

Grace looked surprised, then amused. "It certainly does not. He *likes* you."

"But that's just it!" Marcia said excitedly. "He likes me—when he ought to hate me."

"Ridiculous! Why on this earth should he hate you?"

"Because," Marcia said carefully, "if I were in his place, I'd hate anyone who tried to take my father away."

Grace shook her head. "But that's no *reason*, Marcia."

Marcia looked at her, startled. "No—no, it isn't a reason, is it?" she said then, as if puzzled.

She left Grace early. Alone in her room, she discovered that of all Grace had said to her, the words, "But what you are doing to my son is not fair," were the most vivid in her mind. And as she thought upon them, it began to seem that in some way they expressed the feeling she had had when once she had briefly glimpsed J.W. as a man apart from her and her need of him. She was oppressed with loneliness, as if some subtle force had severed not only him from her but the whole world. . . .

Restlessly she looked again at the message Mrs. Murdock had slipped under her door while she was gone. Professor Grant had come in person and then later telephoned about a book. . . .

She picked up *In Praise of Failure* and idly leafed through it, once more wondering why it was important to him. Suddenly her hands tightened around it. If he were that concerned over it, wasn't that excuse enough for her to go to him with it?

Hurriedly she put on her coat. She could say that she had just finished reading it—or that Mrs. Murdock's message had made her aware that he wished it returned. . . .

But she knew that she would need to say or explain nothing. He would accept her coming as unquestioningly as he had accepted all her acts and words, the unreasonable as well as the reasonable. That knowledge was why she could go to him.

It was not until she was actually at Millie's that she began to seem absurd to herself. If she had found him at the Summit, that would have been one thing—but to have come here, to Millie's. . . .

She sat where Millie had invited her to sit—on the edge of the ornate sofa, surrounded by piles of brocaded drapes. Millie was housecleaning. Windows were bare, and a part of the rug was rolled back. A ladder leaned against the wall, and on the hall table stood a big can of paper cleaner which Millie had set down when she went upstairs to tell the Professor that he had another guest.

A man came down the stairs. He wore a blue cap and had bulging coat pockets. Instinctively Marcia tried to shrink back out of sight, but he looked straight ahead as if long ago taught that what was in Mrs. Winter's living room was no concern of his. At the door he shouted: "G'night, Millie!"

"G'night, Whitey!" she called from upstairs. "Have a good run."

Whitey went out, slamming the door behind him so that it jarred the whole house.

Marcia considered leaving *In Praise of Failure* on the table and following Whitey, but she had waited too long, for Millie was now coming down the stairs. "The Professor's niece is with him," she said apologetically, "but he'll be down very soon." She sat across from Marcia and regarded her with frank interest. "Do you know the niece— Janice?"

"Yes—as a student." Marcia stood up. "If you'll be so kind as to—"

"Oh, that's right." Millie gave her a final head-to-toe look. "I keep forgetting that you're a teacher."

"If you'll be so kind as to tell Dr. Grant that I left this book for him," Marcia said hurriedly, "I'll run along now without disturbing him."

Millie leaned back in her chair and made no effort to take the book Marcia held out to her. "From the way he looked when I told him you were down here, I'd guess that he's going to enjoy being disturbed— if"—she winked—"you get my meaning. Sometimes— Why don't you sit down?—I worry about the Professor. I always say, 'All work and no play—' "

"I did not come to play," Marcia said stiffly. But she had reseated herself.

"Yes, I know." Millie smiled slowly. "You came to see the man about a book."

"I did," Marcia said, trying to sound like Etta Wilson. But she felt herself blushing. Millie wasn't wholly wrong in thinking the book a mere excuse.

Millie crossed her legs and smoothed out the folds of her pink housecoat. It was slightly ripped under one arm and most of the buttons from the knees down were missing, but it was still a provocative garment. "Sorry you caught me in this rag and the place in such a mess, but I'm housecleaning. That's why I had to send Janice up to the Professor's rooms."

"Please don't let me keep you from your work," Marcia said. In spite of herself, she glanced briefly at Millie's legs and saw with a certain sense of disappointment that they were very good legs. Why *did* he live here?

Millie laughed throatily. "I'm always glad of a reason to be kept from it. It took me all day to get the ambition to start, and then I got

354

at it finally only because I thought, if I get this room done tonight, I won't have to do it tomorrow. And then when tomorrow— Oh, here they come."

Grant and Janice stopped at the bottom of the stairs. He waved toward Marcia, but could do no more, for Janice was talking rapidly to him.

Millie made a wry face. "I just don't like it without drapes, do you? Those"—she pointed to the pile on Marcia's right—"go right up there"—she pointed to the arch beyond which Janice and Grant stood —"and they make the room nice and cozy."

"I'm sure they do," Marcia said uneasily. As long as she had been foolish enough to come, why did it have to be on a night that Janice was here?

Millie had moved to her side. "That girl's a leech," she murmured. "She hasn't given the poor Professor a free hour for the past six months."

"She needs him," Marcia said involuntarily. "I can—" She grew aware of Millie's surprised look. "I mean I really don't have to see him tonight." She walked out into the hall. "Hello. I'm sorry I interrupted you two, for I merely wanted to leave this book." She handed it to Grant.

"Have you read it?" he asked quickly. She nodded, and he said decisively, "Well, then, you're certainly not leaving until you tell me what you think of it!"

"I'm going," Janice said shortly. She had avoided looking at Marcia.

Marcia turned to Grant. "Please . . . we can talk about it another time."

But he didn't understand. "Goodnight, Janice," he said almost curtly.

Janice's expression did not change, but Marcia felt what she was feeling, and her mind cried out to Grant: Don't talk to her that way! She saw, however, that he was not only impatient with Janice, but preoccupied and hardly aware of what was happening. He walked away from them into the living room, the book already open in his hands.

At the door Janice hesitated, looking at Marcia for the first time. "Aren't the MacMillans home tonight?" she asked with an insolent smile. She flung open the door and went out into the night. Marcia waited a moment, then moved to the door and closed it softly.

Grant was calling to her. She went into the living room and found him bent over the book under a shadeless floor lamp. Millie was looking on with tolerant amusement.

"Well, what do you think?" he asked abruptly.

She assumed that he was referring to *In Praise of Failure*. "I hardly know where or how to begin. Perhaps if you'd ask me some specific—"

"Professor," Millie said, sauntering over to them, "this is no place to discuss a book. It's all torn up and the drapes are down. Why don't you go upstairs?"

"I'll be glad to come to your office tomorrow," Marcia said quickly.

"Tomorrow?" Grant said vaguely. He looked disappointed.

Millie gave Marcia a look of near contempt. "It isn't as if the Professor had only *one* room. Besides, I intend to go right on cleaning this room." She shepherded them into the hall and stood by the stairs while they went up. "Should I bring you a snack later on?"

Grant seemed not to hear. Marcia looked over her shoulder and said primly, "No, thank you." But Millie's smile reached her. It was self-satisfied, as if she had successfully maneuvered a long needed strategy, but it was also friendly. Marcia smiled back. "We'll not need a snack—but thank you very much."

"So you think it's bad?" Grant walked restlessly to his desk and flung *In Praise of Failure* down upon it. He turned and stayed by the desk, regarding her sternly. " 'Glib and unsound,' you said, didn't you?"

"Why—yes," she said uncertainly. "Shouldn't I have?"

His face did not relent. "I want your honest and objective opinion. Don't spare my feelings."

She looked puzzled. "I don't understand. Is Silas Seabolm a friend of yours?"

He laughed shortly. "Yes."

She was growing confused and a little angry. He had never before seemed so unapproachable. "Well, I still say that it's a superficial treatment of what might have been a very good theme."

"But you *did* understand the theme, didn't you?" he asked carefully. "Understand it and thought it good, so that if another book with the same theme were to come out, you'd think it superfluous, no matter how sound? Isn't that right?"

"I did understand the theme," she said with equal care, "but I certainly should not call another treatment of the same theme superfluous." When he was silent, she said, "Hadn't you better explain why this is so important to you?"

He moved impatiently. "There's nothing to explain."

"I'm sure that there must be. I've never seen you so—so upset."

He looked suddenly contrite. "I'm not being very civil, am I? I doubt if I've even thanked you for coming." He looked at her as if seeing her for the first time that night. "How strange to have you here —yet how natural. That's the trouble. It seems so natural that I have to be reminded that you don't know everything inside my mind."

She smiled. "You're evading."

"Not at all," he said firmly. "I'm through with evasion."

"Are you talking about *In Praise of Failure?*" she asked sceptically.

He laughed. "I am not—and you know it." He picked up the book again. "Maybe I exaggerated the whole thing. Nevertheless. . . ." He shrugged and walked over to her, leafing through the book until he found a particular page; then he held it up for her to see. "Remember this chapter? Well, these twenty pages contain the gist of three hundred of mine."

She began to understand. "But that's incredible! I mean, what a horrible coincidence!"

"Amusing, isn't it?" he said dryly. "Besides, it isn't exactly a coincidence."

She looked unbelieving. "You don't mean. . .?"

"By now I don't know what I mean." He pitched the book back to the desk and pulled a chair nearer to hers. "I saw Si—Silas Seabolm —at the last Literary Convention. At his urging, I talked about my Melville. I didn't particularly want to talk, but the way he put it, I'd have seemed rude not to. So I talked—and now—a year later, he has written and published his version."

"It's hard to believe," she said slowly, "that there are people like that."

"That's it," he said intently. "That's exactly what depresses me. Si and I—well, we were old friends, if not close ones."

She studied him thoughtfully for a moment. "Even so, you know people too well to be especially disillusioned by this—bad as it is. Scott's book didn't shock you. It did me, until I talked to you about it."

"But that was different," he said quickly. "Good or bad, *Sentimental Farce* came from Scott himself. He didn't steal it." He seemed impatient again, and walked restlessly about the room. "If Si were one of Matt's kind, I'd not feel such—well, call it bewilderment. But Si is our kind, of our world."

"What do you mean—our world?"

"There are two worlds," he said, looking down at her. "Haven't you discovered them? There is Matt's world, and there is yours and mine, each with its own set of values."

She thought of J.W. and understood what he meant. "Yes, I've discovered them—and also that each can reduce the other to a cipher."

He nodded. "That's what I meant when I told you MacMillan was only a symbol to me. He's Matt's world, although"—he smiled faintly —"I'm sure that it's Matt who derives from MacMillan's world—and when he tries to impose his values upon the college, I try to fight them—not in Hughes' way, but in my own. However"—he made a helpless gesture—"when someone like Si appears, I don't know how to fight."

She noted that they had been thinking of J.W. at the same time, but that he had spoken of him as if for that moment he had forgotten the personal meaning the name had for them. She was glad of that. "I think," she said suddenly, "that you're wrong about one thing. There are the two sets of values, but they're not neatly divided into two separate worlds."

He looked ready to argue, then changed his mind. "You must be right," he said wearily. "Good Lord! doesn't one ever get beyond being disillusioned? I guess I've assumed—without knowing it—that a man behind books and papers is naturally a good man." He shook his head. "Crooked thinking."

"Or," she said, *personal* thinking."

He frowned. "It's not personal."

"But isn't it because of Matt that you set up the two worlds?"

"Perhaps . . ." He shrugged. "Well, yes. Why?"

"Then it *is* personal. Don't you see?"

He stared at her for a moment, then said half angrily, "I don't follow you. I still say that my reaction to this is no more personal than would be that of any other normal individual." He hesitated, but went on defiantly, "I have a right to some sense of personal injury, haven't I? Si threw that book together on the strength of an idea that wasn't even his own, and he has it published. Do you realize how many years I've been plodding along on my study? Do you realize how. . . ." He walked away from her. "Why is it that I have to be so slow? Why do I—"

"Because," she interrupted firmly, "you are sound, because you work with a sense of responsibility, because you make something more of your writing than a mere expression of personal feelings, because—"

"That's enough," he said with an embarrassed laugh. "I don't blame you for thinking that I needed a few pats on the back. You have certainly caught me at a weak moment."

She ignored this. "I didn't realize that you were impatient over your Melville. I know that there's reason enough, but I didn't—"

"I'm not really." He sat down tiredly. "Most of the time I'm fully aware that the world can get along very well without the appearance of my Melville. It's only that now and then it occurs to me that once I publish Melville, I can give up Oaklands." He seemed perplexed by his own words, and said, "Another crooked thought—but there it is."

"Oaklands? Your summer home?"

"Summer home?" He laughed. "Janice's description, no doubt? Well, Oaklands is the place where we were born—as Matt puts it when he's feeling sentimental. It was a farm, a good one. Matt isn't interested in it as a farm. He wants to own my share so that he'll have sole right to remodel it into the kind of property he wants it to be. You see, property is Matt's stake in the world, and—"

"And Melville is yours," she said.

He grinned sheepishly. "It's beginning to look that way, I admit. I must have had the sneaking thought that publication would prove my set of values as tangibly successful as Matt's. All these years that I've hung on to Oaklands—and it has been nothing but a nuisance for me, actually—I've persuaded myself that my motive was my not wanting good land wasted or robbed of its original purpose. Now I'm beginning to wonder."

"Oh, I'm sure that reason was genuine," she said quickly. "It's just that there was another and deeper reason too. I doubt that any motive is thoroughly known."

"You're very wise," he said after a short silence. "You're what I didn't know existed—a creative listener. I understand more and more what Janice finds in you."

She looked at him in surprise. "Evidently she hasn't told you. . . . Well, that's unimportant. About Oaklands, however, there's a very simple question you could ask yourself as a kind of test. If Oaklands should be completely destroyed in some way, who would lose more—you or your brother?"

"I know the answer, teacher," he said, grinning. "Materially speaking, we'd both lose exactly the same; but if we consider the different values, Matt would stand the greater loss. As property, the place means far more to Matt than to me. I'd even gain a little, for I'd be rid of a trouble and no doubt believe that some obscure justice had struck down Oaklands for the sole purpose of proving that I'm right and Matt's wrong. How's that?"

"That," she said, laughing with him, "is very good. And now"—she pointed to *In Praise of Failure* lying on the desk—"I hope you have no more destructive thoughts about that book—destructive to you, I mean."

He stared at the book. "Did we really start out talking about *that?* I hope you—" He stopped as there was a knock on the door. "Yes?" he called out and went to the door but did not open it.

"Did I leave my book? Spengler." It was Janice's voice.

"You did not," he said and shook his head slowly at Marcia as she started to put on her coat. "You weren't even carrying a book, Janice."

"You can't know that," Janice said sharply. "You weren't paying much attention to me this evening. Let me come in and look around. Maybe it slipped down in the back of a chair."

"If you mean Spengler's *Decline of the West,*" he said grimly, "it couldn't have slipped down in the back of a chair." He hastily surveyed the room. Marcia was also looking. "It isn't here," he said.

"Thanks for looking so carefully," she said sarcastically. "I'll come back for it tomorrow."

"You should have seen her," Marcia said when they heard her start downstairs.

He looked harassed. "I suppose I did sound heartless—but, Marcia, would you believe it if I told you I was certain that girl came back only to see if you were still here?"

She fastened her coat, avoiding his eyes. "I believe it. But—" She moved quickly toward the door when Janice cried out as if with pain.

But he put a restraining hand on her arm. "Yes, I know. Janice has fallen down a few steps, and I'm heartless again. However, I also know that Janice would never fall by accident. You stay here."

"But if she's really hurt. . . ."

He nodded. "If she's really hurt, I'll call you—and then eat my desk." He went out into the hall and shut the door behind him.

She sat down and lighted a cigarette, striking the match as quietly as possible. It was a ridiculous situation, yet she knew with him that it was also serious.

Grant's voice came up to her, then Millie's. "Oh, I'm all right—really I am," said Janice in a plaintive tone that meant she knew she had gone as far as she dared.

The front door closed, and Grant was coming up the stairs. "It was a very graceful fall," he said as he came into the room.

"I must go," Marcia said quickly. "It's very— On second thought" —she gave him a brief, guilty glance—"I suppose I had better wait until Janice. . . ."

He agreed. "But don't look that way, Marcia! We both know Janice, and it's only through her that this has been twisted into something that seems unpleasant. Nothing about her surprises me, but I don't know why she's so intent upon—"

"I do," said Marcia. "She's furious with me. We quarreled. I don't know what she intended to do tonight, but I do know how she was feeling—shut out, deserted. I think that she has felt that way all her life."

He shrugged. "You're right, I suppose. We've said this before about her. Nevertheless—I can't be her father, nor you her mother."

"But remember," she said quietly, "that the feeling is the very nucleus of her life. It controls everything that she does."

He was watching her intently. "Marcia, how do you know so much about Janice—about her feelings? Is it that you see yourself in—"

She looked up at him quickly, and it was a pleading look. "I've been meaning to tell you," she said with deliberateness, "that I sent my Blake off to Hill-Moran yesterday."

He hesitated only a moment. "I didn't realize that you were making such progress with it."

"I had to finish it to get it off my mind. I'm afraid I lost faith in it— but I had to finish it."

"How did you wind it up? What did you add to it that I didn't see?"

"A separate chapter on his engravings." Absently she opened her case for another cigarette. "In a way, it's the best part of the whole thing—I think. Even you might like it. I owe the idea to. . . . Well, it's about the bounding line. Blake believed that a definite bounding line is necessary to all great art. This belief became a principle to him, and certainly he applied it to his engraving, but, curiously enough, he lost sight of it in the major portion of his writing. I re-examined the writings with this as a kind of touchstone, and I . . ."

She put her cigarette out in the overflowing ashtray. "What time is it?"

He leaned back in his chair and crossed his legs. "I find that an exceedingly interesting idea. How did you develop it?"

"What time is it?" she repeated severely.

"Oh." He glanced hastily at his watch. "An awkward hour," he said guiltily. "Four-thirty."

"Very awkward indeed! And what do you propose I do, Professor Grant?"

"Endure a few more hours here," he said promptly. "This is the least awkward place for you to be at an awkward hour. No hour is awkward to Millie, but I have a feeling that this one might be to the Murdocks—or to anyone else in Riverville who might see us strolling up the Heights. If you—" He became suddenly serious. "But what an uncomfortable night for you. And you have classes in the morning!"

"Not very early ones." She smiled, suddenly not caring. It had been a good night. "Herby's will be open in a couple of hours. I'll have breakfast there and still be able to get some sleep before class."

"Truly I'm sorry. I've been very thoughtless."

"No more than I. I should have left when Janice—"

He laughed. "Let's blame it on Millie's housecleaning, Si, and William Blake. Now, how about some pre-breakfast coffee?"

She said that would be wonderful. He went to make the coffee, and she drew her coat around her and curled up in his leather chair. For the first time in many months, she felt at peace, although she did not trust the feeling enough to probe it. . . .

She looked around the room, thinking of Grant in it. *In Praise of Failure* still lay on the desk. She disliked it very much now that she knew it was a dishonest book at his expense, but she also felt grateful toward it. Because of it, she had a new knowledge of him. . . .

New knowledge? Not exactly, for although she now knew that in one small way he had deceived himself in thinking about his brother, her idea of him had not changed. She thought of the ease with which he had admitted his self-deception. One could reach him without penetrating an armor. And she felt certain that no matter how far beneath the surface of his mind she might have cause to go, he would remain Grant to her.

Would that be true of her? Or would there not be found within her another being—selfish, cruel. . . .

"Why do you live here?" she called out to destroy her own thought.

He appeared in the doorway, an aluminum coffee pot in his hand. This was the question that he had planned to answer with a curt reminder that where he lived was strictly his own affair. But now that he had heard her ask it, he found himself carefully preparing an explanation. He liked colleges, but he also liked to live among people who were not academicians. He had a slight fear—abnormal or self-deceptive? He didn't think so—that to be encircled at all times by only colleagues and students would make one lose touch—

"I didn't mean to pry," she said quickly.

Disappointed, he realized that he had hesitated too long. Then he laughed at his own eagerness to tell her. She looked at him questioningly, but he merely held up the coffee pot and said, "This will be ready soon." As he poured the boiling water into the pot, he marveled over his desire to talk about himself to her. He wondered if she knew that her most casual question evoked in his mind the whole dull drama of his life.

Marcia stood up and stretched her cramped muscles. "Herby's should be open by now."

He agreed reluctantly and turned off the electric light. Thin daylight streamed into the room. She took a small comb from her purse and ran it hastily through her hair. "This has been a ghastly night for you," he said contritely.

She laughed, knowing that she didn't have to reassure him that she had enjoyed it. "I look ghastly, you mean."

"I do not. You look as if you had just arisen from long peaceful hours of sleep." He rubbed his hands over his face. "I've grown a beard and no doubt have pouches under my eyes."

She gave him a brief critical scrutiny. "You look fine—much better than when I arrived—I'm flattered to say."

They went quietly downstairs and out on the porch. The April morning was brightening. There were a few distant sounds, but no one was on the street. The air was clean and sharp. "It's beautiful," she said.

"Yes," he said, looking at her. "I don't want you to—let me take you to breakfast."

"If you don't mind, I'd rather be— I mean, I'm going to eat a very hurried breakfast."

"Of course," he said immediately. "But what about lunch? Are you eating in the Cottage? Do you realize, Dr. Anderson, that we have never lunched together in the Cottage?"

She laughed. "I'll see you there today."

He thought she said it too carelessly. Exactly when would she be at the Cottage? How could they be assured of having a table for only two? It seemed suddenly that a host of details needed settling before they could meet, but he knew too that the details had no place in the present moment.

As she turned off the walk, she waved briefly. He lingered on the porch until the MacMillan milk truck pulled up to the curb. Then he returned to his deserted room.

Herby's door was shut, but Marcia saw him inside swiping the floor with a long-handled mop. When she rapped on the glass pane, he shouldered his mop and came to open the door for her.

"Sorry to hurry you," she said, "but I'm starving."

"S'all right. You're not the first one." He jerked his head in the direction of the counter.

Janice sat there drinking coffee. Marcia would have walked away, but Janice turned then and smiled mockingly. "I *thought* you'd turn up here—sooner or later."

"Hello, Janice." Marcia sat down beside her. "Give me everything that you have, Herby—bacon, eggs, toast, coffee." She felt determined not to allow even Janice to spoil her good feeling.

Janice was watching her. "You seem to be in high spirits for so early in the morning."

"Janice, I've been thinking—"

"You'd *better* be thinking."

"I've been thinking that we should be friends again."

Janice laughed harshly. "You're a little late with that idea, aren't you?" She took some change from her purse and threw it on the counter. "And if you think I don't understand why you're suddenly so anxious to be friendly, you're crazy." She swung off the high stool and sauntered out into the street, leaving the door wide open behind her.

Herby brought Marcia her breakfast, then crossed the room and slammed the door shut. "She must think it's July." He stood staring out into the sunshine. " 'Tis warming up, though." He came back to the counter and added morosely, "Before you know it, it'll be *too* hot. That's the way it goes."

"Yes," she said absently. She tried to eat her breakfast to please him, although she no longer wanted it. "How long had she been here?" she asked him.

He shrugged. "That was her third cup of coffee. She knocked loud enough to bring the house down, and I had to let her in before I had my own breakfast."

J.W. smiled at the girl sitting across the desk from him. He was annoyed at the interruption, yet he rather admired the skill with which she had convinced the very efficient Miss Gillroy that she had to speak with him. "I'm interested to meet Matt Grant's daughter. Your father should have made you known to me earlier."

"My father," Janice said coolly, "often forgets about me." She took a small pad and pencil from her purse. "I'm sorry to come unannounced, Mr. MacMillan. Evidently some careless staff member failed to confirm our appointment with you. With your permission, the *Gazette* wishes to do a feature article on you—the man to whom our school owes so much—everything, in fact."

He granted permission. "I am glad to know that someone besides Miss Gillroy and myself is energetically at work at this hour—and of course I'm especially glad to know that it is a John Willard student." He stared thoughtfully at a 1941 sales chart on the wall. "The secret of success lies largely in the time spent in striving for it."

She nodded gravely and marked this down. "And now we should be pleased to have your opinion upon a few other topics of great importance. The war, for example. What do you think of the war, Mr. MacMillan?"

"I think," he said slowly, "that the war is a tragedy. Yet good will come out of it. Necessity is the mother of invention. In this emergency, our scientists are every day making new discoveries that will add to the fullness and comfort of peacetime living. Also, the means of accelerated production perfected by our industrialists will contribute significantly to peacetime economy."

She wrote rapidly, then said: "You are, I believe, a staunch advocate of individualism?"

"I am. Without individualism there is a weakening of the moral fiber—of all character traits such as self-reliance, fortitude, and independence. It is well known that over-protective parents thwart the development of their children. Similarly, over-protective governments destroy the ambition, the aspiration, the originality, and the initiative of their people."

She studied her notes before she said, "Your strong belief in individualism probably explains why you so leniently condone the experiment in morals now in progress on campus."

He looked puzzled. "I consider myself a lenient man, but I have been informed of no experiment in morals."

"Oh." She seemed embarrassed. "I shouldn't have— Please forget that I mentioned it, Mr. MacMillan."

But his interest was aroused. "I am surprised that President Cameron has not spoken to me about this matter. Just what *is* in progress?"

"Really, I . . ." She faltered and nervously fingered her pencil. He watched her, curious and somewhat disappointed. The past minutes had not led him to expect nervousness in her. "Be frank with me, Miss Grant," he said sternly. "As you know, my interest is at one with that of John Willard."

"Well," she said in a low voice, "it seems to be among only the faculty—thus far. Certain—ones have decided that conventions are a needless restraint upon individuality and should be cast aside."

He leaned forward, resting his arms on the glossy top of the massive desk. "How do they intend to cast aside the conventions?"

"By living a kind of Bohemian life," she said carefully, as if painstakingly repeating what she had been told. "By a free intermingling of the sexes. . . . For example, a man feels free to visit a woman's room at any hour, and of course a woman freely visits a man—"

"Miss Grant, you're mistaken," he said decisively. "Or you're grossly exaggerating someone's idle theory. Such a condition could not possibly exist on the campus of John Willard."

"It doesn't exist *on* campus," she admitted, "for it all happens at night—off campus. And perhaps I am exaggerating, for, as far as I know, only two faculty members have practiced this—Bohemianism."

He looked incredulous. "Do you mean that you could, in all fairness and honesty, name two faculty members guilty of such unsavory action?"

She nodded, her eyes wide and fearful. He reassured her. "I certainly do not intend to ask you the names of these people, but"—he pulled a memo pad to him and lifted a long slender pen from its onyx holder—"if what you say has its basis in reality, then of course it must be properly investigated." He wrote a brief note on the pad, his mouth tightened into an expression of strong distaste.

"I shouldn't have spoken." She seemed on the verge of tears. "Uncle Paul is a man of high ideals. I'm sure he didn't—"

"Paul Lewis Grant?" He looked at her sharply. "Professor Grant is one of the two people you could name?"

"But I tell you he didn't mean anything wrong—I know, I know! Nor did Dr. Anderson. She is my best friend."

He replaced the pen in its holder. "Think what you are saying, Miss Grant. Professor Grant and Miss Anderson—those are the two people?"

She sighed. "I'm glad to have told someone—really I am. It has been bothering me. I suppose I'm silly . . . or maybe I'm too old-fashioned. It was only one night."

"Which night?" he asked tensely and without caution.

She studied his face for a moment. "Last night," she said then with insolent confidence. Her nervousness had miraculously disappeared.

He reached for the pen again and made a few meaningless marks on the pad. "Is this a part of the interview, Miss Grant?" he asked in a controlled voice.

She merely shrugged. Her face and attitude and voice told him what he should have perceived in time to save himself—that she had come for the sole purpose of giving him this information. He flushed with anger, and a small tic near his right eye started up. He wanted very much to press a finger against it, but he forced his hand to stay in a seemingly relaxed position on the arm of his chair. "If you publicize the gossip which you erroneously assume to be knowledge, you will make it impossible for John Willard College to retain the services of Professor Grant and Miss Anderson. In short, you will be the direct cause of ending their careers as teachers." He stood up.

"Don't rush me," she said carelessly. "The *Gazette* likes a personal touch in interviews, and so should like to end with this question: Is it true that you will marry Dr. Anderson as soon as your work permits? Dr. Anderson has asserted this upon several occasions, and although we have no reason not to accept Dr. Anderson's word, we should like you to corroborate it." When he said nothing, she nodded wisely. "I understand your dilemma, Mr. MacMillan. You do not wish to corroborate her word, yet you do not wish to appear so unchivalrous as to—"

"This matter," he said then, "as other matters discussed this morning, is none of your business. Nor is it the *Gazette's* business."

She laughed as she scribbled something on her pad. "The *Gazette* isn't going to like that remark."

He stood still for long minutes after she was gone; then he moved abruptly to click on the intercom. "Miss Gillroy, please telephone the office of the *Gazette* to inquire whether the paper had planned to interview me this morning and—yes, that *is* the college newspaper, and it *is* the newspaper that I mean! Also, ask in what capacity Janice Grant is associated with the paper."

He lighted a cigarette and told himself he need not begin to think until he had his first fact. But anger toward Marcia leaped up in his mind like a small, licking flame. Paul Lewis Grant and she. Fantastic —yet he already knew that it was true. Underneath his anger he felt a kind of contempt for her. What a *stupid* thing for her to do! What—

Miss Gillroy was signaling him. "Yes?" At last he pressed his finger tightly against the tic, which was now going at a furious pace. Miss Gillroy had the *Gazette* editor on the line. It appeared that the *Gazette* had not planned to interview Mr. MacMillan that morning, but it was an excellent idea and if Mr. MacMillan would consent, the editor himself—

J.W. cut in with a steely voice: "I wouldn't grant an interview to anyone remotely associated with that paper if my life— Explain that I haven't a free moment for the next six months, and explain it in a politic way, Miss Gillroy. Janice Grant?"

Janice Grant, it seemed, was not connected with the *Gazette* in any way. Perhaps Mr. MacMillan meant the *Young Spectator,* the literary magazine, upon which Miss Grant was quite active.

"Perhaps," he said crisply, and shut off Miss Gillroy. He lighted another cigarette before he noticed that the old one was still going. He crushed out both of them. So the whole interview had been faked.

His mind stayed obstinately on Janice Grant, for when it left her it would have to go on to Marcia. . . . He'd like nothing better than to deal with the girl himself and to mete out her rightful punishment. Yet he noted that he could still admire her. She had been fearless, daring, and clever. He winced as he thought of her maneuvering the seemingly conventional interview so that it reached its calculated climax. He found himself wondering if Russ could handle as delicate a situation as well. He thought not. With that awkward shyness of his, Russ would blunder. . . .

Is it true that you will marry Dr. Anderson. . . ? Dr. Anderson has asserted this upon several occasions. . . .

How dare she! He'd put her and Grant out of John Willard, and in the blaze of such a scandal that they'd never teach again. He'd—

And then they'd all be laughing at him.

As it was now, only three of them were laughing—Janice, Grant, Marcia.

He absently looked around the spacious, soothing office; then more alertly. He thought of his gracious mother in his gracious home—and Russ, his son, who would return to him, whole in body and sound in mind. Next month his solid family would gather around him to honor his birthday. Next year he would be in Chicago.

His was not the kind of life that could be knocked to pieces by the twisted emotions and confusion of other people. There would not be laughing for long.

Marcia needed him. He alone knew the intensity of that need, although he did not pretend to understand its source. Nor did she understand, and so they fought on equal ground. He had strength without softness. She did not have the strength to break away from him.

Yet there remained within him the desire to put an end to the laughing as quickly as possible. He could indulge himself with one rash action—one. He reached for his coat and hat and went to the outer office to tell Miss Gillroy that he would be away until noon.

Miss Gillroy was incredulous. "But Mr. Luther, from Chicago, will be here in half an hour."

"Yes," he said, getting into his coat. He strode through the large busy rooms, sensing that Miss Gillroy was staring after him with shocked disapproval. He felt momentary sympathy for her. There existed a strong mutual respect between them. In seven years she had not missed a day, nor had she by so much as a look indicated that she had a life beyond his domain. He and Efficiency were her gods. She had a right to be shocked.

It would take another seven years of unbroken routine to reassure her. It might be wise, he reflected, to raise her salary and transplant her to the new Chicago office so that she could continue to work closely with him until her complete confidence was restored.

Marcia came down the stairs in a long black robe and salmon-colored mules. Her hair had been hastily combed, he noted. "Hello," she said. "Is there something the matter?" The last three words were blurred by a suppressed yawn. She dropped down into a chair.

He stood over her, irritated almost beyond endurance. That suppressed yawn seemed so very blatant. Yet he smiled and said lightly,

"What makes you think there should be anything the matter?"

"It's unusual to see you so early. That's all."

"Early?" He continued to smile and glanced at his watch. "But it isn't early, Marcia. Mrs. Murdock said that you were still sleeping. I didn't realize that you slept so late. Shall you be a wife who expects breakfast in bed?"

"I've had exactly one hour's sleep," she said. "Why don't you sit down?"

He sat down and regarded her solicitously. "What were you doing all night? Grading themes? Are you still working too hard, Marcia?"

She looked at him thoughtfully. "I was with Professor Grant."

"All night?" he asked, almost taken off guard. He had not expected such immediate frankness.

She nodded. "It was quite accidental, of course."

"Oh, of course." Then he said sharply, "Do you think it was wise, Marcia?"

"It wasn't wise," she said, smiling faintly. "Accidental happenings seldom are."

The smile infuriated him. "What was accidental about it? Why did it happen?"

She closed her eyes, as if trying to remember something. She opened them and said gravely, "Mrs. Winters' housecleaning, Silas Seabolm, and William Blake."

"Marcia!" He stood up abruptly. "I'm willing to be reasonable, if you are. I came here to give a just hearing to your reasons, to—"

"You came here to give a just hearing. . . ." She stared up at him. "You knew about it when you came. That's *why* you came."

Once more he forced gentleness into his voice. "I came to tell you that I understand. I wasn't born yesterday. . . ." He hesitated, knowing that he was saying the wrong words. He was losing control again, as he had for those few minutes in his office. "My only condition is that you never see—that you resign and marry me immediately."

She had not listened. "How did you learn about it?"

"My source of information is unimportant, but perhaps it would give you a rightful sense of shame to know that it was a student. Janice Grant."

Marcia looked away from him, her face sad. The expression puzzled him. He had thought she would be startled and fearful. "I didn't think she would bring herself to do it," she said in a low voice.

"You knew that she had this knowledge, yet you thought you were safe because she would be afraid to speak of it?" There was cold contempt in his voice. "Think of it, Marcia! You know what the shock of disillusionment does to a young mind. That poor girl was almost out of her senses. She could hardly bring herself to talk about it, but she forced herself to do so because her conscience told her that it was her duty to reveal what she had unwittingly discovered. You have betrayed the most sacred trust a student willingly places in a teacher, that serious responsibility—"

"Stop it!" she said with her first show of feeling. "You're wasting a good speech." Suddenly she laughed. "Janice really took you in, didn't she? You see, I know her—quite well."

He wanted very much to slap the amused smile off her face. He drew himself together. "You realize, I'm sure, that this is more than adequate reason to force the resignation of both you and—him."

She looked up at him quickly. "You're not serious?"

"I've never known a more serious moment," he said solemnly.

She sighed tiredly. "You haven't asked for it, but now seems the time to give you my word that my staying in Professor Grant's rooms all night was not an immoral act."

"Why should I believe you?"

She stood up slowly, facing him. "If you loved me, you'd believe me."

"Your peculiar kind of devotion," he said with dry irony, "does not in itself persuade me of your fidelity."

She shook her head. "I didn't mean that. I meant that if you loved me, you'd know the kind of person I am. You'd know I wouldn't lie about a thing like this. If I wanted to do what you think I did, I wouldn't do it this way."

He sneered. "I did marvel at the stupidity of your method. You could at least have left Riverville for the occasion."

She flushed. "Nor did I mean that. Why should I try to convince you?" She shrugged. "Why should I?"

"If you are going to marry me," he said, "you should be interested in convincing me."

She walked away from him. "I'm not going to marry you. I hadn't meant to tell you this way—but it had better be said." She turned to him. "Oh, I'm sorry. Please believe me. I'm largely to blame for the torture we've inflicted upon one another. I know that better than I can explain it."

He ignored this, but came to her and took her hand in his. "Explain last night, Marcia. You haven't, you know."

She drew away her hand. "But last night has nothing to do with it."

"You yourself went to his rooms?"

She nodded. He could see that she was near the breaking point from tiredness and strain. "Why did you go, Marcia?"

"To return a book." She moved away from him again. "Let's stop this."

He followed her. "Could it have been the book you were reading in my home?" He laughed gently. "Last night you were in *my* home also, Marcia. Remember?"

"It was that book," she said tensely. "It was important to Professor Grant."

"So important that you had to take it to him in the middle of the night?"

"It wasn't the middle of the night."

"We'll not quibble over that. You took him the book. He was glad to see you. He took you up to his rooms—"

"Mrs. Winters was housecleaning. That was why we could not stay downstairs."

"I see. Once in his room, you sat down and discussed the book all night?"

"We discussed many things," she said tonelessly. "One thing after another kept me there, until it was so late that it seemed sensible for me to stay until morning."

"Thank you, Marcia. That is a very clear explanation, although a few details still perplex me. Let us start at the beginning. After you left my mother, you rushed to him, of your own volition and without a thought of compromising me as well as yourself and him. And then you—"

"I can't take any more of this," she said warningly.

He stood very close to her. "In his room you talked about the book —but surely even that stimulating conversation must have lagged now and then. What did you do at those times, Marcia?"

She laughed shrilly. "We went to bed."

He felt triumph. "Ah!" He grasped her wrists. "I knew all along, but I had to hear it from you. A man knows the truth about such a thing."

She jerked free of his grasp. "I wish that we *had* done that! At least it would have been real. Do you understand? Real—*real!* I wish that we—"

He slapped her across the face. Then he put his hands on her arms, his fingers digging into her flesh. "I had to do that," he said, "because you were growing hysterical."

"I am sorry for you," she said.

Abruptly he took his hands away from her arms. "I apologize, Marcia. I shouldn't have slapped you. No matter what you have done, I shouldn't have slapped you."

"I am sorry for you," she said again, "because you're in such a trap. You have to be convinced, but you can't believe me. You can't believe me because you don't know me. You want to punish me, but you're afraid of scandal. Why, I'm another Diaz, but you're a little more concerned over me because I come under the heading of slightly more personal property! That's your armor, and under it you have no self —no self to be touched by a wife or a son. . . ." She stopped the rush of words and turned from him. "I don't want to say these things to you. We shouldn't quarrel this way. Please go, Jack."

"If I go," he said softly, "it is for good, Marcia."

She did not answer. He came to her. "You are right, Marcia. We should not quarrel. You are too beautiful to show anger." He forced her to face him and then kissed her roughly, his hand ripping the robe off her shoulder. Her lips stayed passive under his and her body lax until he released her. Then she took a step back from him and adjusted the robe over her shoulder.

"You've tried everything now, haven't you?" she said coldly. "In your mind, there never was any other way of coming to terms with me."

"Don't be vulgar, Marcia." He picked up his hat and coat and looked at her steadily. "So you wish me to go now—knowing that it will be for the last time?"

"I do not want to marry you," she said.

"Very well," he said calmly, and he thought he saw fear shadow her face. He went to the door. "But this time it is final, Marcia. There can be no more vacillation, no more indecision. If I reach the end of the walk without your calling to me, you must know that I am out of your life forever."

She said nothing, but moved so that she did not see him open the door and go out. She heard his footsteps on the porch, and they sounded cruelly slow and deliberate, a death march in her mind. Her heart pounded.

But all I have to do, she thought, is stand here a minute more; it is easy . . . that is all there is to it.

It was a test, she knew. He thought her too weak to withstand it. It helped her to know that it was a test. That made it seem remote from life. It was merely a kind of exercise.

At last she moved and walked quickly to the stairs. She started up them, then changed her mind and went to the telephone. "This is Dr. Anderson," she said to the first person who answered her from the Summit. "No, I don't want anyone special . . . I haven't time. . . . I merely want to say that I'm quite ill and can't meet my classes today. No instructions—just have them dismissed. I'll call again later. Thank you."

She went upstairs and flung herself down on the bed. Sleep was what she needed. She'd be all right after some sleep.

Time. Hurry . . . hurry. The class waits only ten minutes. If only you can put the heaviness aside and move quickly, you can make it on time . . . time. . . .

There is the ringing of the bell. Now find the door, the closed, locked door, with the nothingness on your side. . . .

She turned and put her hand over her ear. She did *not* have to hurry. She had called to cancel her classes . . . *cancel the future. . . .*

The six tenses of time. Not real, but segments of time wrapped up in neat packages. The six ways the pitiful mind dissects the infinite to please its own small self. . . .

What is that, Janice? Oh, yes, there is that foolish hybrid tense called the Historical Present. Past-Present. Difficult to explain, but

371

frequently used . . . when you tell a story, or live. . . . Virginia in the portrait, no, that is Eileen. Understand, Janice? Dr. Anderson to you, please.

We can never live in the present. From a book. The images on our retina are light waves already past . . . the vibrations in our ears are sound waves already past. . . .

The past is pregnant with the present. That's a trite image, Janice. True, but too often said. . . . Beneath your ability. You can write better than that. Besides, you don't want to bear your father's child, do you? Oh, no, oh, my no.

The body devours itself when starving . . . when you live on the past. Now our butter and meat must go to the army—which is right, of course. Nevertheless. It was a bountiful country, until the war . . . and he brought her home. . . .

. . . She was curled up in Martin's leather chair with its mixed smell of paint and cigars. Martin had stepped out to be married. When she said it like that to herself, it didn't seem important. It was really no different from his stepping out to buy candy for her or cigars for himself.

She heard his step on the porch. Quickly she stood up, although she did not run to meet him.

He walked in, a woman beside him. The woman had shoes, gloves, coat, and hat—but no face.

"Marcia," he pleaded, "this is Virginia."

At first she merely stared. She had not realized that Martin would bring home the person he married. Then her stare became rude as it dwelled upon this intruder.

"Marcia!" Her father was still pleading.

For a moment she triumphed in her rudeness; then suddenly her triumph seemed empty. "Papa!" she cried, and rushed to him. He stooped down and held her tightly in his arms. She sobbed fiercely.

The woman reached out and touched her shoulder. She shuddered and moved free of the woman's hand. She broke away from her father's arms and looked up at him accusingly. "You didn't have to bring her *home* with you!" . . .

She sat up on the bed, bewildered and afraid. The sunny room seemed ominous. She got to her feet, feeling drugged. She must have been asleep for hours. Or had she been asleep at all?

She looked at the clock. She had been on the bed only a few minutes. The clock, then, had stopped. But her watch told the same time as the clock.

She walked about the room, telling herself how wise she had been to arrange not to meet her classes. She couldn't possibly face a class today. She was quite ill. She needed to be alone.

Then she shuddered as she thought of the long day ahead of her.

Her mind began to dwell upon the classes she was not meeting—of their impersonal challenge, of the blissful forgetting of self when she stood before them. . . .

She dressed hurriedly. Before she left the house, she again called the Summit to say that although she'd be late for her first class, she would be there, and she'd appreciate someone's asking the students to wait for her.

Chapter Three

THE Inferno was empty. Grant went on up to the Widow's Walk. Marcia was there, standing alone at the railing. She did not turn until he had called her name twice. Then she looked at him as if he were a stranger.

He stood by her side. "Are you avoiding me again because you know what I want to say?"

"No," she said, and then added quickly, "I don't know what you mean."

"I think that you do." He was shocked by her pallor. "Yesterday I waited for you in the Cottage until Miss Schultz grew suspicious. You didn't come back here after your last class, and by the time I got to Main Hall, you were gone."

"You waited for me at the Cottage?"

He was puzzled. "You promised to meet me there for lunch."

"And I forgot." She was very grave. "That was inexcusable of me."

"It certainly wasn't important," he said lightly, although at the time he had thought it important and had been deeply disappointed. But something in her manner stopped him from telling her this or reminding her that he had considered it more than a casual luncheon date. "Are you ill, Marcia?"

She shook her head. "No." Her voice took on firmness. "No, I am *not* ill."

"I'm glad." He hesitated, then said, "I'm afraid that I've chosen the wrong time to say what I want to say, but if I go on waiting, there may be no time. I—"

"We don't choose time," she said as if that were the only one of his words she had heard. "Isn't it ironic, the habit we have of speaking in terms of freedom? We choose a time, we plan a course of action, we exert our will. . . ."

"Marcia," he said gently, "at the moment I'm not interested in discussing the problem of free will. I'm trying to tell you that I love you." Watching her, he sensed that she had withdrawn from him. Her face was not indifferent, but expressionless. There was a strange passiveness about her that seemed to have a power of its own, and he felt a sudden languor of spirit. Under this spell, he was not surprised when she said nothing in response to his words.

He looked away forcibly. It was another sunny, windy afternoon. White clouds crowded the sky. A Cadet squadron marched out of Main Hall and across the Heart.

He turned back to her. She too was staring out at the Heart. He had an impulse to shake her, to force awareness of his presence upon her. . . . It was a short-lived impulse. "Marcia, you didn't hear what I said, did you?"

She gripped the railing with her hands. "I—I— No."

He put his hand over hers. "You came up here to be alone. I'll leave you now."

"No!" she cried, and he was thankful for the life that had come into her voice. "I lied to you just now. I heard what you said. I thought I couldn't bear it—but now I want to talk. I *have* to—" She stopped suddenly, then went on in a strangely formal voice, "You must forgive me today. I'm not good company."

"Good Lord, Marcia! Don't bother to be polite. I don't know what has happened to you, but I'm sure that it's something profound. Profound—that's a strange word to have used, isn't it? Perhaps I mean fundamental."

She looked at him quickly, her eyes bright with tears. Her face was no longer mask-like, but showed hope, even eagerness. "What made you say that?"

He shrugged, keeping his hand over hers. "It's not easy to explain —but a few minutes ago I had a glimpse into your world, or the way you're now seeing it, and it was a dark view." He smiled. "I've never been psychic with any other person."

She groped in her coat pocket for a handkerchief and then hastily dabbed at her eyes with it. "I haven't cried in years." She put the handkerchief back in her pocket and said more steadily, "That's over now. It won't happen again. Please—let's talk."

"Fine. Do you feel like talking about Blake?"

"Blake?" She sounded hurt. "That's what we always talk about when we want to avoid something more—more . . ."

He laughed. "So you've noticed that too? Good old Blake. Well, there's much to his credit. He's interesting, meaningful, and personal or impersonal—whichever we choose to make him."

"But I thought"—she drew her hand out from under his—"I thought you had a—topic."

"I had a very good one—too good, in fact, to be wasted."

She shivered and pulled her coat more closely around her. "I don't blame you for not wanting to say more after you've seen how impossible I—how weak—"

"Marcia! You know I meant nothing of the kind. Actually, I was speaking selfishly. I'm only human and I don't want to take an unnecessary risk. I made a simple statement, and I was going to follow it with an equally simple question. But I'd like to keep that question for a happier time."

"I'm sorry," she said after a silence. "It sounds unreasonable, I know —but I wasn't thinking of a question. It hadn't occurred to me that there would be one."

"There usually is," he said gently. "I'd willingly say, 'I love you,' a hundred times over, but I shouldn't wish to stop with that. Next I'd ask, 'Do you love me, Marcia?' That's not particularly original dialogue, I admit. Nevertheless, I like it because it is fairly universal, simple, and definite."

"But it's a lie," she said violently. "It's all a lie!"

He made a helpless gesture. "There you are. I knew it would be something like that." He folded his arms before him and looked stubborn. "I refuse to hear you, Marcia, and even if I heard you, I wouldn't understand."

She ignored this. "You think I'm incapable of thinking coherently or giving straight answers today. But I tell you that's not true—not true! I never saw things so clearly as I do now; I was never less likely to deceive myself as I am now."

"All right," he said suddenly, "all right, Marcia. Then what is your answer?" He stood very close to her and put his hands on her arms. "I love you. Do you love me?"

His nearness took the planned words away from her. "I—I. . . . My answer to that question is unimportant." She broke away from his hold. "Even if I had an answer—even if I knew that I loved you, I'd not allow myself to tell you."

"But why not, Marcia? Why *not!*"

"Because it might be a lie," she said readily, as if she had been storing up the words. "I have learned that first you need and then you love what—whom you need. You're driven to love only because you need . . ." She shook her head, annoyed with herself. "I'm going around in circles, but it is clear in my own mind. I feel that I can never be nearer to reality." She looked at him almost pleadingly. "Do you understand?"

"Perhaps I'm beginning to understand," he said. He put his hand out to the railing, feeling its sun-hotness. Again he glanced out over the Heart. "I wish that we had waited," he said.

She had not heard him. "Don't you see how it is? Actually we hate what we need, for our need comes from something taken away from us. And so to get it back, we pretend love. That's what I mean when I say that it's a lie. I love you—I need you—I hate you." She shuddered. "They all say the same thing."

He stooped for the pillows lying on the floor and struck them together to shake out the dust. "Sit down," he said when he had replaced them, "and smoke one of your cigarettes. I wish I had one to offer you, but I haven't—as usual." He took out his pipe and watched her obediently sit down and open her cigarette case. He leaned down to light her cigarette. She smoked in a preoccupied way. "That's better," he said heartily. "Much better. It's not that I want to see you always with a cigarette, but today you're too quiet—even when you talk. With a cigarette, you have to make at least a few movements—and they're purposeful movements."

She looked curiously at her cigarette. "Strange—I haven't smoked all day. I forgot about it." Then she smiled with faint irony. "Do you really believe that I should be consoled by having the important purpose of smoking a cigarette? I don't think you're taking me seriously. I understand, however. I must seem too—intense over nothing."

"It isn't that," he said quickly.

"You think I'm wrong, then?"

"I think you're half wrong. I think that what you say does not apply to us."

Her cigarette had gone out. She did not relight it, but tossed it aside. "If you knew how much it applied to me, you probably wouldn't be talking to me. I tell you, once you have seen reality, you can't forget it. It's as final as—well, as death. Yes—seeing it is something like looking at death."

He refrained from saying that she would forget, that the protective memory would see to it that she did. That was the mechanism that prevented mass suicide, that made possible continuity. The pain would become idea—in fact, that had already happened in her. Even the idea would be sapped by time, until its vitality had been reabsorbed in the flux of living.

But he said none of this to her, for he knew to do so would be to interfere with an experience which rightfully belonged to her, not to him, and to mar the clarity of vision to which she was entitled, bitter as it might be. One did not comfort a pregnant woman by assuring her that the son she bore would rush through the brief stages of man and then die to nourish the soil.

He lighted his pipe slowly, ironically amused to note how wise he could be upon so little knowledge. What *had* happened to her? When? Obviously, since he had last seen her and before today. Yesterday then. With whom? Her immediate family—MacMillan? Against his preference, he admitted that the nature of what she had said suggested MacMillan.

Yesterday—MacMillan. The coincidence was too pointed for him not to think that the night before had in some way figured. He very much wanted answers, but he also knew that she would tell him when she was ready.

He sat down beside her. "Marcia, there is something more that I want to say. I've often thought it, but I never intended to say it. However, I believe that there is a place for it now." She turned toward him, waiting. "You see, Marcia, my love for you is free. My life is complete without you. Oh, I should find it dull without you now; but, nevertheless, I should go on. . . ." He stared past her, lost in his own thought, although he had not meant to become so. "Sometimes I've wished that I were of different temperament, so that I might love you as—well, as Kim Duncan might love—wildly, impulsively, desperately. Then long ago I should have forced your awareness of me."

"But if your life is complete without me," she said as he stayed silent, "why do you want to bother with loving me? You've made it seem very unessential—superfluous."

"You've misunderstood." He got up and leaned against the railing, looking down at her. "Let me try to explain, Marcia. I honor my solitary life. Before I met you, I thought a wife would be a kind of perennial guest in it. It never occurred to me that someone could enter my life without changing it. With you, Marcia—with you there would be no change, but richness added. Even now to take you away from it would be to take away the color—the sound—the taste. When you leave me, I feel lonely. Why, I've never before known loneliness. I never—" He stopped with a slight laugh. "But I'm not being fair. I didn't plan to say that. The important thing for now is that you see, as I see, that I am not driven to love you. There is no falseness, no self-deception in my feeling for you, Marcia."

She was quiet for a minute. "I believe you," she said then. "There is no falseness of any kind in you. I've always known that. I am not afraid of you, but for you. I am one of those who—who . . ." She shook her head and started again. "It was you who once said to me that we were so controlled by our needs that it was as if we were born with a net over us. Do you remember? I have been thinking of that all day, and I know it to be true. What is more, we must enmesh other people—"

"That may be true of some," he said firmly, "but not of us, Marcia. We were talking about Carol Leeds when I said that. Yes, it is true for her—but not for you and me. I know you, and I—"

"You *don't* know me!" she cried. "Nothing can be known outside the self. You know me only as I appear to you—not really *me*."

"I'll take a chance with the appearance. I rather like it."

"You're laughing at me—but that doesn't change the truth. What I'm trying to say is that everything outside the self is mere symbol. It's like a dream." She laughed ironically. "Life is like a dream. How trite —how horrible."

He made an impatient gesture. "Well, the symbols are real. Think where they come from. They're not floating about in this world for the sole purpose of deluding us. They come from the self—all the selves—and so have the same kind of reality."

"Then we can't trust them, for the self is deceptive," she said wearily. "That is what I've been trying to tell you. It will do anything to gain its own ends."

"All *right!*" he said half angrily. "And what if you have found a truth, Marcia? What should we do? Sit down and disintegrate? That would be the only honest thing to do. I tell you, Marcia, I have little awe for a truth that doesn't add to living."

She looked away quickly, and he knew that she felt his words to be a rebuke. In the interest of their talk, he had forgotten the despair in her face, and now as he saw it anew, it came to him that what was to him a theoretical idea to be examined and then thrown aside if not found desirable, was to her a reality to which at this moment at least there was no alternative. That, after all, was what she had been trying to tell him.

She stood and said, still not looking at him, "You are strong. That is why you can think and be that way. But I—"

"No, Marcia. In that moment of oratory I was inexcusably smug. Please don't think me so self-satisfied as I must seem."

"You are strong," she said again. "I believe that if the whole world were to collapse around you, you would quite simply start to rebuild it. But suppose"—she faced him then—"suppose you were to discover that you had been living a lie. I don't mean a very small one—like Oaklands. But one that took in your whole life. Would you then be able to go on with confidence? How would you convince yourself that you were not beginning a new lie—or even still living off the old one?"

"What lie do you mean, Marcia?" he asked quietly. "Without knowing, I blunder with words and hurt you. It is time for me to know."

She hesitated only a moment. "Nothing. Nothing more than a quarrel. Everyone quarrels at some time or other." She laughed shakily. "Isn't it ridiculous? I mean—to make so much of a quarrel."

"You quarreled with MacMillan?"

She merely nodded, but he saw her hands clutch the railing so hard that her knuckles went white. "When?" he asked. "Yesterday?" She nodded again. "Because of your being with me?" She did not answer. "You must tell me, Marcia! Perhaps I can help. God knows it was my fault—or, rather, my selfishness and stupidity."

She turned to him then. "I'm glad it happened. The night with you, I mean. Yes, it caused the quarrel—but it was a surface cause. The quarrel had to happen."

"Nevertheless," he said, "I'll go to him. I'll—"

"No! It's over now. It had to be between him and me, and we settled it. Besides, if he wouldn't believe me, he—"

"He didn't believe you?" he asked incredulously.

"It's over now," she said again. "That's the only important thing. You must not go to him. Usually he is a kind man, but he can be very cruel when . . ." She looked at him. "Promise me that you will not go to him. I mean this seriously."

He studied her face for a moment, then shrugged. "Very well, Marcia, I promise—somewhat reluctantly. I hope," he went on dryly, "that he appreciated your honesty in telling him."

She smiled faintly. "I didn't have a chance to tell him."

He stared at her. "Who did, then?"

"That too is unimportant. Oh, believe me, the whole stupid quarrel is unimportant. I don't know why I started to talk about it." Then she laughed shortly. "By way of evasion, I suppose."

But he said grimly, "It was Janice. Of course."

"I wish you wouldn't. . . . In her eyes, she had reason—"

"Ridiculous!" He was very angry. "She can't forever live her life at the expense of everyone else's."

"That's what I've done," she said in a low voice. "Remember our talking about the two worlds—and I argued that they did not exist in space? Now I know that they do not exist even in time."

Again he felt at a loss, for he did not understand. "You mean that Janice and Si Seabolm are of the same kind? Yes—you're right. In fact, once before I had the fleeting thought that she had wandered out of—"

"Perhaps," she said vaguely, and he knew that she had not really heard him. "What I mean is that the needs of the past continue to rule us. That is what makes a mockery of the present."

Once more he put his hand over hers. "You wanted to quarrel with him, Marcia?"

"Not to quarrel—but to end it."

"You didn't love him?"

"I didn't love him."

Hearing her say this, he felt a sudden happiness, although he knew that it was a selfish feeling based upon her unhappiness. "I believe that I've always known that. If that seems smug and arrogant again, I'm sorry—but there it is, and it is what gave me hope."

She shrugged. "Everyone knew it—except me. That's wrong too, for even I knew it, but couldn't acknowledge it because . . ."

"Because?"

"Because of my great need for him," she said with a rush of words. "I took up a part of my life where it had stopped when I was very young. Circumstances helped . . . Eileen . . . Russ. It was the same situation, but this time it was I who was gaining . . . possessing. Don't you *see?*" Her voice was pleading.

"No," he said gently. "I don't see. What part of your life?"

She drew away from him. "I suppose that I've led you to expect some momentous secret. It is so simple . . . so absurdly simple. My fath—Martin remarried at a time when I thought he was wholly mine—when my mother was conveniently reduced to a photograph." She looked at him defiantly. "Now you know how simple it is when put into words. It is a small thing which anyone else could have. . . ."

"So when shut out," he said casually, "you went on searching for a father."

She seemed to be listening to his words long after he had said them. "If it were only that," she said finally, "I shouldn't mind. I hated them all—Martin, my—Virginia, even—him. I trapped them all with my hate, making them suffer."

"I don't believe that," he said firmly. "You are the only one who has suffered. You may have caused them brief unhappiness and disappointment, but not the pain you have inflicted upon yourself. You—Why, Marcia, that follows from the very nature of things that you have been insisting is reality. Only the self could feel its own pain . . . its own hate. You—"

"You are very kind," she said wearily. "It seems to me that I'm always saying that to you. You are refuge, kindness, sympathy. You see"—she looked at him accusingly—"I do have need of you."

"You faced this yourself, Marcia. By the time you began to talk to me about it, you had endured it—all of it."

"Do you really think that's true?" she asked wonderingly.

"I do—I know it."

"I should like to be able to believe that. . . ."

"You have every right to believe it," he said, "but, for now, stop thinking about it. You have been forced to understand too much in too little time, and you're exhausted without knowing it. Get some rest. Lose yourself in the routine of the school. It will help."

"Yes," she said absently, "I must do that."

"Let me walk with you to the Murdocks' now. I'll feel less concerned if I know that you're there."

"Please— I don't want to go just yet. There's no cause for you to worry—really."

He glanced at his watch and sighed. "I have a class."

"You must go to it," she said quickly, almost eagerly, and he sensed that she would be glad to be alone again. He knew by her face that he had to resign himself to walking away from her with nothing more than his old passive reliance upon some future time. It seemed to him that now he had even more to risk, for when they next met she would be feeling the natural anger for having told him what she had told him, and again he would be able only to wait. . . .

"Marcia," he said in a quietly desperate voice, although he knew that she would not understand the desperation, "perhaps one day you will remember what I have said to you this afternoon. It somehow got lost in our consideration of the nature of the universe—and other things, but I swear that it is real—to you as well as to me. I sincerely believe that there is a good life for us together, and a free one. Because it is real," he went on quickly as she looked ready to interrupt, "it can wait forever, if necessary. I am hoping, however, that in a few months

—perhaps when we return next fall—you will—"

"I think that I'll not come back next year," she said as if to herself. She turned away from him and looked out over the Heart. "I am beginning to hate this place."

Once more he refrained from saying what came into his mind, that she hated only herself. "Good-by, Marcia—not until I next see you, but until we are together again."

She did not ask what he meant. She did not even look at him. After a minute he left her and went down to the Inferno, where Mcyerson stopped him to ask about the possibility of selecting a new grammar text.

When his class was over, he went back to the Widow's Walk. She was not there. In his office he called the Murdocks'. She was in her room, Mrs. Murdock explained. "Fine," he said. "No—I don't want to disturb her. I merely wanted to make sure that she was safe."

"*Safe!*" cried Mrs. Murdock, but he said good-by hastily and hung up. Then he called Grace Hall, and when Janice came to the phone, he told her that he would be there in ten minutes for a talk with her.

"I'm always glad to talk with you, Uncle Paul," she said, "but I *am* frightfully busy—studying for an exam."

"I'll be there in ten minutes," he said curtly, and slammed down the receiver.

Walking to Grace Hall, he told himself seriously that he meant at last to deal with Janice in terms that she would understand. Let her be confronted by someone as shrewd and ruthless as herself.

Janice was waiting for him in the lounge, sitting at a study table with a book open before her. He ignored her plaintive smile and pulled shut the large sliding doors. "Tear yourself away from that book," he said, crossing the room to her. "Perhaps it's going to surprise you to discover that you can't forever hide behind books and writing."

She stared up into his stern face and her smile changed. "Well, well," she said as if deeply amused. She closed her book and gave it a careless shove away from her. "I can see by your all too obvious expression that you have come to discuss your nocturnal escapade."

"Good. You're saving us time." He jerked a chair around to face her and sat down. "I thought you'd begin by trying to lie yourself out of it. That's your usual method."

She hesitated a moment, and he sensed that in spite of herself she did not like to hear those words from him. Then he put this feeling aside, for it confused him and weakened his purpose.

"Why should I lie about it?" she was saying coolly. "I'm rather proud of that accomplishment. Even you would appreciate it if you had heard that interview!" She was silent, seeming to review it in her mind. Suddenly she said in a burst of anger, "Why should she want him? It must be for his money. That proves how—"

"I'm not interested in your interpretation," he cut in sharply. "What I want to know is why you went to MacMillan."

"To show her up," she said, still angry. "To keep her from—" She stopped and when she spoke again, her voice was once more cool and guarded. "You're in no position to ask *me* questions."

"What do you mean by that?"

"Oh, I think you know. Mr. MacMillan said that when it's made public, you and—and she will have to leave."

"He's going to make it public?"

"Of course he is! Why wouldn't he?"

He shrugged. "I'm sure I don't know. But I wonder why he's waiting. This is the second day, you know."

"Well, what of it? He's probably planning . . ." Her words trailed, and she avoided his eyes. He saw that she had already guessed that MacMillan meant to keep quiet.

"So you see, Janice," he said quietly, "it's now up to you to act. And I don't think that you're going to do one thing, for you're afraid to act. You may have laughed at MacMillan, but you also know that he is a man of power. If he chooses to stay silent about this matter, then that means he is not going to like the person who publicizes it. I believe that you sense this, even if you haven't yet thought it through, and that is why there is fear in your eyes at this moment."

She sneered. "You're trying to scare me. But you can't stop me. Nothing can stop me—if you don't do what I say."

"Ah—conditions!" He sat back and folded his arms before him. "I thought there would be conditions. Let's hear them."

She looked at him suspiciously, but said, "First, you send—her away. You can do it. You can have her fired."

He nodded. "Next?"

She hesitated, seeming less sure of herself. "You get me a job at Deardorff's." She got up and walked away from the table, her back to him. "I want to earn my own money. I'm sick of being dependent upon— Anyway, I want a job. I'm above selling books, but it's the best thing around here. Besides, Deardorff interests me."

"He'll be flattered," Grant said dryly. "Anything else?"

"Yes. I want to be editor of the *Young Spectator*. You can arrange it."

"Why do you want the editorship? It entails real work, you know."

"It's a key position on the campus," she said.

"Oh, yes—power again. For a moment I had a faint hope that you were genuinely interested in the magazine."

She sat down at the table again and said nothing. "And if I don't fulfill these conditions?" he asked politely.

She flashed him a look. "You know what."

"That's what I wanted understood between us." He stood up as if to leave.

She stared at him. "You mean you *want* me to talk!"

He smiled. "I do—and Marcia does. You see, Janice, there is likely to be gossip, and so we'd both appreciate having the thing brought out into the open. I merely wanted to know your plans before we took steps, for the more I thought it over, the more certain it seemed to me that you would do nothing." He walked around the table and leaned toward her. "Let me explain—"

She shrank back from him. "You're going to kill me! You're just pretending you want me to talk. Tonight you'll come back and kill me to keep me quiet."

"Janice!" He straightened up, shocked in spite of the absurdity of her words. Her terror was real.

"I knew you would," she gasped. "But they'll know. I left a note. It's hidden in my room. They'll find it."

"Stop it, Janice," he said roughly and turned away from her. After a moment, he went on more calmly. "Let me explain what is going to happen. MacMillan is a proud man. When this thing is made known, he's going to feel that people are laughing at him, and that will make him very, very angry. Marcia and I shall be gone. The only one around for him to punish will be you. And your father."

She made a sudden movement. "Matt?"

He nodded. "Yes. Do you think he would stop with you? Matt may be a good advertising manager, but when his daughter makes a fool of—"

"He wouldn't dare!"

Grant laughed shortly. "Wouldn't he? You've misjudged the man. For once you've miscalculated. You've set a wonderful trap for yourself, Janice. Go ahead and spring it. Get yourself expelled, get Matt fired."

She did not seem to realize that he had stopped talking. At last she grew aware of the silence. "If I keep still about it, do you think he'll tell Matt about the faked interview?"

He almost laughed out at the childishness of the question. Only a few minutes earlier she had been talking in terms of blackmail and even murder. . . .

His anger crumbled. He suddenly saw himself as he had been with her, and he knew that he had been talking to her out of his helpless worry over Marcia—and perhaps even his hurt over Si. "I don't know what he'll do," he said. He sat down and faced her again. "Listen, Janice. We've both been play-acting. I don't expect any serious consequences to come from what you've done. That's the odd thing. It merely hurried what was due to happen. But it should make you stop to think. I wasn't fooling when I described the trap you had set for yourself. One false move on your part, and it would go off. You can't probe around in the personal life of a man like J. W. MacMillan and then calmly withdraw. Nor, in fact, can you do so to any other human life. You have intelligence, Janice. Why not turn it upon yourself to see that your hate does not destroy that which you wish it to, but only yourself? Can you not. . . ."

As he talked, the fear left her face. She knew by his tone that he had relented, and to her that meant she was winning. He watched her resume the familiar attitude of shrewdness and insolence, and he felt the futility of his words. But he went doggedly on. "You spoke of your talk with MacMillan as an accomplishment, and I do believe that you carried it off with the same skill and creative imagination that you bring to your writing. What waste! And what about your writing, Janice? I thought that at least was real and meaningful to you." He went over to the round wicker table by the window, on which were lying copies of the *Young Spectator*. He picked them up and came back to her. "You have something in every issue here." He threw them down before her. She kept her eyes on him and did not look at them. "I've followed your writing carefully ever since your first story, 'The Boy.' I have respect—even awe—for it. Some men would go down on their knees for such a talent as yours. Men with lesser talent have sacrificed everything else in their lives for the privilege of developing it. Yet you squander it and—"

"I know I can write." She had risen, and stood with her hands clenched at her sides. "You don't have to tell me that. And I have *not* wasted my talent. I wouldn't be so stupid. It's mine to keep. Nobody can take it away from me—nobody!"

He nodded. "Except yourself. You can live it out—as you did the other night and morning. I've been told that it's possible for a person to live a lie so completely that it is accepted as reality by the self. Yet it is always there, a parasite in the self, absorbing, devitalizing. I think that you—"

"I don't tell lies!" she said. "Not the kind you mean. I always know when I tell a lie, and I tell it for a purpose."

He saw that she had misunderstood his meaning, and he was glad, for he had suddenly realized that he was trying to give to her in a few sentences what Marcia had discovered in years of living. And he knew that he had been wrong to try. "I know," he said with more gentleness than he had yet given her that afternoon.

She was surprised that he should be gentle over her telling lies, and she took it as a sign of further relenting. "I've listened to enough sermonizing, Paul. If you're really interested in my writing, you'd help me get the editorship of the *Young Spectator*."

He went weary at the sound of her voice. The same Janice. Well, what had he expected—a miracle? Marcia was still Marcia, although he knew she thought she had changed. And he was inclined to think that Janice would stay Janice. . . .

He managed a smile. "In that, my girl, I am completely powerless to help you. Clearly you have not read Esther Cornthwaite's will, for therein is stipulated that the *Young Spectator* receive her annual bequest only as long as the editor is elected by a majority vote of the Student-Faculty Editorial Board. Once that procedure is violated, the funds automatically go to the Library. When I first learned of that clause, I thought it a strange and superfluous detail, but—"

"She was a silly old woman," Janice said, shrugging. "I discovered that when I was a freshman."

"But now I am forced, as always, to pay tribute to her foresight. There is, however, another of your conditions that—"

"Never mind the conditions," she said quickly. "I didn't really mean—that is, I withdrew them."

"The idea of your working with Deardorff is too good to be withdrawn. It would be instructive to learn what happens when you try to rearrange his life."

Janice eyed him suspiciously, not knowing whether or not to take him seriously. "But I've changed my—"

"Of course," Grant said gravely, "I'm not sure that we can persuade him to take you on. But if I make a humanitarian appeal in the interest of all the people who are not Janice Grant, he might consider it." He went to the sliding doors and pulled them open. "By the way, Janice, the fact that the editor of the magazine is chosen by honest means doesn't necessarily preclude all your chances, you know. You have a month or more to educate the voters, and for you that should be enough time to turn the national elections."

She wanted to call out after him, but she could not think what to say. When he was gone, she sat down at the table again, staring at the magazines he had put there. She stacked them and placed her hand down flat on them as if to make sure they stayed closed.

Some men would go down on their knees for such a talent as yours . . . yet you squander it. . . .

She swallowed hard, and there was a stinging pain in her eyes. Everything good said to her had been said grudgingly and with an insult tagged on.

You have intelligence, Janice. Why not turn it upon yourself. . .? Her mother once: *Must you be so obvious about your intelligence, Janice? Haven't you yet learned that all those ideas embarrass the boys?* And another time, her father: *What makes you so different from the other kids? All those brains?*

She had opened one of the magazines. She leafed through it until she found her story, and began to read. At first her own writing bored her, and she wanted to fling it far away from her. It was lifeless stuff. What had ever made her think that she could write? For a moment she felt an intense anger for all the people who had encouraged her to think that she could write.

I have respect—even awe—for it. She sneered, but she kept her eyes on the printed words, feeling an ugly pleasure in thus punishing herself. At last she came to "The Boy," and suddenly she was not only seeing the words, but remembering the twisted, jumbled feelings from which she had taken them. Out of chaos, she had brought form and order; out of the dimness, clarity; out of the unknown, that which could be known.

The sketch could easily have become obscure—but she hadn't permitted that! She understood now that the simplicity of words which had at first bored her was the boundary of the pure form she alone had created. . . . Remembering, she could almost feel again the sheer physical exhaustion which had come from the arduous selecting and rejecting, selecting and rejecting. . . .

She carefully closed the magazines and stared unseeingly ahead of her. She was in awe of herself. There was an excitement within her too great to allow her to be still.

She went outside and stood on the steps, looking about her. It seemed to her significant that she should have chosen this moment to leave the gloomy room, for the brilliance of the physical world matched her own exultancy. Buildings were sharply etched and all color heightened by the last rays of the sun.

Even as she watched, a dullness came into the light. It was still clear, but deceptively so. The fine outlines were lost. There was suddenly no distinction between shadows and light, roofs and sky, distance and nearness. She drew in her breath sharply and hurried down the walk.

She was only Janice Grant. The triumph, the clear knowledge, the talent itself—all were accidental and impersonal gifts. Occasionally they would flash through her, but those times would be as brief and impermanent as that wonderful light; and in the long intervals between them, she would be bound to the formless world. . . .

She thought of her uncle and his uncharacteristic firmness. He had struggled to be kind to her in the end. She winced. That impersonal kindness and sympathy people gave her! Without love; not for Janice Grant, but for that aggregate mass of human nature of which she was but a particle. . . . As they gave her clothes and money at home, dutifully remembered birthdays, graduations. . . .

The mythical Marcia-voice: *It is for you alone—because you are Janice—that I care.*

She was in front of the Murdocks'. She had meant to cross over to the Park to avoid going by the house, but now it was too late. She walked on, her eyes fixed straight ahead of her. *I and my talent create the world, and I shall make it sufficient unto myself. . . .*

More tears stung her eyes. Annoyed, she blinked rapidly. Now that she was by the Murdocks', she felt tired and limp, and she had sudden disgust for her aimless walk. She stopped to stare across the street at the short cut leading to town. Should she take it? There was nothing in town.

She shrugged and turned toward the river, going carelessly down the steep and stony path. At the bottom, she stood still again. The river was glassy and reflected the pale yellow sky and gray-green trees. She walked to it and leaned over, seeing herself upside-down. Janice Grant, she thought, but I am the only one who knows it.

She stooped down for a half-buried stone. The dirt around it was cool and moist. She brushed it off and then sent the stone skipping over the still water. It pleased her to break the smoothness and distort the tree-images. She found another stone. . . .

MacMillan—was he really strong? She thought of the tight mouth and the cold eyes. He had barely faltered when he had understood. Some men would have lost control, raised their voice, ordered her out. Yes, he was strong.

Her fear arose again, and she stopped smiling. Would he tell Matt? It was the way he would tell it that she feared. He would say simply that she had faked an interview, and it would seem like a senseless sophomoric gesture—somewhat clever, but mostly foolish. She gritted her teeth. It had been so much more than that!

Matt would be angry, chiefly because she had done it to J. W. Mac-Millan. He'd say: "By God, Janice, if you were younger, I'd give you a good old-fashioned tanning!" In years past, he was always going to give her a good old-fashioned tanning, but he never got around to it. His anger toward her was explosive and brief because she existed in only the surface of his consciousness, like the shallow tree-images in the river. . . .

She threw the last stone, not bothering to make it skip, and walked along the river bank, bored. As the intensity of her thoughts wore off, she became aware of what was outside her, and she saw that a short distance away stood a man painting. It would of course be Kim Duncan, and she felt a surge of anger because of his intrusion. She wanted the river bank to herself.

If she couldn't have it, there was no reason why he should. She moved firmly toward him, intending to destroy the absorption in which he obviously worked. But as she drew nearer, the quiet, intent expression upon his face halted her in spite of herself. He was in profile to her and still completely oblivious to her presence. He frowned against the dimming light, but she knew that he was not really aware of the light or the ground upon which he stood or even the brush in his hand. For him there was only that which he was painting.

Except for the motion of his hand and arm, he was very still; yet she sensed a rhythm that flowed through his body to direct his hand. It was as if, she thought excitedly, the rhythm of the whole world had become concentrated in him.

For one moment a strange hate threatened her impersonal interest. Who was he to know such singleness of purpose, when she—

She thrust aside this feeling, for she was genuinely curious. Here was something new, although half familiar. Quietly she crossed behind him to the large flat rock on which he had set his paint box. She lifted the box and carefully put it on the ground, then seated herself on the rock, still watching him intently. A wind arose and whipped her hair across her face and chilled her bare arms, but she minded only its rocking the easel so that he would soon have to stop painting.

Suddenly he looked up and scowled at the wind; then he stared around him in a dazed way, as if bewildered by the steadily diminishing light. She came within his vision, and he started. "Who in— Oh. Janice Grant."

She nodded. "I've been watching you."

He scowled again. "I don't like to be watched."

"You have a great talent," she said solemnly.

He looked suspicious. "You mean you like it?" The scowl went away. He turned to look back at his canvas. "You think it's good?"

She hadn't looked at the canvas, and now she couldn't see it in the dusk. She knew that he wouldn't understand if she tried to explain that her interest was in him and not the inconsequential result of what she had seen in him; and so she said politely, "It's very good—quite excellent."

He gave her another wary look, then walked to the swaying easel and stood before the canvas for several long minutes. He came back to her. "I haven't done much with the human face."

So it was a face. She glanced around the inanimate world surrounding them. "Wouldn't a model help?"

"Not for this one," he said shortly. He towered above her, hands in his pockets, his lean olive face still not wholly relaxed from the tenseness with which he had worked. "Did you know her?"

"Not by name," she said cautiously.

"Carol Leeds."

"Oh—yes. She was a senior when I was a freshman."

He stared past her for a moment, then shrugged. "Well, I'd better pack up. There's never time enough."

"I have a talent too," she said as he began to take the easel apart.

"You have?" he said absently. The easel was now a bundle of sticks. He carried it and the canvas to the rock.

"I write," she said.

"That's fine." He squatted down and carefully slid the canvas into the paint box. She went on talking about her writing, and he wanted to tell her to shut up, but as he glanced at her, the desire to speak faded. She had leaned back on the rock, resting her weight on her hands and looking beyond him as she talked. He thought of fire and wind. It seemed to him that she had no body, and he knew that if he were to paint her at that moment, he would make even her small pointed breasts a symbol, not of sex, but of the restless driving fire within her. "God," he said softly, "I'd like to paint you."

388

She was instantly quiet and turned her head slowly to look at him. He held his breath, thinking how he would make her emerge from the veil of evening light. . . . "But not because I'm Janice Grant," she said abruptly. And to his horror her face puckered and she began to cry.

He let out his breath in a long sigh. Nothing endured. He took an angry step back from her. She had ruined it! Now she was merely another girl crying. "What in blazes is the matter with you?"

She hid her face behind her hands and went on crying with deep gasps that shook her whole body. He stood by feeling awkward. He supposed he ought to do something for her. He pulled out his handkerchief and tossed it into her lap. She clutched at it with one hand, then buried her face in it. He began to understand that the large, tearing sobs were caused in part by her shame in crying before him. "What's the matter?" he asked with an attempt at gentleness.

He thought she wasn't going to answer, but then she mumbled, "Nobody likes *me*."

He grimaced, knowing that she couldn't see him. The childish self-pity! Yet it was only human to try to comfort her. "If you're nice to people," he said lamely, "they'll like you." He thought she was too upset to notice that those were asinine words.

She quieted, and after a moment she took the handkerchief away from her face and flashed him a look of such contempt that he winced. "You're stupid."

"You spoiled it first," he muttered. But then it came to him that in her eyes he had descended from his pedestal as she had in his. He grinned. "We're a couple of gods—huh?"

She didn't understand this remark, but it arrested her, and she forgave him the earlier triteness. She wiped her eyes for the final time, gave him back his handkerchief, and took a long quivering breath. "You're interesting—different," she said decisively. "When I used to see you up in the Inferno, I thought you immature and conceited. But now that I have seen you painting, I know you for what you are. We have much in common. We are of the same element."

"Elements, you mean," he said dryly. "Fire and wind."

She was pleased. "That's good. Yes." She stood up on the rock so that she was taller than he. "I'm glad that I found you. We shall be friends."

"There won't be much time for that." Abruptly he picked up the easel and paint box. "I'll not be here next year. I've resigned."

"Resigned?" She looked disappointed. "Why did you do that?"

"Why?" He laughed bitterly. "I'll tell you why. This place can't hold an artist."

She considered this seriously. "I understand. I can bear it because I'm a student." She nodded. "You were very wise to resign. I suppose you're awfully glad to have done it."

He had been staring across the river, busy with his own thoughts.

Her words came slowly into his mind. "Glad!" he cried incredulously. "Why should I be glad to give up my job, my security, my—"

"But when you don't have to teach," she said impatiently, "you'll be able to work all day."

He knew that she meant painting, and he almost blurted out that painting wasn't his work; but he didn't, for he was suddenly afraid that if he did, she'd say again, "You're stupid." She had it all wrong, but he wasn't going to enlighten her. He shouldered his easel. "Let's go."

She went up the steep bank easily without help from him. When they reached the Heights, they both stopped instinctively to look at one another. She's seeing me now as ordinary, he thought; for he was seeing her now as the student with the sometimes unpleasant sharpness in her face who was too often in the Inferno bothering Marcia. . . .

"By the way, Mr. Duncan," she said in a politely formal way that would have been incongruous on the river bank, "are you a member of the Student-Faculty Editorial Board of the *Young Spectator?*"

"I doubt it."

"Oh, but you are," she said, annoyed. "Every English teacher is automatically on it."

He tried to look knowing. "Now that I think about it, I believe that I am a member."

"I merely wanted to remind you that the election of the editor is coming up in June and that I'm an applicant. I don't intend to influence you one way or the other, but when the time comes, you might remember that I *am* a good writer, that I'll be a senior next year, and that because of my knowledge of people, I can make them work well for me. Also, I'd appreciate your suggesting to Dr. Anderson that it is only fair to be completely impersonal in such a matter and not be guided by likes or—dislikes." She hesitated, and he was sure that she was briefly reviewing the English Department in her mind. "Perhaps you'd better speak to Dr. Wilson," she went on, "and Dr. Meyerson. They don't know me very well. Dr. Scott will know how to vote. He's had me in class."

"Shouldn't I do some suggesting to Dr. Grant?" he asked, amused. "He's the only one you haven't mentioned."

She smiled and shrugged. "He doesn't need it. I can always count on him—in the end."

Kim waited until she started up the Heights; then he crossed to the short cut and went to the Bijou. She was a queer, mixed-up kid, he told himself. Not very likeable, with that arrogance and shrewdness. Yet she had a certain wisdom that seemed above the unpleasant things. He couldn't wholly forget the look about her that had made him want to paint her. And she had, after all, uttered some memorable words. . . .

You have a great talent. . . .
He'd be a fool to take seriously anything she said.
But when you don't have to teach, you'll be able to work all day.
And she had meant *paint*.

That's how simple it looked to other people, he thought ironically.
You were very wise to resign. I suppose you're awfully glad to have done it.

But she didn't know that he had been practically pushed out.

To paint all day. To know when night came that he had merely to wait for the morning light. Not to have to face classes, to grade papers. . . .

Suddenly he was hurrying. He rushed across the Square, into the Bijou, and up to his room. He threw the easel on his bed and took the unfinished portrait of Carol from its groove in the paint box. Being careful not to look at it, he set it up on a chair to dry. It was too soon to test himself on that work.

From the closet he dragged out a small stack of canvases. After Martin Anderson had seen them, he hadn't kept many of his things. He didn't even know by what process he had discarded some and held on to others. He had done it instinctively, not really caring.

Now he turned on all the light there was in the room and sat down on the floor by the canvases. Slowly and critically he began to look them over, taking them in the meaningless order in which they were stacked. He argued violently against every good thing he thought he saw, but in spite of that he grew excited. He was remembering how it used to be for him. Once he had finished a canvas, it had died. Oh, he had always pretended that he thought it good, but by the time it was dry, he had been unable to pretend even with himself, for the thing never had anything to say back to him.

But tonight the same canvases seemed vibrant with meaning. Why? Obviously nothing could have happened to them—so it must be that he was seeing them differently.

He refused to acknowledge his feeling of elation, although his heart thumped madly as if it had a life apart from his mind. He wasn't, he told himself severely, trying to prove that his canvases were *good*. That wasn't the point. The important thing was that they had taken on meaning for *him*. At that moment he couldn't be daunted by even the thought that they might have no meaning whatever for anyone else in the world. That was all right. Let him worry about that later.

He had reached an old canvas, one that showed the ancient willow tree and a portion of the muddy river. While he was looking at it, remembered words crossed his mind. *What is so strange is the way everything goes on as usual—in spite of change.* The scene followed the words. Marcia had said them. They had been in the Inferno, she standing by the window, and he at his easel, not particularly listening

391

and wishing that she would move away from his apples. And then someone—Meyerson—had said, "Yes. that is the most difficult of all lessons to learn."

Change, yet no change. But that was what his canvas said! There was the ceaseless flux of the river bearing the static image of the willow tree. Change, yet no change. He couldn't have thought it in idea, but he had felt it when looking at the tree and the moving river, and he had put it on the canvas. It was there for anyone to see who wanted to see it—who wanted to see the world through his eyes. He sat very still, remembering exactly how he had felt while painting that canvas. . . .

Soon he piled the canvases together again, then got up and lighted a cigarette. He paced about the small room, recalling the painting of many canvases. Each time had been different, yet there was a sameness binding together all the times; and he saw that he who had felt so powerless had a great power—that of entering simply and directly the world which others had to recreate through laborious thought.

He had never taken seriously the power, for it had been his without effort. It had seemed refuge, a kind of border to his cramped life to which he could escape from time to time, but always to return to the crowded and shadowy center. Suddenly it shifted position and arose in his mind like a sun, lighting the whole, which now appeared limitless. He felt free, but not without a sense of irony, for it seemed to him that he had found his way out of a prison which had never had more than three walls.

Impulsively he grabbed up the canvases and rushed out into the hall. Iris had to know.

But before he reached the stairs, he hesitated. He had gone to her many times, only to have it proved each time that his offering was false. He didn't dare fail again—with either her or himself.

Slowly he went back to his room and dumped the canvases on the floor again. He was disappointed but resolved. He felt chastened and humble. He'd give himself—he glanced at his watch—eight hours. If by morning he could remember with the same sense of conviction what he had thought tonight, he'd go to her. Perhaps that wasn't time enough to test it, but it was all that he was willing to sacrifice. Life was short, and he had wasted a goodly part of it.

He strode around the Heart in the fine drizzle, hatless and coatless. The long walk in the rain had plastered down his hair to look like a ragged skull cap. His coat was wrapped protectively around the canvases he carried. He was as tired and haggard as he looked, although he felt bright and new.

The students on their way to early classes stared after him. He grinned. Let them think him the campus oddity. He didn't care.

He threw open the door to Iris' office. She was at the desk and looked up in astonishment. "It lasted all night!" he cried.

"What? The rain?" She came to him, concern in her face, and put her hands on his cold wet arms. "Good heavens, Kim! You must have been out in it all night too."

He pushed her impatiently aside and dumped the canvases on the couch, his coat still over them. "I'm not being forced out, Iris. I've decided to leave— I *want* to leave. Do you—give me a dry cigarette—understand? Do you see the difference?"

She went back to the desk, tossed him a cigarette, and lighted one for herself. "You mean you want to resign?"

He nodded, relieved to have her understand without more words. Then he led her to the couch. "That's me," he said, pulling the coat off the canvases.

She looked at him wonderingly, then sat down on the couch and picked up one of the paintings. He shook his head and walked away from her. "You don't have to look at them. That isn't why I brought them. I can't say exactly why I did bring them—unless—well, they're the only evidence I've got to show."

"Evidence of what, Kim?"

He turned suddenly, looking at her intently from across the room. "Iris, I love you. That was supposed to come later, but I'm afraid I might not get to the end. Look—it's my peculiar nature to go backward. When I first told you that, I at least had a good job. Now I haven't got that—or even the prospect of one. All I've got"—he hesitated, then went on rapidly—"is the knowledge that I'm a painter—and at present a pretty bad one."

"That's a fine thing to have," she said.

He sighed. "You don't know how much depended on your saying that." He was suddenly aware of his tiredness and sat down in a chair far away from the couch.

She returned to his canvases, and for a while the room was very quiet. "I've never before seen so many of your things together," she said at last. "Why, Kim—they've got something!" There was excitement in her voice. "They're—they're—"

"Don't say it!" he shouted, jumping up. "I'm not worrying about that—yet. Besides, Martin Anderson said they were no good."

She shrugged. "His is only one opinion, after all."

"And a damn good one," he said dryly.

"Well, maybe it is—but it's still only one." She set up the canvas of MacMillan Hall, then backed away to look at it. "What I mean is this, Kim: if I were to walk into a room and see that painting hanging on the wall, I'd be intrigued and curious enough to go up to it, and I'd say to the owner, 'What an interesting work!' And I'd mean it. I shouldn't even think of saying whether it was good or bad. In fact,

393

who *could* say that right off? As you said, worry about that later. But from the point of interest, your work has value *now*. Just think of it, Kim. You can sell a few to—"

"Wait a minute!" he said angrily. "You're going too fast. I'm not concerned about selling anything. It's the experience that's important to me. It came to me last night. When I paint, I see things as they are. At other times, I feel walled in—but when I paint, the walls disappear. . . ." He was suddenly embarrassed. "Sounds crazy, doesn't it? But that's the way it is, and all I know now is that I want a life that allows me to have as much of it as possible."

"But that's exactly what I want for you!" Iris said eagerly. "You don't want to walk right into another prison, do you?"

"What do you mean?" he asked fearfully.

"You've got to earn your living through painting. If you don't, you'll trick yourself into taking some other kind of job. You do have to earn some money, don't you?"

"I do," he said glumly, "although I've got enough for us to live on for a year. In the summers we'll live at Martin Anderson's colony, and—" He broke off impatiently. "But I'm not saying what I came to say. Let's get it over with. You understand why I went to New York, don't you? I had to prove to myself that I was free of her."

"Well, did you prove that?"

"Yes—but not by going off to New York. Good Lord! Why are we always rushing around trying to prove things to ourselves, when all we have to do is . . ." He shrugged. "It was wasted train fare, because what I wanted to prove happened last night—and it didn't have anything to do with her."

"Still," Iris said suddenly, "you wouldn't have been satisfied if you hadn't gone."

"That's it," he said gratefully. "Besides, it— I came back scared and thinking, good old John Willard, my home, my asylum. That was the night—that was the night . . ."

"That Dr. Grant suggested you resign?"

He stared at her. "How did you know it was then?"

"He told me," she said. "He knew you were upset, and he wanted me to know so that if you ever talked to me about it, I could assure you that he did not mean for you to resign if you didn't *want* to leave."

"You didn't tell me!" he said accusingly.

She smiled. "You didn't talk to me about it. In fact, you didn't talk to me about anything."

"I couldn't. I thought the world had turned upside down. Look"— he went over to the couch—"there's one painting you haven't seen. This one." Carefully he pulled a loose cloth off a canvas, which he then set against the couch. "It's still wet."

She looked for a long minute, then shuddered. "You've made her look very cruel, Kim."

"She is cruel." He walked away from her. "Tell me what you see in it, Iris. Don't make up anything. Say only what you see."

She hesitated. "There's not much besides the cruelty," she said slowly. "That's clearer than the features themselves. . . . The face emerges from the background— What is the background, Kim? I can't—"

"Yes, you can," he said sharply. "What does it look like?"

"A big piece—of earth," she said uncertainly. "Perhaps dark moist —no, it's gnarled, isn't it? Perhaps a thick tree trunk."

"Good enough," he said, his back to her and the painting. "It is a tree trunk. I used to see her down by the river against a tree. In my mind only, you understand. It was as if she belonged to all that struggling life down there. On the surface, you don't see it. But it's there. Go on."

"The cruelty is in the eyes and mouth. The rest of the face and hair is indistinct, as if not quite separate from the tree."

He asked quickly, "Does the blurred quality bother you—detract from the clarity of meaning?"

"No. . . . I think not. I shouldn't want to see the face more clearly. It would spoil the . . . Well, I don't know why, but it wouldn't do."

He laughed exultantly. "It seems that once you see the bounding line you can blur everything twice as much and it still looks clear. I suppose Martin Anderson knew that all the time. Well, what else?"

"The cruelty is . . . strange. . . ."

"How is it strange?" he demanded the moment she hesitated.

"Perhaps I didn't mean that. Perhaps it's very natural—natural in that it might express a kind of instinctive fight for life."

He came to her and seized her by the arms. "Do you really see that, Iris, or are you just guessing?"

"I really see it, Kim."

He let go her arms. "I started to paint the thing because I hoped I could paint the hate out of me. I came back hating her and the whole world for letting her live. But as I worked, the miracle happened. I began to see her cruelty as a kind of necessity, and so there was no longer any need for hate. Oh, that's putting it badly—but it's what I was trying to tell you happens when I paint. It's as if everything in the world loses its name and I can see all things without goodness or badness or rightness and wrongness. . . ."

"You could have a very full life," she said suddenly, "without me."

He shook his head. "Maybe I'm selfish, but I want you too. Some people might be happy stacking up canvases, but I wouldn't. What I really mean is that I don't even want the other without you. I found it through you. I—" He stopped as there was a firm knock on the door.

Iris slipped her hand in his for a moment, then went to the door. "Oh, come in," she said blankly, and Dean Briggs gratefully put down his big black umbrella and stepped inside. "Hah!" he cried, giving

Kim a brief survey. "I can see that you've been in it too." He set the dripping umbrella against the wall and stamped and shook his head vigorously, although he was quite dry. At last satisfied, he began to look around him, nodding and frowning critically. "Yes—quite shabby. I see what you mean, Miss Taylor. Of course, I can't . . ."

Iris stood leaning against the door, staring across the room to Kim. He lighted a cigarette, his eyes never leaving her.

". . . war makes it difficult, but you certainly are entitled—" The Dean fell silent, as if suddenly aware that he alone was making all the sound in the room. He looked swiftly from Iris to Kim, then back to Iris. "This *is* the time we arranged, is it not, Miss Taylor?" he asked delicately.

Iris aroused herself. "Oh, yes—of course." Kim muttered something and moved to stand in front of the couch. Her eyes went to the canvases, which he was trying to hide, and her face brightened. "This is exactly the right time!"

"Fine, fine. Now as I understand it, you're more interested in props and production equipment than office furnishings." Dean Briggs smiled as she nodded. "Excellent. I commend your spirit. What, I ask, is a handsome office without—"

"Nothing, Dean Briggs, nothing at all!" she broke in with such fervor that Kim looked at her suspiciously. "You are very kind to consider my wishes for new equipment. In fact, you are so kind that I should like to return your kindness at this very moment." She took his arm and led him toward the couch. "Dean Briggs," she said solemnly, "fate brought you here at this time, for Mr. Duncan happened to bring along the best of his work this morning."

The Dean looked blank. "Fate? No, Miss Taylor, it was an appointment agreed upon by . . ." The upright portrait of Carol Leeds arrested him. He tipped his head to one side. "Very interesting . . . very interesting."

Iris flashed Kim a triumphant smile. He was red in the face. "You're an excellent judge, Dean Briggs," she said.

He shook his head modestly. "Not at all, not at all. I merely know what I like and I like what I know."

Kim winced. "Then you won't like my—"

"Dean Briggs is searching for a painting," Iris said loudly. "A very special painting."

"Not too special," the Dean said quickly.

Kim was eyeing him sceptically. "You're a collector, Dean Briggs?"

The Dean seemed to agree that this idea was absurd, for he laughed soundly. "Not at all, not at all. Mrs. Briggs wants something for over the mantel."

"I never did anything for over the mantel," Kim said stiffly.

Iris frowned at him. "It's a unique mantel, Kim. Tell him about it, Dean."

"I should call it troublesome, Miss Taylor—troublesome. You see, Mr. Duncan, my predecessor, Dean Holcomb, evidently graced the mantel with a picture, which he quite naturally removed with him. Unfortunately, it left its toll upon the wallpaper, which no amount of cleaning will erase. None of our pictures quite fit, and Mrs. Briggs is sore troubled."

Iris reached down the painting of MacMillan Hall. "As I recall the space," she said, standing away from Dean Briggs and holding the canvas before her so that he could see it plainly, "it is about this size."

Dean Briggs was hesitant. "Perhaps. But then again—"

"And of course," she said enthusiastically, "this has the advantage of being local color."

The Dean tipped his head again. "Really? What is it?"

Kim started to say something, but Iris ignored him. "MacMillan Hall, Dean Briggs. I can understand why you didn't recognize it immediately, for you still aren't truly familiar with all our buildings. Think how appropriate it would be to have this painting of the Hall come to rest in the home of our Dean."

"I have no particular fondness for that building," he said a bit drily. "In fact, I consider it a monstrosity—I mean"—he added quickly—"the real structure."

"But that's exactly what the artist—Mr. Duncan—has so effectively portrayed," Iris said. "The monstrosity of the place."

"Yes—yes, I see that," the Dean admitted after another moment of scrutiny. "Quite cleverly too. But that would indicate, would it not, that the painting is not suitable to a living room? Now in a studio or a museum . . ."

Iris had become very thoughtful and did not appear to hear the Dean. "Perhaps I am being too hasty. Kim, is this the canvas Martin Anderson wants for his studio?"

"Iris," Kim said in a choked voice, "what are you—"

"Martin Anderson?" Dean Briggs looked at Kim with new interest. "He executed that splendid portrait of Grace MacMillan now hanging in the Summit, did he not?"

"Mr. Duncan is his protégé," Iris said before Kim could speak.

"Is that so! I didn't realize that you took your painting so seriously, young man. Now I'm beginning to understand your resignation. At first I was disappointed and thought, another one who doesn't know his own mind. But—"

"But now," Iris said quickly, "you can see that he must resign *because* he knows his own mind."

Dean Briggs gave her an appreciative smile. "Certainly *you* know it, Miss Taylor. And, believe me, I am in complete sympathy with your desire to make a sound start."

Iris held the canvas forward. "It is also a great opportunity for those who are in at the start."

Obediently the Dean eyed MacMillan Hall again. "The Scotts have a mirror," he said doubtfully. "Mrs. Briggs admires it very much. However, it was cut to order out of Riverville, and as we haven't yet had the pleasure of meeting Mrs. Scott and as Dr. Scott is very vague about the matter, we have been unable to learn—"

"A mirror!" Iris was contemptuous. "A mirror can reflect only what already exists. A mirror—"

"What price have you set upon it?" the Dean asked Kim hastily.

"I don't think you want it," Kim said flatly, "but if you do, I'll give it to you, of course. I don't sell—"

"What the Dean wants to know this moment," Iris said deliberately, "is at what *price* you'll give it to him."

Kim glared at her, then shrugged resignedly. "Five—six—seven," he said.

Dean Briggs looked happier. "Is that so? Well, I—"

"Five *hundred?*" Iris said concernedly. "Perhaps that's a little high for your Taupe Period, Kim." She smiled at the Dean. "One hundred dollars."

He sighed. "I hope Mr. Duncan appreciates having you on his side." He managed an almost hearty laugh. "You'd make an excellent dealer."

"No," Iris said suddenly, looking at Kim above the canvas. "I like my work here. I'd want to go on with it—for a long while."

"That's all right," Kim said. "I knew you'd want it that way, and I'd already decided that would be all right."

"Truly remarkable," the Dean said, having wandered back to the portrait of Carol Leeds.

Kim shook his head emphatically, and Iris said: "That one belongs to Mr. Duncan's private collection, and is not for sale."

"Oh." Reluctantly the Dean turned back to MacMillan Hall and once more tipped his head. "I'm trying to see this through the eyes of Mrs. Briggs, and I'm still wondering of it's quite the thing for a living room. . . ."

"Then put it in the kitchen," Iris said softly, looking at Kim again.

Chapter Four

DEARDORFF'S was dim and cool. At first Marcia thought no one was in the shop, but then she saw the top of Deardorff's head back of the stacks of books that covered his desk.

"Hello," she said cautiously.

He jumped and one pile of books toppled and fell to the floor.

"Oh, I'm sorry. I was afraid that would happen, but I—"

He had arisen to glare at her. "Can't you find your own book by now?"

"I didn't come to buy a book." She stooped to help pick up the books. "Are you sending out all these books? Orders must be coming in thickly."

"From overseas." He gathered up the last armful and dumped them on the desk. Then he began to brush each one off and carefully restack it. "I have to send them according to poundage, not titles or even subject matter. I have to decide—" He turned to her suddenly, his eyes merry. "On second thought, I'm delighted to see you, for who else but a pedagogue could tell me precisely how many ounces of poetry, how many pounds of history, how many—"

"What I'll tell you," she said firmly, "is what I've been telling you for two months—you need an assistant."

He raised his eyes to the ceiling. "O Zeus!"

"Yes, here we go again. You can't possibly take care of all this"— she waved toward the book laden desk and the piles of corrugated and wrapping paper on the floor—"yourself. You look very tired, and the way you treat the few customers who wander in here is disgrace— By the way, how do so many people overseas know you?"

He seemed amused. "From yonder hill—alumni."

"All the more reason why you should take on a John Willard student now. Janice Grant is—"

"Who's she?" he asked innocently.

She made an exasperated gesture. "But I've mentioned her to you dozens of times! She's the one you need for an assistant."

"Is she now?" He moved to the wall of books and leaned against it, his thumbs curled around his suspenders. "Can she read?"

"She loves books. She reads—"

"Ah, yes. I know these book-lovers. I am to pay her for doing her reading in my shop." He looked curiously at her and tapped his forehead with a grimy finger. "I think I'm beginning to understand. She is another little fly buzzing around your conscience."

She flushed in spite of herself. "I haven't the slightest idea of what you mean!"

He closed his eyes. "I remember . . . I remember a certain little fly you brought in here some time ago. It had been annoying you, and you, having a kind heart, did not swat out its life, but brought it here and allowed it to ruin several of my very best books. . . ." His shoulders were shaking with his silent laughter. He opened his eyes. "Have I not rung the bell, Evangelist?"

"This is quite different," she said wearily. "Much more serious. . . . I promise you Janice wouldn't sit reading all day. She is very energetic and—ambitious. If you don't prevent her, she might even sell one or two of your books for you. She knows books not only as a reader, but as a writer knows—"

He held up his hand in alarm. "She's a writer?"

She nodded. "And a very good one. If you wish, I'll send you some of her things."

"I'd not trust a writer within a mile of my books," he said grimly.

"That's unfair and illogical. After all, writers are necessary. I mean, if you're going to have books, you have to—"

"Nevertheless!" He waved his arms. "Let me tell you this—if she's a writer, she recognizes only two classes of books: those she wouldn't bother to write herself, and those she would. The first ones might as well be marbles; the second ones she devours and gets indigestion from envy." He shook his head emphatically. "Would you set a cannibal loose among little Christian children?"

"Oh, Janice isn't like that," she said uneasily, for she wasn't sure that he hadn't described Janice very well. "Not at all. She's clever and—" She turned as the door opened. It was Grant, and when his eyes could see in the dimness, he came back to them. "Mr. Deardorff," she said, giving Deardorff a pleading look, "has just consented to give Janice a try this summer."

Deardorff grimaced. "Who is safe before the assault of an evangelist?"

"Evangelist?" Grant looked at Marcia. "You?" Suddenly he smiled. "A very good title for you, I think."

She moved away from them, annoyed. "Mr. Deardorff is a fine man with a distorted sense of humor."

Grant watched her for a moment, then turned back to Deardorff. "What are you going to charge Janice?"

Deardorff chuckled. "You have understanding, you have understanding. . . ." He sighed, then said with dignity: "To myself I am calling it a wartime emergency. If it weren't for those"—he pointed to the books on the desk—"I'd not give in to a battalion of evangelists."

"There's another reason why I came to see you," Marcia said, rejoining them. "I want to say—" She felt suddenly embarrassed over having come to say good-by, as if it were somehow an artificial gesture. "If you recall," she went on casually, "I ordered Blake's *Daughters of Albion* illustrations long ago. I had better give you my home address so that you can mail them to me when they come." She tore a piece off his wrapping paper, wrote her name and address on it, and handed it to him.

He waved it away impatiently. "I can't be bothered with two addresses for one customer. Besides, the Blake won't come before fall—and probably not then."

"You don't understand," she said quickly. "I'll not be back in the fall. I've re— I'm—well, I'll not be back."

He gave her a quick searching look. "Is that so? If that's true, then . . ." He took the paper from her hand.

"It's true," she said. She took a step back and collided with Grant, who said nothing but placed his hand firmly upon her arm. "I've en-joyed your bookshop very much, and I thank you for giving Janice at least a trial," she said angrily, for she thought it unfair of Grant to keep his hand remindingly upon her arm at such a time.

Deardorff seemed amused again. "Good-by, then, Evangelist," he said somberly, "until September."

When they were outside, Grant said, "I've tracked you down pur-posely—as you might guess."

"Truly I must hurry. Stephanie is coming this—"

"Even you can spare a few minutes to settle your future." He still held her by the arm and made her walk with him toward Herby's. But when they stood before the screen door, he shook his head. "Too crowded." For a moment he looked desperate, then shrugged resignedly and led her to the plot of grass surrounding Benjamin Willard. "I should like to think that you avoid me so persistently because my pres-ence disturbs you. That would, in a way, be a hopeful sign."

"It isn't that," she said. "You make me feel at ease."

"What's wrong with that?" he demanded.

"I don't trust it."

He said nothing more until they were seated on an iron bench, which was hot and uncomfortable in the sun. He turned sideways to see her face. "You tried to say good-by to Deardorff. Are you still de-termined to leave?"

"I think you have my letter of resignation," she said stiffly.

"Why do you want to leave, Marcia?"

This broke her unnatural calmness. "I've told you that I hate the place! Now I understand how Cliff Hughes felt." She looked at him defiantly. "Meyerson has not been asked to return, has he?" When he merely shook his head, she went on eagerly, "And Kim and Scott. They—"

"Not so fast," he said. "You can't blame their leaving on John Willard."

She ignored this. "I was gullible and blind, but now I see clearly. When I think how Cliff Hughes and Meyerson were sacrificed to a man like Diaz! Oh, I tell you it's all pretense and hypocrisy glossed over by President Cameron's noble Philosophy of Education."

"You're partly right, of course," he said mildly, "and it's good to be aware of it. When you leave, there will be one less teacher with that awareness—and that is a great loss."

"A great loss," she repeated ironically. "I've contributed only blun-ders. I blundered teaching Blake, I blundered teaching the Cadets, I . . ."

"It would seem," he said when she did not go on, "that your sense of failure is greater than your hatred of the college."

She shrugged. "Perhaps so. Certainly my list of failures is impressive. I failed even in writing about Blake. My manuscript came back yesterday."

"I'm sincerely sorry about that, Marcia—and disappointed in Hill-Moran."

"Don't lose your sense of judgment," she said impatiently. "Hill-Moran is right, and you know it. You of all people know it, for they told me essentially what you told me, although their way of telling it was much less kind than yours."

"I'm sorry," he murmured again. "A flat rejection?"

"It amounted to that. They did say that the last chapter had possibilities. They suggested that I expand it and—" She laughed shortly. "What difference does it make? I'll never do anything more with Blake."

He was silent for a moment, then asked lightly, "What other failures, Dr. Anderson?"

"Carol Leeds," she said quickly.

He shook his head emphatically. "That's absurd."

"Well, Janice, then."

"Why," he asked abruptly, "were you seeing Deardorff about Janice?"

She stared at him, puzzled and hurt. "You told me you thought it would be a good thing for her. . . . I thought I was helping."

"Janice should have had to approach Deardorff herself," he said more gently. "More importantly, you should not—for your own sake—assume such personal responsibility for her. For some reason or other, you've identified yourself with Janice, and that's why you can't keep her in her proper place."

She seemed ready to deny what he had said, but suddenly she sighed and leaned back against the bench. "All right. I *did* read myself into Janice. I knew it all along—yet didn't know it. And now—and now she hates us both."

He smiled briefly. "We can bear it. I may be sanguine, but I have some hope for Janice. She is amazingly honest in her writing, and perhaps one day will meet herself face-to-face in it."

"Then you believe," she said slowly, "that my sense of failure is exaggerated?"

"I do. Good Lord, Marcia, you're too intelligent to think that things such as you have named can be called failures or successes. We'd have to be up there with the sun looking down on the whole of time and space to be able to judge human relationships that way."

She was impatient again. "What *do* you believe about me, then?"

He took a long while to answer. "I believe," he said finally, "that you were much more honest in April. Then you saw that the anguish and the sadness were within you . . . dependent upon you."

She made a helpless gesture. "But why . . .?"

"And I believe," he went on, "that the pain of such a truth was too great to bear, and that now you have manufactured scores of reasons to explain your hate, which is really . . ."

"Hate for myself," she said quickly as he hesitated.

"I suppose so," he said reluctantly. "Of course, I believe that too is unfounded."

She ignored this. "Yes . . . that's it. I've sensed it all along. Yes, it's my own hypocrisy that I can't face. I tried to tell you about that once before," she went on excitedly, "but I couldn't, for I didn't understand it myself then. You thought I meant it came from ideas and values— I mean, you thought it was that I had discovered his values to be different from mine. But, you see, that was really very superficial. What I felt was much deeper. And then I discovered that the reason . . . the reason . . ."

"Was that you were living a lie," he said. "That is the way you put it when we talked in April."

"Yes, yes," she said eagerly. "But don't you see that the lie went far beyond—him? There's no reason to believe that it does not include everything in my life since—since Virginia entered it. That would mean my studies, my interest in Blake, my teaching. . . . That would make them all unreal."

"I thought it was something like that," he said after a minute. He looked at her. "You are a *real* teacher, Marcia. That I know. How can I convince you? Day after day you went on teaching in spite of the weight of your own problem. Humanly speaking, you had a right to leave in April. But you didn't rush away then. You didn't even ask for help—"

"You don't know how near I came to doing all those things," she said.

"But you didn't. That's the telling fact. You have an inner strength which apparently you don't even know you possess. I saw you use it and allow others to draw upon it; I—"

She stood up. "I couldn't come back. It would be like living among ghosts. In the Inferno I'd be conscious that Kim and Cliff and Meyerson weren't there and that Diaz was. I'd—"

"You wouldn't be in the Inferno. You'd come back as an assistant professor, and you'd have Scott's office in Main Hall. You'd—" He laughed at the look she gave him. "No, these are not bribes, Dr. Anderson. The promotion and change of office would have occurred in any event."

"I really must hurry," she said, glancing at her watch. "Stephanie is coming home this afternoon."

"And you have to be there to greet her," he said dryly, "or she'll be branded with hurt and neglect for the rest of her days."

She flushed. "Well, she does expect me to be there, especially as I'm leaving tomorrow. Besides—"

"Besides, you don't want to make the only decision there is to make after my eloquent proof. All right—but, Marcia, I want to hear your final word about your resignation by the middle of August. Will you remember that?"

"Yes—but won't that be inconvenient for you? Why not take my answer now?"

"For one thing, I'm obstinate. For another, the situation merits a little inconvenience."

"I'll write," she said, "but I do think you're causing yourself unnecessary trouble. I won't change my mind. I deliberated fully before I resigned. I'm not strong, but I'm not so weak that I'd vacillate in a matter like that. I'd—"

"For God's sake, Marcia, don't refuse to change your mind out of pride!" He spoke angrily, as if to arouse her, for he felt that she was withdrawn and that his seriousness could not reach her. "I've purposely stayed impersonal today," he went on more quietly, "but surely you must know that I do so with effort. Often I've been tempted to say, 'Let the teaching be hanged. All I want to know is whether you love me and want my love.' But I knew that would be false. You must decide the other first, and you must believe that coming back to John Willard doesn't necessarily mean that you're coming back to me. Naturally, however, I'm hoping—" He broke off with a laugh. "In short, Dr. Anderson, when you write in August, will you include at least a postscript concerning the more personal aspect of the total situation?"

"Of course," she said quickly and, he was afraid, perfunctorily. "I'll do that." She moved away from him then, but at the curb, she hesitated and looked back, as if she herself were suddenly aware that she was perhaps walking away from more reality than she could feel at that moment. "Thank you," she said, "thank you for—" But the words must have seemed inadequate even to her, for without finishing the sentence, she turned and hurried on.

Stephanie had brought home a friend, one Chester Jones, who brushed aside her faltering introductions and sorted and filed the people for himself. "Aunt Madge!" he cried, gripping her hand. "Uncle Justin!" He added three smart raps on the arm for Uncle Justin. He turned his bright, direct look upon Marcia and allowed it to drill steadily for a moment. "And you're Dr. Anderson!"

He helped Aunt Madge to a chair and then seated himself on the sofa beside Stephanie. Sitting, he appeared taller than she. He had ruddy cheeks but a pale forehead topped by bristly black hair.

When he had given Stephanie a brief but reassuring smile, he turned to Justin and said in a commending voice, "You have fine orchards, sir. We stopped to give them the once-over on our way here."

Justin closed his mouth. "You did, did you?"

"However"—Chester shook his head dolefully—"I noted a few

signs of the codling moth. No doubt you're aware of its existence."

Justin grasped the arms of his chair and eyed the upstart. "Mr. Jones, I've been a-fighting that pest for some years."

Chester frowned sympathetically. "You're using an arsenical spray, of course."

"I am not. They can't sell me arsenic—though they've tried."

Again Chester shook his head. "Obviously, Uncle Justin, you're uninformed—or *mis*informed. It's foolhardy to attempt to combat the codling moth with any other preparation."

Justin merely stared. Stephanie said humbly, "Chet knows all about insecticides."

Chester frowned in the manner of a man who desires to keep everything in its proper place. "But as you know, Baby, arsenical sprays are merely a hobby of mine. My field of concentration," he explained to Mrs. Murdock and Marcia, "is oil emulsions. Colloidal chemistry."

Mrs. Murdock fluttered. "Imagine that!"

Justin turned his stare upon Stephanie. "*Baby!*"

She flushed but said defiantly, "That's just a nickname."

"However," Chester said, "I'm taking post-graduate work in soil nutrition. In this day and age, you have to specialize, but I want to round out my knowledge as much as possible, for I intend to have my own orchards—some day." Openly he turned to smile again at Stephanie, and for a moment the others were silent while some mysterious communication occurred between the two. When it had ended, Chester regarded Justin. "Orchards on the order of yours, sir—but of course on a much larger scale."

"Dinner!" cried Mrs. Murdock hastily. "We should go in to dinner!"

At the table, Chester carried the main theme of conversation. Justin ate steadily and cocked one eyebrow as a sign of unrelenting scepticism for whatever he might hear. Finally, in spite of himself, he grew interested, and the eyebrow slipped down to its natural level.

"You didn't happen to look at my soil, did you now?" he asked cautiously.

Mrs. Murdock coughed warningly, for, like Marcia, she sensed that he was inviting trouble. But he glared at her and repeated his question.

Chester laid down his fork and cleared his throat. "I did, sir."

"You did, did you?" Justin cleared *his* throat. "What do you think of it?"

There was a telling silence. Stephanie giggled from the strain.

"Baby!" said Chester reprovingly. Still looking at Justin, he drew a white sealed envelope from his inside coat pocket. He shook it, precisely ripped open the top end, and turned it upside down until a little mound of dark dirt had formed on the tablecloth. "*Looks* rich, doesn't it?" he asked pleasantly.

Mrs. Murdock eyed the pile of dirt and fought for control. "Yes," she said tremulously, "but, even so, I don't think it wise to mix it with your food—do you?"

Justin sucked in his cheeks and waited.

"But looks aren't everything," Chester informed them. He picked up some of the soil and allowed it to trickle through his fingers. "Uncle Justin, your soil strikes me as being too rich in certain properties and deficient in others. You know, soil is like people. . . . Too much heartiness may lead to apoplexy, and"—he laughed a little—"a ruddy complexion may hide a heart condition. Looks aren't everything, Uncle Justin."

"I see," Justin said with dangerous calmness. "What do you suggest that I do, Mr. Jones? Fertilize with arsenic?"

Chester chuckled admiringly. "You're a wit, Uncle Justin. Now, of course, I've made only a preliminary diagnosis. With your permission, I'll give this sample a laboratory analysis when I go back."

"When *are* you going back, Mr. Jones?" Mrs. Murdock asked politely.

Chester regarded her thoughtfully, seeming to consider something. "Oh," he said then in a noncommittal way unusual for him. Carefully he spooned up the soil until every grain was back in the envelope and only a faint smudge remained on the tablecloth. He wiped his spoon on his napkin, brushed his hands together, and looked gravely at Stephanie. "Tell them, Baby. It is time."

Sheer fright came into Stephanie's face. She shook her head quickly, but he was nodding his with deliberate emphasis. "It is time," he said gently and smiled.

Stephanie turned to look first at her uncle, then at her aunt, and at the last her gaze rested upon Marcia as she said, "We're married."

"So I figured," Justin said mildly. "Nothing else could explain that 'Baby.' "

But Mrs. Murdock was staring wide-eyed at Stephanie. Suddenly her eyes glistened and she said chokingly, "But why didn't you tell us? You shouldn't have married away from here. . . ." She covered her face with her hands and rushed to the kitchen.

Justin looked sternly at Stephanie. "You've gone and hurt your Aunt Madge."

"I wanted to do it properly," Chester said quickly, "but Ba—Stephanie wanted it this way—although I still don't understand why." For a moment he looked both baffled and irritated. Clearly he was a man who had no liking for what he didn't understand.

"I knew that Aunt Madge would make a big fuss," Stephanie said miserably. For the first time that day she sent a pleading look to Marcia.

"We understand," Marcia said, smiling. "And so will your aunt—in a little while. I think it's wonderful." She turned to the groom. "Congratulations!"

"Thank you," he said solemnly. He regarded Justin anxiously. "Sir, it disturbs me to think that you might suspect me of trying to slip into your family in an underhand way. If you would care to step into the next room, I'll show you certain credentials. . . ." His hand again went to his pocket and came back clutching a wallet, a small notebook, and several letters.

"A man is his own credentials in this house," Justin said easily. He waved his hand sweepingly, as if to indicate that an endless flux of humanity without credentials passed in and out of his doors.

Stephanie stared incredulously. "Aren't you even angry, Uncle Justin?"

Justin shrugged. "Why should I be? Almost everyone gets hitched—sooner or later. Madge!" he shouted. "Let's have some dandelion wine!" He listened, but there was no coherent answer from the kitchen. "Madge! If you don't come right back here, I'm not a-going to leave that money to—" He broke off, caught Marcia's eye, and grinned sheepishly. He pushed back his chair. "I better see about that wine myself."

He disappeared into the kitchen, and there were new muffled sounds from there. Soon Mrs. Murdock returned quietly to her place. Her face was tear-stained, but there was a small, unsteady smile upon her lips. She looked shyly at Stephanie. "Everything is going to be all right, dear." Then she turned to Chester. "He has taken to you. He *really* has taken to you!" There was wonderment in her voice, and she stared at the smudge on the tablecloth. "You see, the orchards have never before come right to our table!"

Stephanie soon followed Marcia up to her room. She closed the door and stood with her back against it. Her attitude was accusing. "You're not married!"

Marcia was casual. "Oh, you know how it is, Stephanie. The best laid plans of mice and men. . . ."

Stephanie flushed angrily. "You just *told* me that you were getting married! You just told me that so I'd—"

"Nonsense," Marcia said firmly. "Whatever the reason, it's right for you and Chester to be together. I can see that."

"Honestly?" Stephanie forgot her anger. "Do you know what? I think Uncle Justin wants us to come back here when we've finished school! They're downstairs arguing now. Chet has always planned to settle in the Finger Lakes region, but Uncle Justin keeps saying, 'What's the matter with Ohio?' I wonder if . . ." She looked up at Marcia, seeming afraid to believe what she thought.

"That doesn't surprise me," Marcia said. "Your uncle would like nothing better than to have you work with him. It took him a long while to learn that it was possible—that's all. Would you like coming back here, Stephanie?"

"Yes," Stephanie said slowly, "yes, I would. Aunt Madge could help me take care of Chet."

"Take care of him? Does he need special care?"

"He has a heart condition," Stephanie said almost proudly.

Marcia moved to the window. "Then you'll have to keep him away from strenuous work."

Stephanie shook her head matter-of-factly. "Oh, no. You see, it's his nature to be strenuous. Besides, he says that now it's his way of making up for not going to war."

Marcia stared at the neighboring roof. She was angry with Stephanie and wanted to cry out, "Why did you have to meet this Chester Jones with his heart condition and his desire to work himself to death for not going to war? I have tried to make things *right* for you, but you are making another failure for me. . . ."

Stephanie had been watching her intently. Now she asked pleadingly, "Aunt Madge *can* help me, can't she?"

"Of course," Marcia said with quick reassurance, and turned back to Stephanie.

Stephanie seemed relieved. "Well, I'm glad it's all over—coming home, I mean." She gave Marcia a shy look. "We're going to the orchards early this evening. Chet says it's all right for you to come along. He likes you."

Marcia smiled. "Thank you very much, but I must pack."

Stephanie's look became pitying. "That's too bad! I wanted you to see him actually *in* an orchard."

Marcia went downstairs to find Mrs. Murdock. Justin and Chester Jones were talking in the living room, and did not see her pass. Mrs. Murdock was in the kitchen, whipping up a cake, although the dinner dishes were still stacked unwashed on the sideboard. She paused for a split second to turn her flushed and shining face toward Marcia. "I can't stand not to do *something* special."

"It is wonderful, isn't it?" Marcia said sympathetically. "I don't mean to disturb you at this time, Mrs. Murdock, but I did want you to know that I'll not return in September."

Mrs. Murdock beat the creamy batter with slightly less enthusiasm. "School opens late?"

"No, no," Marcia said, annoyed. "I mean I'll not be back at all. I've—"

"I won't hear of it!" Mrs. Murdock cried as if suddenly enlightened. "There'll still be space for you. Stephanie's room is plenty large for both of them, and if they want it, they can have the back sunporch too."

"You don't understand. I'll not be in Riverville. I'll not—"

But Mrs. Murdock had returned to the beating with her original fervor, and she shouted above the noise: "*Nothing* could take that

408

room from you, Dr. Anderson. Why, we consider you one of the family. Even Justin. You've been through the bad time with us, and we wouldn't think of letting you miss out on the good one!"

"You're very kind," Marcia murmured resignedly. She would write Mrs. Murdock a letter when she was at last safely out of Riverville.

In the early evening, she wandered back to Main Hall, morbidly curious to look into the office that would be hers if she were to come back. The building was lighted and being thoroughly cleaned for John Willard Day. She found Charlie, who unlocked the door for her.

She clicked on the light and closed the door behind her. Scott had taken away most of his books, but had left behind a few complimentary copies of grammars and literature anthologies. The surface of the desk was cleared except for a much-used green blotter.

She went to the window and stood looking out at the Heart as she had so often seen him stand. She wasn't coming back, but if she were, this would be a good office. There was perhaps a ghost even here, but it was an elusive, impersonal one that would soon cease to bother— She started as the door opened abruptly.

"Well!" Scott was as surprised as she. He set down his Gladstone bag and took off his hat. He looked very neatly and carefully attired. "Have you graduated to this office?"

"Yes. I mean—no, I merely—"

"Oh, you needn't apologize. It's quite logical, but I didn't expect you to move in before I was gone."

"I'm not moving in. In fact, I'm not—"

"Believe me"—he gave her a thin smile and waved his hand—"it's *quite* all right—quite." He went over to the bookcase and frowned at the remaining books. "I've misplaced a Pope, and I thought I'd make sure I hadn't left it here. You didn't happen to see a Pope, did you— in a drawer or some obscure corner?"

"I didn't see a Pope," she said, standing by and feeling in the way, "but then I didn't look around very carefully."

"Really?" He shrugged and turned away from the bookcase. "It isn't here."

She moved to the door, convinced that he had come to the office for some reason other than to look for a book. "I'll go now," she said quickly. "I still have the most of my packing to—"

"Oh, but no!" he cried, reaching for his bag. "I shouldn't think of running you out. I had no intention whatever of intruding."

She forced a smile. "I'm glad to see you tonight, for I haven't yet had a chance to say a decent farewell. I do hope that you'll like Coningsby."

His eyebrows went up. "Do you know of any reason why I shouldn't?"

"Of course not. I merely—"

"Coningsby," he said seriously, "is everything that I wish John Willard could be. Even so"—he gave a final look around the small room—"I shall always retain a certain fondness for the old place." He shook his head sadly, and his words became a dirge for those left behind in the old place. But after a moment his face clouded and he seemed lost in a thought that had no relation to what he had said. Suddenly he set down his bag again. "This *is* farewell, isn't it?" he said then in a tone of surprise.

"Yes, it is." She hesitated, wanting to say something about Judith and him but not knowing how. She decided against trying, and held out her hand. "Good luck—and happiness."

And happiness! Scott thought ironically as he walked rapidly around the Heart. *Happiness is a perpetual possession of being well deceived.* Jonathan Swift had said that, and he, Owen Scott, had found no cause to doubt the essential accuracy of the definition . . . *the serene peaceful state of being a fool among knaves.* Yes, Swift was right about that too. That belonged to the definition.

He wondered what irrational impulse had led him back to the office. Perhaps it was in the nature of man to linger over the scenes of unhappiness. And certainly it was characteristic of his own perfidious fate that he go back at the same moment Marcia Anderson was taking possession.

At the tip of the Heart, he paused almost against his will to look back at the Summit. He hadn't stayed around long enough to come into a Summit office. Had he been wrong? Had he—

He turned sharply and went on. He hadn't been wrong. In another year, he might have become an associate professor, and finally, when he was old and senile, they might reward him with a full professorship —the way J.W. handed out silver watches to his factory employees who had endured four or five decades of service. Grant was the Big Man here, as solid and firmly entrenched as a stone wall, against which he'd be butting his head to the end of his days.

When he reached the Heights, he purposely crossed over to the Park side, but he could not prevent his looking across the street to see his house. Light from the setting sun had transformed the ugly gray stucco to a soft pink. The windows on his side looked black, but the Holcomb windows were cozily lighted from within and he could— No, not the Holcombs—the Briggses. But the Briggses weren't real to him. The past year was a long blur, filled with dimly moving figures and pain. . . .

He set down his bag and closed his hand tightly around his left arm above the elbow. His right arm ached too, but he had, for some obscure reason, developed the habit of holding only the left arm. Of course, bending the right arm at the elbow gave it some relief, so that the one gesture accomplished—

He laughed grimly and bent down for his bag. There wasn't a nerve or muscle in either arm with which he didn't have an intimate acquaintance.

When he came within sight of the station, he realized suddenly that he must look as tired and hot and dusty as he felt. Irritated, he threw down his bag once more and pulled out his handkerchief. He had meant to board the train looking fresh and brisk. But for a while he stood motionless, staring abstractedly ahead of him. He was thinking that it would be good to be on a train among people whom he didn't know and who didn't know him. . . .

A pink house with black windows. Fantasy house . . . unreal. That would be the way he'd have to remember it, that would be *this is the way the world ends*.

Damn that line—always clogging up his thought.

He moved quickly then. He took off his hat and rubbed the handkerchief hard against his forehead. He ran a pocket comb through his hair. At the side of the road, he stooped and pulled out of the ground a fist full of dandelion leaves. With these he wiped the dust off his shoes. The leaves were cool in his hot hand and he reluctantly threw them aside.

He rested a moment longer, but his mind raced over what little he knew about Coningsby and the English people he had met there. Beagle, the Chairman, was picturesque but not important. Of the Old School . . . white hair and Vandyke . . . gentle eyes turned lovingly upon the past . . . Addisonian English. There was a younger man— James B. Carmichael—the real force in the department. He had sensed that immediately. Thank God for his intuitiveness about such matters. Carmichael was the man to watch. He'd be friendly with James B. Carmichael, but wary. . . . He'd get along.

Besides, he had another book in mind.

He grabbed up his bag and moved on, but when he came to the platform, he halted again. A man was standing in the middle of it, his back to him, but there was something so familiar about the back that he was sure he knew him. He was deeply disappointed, for this meant that his comfortable anonymity would be gone. All he needed were a few hours alone before he reached Coningsby . . . a few hours to remove the last doubts so *this is the way the world ends*. . . .

He cursed inwardly and took a violent step up on the platform. At the sound of the step, the man turned so that he could see that it was J. W. MacMillan. His fury and disappointment slid away from him. "Good evening," he said cheerfully. "Could it be that we are taking the same train?"

J.W. slipped a white envelope into his pocket. "Good evening, Dr. Scott. We probably are—if you are going east."

"I am," Scott said, pleased to hear MacMillan call him by his name so readily. "I'm on my way to Coningsby, you know."

"Coningsby?" J.W. frowned slightly. "Oh, yes—a college. That reminds me, Scott— I'm glad of this opportunity to tell you personally how sorry I and the other trustees are to see you leave John Willard. We consider it a great loss to us."

"Thank you," Scott said solemnly, although his spirits soared. "I trust that you understand that I make this move only after the most serious consideration."

"So you mentioned," J.W. said with a faint smile, "in your letter of resignation. Incidentally, I've also been meaning to congratulate you upon your book, *Sentimental—Sentimental—*"

"*Farce,*" Scott said after a modest wait. "*Sentimental Farce.*"

"Of course. I looked into it and found it decidedly entertaining."

"Thank you again." Scott sighed. "It is a much misunderstood book, Mr. MacMillan, and I find it a pleasant change to talk with one who has the rare ability to enter into the spirit of intellectual satire."

"I liked it," J.W. said simply. "I particularly enjoyed your interpretation of women scholars. In fact, I recommended it to my uncle— Philip Willard, the poet."

"Ah, yes—the poet," Scott murmured, racking his brains to fit a poem to Philip Willard. He was unsuccessful and so decided it wiser to be done with the matter. "I use satire in the manner of my eighteenth-century predecessors. To me it is ridicule with the purpose of correction. A man fears ridicule more than he does serious admonishment. Hence, I seek not only to expose, but to reform; not only to—" He stopped, aware that J.W. had made a restless movement.

"Very interesting," J.W. said, and looked bored.

"I must see about checking this thing," Scott said hastily, reaching for his bag. "I should be only a minute or two."

J.W. watched the tall young man step briskly into the station, and now that he was alone, he allowed his annoyance to show in his face. Scott had a crisp, confident air about him that he liked, but underneath even that breathed the pedagogue, which was bound to appear every now and then—as witness the address on the satiric spirit to which he had already been subjected. Thank heavens for reserved seats on the train. It was extremely unlikely that they'd be sitting together.

Absently he lighted a cigarette, wondering if he had time to look over Russ's letter again before Scott came out of the station. He moved nearer to the lighted window, but decided not to risk it. For one thing, it was a very long letter, and for another, he knew it now as well as he would ever know it.

His hand touched the pocket that held the letter. It was a queer letter and in many ways an unsatisfactory one; yet Russ had at least ended his long and confusing discourse with the remark that *therefore* he had decided to return home and to the John Willard Tractor Company after the war, and to stay until his mind told him to do otherwise.

He didn't understand the *therefore,* and the restrictive time clause irritated him; but the rest of it justified his steady conviction that Russ would return to him.

He glanced in the direction of his plant. Twilight obscured the lettering of the big sign. Strange that it had never occurred to him that it was dead at night.

John Willard Tractor Company. John Willard College. And tomorrow was John Willard Day. He admitted to himself a certain disappointment in being absent from the ceremonies. He enjoyed his annual appearance. . . . But he needed a vacation badly, and leaving tonight would give him one extra day in Maine. As it was, he had only two short weeks before he had to go to Chicago, where he would be in the thick of it again. Without doubt, it was good for him to manage his leaving exactly as he was managing it. Without doubt. . . .

He began to walk suddenly. The tic by his eye had given a faint throb, and he had discovered that abrupt motion sometimes stopped it. At the end of the platform he turned and started across it again, but by the window he halted, realizing that Scott might come back at any moment and find him pacing nervously. The tic had subsided obediently, but that small area of his face remained sensitive, as if to remind him that it had a will of its own and would start up again whenever it wished.

Deliberately he selected a safe topic for his mind. Why had Briggs bought one of Duncan's things? He distinctly remembered Martin Anderson's saying that Duncan couldn't paint. Still . . . Briggs wasn't a man to throw away a hundred dollars. Perhaps Duncan had developed. He could of course write Martin Anderson to ask for his estimate of Duncan's future market value. . . .*Anderson.*

The tic was now going fiercely. He didn't try to stop it. He didn't try to stop his thought. He turned to stare at the corner of the station by the road, admitting at last that he had been hoping that in some miraculous way she would have heard of his leaving on this particular train and rush to him, begging to be reinstated in his life. . . .

But the space was empty and still, and he looked away, angry. Why couldn't she have been content to be pure woman?

Yet even under the anger he had the disturbing knowledge that as time went on, he would forget the quarrel and the uneasiness, and remember only her beauty as she had first appeared to him, when he was still unaware of the senseless complexity of her nature. He was surprised to note the enduring strength of his physical desire for her, and he knew that for a long while he would think of her at unexpected moments when he was least armed against her and when—

"Sorry," Scott said apologetically as J.W. started. "I thought you heard me. You have remarkable powers of concentration."

Ignoring this, J.W. looked down the tracks. "Our train's coming, I believe."

Scott looked too and said, "Excellent!" But he was sorry. He cursed the stupid baggagemaster who had kept him inside the station arguing that it was too late to check his bag and who had therefore shortened his time with J.W. For it had occurred to him that it was indeed fitting for him to be leaving with J.W. Two successful men—

The train roared by and slid to a stop. The great noise filled him with an excitement, and he eagerly hurried after J.W. to the nearest coach. The brakeman swung down, his feet making a soft thud on the ground *not with a bang but a whimper.*

He stopped in sudden fear. What were those words? And then he understood that they were meant to follow the ones that had been haunting him.

> *This is the way the world ends*
> *Not with a bang but a whimper.*

His mind worked fast and automatically. "The Hollow Men," T. S. Eliot, 1925. A real—

He looked blankly at J.W. as he gave him a gentle tap on the arm and said, "After you."

"Oh, yes—yes, thank you." He went up the steps and waited inside the coach. J.W. joined him, examining his ticket and saying, "Wouldn't it be a coincidence if we should happen to have seats together?"

"Yes—oh, yes." He fumbled for his own ticket and brought it out into the light. "B-13," he read.

"Mine," J.W. said after a moment, "is B-12."

Scott smiled, suddenly aware of what was happening. He was going to be sitting with J.W. Two successful men leaving Riverville. His moment of panic was over. "Evidently we reserved our seats at the same time."

"Evidently," J.W. said, and led the way down the aisle.

Chapter Five

IMPATIENTLY Marcia readjusted the pillow between her back and the wall, wondering why she had ever thought it enjoyable to sit on the floor and drink coffee. The room irritated her, and with a shock of guilt, she realized that even Dr. Ware's sharp voice irritated her.

"Or didn't you read it?" Dr. Ware asked abruptly.

"No, I didn't," she said defiantly. And the talk bored her. Books, books, books!

Dr. Ware arose for more coffee and seemed surprised when Marcia declined a second cup. Resettling herself on the floor, she said cheerfully, "So you've been too busy teaching to read. That must mean that you've found yourself at John Willard—that you've come to like it."

Marcia thought she sounded smugly satisfied, as if she were really saying: You see how right I was to send you off to John Willard? You see how fittingly I arranged your life?

She said flatly, "I'm leaving John Willard."

"Oh. Does John Willard know it?"

"Naturally," Marcia said, suddenly angry. She had expected Dr. Ware to show more feeling. "That is—well, I resigned last spring, but . . ." She hesitated, feeling confused, and Dr. Ware seemed amused. "For reasons too complicated to explain," she said stiffly, "I have another week in which to make my final decision, but in my own mind it's quite settled."

"I see." Dr. Ware considered this as she lighted a cigarette. "What an odd procedure. They must like you."

"You don't *understand!*" Marcia cried, although she had meant to stay cool and distant. "I'm through with John Willard—teaching— Blake. Everything."

Dr. Ware regarded her silently, then said again, "I see. I'm sorry, Marcia, but"—she shrugged faintly—"it's your life, of course."

It's *my* life now, Marcia thought ironically—now that you've discovered that it is the wrong life for me. "I'm sorry too—sorry to have wasted so much time. It's difficult to understand why you thought I'd make a good teacher."

"Teacher?" Dr. Ware frowned judiciously. "I don't recall that we ever discussed your capacities for teaching, Marcia."

"We didn't," Marcia said bitterly. "You hardly mentioned teaching. You led me to believe that it was a kind of afterthought to scholarship."

Dr. Ware seemed amused again, but her smile was sad. "They always come back accusingly. Isn't it strange?"

Marcia ignored this. "You said that teaching was simply a means of earning a living while one worked as a scholar."

"Did I?" Dr. Ware put down her cup and leaned back against the wall as if suddenly very tired. "Yes, I suppose that I did. I'm not infallible, as you"—she laughed brusquely—"are certainly in the process of discovering. You know, I still think of myself as a potentially great scholar bogged down by teaching." She was silent and thoughtful, then added: "I had a leave last year."

Marcia thought this irrelevant. "I'm glad," she said politely.

Dr. Ware looked at her as if she had read her thought. "There's a point to this, my child. I had pinned my hope on that leave for years. At last the scholar in me was to be born. I was going to write the kind of book that gets set up on special reference shelves and is read by a few honest souls out of a stoic sense of duty." She laughed again as she bent forward to stub out her cigarette. "You've guessed it. I didn't write it."

415

Marcia was vaguely embarrassed. Dr. Ware seldom talked about herself. "I am sure," she said, "that you were too tired to write."

"Hell! I wrote." Dr. Ware got up and went to the great desk. She jerked open a drawer and lifted out a thick bundle of typewritten pages. "And this is what I wrote." She read from the top sheet, " 'How To Teach the Course Commonly Called Survey of English Literature.' See what I mean? I couldn't take a leave from teaching."

Marcia looked up at her, puzzled. "You mean that you discovered you preferred teaching to scholarship?"

Dr. Ware smote the manuscript with her fist. "This," she said indignantly, "is a *scholarly* work, Marcia Anderson." Then she gave it a gentler pat. "It's even going to be published. All I have to do now is shorten the title."

Marcia said nothing but watched Dr. Ware carefully put her manuscript back into the desk drawer. She found herself wondering why 'How To Teach the Course Commonly Called Survey of English Literature' should be published and her Blake rejected.

"The mistake I made," Dr. Ware said, sitting down again, "was separating the two—teaching and scholarship."

"But they're not the same," Marcia said.

Dr. Ware nodded. "Right—and I didn't say that they were. But they go together. Scholarship is a method, a way of digging out truth. It's not a subject matter. It should be a verb, not a noun. And teaching is a way of pointing out what you've discovered. Why, you can't *keep* them apart—any more than you can prevent a living thing from wanting nourishment."

"Yes—yes, I think that is right," Marcia said in spite of herself. "I have come to—" She stopped, remembering that she had no right to be interested. "It doesn't matter," she said, her anger rising again. "You were wrong about me and scholarship too! You said I had objectivity—but everyone who reads my work on Blake says that it's too *subjective*. You see, you were wrong again!"

"I tried to discourage you about Blake, Marcia."

"This has nothing to do with Blake," Marcia said, leaning forward intently. "It's my approach that's wrong. I would have made the same mistake with any figure I might have chosen to study."

"Good! You've learned a big lesson." Dr. Ware reached for another cigarette, but suddenly pushed it back into its package. She got up again and walked restlessly before one of the big bookcases that still served to partition off sections of her room. "How could *I* know that you were to lose your objectivity in your work!" She ran her knuckles sharply across a long row of closely packed books. It was an angry gesture.

Watching, Marcia felt a sense of triumph, as if she had been waiting for that anger. Now they were face-to-face—Alice Ware and Marcia Anderson.

"I could not guess that you were not what you seemed to be," Alice Ware said then. "You seemed remote, independent, aloof. You didn't appear to need people; you didn't seem drawn to them in any way. But you were drawn to books, and you had a mind that could cope with them. So I thought to myself, here is one with all the wrong qualities for common happiness. Yet if those same qualities could be directed toward scholarship, how fine it would be."

Marcia sat very still, her small triumph gone. All those years ago, when she had felt secure under the protective friendship, Alice Ware had thought of her as a problem student, a case. . . . "And all the time I thought you liked me," she said, some force dragging the childish words out of her, although as soon as she heard them, she wished with her whole being that she could recall them.

Alice Ware accepted them calmly. "I did like you, Marcia. I was downright flattered when you listened to me and talked with me. Yes, I remember those talks—without half trying. And there's another thing that you're ready to know now. When you went to John Willard, there was an opening in my department which you could have filled. I deliberately did not tell you about it, although I should very much have liked having you."

"I don't understand," Marcia said, still hurt.

"I did not tell you because I knew that what is happening now was bound to happen, and that if it came when we were working together, it would come explosively—perhaps disastrously."

Marcia looked up fearfully. "What is happening now?"

Alice Ware laughed. "Something perfectly natural. Don't look so scared. You're shifting relationships—that's all. Today you're not looking upon me as a student looks upon a teacher, but you're seeing me simply as a human being—and a very ordinary one at that. That is why you are so critical of my every word; why I bore you, why even this room—"

"That's not true!" Marcia cried.

"How do I know that this has happened?" Alice Ware went on as if she had not heard Marcia. "By the fact that you came laden with accusations. Something has happened to you, Marcia—something that has caused you anguish, and you seek to blame me because it was I who gave you the first little shove to where you are now. But let me tell you this: you would not be able to think of me as a meddlesome and blundering agent in your life if you had not first stopped thinking of me as your teacher."

"You're wrong," Marcia said because she thought she should say it. "I'm sure that you're wrong." She wanted to leave quickly, for it seemed to her that something had ended and it was time to leave. But a strange and heavy sadness kept her there. It was not the feeling she had expected.

She did not look at Alice Ware, but she saw her with new clarity

417

. . . saw her growing old among students and deliberately sending away those whom she liked. This was Alice Ware, who had once appeared efficient and enviable because she managed her life without personal ties. . . . "Oh, I'm sorry," she said involuntarily. "I'm so sorry!"

"You mean for me, don't you?" Alice Ware said sharply. "Yes, I can see that in your face. Sentimental rubbish! When I crawl into my grave, I intend to call it a good life spent."

Marcia flushed. "I didn't mean—"

"No matter. Run along and shed a few tears for me. They'll make you feel better. If after a year or two, you find that something has outlived the need that used to bring you to me, well, then perhaps . . ."

"I'll be back very soon," Marcia promised hastily, although she thought that she would not want to return for a long while.

Marcia went home thinking of herself as Alice Ware had once seen her. *You seemed remote, independent, and aloof.* . . . Alice Ware had seen the shield against Martin and Virginia.

She entered the house and stood by the door, looking around her and seeing every object with new significance. She had been wrong to go to Alice Ware, for she had nothing to do with the lie she had lived. Nor had even J.W., she thought suddenly. She had lived it out with him, but it had begun in this house and with the people in it. Here, then, it must end.

Impulsively she went to the studio door. *Martin, I understand now. You did me a grave wrong by forcing Virginia into my life, but you as an individual had that right, and I forgive you.*

She knocked rapidly on the door and opened it without waiting for him to call out. He only half turned away from the canvas before him and looked at her blankly, still absorbed in what he had been thinking as he studied his new painting.

"Martin, I—"

He moved suddenly and smiled. "Why, hello, Doctor! What brings you?"

"I want to—" She stopped, thinking of the shocked surprise that her words would cause him and the endless, tortuous explaining that would be necessary. She had been wrong to plan to say it so quickly; she would lead up to it carefully. . . . "I want to go on with the portrait," she said.

He took off his glasses and stared at her. "What portrait?"

"The one you started a couple of years ago. Or didn't you keep the sketches?"

He shrugged. "I never destroy a line from the hand of Martin Anderson. They're filed away, but they won't do us any good."

"You mean I've aged that much?"

He gave her an expressionless scrutiny, and she moved uneasily

418

away from it. "You've matured," he said, "and don't let me think you so shallow-brained that you want that maturity concealed."

Matured, she thought ironically. She went to the dais and sat on the straight chair. *Look, Martin, I've been through a very special kind of hell, and in a way you put me into it; but I want you to know that I understand and forgive. . . .*

But now was still not the time. Half his mind had stayed on his painting. She glanced at it casually, but then lingered over it. The portrait was of a girl not yet in her teens. She was thin and big boned, with straight light hair pulled back carelessly from her face and held in place with bobby pins. The hazel eyes were eager or perhaps greedily expectant. The decided arch of the brows and the flaring nostrils gave to the face a kind of wild beauty, but they might also mean cruelty. She sat forward in a cane chair obviously intended for a much older woman, and seemed on the verge of making a great discovery, although it was clear that she did not have the least idea what it was she was about to discover.

Martin had got himself a pad and charcoal and now dragged the stool into position. "Ah, yes," he said, sitting down and looking at her again, "your face is much better adjusted to my art than it was— By the way, do you realize that you very rudely did not permit me even to start that portrait?"

"You went away," she said quickly.

"But I didn't stay away for two years—as you did. And if that's a reason, there's no use working now, for I'm going back to the Colony tomorrow."

"But this is different," she said significantly. "We'll finish *this* portrait."

"Is that so?" He gave her a quizzical look and adjusted the pad on his knee. She saw that he had not even noticed the significance. He thought merely that she was in a mood.

"As I recall," he said, the amused look leaving his face as he became absorbed in his sketch, "your face was then too mask-like. I had to make you grimace and laugh like an idiot to be able to see the possible mobility. But now"—he flashed her a genuinely admiring look—"but now, Marcia, your beauty is at its height."

"I'm not flattered," she said dryly. "You make it sound as though I'll begin to fade tomorrow."

He smiled complacently. "Not tomorrow, my dear. You have at least five good years—and probably more."

Five good years. She shuddered. Rushing time, and so much of it had been taken away from her. *Martin, you must understand immediately, for there is to be a new beginning, and it is already late for me to start over. When you brought Virginia home with you, time stopped for me, so that even when I grew to adulthood, there was always with me that defeated child. . . .*

419

"Martin, we had a good time together when there were only you and—when I was very young, didn't we?"

"Uh-huh," he said absently. "I spoiled you, however, and you had temper tantrums which—"

"Not until Virginia came," she broke in quickly.

"Well, that's good, then, for she could cope with them, I'm sure. I couldn't."

For a moment the old fury flamed up within her, and she turned her head abruptly.

"Marcia!" he called out sharply.

She turned back then, her face calm. The return of the old feeling had been a warning. She had come to Martin in the wrong spirit. *I trapped them all with my hate, making them suffer. . . .* Those were her own words, said to Grant, when she had perceived and understood clearly. Yet today she was offering forgiveness.

There was nothing to forgive. There should be only acceptance— but not from her alone; from him too. He owed her at least that. . . . *It was through J.W. that I discovered . . .*

"Martin, do you remember the MacMillans?"

"Remember the MacMillans!" he repeated incredulously. "Why would I forget one of my most successful portraits?"

"This has nothing to do with Grace's portrait," she said impatiently. "Do you remember that there is a son, whose mother is dead, and there is J.W., his father, who—"

"I *knew* there was something I wanted to tell you!" he exclaimed triumphantly, holding the charcoal arrested over the pad. "I received a letter from J. W. MacMillan yesterday—a most impersonal epistle that contains not one reference or even remote allusion to you." He waited a moment, then went back to the sketch. "Do you know what I expected when I saw the envelope? A formal request for your hand, signed by two witnesses. After all, Marcia, you gave us some reason to believe . . . Well, it seems to me that your methodically spending all legal holidays in his home would be more than adequate grounds for marriage to a man like MacMillan." As she still said nothing, he looked up again. "It didn't work out?"

She shook her head. *No, Martin, it didn't work out. There were many reasons, but perhaps the real one was that I discovered that he himself was never real to me. It was you—*

He sighed. "I never felt at ease over that prospective alliance, although, all things but feelings considered, it should have been a fortunate one—Anderson brains, talent, and beauty, and MacMillan money. Ah, yes . . . Beauty and the Tractor."

"Don't be flippant! You bore me. You—you . . ."

"Oh, I'm sorry, Marcia," he said quickly. "So it was a painful experience?"

She nodded slowly. *Painful, yes; but also the means to the begin-*

ning. "Martin, I can't explain it very well, but I—"

"Of course not," he said kindly. "I didn't mean to be such a clumsy fool. There is no reason in this world why you should be made to talk about it. At least wait until the pain is gone."

But, she thought desperately, when the pain is gone, so is the clarity. It is already dim for me now. That is why I must—

"I'll tell you what the letter did say," he went on briskly. "He wants me to predict Duncan's worth in twenty years."

She was silent for a minute, then asked resignedly: "How are you going to answer him?"

He brandished the charcoal. "There is only one answer possible. Duncan is an artist, and artists are unpredictable."

She smiled faintly. "He won't like that answer."

"I hope not. I don't like his letter. And I have no intention of hanging a price on my friend Kim."

Seriously, Martin, you have no right to draw the talk away from what I have to say to you. . . . "Seriously, Martin, what do you think of Kim's work? You called him an artist. There was a time when you hesitated to do that."

He shrugged. "He has developed a sense of form. He already had the feeling. Of course"—he looked at her defiantly—"of course, I do not find it in my heart to endorse his kind of art. He and I shall never agree. If his painting mirrors the world, then his world is not mine." The pad slipped to the floor and he did not move to pick it up. He turned from her and stared at his portrait of the girl. "I wonder"—he got up and went to the portrait—"I wonder how many people see his world and not mine."

She watched him curiously. His manner was solemn, and on his face was a puzzled, questioning look. Suddenly she understood that working side by side with Kim had brought him a challenge, and that for this fleeting moment at least he was confronting his work in doubt.

She was saddened, for she knew that he was not one to sustain doubt. It seemed to her that she was seeing not Martin, her father, but a man unknown to her—a man who was used to being confident and clear-sighted, but who now looked at the work of his life and found cause to wonder.

Her eyes went once more to the portrait, seeing the boldly definite line, the exact and significant detail, the fulfilled intention. . . . "It's a magnificent portrait," she said.

He started guiltily. "Naturally. But I am glad to have your approbation, my dear." He reseated himself on the stool and bent for the pad, and when he straightened, there had returned to his face his habitual expression of intelligent self-approval. "However, as I remember, my dull realism usually evoked from you a certain—shall I say—unsympathetic response."

You are right, Martin. That was part of the pretense. But in the

421

moment past I saw you as a man unrelated to me in any way—free of my love and hate. I am glad of your freedom, and through it I shall perhaps gain some for myself.

She smiled wearily as she thought how these words would startle and embarrass him. She put them aside and answered him in the half serious, half light way in which he liked to talk with her: "Oh, I've acquired tolerance for all forms of painting, Martin."

He chuckled, appreciative of the spirit in which she had spoken, and contentedly began a fresh sketch.

But once in her own room, she admitted to herself that she felt dissatisfied. It was as if she had been cheated of something that should have been rightfully hers.

She allowed herself to think of Grant and acknowledged the aching loneliness she had for him. He alone in the world cared what she felt and thought. . . . She had come home, but without him she seemed among alien people.

Suddenly she took up the photograph of her mother from her dresser and put it in the bottom of a drawer. She was done with empty symbols. She thought of Blake, and brought out the boxed manuscript. Settling on the floor, she opened it and slowly and ceremoniously tore up the title page. She went on page after page, pretending satisfaction, although she was aware that it was a meaningless rite, destroying nothing and signifying nothing real. . . .

Virginia called to her from the hall, and when she had answered, cautiously opened the door. She stared at Marcia and the growing heap of torn paper beside her.

Marcia barely looked up. "Well, ask me."

"What *are* you doing?" Virginia asked obediently.

"It's obvious, isn't it?" she said in the tense, curt voice she habitually used for Virginia. "I'm tearing up Blake. I'm—" Then she remembered that she felt differently toward Virginia . . . understanding and forgiving. "I'm tearing up Blake," she repeated in a soft and gentle voice.

Anyone but Virginia might have thought the sudden change of voice queer, but she accepted it unquestioningly and said simply, "That's a pity, Marcia."

Marcia sighed inwardly. If she were to start eating the paper, Virginia would accept it calmly. "Won't you sit down?" she said.

"If you're sure I'm not . . ." Virginia pulled out the desk chair and sat down quietly, still watching Marcia at her strange task. "I'm sure that you know best," she said hesitantly, "but it does seem such a waste. You worked at it for so many years."

So you remember those years too? You remember how I locked myself away from you and Martin. . . . "I wasn't a very sociable being to have around the house, was I?"

"Well, who could be sociable and accomplish what you have!" Virginia said indignantly. "I always admired your perserverance and love of work. Even when very young you had those qualities. Of course, I sometimes wondered . . ." She seemed to decide not to finish what she had been saying. "Oh, well. It is over now, and I can't see that any harm has been done."

"What did you wonder?" Marcia asked intently. Wasn't it, after all, with Virginia that her score was to be settled? Perhaps it was right that she had failed with Martin.

"Nothing that matters now," Virginia said apologetically, "but I used to worry that you'd injure your health by working so hard . . . and then it seemed such lonely work for one so young." She laughed. "But it's clear that you're in very good health, and I guess you wouldn't be Martin's daughter if you didn't have the capacity to lose yourself in your chosen work. You're very much like him in many ways, you know."

"I'm like my mother," Marcia said out of habit. Violently she ripped a page in two. What lack of understanding—what *complete* lack! How could she make a fresh start if no one helped her?

Virginia had said nothing to her remark. She was used to it and would have been surprised if it hadn't been said.

Conspicuously Marcia glanced at the vacant spot on her dresser where the photograph had been. Why didn't Virginia notice that it was gone? But she didn't even turn to look. "Nevertheless," she was saying, "I was very glad when you seemed to relax and enjoy yourself with your friends the MacMillans. . . ." She hesitated, then went on rapidly, "I'm no good at pretending, Marcia. I came to your room deliberately to ask . . . Well, the minute I came into the house, Martin told me about you and Mr. MacMillan. He is very concerned . . . said that he was sure it had been a painful experience for you. Marcia, you seldom take me into your— But if there's anything I—we can do to help. . . ."

You can listen to me, Marcia thought, and understand. Carefully she once more selected the words. *I never loved J.W., but I was bound to him by the unsatisfied desire that filled me with hate when Martin brought you into our lives. The loss of him, who was really Martin, would have meant utter desertion again. . . .*

"Forgive me, Marcia," Virginia said, misunderstanding her silence. "Anyone should know that you wouldn't want to talk about it yet. It's just that I became overanxious and thought perhaps . . ." She was silent for a moment, then said firmly, "However, Marcia, there is one thing that I am determined to say, although it too may sound insensitive. I am glad—yes, happy—that you are not going to marry him. It is not easy to be a second wife."

Marcia looked at her, startled. *It is not easy to be a second wife. . . .*

Virginia did not seem to know what she had said, for her face showed no sadness, only a kind of concern, which was for her, Marcia.

She had come from the beauty parlor and held her straw hat in her lap. Her hair was in neat waves, which by tomorrow would be not quite so neat, for she still had no knack of fixing her own hair. There were the broad brow, the gentle but alert eyes, and the firm mouth that Marcia knew so well yet did not know, and there was about her very presence that air of calm capability that was so necessary to Martin's self-confidence. . . .

She realized suddenly that she had not seen Virginia for many years. Virginia, a second wife to Martin, who was constantly preoccupied with his own work; stepmother to the remote and unrelenting Marcia. . . .

"I understand," she said, pushing aside the papers and rising to her feet, "oh, I understand how hard it has been for you. Martin has always been selfishly engrossed in his—"

"Marcia!" Virginia rose too, shock in her face. "Surely you didn't think that I was *complaining!* I was thinking of you—"

"And I've been impossible," Marcia went on excitedly. "For once, let's not pretend, Virginia. I was a hundred times more selfish than Martin, but now I understand why, and at last we can begin—" She stopped abruptly, for even through her eagerness she was aware of the fear that had come into Virginia's face.

"But Martin's work and you are my life," Virginia said, striking her fist gently against the back of the chair. "I have made them that, for that is the way I wanted my life to be."

Marcia said nothing, for she knew that Virginia was talking more to herself than to her. And I was about to take half your life away from you, she thought, by carefully explaining to you how and why you made me so damnably unhappy.

She shrugged and made her face indifferent. "Well, all right, Virginia. I'm certainly not going to force sympathy upon you." That would sound more natural to Virginia, and she winced inwardly at the relief that surged into her face.

Virginia laughed embarrassedly. "What a strange topic. How did we ever . . .? Oh, yes, But now you do believe me when I say that my life is full and happy, don't you, Marcia? I've often thought that I have more than my share of good things."

"I always did believe that," Marcia said dryly.

Virginia lingered by the door. "If ever you feel like talking . . ."

"It was just one of those things. There's no need to drag it out in words."

Virginia nodded understandingly. "Yes, I'd feel that way too." She gave another worried glance at the Blake papers. "I wish . . . I mean, it *does* seem a great pity to destroy so many words. Still, I suppose"— she brightened over her own thought—"it's something gained to have all that out of your system. "

Marcia laughed suddenly. "Virginia, that's the most encouraging thing ever said to me."

Virginia smiled, pleased. "Dinner at six-thirty, Marcia." She went into the hall, closing the door after her.

Marcia stared at the closed door. It seemed symbolic of some finality which she had accepted but did not yet understand.

Abruptly she turned away from it and looked down at the torn Blake papers. Wastepaper . . . wasteyears.

She was not to be permitted to create a new beginning. Her father and Virginia had unknowingly refused to accept her new self. It was as if nothing had happened to her.

She had tried to hate and to blame, to forgive and to thrust her new awareness upon others; yet she had effected no change.

Fearfully she glanced again at the door. Was that what she had sensed when Virginia had closed it, leaving her alone—a return to herself, the trap of the past?

Yet she felt within her a calm acceptance which did not match her thoughts. Did that—the accepting without struggle—signify final defeat?

She thought it strange that defeat should bring peace and lightness. Her laggard mind did not understand, but her body had found some mysterious answer of its own, for the tiredness that had oppressed it for many months was gone. It was as if a danger had been narrowly averted and she could now relax.

She moved to her desk and took up the sealed letter she had written to Grant weeks ago. It would be mailed tomorrow. . . .

Suddenly she ripped it open and reread it. The words were formal and merely repeated her wish to resign. When she had written them, they had seemed right and inevitable. Now she knew that she would have to test and measure their meaning again before she could send them on to him.

She stood holding the letter and thinking of him, until it seemed that he was in the room with her. It had always been easy to reach him with her thoughts. She had never doubted his reality, even when Janice had tried to keep them apart with her insinuations about Millie . . . even when she had been most confused about every other person and thing in her life.

And even knowing about J.W., he had not withdrawn. His love for her had grown in the very midst of the lie she had lived, and yet it was real. . . .

Without thinking, she tossed the letter down on the scattered Blake papers, and, when she realized what she had done, regarded it there in surprise. Well, that was all right. She would write another letter, a friendlier message, at least.

Wasteyears? Could they be called that when his love for her had come from them?

She wondered then if it were not as it should be that she had failed to make her father and Virginia see her as someone different from the Marcia that they knew. For she was beginning to understand that her present self had not suddenly and miraculously come into being, but had emerged from the aimless but relentless accumulation of past moments, not one of which could be set aside or annulled. They led to Now, and she had no self apart from them.

Curious, she knelt impulsively beside the papers. Could Blake too be real? She took up one of the still untorn pages and read a passage of her own writing.

> Love, Blake meant, is at once the fulfillment of self and the death of selfishness, for it alone is the sole and tenuous line between the tightly enclosed self and the other selves. It is through love that the self comes home, that the individual takes his place in the world. . . .

As she pondered these wise lines which she had written without wisdom, she thought beyond herself and Grant to students—not merely those who had forcibly impressed themselves into her life, but the long succession of individuals, some named and some unnamed in her memory, who made up the impersonal classes for which she had learned to be grateful. Long ago she had known that they served to draw her out of herself; but now she found it possible to believe that she also had given of herself to them.

Blake meant, she knew then, not only the love that went from individual to individual, but a great impersonal force that could embrace the whole world without losing strength. She remembered drawing near to that thought before, but not near enough to keep it as her own.

She knew now that she wanted to return to teach, and that not to return would be as meaningless as her other attempts to break the continuity of herself.

But would she also return to Grant?

She wanted him . . . she needed him. To admit that freely was like food and drink after hunger and thirst. . . . But she was still afraid of need, for it had been need that had driven her to J.W. Could she risk beginning another cycle of deception?

She didn't know. She could no longer think clearly. She would wait until she returned to John Willard; then she would decide. He would understand. . . .

After a minute, she went on tearing up the manuscript. It was no longer a meaningless rite, but an act of purpose. The work had merit as it was now, but she thought that she had the power to give it soundness and clarity too. With Blake at least she could make a completely fresh start.

She worked diligently, but when she reached the last chapter, she hesitated. She smiled then, amused with herself because she did not have the heart to destroy that chapter, which had, as the man from Hill-Moran had written her, "distinguished possibilities, and my suggestion to you, Miss Anderson, is that you expand this section at your earliest convenience. . . ."

She crammed the torn paper into the wastebasket and then carefully placed the still whole chapter into a manila folder, which she labeled and put in the top drawer of her desk. . . . .

The meeting was already in progress when Marcia entered the big room. Only President Cameron saw her as she stood for a minute at the back of the room. He sat alone in the front row and had turned his chair so that he could give one eye to the presiding Dean Briggs and the other to his faculty. Arnold Cunningham had the floor and was issuing detailed and familiar instructions on the forming of the academic procession for Convocation the next morning. Miss Schultz earnestly took minutes, but the other listeners appeared bored and restless. Colley openly read and rattled a newspaper. Dexter scribbled on a white pad. Webb was deep in a book, and Medora Day stared abstractedly at her quietly folded hands. . . .

Still Marcia hesitated. Had she been wrong to come to the meeting? She had gone straight from the station to her Main Hall office, thankful that everyone was busy with registration at the Summit. When she had found the notice of the unexpected meeting, she had decided that it would be a good thing to attend and thus see everyone first in a group. . . .

Everyone? Grant, of course. She had seen him the moment she entered the room. He was sitting in a middle row. Etta Wilson was on one side of him, Diaz on the other. He had not turned.

As she looked again over the roomful of people, she felt sudden contempt, for in that moment it came to her that they could not be different from her. Adults—although they posed so convincingly? Impossible. They too must be parasites living off childhoods, even as she had been one. . . .

But instinctively her eyes went back to Grant, and her thought took new form. Whatever else they might be, these people were also the essence of the multitude of endeavors and aims, successes and failures, that had come to be called John Willard College. Perhaps some did remain only out of weakness or fear, but there were others who struggled with awareness to stay and to belong. . . .

The large electric clock above her head clicked off a minute, and she quietly took a chair in the last row, between Dean Haskins and a small man whom she did not know. He had a frail, ascetic face that

427

looked incomplete without pince-nez on a black ribbon, and his hands clutched a John Willard catalogue. When she was seated, he leaned toward her and whispered, "I find these directions"—he gestured toward Cunningham—"distressingly complicated, but I suppose that someone will be on hand to help me when the time comes. I'm completely new here, you see. Dr. Gregory Smyth"—he held out a delicate hand—"that is Smyth with a *y*. English Department."

She shook his hand, but was uneasy. English Department? Could it be that Smyth with a *y* was replacing *her*? Had Grant not waited for her answer? Or had he at last become angry when she failed to send a personal message with her reply? Had he—

Then she remembered that both Scott and Meyerson had to be replaced, and she gave Dr. Smyth a sudden smile. "I'll be glad to help you when the time comes. I'm Dr. Ander—"

"Anderson!" Dr. Smyth finished before her. He wagged a finger at her. "Blake! Now, don't deny it. Dr. Grant has told me all about it. Have you not noticed a certain similarity between him and the seventeenth-century mystics? But perhaps"—he leaned toward her again, his voice almost whistling in his excitement—"I should explain that the seventeenth century is *my* passion—"

Dean Haskins caught the word and sent him a sharp look. "Later," Marcia whispered to him, and he subsided.

She stared at the back of Grant's head. It seemed incredible that he did not know she was in the room. She moved her chair, but the sound did not draw his attention. She cleared her throat and then coughed gently, and Dean Haskins hastily reached for her fresh linen handkerchief to ward off possible cold germs. Still Grant did not turn.

She caught a whiff of lily-of-the-valley fragrance from Dean Haskins' handkerchief, and it was this small thing that made her aware that she was actually back and glad to be there. She had an impulse to tell someone how she had almost not returned. "I'm so glad to see you," she whispered to Dean Haskins. "I was afraid you might not return."

The Dean looked stunned. "And why shouldn't I have returned?"

"I thought—well, I thought perhaps Dean Holcomb's leaving would—"

"I should choose larger footsteps to follow, Dr. Anderson. Furthermore, I should not think of leaving before completing my ninth year, and this . . ."

But Marcia was no longer listening to Dean Haskins. Words from Dean Briggs had floated into her consciousness. ". . . in brief, is Mr. MacMillan's suggestion . . ."

The mere name *MacMillan*. It was the first ghost that she had met since her return. She had known that it would come, but she had not thought it would be this soon. She was not yet prepared. . . .

Grant, she saw, had risen. "I should like to make certain," he was saying, "that I understand the proposal. It has been suggested that we accept an eight-hundred-dollar salary increase to teach a ten-week summer session. Is that correct?"

Colley folded his newspaper and snickered. "Nothing abstruse about that."

Dean Briggs tapped disapprovingly with his gavel. "That is correct, Professor Grant."

"One more question," Grant went on quickly as there was restless stirring in the room. "According to the proposal, is summer teaching to be *compulsory?*"

The question was almost lost. Iris had tiptoed in, carrying a suitcase, and as she found a chair two rows ahead of Marcia, people turned to watch her. Marcia watched too, as if life depended on her remembering every move that Iris made. When there was no longer excuse to watch, she stared out of the window into the expanse of soft, hypnotic sky. Her mind seemed as empty as the sky, and she was suddenly very sleepy.

As in a dream she heard Dean Briggs give Grant an answer and Grant say something more. All she knew was that Grant was dissatisfied, and she thought this foolish of him.

She wasn't sure why he was dissatisfied, but that didn't matter. Didn't he know that it was meaningless to move against the old pattern of J.W. and her and—

She started as Dexter's voice blasted forth, ragged with impatience: "Motion! Let's hurry this thing along. I move that we accept—"

But Cameron was on his feet. "It occurs to me that Professor Grant is raising this Question: If this Faculty should accept the Proposal, would the Individual Teacher be left free to choose between Accepting the additional salary and summer teaching and Rejecting the additional salary and summer teaching?" He turned to Dean Briggs. "I believe, Mr. Chairman, that the Question deserves an Answer."

Grant smiled and sat down.

"Now that *that's* settled," Dexter said desperately, "let's proceed! This is regis"—his voice broke—"tration, and I'm the Registrar; yet I'm made to sit here and play questions-and-answers. I move that we accept—"

"But *what's* settled?" Iris broke in. She returned Dexter's glare defiantly, and went on: "I admit that I'm lost because I came in late, although my coming late isn't my fault. I certainly didn't expect a meeting today, for we've never before had one during registration. Well, we'll skip that small point—but if this is a matter of voting my summers away, I want to know more about it before there's a motion on the floor."

Marcia listened to her in mild surprise. So Iris was like Grant, intent upon making a futile gesture. . . .

And then she was aware that Grant was looking directly at her. He had turned to see Iris as she spoke, and he had found her.

If only he had found her earlier. This was not the time. But as she met his look, it seemed to her that he was saying, "The time is now. There is no other time."

She tried to smile. She tried to put expression into her face, to make it as she had intended it to be when he first saw her. She had meant to make him understand that she had not yet decided. . . .

But she knew that her face stayed blank and apathetic. The absurd sleepiness was like fog in her mind, and her heavy-lidded eyes closed against her will. But even as she shut him out of her vision, she thought he said loudly, "Wake up, Marcia! You're not sleepy. You're under the old, rotten spell; and no one but yourself has put you there."

She glanced around her quickly, so vivid had been the illusion of his voice. But no one was paying her any attention, and he had turned back in his chair so that he could not see her.

She began to struggle against her apathy in earnest, and listened closely to Briggs, who was concluding his answer to Iris. ". . . idea occurred to Mr. MacMillan when he observed how successfully we managed our all-year-round teaching of the Cadets. In short, if we could do it for the Cadets, why can't we do it for civilian students?"

"And why can't we?" Colley demanded. "Perhaps it's the threatened salary increase that bothers some of you. Well, I suggest"—he stood and solemnly surveyed the room—"that those who are afraid they'll be *compelled* to accept a raise leave the room to escape all possible intimidation."

An undertone of laughter spread through the room as Colley re-seated himself. Marcia saw, however, that a few people did not look amused. Medora Day had become alert. Dean Haskins was unsmilingly thoughtful, and Dr. Smyth shook his head in an emphatic negative. Even Webb was now listening.

Etta Wilson seemed tensely ready to speak, but before she could do so, a History man in front of Marcia rose. She had never before heard him speak. "I should like to move," he said in a small voice, "that we accept the proposal as presented to us by Dean Briggs." As heads nodded in agreement, he gained courage and went on with a self-conscious little laugh: "I might add that I'd never be able to face Mrs. Stanford if for any reason I voted against a motion that increased my salary."

There was more appreciative laughter over this, but Grant stood quickly. "Yes, Stanford, that is exactly—"

"Gentlemen!" cried Dean Briggs, horrified. "There has been no second to the motion. How can we proceed with civilized discussion without—"

"I'll second it," Dexter said wearily. "I'll third, fourth, and fifth it. I'll do anything to end this meeting."

Grant had waited quietly. Now he said, "I sympathize with your impatience, Dexter. This is an unfortunate meeting time, and all of us"—he allowed his glance to rest briefly upon Marcia—"have urgent matters awaiting us. However, I still want to take another minute to maintain that in these days it is unfair to offer a man a goodly sum of money in exchange for a part of his freedom. My original question received no real answer; but I have been led to assume that if the faculty vote in favor of the motion, the individual instructor will no longer be free to choose not to teach the full year."

There was a silence; then Vincent Diaz spoke in a casual, off-hand manner and to no one in particular. "Being somewhat—familiar with Mr. MacMillan's ways of thinking, I know that the principle which regulates his decisions is efficiency. Surely it can be seen that *optional* summer teaching would not produce an efficient summer school. If you . . ."

Marcia forced herself to lose the sound of Diaz's voice, for it brought J.W. even nearer to her . . . and the threatening inertia. To help herself, she imagined what she would say to Grant if she and he were alone in this. "Don't you understand," she would say, "that all these words are futile? Words never matter to him. And can't you see that the thing he has done is personal? He is very angry with me and with you, and he knows that you'll fight his plan—and lose, because no one else cares enough."

And in her mind she listened to what he would say to her: "Personal? Yes, I understand what you mean, and I think it possible that his anger did play a small part in this. However"—he would smile slightly—"I think that he has merely confused students with tractors. That is more like him, you know. And, remember this, Marcia—whatever the motive, the issue for *us* can be—must be—impersonal. . . ."

Her thought was broken by the sound of Grant's real voice as he actually spoke. "Efficiency is fine," he said, looking at Diaz, "but do you really think that the efficiency of a college is to be measured by the mere number of students turned out on the academic assembly line? Isn't it possible that Mr. MacMillan has confused students with tractors? If we are to . . ."

Marcia leaned back against her chair, suddenly weak with a heady happiness. Some day she would tell him about this strange coincidence of words and thought. Coincidence? She didn't really believe that.

She wondered then where her fear was, and it came to her that she had discarded it long ago and had been haunted only by its echo. Why fear a need that she understood and accepted? The old need had been hidden and had driven her on in ignorance. . . .

Diaz spoke again, and she listened now without trying to withdraw. "Then you would deny education to the masses?" he said as if amused. "That is regrettable, Professor Grant, for I have been told that veterans will eventually come to us in great masses."

Grant smiled, but Marcia knew that he was holding back anger. "I assure you that I heartily approve of the G.I. Bill of Rights—and even summer sessions, if they are staffed by those who freely choose to teach them. But let's not be sidetracked again. I wish merely to point out that to give up the traditional summer vacation is to relinquish also the opportunity to continue the scholarship that prevents teaching from becoming shallow."

"We can't *all* pretend to a genuine interest in scholarship," Colley said with sarcastic politeness.

Grant shrugged. "Perhaps not. But that doesn't change my view, and I'll even generalize my contention. The individual should be free to teach all year *or* to forego the larger salary and spend the time as he sees fit."

"As he sees fit?" Dean Briggs repeated sceptically. "But what if he saw fit to fish all summer?"

Grant smiled again. "Fishing has produced some noble literature, and, I should guess, some good, sound thinking."

"What's wrong with fishing?" someone asked belligerently.

"Nothing, nothing," Briggs said hastily. "I like to fish myself. My one concern, however, is that we protect ourselves against the accusation of laziness. Personally, I admire hard workers. My father was a country schoolteacher and he never had a vacation, and his father . . ."

"Oh, my," murmured Dr. Smyth, his face drawn with worry. "This is horribly serious. No one seems to realize . . . If I had known this was going to happen, I should have never left . . ."

Marcia kept her eyes on Grant. Something about his attitude told her that he did not intend to speak again. She thought of the impersonal manner in which he had spoken, and how he had not mentioned the tortuous way in which he had been forced to pursue his own scholarship. She understood that now he was deliberately leaving it up to the rest of them, and she felt that he was waiting and listening. . . .

"You've quite missed the point," she said loudly, cutting into Dean Briggs' words. Everyone turned to stare at her, and she didn't know what next to say. But she arose and stood behind her chair. "Teaching must leave time for scholarship. The mistake is in trying to separate them," she went on with sudden ease, and offered up a silent prayer of gratitude to Alice Ware, who had given her words which she could now use with sincerity as her own. "Scholarship is a means of digging out truth, and teaching is a means of communicating it. Scholarship is a method, not a subject matter."

She hesitated then and looked fully at Grant, who, with the others, was watching her. He was pleased, she could see; but that did not satisfy her. It seemed wrong that she should have to speak to him first in this impersonal way, and she wondered how much meaning she could make him take for himself. "I was wrong," she said suddenly, still looking at him. "We don't make decisions with the mind. We live them . . . making them in every move and idle thought. To decide is merely to understand what we are and what we have already done. . . ."

She knew that he understood, for his eyes met hers in certain recognition.

She wanted to be done with words then, but grew suddenly aware that the rest of the people were still listening attentively. "What I mean," she said hastily, "is that scholarship, being a method, can be applied to everything—to life itself, I suppose. Why not? For if we do not have the time and means to understand ourselves, then our teaching too will be ignorant . . . and twisted. That is why it's impossible to estimate the value of any person's free time. I believe—yes, I believe that one could spend a whole summer destroying a work already accomplished and yet call the time spent valuable. It—it all depends," she concluded defiantly, and sat down.

"Excellent! Excellent!" Dr. Smyth whispered fervently. "If I were not so new, I should carry on, oh, I should carry on!"

Etta Wilson had stood up abruptly. "I wish to endorse Dr. Anderson's words—at least those relating strictly to scholarship. I did not say them myself only because I assumed that our Profession required no defense of scholarship—especially in an institution with which the name of Esther Cornthwaite has long been associated." She sat down with the satisfaction of one who has eloquently pleaded a cause.

Colley was trying to say something, but Dr. Day was given the floor. "I should like to add that to teach is also to serve. When on campus, we cannot lock our offices—or even our homes—against the student who might need us. In my work, I do not consider myself an original scholar; yet if I did not have time for quiet and undisturbed study, I should not be able to keep abreast with the year-by-year advance of my subject."

"And my travel!" Dean Haskins exclaimed as if she had been arguing about it for a long while. "When should I do my traveling if I spent twelve months in Riverville? How should I broaden myself?"

No one ventured an answer, but within a moment a young Science teacher stood and said in a shy, low voice that they had to strain to hear: "In the summers I do research with the Byson Chemical Company of New York. If this privilege were withdrawn from me, I should be stopped completely, for in no other laboratory is the necessary equipment . . ."

As each one arose to speak, Cameron turned his chair so that soon he faced them almost directly. His manner did not vary from that of an impartial judge, but Marcia decided that he was pleased.

". . . and I wouldn't attempt to direct," Iris was saying, "without my acting experience in summer stock companies. That's why I insisted upon knowing what all this was about before I voted one way or . . ."

"*Question!*" Dexter shouted hoarsely

But Webb was already on his feet, and everyone stared at this phenomenon, forgetting that the question had been called. "I have been listening," he said in his dry, thin voice, "in utter amazement— in utter amazement. Is it possible that there are those among us who find the issue controversial? And no one has yet remarked that a teacher quite simply requires time to *think*. If in a college there is to be no time for pure thought, where in this life is it to be had?"

"I'm not so sure," Colley said, "that it would be such a great loss to be without *pure* thought. I don't mean to be personal, Webb, but it occurs to me that you've thought through dozens of summers and even some sabbaticals, and I haven't noticed any momentous results."

"At the end of this very summer," Webb said with dignity, "I found my Premise."

Colley gaped. "Premise for what?"

"For the existence of all things," Webb said in the unperturbed manner of one who without arrogance is convinced of the value of his work. But suddenly he cackled and pointed a bony finger at Colley. "You may not feel any immediate effect, Professor Colley, but one day, when you confront the mystery of which you—yes, even you, are a part, you may feel belated gratitude for my having proved that you are something more than a shadow drifting across the sunlight of reality."

Only three of them voted for the motion—Colley, Diaz, and Dr. Stanford, whose anxiety over Mrs. Stanford's opinion persisted. When the result was apparent, Grant arose, and Marcia watched with a deep sense of excitement as he approached. He stopped by her row and whispered something to the person on the end. The message traveled to Dean Haskins, who turned to Marcia and said in a sceptical voice, "Professor Grant wishes to remind you that you and he are due immediately at a Relationships Committee meeting."

Marcia thanked her and quietly pushed back her chair. But the Dean was not put off so easily. "Is this a meeting I should know about? I wasn't even aware that we had a Relationships Committee."

"It's—it's quite new and small," Marcia said hurriedly, "and there are no deans on it."

Dr. Smyth, who had heard the message, was watching her in consternation. "Tell me, is this the—er—usual rate of meetings per day?"

She assured him that they quieted down after the first few days, and then went toward Grant. He touched her hand briefly and walked on. As she followed him out the door, she heard President Cameron's sonorous voice: "It is wise and fitting that at this time, the Beginning of a new Academic Year, we should gravely consider our Responsibility to the coming Veterans, who will provide us with the most remarkable Educational Opportunity that History has ever presented to Man. . . ."